D1015016

What Readers are saying about

Henry Ripplinger's

First Three Books in The Angelic Letters Series,

Pewter Angels
Another Angel of Love
Angel of Thanksgiving

"… The best books I have ever read. Absolutely wonderful stories and so much to learn from each one. I literally could not put the books down."

MARJORIE

"… I just finished reading 'Angel of Thanksgiving' It was amazing!! What an inspiring, thought provoking, spiritual and emotional roller coaster!! I loved it!! I laughed, cried and had to think really long and hard at some of the situations in this book! I just can't get enough and can hardly wait for Book 4 to come out!!"

CATRINA

"… I just wanted to thank you for writing such an inspirational book. I was glued to this book and it was full of life lessons. It is quite refreshing to read a book devoted to God. You truly have God given talent. Thanks."

JENNIE

"…It is so inspiring to read books that can be enjoyed by all ages. I am not a religious person, but am truly touched by the references to scripture in the books."

PAULA

"… I am anxiously awaiting Book 4 –Love, love, love your books. I hope the series continues forever as I can't get enough of them."

JOANNE

"…Oh, I(we)can't wait much longer...we all want Book 4,The Angelic Occurrence. Could you let me know when it will be available, hopefully soon, I need it! I've started book 1 again,and will go on to 2&3. They are the BEST, great author! God Bless You,"

RACHELLE

"… I don't think words could ever express what your books and your words have done for my life. So thank you from the bottom of my heart."

ANGELA

"… I loved all three; where I got my 82 yr old Grandmother to read them and another friend of mine to read them. . I and the others are wondering when book 4 will be out. We are all so impatiently waiting:) "

CHERYL

"… I just read 3 books in your angel series and it is one of my favorite books of all time. I am passing them on to many of my friends and they feel the same. Thanks so much for all your inspirational words in those books."

CHRIS

"…I lived with your characters…I loved your characters…..I was at the weddings…I was at the funerals….I cried.. and I laughed…it was all so good. I feel so RELATED to these families. It was such a pleasure to have met you."

DOROTHY

"…I have read literally hundreds of books in my lifetime and none have kept me hanging on every word as your series. I could not put them down and when I did I picked them up again within a few minutes."

ANGELA

"… I have finished reading Pewter Angels and have just started Another Angel of Love. I have to tell you that your writing has added such a joy and peace to my life. ….You and your words are truly God sent. You will never know how these books have impacted my life and inspired me to be a better wife, mother, and person. Thank You from the bottom of my heart."

JENNIFER

"… I absolutely loved the book 3!! Life just rolled off the pages and I was so taken into their lives and cannot wait to see where we all go next. I have drawn strength, faith and renewed my belief in my guardian angels….. So again Thank you Henry . I love the roller coaster of life, faith and emotions your storytelling takes me on and I eagerly await the next book."

ELAINE

"… The Angel of Thanksgiving was by far my favorite, I could not put it down. The plot was amazing, I loved how you connected the characters in the end. ….. Your very inspirational, and I just love how your books come from your heart, and change the lives of every one who reads them! I can't wait to see where this story goes, I'm trying to predict it!

NEELY

"… My grandma is in love with your books… We gave book one to her for her birthday and she read it in like 4 days, then we bought her book 2 for mothers day and she read it in 4 days as well… We saw you there and we bought book 3 from you….She finished the book in 5 days this time…. when book 4 will be out…?"

ASHLEY

"… Thank You for the beautiful books, They are truly inspiration and I hope to share them all with my bible study group in the fall. May God bless you." LINDA

"…I have just finished reading your third book in the Angelic Letters series and would like to tell you that I have never read another book that has moved me as much as your has. I think that every man, woman and child should read your books then maybe this world would be a better place." ELLY

"… I have read all three of your books. They are absolutely fabulous! They capture your mind as well as your heart. I am an avid reader of a lot of different types of books but I have never been captivated by any series as much as I have with the Angelic Letters Series." DEBBIE

Oh, how I enjoy these books!!!!! There's no words to describe how much I've enjoyed book 1-2-3. I have read each one twice now and absolutely will read them again! Just can't get enough of them!! Also tell my friends and they buy them too. Could you tell me when book 4 "The Angelic Occurrence" is available? In my 68 years they are the BEST!!!!!!! God Bless You!" RACHELLE

I have never enjoyed reading a book (s) like this, I just can't get enough. Please let me know when the next one comes out,"

MICHELLE

"… WOW, all I can say is WOW.... my 2 granddaughters and I met you in Costco about a week ago. I have finished the 3 books we purchased that day. My oldest grand- daughter is on book 2. We are totally blown away. My youngest granddaughter is nearly done with book 1. You are an extremely talented author. I can hardly wait for book 4. Absolutely love the series." ANNETTE

"… There are 3 generations of our family waiting for the next book. Can you give us some idea when we can expect it to be available?"

NORMA

Please write to Henry at: henry@henryripplinger.com or visit www.henryripplinger.com for more information about Henry's work and art. Or join the conversation on Facebook at www.facebook.com/henryripplinger or on Twitter @HenryRipplinger We would love to hear from you!

THE
ANGELIC
OCCURRENCE

"THE ANGELIC OCCURRENCE"   H. RIPPLINGER/2013

Also by **Henry K. Ripplinger**

THE ANGELIC LETTERS SERIES
Book One....Pewter Angels
Book Two....Another Angel of Love
Book Three....Angel of Thanksgiving

OTHER WORKS
If You're Not From the Prairie...
(Story by David Bouchard, Images by Henry K. Ripplinger)

Coming soon from Pio-Seelos Books:

BOOK FIVE OF THE ANGELIC LETTERS SERIES
Angel Promises
Fulfilled

THE ANGELIC LETTERS SERIES,

Book Four

— ✶ —

THE

ANGELIC

OCCURRENCE

1986 -1988

HENRY K. RIPPLINGER
Best Selling Author of Pewter Angels

Library and Archives Canada Cataloguing in Publication

Ripplinger, Henry
The Angelic Occurrence / Henry K. Ripplinger.

(The Angelic Letters ; bk. 4)
Includes bibliographical references.
Issued also in electronic and audio formats.
ISBN 978-0-9917102-1-8 (bound).

I. Title. II. Series: Ripplinger, Henry. Angelic Letters series ; bk. 4.

PS8585.I565A835 2013   C813'.6   C2013-900844-6

Author photo: Bruce Vasselin, Designer Photo
Cover concept and design by Henry K. Ripplinger
Cover production by Brian Danchuk Design
Page layout by Human Powered Design

PIO-SEELOS BOOKS
Ph: (306) 731-3087, Fax: (306) 731-3852.
E-mail: henry@henryripplinger.com

Printed and bound in Canada by Friesens Printers
April 2013

This novel is dedicated to my children

Kenneth, Tracy, Jody and Jason

and

their families!

Acknowledgements

Thank you, Joan for your support, friendship and love. Thank you for proof-reading, assisting with the editing and being a sounding board. Thank you, for being you!

Proof-reading is critical to an author. The importance of fresh eyes scanning a lengthy manuscript to catch errors in spelling and punctuation cannot be over-estimated! Thanks, Tracy for once again finding the time to read the novel and your helpful suggestions. And thank you too, Darlene for proof-reading the book as well! Much appreciated!

To my daughter, Jody, it's amazing how you found time to assist with the editing of the first part of the book and reading through the manuscript while at the same time tending to three young children and also beginning your graduate studies full time. Thank you for your suggestions!

To Gail Jansen-Kesslar, thank you for editing, proof-reading and your helpful suggestions and for always being there for me! It was a pleasure working with you on this book.

Once again to all of the above, my heartfelt thanks for making my writing the best it can be!

With each passing year and the release of another book, it becomes clearer not only to me, but to the readers as well, that I may have held the pen but it was led and guided by the Holy Spirit and my guardian angel. I thank God for this wonderful miracle in my life.

PREFACE

Wow, what a journey writing the Angelic Letters has been so far! I never would have believed that at this point in my life I would be starting a new career. I thought my life-long dream to write a self-help book or any novel for that matter was over. How wrong I was!

Seven years have elapsed since I first put pen to paper. It seems like only yesterday that I was sitting in the sun-room of our farm in the early morning hours of June 2005 when, all of a sudden, it came to me like a lightning bolt, that the unbelievable experience I had five years earlier had its origin in a love story involving guardian angels and miracles.

My initial purpose was to write a book about this extraordinary experience which I now call *The Angelic Occurrence*. However, within a matter of weeks the book began to take on a life of its own. The characters came alive and I followed them and their lives; we talked and laughed and cried together. They took me in directions that I never would have thought of on my own. They led and I followed.

After several months I began to realize what was happening. Through the lives of the characters in the book, I was writing a self-development book that I had aspired to write when I was in my thirties as a high school guidance counsellor. I was amazed by the revelation that life lessons and insights are far better absorbed intellectually, spiritually, and emotionally when revealed through a story than listing a series of do's and don'ts. By writing it in a story format, readers would be able to identify with the decisions that characters made and witness themselves, the consequences of their actions. Countless e-mails from readers since, have told me how the lives of the characters seemed to have intertwined with their own and how helpful and inspirational these books have been for them.

The story line couldn't have been made up of a more perfect combination. On the one hand we have a tender-hearted epic love saga that has blossomed into an intriguing plot, captivating the hearts and minds of so many readers. But on the other hand, we have the real essence of the story which are the life lessons revealed to us by the characters. Especially, Mr. Engelmann, an endearing and wise mentor who is living out the word of God. He has not only become a special person in Henry's life but in the reader's lives as well.

Very early on I realized that the story was a gift from God. I am still amazed by the effortlessness with which the story emerged and continues to do so. The chapters, their order and all the key elements seem to be guided. Thoughts seem to come out of nowhere, and everywhere, all at once. Countless times I wake up in the wee hours of the morning thinking about the story and a different plot, or some event happening to one of the characters. When this happens, I immediately get up and write it down lest it be gone from my memory by morning. Frequently I will write 8-12 pages and then go back to sleep. When I read it in the morning I am amazed at what I wrote and how it changes the story. Similarly, at times, after a long day of writing I shake my head over what I wrote. It goes way beyond just the creative gift and talent that the Lord gives to each and everyone one of us. I may be holding the pen, but it is led by my guardian angel and the Holy Spirit. Often times, I am like one of the readers waiting for the story to unfold, who can't wait to see what comes next!

In the Lord's perfect timing He not only answered a long held dream and prayer of mine to write a novel, but He waited until I was ready and had drawn closer to Him. I would never have been able to write a story of such epic proportions at a younger age. And while much of the story contains my own life experiences and the challenges that I have either personally gone through or have had the opportunity to witness others going through, the rest is the creative imagination the Lord has gifted me with.

As I look back on what has transpired, I am amazed that it took three books to finally write about the experience that initially motivated me to write in the first place! At the time, it was clear that the *experience* or *angelic occurrence* was the main story and what would appeal to readers, and yet the story resulted in a series that has been overwhelmingly responded to by readers. The social media responses, the quantities that have been sold, the medals the books have won, all testify to the large appeal of the books in the series thus far. I would never have imagined that when I wrote the first sentence that I was about to begin such an epic journey. But then this is something I have learned over the years that if we step out in faith and act on a dream or a compulsion amazing things happen in our lives. Things like this that go beyond the abilities and gifts the Lord gives us; *its faith building because we know its God at work in our lives.*

When I tell people that I was guided to write this story, many don't understand what I mean, One example was the idea of Jenny being raped and conceiving a baby. This idea came after I had finished writing the first draft of book one, Pewter Angels. As I began to read it over and came to the part where Henry and Jenny were walking home after the movie and were confronted by several boys, it came to me in a flash that the boys returned a second time and took Jenny to the park where she was raped. I knew such a change would literally take months to rework and weave into the entire story but I realized too, how much richer the story would be and create so many twists and turns and new possibilities! I immediately set about to incorporate this major new happening into the existing plot.

The consequences of this change become obvious; the conflict it sets up for Jenny to give her baby up for adoption and how she longs to reconnect with her daughter. It keeps Jenny and Henry connected through the series in a special way and also introduces a powerful way to bring Camilla into the story by meeting Henry's son! In the final books yet to come, still further effects from this one change will become evident. This is just one example of an insight that comes along and takes the story ahead in a far stronger direction and has profound effects upon all the characters in ways we could never have imagined.

I believe that our own actions can have a similar ripple effect and touch so many people's lives in ways we may never know, too.

Seeing this come to life in the Angelic Letters Series may give us pause to reflect that our every thought, word and deed has consequences not only in our earthly lives but also our eternal lives as well. Accompanying such awareness changes us. We live with greater purpose and meaning because we know that everything we do matters. It is my personal believe that acts of love such as kindness, forgiveness, patience, compassion...last forever.

I realize it's difficult for a reader not to have full closure in a novel. But I assure you the length of time between books is really a godsend. These times in between are when the story has strengthened and become much deeper, richer, and more powerful. Further, this time in between has allowed me to mature as a writer and improved my ability to express more clearly the purpose that the Lord had in mind when this all first began back in 2000. He wanted me to remind everyone of His words, and how they are not just words in a book, but "*living*" instructions as to how we should lead our lives, and "*living*" words of hope and healing for those who need it.

What I want you to know, dear reader, is that my connection to you through these books has been a treasure from God for me. I know that my life has been the richer for this experience. Not only have the Angelic Letters fulfilled a life-long dream to write, but they've also fulfilled a life-long dream and passion I've had to help others find meaning, direction and purpose in their lives. Not by me, but through me, as God works towards a far greater purpose than me or my story.

Henry K. Ripplinger
March, 2013

"Where your treasure is, there will your heart be also."

MATTHEW 6:21

"No one can be a slave to two masters: he will hate one and love the other; he will be loyal to one and despise the other. You cannot serve both God and money."

MATTHEW 6:24

"The eyes are like a lamp for the body: if your eyes are clear, your whole body will be full of light; but if your eyes are bad, your body will be in the darkness. So if the light in you turns out to be darkness, how terribly dark it will be.

MATTHEW 6:22-23

"Do not lay up for yourselves treasures upon the earth, lay up for yourselves treasures in heaven."

MATTHEW 6:19-20

"What did we bring into the world? Nothing! What can we take out of the world? Nothing! So then, if we have food and clothes, that should be enough for us."

1 TIMOTHY 6:7-8

"But those who want to get rich fall into the temptation and are caught in the trap of many foolish and harmful desires, which pull men down to ruin and destruction."

1 TIMOTHY 6:9

For the love of money is a root of all sorts of evil. Some have been so eager to have it that they have wandered away from the faith and have broken their hearts with many sorrows.

1 TIMOTHY 6;10

"It is much harder for a rich man to enter the Kingdom of God than for a camel to go through the eye of a needle."

LUKE 18:25

"For what shall it profit a man, if he shall gain the whole world, and lose his own soul."

MARK 8:36

"Do not love the world or anything that belongs to the world. If you love the world, you do not have the love for the Father in you. Everything that belongs to the world—what the sinful self desires, what people see and want, and everything in this world that people are so proud of—none of this comes from the Father; it all comes from the world. The world and everything in it that men desire is passing away; but he who does what God wants lives for ever."

1 JOHN 2: 15-17

PROLOGUE

A THOUGHTFUL MAN ONCE said that where a man's treasure is, there his heart will be also. I contemplate the truth of these words as I watch the dawning of a new day begin in the valley. I am sitting on the deck just outside of my closest friend's prayer house. For several years I have come here to renew my spirit and draw closer to God. It is a retreat I highly recommend to each and every one of you. It is as the Lord promises in Psalm 23:2,3: He maketh me to lie down in green pastures: he leadeth me beside the still waters. He restoreth my soul."

Ever since I returned from my stint on the other side I have thought much about what I had heard and seen. In less than a blink of the eye my dear friend and protector, Zachariah, permitted me to see so many powerful visions and glimpses not only of my own life and those of my close friends, but also of all mankind.

From that heavenly perspective, it was easy to see in the preoccupations of man's thinking and the major thrust of his efforts and energy, what treasures lay in his heart. Even a cursory glance showed that for all too many people their heart was in the wrong place. So many of mankind have been duped into believing that the accumulation of wealth and material possessions will bring peace and happiness. We have come to believe that our worth is equal to our wealth, our bank account, the size of our home, the number of cars we own or which particular model. The list is endless.

For all too many, riches, recognition, honour, glory, the ingredients of bolstering our pride is the food that Satan wants to continuously feed us. He tries to hide the fact from our awareness that what we are so in love with is nothing more than a fleeting illusion that has no lasting value. It's temporal, fleeting, and each new item we work so hard to buy begins to rot, decay and rust out no sooner than we take it out of the store or drive it off the lot. What we thought would give us peace and joy and fulfillment is here today and gone tomorrow and of absolutely no value in the eyes of the kingdom of God.

Sadly, my friends, at times many even seek personal gain at the expense of dignity and integrity, forsaking honesty, stealing, taking advantage of others, manipulating situations and wrongfully placing work over and above family and friends. It's little wonder at the end of the day we feel emptiness and lack of fulfillment. Never before in the history of mankind has man lost his way, his freedom, his purpose and meaning of life.

When wealth and materialism are seen for what they are and put into proper context, they become good and necessary, like anything the Lord provides. It is when we make these earthly possessions our gods and the treasures of our heart, that they are no longer good for our soul. Man cannot live by bread alone. Neither can he serve two masters. He will either love the one or hate the other. As long as that happens, man's love of the Lord will always be secondary, if at all.

As I envisioned these things when I was on the other side, my dear friend and protector, Zachariah, not only read my thoughts but summed them up so wisely: "What does it profit a man if he gains the whole world and suffers the loss of his soul in the process?"

I nodded sadly in return, "Yes, Zachariah, all that man works for so stringently has no eternal reward. It's also easy to see from this heavenly perspective the underlying motive that drives man's heart in such pursuit of wealth and possessions. We are in a constant state of discontent, never satisfied with what we have."

And before my wise protector could reply, I rambled on. "The propaganda toward that end is endless. Televisions are blasting away at us daily with a constant stream of advertising, so too are newspapers and promotional flyers in our mailboxes all are bent on constantly revving up our minds to buy. We are continuously moving, distracted, our minds thinking endlessly how to make more money so we can buy more. It's like we are caught up in a wheel of fortune, ceaselessly going around in circles, moving us so fast in this secular world that the centrifugal force of our busy lives and preoccupations upon us hurtles us constantly away from the true source of life and what really matters."

"That is all very true," Zachariah said, acknowledging my insight. Then he continued, "The apostle Timothy warned man of his insatiable desire for more and advised him to be content and appreciative of what he has. It has been easier for you to see and do because you have always been satisfied with little and your main focus has always been the Lord. But look closer and you will see a dangerous oversight in man's thinking."

"Ah, yes, Zachariah." I could see what it was that sustained man's drive for ever more wealth and materialism, and his eyes brightened at my further understanding. I suddenly saw what my angel saw daily in the lives of men.

"All too many people think that life will go on forever. So many live under the illusion of the permanence of life thus staying trapped in the values of the world. We do not stop long enough to see that one day, sooner or later, we will die and be caught unprepared for the Lord's judgment and our acceptance into His kingdom. Our false sense of dependence on the bounties of the world have puffed up our pride to the point that we have no need of God!"

As I recall our discussion on that memorable day, a restlessness begins to stir within me, drawing me back to the moment. I get up and walk to the edge of the deck which touches the water. In the twilight of a new day the soft glow of light began to illuminate the valley.

Across from me the tall grass, bulrushes and lush green hills and trees reflect so soothingly on the still waters of the pond. I marvel at how accurately a bird zips to the surface of the water for an insect or two for its morning breakfast. In the distance I hear a Whippoorwill, and coming out of the brush to my left is a doe with her little fawn at her side. I am filled with peace as I drink in the stillness and beauty before me.

Not only does the beauty of nature speak to us, but the One who created it does, too. I felt an expectancy of something the Lord wants to share...

The sun is rising higher now, burning into the edge of one of the hilltops in the east. As the first warm rays strike my face I am reminded once again of perhaps the most illuminating vision while I was on the doorstep of heaven; a glimpse into the unseen workings of the angels.

The light was staggering. Heavenly angels were aglow and filled through and through with light. They were saturated with God's love. They had yielded their will to their Creator and in return it was easy to see what treasure lay in their hearts. They were filled with the power and joy of God's love. With my own eyes I saw how they live in the brilliance and purity of a light that words cannot even begin to describe. They are filled with a reflection of what they constantly see and adore: the face of God.

And now, watching the sun rise above the valley, I know what it is that God wants me to further comprehend. The words of the apostle John in 3:19 shine before me with full understanding: "The Light has come into the world but men love the darkness rather than the Light."

Yes, yes, my friends, although we live in the sunlight, our hearts live in the dark. It was so poignant to see the angels helping to lift mankind daily from the darkness in their hearts to the Light. Can you not see the wisdom of it all? Are you not beginning to see the truth of the Light? It is all about the Light my friends! The Light of Jesus Christ who came into the world to save us!

No sooner had this exhilarating thought entered my mind then a glow of intense light hovered over the still pond. And there before me He appeared in all His resplendent glory standing on the mirror like surface of the shimmering water: the son of God. He came to show me what treasures lay in His heart. One would expect to see all the honours and all the glitter of gold and gems befitting a king to shine magnificently therein. But no! The treasures of our Lord's heart was filled with love for mankind. And He did the ultimate for us to show the depth of His love.

There he stood with open arms His hands revealing the wounds and suffering he endured when he was crucified for our sins; His heart radiating love, forgiveness and a sea of mercy. The sight was staggering, overwhelming, breathtaking, my heart filled to overflowing with so much praise and gratitude.

Instantly, alongside the heavenly angels I praised our God. The Holy Spirit filled my spirit to overflowing with pure love and I fell prostrate before my Lord and saviour and redeemer.

My dear, dear friends, the mercy and love of our Lord's heart is boundless. If only we could trust what awaits us if we choose to live for Him; to replace the earthy treasures of our hearts with treasures that have eternal value in heaven; to take the time to shed what binds us and that which keeps us captive in the dark, we would all be rich beyond our limited imaginings.

As I lay upon the deck feeling the love and mercy of my Lord and Saviour, it comes to me the reason behind all of our failings…We have forgotten who we are; we are children of God. We have forgotten that we were put on this earth out of His love for us and to develop a relationship with Him, our Father, and to Jesus, His son and to the Holy Spirit. He so desires that we come to Him. That we love Him above all else; that we are here to serve Him and our neighbour, to yield our will to Him so we can be used for His purpose to save all mankind and spend an eternity of happiness with Him in heaven.

The depth of my understanding overwhelms me. If we were to fully realize the reason for our existence and our purpose, all else would fall into its proper perspective in our lives. The scripture summarizes it perfectly:

"But seek ye first the kingdom of God, and His righteousness; and all these things shall be added unto you." Matthew 6:33

I slowly get up as if lifted by my heavenly protector. I can feel the warmth of Zachariah's presence and I picture him so clearly: his warm, brown, twinkling eyes filled with joy at my understanding.

As I gaze out again across the pond and watch the rays of the sun shimmer on the gentle ripples, it comes to me that just as the grass and flowers need sunshine and water to grow and flourish, giving beauty to the world, so too do we need the light of Jesus in our hearts to make our faith grow. If we water our hearts daily with His Word, others will see the beauty in us just like the breathtaking beauty of God's creation.

As the shimmering water before me sparkles like diamonds under the rising sun, I proclaim to the whole world,

"Yes, yes oh my Lord! Let us see that each and every Word you speak are like diamonds, too, jewels that we place in our heart each day. These are the treasures we must seek. The light and truth we gain from Your Word will make us sparkle, too, and has far more worth and lasting value than all the gold and silver of the world."

So much passion and love for the Lord floods me that tears of erupting joy blur the glorious, sunlit valley before me. I can feel the gentle touch of my guardian angel's hand on my shoulder and the warm, morning breeze moving across the pond toward me, carrying the sweet voice of my protector.

Lovingly, soothingly I hear Zachariah whisper…

"For to the man who pleases Him, God gives wisdom, and knowledge and joy!" Eccl. 2:26

CHAPTER ONE

WHAT AN AMAZING career you've had, Mr. Pederson. Or, should I say careers? You seem to be successful at almost anything you do. You're a carpenter, a teacher, a guidance counselor, an entrepreneur, a curator of an art gallery, a professional artist and a very successful businessman. This may seem like an odd question to ask, but who are you really? Will the real Henry Pederson please stand up?"

Henry leaned forward to rest his elbows on the table, his fingers intertwined. Henry knew how he answered would reflect his character both in terms of the interview and in terms of the feature the Regina Sun planned to print in one of their Sunday magazine issues. Brenda Oakley was right. It did appear to everyone that he was successful at many things – otherwise he likely wouldn't be doing this interview. But did any one of those things truly reflect his heart?

"Well, Brenda, I guess I am all the things you just mentioned. I have never been able to do just one thing. I am always looking for a new challenge and will use all the expertise I have acquired to date to meet it. If I'm lacking in a certain area then I will learn the skill or knowledge needed for the situation. I may not be one hundred percent successful at the start, but I know within a short time I will have the necessary skills to meet the challenge. That's just the nature of the beast. I am a very hands-on type of person.

"Unfortunately, doing so much does sometimes distract me from doing just my art, or carrying on just my business or spending the time I'd like to with my family and grandchildren. I do have a tendency to spread myself too thin at times. But once I get an idea how to improve something – whether it's a business strategy, a painting or renovation – I'm driven to make it a reality."

"Yes," Brenda replied, "it's difficult to slot you into an easily identifiable, one-dimensional role. It's like trying to put a round peg in a square hole. It just can't be done!"

Henry laughed.

"That's an interesting way of summing up my character, but I guess what I do and the way I operate is what has helped me to become successful. For example, in establishing the art gallery, I blended several skills I had acquired over the years; my carpentry abilities, my pursuit of art and love for dealing with people are all skills needed in business.

"I mentioned to you yesterday about how Mr. Engelmann and I worked together to turn a failing business into a successful one in a very short time. I combined what I had learned from that four years of experience with my other skills and have made our gallery a very successful business that just keeps expanding. We went from being just an art gallery, to include a café, a card shop, a ladies boutique on the second level, as well as several other boutiques."

"Whew! Just listening to what you have accomplished makes me tired. How on earth do you manage to get it all done?"

"Well, there is a trick," Henry said, with a smile and tongue in cheek. "You have to be disciplined, committed, and prepared to work hard and long hours. There are no short cuts to being successful. You have to pay your dues."

"Well, you certainly have, Mr. Pederson. It's very impressive what you have created for the city."

Brenda flipped through her notes. Her eyes brightened as she reread a note she had made earlier.

"So, tell me a little bit more about Mr. Engelmann and how he fits into this picture? You mentioned him several times during our last two meetings and then again, just now."

"The good Lord gives each and every one of us certain aptitudes and abilities. These inherent tendencies, however, must be worked at and developed to realize them."

"Like your skill as an artist."

"Yes, that's right. I love to work with my hands and I love to create, but to paint landscapes and beautiful paintings, I had to work long hours to develop the inherent skills I was gifted with. If I hadn't taken classes and painted hundreds of paintings to come up with really good ones, it would never have happened. The gift the good Lord gave me would simply have laid dormant or died with me, never to be realized."

"What has this all to do with Mr. Engelmann?"

"Well, it is to him I attribute the discovery of many of my aptitudes and skills, such as relating to people, my business skills, my wanting to be a teacher and then a counselor, and even an artist."

Brenda wrinkled her forehead as she studied him for a long

moment. "How can one person trigger so many interests and skills?"

Henry sat back in his chair, sipped his cooled herbal tea and allowed his mind to drift back almost 29 years to July 7, 1956 when he started working for Mr. Engelmann. Henry was about to share that day with Brenda, when his mind somehow drew him into the day before. That memorable, unforgettable day when Jenny, his very first love, moved into the neighbourhood, three doors down from his house. His mind pictured it vividly, as if it were yesterday.

...How she had captivated him as she strolled past his house... how he'd followed her to Engelmann's Grocery Store. Henry had never forgotten the moment he had knocked over all the salmon tins when he first looked into her cerulean blue eyes. It truly was love at first sight, a magical, spiritual moment, there was no other way to explain it.

Without realizing it, Henry had thrust his right hand out towards Brenda as he reacted to the memory of that wonderful phrase Jenny always said as they crossed busy streets, "Quickly, hold my hand." It was as if Jenny were there beside him. An electrifying thrill coursed through him as it had that day when their hands engaged and every time he thought about it since.

Henry's heart warmed as he recalled that summer. How he and Jenny had grown closer together. How they dated and almost made love in the park. And then, just two weeks after high school started, it ended. Jenny and her parents moved to Ottawa and he never heard from her again.

He recalled packaging up over 40 letters and mailing them to her father's business, but she had never responded. It was as if she'd vanished from the face of the earth. Henry's hand landed on his chest as his heart ached.

"Mr. Pederson...? Henry, is everything okay? You drifted so far away."

"Oh, I'm very sorry, Brenda," Henry said, as he shook his head to snap himself back into the present. "As I thought back to how I got started with Mr. Engelmann, I somehow began thinking of a very special person that also came into my life at that very same time—"

"It must have been a girl to put you into such a deep trance so quickly," Brenda interjected with a smile.

Henry looked at Brenda and smiled back.

"Yes, it was a girl, she was my very first lo—" He stopped. It was too private, too personal, to share with a reporter he hardly knew.

Henry couldn't get over how quickly and utterly absorbed in the past he still became when he remembered Jenny and how immediately he felt the pain of their parting. It took considerable effort on his part to let go of the momentary grip it had on him. He shook his head again and said, "Oh, I better not go there, Brenda."

Henry sat up trying to shake off the reverie that was still trying to draw him back. Brenda looked a little disappointed that he wasn't going to share where his mind had so strongly drifted to.

"Well, let's get back to your question which I believe was, how did Mr. Engelmann influence me, my skills and my careers in so many ways?"

Brenda nodded.

"Well, Brenda, he not only touched my life, but the lives of many, many people in the neighbourhood. Let me see now...Mr. Engelmann...What can I say in a few words that would capture the essence of the man? Perhaps I'll start by giving you a little background and then share examples of what I mean.

"It was 1956 and I had just finished Grade 8. I was starting my summer holidays when Mr. Engelmann called my parents and asked if it would be okay for me to work for him during the summer. It was okay with my parents, but it was I who wasn't sure if I wanted to work for him. I had always perceived him as sort of a grumpy old man, who usually gave us boys a stern look when we entered his store. Not that he was unjustified in doing so, our intent most of the time was to snitch a chocolate bar or two.

"Something told me to work for him anyway, and in a matter of days, I began to respect Mr. Engelmann and soon came to love him like a dad or grandfather. Soon, I began to see him as one of the greatest and wisest persons I ever knew. And, I might add, my opinion of that judgment hasn't changed one iota over all the years. In fact, it has only deepened."

Brenda looked intrigued and nodded for Henry to go on.

"Well, let's see... Mr. Engelmann's business was failing and on the verge of bankruptcy. He owed money to his suppliers and was behind in paying his taxes. His wife, Anna, was very ill and could no longer help her husband with the business. Gradually Mr. Engelmann became overwhelmed by the daily grind of looking after both the store and his wife. They hired me to help out and that's what I did."

"Why someone so young and inexperienced?"

"Well, perhaps it was all they could afford. In fact, I never received an hourly wage. On Saturday night after the store closed, Mr.

Engelmann would give me a five or ten dollar bill from the cash register, whatever he could afford. But you know, Brenda, I would have worked for nothing. I derived so much joy and inner satisfaction from helping Mr. Engelmann fix up the store and get it back on track. Also the joy it gave to both he and his wife to see it all happen so quickly, was more than payment enough. Within six months, the store was back on track and making money again. All of his debts were paid within a year and his savings account was growing."

"That's wonderful. So, what exactly did you do?"

"Nothing out of the ordinary. I started by organizing the shelves and the stock. I painted the basement, and then the upstairs store and then the exterior.

"Seeing something so deteriorated and disorganized drew out my characteristics, aptitudes, and potential ability. Seeing the improvements and the joy the results gave to Mr. and Mrs. Engelmann and to the customers was so satisfying it just motivated me all the more. I kept the shelves well stocked all the time, developed a delivery service, remembered people's birthdays, organized coupons and sales, and so on. Mr. Engelmann treated me as if I were an adult, an equal, almost a business partner. Things which we developed back then, I have implemented in my business today."

"That's really something," said Brenda.

"But, Brenda, that is really the least of what I had learned while working for Mr. Engelmann. The biggest and most important part is what I had learned about life."

Henry sat back in his chair again. Brenda followed his lead and sat back in hers assuming a more relaxed position.

"Shortly after I began to work for him, I developed such a deep respect for him that he became my closest friend, counselor and mentor. Over the months and years that followed, I shared everything with Mr. Engelmann."

Brenda remained silent. She sat up in her chair, encouraging him to go on.

"Perhaps the main reason why I so readily opened up to him was because he accepted me unconditionally. I never had to be defensive because he never criticized. He always took me exactly where I was at and helped me talk and work through any concern or problem. Out back behind the store, Mr. Engelmann and I would sit on two old grey crates, drink soda pop, and talk. This was Mr. Engelmann's classroom, what he referred to as his 'school of life.' It was there, behind an old grocery store, that he not only helped me meet life's challenges, he also imparted to me very valuable principles of life to live by."

"Hi, Henry," called a customer as he passed by.

"Hi, Nick." Henry turned and waved.

"I need to get another one of your paintings. My secretary is retiring."

"Shelly is in the gallery right now, she can help you out."

"Great. I'd like you to personalize the painting to my secretary, though."

"I will be happy to, Nick."

Henry waved Nick off and turned back to Brenda. "Now, where was I?"

"You said Mr. Engelmann taught you the principles of life."

"Ah, that's right. In helping me solve my personal problems and concerns, he also explained important lessons surrounding it all; accepting others and their weaknesses; forgiveness; living with integrity and never to compromise honesty; truthfulness; kindness; to separate the person from their acts, and to live in the present moment."

"Live in the present moment?"

"Yes. Most of us are only half aware of life and our surroundings in our moment-to-moment functioning. Most of the time, we live in the past, worried about something that happened to us, reliving a regret, angry over someone who hurt us, and anxious about it all. We literally drag into our present moments the concerns and worries of the past, which is such a waste of precious time. We are also guilty of worrying about the future, being apprehensive about upcoming events or happenings, worried that this or that might happen. In short, we fill our present moments, the only real reality of life in which we could be fully alive, with a lot of yesterday's garbage or worries about tomorrow."

"Oh yes, I have seen several books on the market about that subject."

"Yes, that's true, but back then it was just coming into discussion and consideration. Anyways, you can see how Mr. Engelmann influenced me to be a teacher and then a guidance counselor."

Brenda nodded with a smile.

Henry sat up and sipped his tea.

"What developed my character perhaps more than his words and teachings, though, was that I saw him walk the talk daily, without fail. He never missed an opportunity to show kindness or love. He always encouraged me to reach out to others, to give of myself, my time, and act out of kindness. To always do it when the opportunity presented itself as you may never pass that way again. That is what our Lord will judge us on – how we have lived. How we have loved."

Henry looked intently into Brenda's eyes and continued, "What I realized over time, Brenda, was that both he and his wife, Anna, were not so much selling groceries and trying to make a living, as they were using the store as an avenue to carry out their mission in life; to reach out and serve their fellow man."

Henry stopped for another moment and sipped his cold tea.

"I so desired to emulate him, but not without a lot of bumps and hard knocks along the way. It wasn't until I followed another one of his precepts that I finally started to make some progress."

Brenda leaned forward and closer to the edge of her seat. Her actions reminded Henry of himself seated on the edge of the old grey crate behind the store waiting for Mr. Engelmann's next tidbit of wisdom.

"What helped me to grow and follow somewhat in Mr. Engelmann's footsteps was when I began to acquire the habit of daily meditation and prayer."

"Do you mean being on your best behaviour at all times so as to be an example to others?"

"Well, that's very important and we so need people to be models in this day and age. But what I was getting at was the importance to continually examine your life and prepare for the day. Perhaps you meditate already, Brenda, and realize this."

Henry studied her for a brief moment, but Brenda didn't respond.

"Unless one examines his or her life continuously, and checks the direction in which one is heading, one can easily get stuck in a rut, get caught up with just trying to live out the day, then go to bed, get up the next morning, only to think basically the same thoughts and perform the same actions and behaviour all over again. Many of us spend our lives this way, as sad as it may be, it is a fact. I know I was guilty of it and still am many times."

Brenda was about to say something when Henry blurted out, "It all comes down to how one starts each and every day. The heart must be fueled daily with a restful solitude, meditation, thoughts of gratefulness and faithful prayer. Without this, success is difficult, the road a struggle. We spend day in and day out with the same self-defeating behaviours and thoughts."

They both sat in silence, sort of staring at one another. What was supposed to be an interview to learn about Henry's business and his background had somehow turned into a philosophical and spiritual dissertation.

"Well, Brenda, this is really not getting you any further in your interview about the article you want to write. You can see, however, how all this influenced me and the choices I made throughout my life."

"Yes, I can definitely see that, Mr. Pederson, and it's all very enlightening." After a further reflective thought, Brenda added, "It is so true how easy it is to get stuck in the process of daily living and not really grow. And it is true that we do have a tendency to think the same thoughts over and over."

"After learning so much about human behaviour and helping others from Mr. Engelmann, I was motivated to become a teacher, and then after four years of that, I went on to become a guidance counselor. After that, it was time to pursue my love of art and then business. My four years working with and for Mr. Engelmann very definitely led me to do and realize all these career choices."

"Yes, I am beginning to understand and for sure, I see what you mean. He has been a big influence on your life…" Brenda's voice trailed off, like she didn't know what to ask next.

"You know, Brenda, an article about Mr. Engelmann would indeed be highly interesting."

"Is he still alive?"

"Well, yes, he is. In fact, around 1960, shortly after his wife died, he decided to enter into a new career, a natural for him."

"He became a psychologist?"

"Well, in a way he did, but he became someone even better, at least I think so. He went into the seminary and became a priest."

"Really? That's fantastic."

"Yes, it certainly is. And would you believe, he is still active as a priest today, at St. Mary's Church. I think he's somewhere in his eighties, looks like he's in his late sixties and acts like he is in his forties. The Archbishop has been trying to get him to retire for years, now, but he always says, 'next year.' He maintains that his flock still needs him and that he, the shepherd, is still able to walk the hills and valleys."

Henry smiled and quickly added, "But I do think he is beginning to think seriously about retirement of some kind. Last Sunday after Mass when I talked to him, he mentioned that he might want to move into a care home. He sees all too many lonely people in there when he visits them, living day in and day out just waiting to die. 'Perhaps I can help,' he said to me. So, he has something up his sleeve."

"So, what is next on the agenda for you, Henry?" Brenda popped the question with a sparkle in her eyes.

"Well, Brenda, I have always wanted to write a novel, but that is on the back burner for now. At the present time I have a crew that is completing several major renovations to other revenue property I have, including an office building just down the block."

"So, you're a developer, too!"

"Yes, sort of. Like I told you before, I love renovating. I acquire houses, fix them up and either sell them or rent them out as another source of revenue. I love doing that. I derive great satisfaction out of taking something that is run down and turning it into something beautiful. That is what motivates me in my painting and everything I do. Starting with a blank canvas, for example, and turning it into a beautiful prairie landscape, taking an old house and turning it into a work of art, just as we did to the gallery and then the café and so on. I've always been like that.

"In short, Brenda, I like to make the world a better place. I get a lot of satisfaction when people come into our business and tell me how much they love it here and how good it makes them feel. That's what it's all about."

"It's amazing how you still manage to find time to paint as an artist."

"Yes, I hear that all the time. But like I said, it requires commitment, hard work, and long hours. It's like they say, if you want to get something done, give the job to a busy person."

"Hmmm, that's interesting. A busy person doesn't procrastinate and gets on the job right away," Brenda analyzed.

"I certainly don't paint as often as I used to. In most cases I just do it and get at it in a very committed way, so in a way you are correct," Henry replied, "but I must admit I am guilty of procrastination. If I overcame that, I would really get a lot more done."

Brenda's eyes grew wide with a look of disbelief. "As I listen to you, you have really accomplished what most people only dream to do. Most of us fail to act on our dreams and visions."

"That's so true and a very sad state of affairs," Henry said with a nod. "Perhaps one of the biggest factors why people don't do things or act on their ideas is the fear of failure. I have seen it over and over again, not only as a counselor, but also talking to people who tell me how they envy my success. Perhaps they always dreamed of opening up a café, but for them, all it was was a dream; they never acted on their vision. When we decided to open a café, over and over business people advised me that a café would never work…"

"Yet, you still went ahead," Brenda interrupted.

"Yes, I believe when you do something, do it to the best of your ability, don't cut corners, do it right the first time and just believe that it will work. Wasn't it William James, the well known psychologist, who said 'our belief at the beginning of a new venture is the one thing that insures the successful outcome of your undertaking?'"

"I'm not sure who said that, but it's true. We do tend to attract what we think."

Henry nodded with a smile.

Brenda looked up. "I really must say I am very impressed by your total commitment to life."

"Thank you, Brenda, that's very kind of you to say. But really, if I can do it, so can anyone. I'm just an average Joe. I suppose that's what I have learned is that to make it happen you must do one very important thing."

"And…?"

"You have already alluded to part of it earlier when you said one must 'act' on it. To achieve anything in life, to realize your vision or dreams, you must begin to do it and keep at it until it's done. So many of us have great ideas, profound visions, but instead of acting on them, we snuggle into our security blanket of safety and comfortableness, afraid to act. Slowly we watch one dream after the other whither and die or see it realized by another who dared to act."

"You said that's part of it, what is the other part?"

"Dreams, ideas, and visions all have to do with the mind, Brenda. It's the heart, however, which realizes them."

Brenda looked at Henry quizzically for a moment, then her eyes brightened.

"The heart must always follow the idea, push it, be committed to it, desire it with fervour and passion. It is the heart, the inner vision that keeps one focused and motivated until one's dream or goal is accomplished. That is what makes all the difference in a person's life and being successful in achieving their dreams and goals. *Action and passion are the key!*"

It was now Brenda's turn to just nod. After a long moment, she asked, "But, what if your project or venture fails? No matter how hard you try or as you say, how much heart you put into it, it just may not be in the cards to succeed."

"I think I answered that question, earlier. I don't believe in failure."

Brenda looked puzzled, but remained silent.

"We learn from everything we do, Brenda. If something doesn't work it doesn't mean we have failed, it just means we have to try something different, perhaps another approach, a minor adjustment to what we are doing. If what we have done isn't quite working, then I am thankful that I know, so I can shift gears and get going again. Look at the great inventor, Edison, when he invented the light bulb. He had many setbacks before he achieved his goal, but he learned from each setback and then opened another door.

"So often, Brenda, we are at the door to success, so close and we give up. I carry around a little poem in my wallet that I have had for years and years. I came across it when I was a guidance counselor, it's entitled, 'Don't Quit.' I gave it out to all my students and I follow its lesson to this very day: Stick to your dream or goal until it's done."

Brenda shook her head slightly, raised her eyebrows and smiled broadly. "Well, Mr. Pederson. It's clear that you have followed that creed your entire life. You're the epitome of success."

Instinctively, Henry humbly averted his eyes at the compliment and cast a glance around his busy café. Brenda was clearly impressed by Henry, yet, a feeling of smugness tugged at his stomach. Or was it a twinge of guilt and hypocrisy. He had all the answers and knowledge of how to succeed in the world. His gallery, café, wealth, and all the property he possessed was evidence of that. But was he *really* successful?

Sure, he'd used his skills to bring beauty to the world around him. Sure, he'd used his business to serve others and help those in need. Yes, his accomplishments were many. However, deep within, Henry also recognized that his success indirectly kept him in bondage to worldly distractions. Instead of gaining freedom, inner peace and happiness that he thought would come with wealth; he felt an uneasiness, a void that could only be temporarily filled by accomplishing and accumulating more. Over the years, his skills and aptitudes gained him recognition and status which he had come to enjoy and depend on, but he had also bought into the false belief that the more he had, the greater was his worth in the eyes of others.

Henry recognized that his striving and desire for more outweighed his wisdom. He knew better, and he had been taught better. Henry clearly saw in Father Engelmann, what it was that he lacked. Father was free of all attachments. He knew his purpose in life and his place in the scheme of things. He had a single-minded devotion to only one Master and one Master alone and that was his Lord. His Lord was at the centre of his life, whereas for Henry his worldly success was at the centre of his. He knew he could not serve two masters.

Somehow over the years, especially after Julean's death, he had become duped into the illusion of believing more in his independence and success and less on his dependence on his Lord and placing Him in the driver's seat. The pursuit of abilities and honours and riches had kept him from coming totally to his Redeemer.

Brenda was staring at him quizzically, again. She was probably wondering if he'd returned to his earlier reverie about his girlfriend.

Henry shifted uncomfortably in his chair. The thoughts he was entertaining were unsettling. The Lord was asking too much. For too long he had felt the comfort and security of wealth. For several years now he had been struggling with this issue. He knew where the treasures of his heart really lay. His integrity – the need to be forthright and honest – weighed on him. He didn't want to leave Brenda with a false impression of where he was really at in his life.

"You know, Brenda, I don't want to mislead you. I may be a success in the eyes of the world, but true success is when one's main goal and ambition in life is to love and serve his fellow man. Father Engelmann is the only person who I know that has achieved that goal. I don't want this to end as a sermon or a spiritual dissertation, but there is a scriptural passage that Father Engelmann talked about several weeks ago in one of his sermons that keeps coming up in my mind. It's the one about a rich man who asked Jesus what he needed to do to gain the kingdom of Heaven. 'Sell everything you own, give it to the poor, and come follow me,' was His answer.

"Now, if we take that literally, how many of us could do that? How strong and deep is our attachment to the world? Could I really place my trust completely in Him and not in my wealth and possessions? Where would the treasure of my heart really be?"

Henry paused. "A little further in that same scripture the Lord goes on to say that it is truly easier for a camel to go through the eye of a needle than it is for a rich man to enter the kingdom of heaven."

Henry knew his thoughts surprised Brenda. She and everyone he knew thought he was on top of the world with his success and, yet, he still struggled in a way he knew many people had never given much thought to.

"We work and strive so hard to be a success in the world and lose sight of the fact that nothing is really ours. We are simply stewards of God's blessings upon us. At the end of the day, of what value is wealth, possessions, talents, and gifts if they are not used for others? That is the kind of life that has lasting value and one that will be truly rewarded. To fully recognize that and be totally free of our attachment to things and the ways of the world – that is to be successful."

Henry winked at Brenda and smiled. "I'm still working on it."

Brenda and Henry fell into a reflective silence. The morning sun streamed through the south windows and flooded the patio just outside their window. It was a beautiful day and customers were taking advantage of outdoor eating, a luxury that prairie folk have for a very limited time during the summer. If it wasn't the wind making outdoor dining a nuisance, it was the wasps or the coolness in the air. Today was perfect to be outside, however, and customers were coming early to beat the noon-hour rush to the patio.

"So, one final area I want to be clear on. This is a family business?"

"That is correct. My wife was a graduate nurse, but she never really pursued it after we married. She wanted to stay home and raise the children. She did however help out with the gallery when it first opened, but shortly after, she contracted meningitis and passed away. "

"Oh, I'm sorry to hear that," said Brenda.

"Yes, it happened suddenly. I miss her very much. I still haven't gotten used to it. We have four children. My oldest son, Jeremy, looks after the café along with my oldest daughter Allison, who manages the gallery. The two pretty much help me operate the business. My other daughter, Lauren, helps out in the boutique shops upstairs and is also a waitress when she isn't in school. And my youngest son, Justin, who came into the family much later in our marriage, helps out with odd jobs in the kitchen and gallery when he isn't in school. So, it is as you say Brenda, a family-run business."

"Well, I guess that just about does it. I have more than enough material. It has certainly been a pleasure talking to you Mr. Pederson."

"Think nothing of it, Brenda. And please, call me Henry; after all, that's the guy who owns this place."

"Well, this has just been great, Henry. If I have any more questions as I write up this interview, I will call you. In any case, we will get it into print and out in a month or so. Thank you, again, for your time, I appreciate it very much."

"You're welcome, Brenda. And, as a special treat, I would like to offer you our house specialty 'Henry's Oh-so-creamy Cheesecake.' It is, without question, the best cheesecake you will ever have."

Brenda's eyes opened wide in anticipation. "I can hardly wait to taste it."

Henry signalled a tall, handsome young man in his twenties who had just finished seating some customers.

"Jeremy, I would like you to meet Brenda Oakley, the reporter from the Sunday Sun..."

"Hi, nice to meet you, Brenda." Jeremy extended his hand and gave her a warm smile. Brenda could see the family resemblance.

"Yes, it's a pleasure meeting you, too. Your dad tells me you run this place."

"It's a joint affair, actually. Most days Dad is in the trenches right along next to us," and turning to his dad, he continued, "Tamara phoned in sick at the last minute which is why I'm seating people until Zack gets in. I want to check how the kitchen is doing, I think with the weather being so nice we're going to get slammed today. Oh, and I'm expecting Camilla and Joshua any minute; tell her to go into the gallery..."

"Actually, Jeremy, here they come now," announced Henry, who was seated facing the front door to the café.

Brenda turned to see a beautiful, blond haired woman and a small boy enter the busy room. The woman took a look around, spotted Jeremy and Henry, and with a smile that was brighter than the hot June-day sun, gave a small wave.

"Oh my," said Brenda under her breath and then more audibly, "Isn't she just as lovely as an angel..."

"You'll have to excuse me, Brenda," Jeremy said, "it was nice meeting you."

"Yes, that goes for me too, Jeremy."

As his son was leaving the table, Henry remembered why he had called him over in the first place.

"And Jeremy, send over a slice of our house special dessert for Brenda."

"You got it, Dad!"

Jeremy made his way to the door to meet his wife. The young boy freed himself from his mother's hand and ran to Henry yelling, "Hi Grandpa!"

"Hi Joshua, how's my boy?"

Henry stood just in time to scoop up the two year old, then turned to Brenda. "Well, I better start helping out, Brenda, but... if I can just add one more thought for the record before I leave..."

"I'm all ears, Henry."

First turning to Jeremy who was just giving his wife a peck on the cheek and then back to Brenda, Henry said, "Given everything I've said over the course of this interview, this is the most important: Never take life for granted. *Never.* Never in a million years would I have expected that blond haired, blue-eyed young lady to enter into our lives and become... my daughter.

"*Never!*"

CHAPTER TWO

"And you saw her kissing the owner of the bookstore?"

J.J. cast a long convicting look at his mother and then turned his gaze back to his father's lawyer.

"Yes. Yes, she was. She betrayed my father—"

"Objection!"

"Sustained. Please ask your witness just to answer the questions," said Judge Gerian.

"Yes, your Honour."

Jenny stared at her son in disbelief, hardly believing her ears. His remark after seeing John kiss her cheek that day still stung. Over the years she had tried to explain, but he wouldn't listen to her side or to reason. He accused her of being unfaithful and claimed she was totally to blame for breaking up the marriage and the home. He was completely supportive of his father and totally overlooked his father's input into the demise of his parents' marriage.

She should have known this would eventually happen. Almost from the moment J.J. was born, James set out to take him away from her. He had made it his mission to make J.J. a clone of himself, only better and smarter. The moment J.J. was able to walk, James took him to the office to prepare him for his eventual role as president. When J.J. was at home, James continuously took the opportunities of raising and bonding with her son away from Jenny. She and her son hardly had any time together or time to get to know each other.

It was no mystery how over time, J.J. acquired all the habits and idiosyncrasies of his father. J.J. walked like his father, stood with the same tilt to his back, and even folded his arms across his chest when talking to others. But most important, J.J. thought just like his father, as well. And now, James was reaping the reward of his training. He had succeeded in turning his son against his mother.

Even though Jenny was there in body, she no longer heard the questions the lawyer asked her son. It was all a blur...

"Mrs. Hamilton, please take the stand…Mrs. Hamilton…"

Jenny's lawyer, Mr. Neels nudged her … "Are you okay?

Jenny was in a daze. Her lawyer quizzed her over and over how to respond to reveal her side of the story. How estranged and lonely her marriage was. How she was warned even before they got married that troubles were impending. She had seen all the signs how deeply James was immersed in his company's interests. Even her father had cautioned her in that relationship. But she hadn't listened to her dad, or her instincts, or all the other obvious signs of James' neuroses. She chose to get married, thinking and hoping it would all change or improve somehow. She soon realized however, that James was married to the corporation and not to her, and that his obsessions were too deeply rooted to go away.

In parts and pieces she heard her lawyer's questions, the objections by James' lawyers and the judge ruling "sustained" over and over. Mr. Neels was asking questions in such a way to give the answers. Clearly he was leading and coaxing her but Jenny couldn't respond. It was against her nature to condemn others and to do so against J.J.'s father was unthinkable. She couldn't bring herself to condemn James in the presence of her son or discuss any of her feelings toward her marriage. Mr. Neels shrugged his shoulders and shook his head. He wasn't getting anywhere and wasn't making any case for her defence try as he might.

Even though Jenny disagreed to bring up the fact that James was cheating on her, her lawyer had no other choice but to try and force his uncooperative client to speak up for herself. He knew what he was about to say would be objected to but he simply wanted to get it out there that James Hamilton was an unfaithful husband and …!

"Mrs. Hamilton, tell the court about Mr. Hamilton's relationship with female staff, in particular…"

"Objection, leading the witness."

"Sustained. Mr. Neels, please rephrase the question."

Jenny stared straight ahead, reluctant to express her belief that James was having an affair with another executive, a very attractive lady whom Jenny had met at one of the social affairs that the company held several times during the year. Her name was Susan Evans. After J.J. was born James never took her to the staff parties any more. Jenny always suspected her husband took his office manager, Susan. But what bothered Jenny even more deeply was that J.J. had bonded more to Susan than to her. It was Susan who tutored J.J. at the office all the time as he grew up. It pained Jenny each time her son raved about the new things he had learned from

Susan at the office.

Unable to get any kind of reply from Jenny, her lawyer raised his hands in frustration and sat down.

Having made the insinuation that James was cheating on her, James' lawyer quickly tried defuse that issue. "Mrs. Hamilton, suspecting that your husband was seeing another woman is hearsay. Do you have any witnesses to corroborate this?" asked Mr. Roberts, one of the several lawyers representing James.

Jenny simply shook her head negatively. She could have said that J.J. more than likely saw them kissing and being together, but she would never have her son get caught in between.

"Do you have any photos or proof of any kind by an outside agency you may have hired?"

Jenny looked at James and then back to the lawyer and stared blankly at him.

"Your lawyer suggested that you were suspicious and had good reason to believe that your husband may be seeing someone else." And then moving closer to Jenny and leaning towards her, he continued, "Mrs. Hamilton, a woman's intuition has to be substantiated with fact. Hard evidence. This is a court of law and what we say has to be substantiated."

Mr. Roberts stared intently at Jenny waiting for some response then pivoted on his heel and returned to the table. "I have no further questions of Mrs. Hamilton, Your Honour."

Jenny, completely absorbed in the deplorable situation she found herself in, just sat in the witness stand. Her mind was swirling... how is this all possible? Perhaps if she had been firmer, more demanding, right from the start...? But that would have gone against her nature. And then when J.J. was born it was too late to leave. She decided to stay in an almost intolerable relationship and environment. She had hoped her presence in the home would give J.J. some sense of a normal upbringing, but she never had a chance. And now James had won the ultimate victory, his coup d'état. He had finally found a way to get rid of her and the weapon he used to do so was...her own son.

THE AFTERNOON SESSION proved to be even more disconcerting for Jenny as the questions turned to money matters.

"Is that your signature on the Inter-Spousal Agreement?"

"Yes," answered Jenny cautiously.

"Were the contents of this document fully explained to you?"

Jenny hesitated to answer. Mr. Hamilton Sr. had explained it to her and so did the lawyer the next day at James' office. She clearly knew by signing the agreement she would relinquish all rights to the company's assets.

"Yes, it was explained, but surely I am entitled to James' share or his personal savings, am I not?"

"Well, let's take one thing at a time. First, it is clear that you agreed to give up your rights to the corporation's financial assets and holdings. Now, since the estate, which includes the house you live in, the cars you and Mr. Hamilton drive and all furnishings, belong to the company, it is also evident that you have no ownership or rights to these assets, either. Do you understand that, Mrs. Hamilton?"

"Ye-yes."

"Now, in regards to Mr. Hamilton's savings and assets, it is much like yours. The small amount he drew as wages, he gave to you to run the household over the years, as a good provider should. There is a substantial trust established for your son, James Junior, but it does not include you nor do you have access to it. The condo Mr. Hamilton lives in is also owned by the corporation and most expenses are paid by the corporation, as well."

"But, James told me after I signed the agreement that he would make certain I was well looked after. Does this mean that after all these years I am entitled to nothing?"

Mr. Roberts gazed at Jenny for a long moment. He was almost hesitant to say what he had to. His employer had made certain through trusts and legal manipulations that Jenny would be entitled to nothing.

"I'm afraid that's the case, Mrs. Hamilton. We want to make certain you and your counsel fully understand our position in this regard."

The lawyer stopped for a brief moment, allowing Jenny to acknowledge what he said and then he added, "Mr. Hamilton however, has always been an excellent and faithful provider. When we submit our offer of settlement to the court, I'm sure you will be well-provided for."

When the settlement was given to Jenny's lawyer, however, James' penny-pinching frugality and lack of consideration for her future was very evident. James' corporation was worth billions. Since diversifying into computer technology and several oil company holdings in Australia and the Middle East, the company's fortunes had skyrocketed. In spite of the wealth James had access to he was prepared to offer a divorce settlement of $250,000. His legal staff was quick to point out that this was a very generous offer since Mr. Hamilton wasn't obligated to give her any more than what he had in his name.

Neither Jenny nor her lawyer could believe how hard-nosed and uncaring James was for Jenny and her future. James' vindictive spirit coupled with his possessiveness for his money was now clearly manifested in the meagre settlement.

The court proceedings finished earlier than expected. Jenny didn't have any witnesses, damaging or supporting evidence to submit to the court other then her own testimony. She could have asked or subpoenaed Matilda to take the stand and perhaps even Charles or Thomas. They knew the real story in the household and the abuse James had subjected her to. But Jenny would never subject Matilda to this and James knew full well that Jenny wouldn't. And calling Charles to testify now that he looked after the condo would certainly mean termination of his employment, and Jenny couldn't in good conscience do that or even contemplate to use others in such a manner.

Mr. Neels also tried to convince Jenny to ask John, the bookstore proprietor to testify that their involvement had been nothing more than a friendship, but she didn't want to involve Patrick or his wife in her divorce proceedings, either. In the end, true to her nature, Jenny accepted full responsibility for her decision to marry James. She could have left years ago, but instead chose to stay for the welfare of her son and to be with him.

Judge Gerian broke into Jenny's train of thought.

"If there are no further witnesses or considerations before the court, there is still time this afternoon for closing arguments. Are you prepared to present your summation… Mr. Roberts? Mr. Neels?"

Since both lawyers agreed, James' attorney went first. Jenny could have easily predicted what they would say. Mr. Roberts gushed about James' generosity and how well he provided for Mrs. Hamilton. Since he spent very little time at the estate, he could have down-sized their home and moved Mrs. Hamilton into an apartment or condo. He chose, however, to leave Mrs. Hamilton in a very comfortable estate, well looked after by a large staff. His company also paid for all the antique furniture his wife wanted even though the home had brand new contemporary furniture. Each year, Mrs. Hamilton was provided with a new car.

Mr. Roberts asserted that very obviously Mr. Hamilton had exceeded his responsibility to his wife. And perhaps more importantly, it was Mr. Hamilton who brought up their son and looked after him in every way. His son on the witness stand confirmed his father's devotion to him and further attested to his father's commitment and faithfulness in the marriage. It was his mother who broke the vows and was the cause of the marriage breakdown by seeing another man.

At the end of the day, the lawyer argued, even if Mr. Hamilton had participated in the demise of the marriage by his absence, Mrs. Hamilton by law, had no rights whatsoever to any of the assets. Everything, absolutely everything, was owned by the corporation and the Spousal Agreement which Mrs. Hamilton had signed prior to the marriage, completely relinquished any rights she had to the firm's assets or James' shares in the company.

Jenny could no longer listen. As had happened to her that morning, the words in the courtroom faded into the background. She visualized herself living in a small apartment, all alone. She would miss the landscaping staff, the grounds, the wildflower garden and her gazebo. And, what about the Angel of Thanksgiving? It was hers, right? Or, did it belong to the corporation, too? Even though it had been a gift from the staff, she had no doubt that James would find a way to keep that as well. Anyway, what would she do with it? It would be too large to move to an apartment. And the antique furni—

"Thank you, Mr. Roberts. Mr. Neels, you may proceed."

Jenny sat up trying to refocus on the proceedings. She wondered what her lawyer could possibly say to sway the judge in her favour. She had severely handicapped her case by instructing her lawyer not to bring up the matter of her rape or her daughter and James' neurotic reaction to it. James would simply deny the rape as further evidence of her promiscuity, which would only support what her son saw and testified against. Why bring up all these issues when at the end of the day it probably wouldn't make any difference in securing further compensation?

She and her counsel knew their hands were tied and at the mercy of James' lack of generosity and his willingness to give whatsoever he desired. James had the law behind him and all Mr. Neels could do was to present a case that might indirectly move James' cold, hard heart to be more equitable in his holdings.

"Thank you, Your Honour." Mr. Neels rose from his desk and stepped towards the bench. "In 1966, Marjorie and James were united in matrimony. They both had just finished university and were eager to begin their life careers and marriage. They both had very little personal wealth except for what their parents had.

"Normally, during a lifetime together, in this case 22 years, a professional couple such as this would have accrued a sizeable estate. A home, automobiles, investments and a savings account would be more than reasonable to expect. Unfortunately, this case is not normal. Prior to this marriage, my client was asked to sign a spousal agreement relinquishing her rights to Mr. Hamilton's family business and assets.

"We concede this is not out of the ordinary, but what isn't common is for the husband, in this case Mr. James Hamilton, to keep everything within the company and virtually nothing as personal wealth. And, through trusts, legal manoeuvring and salary control, Mr. Hamilton kept his personal wealth, to which his wife would have had access, to virtually nothing.

"It is true that my client's sense of business and unquestioning nature didn't cause her to look ahead and think more of her future should problems arise. Rather she went on year after year trusting in her husband and in his sense of fairness to do the right thing. She only knew that in most marriages everything is shared, and never once conceived that it would all come down to this – legal papers, agreements and lawyers deciding the fate of her entitlements."

Mr. Neels walked back to the desk, his shoes tapping on the wood floor, and picked up two sets of papers.

"When we look at Mrs. Hamilton's savings account and the RRSP's she has invested in, it comes to a total of $87,000. She could have saved more if she hadn't contributed much of her salary to the running of the household and buying groceries. It is inconceivable that a man owning a company that is making millions of dollars a week did not provide his wife with sufficient funds to run the household. That she had to use her librarian's salary to subsidize the estate is astounding!

"The settlement offer of $250,000 will not even buy a small home in a respectable area of the city or a condo downtown. If Mr. Hamilton were not a man of means this offer might seem reasonable. But last year..." Mr. Neels put down the papers and picked up a glossy annual report and waved it in the air, "...according to page 18 of the company's annual prospectus, it is mind staggering to note the company's worth was $28.2 billion. Yes, $28.2 *billion*.

"Who would think that a man of such wealth and means would consider such a meagre payment to his wife after 21 years? After giving birth to his son, putting up with an estranged relationship, giving up the prime years of her life in faithful service, this is her reward? How fair and considerate is this? She is now forced to give up a home and style of life that had at least given her some solace in this highly unusual relationship, to live in a small apartment and make ends meet with the small pension she receives from the Teachers' Superannuation Fund.

"In 1966, when Marjorie and James were married, Mr. Hamilton made a commitment to honour, love and look after his spouse. I ask this court, has James Hamilton lived up to his commitment and responsibility? At this crucial point in Mrs. Hamilton's life, where is she at? She has no home, no car, little savings, a small pension that *she* paid into. She is no longer a young woman that can start over. Does the settlement offered show any consideration for Mrs. Hamilton's future and welfare?"

Mr. Neels stopped for a long moment shaking his head from side to side. "The answer is clear. Mrs. Hamilton was only important to Mr. Hamilton insofar as providing an heir for his company. The claim that Mrs. Hamilton inappropriately kissed another man, when she only received a kiss on the cheek from a married friend she had known for years was completely blown out of proportion and used as fodder for Mr. Hamilton to divorce his wife."

Mr. Neels walked right up to the bench and looked directly at Judge Gerian, "I ask this court to find that Mr. Hamilton honour the settlement we have asked for of $5 million dollars. In a matter of minutes, Mr. Hamilton could easily write a cheque for that amount and give his wife just a small portion of her due and fair share.

"$5 million would help Mrs. Hamilton adjust to her new life, help her accrue what she lost over the years and, at the very least, help to compensate her monetarily. Most of the board members of Mr. Hamilton's company make two to three times that amount in any given year. Two made over $20 million last year. Some have only sat on the board for two years and what have they done in comparison to Mrs. Hamilton's 20 years?"

Mr. Neels turned and gazed at Mr. Hamilton. "What has happened to Mrs. Hamilton is shameful. It cannot be stressed enough what has occurred here. Mr. Hamilton has seriously taken advantage of his wife's naïve business sense and her trusting attitude.

"Her mind does not entertain suspicion, especially of a husband. She was completely unaware and unwary of Mr. Hamilton's financial and business affairs and his intentions. She had no idea that he never had any intention of being fair and equitable with his money. We sincerely hope Mr. Hamilton will honour his responsibility to the mother of his son and look after her accordingly."

He turned back to the judge. "Your honour, we ask for your understanding and consideration of the abnormality of this marriage relationship and the arrangement of the finances and assets and do all within your power to right such a serious wrong."

Having heard both sides, Judge Gerian simply looked at both parties. His face showed no expression of siding with either.

"I will deliberate on the submissions and what I have heard and witnessed in this courtroom. We will reconvene Thursday morning at ten o'clock. At such time I will render my decision." With that, he rapped the gavel on the rubber-padded board.

"Court is adjourned."

CHAPTER THREE

"Hɪ, Mᴏᴍ. So family dinner is postponed for the Sunday after next?"

"Yes, Father can't make it this Sunday as a touring missionary is speaking Sunday evening. I would like to attend that and Jeremy and his family are busy this Sunday, too."

"Well, I can hardly wait until then. I can smell the roast beef already!"

"It won't be roast beef, Son I came across a recipe for beef stroganoff that looks very good and instead of potatoes it calls for broad noodles sprinkled with poppy seed. I hope you won't be disappointed."

"Anything you make is great Mom! I'm just looking forward to one of your home cooked meals."

"You can come as often as you want, you know."

"I know, Mom, but with Julean gone, the girls in school, working at the store, and spending time with Justin, it's just too difficult to get there more often."

Mary hesitated for a brief moment and then forged ahead with a question weighing on her mind.

"Are you going to bring your new lady friend on Sunday? The kitchen is crowded, but there's always room for one more?"

Henry was silent for a moment as well before answering.

"I don't know, Mom, I'd be too uncomfortable with Ivania there around the kids...you know."

"Well you have gone out with her several times and the children are aware of her and I would love to meet her."

"Perhaps some other time, Mom."

"And how do you pronounce her name? Is it Ivan-ia?"

"Not quite. Combine the "ia" so the ending sounds like "yuh," Ivan-yuh, not Ivania."

"Oh, I'll get the hang of it. It took me a little while to get the correct pronunciation of Julean's name as well. For the longest time I called the last part of her name "Ann" instead of Ju-lee-un."

"Yeah, I always loved the sound of Julean's name and I must admit Ivania sounds interesting as well."

"I believe you told me she was from Russia?"

"Yes, she came to Canada with her parents and two brothers when she was 7 years of age. She told me she was named after her Czechoslovakian grandmother who had married a Russian man during the First World War."

"Well, Allison has seen her both in the café and at the gallery and your daughter tells me that Ivan-yuh is a very attractive lady." Mary said with a strong emphasis on the correct pronunciation of the name.

"She is all of that, Mom and twelve years younger than I."

"Age isn't a major factor, son, as long as you care for one another. Look how much in love Jeremy and Camilla are and there's a large age spread there as well."

"I suppose you're right, Mom … it's just that I'm not interested in getting too serious at this point in my life. I know it's been three years yet the memories are still so fresh and I still …" Henry was going to say that his heart still ached for Jenny, but thought better of it.

It didn't matter anyway as Mary already finished the sentence in her mind. The last letter Jenny sent to Henry with the Pewter Angel inside that she had hidden inside her treasure chest had been on her mind lately as well. Henry's next words broke into her thoughts.

"And like I said, I'm a little uncomfortable to bring her around the kids. You know, what would they think of me going out with another woman? … I just don't know… Father Engelmann encouraged me to go out, too. We'll see. Let's see how this develops. By the way did Camilla's dad go back to Victoria?" Henry asked, wanting to change the subject.

"Yes, I was talking with Camilla this morning. She called and asked if she could bring anything over for dinner on Sunday. I told her immediately that her Caesar salad is amazing. I love the garlic and anchovies she adds. It gives it such a nice flavour."

"Yeah, it's a great recipe. So I'll have that to look forward too."

"Every time I see that girl, she looks so familiar—"

"It's Jenny, Mom. She's the spitting image of Jenny the girl that lived three doors down the street when I started grade nine. Do you still remember her?"

It was as if the phone went dead. Henry could hear his mother's gasp followed by heavy breathing.

Mary started out slowly. "My gosh, Henry, yes, … yes, that's exactly right. Isn't that silly of me not to make that connection over the past two years? Yes, she does look like Jennifer…the blonde hair and blue eyes and just every bit as pretty as Jenny was. Same oval face I might add too."

"Seems to me you recall Jenny quite well, Mom. The first time Jeremy brought her home I nearly fell over. I thought I had traveled thirty years back in time and Jenny Sarsky was walking through my door."

"It's true, Son, now that you have jogged my memory, Camilla's resemblance to Jenny is striking."

"I bet you, Mom, I've played that dinner scene the day I first met Camilla over in my mind a thousand times. I sat on the edge of my chair when I asked her, 'Camilla, tell us a little about your parents. What do they do? And…what is your mother's name?' I fully expected her to say Jenny, …but when the name Valerie tumbled out of her mouth it was like my world collapsed. Impossible! There must be some mistake. I asked her again, 'Did you say Valerie?' She looked at me quizzically and nodded, 'Yes, Valerie and my Dad is Stanley…Valerie and Stanley Breckhart.'

I couldn't believe it, Mom, and when I met the Breckhart's I was blown away again. I fully expected that at least one of the parent's would have blonde hair and Camilla's features, but there was no resemblance whatsoever."

"Yes, I noted that when Jeremy and Camilla married and I first met her parents. I was surprised how the Breckhart's are short and stocky and big boned while Camilla is slim and taller. Her complexion is so fair while the Breckhart's is ruddy and… and her hair colour doesn't have a bit of black in it like her parents."

"See? That's exactly right! I am so glad Mrs. Breckhart was alive up until last year, so we could see first hand how completely different both parents are from their daughter. Camilla's hair is as blonde as …as… Jenny's." Henry's voice trailed off softly as he whispered his first love's name.

Mary was silent for a moment. She had to admit that she came to the same conclusion. Henry broke into her train of thought again…

"And I don't know if I ever told you, Mom, but I always thought Jenny had a baby…"

"Yes, I do recall you sharing that with me. Some boys overcame you and Jenny and took her to the park."

"Yeah, I always had felt over the years that Jenny was raped that night and later gave birth to a child. One of Eddy's friends, Pete was one of the guys involved and apparently he dreams of that night as well. He told Eddy that he thinks Jenny gave birth to a baby girl with blonde hair and blue eyes that he fathered. It's all so weird. When I saw Camilla for the first time everything sort of came together for me: what Pete said, my intuition that she was raped and became pregnant, the name Camilla …and that, Camilla was Jenny's daughter."

"But she isn't, Son. Camilla claims that Valerie and Stanley Breckhart are her natural parents."

"Yes, I asked Jeremy on several occasions about Camilla's background and he too confirms that Mr. and Mrs. Breckhart are Camilla's parents, but it just doesn't seem right somehow…"

"It's true, Son, Camilla's resemblance to Jenny is striking." Mary said cautiously. She remembered only too well that conversation she'd had with Henry shortly after Julean's death when Henry told her of his love for Jenny, how Julean knew everything, and how even after knowing all that, Mary still had opted not to share Jenny's letter with Henry.

"And to think, it turns out that it's not Jenny who Camilla is related to, but Julean!"

"Did I hear you correctly? Did you say Camilla is related to our Julean, your wife!?"

"You heard me correctly alright, Mom. Before Camilla and Jeremy got married I talked to Stan about his family background and nationality. I couldn't believe it when he told me that his great-grandparents were Mormon. Apparently there was quite a ruckus over the multiple marriages of their founder, Joseph Smith. I recall Julean telling me about that, too. I think it was in the late 1800's that the practice of multiple marriages was banned and the community started to split up. Stan's great-grandparents were the first to move away from the Utah community to go on their own. Apparently Stan's great-grandparents moved to Cardston, Alberta, where Julean's parents were from, where they raised six boys. I can't remember the exact details anymore but I think Stan was an offspring from one of the six boys. I'll have to ask Camilla how they eventually got to Ottawa."

"That sounds interesting, Son but it doesn't really give any clue as to why there is such a dramatic difference between them and their daughter nor does it explain how Julean could possibly be related to Camilla!"

"That's exactly what I was leading up to, Mom. The Breckhart's are related to Julean's Aunt Netta and Uncle Jacob. Seems to me Stan said they were the third or fourth distant cousins and I suppose if we go back enough, Julean would also be related to Camilla somehow."

Henry was silent for a long moment and spoke in such a soft voice,

Mary strained to hear what he said.

"And I was just thinking, Mom, about Camilla and Julean and Jenny and how crazy it all seems. Even though I know that Camilla isn't Jenny's daughter and that she's a long-lost relative of Julean's, it still just blows me away that Camilla came into our lives, married Jeremy and indirectly became my daughter! It's all very strange…supernatural…"

"Oh my, Henry it is quite something and, you're right …it would have been even more so had Camilla proved to be…Jenny's daughter…" Mary's words trailed off again revealing that she too still had some doubts about Camilla's upbringing and past.

Henry knew what his mother had in mind.

"I know, Mom. The resemblance is uncanny and her background fits into so many things that happened in the past. Jenny said that she would call her first daughter, Camilla. And… and if we calculate back from Camilla's present age, she would have been born in 1957 the exact year that Jenny would have given birth had she been raped and impregnated and…it was also the time I always had such severe stomach aches which all of sudden stopped that spring. It's so uncanny and yet if the Breckharts are Camilla's parents then something extremely coincidental has happened. In fact, Mom, there are just too many coincidences for this all to be a coincidence…if you know what I mean."

The phone went silent for a moment before Mary came up with something positive that could come out of all this…

"Well even so, Son, if Camilla can't be Jenny's daughter then at least she is related to Julean in the distant past which makes us all family somehow."

"Yeah, I suppose you're right, Mom. It's what makes life so interesting. One just never knows what life is going to toss at you next…"

"Yes, Son,"

This time it was Mary who changed the subject. "I am so looking forward to have everyone come for dinner Sunday night. Are you picking up Father on the way or is Jeremy?"

"No, I am picking him up. And yeah, it will be great to have all of us together. Soon the kids will be moving out and going on their own and these special times will become less and less."

"Yes, it brings tears to my eyes just to think on it. I hate to see Allison move to Radway, Alberta this fall but her choice of career is so worthy."

"That's right. She struggled with her faith when Julean died. She was so angry with God. Yet, she got over it and is attending the bible college there. I wonder where this will lead to?"

"It's up to the Lord. I'm sure she is following the plan that He wills for her life."

"Well, Mom, I better go. I haven't had breakfast yet and I want to take the dogs for a run in the valley later."

"Oh, I'm so glad you have taken a day off! You work far too much, son. Ever since that dear wife of yours passed away you've immersed yourself much too much in all the things you do."

"Yeah, I know you're right, yet it's just my nature to have four or five things on the go."

"Well, take the time to enjoy and appreciate all you have been blessed with. Just the sight of the valley with the prayer house and wild-flower meadow surrounding it takes my breath away. And yes, I better run too and let you enjoy your day off."

"Bye, Mom, love you."

"And I love you too, Son."

MARY HELD THE phone for a long time as her mind swirled over the conversation with Henry. She knew that she had to give Jenny's letter to Henry. She held back for the longest time over her concern that Jenny was married and it would all be for naught anyway… It would only upset Henry, and yet Mary's guilt and the glowing light around her treasure chest was simply not going away, but getting stronger by the day.

If she was ever going to have peace, Mary knew she must be truthful with her son, regardless of the circumstances. *Oh, but now he has met a new lady friend… It may be healing for Henry to start his life again. What good could it bring to give him Jenny's letter now …?*

Mary felt confused and more guilt-ridden than ever. She hung up the phone still thinking what would have happened if she had given Jenny's letter to Henry just before he and Julean married? Where would destiny have led everyone to this day? Would Julean have wed another? Would she be alive today?

Oh, my dear sweet Jesus, I have played God for all too long. I have tried to do what was best for all, but…please, Oh dear Lord, give me the wisdom and strength to do what is best. Forgive me, Lord.

CHAPTER FOUR

HENRY SLOWLY HUNG up the phone his mind still so focused and preoccupied on the possibility that Camilla was Jenny's daughter. An eerie feeling crawled up and down his spine.

"What do you make of all this Julean? And what about Ivania, where does she fit in?" Henry silently muttered as he made his way into the sun-room and gazed out of the window into the valley below.

Henry mulled over the interview he had with Brenda. He wondered when the article would come out. Since he lived out of town on an acreage near Lumsden, the Sunday Sun would not be delivered to their place. He'd have to keep an eye out for it. He hoped Brenda would mention Julean's name in the article and how she had helped out in the gallery when it first opened.

It was hard to believe that his dear sweet wife had passed away over three years ago. It seemed like yesterday; his feelings for her were still so deep and strong. He reached into his trouser pocket and pulled out Julean's rosary and his hand automatically fingered one crystal bead and then another. It was her last gift to him. Henry still marvelled how easily her fingers opened, giving him her rosary, her most treasured possession, as she lay there in the coffin. He was glad that he had accepted her gift as it always gave him solace. At times he felt certain he could feel the warmth and comfort of her hands emanating off of it.

He carried the rosary with him every day, and at night before he undressed he would take the rosary out of his pocket and toss it on the bed. Upon retiring, Henry would pray the rosary again and dream that he was snuggled up to her with his arm around her, his fingers intertwined in hers. Some nights the aching and longing for Julean was so intense, Henry would cry himself to sleep.

Those first hours, days and months were so difficult without his dear sweet wife at his side. It was a good thing Father Engelmann was there to help him through. He always seemed to be there like an angel ready to help, minister and console.

Father was there for Henry when Jenny left, too. Incredibly, his feelings for Jenny had never left him over all those years. He was thankful that Julean was so understanding of the memories he held of his first love. Hours before her death, she even encouraged him to seek Jenny out and said she would help him. Her words stayed with him to this day, "When I get to heaven I will pray for her or someone else like her to return to you. A man like you should marry again and not be alone."

Henry believed that it was possible for Julean's spirit to guide him in the same way he believed in the guidance, promptings and protection of his guardian angel. He recalled when he was at the cemetery shortly after her death how she had appeared beside John McBryne and helped him to forgive the very man that caused her death. And for months now his feelings for Jenny seemed to have been strengthening along with the star of the east that he and Jenny shared.

He wouldn't have been aware of the star had he not seen the spirit of Julean standing on the deck of his farmhouse outside of the sun-room earlier that past spring. He remembered feeling prompted to make a cup of tea and as he passed the patio doors, he looked out and there was Julean, gazing towards the eastern sky. He rushed outside, but Julean disappeared, leaving in her wake the brilliance of the star of the east which immediately touched his heart.

He felt Jenny.

The love radiating from the star was *unmistakable*. It was like feeling Jenny standing next to him. Well over twenty years had elapsed since he had felt those wonderful feelings of his first love.

And just this past July 6th, the anniversary day he and Jenny had met, his dreams of Jenny were so vivid and real. He even woke up to catch himself calling out to her early that morning. How difficult it must have been for Julean to hear him whisper loving thoughts to another in his dreams.

But that night as well, the evening of their anniversary, Henry made a point of looking to the east at twilight and sure enough, the first star of the east shone in all its glory. There was no mistaking it; the star's warm rays of love penetrating his heart were *Jenny's*.

Henry was filled with hope, yet did it really have any significance? Was his dear sweet wife leading him back to Jenny or was it to another?

Henry had first noticed Ivania shortly after he opened the gallery and café. Julean was still alive at the time and on several occasions he noticed her briefly chatting with Ivania when she paid her lunch bill at the cashier's station. One day however, Ivania was not there for lunch but for business purposes. She came into the gallery and presented Henry with her business card along with a short description of her occupation.

"Good afternoon, Mr. Pederson, my name is Ivania Gorbachov." She presented Henry with her business card and continued, "I'm a financial advisor and estate planner. I would very much like to meet with you and Mrs. Pederson to discuss your long term plans ..."

Henry recalled he didn't much listen or pay attention to the rest of her spiel but had to admit that her accent and stunning facial features captivated him. He had seen her in the café many times and only exchanged greetings. But that day Henry could see that the woman wearing a two piece banker grey suit standing across the counter from him was a very intelligent, sophisticated and attractive lady in her thirties.

Her hair was neat, tightly combed from the front of her forehead to the back and coming together into an impeccably curved bun. What interested Henry was the streak of blonde that was nestled into her dark brown hair just off centre to the left side of her head. It was odd and yet striking…It drew one's attention.

But what captivated his interest even more was her European accent. He recalled Julean telling him that Ivania came from Russia when she was just seven years old. But even though Ivania had grown up in Canada her spoken English retained a light Russian articulation that was clearly evident when she said certain words. Henry suspected that it was purposeful; that Ivania was aware that it made her more attractive and intriguing somehow.

Perhaps what affected Henry most powerfully was when Ivania spoke his name. It was then that her light Russian accent turned heavy. She pronounced his name with a "d" just in front of the "r"… Hen-dry. Henry liked the sound and whenever she spoke his name it sent a tingle through him.

Ivania's Russian background together with her stunning figure and attractiveness always brought a sense of intrigue into Henry's mind every time he saw her in the restaurant. Often times as he studied her he thought that Ivania would make the perfect spy. She would be able to lure even the most cautious politician into a scandalous affair.

Despite Henry's intrigue with Ivania, their relationship was always on a business and professional level. Even after Julean passed away. One day however, that all seemed to change when Ivania came into the restaurant on her day off. It was a busy lunch time rush, and Henry was assisting the hostess in seating customers who were waiting in line. Suddenly Ivania appeared before him and Henry barely recognized her! She was wearing a bright yellow and green summer dress, as opposed to her usual business suit attire. Her hair, usually pulled back quite severely, albeit strikingly, was now down and flowing well beyond her shoulders. The blond streak in her hair had expanded at least three to four inches and drew even more attention to her strong attractive features.

Henry was momentarily speechless, frozen in the moment.

Standing before him was another side of Ivania that he had never envisioned! It was like seeing another woman altogether and ... *Something within him stirred.* He never thought another woman besides Jenny or Julean could ever excite him... *But he was wrong.*

"Is that you, Ivania?" Henry asked, with total surprise in his gawking eyes.

"Yes, Hen-dry, it is me, Ivania. I do let my hair down on occasion."

Henry chuckled nervously. In a way, Ivania's brown hair with the blonde streak reminded Henry of both Jenny and Julean. Ivania captured both of his loves. He could see Jenny's blonde wheat coloured hair softly nestled in the brown colour of his dear wife's hair.

"Well, are you going to show me to a seat in your café Hen-dry or must I do it myself?"

"Yes, yes, of course...It's just that I have never seen this side of you Ivania and I must say... *it's very nice!*"

Not often did Ivania blush at the words of a man, but at that moment her luminous white skin revealed a hint of pink, as she cast her eyes uncharacteristically downward.

Henry showed Ivania to a table beside a window and felt compelled to join her. He fingered Julean's rosary in his pocket as if to ask his dear wife permission to do so. It was an awkward moment but Henry sensed Ivania wouldn't mind. Her soft, dark hazel eyes seemed to welcome him.

"Do you mind if I sit down?" Henry asked coolly, feeling a little silly at his teenager approach.

"No, I would love for you to. Please Hen-dry, by all means, sit."

Henry sat opposite her beside the south window. As the sun streamed in and struck Ivania's face, Henry was reminded of Anna Engelmann, reading the bible by the south window in their living quarters above the store. There was a similar elegance and sophistication about Ivania that was hard to pin point.

Was it the way she held her head and wore her hair up like Anna did, Henry analyzed? Or was it her graceful stance and the way she moved her arms? Then again, perhaps it was all of those things... Henry was surprised how much he had already taken notice of this particular patron.

Ivania smiled, waiting for Henry to speak but Henry just blushed; he was so out of practice speaking to a woman for whom he had feelings, he was unable to come up with that first line. And then Ivania, just like Jenny would have, naturally started up the conversation.

"I hope the kitchen has the Minestrone soup on today. It's delicious and so is the grilled cheese with Pesto and tomatoes. I would never have thought up that combination."

"Matthew is a good cook and a creative one at that."

As Ivania continued to talk about another dish she enjoyed, Henry checked her hand and didn't see any ring. He had noted that the last two times she had been in, but wanted to make doubly sure once more as his heart was beating fast at the thought of perhaps asking her out for dinner. To the best of his recollection, Ivania had never mentioned that she was married. He could tell she was a lot younger than he was, but the way she looked at him when their eyes met simply said, *'I'm interested in you.'*

"I noticed that you haven't been in for awhile, Ivania."

"Yes, the man I have been seeing for the last four years had a tragic and fatal accident over two months ago. He was a mining engineer and he along with two of his colleagues and the pilot were killed in northern Saskatchewan when flying up there to inspect a Uranium mine. The plane crashed in the wilderness and it took the search party over two weeks to locate them. There were no survivors."

Ivania's eyes teared up and she softly whispered, "We were to wed in the fall."

"I'm so sorry to hear that, Ivania." Henry wanted to reach over and touch her hand, but wasn't sure if it was appropriate. He noticed the line up at the door and thought he better start assisting the hostess.

"Thank you for letting me join you, Ivania. I better help seat the customers. I'll send a waiter over right away to take your order."

Henry reached forward and touched Ivania's hand, turned and left.

From that day on, the relationship between Henry and Ivania changed.

While Henry considered it more of a close friendship, he sensed that Ivania considered it more seriously.

Henry shook his head as he recalled how Ivania had come into his life, almost at the same time as feelings for Jenny had started to resurface. What did it all mean? It was all so confusing. *I don't know what I'm feeling anymore.*

CHAPTER FIVE

TWO DAYS LATER, Jenny and her lawyer waited in the courtroom. James and his entourage had set up shop at the table opposite. It bothered Jenny deeply that their marriage had come to this. What hurt her even more was the presence of her son sitting next to his father; such a defiant act against her. At least the other day when J.J. was called as a witness, he sat in the public pews, but today, he sat at the same table as his father. The sight of seeing her son put in such a position that he would have to choose between his mother and father was almost too much for Jenny to bear.

What have I done wrong for my son to have such a blatant disregard for my feelings? I tried to be a good mother in the little time I was allotted with him. Jenny swallowed hard trying to hold back her tears.

Jenny saw J.J. cast quick, furtive glances her way. She could sense that underneath his bold exterior he was troubled by all this. She felt for him and loved him deeply. He was so much like James and, yet, what was their relationship really like? Was it really love and loyalty that J.J. felt towards his father or was it fear? That was how James controlled everyone around him: he instilled fear.

J.J. had witnessed what happened to executives who violated their loyalty, how quickly they were terminated and at times, even black-balled from ever finding another job in the city. Jenny felt certain J.J. would never cross his father out of fear that he would meet the same fate as these unfortunate men.

It was just a natural spillover from everyday observation of events, but then again, J.J. knew his ultimate destiny and purpose in the whole scheme of things. He knew he had been groomed from the day of his birth, like some prince born into a royal family; he knew that his destiny was to take command of an empire. And every fibre of his body knew that he could never jeopardize that utmost goal and consummate expectation of him.

"All rise. His Honour, Judge Gerian presiding."

The judge entered from a door behind the bench. Everyone stood until His Honour was seated.

"Please be seated," directed the court attendant.

Judge Gerian waited until everyone had taken their seats and all the shuffling had died down. He started to speak, then stopped and looked at James' table and then at Jenny's for a long moment. He seemed almost hesitant to state his decision. He looked down at his notes, tightened his lips then slowly looked up.

"The decision I have made, comes after much thought and deliberation. What didn't come out in the proceedings was why the relationship was estranged and why Mrs. Hamilton didn't leave earlier on. I assume Mrs. Hamilton stayed for the sake of her son. In this case, however, such information or knowledge would not have helped the court.

"Normally in divorce proceedings an equitable division of assets is sought which is fair to both parties. This should be the case for a marriage that has gone on for over 21 years. As a result I would be remiss if I didn't come to a decision which was favourable to you both.

"However, as Mr. Neels pointed out in his summation and I have already alluded to as well, this marriage relationship was not normal. It is hard to believe that no assets were accumulated outside of the company in both your names and for Mr. Hamilton not to have acquired a large savings account, shares outside of the company or personal investments. It is unfortunate that Mrs. Hamilton did not question this earlier on and the way in which the Spousal agreement was structured to shelter Mr. Hamilton's shares. Better yet, had she the foresight that her husband would keep everything within the business and trusts, it would have been wise on her part not to have signed the Spousal Agreement. "

James' lawyers started to talk and laugh amongst themselves. They could see where the judge was heading and smugly congratulate James.

"Order, order in the court!"

Silence prevailed at once as Judge Gerian looked compassionately at Mrs. Hamilton and went on. "I thought that I could make the division of the estate more equitable by making a claim on the property on which you lived. However, I know that if I were to decide to make such an order, Mr. Hamilton would immediately appeal my decision based on the law surrounding the Spousal Agreement you signed prior to your marriage. Should he lose, again, it is my sense of human nature, that Mr. Hamilton will appeal until the court decides to grant him his due rights under the law. It is my regrettable decision therefore, to save you further heartache and expense—"

James Hamilton's lawyers chattered amongst themselves and shifted noticeably in their seats. Judge Gerian immediately restored silence with the wave of his hand.

Returning his gaze to Mrs. Hamilton, his voice once again compassionate, the judge continued.

"To save you from further grief and expense, which you will now find yourself very limited to, I cannot order Mr. Hamilton to give you any more than the settlement he has offered. It is my sincere hope that some understanding and consideration will be extended to you by your husband and he finds it within him to be generous and fair towards you.

"Certainly after 21 years, there must be some feeling towards each other, some obligation, some debt, some commitment, and some responsibility. I ask you both to work out a solution which reflects what I have just said and to reach within your hearts to be kind to each other."

The judge's sympathetic look for Jenny turned into a stern gaze as he rested his eyes on Mr. Hamilton. He seemed to want to say more, but thought better of it. He picked up his gavel and reluctantly, weakly let it fall, its sound so soft it was barely audible. In a tone which carried dissatisfaction with his decision, he almost disgustedly declared, "Court is adjourned."

As Judge Gerian left the bench, the hooting and hollering resumed at James Hamilton's table. Jenny had tears in her eyes, as she looked over at the scene. It was her son placing his hand on his dad's shoulder, patting it as if to say, "Way to go Dad" that pierced Jenny's heart as if with a knife.

Jenny's lawyer turned to her and apologized for the outcome.

"My hands were tied, if it weren't for the Spousal Agreem—"

"Shush," interrupted Jenny, "it's okay, I was too naïve and trusting. But isn't everyone when they're young and in love?"

"It's that no-good husband of yours. He has no heart, never did, and never will. You're better off without him."

As soon as her lawyer said those words, Jenny recalled the heeding her father gave her years ago. It seemed like forever, now. "Go out with other boys. It's the only way to compare hearts, Jenny. You may see things in others that are not in James. I have seen too many business types like him…" He had tried to warn her of what was to come. He had seen it. Unfortunately, she had just laughed off his prophecy.

"It's all too late now, Dad," she muttered under her breath.

"What was that, Mrs. Hamilton?"

"Oh, it's nothing, Alan. Just thinking about some advice a very important someone in my life once gave me and foolishly, I didn't heed it."

As Jenny walked to her car, she couldn't shake her father's words of encouragement for her to go out with other boys.

"Why didn't I?" reflected Jenny. "Come to think of it, there were only two men in my life, James and Henry."

Jenny always felt guilty when her mind drifted back all those years to when she was young and so much in love with the boy next door. She now allowed her mind to go there. There was no further need to suppress those thoughts and remain obligated to James. There was no more James in her life. In a way Jenny felt relieved, she was free again.

As Jenny slipped into her car, the liberation she felt moments ago was replaced by loneliness. She needed a hug, to feel she was loved and the only person who immediately surfaced to her mind yet again was Henry, her first and, yes, her only real love.

"I know he is married, has a family and is happy. And yet, I wonder why he never answered any of the letters I sent him? I thought we were so in love."

Jenny leaned back against the hot leather seat warmed by the afternoon sun. She recalled how they first met in Mr. Engelmann's grocery store. She had seen him come in and duck behind one of the aisles so he wouldn't see her stare. She smiled as he knocked over the stack of salmon tins at the end of the aisle and thought how it would be a perfect way to meet him by helping him pick up the tins.

"I think from the moment I looked into his green eyes, I loved him."

Jenny thought about the dates they'd had, the notes they wrote to each other and how their love grew deeper and deeper as the summer passed.

"And poor Mom, how concerned she got about us, getting so close, seeing too much of each other, worried that I might get pregnant..." Jenny whispered. She smiled as she recalled the time they nearly made love in the park.

"Oh, how I wish we had! Perhaps then, things might have been different. Perhaps then, Henry and I would have eventually married and... Oh, Jenny! Those days are over and long gone. This is all just wishful thinking now."

Jenny put the key into the ignition and started the convertible.

And just before she put her – or, rather, James' – BMW into gear, she thought about the letters.

"When we moved to Ottawa, Henry and I promised to write to each other. I kept my promise. I wrote so many letters to him and he never answered one of them. Not even one."

She stomped on the gas so hard that the tires squealed as the car thrust backwards with a sudden burst of acceleration. She sensed a release of pent up emotions as frustration and anger came to the fore. She wasn't sure towards whom she should direct them? James? Her son? Herself? Henry for not writing? If only he had written, things might have been different.

"Life can be so cruel."

Such a thought was usually alien to Jenny. She loved life, but somehow life hadn't reciprocated. She took a deep breath and as she expelled more tension, a tear rolled down her cheek and then another. All the suppressed emotions from the last few days surfaced. But it was the thoughts of Henry, her realization that her first love still lay buried deep within her heart, that brought it all to the fore. If only he were not married.

Jenny slowly drove home, sobbing uncontrollably, helplessly. She so needed to love and be loved. Her only solace was to immerse herself in feelings of nostalgic regret over a love that should have been.

THE NEXT DAY, Jenny got her diary from the secret drawer in the living room and made her way through the kitchen to the grounds out back. The house seemed so empty and lonely since Matilda and Charles had left. For days and months after, Jenny's heart yearned to have them back. But, true to form, James had taken away from Jenny anything and everything that gave her joy.

Matilda had been an especially loyal and close friend. They would have conversations that sisters would share. Matilda knew about Jenny's diary. Jenny shivered when she remembered the morning when, in her haste to get ready for school, she'd left her diary on the end table in the living room intending to put it in the secret desk drawer after her shower, but forgot. Later that afternoon James had popped in unexpected, saw it and picked it up. Matilda came into the room just as he was about to open it.

"Oh, that be mine, Mr. Hamilton," Matilda quickly intervened. "I be keepin' my favourite recipes in there. I was showing some of them to Mrs. Hamilton, just this very morning." She bravely walked over and took it from James' hand and dashed back into the kitchen.

They'd nervously laughed over that incident so many times. Had James opened the diary he would have known so many of her secrets. It would have been catastrophic for Jenny and Matilda if James had read the diary.

Jenny stepped out into the morning air and was greeted by a swarm of Monarch butterflies. Their wings seemed to be fluttering more rapidly just at the sight of her. To Jenny the Monarchs were like angels flitting about. She often thought that one of them was her friend, Tammy, coming in disguise to pay her a visit. She reached up and one quickly settled on the palm of her hand. Perhaps this one was her friend, Jenny mused. In a few short weeks the Monarchs would begin their long trek back to Mexico and she would be leaving too. Not as far, but she would miss the beauty of it all.

If it had not been for the grounds with its array of flowers, the butterflies and beautiful landscaping, she would have left long ago. However, the pleasure and peace of nature, the scent in the air filled with the natural perfume of all the flowers and pungent smell of herbs still gave her enough comfort and relief to stay. And at the heart of it all was the Angel of Thanksgiving. She never failed to fill Jenny with peace and joy. How many times when the storms of life were closing in on her was she lifted back into the light by her angel? She could never thank her father enough for commissioning such a beautiful gift for her. Whenever she sat in the angel's presence, she felt her father's love.

Jenny loved to walk along the winding path feasting her eyes on the beauty before her. Wherever she turned, different plants and flowers bloomed. Just as one flower stopped flowering another would bloom to take its place. From early spring to late fall the grounds glowed with the scent and beauty of a kaleidoscope of colours. Thomas was an artistic landscape genius. He knew God's creation better than his own name.

She wondered where Thomas was?

"Oh, I hope and pray James didn't let him go, too," Jenny muttered. She felt instant relief to see the top of his head bobbing up and down as he trimmed one of the hedges. She loved Thomas as much as Matilda. They both had such a kind manner and way about them. Their words were so calming and peaceful. They truly were special servants of God.

The wildflower patch never looked better. Her spirits lifted at the sight of the morning dew glistening with the healing essence of the flowers. Jenny bent down and picked a buttercup before entering the gazebo. She smelled the flower and, like the butterflies, licked the moisture off its petals as she sat in her chair and began to swing.

The Angel of Thanksgiving looked so brilliant, too, as the sun bounced off the gleaming white marble. She thought of the morning she first saw it and how it had emerged out of the mist as a luminous apparition. She thought for sure she had died and gone to heaven. It was such a precious gift from the staff to show their love and support for her. It was so amazing how the statue had found its way back to her. Tears filled Jenny's eyes over the miracle of the statue seemingly created and brought to her out of the love and friendship of those around her. A tear fell from her cheek onto the open diary. She brushed it away with her finger and wrote:

Aug. 3, 1986

In another two days I shall leave this beautiful garden. Thank you Lord for all the joy and solace Your creation has given to me. I shall especially miss the people here and the support and comfort they have shown. Thank you too for James, the comfort of his home, this heavenly garden and our son. Someday perhaps, James will stop his race to own the world and enjoy the treasure that is right under his nose.

Jenny rose, still holding that latter thought in her mind, and picked a beautiful array of flowers from the wildflower patch. She especially loved the Blue flax, Baby Blue Eyes, Cornflower, and Sweet Alyssum in the mix.

"Oh, I better add a Forget-Me-Not. There. This looks so lovely, perhaps the best combination I have ever put together." She placed the bouquet in the angel's basket. "This is for you, James. Thank you for allowing me to share your garden. This is truly the best gift you have given me in all the years of our marriage. Above all else, I choose to remember this part of our relationship. I offer it up to you now in thanksgiving and pray that someday you will derive the great joy and happiness it has given to me."

Jenny rested her hand on the angel's arm for support and stood on her tiptoes to kiss the angel on the cheek. She allowed her hand to slide down the smooth arm of the angel holding the basket, her hand eventually falling on the flowers she had just put there. She patted the bouquet and softly and ever so gently whispered, "For you, James, just for you."

Jenny wandered along the interconnecting paths. It was approaching noon and the warm sun soothed her troubled spirit. Now that she and James were officially divorced, she would have to get ready to leave. She had anticipated this day for a while and had looked at a few apartments on the west side. There was one in particular that drew her back. She really didn't care for the size of the apartment; it felt confined after living in such a huge mansion for all those years. What appealed to her was the courtyard and the beautiful array of flowers it displayed.

In the centre was a small trestle, four concrete pillars with boards spanning across the top to provide some shade from the sun with a bench below. It wasn't like the gazebo she was used to, but she knew she needed a little getaway and to be surrounded by the things she so loved that had comforted her all the years while she lived basically alone.

She strolled through the grounds for over an hour. She had retraced her steps several times, but she didn't mind. It was like opium to her. She could never get enough of the beauty of nature. Just as she gently reached into the sky to entice a butterfly to land on her hand her beloved gardener came up the walk.

"Good afternoon, Mrs. Hamilton," said Thomas, "A pleasant day to be strolling about."

"Yes, it certainly is, Thomas. By the way, I shall be leaving soon…" and for a moment Jenny found it difficult to speak, "and…I just want you to know how much I love the way you look after the garden and all the flowers. I know you love what you do. It shows, Thomas."

"Why, thank you, Ma'am. I do enjoy what I do very much, and I must say, it gives me great pleasure to see the joy you derive from all this, as well."

Jenny smiled.

"Will you be gone for long, Mrs. Hamilton?"

Jenny was taken aback by his question. Should she tell him what was going on or just wave it off? She thought about it for a moment. He would be the first one to share this with.

"Thomas, Mr. Hamilton and I have seen it fit to end our marriage. I will be leaving within a few days and I doubt very much that I will ever be back."

"Oh my. Oh my. Mrs. Hamilton, what can I say? That is such sorrowful news. I will truly miss you. Oh my, this is so sad to hear. Is there any chance that…?"

"No, Thomas. I'm afraid it is indeed over. It was official, yesterday." She looked lovingly into Thomas's eyes. They were filled with compassion, almost as if he wanted to hug her and hold her. His eyes usually so white against his dark skin and added tan from working in the sun all day, slowly turned red as tears welled up in his eyes.

Jenny approached him, ignored his dirty hands, his soiled clothes and hugged him tenderly.

"Thank you, Thomas, I shall miss you." She released him, then turned and headed back towards the house.

It was approaching mid-afternoon and she still hadn't had her lunch. Perhaps she would go out for an early dinner to her favourite café before going to see her mother. With all the goings-on over the past few days, Jenny hadn't had a chance to visit her. Jenny had called several times, but she was either asleep or not well enough to come to the phone.

Before she entered the kitchen, she turned and looked at all the beauty she would have to leave behind. *Unfortunately, all the beauty was out there, and none was ever inside of our marriage.*

AFTER A GLASS of Chardonnay, Jenny's appetite somewhat revived, she ordered a light mushroom vegetarian dish. Her favourite waiter was on duty this evening, which helped pick up her spirits.

All the male servers in the restaurant envied Keith as Jenny always sat in his section. The café was brighter than on her usual evening visits and, as the late afternoon light streamed through the window, it gave a glow to Jenny's skin. At 45, she looked 35, perhaps younger. As soon as she entered the café, she felt the gazes of the other patrons follow her.

Jenny's mind was just beginning to wander back to the judge's final words in the courtroom the day before, when Keith arrived with her order.

"Oh, that looks delicious, Keith."

"Enjoy, Mrs. Hamilton."

Jenny sipped her wine, then delved into her meal.

"Mmm, this is good," Jenny muttered under her breath as the sauce tantalized her taste buds. She was so glad she had stumbled across this café over a year ago. She had taken the wrong turn to a near by Mall and noticed the sign advertise French cuisine. She was glad she had stopped and tried the restaurant out. The owner who was also the chef was from France and the sauce he put on every meal she tried, was absolutely delicious. She liked the quaintness and charm of the café. It sort of reminded her of being in Paris or some equally romantic place. Perhaps she would travel there some day instead of just reading about it.

As she ate, her mind reflected back upon the court scene. She so regretted how hurt and blaming her son looked when asked if he'd seen her kissing a local bookstore owner. J.J. simply didn't understand what was going on there at the time. It was the first and the last time Jenny kissed John. In fact, it was John who kissed her, and it was on the cheek; nothing more than a farewell kiss, as far as she was concerned. But J.J. refused to hear her side of it.

J.J. had kept the secret for two years, until one day when his guard was down he related the incident to his father. It was exactly what James had been looking for to proceed with divorce.

By the time Jenny left the café, a pleasant summer evening had settled over the city. As she got into her car, she was reminded that it had never really been "her" car. She had thought it was until yesterday, when the judge said that everything belonged to James' company. How could she have signed away all her rights to everything? She wondered if James would leave the car to her.

"Oh, it doesn't matter, anymore. It's all for the best. My only hope and prayer is that J.J. will someday see that money and possessions are not everything and realize how much his mother really loves him."

Chapter Six

THE MAN ENTERED the dark cubicle and closed the door behind him. He knelt down and thought about the sins he had committed. He was ready to get up and leave when the door to the wooden grille screen slid open.

He lowered his voice in an attempt to camouflage his identity and moved his head further into the darker corner of the cubicle.

"Bless me, Father, for I have sinned. It has been six months since my last confession and these are my sins: I swore, used God's name in vain, told a lie…twice…" and then the words "…I…had impure thoughts…" tumbled from his mouth, followed more slowly by, "I missed mass once on Sunday and talked badly about one of my co-workers. I think that's all, Father. For these and all the sins which I cannot remember, I am very sorry."

Father smelled Bud's perspiration and heard his heavy, nervous breathing. He knew Bud had tried to conceal who he was, but Father always knew. For years, Bud had repeated this struggle many times, and he was not the only one. What surprised Father when he first started listening to confessions was how prevalent this sin was amongst women as well. Father often thought that God should have made man differently or that passion should only come along with the sacrament of matrimony. But no, once passion is experienced it soon gives way to lust, adultery and soon runs rampant.

What surprised Father even more though was Bud's connection to Henry and the incredible workings of God's divine providence to deal with unforgiveness. It was only after Henry had opened up the Gallery that Bud came into the shop to meet Henry and inform him that it was he and his wife who had purchased Henry's home in Whitmore Park when they moved out to their acreage.

Part of the reason for Bud's purchase was the studio on the second floor. Bud too was an aspiring artist and had come in to ask for Henry's help and some painting tips. Henry agreed to visit Bud and pass along some of his artistic skills and knowledge.

Even though Bud and Henry had both moved away from the east end of Regina, they still attended mass at St. Mary's on Sundays. Over the months they had become good friends and after Mass on Sundays they engaged in conversations.

It wasn't until one Sunday when Eddy Zeigler attended church that he remarked to Henry that he was glad to see that he had become friends with his high school pal, Bud, along with John McBryne and that third boy, Peter.

Miene leiber Gott, Father said silently and shook his head. He would never forget the look on Henry's face when Henry learned that he had become friends with another one of the boys that had harmed him and Jenny and who had taken Jenny to the park back in Grade 9.

Fortunately, Henry was more forgiving of Bud as he recalled Bud was the one in the car who had tried to encourage John and Pete to leave he and Jenny alone. Fortunately, Henry decided to bury the hatchet and forgive Bud as he had John.

Father momentarily thought of Peter and how Henry was dealing with that when his reverie was broken by Bud's coughing and question, "Is there anything you want to ask me, Father?"

"Yes, yes, I am sorry. It seems to me that you are struggling with impure thoughts. Is that it, just impure thoughts or is there more to it than that?" Father probed, sensing there was more and at the same time trying not to reveal his knowledge of the magnitude of Bud's sin from the past.

"Yes, Father, there is more." Bud replied reluctantly. "I have been casually going out after work to the bar with a co-worker. Last time she joked about having a drink at a motel. I would have, if it had not been for the fact that I had to drive my son to his hockey game—"

"Is she married, too?"

"Yes, she is, Father."

Father moved his head closer to the screen wanting to make certain he heard every word. "Have you had an affair, sexual relations, with her yet?"

"No, our last outing was the first time that it was suggested."

"So, this is more serious than just impure thoughts."

"Yes. Yes, it is, Father."

"And your marriage, is it failing, or in any way the cause motivating you to do this?"

"No, Father—my wife and I get along fine and I love her very much… It's just that I entertain these thoughts and give in to my temptations."

Father fell silent for a brief moment, asking the Holy Spirit to guide him in his words to this man who was not only troubled, but in grave trouble.

"Adultery is a serious sin, my son. It's a breaking of your marriage vow to be faithful to your spouse. It can only lead to more sin and put your marriage and family in jeopardy and all for a fleeting moment of pleasure."

"Yeah," whispered Bud almost inaudibly, "I feel so guilty and ashamed I can't look at myself in the mirror."

"It all begins with your thoughts, which lead to feelings and then actions. Passion, sexual desires, impure thoughts are a great temptation and if one is not careful, one can quickly become a slave to one's thoughts. We must come up with a plan to deal with our thoughts before our feelings are aroused. We must have new thoughts and be prepared. You are sorrowful, now, but as soon as you go out into the world, you will be bombarded by sex all around you again and if you are not prepared to deal with it, you may soon again fall prey to it. Do you understand?"

"Yes, Father. I pray about it, but it doesn't seem to help. It also doesn't help the way women dress: short skirts, open blouses, and tight sweaters and slacks. They almost encourage men."

"Society has taught us to behave this way, to be, as you say, sexy. To wear this or that. This is a tough world we live in. But we must be tougher and use the intelligence God gave us to be cleverer than all this exposure of sex that is inflicted upon us."

"So, how do you deal with it? Like I said, prayer doesn't work."

"First, my son, you must really want to deal with it, to desire to stop this more than your desire to think or engage in it. Can you really commit yourself to a plan to deal with this?"

Father recalled putting this very question to Bud several months ago and, yet, he'd returned even worse off.

"Yes, Father, I really want to. I came too close last time to making a really big mistake."

"Yes, that would have been a big mistake, but it's all the little mistakes leading up to it that we must deal with. Toying with impure thoughts, lusting after women, desiring another's wife, watching sexual movies or reading books with sexual content and so on. This is the way we become slaves to our passions. Remember, thoughts lead to arousal of sexual feelings and once it gets into that arena it is very difficult to stop us from sinful actions."

"But what can I do, Father?" Bud asked helplessly.

"We must transform our minds, always have a plan in place and change the way we think about women. They are not objects, to be used for sexual gratification.

"Begin to look upon women as beautiful children of God, not as commodities for our entertainment or gratification. See them as your sister in Christ or as your daughter and think about how you would like to see them be respected by men. Pray to Mary, our Holy Mother for a pure mind. Visualize her standing behind or beside women you see. Remember, sex belongs in the marriage setting. There, it is a safe, loving experience. There, you are free to carry out what God intended. You must continually change your thought pattern and break the habit that has such a stronghold on you."

"Yeah, it's like I'm still a teenager and haven't grown up."

Father paused for a moment. "Yes, it is a matter of maturing and becoming more responsible in the thoughts we allow ourselves to think about. You are not alone, Bud, in these thoughts. Temptations and amoral thoughts confront man all the time—it's how we deal with them that is vitally important.

"Every time a temptation comes along, don't panic. Instead, give thanks and praise to God and He will give you the strength that you need."

Bud raised his eyebrows and looked at Father through the screen. "Give thanks for temptation?"

"Yes, temptation can be seen as a wonderful gift from God as an opportunity to do good and follow His will. You must activate your will. It's a moment of choice, an exercise in free will. But once you chose to follow His will, then always choose His strength over yours, it will renew your spirit. As I asked you before, if you really want to overcome this thing and grow more responsibly, don't rely on your will power alone. You know the results to that.

"If you choose the Lord's strength you will grow in character and confidence and strength. You will walk in a manner that glorifies God. Just as you want your children to obey you and do good, so too as a child of God you want to obey Him and improve the world. You will be proud of yourself and you will just naturally praise the Lord as you see His power work through you. 'I can do all things through Christ who strengthens me' is a powerful scripture. It is at such a time, my son, you can gain freedom."

Father paused for a few moments, allowing what he said to sink in and then added, "This is not to say we should go out of our way to be tempted. But to recognize the opportunity you have to seize the moment and make

Jesus smile and your heart glad. His Holy Spirit is there to help you, to give you strength. But you must ask, give Him your permission or else He won't infringe upon your free will."

"I never thought about it in that way, Father. I know my way sure doesn't work. I usually end up giving in to my thoughts."

"To also help you draw on the strength of the Lord, it helps to keep reminding yourself that you are a married man. Think, do you want self-gratification over being loyal to your wife and family? If you choose for self you gain a fleeting moment of pleasure, but can you honestly look into your wife's eyes after and say, 'I honoured the vow we made'? Can you look into your son's eyes and say, 'I am a committed father' and be an example to him? And, as you said, you don't want to look in the mirror and see what you are ashamed of.

"Look down at your ring. Do you remember the vow you made to your wife when she gave you that ring?"

Bud's heart beat faster and the hand holding his wedding band glistened as his fingers trembled in the dim light. He couldn't answer, yet Father heard him. The odour of Bud's tears was answer enough.

"These are the thoughts you must think about, not how to go to bed with another man's wife. You must lead others, be an example. We so need mature people of strength and character in this world. Others will see you and respect you for how you speak about and act with women. You will help others in this way without even realizing it. Perhaps there are many men at work who are failing in their marriage, too. If they see you as strong and committed, it will help them just as I'm helping you. Remember, the blind cannot lead the blind lest they both fall in the ditch. Do you understand?"

"Yes, Father, thank you, this will help. I know I need to pray more and seek God's help. And … what keeps coming through Father, is that I need to think and act my age and be a good example."

"Did you know, my son, that God needs you as much as you need Him to make a better world? Every choice you make either hinders or improves the earth. Because you have free will, you are called upon to be a collaborator with the good Lord. That's why it's so important as you said, to be a good example to others and make mature, wise, godly choices, and call on His help."

A long silence fell as each man thought about those words.

Father broke the stillness. "You know, there is one thing, which you may already be doing in your marriage and I often wish I would have done more of it when I was married to my Anna."

Bud looked at Father through the wooden grille and saw tears roll down his cheeks.

"I wish I had let her know more often how much I loved her. As a marriage goes on we take each other for granted and we assume that our partner knows our feelings for them and at times we think the grass is greener on the other side. Perhaps even more important than what we have discussed is this: when you look at your lady friend at your work place, instead visualize your wife, the girl you made a promise to, the girl you vowed to honour and be faithful to. And when you come home, go to her, look in her eyes without guilt or shame and see the woman you really love. And tell her so.

"Tell her how much you appreciate her and ask her out for a date on the weekend, or surprise her with an outing during the week. Take her to a fine restaurant or to a movie or the theatre. And, you know, I will tell you right now, my son, that if you do that regularly, that wife of yours will make love to you that's honest and good and real and will outshine, outperform and outdo anything that lady at work will do. And what's more, is that you will feel true love and not shame and guilt. Do you hear me?

"You have to constantly remind yourself of the gem you have, keep polishing it with kindness, appreciation, encouragement. That is the meaning of love and how to grow deep in your relationship. Then you won't need to go elsewhere or ever deal with all the terrible problems that infidelity can bring to a family."

Father reached forward to a filing board he had screwed to the back of his confessional door. It was made of five separate slots, each containing sheets of paper with scriptural passages that applied to various common sins. Father took out one of the sheets of paper, rolled it up and slid it through one of the squares in the screen.

"For penance, I want you to memorize the scriptures on this page. They have to do with the Lord renewing your spirit, transforming your mind, giving praise and thanks for his blessings and turning all things into good. Trust Him. Try to get up earlier this week, go on your knees and pray and read other passages. Prepare yourself and focus yourself on the day and the task at hand. This is a tough battle you face. You must put on the whole armour of God.

"Try to come to church as often as you can, receive Holy Communion and pray to God in the presence of the tabernacle. Also, ask the Holy Mother to help and guide you to a pure mind and heart. And for the next month, I ask you to come to confession every Saturday to discuss your progress. You are not alone in this battle. Together and with God's help we can deal with this.

"Remember, my son, it takes a lifetime to develop character. Every time you obey the words of God to do what is honest, good and right you become a stronger and more mature person. And not only that, every thought and action we have carries with it eternal consequences. It's your character at the end of day, when all is said and done, that God will judge you on and reward you accordingly. Were you loving, kind, honest, faithful, generous, and serving of God and others?

"This is what you carry with you at that instant of transition. At that moment, there will be no time for character development. So, make every action, deed, and thought count. It's a sure way to be happy on earth, to be an example and of service to others, and ensure your happiness in the next. Do you have any comments or questions?"

"No, Father, and thank you. I will do as you suggest."

"It's up to you now to choose wisely. Earlier you said you could hardly look at yourself in the mirror. If you do the things we discussed, what would you then see reflected in the mirror, my son?"

"A happy man, Father." Bud chuckled through his tears. Father did the same.

Father gave Bud absolution for his sins and then added, "Go in peace, my son, and desire to sin no more. In Christ, you can be free from all bondage."

Bud rose and exited the confessional booth feeling like a soiled glass that had gone through a dark dishwasher and had come out clean, clear, and sparkling into the light.

Father closed the sliding door to the grille and prayed silently before opening the screen door on the other side of the confessional booth. He thought about Bud and the many other parishioners who came to him for this very sin. How strong sexual desires took hold and how easily Satan caused men to sin in this area. Father not only recalled his own struggles with it in his youth, but also about the first person he ever talked to about sexual concerns.

Even though it was many years ago, he could clearly visualize himself and Henry sitting on the old grey crates behind his grocery store, talking about that very subject. Father smiled as he remembered young Henry's desire to have sex with that new girl who moved into the neighbourhood.

Such a pretty young girl, that Jenny. Henry had suffered such pain and heartache when she left and never wrote. Many times he, himself wondered what had happened to her, too.

Well, it no longer mattered. God gave Henry another beautiful woman. It was so unfortunate God took Julean so early and that once again, Henry had suffered much. Fortunately, it seemed to Father that Henry had adjusted to life without her. Father remembered only too well when his Anna passed on to her Lord. How he had grieved for her, and still did to this very day, even though he knew she was happier now to be with her Lord.

"Oh Lord, I cannot wait until the day I will be with you, too."

Father opened the sliding door to the other confessional booth to make sure no one was there. His eyes had so adjusted to the darkness that he easily saw the cubicle was empty. "I guess Bud was the last one."

He rose and left the confessional. He had been listening to confessions for over three hours and was stiff and tired. He slowly stretched his legs and took a deep breath of fresh air. He left the door open to let out the odour of sweat and tears. The odour of guilt, shame, remorse. The odour of sin. Instead of finding the odour repugnant, however, Father actually welcomed it, almost loved it. Along with the smell came forgiveness, freedom, and release from the bondage of sin. He was so thankful for the gift of absolution, that he was one of God's shepherds, ordained to forgive the sins of his fellow man. To give them a fresh start, a new beginning to live for Jesus. To grant them peace for however brief the time until they sinned again.

"Aah, such is life," Father said with a sigh, "each and every moment we make a choice … to live for Jesus or ourselves."

An elderly lady kneeling in the front pew of the church turned towards him as his words echoed through the large, hollow ceiling. Father nodded sheepishly and went over to the side of the church where a statue of the Holy Mother was supported by a wrought iron stand containing dozens of candles on a tiered shelf near her feet. Over half of them were lit, each burning with some request. Father lit another for Bud and then another for the other people who had come to him for confession. Father knelt before his beloved Mother and silently prayed.

He was weary and knew he would soon have to go on one of his mini-retreats to the prayer house in the valley at Henry's farm. It was a small hut situated by the creek that meandered through the valley floor. The soothing sound of the rippling stream, the solitude, the prayerful encounter with his Lord never failed to replenish his spirit that was constantly being drained of energy. Henry called it his Poustinia and yet, strangely, he never used it.

CHAPTER SEVEN

A<small>T THE AGE</small> of 68, Edith Sarsky's health was failing. In 1983, only a year after moving out of the estate and into her new apartment, she entered a care home. Since then, she had moved three more times into homes which provided progressively more care. She had difficulty walking now, and often Jenny arrived to see her in a wheelchair. It pained Jenny to see her mother's deterioration. She had always been such an active and strong person.

Edith was also beginning to accumulate excess fluid in her system. Last month, they had discovered cirrhosis of the liver, so once a month she had to go to the hospital and have the fluid drained off, as her liver could no longer do it on its own.

"Good evening, Jenny."

"Hi," Jenny responded to the duty nurse.

"As soon as we saw you pull into the parking lot, we told your mother, 'here comes your medicine.' It was the first time your mother has smiled in days. She really missed you and is anxious to see you."

"Yes, I have been very busy the past few days. But I have dealt with that and should be able to visit more often again."

"Oh, that's good. We all so enjoy having you come, you seem to cheer the whole place up."

"Why, thank you, Millie. I really needed that."

Her mother's eyes brightened and widened when Jenny entered her room.

"Hi, Mom, how are you feeling?"

"Oh, much better now that you are here."

Jenny kissed her mom's forehead. "Yes, I have been quite busy this past week."

"So, what have you been up to?"

Jenny stared at her mom, debating whether she should tell her? *Perhaps tomorrow.* Edith hadn't seen her for almost a week and she didn't want to dampen her spirit right away with such sad news. "Oh,

I have been sorting things out at home and making a lot of changes."

"Well, surely it can't be that important that you can't take an hour or so off to see your mother."

"You're right, Mom. I won't let it happen, again. I promise to see you regularly from now on."

Her mother seemed to be fine with that response because she began telling Jenny about the doctor's visit and his assessment that her liver just didn't have the oomph to remove the fluid as fast as it should and that she would have to go to the hospital twice a month, now.

"Oh, Mom, I'm sorry to hear that."

"Well, don't be. I can't tell you how much better I feel after I have the fluid drained. I feel so bloated, almost like a helium balloon."

Jenny laughed. "I'm glad you haven't lost your sense of humour."

"So, tell me how are James and J.J.? That grandson of mine is turning out to be just like his dad."

"Yes, he sure is," Jenny responded.

Jenny had never really complained to her mother about how lonely she had been in her marriage and most of the time put on a front that all was well and okay. Jenny knew her mother would not be prepared for news of the divorce. Perhaps she should have been more open with her over the years.

"To be honest with you, Mom, James and I haven't been seeing much of each other for a long time. He's so absorbed in his work that he is hardly at home." Jenny thought that she would start to prepare her mother for the inevitable news.

"Oh, Jenny, your father was like that, too. They get so caught up in their work they forget who they are married to."

Jenny looked at her mother. "Well, Mom, it seems more than just work with James and me."

The expression on her mother's face told Jenny that she had her mother's attention.

"James and I have drifted very far apart—"

"Oh, Jenny, that's foolish talk. It's all in your mind. Start to cook him some of those favourite dishes I taught you. The best way to a man's heart is through his stomach."

"No, Mom, no amount of cooking is going to tantalize James. I'm afraid I don't have the right recipe any more."

"Shush now, Jenny, I don't want to hear anymore of this kind of talk."

It was precisely the response she expected from her mother, though she got the feeling that her mother knew exactly what she was talking about. But, as always, she just didn't want to discuss it.

"Tell me, how is J.J. and that girlfriend of his? Her name is Nora, isn't it?" And before Jenny could respond, Edith went on, "And what is this talk of marriage? Surely they're not thinking of getting married. He's much too young."

"Like I told you, Mom, I don't see much of either James or J.J. anymore, but last time I spoke with Matilda she said she thinks Nora is pregnant and that she and J.J. are thinking of getting married."

"Oh my, Jenny, he's only 17! Way too young to take on such a responsibility. He's still a boy and between you and me, a very immature one at the best of times."

"Matilda said that Nora is a couple of years older and seems like a sensible young lady but still, I agree with you, J.J. is too young."

As silence and darkness settled over them, Jenny thought about J.J. and how similar he was to his father. She couldn't help but feel sorry for his girlfriend. If their marriage is anything like the marriage between her and James, it's doomed to failure. As Jenny recalled the shocking conversation she'd had with James' own mother so many years ago, she almost felt compelled to warn Nora not to marry her son… Or at least to be leery about him.

Click.

Jenny and her mother blinked in reaction to the sudden bright light.

"My gosh, you two, it's so dark in here. How on earth can you see each other?" Donna said, as she bustled in.

"Oh, we just glow in the dark," quipped Jenny.

"Well that may be, but we need a little more light to do our work when the sun goes down." Donna turned to Edith. "Well, Edith, it's time for your medicine. I'll bring it in as soon as your daughter leaves."

"Oh, I don't need any medicine when she's here."

"Now, Mom, the nurse is right, I better go. I don't like driving at night. I'll stop by around 2:00 o'clock tomorrow afternoon. There is something I wish to tell you."

"Well, tell me now. I'm getting too impatient in my old age."

"Oh, Mom, I really have to go and it will take a little time for me to tell you what I have to say."

Edith looked at her daughter and furrowed her brow, again. "Very well then, darling, I'll just have to wait, I guess."

Jenny stood and went over to her mom and kissed her cheek.

"Goodnight, Mom, I love you."

"I love you, too, Jenny."

"Goodnight, Jenny."

"G'night, Donna. See you, tomorrow."

"Oh no you won't, I'm off for the next two days."

"Oh, that's nice; well, you have a nice holiday."

"Yes, Timothy and I are driving to Toronto, tomorrow, and taking in *Joseph and the Amazing Technicolour Dream Coat*."

"I've heard it's a great musical. Have fun and have a nice time," Jenny said, as she walked out the door.

On the way down the hall, Jenny realized that in her 21-year marriage to James, they hadn't once seen one single play together.

As Jenny made her way to the car she felt prompted to gaze into the early evening sky. There, off to the east was the first star shining bright as ever. For the first time that day her feelings lifted as pleasant thoughts of Henry began to fill her mind.

For a moment Jenny wasn't sure if it was her overwhelming thoughts of Henry that were sweeping through her or was it really loving rays from him coming to her from the star? For years that loving feeling from the star was gone as if shielded by a cold block of ice. The rays were still there but the warmth had been gone until these past few months. She had first felt it again that past July 6th, their anniversary, as she had poured over her old diary late into the night, reading rapturously and reliving her experiences from that first summer they had met. She was certain the warmth was returning more and more regularly. Could her loving thoughts for Henry be thawing the barrier? Or could it be Henry's love directed to her that was melting the shield…?

Jenny gazed into the star-studded sky and whispered the closing sentence she'd written in the last letter to Henry containing the pewter angel. She would never forget that loving thought:

"Even though we are far apart, you are forever in my heart."

JENNY WOKE EARLY the next morning, so overwhelmed by all she had to do. The kettle whistled and steamed as she searched the cupboards for more of her favourite tea. Ever since Matilda left, Jenny had difficulty finding things.

"Ah ha! There you are." Jenny reached into the far back of a bottom shelf and retrieved a full box of herbal tea. She placed a chamomile tea bag into a small tea pot and poured the steaming hot water into it. She carried it along with a china cup and saucer out to patio.

"Oh my," she exclaimed, "what a glorious day! It's so beautiful here,

I will miss all this very much."

Everything looked so serene, almost like a paradise. Thomas was already about his work and turned on the sprinkler at the far end of the lawn.

Jenny placed her right hand like a visor over her eyes and gazed at the grounds before her. The sun, still low in the morning sky, streamed across the glistening dew-speckled grass. The outer mist of the water in the air surrounding the sprinklers danced and sparkled as the rays of the sun bounced through it. She loved that sight. It always reminded her of millions of tiny diamonds shimmering in the light. The grass looked so erect and fresh, almost edible. The falling droplets of water rolled off the tips of each blade, cascaded down into the soil hidden by the evergreen carpet, giving drink and nutrients to the thirsty roots.

No wonder Thomas was so gentle and relaxed. Working with the soil and nature with all its beauty all day clearly had a therapeutic effect. With her love of gardens she realized she could just as easily have been a landscaper or gardener rather than a school librarian.

"Morning, Mrs. Hamilton," Thomas said, startling Jenny out of her reverie.

"Oh, good morning, Thomas. Up early and at it, I see."

"Oh yes, Mrs. Hamilton, this is the best time of the day. There's something about the early morning that's sacred. Just so peaceful and still."

"Yes, I was just thinking about that. It seems to fill you with an inner calm to face the day. I just love it."

"I do, too. I thank the Lord every day for allowing me to care for His creation."

"What a beautiful thought, Thomas."

Thomas just nodded. "I told my missus last evening that you were leaving and how much we will all miss you."

"Yes, I hate to leave, but sometimes life hits you with a curve ball and strikes you out."

"Well, I don't believe you will ever be struck out, Mrs. Hamilton. I'm sure all will turn out for the good for you. I will keep you in my prayers."

"Why thank you, Thomas."

"That's a fine group of flowers you placed in the angel's basket, Ma'am."

"I thought so, too, Thomas, when I picked them, such a beautiful combination. I hope you won't mind to water them."

"I already checked this morning, and they seem fine, fresher than yesterday, it seems. Perhaps they will last as long as the bouquet we picked for you when we gave you the angel statue as a gift." Thomas paused then added, "I have a feeling they will last a long time as a remembrance of you and your love for nature."

"That is so nice of you to say, Thomas, but I didn't place them in the basket for me. I placed them in there for Mr. Hamilton as my thank you for letting me share this beautiful garden."

"Oh my, Mrs. Hamilton, you truly have such a kindly heart." Thomas could say no more, as tears welled up. "You have a nice day now, Ma'am."

"And you, too, Thomas."

Thomas hummed as he walked off with the shovel he retrieved from the storage shed. Jenny couldn't help but compare the inner peace and joy of Thomas to that of James.

"One can be a millionaire and not have a cent," she mused. "Well, Lord, please help me carry into today, the peace you have instilled in me this morning. Thank you, too, for Thomas and all the gardeners, your special workers, making the world so beautiful, feeding our troubled souls with a spiritual sustenance. And please, dear Lord, help me tell Mom about the divorce. Give me the right words to say so she won't be too upset. She has enough on her plate without adding my concerns and worries to it."

With that Jenny stood and walked into the house to start packing.

By noon, she had filled several boxes with personal items she didn't want the movers to touch. One was the large Manila envelope that contained all the notes Henry had written to her and attached to the fence post just outside the front of her parent's home in Regina. She wanted to make certain that those loving thoughts were never lost.

Jenny surveyed the front living rooms and wasn't sure what she was allowed to take. She loved the antiques she had collected over the years; several chairs, round tables, Victorian tables with bronze clawed feet. And the dining room set with an accompanying sideboard and curio cabinet with the curved glass door was just so beautiful. It was almost like new. Jenny loved its unique ornate design and rich walnut colour. It was a small set, too small for the dining room of their huge house, but Jenny couldn't resist. It would fit better into an average sized home.

"I so hope James will allow me to have these antiques. He's more into modern furniture and glass." Jenny picked up the phone and called James' office, again, but as before, James was in a meeting and unable to come to the phone.

Still holding the phone Jenny decided to give Matilda a call. They had become quite good friends and frequently went out to movies or dinner.

"Hello, this be Mr. Hamilton's residence."

"Hi, Matti, it's Jen. I'm going to visit Mom shortly, but thought I would give you a call since we haven't chatted for a few days."

"Oh, Miss Jenny, you brighten up my day just to hear your voice. How is Mrs. Sarsky doing?"

"I saw her last night, briefly. She isn't doing that well, her liver is failing, but her sense of humour is one hundred percent." Jenny chuckled.

"Well, you be giving her a hug for me and that I say an extra prayer for her when I talk to the Boss tonight."

Jenny laughed. "I was packing all morning and will be leaving the estate in a day or so. I called James at the office to ask if I could take the antique furniture, but he was in meetings."

"Meetings! Huuumpt! Him and his meetings and activities. He best be giving you that fine furniture. Never in all the years I be there did I see the man sit on one of them beautiful chairs. He never was one to see beauty under his nose. Oh, I'm sorry for going on so, I'm still upset at the two of them hootin' and hollering and laughing over the court happenings yesterday. Sounds like the settlement be favouring them?"

"Yes, Matti, James and his lawyers are very skilled at making money, retaining it and amassing more. But money isn't everything and it can't buy happiness."

"Seems to me the more you got, the bigger are your headaches. Maybe that's why Mr. Hamilton be walkin' around ready to explode all the time. Oh, here I go fussing again, Miss Jenny. I jus be so sorry to see you leave that beautiful estate. I know how much joy the garden has given you."

"Yes, I will miss that for sure, Matti. And I wish now that I am officially off the premises, that you start calling me, Jenny, or even better yet, Jen. I recall you saying once how much you like being called Matti as opposed to Matilda, that there is more affection surrounding the nickname. And after all, Matti, we have become such good friends."

"That be true. It was a big step to go from calling you Mrs. Hamilton to Miss Jenny. Now to go another step seems to me I would be losing something special."

"What do you mean, Matti? To me it would be more special, wouldn't it?"

"Here's how I see it. If I call you Jenny, it be like all my friends. But I never want to forget that someone as gracious, kind and important as you is my friend…"

"Now Matti," Jenny cut in, "What you're saying is that you consider me being more important and better than you and being my friend makes you feel better about yourself and more important, too. And by calling me Miss Jenny it helps to feed into that kind of thinking that separates people from one another, especially true friends."

"Now Miss Jenny, you be seeing into my heart…"

"No, Matti, I'm seeing into your mind. But it's your heart I want to be in."

Matti remained silent and Jenny continued. "Take your sister Coreena, for example. You love her and think of her as your equal. You feel completely comfortable around her and would never think of addressing her as Miss Coreena, would you?"

"Heaven forbid, no! She already be thinking that she's God's gift to mankind!" But Matilda quickly added, "But you be different, Miss Jenny!"

"But that's just the point, Matti. I don't want to be different. I don't want you to put me on some kind of a pedestal; I need a friend, Matti. A real friend…a sister friend, just like… like…Tammy was…"

Jenny's voice trailed off into a long silence on the phone. Jenny hoped she didn't offend her friend. And then Matilda spoke the most beautiful words that Jenny ever heard.

"My sweet Jesus and me know what you be sayin' is the gospel truth. But never in my lifetime did I ever think I could be living it… Jenny… you truly be my friend and I love you just as if you be my sister."

Once again there was a long silence. Long enough to swallow the erupting tears of heartfelt joy and true friendship.

"Talk to you tomorrow, Matti."

"I be looking forward to it… Jen."

CHAPTER EIGHT

I T WAS EARLY morning and Henry was glad that he had decided to take the day off. He took in a deep breath of fresh air as he stood on the deck overlooking the valley. Everything looked so green and peaceful and helped dissipate the confusion and turmoil he was feeling. It was a beautiful summer day and he just wanted to spend some time alone, maybe work on the painting he had started and take the dogs for a walk. He might even spend some time in the prayer house by the side of the pond that was fed by a meandering creek through the valley bottom.

He loved the reflection of the prayer house. He felt twinges of guilt that he hadn't used it since he built it the summer after Julean died. It was intended to provide solace and meaning, but instead he had immersed himself in his work and property development, finding it too difficult to spend much time alone. It was a good thing Father Engelmann was making use of it.

Perhaps, some day...

Henry placed his left hand into his trouser pocket and searched for Julean's rosary. Even more than repeating bible passages, saying the rosary was the one thing that helped him to cope with his loneliness and the aching longing for his dear, sweet wife. It helped that it also drew him closer to the Holy Mother. Henry identified with the deep sorrow she must have felt when her son was crucified, and he knew the Blessed Mother understood his sorrow over the passing of his beloved, as well.

He always admired the love and close relationship Julean had with Mary, the mother of Jesus. It reminded Henry of what Father Engelmann always said: that we each should strive to be examples of strong faith so as to instill hope and faith in others. Henry could now see that in himself through Julean's example. In witnessing her strong faith, he had grown closer to the blessed Mother and Jesus, as well.

Henry began to recite the rosary as he turned and sat down in his favourite chair next to the window overlooking the valley. The letter Julean had written to him before she passed away lay open on the end table. He picked it up and marvelled how it came to him in much the same way Jenny's last note did when his life looked so bleak and dim.

Two weeks after Jenny's departure he had found a note attached to the fence gate leading to her house. It was a godsend! To this day Henry believed it was their guardian angels that protected the note from winds and rain until he was led by them to find it.

For years after that moment he had read it over a thousand times and more as it was the only way he could sustain himself and help him cope with the days and days of silence that had followed. He pictured the note now as if it was yesterday and as he gazed out into the valley he whispered Jenny's tender words once more:

"Oh, Henry,"

My heart just aches and I feel like it's being torn in two. Being with you has made this the happiest summer of my life. The thought of not seeing you anymore is more than I can bear.

Always remember:

True love lasts forever, it never says goodbye, for you and I have a guardian angel on high with nothing to do but to give to you and to give to me love forever true."

Jenny

P.S. If you were a heart, I'd want mine
       To beat inside yours.

HENRY REMEMBERED HOW consoling the note was, as if she were right beside him each time he read it. He could hear her singing the words from their song, *True Love.* And as he hummed the words…"For you and I have a guardian angel on high with nothing to do but to give to you and to give to me…" thoughts of Julean entered his mind. She had asked him to promise that whenever he sang or heard that song to make her a part of it, too. Julean knew that it was the song that Henry and Jenny shared. Julean wanted to be remembered as his one true love as well as Jenny.

Henry shook his head, amazed at how Julean had always known about his undying love for Jenny and how she supported him even though it took love that belonged to her away from her.

"Oh Julean," Henry whispered, "your love for me was so great that you sacrificed your own happiness so that my heart could be appeased."

Henry marvelled at Julean's acceptance and understanding of this almost unbelievable connection that simply would not go away. Julean understood the supernatural nature of it all.

Unbidden tears came to Henry's eyes as he thought about his two loves and how similarly both had reached out to him when he so needed them near. Just like the note Jenny had left for him on the fence post, incredibly Julean had left a letter for him, as well. It came right when Henry felt he could no longer go on.

Staring at Julean's letter in his hand, Henry shook his head as he recalled how the angels once again had come to his rescue…

Almost a year after Julean's death, while things appeared to be returning to normal in the Pederson home, Henry's heart was filled with such a deep loneliness. Making peace with John McBryne, the man responsible for his wife's death and the kids adjusting to their mother's absence definitely helped, but the aching and longing for Julean overwhelmed him so much that some days he didn't want to get out of bed or live for another day. Even Father Engelmann's friendship, guidance and wisdom-filled words provided little solace for Henry. If it had not been for the warm touch and love he felt from Julean's rosary, he would have died.

On the day that life no longer held any hope, he received a phone call from a nurse who had been on duty during the last days of Julean's illness before her death. Henry wiped away a tear rolling down his cheek as he remembered the call from that dear nurse once again:

"Is Mr. Henry Pederson in?" asked the soft feminine voice.

"Yes, I am Henry. What can I do for you?"

"My name is Susan Miller. I'm a nurse at the Pasqua Hospital and I have something for you. Something I was supposed to give you from your wife."

"You must be mistaken, Miss, my wife passed away over a year ago…"

"Yes, I know. But let me explain. I was on duty during the time your wife was critically ill. She awoke one night while you were sleeping on the cot next to hers. She said she was dying and was afraid that she might go into a permanent coma and not be able to tell you what was in her heart. She refused to wake you at the time knowing how exhausted you were. She had written you a letter and gave it to me with the promise that I only give it to you should she die. I took the letter and placed it in my locker. The next day, I was transferred to another ward. I checked on your wife's status for a day or two after that but then got so involved with the patients and work in my new position, I forgot all about your wife and the letter.

"A day ago I spoke with a colleague of mine who frequents your café and mentioned how unfortunate it was that your wife had passed away. It immediately brought to mind the letter and I hoped I still had it in my locker. Sure enough, under all the papers and reports that I had to fill out, there it was. So, this is the reason for my call. I would like to fulfill my promise to your wife and give you the letter that she wrote to you."

Henry recalled that he couldn't speak for the longest moment. His heart nearly stopped, his words caught in his throat. A surge of much needed joy filled his being and his spirits soared like an eagle high into the prairie sky. He immediately rushed to the hospital and picked up the letter. He had the nurse go over the conversation she had with Julean, wanting to remember and savour every word his dear, sweet wife had uttered.

From there he went directly home and just like the time he took Jenny's letter off the fence post and sat on the front steps of her parents home, Henry sat in the chair in front of their farm home next to the one that Julean had always sat in when basking in the sun. Henry recalled vividly that first day he had opened and read the letter:

My dearest darling, Hank

I see you sleeping on the cot beside me and I long to be in your arms. I do not know what the future holds for me. But I know how this disease works especially the bacterial kind and I could slip into a coma at any time. For this reason, I want to write a letter to you in case I cannot share my deepest innermost thoughts and feelings.

My dear sweet Hank, you have made my life so complete and all my dreams come true. Each and every day is so exciting and an adventure living with you. You are a good man Hank, solid and true. You have always reminded me of my Uncle Jacob.

It is good for you to know that I am aware of another love in your life. I have known it from almost the beginning of our relationship. The look in your eyes and your momentary flash-backs of memories that took you from me were the first clue. But it was on the day we wed that very first night together our marriage was conjugated that you introduced me to your first love, Jenny in your dreams. And from that time until to this very day I have shared my life with her and you.

For many women this may be hard to understand and accept how I have allowed this. For sure, it is my background in which I have seen other women share the same man that has helped my understanding. But most of all it's your faithfulness, strength, love and commitment in our marriage that has filled my heart to such overflowing that it gave me the strength to allow your sweetheart into our marriage. For all the joy and happiness you have given me, it was very little in comparison that I could give to you in return.

Please do not feel guilt or shame for harbouring such thoughts. I understand how this can happen and if you need my forgiveness I give it to you from the bottom of my heart. If this disease should take me home to Jesus I want you to feel free to marry again. You are such a good man and should not be alone. You have too much love to give and it is good for the children to have another mother in the home. When I go to heaven I will ask the good Lord's permission to guide you to another love and perhaps the girl of your youth is waiting for you. I pray that this is the case and I will do all I can to bring her back to you.

I feel so tired and sleep wants to overtake me and so I just want to share one more thing. I know that True Love is a song you and Jenny shared. When it plays, I see the love in your eyes and the joy it brings to you. That is why I bought the record so you can freely listen to it with my approval. I only ask that you make me a part of that song when you hear it. That I am part of the love you feel and that it brings memories of me into your heart, as well.

And lastly, one evening before I met you I heard Elvis Presley sing True Love on a TV show that was being shown all the way from Germany when he was in the army. It was followed by another song that captured my heart and I knew someday that a man would come into my life who would love me tender, love me sweet… make all of my dreams come true. And you have, my dearest darling…. you have.

HENRY COULD NO longer see the words. Tears fell on the page. It was all so incredulous that Julean was watching Elvis Presley the same night and time that he was. He remembered Elvis singing *True Love* and then just the first part of *Love Me Tender* before he got up and went to his room to savour the song that he and Jenny shared. It was a miracle that the other Elvis Presley song would find meaning in his and Julean's heart as well.

Henry got up and made his way to the record changer and pushed the button. Two records would play in the next few minutes that would carry him away into a dream land of his two loves. First it would be *True Love* followed by *Love Me Tender*. He played the songs every day; the lyrics had become a part of his life and gave him solace when he came home from the gallery or when painting. He already wore out six 45 rpm record singles of each song.

Henry made his way back to the sun-room and gazed out the window. He usually stood there and hummed along with the songs allowing loving thoughts of Jenny and Julean to fill his heart. But long after the second song had played Henry suddenly became aware of the irritable scratching noise of the record player needle moving gently up and down as the finished record rotated round and round. Surprisingly his thoughts were neither filled with Julean or with Jenny. Rather it was of the third woman coming into his life.

"Ivania," Henry muttered. "Yes, Ivania, where do you fit into all of this? Is there enough room for you in my heart?"

CHAPTER NINE

A s Jenny went to get ready to see her mom, the phone rang. It was Chloe.

"Hi, Chloe, it's so good to hear from you! I was actually going to call you this evening."

"It's been almost three weeks since we talked and Dad and I were wondering how the court proceedings were going and how you are holding up in all this?"

"It was over yesterday, Chloe. It didn't turn out too much in my favour but I'll manage. And yes, it is stressful when a husband and wife have to go to court and fight each other especially when children are present…in any case it's over."

"Will you be leaving the estate, Auntie?"

"Yes, I'll be moving to my apartment early next week. It will be quite an adjustment for sure. But I'll take one day at a time and see what happens."

"Have you and J.J. resolved your differences yet?" Chloe wanted to know.

"No, I'm afraid not. He blames me for the demise of the marriage and won't listen to my side of the story. I just don't know what else I can do when he seems so reluctant to even discuss it."

"Oh, Auntie, things are piling up on you lately. I hope J.J. sees how foolish it is not to try and resolve this and develop a closer relationship with his mother."

"I do too, Chloe. But enough about this! How are you and Robbie doing?"

"We are doing fine. Dad is on the planning committee for a Campus Crusades Conference coming up in November and I'm really enjoying my PhD studies in Clinical Psychology. Also, I am volunteering at a pregnancy centre where women come for counseling and to discuss their options when faced with an unwanted pregnancy. We also help women who have had an abortion and are regretting their choice. I'm learning so much and gaining more confidence in understanding some of the problems many women have who have had an abortion. It's not just the secrecy, guilt or shame they are dealing with, but it can take the form of depression, anxiety, eating disorders and so many other symptoms."

"Yes, I can see how complex post-abortion trauma can be, Chloe. Especially the struggle many women have deciding an abortion is the solution to their problems, only to find out the tragic and devastating consequences of their decision."

"That's right, Auntie. There are so many hurting women who are not only struggling emotionally but spiritually, physically and relationally with their boyfriends, husbands and family."

"That's wonderful that the centre is providing help for women in both cases."

"Yes, it's so important for women who have had an abortion to know that we are here for them, with love and compassion, to help them. So many girls feel bad about themselves and try to hide what they did. We are not here to condemn them, but to accept them and help them to heal, to bring their wounds out into the light, and let them know that they are not alone."

"Oh, Chloe, how do you begin to help someone who is deeply troubled by the past like that?"

"What we are finding is that one-to-one counseling is not sufficient and so many women are afraid to bring it out in the open to even talk about it. There is a wonderful ministry called Rachel's Vineyard* that is rapidly spreading across the country. It's a weekend retreat program that uses a group approach to dealing with the trauma of abortion. The group consists of a caring team of women and men who have experienced abortion, counselors, clergy and others who share the love and mercy of Jesus with the retreat participants. It's proving to be very effective at treating the emotional and spiritual wounds left by abortion."

"I can see that it is a more collaborative approach. And I suppose when a participant shares their story it encourages others to identify and is able to help them bring their pain to the surface, as well."

"That's exactly right, Auntie. The entire support group is right there to help and compliment each other in assisting each person in the retreat."

"It sounds wonderful, Chloe. Have you been to one of the retreats?'

*Rachel's Vineyard was established in 1996. Time-line has been changed to draw awareness to the outreach program.

Jenny wanted to know.

"I was at one a month ago and I haven't been the same since. I finally understand what Dad has been telling me for years, that it's experience in the world that makes what you have learned or are studying hit home and make sense in a whole new way. This was such a profound experience for me. While I counseled women for months and still did not really help them at a core level, in a matter of a three day weekend I saw how this group approach, using the healing and loving power of Jesus and His teachings immediately brought about an amazing change in their lives. They began to see and understand how many of their thoughts and actions were motivated by the deep hidden pain. It was unbelievable how their relationship with their aborted baby, with themselves, their husbands and others changed dramatically, if not miraculously!"

"That is so beautiful, Chloe. To be in such a safe environment and surrounded by a loving team of people. And I like what you said that the mother develops a new relationship with their aborted child; that the infant was not just some "thing" that was destroyed, but their child. I think it would be so hard for a mother to find any meaning in what was done without this suppressed *truth* surfacing to the fore. "

"That's the key, Auntie. For many women the act of abortion seemed like the right thing to do at the time. They soon realize however, after the fact, that it was senseless and cannot find any justifiable reason for having had an abortion. And as I said, many women feel remorse, guilt, shame and try to hide what they did. The retreat operates on such a deep emotional level that the mothers see an entirely new way of responding to their aborted child. They find meaning in something that was meaningless. They discover and encounter the truth of God's love and forgiveness. The mothers discover the truth of the love they denied in their hearts for their own child and also the truth of the love and forgiveness that their child in heaven wants to return to them."

"That's so healing, Chloe, it touches my heart."

"It's an incredible retreat. The women throughout the encounter are accepted and loved and forgiven. Jesus is present through the acceptance and love of others. I now understand why Dad is so committed to Jesus. He not only had a personal healing experience himself but has seen it in many others as well."

"Yes, I remember that happening when your dad and Tammy or rather your mom were dating."

Jenny was so impressed by Chloe's growth and understanding and desire to help others. What a beautiful difference she was making.

Chloe gently broke the silence with a sharing that lay on her heart. She began softly. "Two weeks ago at one of my counseling sessions I met a lady that knew Mom. She said that Mom had convinced her to carry her child and not abort it. What convinced her more than anything was when Mom shared with her her own pregnancy and at one point in her life she too considered abortion as an option—"

"But Chloe, your mom was under tremendous pressure and abortion seemed like such an eas—"

"I know what you're going to say, Auntie, and you don't have to defend Mom's position on that. I totally understand and I talked to Daddy about it too. He admitted that he was the one trying to pressure Mom into doing it. But he was so wrong and to this day feels such regret for even thinking about doing such a horrible thing."

Jenny often thought about that too. If Tammy had carried out the abortion, Chloe would only be a memory of a horrendous act that was done. How many Chloe's are out there that never survived and could have made such a difference to the world had they been born?

Chloe broke into Jenny's thoughts, "I see what Mom went through in the girls that I counsel all the time; they are in a crisis and have tunnel vision. They see abortion as the quick and easy solution and don't foresee the long term consequences of their actions. In the pressure of the moment, they don't realize that the guilt and shame they feel now is nothing to what they will feel for terminating their child's life. For many they either rationalize or have been told that a fetus is not human or a real life until it is born."

"It's hard to understand how we can dupe our minds into thinking that the infant growing in our wombs is not a real human life!"

"Yes, it's amazing the rationalizations we come up with. But what I wanted to talk to you about and... oh, Auntie Jen, I hope you don't mind me saying this but when I talked to Daddy about all this he told me that you too were once pregnant and had a baby girl. He wasn't sure because it was such a long time ago when Mom shared it with him, but he thought your little girl's name was Camilla? Is that right?"

Tears were surfacing in Jenny's eyes. She had wanted to share Camilla with Chloe so many times and how she had pretended to bring up her little girl vicariously through Chloe. It was the only way Jenny knew how to keep the memory alive and what it would have been like to raise her daughter.

"Yes Chloe, I did have a little girl and I was too young to raise a child and my mom didn't feel that she could do it at that stage in her life. But I hope some day to see her. She would be two years older than you and so I often compared her to you and how you've grown and developed into such a fine young lady."

"Have you had any contact with her, Auntie?"

"No. I wish I knew where she was. I would contact her in a heart beat. At times I just ache to see her and hug her and tell her how sorry I am that I couldn't raise her myself."

"Oh, Auntie, it must be so hard for you. I can feel the pain and sorrow in your voice. It's similar to what I see in the eyes of so many mothers who have had an abortion and regret having done so. At least in your case you gave life to the child and a right for it to live and hope that one day you will be reunited."

"Yes, Chloe, I believe that with all my heart that one day we will…"

The phone went silent as thoughts of her sweet daughter crossed the screen of her mind. It wasn't just thoughts of her daughter that overtook Jenny, but also of her first love. Henry was there the night she had conceived and how often she had wished that it was Henry who was the father! The thought of she and Henry being married and raising Camilla was a fantasy she had played out many, many times. Jenny still believed that one day they would all be together.

Chloe broke into Jenny's thoughts again, "Can I ask you something? If it's something that you'd rather not talk about just say so…"

Jenny remained silent…

"Do you ever think of the man that fathered Camilla …?"

Jenny was a little startled by the question…

"Yes, Chloe I often think of him and wonder if he knows somehow that he fathered a child that night…" Tears surfaced into Jenny's eyes again and her words trailed off.

"Auntie… have you forgiven him for what he did?" Chloe wanted to know.

"Yes, Chloe, I have. I don't want any negative thoughts to surround Camilla and the circumstances of her conception or birth. I know the father was drinking that night and perhaps if he had been more in control of himself, his actions may have been very different. But for some reason it happened and I have accepted it and forgiven him. I harbour no ill will and I pray for him often. I prefer to think of all the good that is yet to come out of this."

"Oh Auntie, you are such an angel. Mom was so right about you. You accept things with such peace. A few of the girls that have come into the centre were raped as well and have such a difficult time forgiving and coming to terms with it."

"It is very difficult to deal with, Chloe, and as you know, we are all different and have different tolerance levels. If you can help them to forgive, it's so important that they free themselves of that past hurt. If at all possible, I recommend that they see their pregnancies to full term and give up their child for adoption, like I did. I know if I had aborted Camilla, the pain and sorrow that would be in my heart and soul for having terminated her life would have been devastating."

"The other day a mother who had considered abortion came into the counseling centre with her three week old baby. She was radiant, Auntie, and so happy she had decided to give birth. The infant was tucked in a cloth sling hanging from her shoulders. It was covered over with a blanket and hanging just below her heart. It looked as though she were still pregnant with the baby. As she stood in front of me she uncovered the baby's face bringing it into view. Oh, how my heart and eyes lit up at the sight of this beautiful newborn."

"What a sight that must have been, Chloe! I can just picture its sparkling little eyes peering out at you."

"It was so cute, but, Auntie, it was so symbolic of a baby still in the mother's womb and then delivered out into our presence. It occurred to me that that very child could have been in her womb on the table waiting to be aborted! The blanket was just as symbolic as the mother's skin!

"If only mothers could lift the blanket of their skin and see the little infant they are about to have destroyed. It's a little human being that wants to live, to be nurtured and to be loved just like they do. Its heart is beating just a few inches away from theirs. They would see a little bundle tucked in feeling so safe, warm and protected just like the three week old baby was tucked in so snug in the cloth sling…"

"That's a beautiful analogy, Chloe. And you are right, there is no difference in the feeling of security both infants feel but there is a night and day difference between the mindset of the two mothers. In the one, there is a deep love and caring and an ever ready willingness to defend and protect the infant with her life. *While in the other mother I think there must be so much fear and confusion and pressure and lack of accurate information and unfortunately it leads to the conclusion for her that her life will be terribly, adversely affected. Unfortunately it comes down to considering only her life and the way she wants to live it even if it is to the detriment of her own child within their womb.*"

There was a long silence between the girls. What Jenny concluded from Chloe's astute comparison of a new born baby under a blanket to that of a baby in a mother's womb under her skin hit them both to the core.

"I've seen film clips of the different ways abortion is done and I still can't get it out of my mind; it's such a horrendous act. I wish that the mother's womb was transparent like a glass dome and both the mother and doctor can see how the limbs are torn from the infant's body, their heads crushed so it can be removed from the womb. It's not surprising Auntie that so many women who make the choice of abortion regret what they have done. As I said earlier, it's manifested in so many ways. There is not only the personal pain and suffering but it can have devastating effects on all those around them; husbands, children and work place. It just seems so needless and sad.

"It's hard to understand how a doctor can advise a woman it's okay to have an abortion without that understanding. Surely they must see the detrimental affects of it all the time."

"Yes, Auntie, I just don't get it. Men and women choosing careers in medicine train for years to learn how to save lives and then specialize in killing the lives of innocent, defenceless children. Imagine terminating the lives of countless infants at the request of mothers who would find a child in some cases as an inconvenience or terminating as a form of contraception or because it interferes with their life style."

Jen thought how mature and purposeful Chloe was. It was amazing how the very girl who was on the verge of being aborted was now championing a cause to prevent it. Tammy and Robbie would have suffered so much had they gone through with the abortion. And to think that this beautiful girl would never have been anything other than a painful memory of guilt and sorrow.

"One would think that the safest place for a baby is in the mother's womb and yet, in all too many cases, it's becoming the most dangerous place. It's unbelievable, Chloe, that I should even make such a bizarre, senseless statement!"

"That's so true, Auntie. When Mom was alive she used to say all the time that a woman is given the awesome blessing to carry and house the gift of life from the moment of conception."

Chloe remembering her mother's words began to cry. She could barely utter the sad words which followed, "Instead of smelling a newborn infant ready to be cradled in her arms, the odour of death fills the air and empty arms reflect the terrible deed that was done."

Jenny was feeling the heaviness of the conversation. She too, missed her friend so much. She too recalled the many times Tammy would say that we should rejoice and celebrate the miracle of life not its termination. How was it possible that the world should have come to such a place in our evolution that we have legalized the killing of millions and millions of children? It was as if Chloe had read Jenny's mind.

"How could such an evil practice become legal? How could intelligent judges in their wisdom make such a ruling that legalizes the killing of millions of innocent, helpless infants!? Could they not foresee the devastating consequences upon the mother's that do that, too? How can they sleep at night? It's all so senseless! I've been involved in this for as long as I can remember starting with my mom and I still can't understand it. What is it that I am not seeing, Auntie?"

Chloe began to cry and the phone grew silent. Tears filled Jenny's eyes too. She had no answer. It was impossible to make such a deep, terrible wrong appear right, a gross injustice appear just, it was an evil that must be stopped.

"People around the world must see it for what it is. A holocaust in our midst!" blurted out Chloe. "Every minute of every day, many defenceless babies' lives are terminated through abortion and all the while we stand idly by and let it happen."

"I think the majority of people know that it's wrong and a horrible thing but they remain silent because it's legal and they don't want to appear to be condemning of women who had an abortion."

"But Auntie, the law needs to be changed! And people need to realize that it is not a matter of choosing pro-life over women who have had an abortion. We condemn the act... not the woman! We welcome them and love and care for them and want so much to help heal their pain and sorrow.

"That's what people need to know and understand, Chloe. Remaining silent only perpetuates the evil of abortion, it doesn't change the law. No one is condemning the women, but rather the act of terminating a baby's life."

"Oh, Auntie Jen, I hope people will begin to speak out. They just have to. It's clear that politicians will never act on their own. Most, if not all, sit on the fence waiting to see which way the wind blows. If only more would have the courage to stand up to this inhumanity!"

"It's like we said, Chloe, politicians will only act when it affects their votes. If the silent majority ever begins to speak up, watch out, Chloe. There is tremendous power in the voice of the people."

"Yes, I saw evidence of that all this week. Perhaps you saw it in the news as well about a mother and father who abused their daughter by locking her up in a room in the basement for days on end when she disobeyed. There was such uproar by the public in the newspapers, radio, TV… as there should be…"

"And I know exactly what you are leading up to, Chloe. How is it that so many speak up when they see abuse of children and yet remain silent and ignore the daily killing of innocent helpless infants?"

"That's exactly right, Auntie!" Where are all those people now? *Is the killing of infants considered less than the abuse of a child?*

"Well, Chloe, the more you talk and champion this cause the more people will come onside. I certainly let my member of Parliament as well as the prime minister know that something must be done."

"Did you know Auntie, that out of the millions of infants that are aborted each year, less than 1% of the babies are due to rape and incest?"

"Oh Chloe, your reasoning is so clear, simple and honest. I have to agree with you, Chloe, that the reasons for abortion in my opinion, are not necessary and in most cases aren't justifiable if at all. Unfortunately they are legally allowed to have an abortion and all too many doctors are willing to do it."

"Yes, that's the part I just can't get, as you said, Auntie, to understand how a doctor can terminate the life of a baby one minute and then in the next try his hardest to deliver an infant! Surely they can see what they are doing; that in both cases it's a human life that they are dealing with."

"Exactly!"

"You're right, Auntie. It just seems like such an uphill battle. Maybe Dad's solution is best of all. He says what the world needs now more than anything is prayer. God answers prayer. If enough people get down on their knees and pray, he believes God will change hearts. He will fill people up with his Holy Spirit so that when they rise off their knees they will be filled with such power and courage that they will shout from the roof tops to stop this insanity."

"You know, Chloe, I think your dad is right! Prayer is what is needed in the world. It's what we have turned our back on. The prayers of those who realize its importance are always answered by the Father. And He will change those who don't. God is the one who can change the heart of those who now don't understand and will help stop the terrible things we do to one another."

"One of the things I remember Mom always telling me when I went with her to the counseling centre was to always remind the ladies who have lost their way in life and come there for help, that Jesus loves them and wants to heal them and that He forgives them. The wounds he suffered on the cross do not reveal condemnation but His great merciful love for them." And after a moment of silence, Chloe added, "I finally understand what Mom meant."

"Chloe, that is a beautiful way to end this discussion. Let's make sure we don't leave our talks three weeks apart again."

"For sure, Auntie, but before you go I just wanted to say that I will never forget that day we strolled in the garden after Mom died and a butterfly followed us. Do you remember how it rested on my hand when we sat down on the swing in the gazebo? I believe it was Mom's spirit."

"I do too, Chloe. It was late in the fall and all of the Monarchs had left for their trek back to Mexico and that one stayed behind for some reason."

Jenny could hear Chloe crying. She missed her dear friend, Tammy, so much too.

In between sobs, Chloe continued, "I'll never forget how we said the Guardian Angel Prayer, the one you taught Mom, and she passed it on to me. Can we say that together now?"

"Yes, Chloe, and let us add your Mom's deepest prayer that all of God's children have the right to life. May her spirit touch the guardian angel of all mothers the world over to ever prompt their charges to never consider abortion as an option but to give life to the precious gift within their womb as God intended from the beginning of all time…

> *"Oh Angel of God my Guardian dear*
> *To whom God's love commits me here.*
> *Ever this day be at my side*
> *To light and guard, to rule and guide.*
> *Amen.*

> *"I love you dearly, Chloe."*
> *"I love you too, Auntie!"*

CHAPTER TEN

A FTER A LIGHT lunch, Jenny left to visit her mother shortly after one o'clock. It was Saturday afternoon so she didn't have to contend with the weekday noon-hour rush. Her mother's care home was only fifteen minutes away. They'd purposely chosen it for that reason. However, with Jenny's plan to move to an apartment in the west end, it would take at least thirty minutes to make the trek.

"Oh well, I'll just have to try to drive over when the traffic is not so busy," she reasoned.

Her mother was sleeping when Jenny entered. She looked so peaceful and at rest. Jenny tiptoed over to a nearby chair and sat down. As she waited in the silence, she thought about how her mom's life hadn't been so fulfilling, either. Her father had been both a workaholic and an alcoholic. Though her mother had never shared her feelings, Jenny knew it had to be painful to see both conditions eventually kill his body and spirit. He had given so much of his life to his company and in the end, it was all for naught; he was forced to resign.

Jenny slipped into one of those rare philosophical times she allowed herself. Life had been so cruel to her on the outside, but really, many of the things had happened because of her thoughts and choices. She hadn't heeded her father's advice and lived 22 years in a loveless marriage that had come to an end.

"Oh, Jenny, don't be so morbid about it all," she chided herself. "Sure you've made some foolish choices, but it's never too late to start over. Each and every moment in the present is an opportunity to begin again. Each and every day is a new day. Look how well you started out today. Just get on with it, create your own future by living fully in each and every moment. You are now free of James' hold, you are still young, just make the best of the time you have left." And then more audibly she added, "Amen."

Her mother's eyelids fluttered open and her gaze fell upon her daughter sitting in the chair off to the side. She smiled as she took in her daughter's beauty. Jenny's eyes drifted back towards her mother's bed.

"Oh, hi, Mom. I see you are awake."

"Yes, I was just admiring my beautiful daughter. You look lovely in yellow, Jenny. It so compliments your golden wheat hair."

"Thank you, Mom. You looked so peaceful I didn't want to disturb you. I thought I would just wait until you woke up."

"Oh, please don't in the future. I so look forward to your visits and am sad when you leave. Every moment you are here is precious to me, so please wake me should I be asleep."

"Okay, Mom."

"I couldn't get to sleep last night. I began to think about what you were going to tell me today. It has to do with James and you, doesn't it? You said you and James had drifted apart."

Jenny sat there motionless and emotionless, staring back at her mother. Thoughts about how she would tell her mother had consumed her on the drive over and now, her mom opened the door for her. Jenny made up her mind to be totally open, to allow her mom to enter her real world.

She let it all out. Tears flowed down her cheeks as she revealed her real life with James. She held nothing back, not even what J.J. had said at the bookstore.

"Oh, Mom, I feel partly responsible for not telling James from the beginning about Camilla. But then, James could have been more understanding, too. Another man would have easily accepted it."

Her mother motioned for her to come closer.

Jenny shuffled her chair nearer to her mother without getting up. When she was near enough, her mother extended her hand and Jenny reached out to receive her mother's compassion and understanding.

TEARS WELLED UP in Edith's eyes, as well, as slowly the sorrow of what her daughter was going through registered in her mind. She recalled only too well that Sunday evening during dinner when she had unthinkingly revealed Jenny's rape. James reaction was terrifying.

Oh, my sweet Jenny. What have we done to you? If only she and Ted hadn't interfered with Jenny's relationship with that boy in Regina. Jenny had just been so young and they had never realized how much in love they both were. They had thought they knew what was best, but that "best" had ended in disaster. Ted had been right, and Edith realized her husband suffered so much by following her decision. Although Edith never had any doubts about it from the start, she couldn't deny over the years the anguish her decision had caused.

How unhappy my little girl has been over the years, marrying someone I approved of, someone I thought could buy prestige and happiness. Oh, how wrong I was.

A sharp pain of regret clenched around her. She tightened her grip on Jenny's hand, trying to squeeze out some measure of forgiveness, without having to tell Jenny the horrible truth of what they had done. How they destroyed all the letters that she had written to Henry and all the letters that Henry had written back to her.

No… not all the letters. There was still one left. Edith wondered if Mrs. Pederson had saved the one for Henry, too? She recalled the pact she and Mary Pederson had made back then, to keep the letters from their children. Edith remembered that at the time, Henry was about to be married in a matter of days and Jenny was planning to marry James the following spring. The revelation of the letters would have complicated things too much and hurt too many people. Had they been wrong in keeping the letters from their children? Would it have been better to bring everything out back then? Just looking back at the years of heartache Jenny had gone through since seemed to confirm that and more.

And what about Henry, Edith wondered? How had his marriage turned out? How many lives had they ruined by their decision to control the lives of their children?

Jenny's eyes looked red and puffy as she sobbed. Sharing her life and divorce had brought with it so much buried emotion. Edith was glad Jenny opened up to her. This was perhaps the first and only real conversation they'd had as a mother and daughter for years and years, if ever.

Edith no longer wanted to control or convince Jenny that she was wrong, or suggest some quick advice. She finally listened with her heart, instead of her head. Edith chastised herself for not doing so long ago.

"Well, Mom, there it all is. Not very happy news, is it?"

"Oh, Jenny, I truly am so sorry for it all. Please forgive me for not really listening to you sooner. You have carried this all alone for far too long. Oh, where have I been? Please forgive me."

"It's not your fault, Mom. You tried your best, and your life hasn't been easy, either. You have had enough to bear, without me adding to it."

"But, Jenny, it's easier to carry a load together than alone. Had we been closer, perhaps we could have talked things out and helped one another."

"Well, that's in the past, Mom. What is done is done. What has happened has happened. Hopefully, we have learned from our past and it will make our futures brighter and happier."

"So, what are you going to do now?"

"Well, I'm moving out the first of next week. I called the landlord of an apartment I saw two weeks ago and he is holding the suite for me until I put down a deposit. And then, after that, I just don't know. I guess I'll just take one day at a time as the saying goes."

"Yes, perhaps that's all you can do for now," Edith concurred. "What about J.J.?"

"I just don't know, Mom. He's so upset with me and blames me for destroying our marriage. He is so blinded by it all, and so esteems his father, he just won't listen. And I feel trapped in a way. I don't want to turn him against his father by trying to convince him to be more understanding and considerate of what I have been going through, how lonely I was and that I had no life at all."

"Just be patient with him. He'll come around."

"I hope so, he's all I have left and I do love him so." And after a long moment, she added, "There is Camilla, too. She was 29 years old this past May 24th. I was thinking about calling up the welfare agency to see if there is any chance I might find her. I'm afraid that she has found out she was adopted and hates me for giving her up."

"Oh, Jenny, you have such a tender heart. Come here."

Jenny bent over enough to fall into her mother's extended arms. They warmly embraced one another as Millie walked in with mid-afternoon tea and a plate of cookies.

"My, my, isn't this a pleasant sight to see. Mom and daughter hugging one another."

Jenny and Edith separated.

"Oh hi, Millie, just what we both need, a nice cup of tea," said Jenny.

Millie didn't linger, but rather walked to the far end of the room, placed the tea and cookies on a table with wheels and then rolled the table between them.

"Thank you, Millie," said Jenny.

"Oh, you are so welcome, my dear," replied Millie, as she bustled out.

Edith and Jenny quietly sipped the hot tea and munched on oatmeal cookies.

"These are sure good," Jenny said, trying to change the subject to something cheerier.

"Yes, I like the way the cook makes them so soft and chewy. I never could get mine that way. Always so hard just like me," she muttered.

"What was that, Mom?"

"Oh, nothing, Jenny. I'm just angry with myself for not being more observant. I guess I always felt things were not right between you and James, but I always swept it under the carpet, afraid to really look at it, afraid of what I might find and of not being able to handle it; to deal with the truth." Edith groped for words she was not used to expressing.

"Please, don't blame yourself. It's my doing, I could just have easily told you."

"Well, from now on, no more secrets between us. Everything out in the open," Edith said, with a tone of conviction.

Thoughts of truth, openness and honesty formed on Edith's lips. She was getting ready to tell all, but nothing would come out. She had lived a lie for so long. The truth in this situation was too alien to her. She so feared the consequences of what might happen. What if Jenny never forgave her and never wanted to see her again?

"Is there something wrong, Mom, you look so flushed?" Jenny studied her mother and a thought from the past popped in her mind. "It reminds me of a time so long ago, when we were sitting in the kitchen of our home on the estate shortly after Daddy died and there was that brown paper bag sitting on the kitchen table. There was some- thing inside it that you didn't want me to see. You have the same look on your face now, as you did then.

"What was in that bag, Mom? I've always wondered about it." Jenny looked at her mother, waiting for an answer.

Edith's heart jumped to her mouth, she was speechless and didn't know how to answer. She was trapped between truth and consequences. Convicted by her own words just moments ago.

"Mom, what is it? Please, you just said we should start to share all."

Edith stared at her daughter, trying to think of the right words to say, words that would soften the blow, words that would carry enough sorrow to elicit forgiveness, words that would evoke and draw forth understanding, words that would justify their reasoning as to why they did what they did. But those words failed to come to mind. For the first time in her life, Edith found herself speechless. She was sick of the hollow words that carried no feeling or truth from her heart and, yet, she just didn't know how to express it. This was an area of life that was foreign to her and she felt lost and alone. Tears flowed from her eyes as the gush of her wrongdoing flooded her being. She became too overwhelmed to speak. It would have been the perfect time to share what had happened and what she had done, but she was so afraid of Jenny's reaction.

"Please, Jenny," Edith said, her voice cracking and trembling, "I just can't share that with you, today. Please forgive me. I need time to think it all out."

"But, Mom," Jenny pleaded, "We just vowed to tell each other the truth, to tell all. I've shared my soul to you and now it's your turn. Please, Mom."

There was a long silence. "Oh, Jenny. My dear Jenny. I just can't today. But I promise I will in the very near future. I just need time. Please grant me that. You will soon understand why I have withheld this from you for all these years."

Jenny was at the peak of her inquisitiveness. "I just have to know, Mom!"

Millie stuck her head in the door. "So, how are the two of you doing? Oh my, Mrs. Sarsky, you look so upset." Millie walked further into the room, keeping her gaze on Edith. "I don't mean to interfere, but remember what the doctor told you, to rest and stay calm. Would you like a pill to settle you down?"

"No, I'm fine; it's just something Jenny and I are discussing."

"Well, I don't mean to end this, but you should be getting your rest. Perhaps, Jenny, you should go now and come back tomorrow, if you can."

"Yes, yes of course. I'm sorry, Mom, I didn't mean to upset you."

"Yes, I know that. Millie is right, though, it's been quite a day for the both of us. Tomorrow is another a day and perhaps, then, I shall be up to the task." Thank goodness Millie had happened along when she did.

Jenny stared into her mother's eyes, searching for some clue as to what she was hiding from her, but nothing came to mind.

I wonder what it could be?

"Mom, you just have to promise me that you will tell me the secret tomorrow."

"Yes, Jenny, tomorrow I will tell everything… I promise."

Finally feeling satisfied with some sense of closure, Jenny stood and kissed her mother.

"I love you, Mom."

"I love you, too, Jenny."

After Jenny left, Millie gave Edith a sedative. It normally put her right to sleep, but no medicine could erase the thoughts churning through her mind. The glaring truth of her wrongdoing stung sharply in her heart. She had done an unforgivable wrong to her daughter and now had to the pay the price. The cost of telling the truth was too high at the moment when Jenny was there. Edith just couldn't afford the possibility of estranging her daughter. She would be so lost without her, yet her deceit stung and her stomach churned away at her.

Once again, Edith grew angry with herself for only thinking of herself. Jenny had the right to the truth, and Edith knew she deserved any reaction Jenny was sure to throw at her. It would serve her right if Jenny left and never came back to see her. Perhaps the punishment might pay for the all the heartache and pain she'd caused her daughter.

As drugged as she was, Edith got out of bed and walked to the closet. Her hope chest, one of the few things she had kept and brought with her to the care home, was on a low shelf. There was still an aura of light around the chest, but over the years Edith had become used to it. Every now and then, the staff would comment on the brightness coming from the closet. Edith usually commented that it was the reflection of the sun's rays that somehow caused it.

As she picked up the chest, it felt especially warm and she became aware again of the shimmering light growing brighter. The key was still in the keyhole since she was afraid she would lose it or forget where she put it should she store it some place else. She carried the small chest to her bedside and placed it on the table beside the empty cups of tea and plate of leftover cookies. She sat down on the edge of her bed, waiting a moment to catch her breath and recoup some strength to face the secret she had hidden from Jenny for 24 years. Edith sighed as she sat there. She felt tired, not just from her sickness, but of life itself.

"Oh, how foolish we can be, and how cruel we can be to our loved ones. It is so true; we reap what we sow. We make our own bed, and now we have to sleep in it. Yes, from the very bed I sit on, I once again withheld the truth from my little girl today. I can no longer live with myself if I don't disclose everything."

Edith turned the key and the latch popped open for the first time since placing Henry's letter to Jenny in it. Edith raised the lid and looked inside for the letter and then she remembered burying it at the very bottom hoping to never see it again. She moved some of the papers and photos aside and dug down to the bottom and knew instantly when she felt Henry's letter. It was very warm.

She took hold of the letter and brought it out into the light of day. "Yes," Edith muttered, "all hidden secrets eventually come to the light of day. Especially secrets that have caused harm."

Edith stared at the letter and remembered that there was something heavy inside. It had frightened her enough back then to not throw it into the fire, but now…it filled her with a sense of peace. She wondered what was in the letter.

She had never told Ted that he had talked in his sleep about the angels inside the letters. She'd never shared that with Ted when he awoke as she didn't want him to remember the letters, but rather to forget about them. At the moment of his death he had cried out: "deliver the letters, the angelic letters." Edith always felt that the letters she and Mrs. Pederson had received were the ones that Ted had spoken of. But what did they have to do with angels? Did the object inside the envelope have something to do with them? Well, she would know soon enough.

"Oh, I'm sorry to you, too, Ted, if you can hear me," Edith softly cried out. She hung her head as the truth continued to confront her. "You were so right. I see it all now so clearly, we should never try to control the lives and destiny of others. They must be left free to choose. We can only be guides, beacons, supportive, and at best, live a life that reflects the integrity which you so strongly tried to live by.

"I made you take a detour from your commitment to be honest and truthful. I caused you to live a lie and carry out actions that went against the very core of your beliefs, your being, your heart and soul. Oh, Ted, please forgive me, too." Edith cried out again in anguish, "I was the cause of your drinking, I see it, now. Oh, Ted. I caused your death. Please forgive me."

If it were not for the medication that softened the harshness of her awareness, her realization of what she had done to Ted and Jenny, she just might have had a heart attack. She was totally immersed in self-condemnation, now spilling out in tears; the only way the body knew how to relieve an aching soul.

Edith reached for a Kleenex on the end table and wiped the blurriness from her eyes, but the tears streamed out relentlessly. All the guilt she suppressed, the knowing which she withheld from her conscious mind erupted and she could no longer hold it back or lie to herself. What Edith didn't realize was that in facing the truth of her sins, that within her anguish and turmoil, she was also planting the seed of peace and that the truth would set her free.

Around 3:30 in the morning, Millie checked on Edith. When Millie entered the room, she was taken aback by what she saw. Edith was asleep. The chest on the table beside the bed was opened. Edith was holding an envelope in her left hand resting on the bed beside her. Several wet Kleenex lay on her bed, the night table, and the table with the chest.

"What on earth is going on here?" Millie muttered. Millie took the envelope from Edith's hand, wondering if that was what had upset her. "Oh my, it feels so warm. Could it be from the heat of Edith's hand?"

Millie brought the envelope to the open chest, placed it back in the chest and closed it, turning the key in the lock.

She picked up the chest and put it back in the closet.

"Out of sight, out of mind," muttered Millie.

Millie stopped and took one last look at Edith before leaving. She wondered how on earth Edith had made her way over to the closet by herself. She had been bedridden for two weeks, not even able to make it out of bed to go to the bathroom. And then, to carry that heavy chest back to the bed?

Something very powerful must have motivated her to do that.

Chapter Eleven

Jenny could hardly wait for morning. What could her mother have to tell her? It seemed so painful for her. Her only clue was that whatever it was had something to do with what was in that brown paper bag. But how could something that happened 23 years ago back when she and James had decided to get married have any bearing on what was making her mother upset now?

Shortly after one, Jenny drove over to the care home. Anxious to see her mother, she pulled into the parking lot five minutes earlier than usual. Jenny turned the car off, but sat silently for a few moments before getting out. She took a deep breath and slowly exhaled. She knew something was about to happen, but didn't know what.

"Well, whatever it is, I'm ready to face it and deal with it." Jenny hopped out of the car and walked briskly into the care home and down the hall towards her mother's room.

Jenny found her mother wide awake when she entered the room. The top half of her bed was cranked up slightly, which made it appear as if her mother was sitting upright. Jenny could tell by the look in her mother's eyes and her posture that she, too, was ready and determined to reveal her secret.

"Hi, Mom," Jenny said, as she studied her mother.

"Hello, Jenny," her mother responded, with a little bounce in her voice.

Good. Her voice was energetic and she sounded well enough to go ahead with it.

"Jenny?"

"Yes, Mom?"

"Before you sit down, I would like you to do something for me."

"Of course, what is it?"

"If you go into my closet you will see my keepsake chest on the shelf. You know the one I inherited from my mother after she passed away."

"Yes, I know the one. You told me that you put important papers and documents in there such as wills and deeds."

"Yes, that is true, but I also keep other things in there that are very private. I must caution you, Jenny, that what you will find in there will be very painful, and I ask you to please be very understanding and forgiving. Remember, I too, was young once and lacked good judgment at times."

Jenny looked at her mother then rushed to the closet. Her first inclination was to look up to where a shelf in a closet would usually be, but in this care home the shelves were purposely put just above the shoes on the floor so that residents could have easy access to them. Jenny bent down and picked up the chest before carrying it to the bedside eating table.

"Turn the key and open it. It holds a secret I have been keeping from you for many, many years. I realize now, I was wrong to do so and I ask you once again to please, please forgive me for my wrongdoing."

Jenny's heart galloped as she studied her mother's face. She was excited to open it and, yet, from her mother's cautioning and pleading for forgiveness, she was afraid of what she might find. A sense of foreboding swept over her, as she reached for the key.

She turned to her mother whose eyes were already filled with tears and pleading forgiveness.

"Is what was in that brown paper bag in here?"

"Yes."

Jenny turned back to the chest. *It can't possibly be that terrible if it could be held in a small paper bag.* Jenny's rationalization helped ease the tension. But the fear in her mother's eyes and her pleading for forgiveness seemed to intensify with every move Jenny made…

Jenny's fingers trembled as they turned the key and the latch snapped opened. She slowly raised the lid. A letter lay on top.

"Is it this letter, Mom?" asked Jenny, trying to brace herself.

Her mother's response was the obvious apprehension in her eyes and furrowed brow. Her face was contorted so much, Jenny almost didn't recognize her. Jenny reached for the envelope, which lay face down. The instant she touched it, a warmth spread through her being, and she instantly knew who it was from. She raised her head and looked into her mother's eyes.

"It's a letter from Henry… isn't it, Mom?"

Her mother didn't answer. She didn't even nod her head.

Jenny returned her gaze to the envelope as she slowly turned it over and read the return address on the top left hand corner. It was as she had thought. It was from Henry.

Jenny's eyes widened as she read the addresses again.

"It is from Henry. But it's addressed to Daddy's business, which means… Henry didn't know our home address. But I sent him many letters with our home address on it?"

Jenny gasped.

"He never received any of my letters. Why didn't Daddy bring the letter home to me? Why? Every day I asked Daddy if there was a letter for me from Henry and every day he said no. But, why?"

Jenny looked at her mom in disbelief, pure shame was written all over her face. Her mother clutched at the bedspread covering her body and gathered it under her chin as if to protect herself from her daughter's impending wrath and anger. Jenny's knees wobbled and finally buckled, she collapsed into the chair next to her mother's bedside.

"Oh, Mom," Jenny said, in a tone that left no doubt as to her pain. "How on earth could you and Daddy have done this to me?"

Her mother didn't answer, she was frozen with guilt.

Jenny looked back at the letter, her mind churning to fit the pieces together and make some sense of it all.

The more she thought about it, the more she thought she understood what had happened. But her revelations brought her no solace. Her mom had been worried about how close she and Henry had become. They'd deliberately sought to keep them apart.

"You and Dad kept Henry's letters from me and my letters from Henry, didn't you?" Jenny searched her mother's eyes.

Her mother ducked behind the covers and nodded.

"Oh, Mom…"

Anger and hurt vied for control of Jenny's feelings. She couldn't understand how her mom and dad could have done this to her. How could they have kept Henry's letters away from her, knowing how much she longed to receive them? How they could have lied to her all these years? Lied about having mailed her letters. Lied about having never received any letters from Henry.

Hot tears rolled down Jenny's cheeks, the streaks burning against her flushed red face. The grip of despair wedged itself in-between her anger and hurt, overwhelming her. She looked up at her mother through blurred eyes, not knowing how to react. She reached up and wiped the tears off with the back of her hand but they just kept coming. All the bottled up disappointment and feelings of rejection she'd suppressed over the years, finally surfaced. Jenny sat there, helpless to control her emotions, at the complete mercy of the truth that had been denied her and was now staring at her squarely in her mind, heart and soul.

Gradually, Jenny's sobs subsided until she sat quiet and still. Jenny reached for the Kleenex box on the end table beside her mother's bed and half-heartedly tugged several sheets from it. She wiped her eyes, blew her nose and then dropped her hands to her lap completely, emotionally, physically and mentally exhausted. First, the divorce proceedings, then learning her mother's secret.

Aloneness and abandonment washed over her.

All those whom she had thought were close to her, truthful to her and trustworthy were no more. James had failed her. Her son had abandoned her, and the persons who had given her life had taken it away from her. Jenny would never have imagined in a million years that she would reach a moment in her life when all she felt was consumed by utter emptiness.

She looked up at her mother. The pain and anguish in her mother's eyes appeared even greater than what Jenny herself was feeling. The forlorn image before her, tugged at her spirit of compassion and forgiveness. A sense of acceptance and reason crawled back into Jenny's mind. Even if she had the strength to lash out at her mother, what good would it do to be angry at her now? The damage had been done and now they must live with the consequences, as painful as they were.

"We thought…we thought it was for…the best," her mother squeaked out between sobs.

Jenny had never seen her mother look so sorrowful. Feelings of empathy strengthened as Jenny felt pity and love for her mother more than anger, understanding more than vengeance. It was against Jenny's nature to be vindictive and she intuitively knew that to harbour a spirit of unforgiveness towards her mother would simply perpetuate this entire tragic affair and keep them both trapped. She managed a slight smile and immediately Jenny sensed her mother's relief as she cried all the more.

As her mother sobbed and looked on, Jenny picked up the letter and stared at her name written in Henry's handwriting: *To Jenny Sarsky.*

Henry had kept his promise.

She was about to open the letter when it dawned on her: what about Henry? Did he know she had kept her promise, too? If he never received any of her letters, he was probably still under the impression that she hadn't written to him.

"Oh, God," Jenny blurted out as once again pangs of pain stabbed at her heart at the full realization of the consequences of her parents' withholding of these letters hit her. Tears welled up again. She wiped them with the back of her hand and looked down at the envelope once more… in no hurry to open it. There was no urgency, now. It was all over between them. Jenny almost didn't want to know if Henry still loved her; that it all could have been so different.

If only… Jenny's thoughts drifted off to what might have been, but she reigned herself in. She didn't want to go there. It would be too painful to dwell on that possibility. She would only drown in thoughts of regret. Decisions were made on her behalf a long time ago and the years of time had done their damage. It was too late. She knew that Henry was married and had four children and was a successful artist.

It could have been me at his side, if only… No, Jenny, it's too late for "ifs" or what might have been, and it's too late for blame. What is done is done.

Once again, her gaze rested on the envelope. She turned it over and over until she noticed the stamp. As she studied the stamp, she noted that it had their home address on it, but the date stamp behind it read differently from the special delivery stamp.

"Oh my," she said. "Henry sent this letter just before Christmas in 1956, then, almost seven years later, just after Daddy died, it was sent by special delivery to our home…" Jenny looked at her mother. "How did this happen, Mom? Who could have sent this letter to us after Daddy's death?"

Once again, her mother was too choked up to speak. She just shrugged her shoulders and shook her head.

The letter had been kept from her not once, but twice. Another realization struck her that she had been home at the time the letter was delivered! Jenny snapped her gaze back up at her mother.

"The brown paper bag! The letter was in it. You hid it in there the day it was delivered, didn't you?"

Her mother stared transfixed at Jenny.

Jenny was on the trail of discovery, but the truth would not bring her satisfaction or any consolation, rather it was all a trail of sorrow. Her mind flashed back in time as she vividly recalled the scene in the kitchen.

"It was right there on the kitchen table, the brown paper bag folded over at the top with Henry's letter hidden inside. I even picked it up and held the bag in my hand. It was just inches away. And then…," glaring at her mother, her voice raising, Jenny concluded, "you snatched it away from me. Mom, you took away my life, my hopes, my dreams! Sure, I was engaged to James, but we still were a long way from being married. There was still time… time to correct it all."

Her mother shook her head.

As Jenny looked down at the letter, she thought about the last one she'd written to Henry. It too was sent in December, a week before Christmas! Both Henry's letter and hers were sent almost simultaneously!

As she brought the letter closer to her, she felt something heavy shift inside. She shook it from side to side and as she did, the memory of her weighted letter flooded back.

"Mom, when I sent my last letter to Henry just before Christmas, I put a pewter angel inside as a Christmas present. Could it possibly be that Henry sent one to me, as well? At the same time? Oh, Mom, could this be possible? And, is that what Daddy was referring to? 'The letters, the angels. Deliver the angelic letters', just before he died? I still dream about that, Mom."

Again, Edith didn't respond.

Jenny now desperately wanted to open the letter. She had to know. She slipped her little finger into the slight opening at the end of the envelope. She visualized Henry sealing the envelope and tried to feel his lips and the moistness of his tongue as her finger slid along the edge of the envelope flap, gradually tearing it open. Jenny's heart hammered against her ribs, as her hand moved away from the open envelope and looked inside.

She gasped!

Jenny was speechless. She looked at the angel in awe. She tilted the envelope and the angel flew into her waiting hand. She set the envelope on her lap and studied the angel more closely.

"Mom, it's identical to the one I sent Henry. This is unbelievable, what are the chances of this happening?" The angel felt so warm, almost as if it had just left Henry's fingertips. She knew he had kissed it, sending along his love. They had both believed their guardian angels would look after them. She brought the angel up to her lips and tenderly kissed it.

Oblivious to her mother's presence in the room, Jenny closed her eyes and whispered, "Oh, Henry, how I longed for this moment to receive your letter and now it is here, but… *it's all too late.*"

Edith looked on. She could only imagine what was in her daughter's heart. Edith wanted to reach out and hold her child, to console her, but she couldn't. She had alienated herself from that privilege as a mother long ago by the dreadful decision she had made. She had been the cause of it all, and was now paying the price of her actions.

Jenny's chest heaved under the weight of her grief and distress. The sight of her daughter's forlorn figure stabbed pangs of guilt and shame into Edith. But would this act of self-condemnation be enough to pay for the price of her wrongdoing? Would she lose her daughter along with her self-respect? That question burned through Edith's mind and heart as she sobbed again.

Jenny cupped the angel in her hands and brought it to her chest. She bowed her head and closed her eyes, savouring the gift and miracle revealed to her. *The same angel.* Identical! The inscription on the bottom edges, exactly the same: "*Watch over my beloved.*" Unbelievable!

As memories of Henry flooded back into her mind, Jenny sat motionless, as still as statue, frozen in time, reliving all those precious moments they'd had together.

A peaceful aura grew within the room. Jenny knew it was her closest friend coming to comfort her.

"Thank you, Lord, for giving us the warmth and peace of the sun," whispered Jenny. Even though her eyes were closed, she knew and felt the intimacy of her consoler. The sun had moved further to the west and streamed in through the bedroom window. It streaked across Jenny's face, highlighting her golden hair and shimmering upon her white skin. She looked as angelic as the angel she held. Jenny so loved the sun; like nature, it soothed her and gave her life. She now likened its warmth to that of Henry's touch, its light to Henry's love. The air she was breathing sweetened.

Knowing that at the very least, *Henry and she had kept their promise to each other,* a sense of consolation filled her. Jenny opened her eyes, again, and looked directly at her mother who stared back, her eyes pleading to be forgiven. Her mother looked so spent, Jenny was unsure if she should go on. But she had already waited too long for the truth, she just had to know one more thing.

"Mom, do you think Henry received my last letter with the angel in it, too?"

"Yes, Jenny, your letter was sent to Henry's home, too."

"Then, Henry must have received it. Then he knows I kept my promise to write, too!"

"Unfortunately, Jenny, Henry's mother didn't give the letter to Henry, either."

"But why!? Why on earth would she do that?"

"Because at the time, Henry was two weeks away from marrying another girl."

"Oh, Mom… Oh, Mom," was all Jenny could say. She understood their reasoning. *But was it too late…?*

"You and James were scheduled to be married as soon as you both finished university and so we both agreed not to show the letters to either you or to Henry."

"Oh, Mom," Jenny lamented.

Wanting to get it all out, Edith continued, haltingly at first, but then once she started, the words came out in a torrential rush.

"Mrs. Pederson and I made a pact never to show you and Henry the letters we received. And yes, Henry's letter was delivered to the house the same day you walked into the kitchen and saw the brown paper bag on the kitchen table. I had just finished speaking to Mrs. Pederson. We had just made the pact and I couldn't let you see the letter. Henry was about to marry someone else and with you engaged to James…" Edith was repeating herself desperately trying to get Jenny to understand their motive…

"Don't you see, Jenny? We both thought it was for the best. It should never have happened. I was so concerned about you and Henry at the time, that you would get pregnant, that we moved so many times and that your relationship with Henry would go nowhere. Please understand, Jenny. I know we did wrong, but at the time, I was so sure it was the right thing to do. It was not your father, it was all my doing. I made him go along with it and he suffered so much for it."

Edith's voice cracked and trembled as the horrible truth poured out. The confession became for Edith a full and complete catharsis of the mind and heart. All the old, dark, evil things she'd kept secret gushed like fresh blood where they had become congealed, effectively blocking the passage of any personal peace for too long. But even after having revealed all and completing her confession, where a look of deep relief should have appeared on Edith's face, there was only fear. Would her daughter, sitting in judgment before her, find forgiveness in her heart? Edith hung her head, no longer able to look into her daughter's eyes, and sobbed uncontrollably.

"Oh, Mom," Jenny said, shaking her head, "how could all this possibly have happened? I wonder what Henry would have done if he had been given the letter? What would I have done? Yes, it was seven years later. We'd both found new partners, but still…"

Edith looked up at her daughter. She knew what Jenny was thinking, but couldn't say a word. What else was there to say?

Finally, Jenny looked down at the letter still resting on her lap, waiting to be read. She laid the angel on her lap and picked up the envelope. She took out the letter and unfolded it as she knew Henry had imagined she would when she received it. Slowly, very slowly, Jenny read what Henry had written to her over 30 years ago…

Dear Jenny,

It's almost Christmas, and just about four months since you left. I was thinking today that the only gift I would ever want for the rest of my life is to receive a letter from you.

I sent a box to your dad's company address almost a month ago. It was filled with all the letters I've written to you since the day you left. I hope you received them. If you did, could you please tell me why you haven't written back? Even if you no longer care or have found someone else, just let me know. It is so hard not to hear from you.

I wanted to send you one last letter, along with a little Christmas gift. I'll always remember how much you loved your guardian angel. I went shopping after school today and as I walked past Eaton's, I saw this angel shining underneath the star at the top of their Christmas tree. It was exactly what I was looking for— a guardian angel to protect you always and to remind you of my love for you. I hope you like it and will wear it around your neck all the time.

How do you like living in Ottawa and how are you doing at your new school? Have you made a lot of friends? I like Grade 9, and maybe you won't be surprised to hear that of all the subjects I am taking, I like art the best.

Oh, Jenny, I sure miss you. I miss your smile, your sparkling eyes, the way you talk and the way you walk. I especially miss holding your hand and just walking along with you. I often find myself dreaming you are beside me as I walk to school, but it's just a dream and so empty without you.

I am looking forward to the Christmas break and working full-time in Mr. Engelmann's store. I just love working there and seem to keep coming up with new ideas to increase business.

Mr. Engelmann is great to work for and I am learning so much from him.

I made a special wish to the bright star of the east tonight, to send out my love to you. I hope and pray that you get this letter and my gift. Every night I pray for my guardian angel to talk to yours, so that together they can find a way to bring us together again.

Even though we are far apart, you are forever in my heart. I will love you always. Have a merry Christmas!

All my love,

Henry

Jenny had to stop reading several times before she finished the letter. Henry's words of love and longing touched her heart so deeply. Tear after tear fell on the letter as she read words that she'd longed to hear for such a long, long time.

Oh, Henry, I love you so much, too.

Her heart ached to be held in Henry's arms and to tenderly kiss his lips. If only they could go back in time and change it all.

Edith watched her daughter read a letter she should have received when she was 15. It would have been her first love letter, a letter she was entitled to. Edith's own first love letter rested in the very same keepsake chest that she'd hidden Jenny's letter in. Yet, she had denied her own daughter that same joy and memory, until now.

Watching Jenny as she read her cherished letter, she ached as her daughter pined, or cried out in sadness or smiled through her tears. As the full reality of her actions came over her, Edith felt her daughter's pain, her sorrow, and her regret perhaps even more so than Jenny herself.

Regaining some composure, Jenny read and re-read Henry's letter. She couldn't get over the wonder of it all. Not only was the pewter angel the same as the one she had sent him but, unbelievably, the very last paragraph was identical as well! After all those years, Jenny still remembered almost every word she had written to her loved one.

She heard him say the words as if he were there, as if she were looking into his eyes:

Even though we are far apart, you are forever in my heart. I will love you always. Have a merry Christmas!

How she longed for his touch, for his lips touching hers, for his heart beating next to hers…

Oh, how cruel life can be at times with all of its twists and turns. Jenny folded the letter and carefully slid it back into the envelope. She picked up the pewter angel, brought it up to her lips, again, and kissed it, knowing immediately that she would retrieve the silver chain she wore when she was fifteen and put the pewter angel on it.

I will wear it always, as a lasting reminder of our love.

She dropped the angel into the envelope and then slipped the letter and its precious contents into a side compartment of her purse where there was no danger of the angel or letter coming out. She would protect this letter for the rest of her days.

She set the purse on the floor beside her and straightened on her chair. She then slowly looked at her mother.

Edith had watched her daughter's every move. She could see and feel the deep love Jenny still had for Henry, a love she'd cut off and tried to destroy, but all her attempts had been futile.

While they had succeeded externally, internally it was still there, yearning to come back. Ted had known the entire time. *He was so sensitive to it and could see it in Jenny's eyes where I was blind to it all.* The hurt, guilt and shame of what they were doing had killed him. And now, as she gazed at her daughter, she hoped and prayed that she had done the right thing in telling her. That her daughter would understand what she did and find within her heart the compassion to forgive her.

Jenny's first reaction was deep disappointment and anger towards her mom and dad. She wanted to express it more than she already had, she still felt so much hurt and regret. But once again her forgiving nature took over. What good would it do? Her father was dead. Her mother was on in years and nearing her death as well. Enough suffering had been caused by all this already. It must end somehow, here.

At least she knew the truth, that Henry hadn't abandoned her, that he still loved her.

Finally, Jenny spoke. "Well, Mom, you did what you thought was the best at the time. We all do things we regret later. I know I have done my share."

It was difficult for Jenny to utter these words of understanding, but she knew it was the right thing to do. She had never been a vengeful or merciless person. She couldn't hold grudges or stay angry for long. She loved life and people, and always sought peace and understanding. She ignored her anguish and continued with a reconciliatory tone in her voice.

"Thank you for giving me the letter. You did the right thing. I know how hard it must have been for you to do so. It would have been best from the start. But, what is done is done. It's over. It's okay, Mom."

"Oh, Jenny, thank you, thank you," Edith blurted out, as tears of relief washed down her cheeks once more. She opened her arms wide.

Jenny could see the freedom she'd brought to her mother and in spite of the sorrow still lingering in her heart, she rose then bent down towards her mother and whispered tenderly and sincerely into her mother's ear,

"I forgive you, Mom, and I love you."

Each word Jenny uttered lifted Edith upwards. They were gems; jewels in her heart that she would treasure to her dying moment. The adrenalin rushing through her body gave Edith such strength that she crushed her daughter against her chest so fiercely it took Jenny's breath away.

"What's the matter with you two? Not at it, again!" exclaimed Millie with a stern voice, as she walked into the room. She looked at Jenny and in a tone which bordered on an impending scolding, continued, "It's too hard on your mother, Jenny."

"Oh no," blurted Edith, in defence. "This is the happiest day of my life." *I feel so free.*

"We are not upset with each other, Millie, we are *loving* each other," Jenny replied, her tone devoid of any defensiveness.

Millie looked at both of them furrowing her brow, somewhat puzzled by it all.

Jenny looked tenderly into her mother's eyes and said, "It's really love, Millie. True, honest-to-goodness love perhaps for the very first time in years and years."

CHAPTER TWELVE

F ATHER ENGELMANN AND Henry got out of the car and made their way up to Henry's parent's home. The screen door was open and the aroma of Mary's beef stroganoff wafted out to the men, whetting their appetite immediately. Mary heard their laughter and ran to the front door to meet her favourite guests.

"Hello Father! Henry! Oh I could hardly wait to see you!"

"I was looking forward to coming as well, Mary."

"Hi Mom," Henry said as he kissed Mary's cheek. "I see Jeremy's Jeep—"

"Yes, Camilla and Jeremy are in the living room."

"Hi Grandpa," yelled Joshua, as he heard Henry enter the house.

Henry picked up his grandson and gave him a big hug. "How is my big boy doing?"

"Come and see the Tonka truck that Nana gave me."

Henry set Josh down and was led by the hand into the living room.

Camilla was already up and rushed to Henry. "Hi, Dad, so nice to see you. You must be spending a lot of time outdoors at the farm. You have a great tan."

"Hi Dad," said Jeremy as the two men shook hands and then hugged.

"Yes, I was doing a little work outdoors, trimming the shrubs and boy there sure are a lot of Monarchs this year, especially down near the Poustinia."

"You know, Dad, we have been out to the acreage several times this year and haven't made it down to the bottom of the valley to see the prayer house, yet. That's what you're talking about, right?"

"Yes, I got the idea from a book I read by Catherine Doherty. She's a lady from Russia who came to Canada in the 1920's. She was called to work with the poor and started up the Friendship House in Toronto and also in Harlem, New York. People were drawn to her faith and love of the poor in much the same way people flock to Mother Theresa in Calcutta. Anyway, in the forties, she continued to help the poor by founding a farm community in Combermere, Ontario, which came to be called Madonna House. The Marion Centre in Regina is one of the missions they have established across Canada. They are houses of prayer reaching out to the poor, feeding them and providing for them—"

"Oh yes, we just took some of our clothes and Joshua's toys down there a month or so ago. Isn't that interesting? How is this tied to your prayer house?"

"Yes, well as the story goes, one day Catherine discovered an old shed or granary on their land and it reminded her of the prayer houses back in Russia which are called Poustinia's. They're just a basic simple one room house with a cot, table and chair, a bible and enough water and bread to make a mini-retreat of prayer and fasting and coming to the Lord. So to make a long story short, she had the shed fixed up and it became the first Poustinia in Canada. The idea was so popular that she had several more built on the property for that use."

"Now you really have my interest, Dad. I would love to see your prayer house in the valley," Camilla said.

"Yeah, but Dad's idea of a prayer house is probably more like a five star hotel compared to the one room sheds that Catherine has!" chimed in Jeremy.

"I'm afraid Jeremy's right, Camilla. Mine did start out as a one room structure, but then I decided to put an addition to each side of the room. To the front, a living room was added with patio doors facing the pond. To the back, a bedroom was attached. That's where I put a cot, desk, chair, bible and a large picture window facing east and a view of the hills and meandering creek that feeds into the pond. To one side a small kitchen was built and to the other side is a bathroom and foyer entrance to the house. When you look at it from the top of the hill it has the shape of a cross."

"Yes, yes," said Father Engelmann, "The setting is a paradise. I am looking forward to spending a week there when my holidays come up next month. It reminds me of the 24th Psalm: He leads me beside the still waters, He restoreth my soul…"

"Yeah, I'm sure glad Father has been using it—"

"Let's continue this conversation at the table," interjected Mary, wiping her hands on her apron. Supper is ready and I was so hoping the rest of the children would be here."

Henry twisted his wrist to catch some light in the dim living room… "Allison said she might be late…oh, I think I hear them now."

The sound of laughter and muffled voices drifted in through the screen door and then Justin burst into the house followed by Lauren and Allison.

"Hi Grandma!" Justin rushed over to greet Mary who had her welcoming arms open.

"Sorry we're late," the girls said almost in unison.

"Well, no matter, you're here and just in time. Dinner is just about all on the table."

Mary went in first because she knew she would never be able to get over to the stove once everyone came in. After much shuffling of the chairs and squeezing they finally were all seated. Mary could barely turn around to get the potatoes and vegetables from the stove.

"It's already getting cold, please say grace, David."

"Yes, yes!" Father extended his one hand to Allison and the other to Justin. Everyone followed his lead and soon all those gathered around the table were holding hands.

"Bless us, oh Lord, and these thy gifts, which we are about to receive through Your goodness and bounty. And a special blessing to Mary not only for the food she has prepared but for the loving home she has created for Your honour and glory. We ask this through Christ our Lord."

"Amen," everyone said.

Justin was the first to dig into the broad noodles while Henry placed the large casserole dish containing the beef stroganoff before him and started to dish out a portion on each of the plates as they were handed to him.

Soon everyone's plates were filled and an unusual quiet moment settled over the room except for the occasional "mmmmm" and "is this ever good."

"Absolutely delicious, Mom," said Henry, and everyone else chimed in with similar comments to express full agreement.

"So your dad left to go back to Victoria?" Henry asked as he looked at Camilla.

"Yes, it was so nice to see him. A week stay goes so quickly. It seemed a bit different without Mom being here. But I am so happy she came last summer and saw our new home and was able to enjoy the backyard and the sun, which they don't always get on the west coast. Dad misses Mom so much… it just doesn't seem the same since she passed away…" Camilla's voice trailed off.

"I know what you mean, Camilla. I still am not used to living alone without Bill. It's been six years since he passed away and I still miss him."

"Dad was so impressed with how you came over and blessed our home for us, Father."

"It was my pleasure, Camilla. And I have to say you and Jeremy have such a beautiful home and backyard. It is so large and filled with so many flowers. My Anna would have loved a yard like that."

"Yeah, she sure loves flowers alright," interjected Jeremy. "Especially those wildflowers that seem to be attracting so many butterflies. Just one more item is needed to literally fulfill her dreams."

"What do you mean?" asked Allison.

"Camilla, for the longest time now has dreamt of wildflowers surrounding a gazebo. We tried to hire a carpenter to build one in the yard but the fellow we wanted was too busy this summer so we booked him in first thing next spring. If the weather is nice it will be built in time for her birthday."

"Wow, isn't that romantic," said Allison and then continued, "There are so many Monarch butterflies out at the farm. I just love their orange and black wings!"

"It's the milkweed plants that attracts them," informed Henry.

"That's right!" said Camilla, excitedly. "Last spring when I was at the nursery buying some Lilac shrubs, which is one of my favourite spring flowers, I asked the gardener there which plants attract butterflies. He talked me in to buying a dozen Astelias plants. He said it's the Latin name for milkweed plants and that they are sure to attract the Monarchs."

"And boy did they ever!" chimed in Jeremy once again. "It seems like every butterfly in the whole area around our place is in our backyard."

Henry couldn't get over it. The more he learned of Camilla, the more connected she seemed to be to Jenny. Jenny loved Lilacs and the fragrance so much that it was her favourite perfume. And the next exchange between Lauren and Camilla confirmed it all the more!

"Butterflies remind me of angels. I just love watching them fly about in the air," said Lauren.

"Yes! Me, too!" remarked Camilla, her blue eyes sparkling. "And I love the guardian angel prayer Jeremy taught me shortly after we got married. I think it's the prayer that has made me so much more aware of them."

"Mommy and Daddy and me say that prayer every night when I go to sleep, don't we Mommy?" said Joshua, as he turned to Camilla.

Camilla hugged Josh, "Yes, we do, Josh. Each and every night to watch over you!"

Henry was stunned! Jenny loved butterflies and thought they were angels, too! He recalled how Jenny used to chase butterflies when they walked, especially near the outskirts of city in the east end. And how she told him that at night, when she was a little girl, butterflies would come into her room and she would see them as angels singing to her.

"We all have an angel," said Father, "it's a wonderful gift God has given to each and every one of us to guide, comfort, protect and help lead us to the Lord."

Justin swallowed his food and said, "That was the first prayer Mom taught me, too..."

The kitchen fell silent as the family recalled Julean. Softly, Justin began...

Guardian angel my guardian dear...

and quickly all those present at the table joined in to recite the beautiful prayer...

To whom God's love commits me here,
ever this day be at my side
to light and guard, to rule and guide
my life forever and ever.
Amen

As Henry's eyes welled, he noticed a tear in Allison's eyes as well as memories of Julean came rushing back to them all.

As Lauren began talking about the preparation she was making for her upcoming dance number with Saskatchewan Express, Henry couldn't help but to be mesmerized by Camilla and how much she reminded him of Jenny. It wasn't just her looks and mannerisms, but everything she revealed about herself. And... how different she was from her parents. Henry shook his head almost imperceptibly as he gazed at his daughter-in-law.

Camilla caught his gaze for the umpteenth time and asked, "I always get the feeling, Dad, that I still remind you of someone you knew. I remember when Jeremy first brought me to your home, you seemed so surprised to see me and said that I reminded you of someone in your past. I am really interested, Dad, tell me who it is that I remind you of?"

Henry blushed slightly, a little embarrassed for staring so much at Camilla. "Oh, that goes back a long time to when I was 15 years old.

I finished Grade 8 and was just beginning summer holidays when a family moved in three doors down the street—"

"And they had a daughter who was also 15 years old that looked like Camilla!" Jeremy blurted, teasing his dad.

"Why yes, that's right, son…" Henry replied a bit surprised by his son's insightful remarks. "We spent the summer together …"

Mary could see that Henry was uncomfortable talking about Jenny and the conversation was also unsettling to her as it reminded her of the letter; something she wanted to forget about.

Mary interjected, "Yes, Henry and the girl next door spent the summer together, and two weeks after high school started she moved with her parents to Ottawa and was never heard from again. But what I can't get over is how your father is related in some distant way to Julean's Aunt Netta and Uncle Jacob in Cardston, Alberta."

Henry looked at his mom, surprised by her uncharacteristic interruption. Camilla looked at Henry, still wanting to pursue the discussion of the girl in his past life, but then turned to Mary and replied, "Yes, I was quite surprised too that Dad stemmed from a Mormon heritage. It all came out when Mom and Dad saw Netta and Jacob at our wedding. I suppose if we go back far enough in some distant way Jeremy's mom is related to my dad's family."

Camilla turned to Jeremy, "I'm glad it's distant, I wouldn't want to have married my first cousin." Jeremy and Camilla nervously laughed.

"Perhaps my next question or two is known by most of the people here, but I am always interested in God's divine providence and how people come together. So how did your parents get to Ottawa and how is it that you settled in Regina?" Father wanted to know.

"I could only have answered part of your question before last week, but since Dad's visit he filled me in a bit more on the family history. "Apparently my dad's great-grandparents moved from Utah in the United States in the early 1900's to Cardston. They had six children and all were boys. Of those six, one was my dad's father. At that time, a lot of the people in the community were moving out. Some went to B.C. and some went to Calgary, and that is where my father went after he finished high school."

Camilla looked at everyone, "I hope I am not confusing or boring you with all this?"

"No, not at all, please continue, Camilla," said Father.

Henry nodded, as well, for his daughter-in-law to continue.

"Well, Dad got a job at Eaton's and worked his way up to be the department head of the furniture department. That is where he met my Mom, Valerie. She was a saleslady in another department. Anyway, in the early fifties, Dad was transferred to Ottawa. In 1963 he was transferred again to Saskatoon as manager of the furniture department, and then his final move was in 1975 to Regina. That's when I started university, as well. Five years ago, Dad retired and they moved to Victoria. Since I had started university and had a job I liked and good friends, I decided to stay and finish my degree. And I am so glad I did! Otherwise, I would never have met Jeremiah!"

Camilla turned to Jeremy and both looked lovingly into each others eyes as if they were still newlyweds.

"Thank you for sharing that with us, Camilla. That was interesting to know how you were led here and into this family." And then Father turned to Allison, "So, Allison, your dad tells me you are going to attend a bible college this fall?"

"Yes, it's in Radway, Alberta. I heard about it from a friend of mine and was immediately excited about it. I wrote away for information and an application form. It looked great, so I applied and got my letter of acceptance two weeks ago."

"I'm going to miss her at the gallery. She ran the shop first rate," said Henry.

"Well, Justin is doing a great job and for his age, his framing skills are excellent! The framer can't get over how well Justin was learning to cut mats and he must have your eye for colour, Dad. His selection of mats for paintings and photos is excellent. If I were the framer I would be worried of being replaced by Justin." Allison winked at Henry.

Justin smiled, "No way, Doug is the best, I'm learning so much from him. Even putting up shows, he's got such a good eye for hanging pictures."

"And you're even good at matching which pottery compliments which painting the best," Allison added.

Well, let me get out the lemon pie," said Mary as she got up and picked up her plates and cutlery. The girls wanted to help clear the table but there was no room, so everyone passed their plates to Father who turned and piled them up by the sink.

"Well, maybe it's best to go into the living room and give the girls a chance to organize things in here," suggested Henry.

Soon everyone was seated in the living room. Justin wanted to turn on the TV but Henry quickly corrected him. "No TV tonight, Justin."

Father Engelmann sat in Bill's leather chair while Henry sat opposite the room on the couch. He wondered if his Dad's spirit was with them. He knew Julean's was. He could feel her presence. And just as Henry was thinking a bit more about family and how things change over time, Father's next comments, as usual seemed to sum up what family was all about.

"You know, we were talking earlier about Henry's prayer house in the valley and what a wonderful place it is to go and rejuvenate and come closer to God, and yet a home is the greatest prayer house of all."

Father looked at Mary and continued, "What you and Bill have done, Mary, is placed Christ at the centre of your home and marriage. Your close personal relationship with Jesus has been such a powerful example of faith to your son and grandchildren. You have created a home that is built on a rock that doesn't get washed away in the raging rivers of worldly values.

"Sadly, more and more families have both parents working, stores open all days of the week and soon I predict till all hours of the night! Society has lost respect for the Sabbath and the healthy order of family living.

"Yet, in spite of a world that is moving faster and attacking our moral fibres. You and Bill have been the beacons of light for Henry and his children. It is so true that the family that prays together stays together. Jesus said, "that where two or three are gathered together in my name, there I am in the midst of them.' Christ must be at the centre of a family and children witnessing this daily. We are there for one another to encourage, uplift, support, love and pass on the faith.

"And what better way to do this than family dinner? In the hectic pace of our lives, besides daily prayer in the home, I would also place high on my list to keep family dinner a sacred time. It is that one time in the day we must be together and share our lives. I have always thought it so commendable that television or any other distraction never disrupts the conversation in this family. How the meal time gathering always begins in prayerful thanks and is never rushed. It is so clear to me that this is how we learn to listen and communicate with each other. This is how we stay in touch; keep the bond of the family alive. This is the time we share our joys and sorrows and laughter and instill family values.

"Over and over just like this evening, I see the power of family dinner. How all of our cares are washed away by the sharing, laughter and support we give to one another."

Then gazing at all those present, Father said, "It is important for the children to realize what is going on here and how important family is. It is through our faith and love for one another, our care, respect and kindness to each other that extends beyond the home to the church and community touching the lives of all we meet. Jesus is the vine and we are the branches.

"Mary, I must say again, you have created a place of peace and safe refuge from the outside world to prepare us for the world. What a beautiful plan the Lord has created where a man and woman come together in love and through their oneness create a family with their Creator at the centre.

"Yes, there is nothing like a home…'Home Sweet Home'…is very true, indeed!"

CHAPTER THIRTEEN

IT WAS TUESDAY morning. Jenny had spent most of the previous day packing, trying to stay focused on the job and not allowing herself to delve into self-pity or resentment. Not only could she still not believe that what she had thought was her home, never really had been, but now she also knew the truth about Henry and their letters…

She forgot the number of times she had read and re-read Henry's letter since her Mom gave it to her. So many times she was angry with him for not writing and all along he had kept his promise just like she had kept hers to him. Jenny found it hard to believe what her parents had done. But she didn't want to go there, neither did she want to dwell on regrets of how her life might have been so much different.

The blessing in all of this was that now she knew the truth and it brought some semblance of closure. Jenny wondered if that was part of the reason she could never let go of the relationship they had shared. It was such a spiritual connection and for Henry to have simply left and have intentionally chosen to just end their relationship was unthinkable. Jenny just knew in her heart that there was some reason why he had not written. Now she knew the truth, and knew that she had been right. Henry had loved her as much as she did him.

Was it possible that Henry could still feel the love in his heart for her that she still felt for him?

Jenny struggled to keep her focus off Henry's letter and deal more with the move on hand. Her things were all packed and ready to be moved to her new apartment in the west end. The one thing she couldn't pack, however, was the antique furniture she had collected over the years. She loved every piece and was hoping that James would let her take the furniture with her. She'd called James several times over the past few days to ask him, but was unable to get through to him. She'd lost track of how many messages she'd left with his two secretaries; calls that he hadn't returned.

The furniture was the only thing she treasured in the entire house.

Looking around the house, she was flooded with memories; every single piece of furniture held a story and she could remember vividly how she came to own each piece. As her eyes settled on the dining room table, she smiled just thinking about it.

She was very fortunate to have been at the antique shop just when the dining room set came in from an estate sale. She had purchased it immediately along with the upright curio cabinet with the curved glass door. It was perfect to hold all of Jenny's favourite china and glass ballerinas she had collected over the years.

Jenny had bought each chair in the living room at different times. Each purchase was carefully considered and each had its own special appeal: the hand-carved arms and legs; the high Victorian back. One of her finds went back to the mid-eighteenth century and the needlepoint covering on the seat of the chair was still well intact.

Another of her favourite acquisitions was the round table in which she hid her diary. It had a secret compartment in the back of the drawer. She had discovered it in an antique shop in Minneapolis. A year later when she made a return trip to the same antique shop she was elated to come across a matching coffee table. Its three legs tapered down, as well, but stretched out much further along the floor like tentacles, providing firm support for the elongated, oval shaped table-top, but it had the same exact brass-clawed feet.

Perhaps, one of Jenny's most prized possessions of all was the tea wagon. She had responded to a tiny ad in the paper. When she called about it, the address was in the older part of the city. Her instincts told her to check it out. She was very glad she did. An elderly lady planning to enter a care home had slowly been selling off all her furniture, piece by piece over the preceding year and a half.

Jenny immediately hit it off with the lady and had high tea with her. Jenny's heart raced with excitement when the lady pushed the wagon into the living room. It looked brand new. The back wheels, covered with a narrow band of black rubber, were about a foot in diameter and had hand carved wooden spokes. The front wheels were much smaller and easily turned this way or that as the lady pushed it along by its ornate handle. On top of the gleaming walnut table-top rested a sterling silver tray upon which was a tall silver teapot and matching sugar and cream holders. Beside them sat fine bone china teacups and saucers with tiny sterling silver spoons.

The second shelf of the wagon held another tray. This one was all wooden with an oval glass bottom. It held the dainties and finger sandwiches. Jenny had been taken by the manner in which the lady so elegantly wheeled the wagon to where she was seated then raised one of the table leafs. She then set the tray with the sandwiches and dainties on top.

By the end of her visit, Jenny purchased the wagon, the sterling silver tea set, a half-dozen bone china tea cups and saucers, all different and unique in design. She also purchased a hand-carved, petite bedroom rocking chair. Jenny had not seen anything like it before or since.

Jenny studied each of the antiques in her collection, recalling how and where she'd acquired them. While she so loved each piece, James looked upon them with disdain. Just old garbage that should have been thrown out long ago.

"Frankly, they give me the creeps," he would often say and lecture her each time she made another purchase. She'd allowed James to control every other aspect of her life, but she stood her ground when it came to her antiques.

She never really understood why he had relented and allowed her this pleasure, but she was thankful to him for this one exception to his orders and demands. Jenny knew he wouldn't want this furniture, but as he hoarded everything he or his corporation possessed, she knew he would be reluctant to part with any of it. James knew that the antiques were valuable and Jenny feared that he may want to retrieve the money the company spent on them rather than just give them to her.

Another hour ticked away and still no answer from James. Jenny thought she would try one last time. If he didn't answer, she would just leave. She felt and knew in her heart that James knew why she was trying to reach him. Perhaps the fact that he wasn't returning her call was his answer. *Just leave and get out of my life.*

She reluctantly picked up the phone and dialed James's direct line number one last time.

"Cismo Corporation, this is Rita, how may I help you?"

Some direct line.

"Yes, this is Marjorie Hamilton."

"Oh, hello, Mrs. Hamilton."

"Hello, Rita, is James in?"

"Please hold, I will see if he is available. I'll just be a moment, Mrs. Hamilton."

"Thank you, Rita." Jenny heard a click as she was put on hold, and sat there listening to the deafening silence. Every time she talked to James she felt like she had a split personality. He called her Marjorie. Everyone else called her Jenny. He said it sounded more sophisticated and advised her always to use it for legal purposes and signing documents. Not that it mattered what name she'd signed. She still ended up with nothing.

One minute, then two, then five minutes passed. Hurt and anger wedged their way into Jenny's psyche and feelings. They were already crowded with other unsettling thoughts. How could James be so rude and mean, not even calling to say good-bye? All she had ever been to him was the producer of the heir to his empire.

Jenny reached up and took hold of the pewter angel hanging on the end of the silver chain around her neck. As soon as she got home from visiting with her mother, she put the angel on the chain and immediately began to wear it as Henry wanted her to. It soothed her troubled spirit.

She was about to hang up when she heard another click.

"I'm sorry to keep you waiting, Mrs. Hamilton. Mr. Hamilton just finished his appointment and will take your call now. Please hold while I transfer you."

Jenny's heart raced. She hadn't talked to James in months; the only communication she received was either through J.J. or one of James' numerous lawyers or secretaries.

"Hello, Marjorie," James said, with a tone of annoyance.

Thank God, this may be the last time I have to hear him call me that.

"Yes, it's me, James. I was hoping you would be able to drop by before I leave."

"I'm too busy for that. What is it you wish to talk about, Marjorie?"

"James, the movers are coming first thing in the morning to pick up my things. I would like to take the antique furniture with me. May I have it?"

There was a long silence, and Jenny could almost hear James' mind churning, how to avoid giving anything up.

"You know I can't make that decision, the house and all of the contents are owned by the company."

"I realize that, James. If you want, I will pay you for it or the company or whatever. I can't afford what it's worth, but—"

"Let me think on it. When did you say the movers were coming?"

"This afternoon for the small things and tomorrow morning for my bedroom set. I'm sure you aren't interested in that, are you?"

There was just silence at the other end, James once again not agreeing or disagreeing.

"I was hoping they might bring the antique furniture along at the same time. It's really too small for this house, and I know how much you like modern furniture…and it will all fit into my new apartment."

Though she'd promised herself she wouldn't beg, she found herself almost doing it.

"Yes, I know all of that," James said sharply. "Just take the damn furniture, Marjorie. I never could stand the stuff. All that old furniture coming from God knows where…always did give me the creeps."

Jenny ignored James's comments. All she heard was that she could keep her treasures.

"Thank you, James. And I will return the car to you before the end of the week."

"Keep it too Marjorie, I don't want it back, either." The phone went dead…as dead as their relationship.

Jenny listened to the dial tone, trying to regain her composure. The phone clung to her damp hands. She almost had to shake it loose from her grip.

"I'm so glad that's over," Jenny said, as she shook her head.

Jenny got up and walked towards the patio. She wanted to have one last look at the garden estate. The afternoon sun was flickering off the green leaves of the low surrounding shrubs. The white daisies and geraniums glistened in the light. She looked towards the gazebo and thought about the many hours she'd spent there reading and writing in her diary.

The Angel of Thanksgiving! She'd forgotten to tell James that if she ever acquired a home she would send for it. She would have to drop him a note about it after she'd settled into her new apartment.

On her last walk around the gardens, she'd hoped to say good-bye again to Thomas, but she saw him unloading some sod. The flowers she had placed in the angel's basket last week for James were still as fresh as ever. Thomas had assured her this morning that he still hadn't needed to give the flowers any water.

Truly amazing.

Thomas must have sensed her watching him, as he turned and gazed at her. Jenny waved and blew him a kiss. Thomas stood there for a long moment and then throwing caution to the wind, he brought both of his hands to his mouth, touched his finger tips to his lips and then thrust them out towards her.

"God bless you, Miss Jenny! I shall miss you dearly," he shouted across the grounds.

Jenny smiled from ear to ear. "Thank you, Thomas! I shall miss you too!"

"Oh Miss Jenny, there is one more thing." Thomas dropped the roll of sod he was about to pick up and hurried towards Jenny.

"There is one thing that has always bothered me from the first day you came to Greystone Manor."

Jenny studied the concerned gardener and tilted her head slightly as a sign for him to continue.

"Do you recall that first morning when we met right here and discussed your plans for the improvement of the garden."

"Yes I do!" replied Jenny excitedly, "You told me how you were going to plant milkweed plants strategically throughout the garden, most of all around the gazebo so that wherever I looked I would see the abundance of beautiful colour and life."

"Yes, Miss Jenny, that is exactly correct. I have played that conversation many times over in my mind…and if you recall I also said that butterflies would abound and it will seem as if you were surrounded by angels."

"Oh Thomas, you did all that and more. Most days I felt as if I were in paradise!" Jenny stopped talking trying to ascertain why Thomas was concerned. Her forehead wrinkled slightly with a puzzled gaze.

"It's what you said next that has always weighed heavy on my heart. You asked me if I liked butterflies and angels. I told you that I did believe in angels and that we all have a guardian and that I say a prayer to mine every day since I was a child."

"Yes, yes, Thomas I remember that too and I asked you to say your prayer."

Thomas's eyes reddened, "I was too shy to say my prayer in front of you and you took the lead and said yours…it was the very same one I said."

"Jenny took Thomas's hand. So what is troubling you Thomas? The prayer was the same as yours?"

"Since the day you arrived on the estate you have always shown us to stand up for what you believe and to be true to yourself and that morning I was afraid or too shy to say the prayer in front of you but…I would like to now if I may, Miss Jenny?"

"Oh, Thomas, that would be wonderful." Jenny took both of Thomas's hands into hers and said, "May I say it with you?"

Thomas simply nodded and then the two of them with butterflies seemingly to come from everywhere in the garden flitted about Jenny and her dearly beloved gardener as they said the *Guardian Angel Prayer*:

Angel of God my guardian dear,
To whom God's love commits me here
Ever this day be at my side,
To light and guard, to rule and guide.
Amen

Jenny let go of Thomas hands and pecked him on the cheek.

"Thank you, Ma'am, and may angel blessings be always with you!" Thomas softly whispered, and then turned and strode down the walkway.

What better way to leave this lovely estate than with such a blessed farewell.

Jenny stepped back into the kitchen doorway reluctant to close the patio door. Slowly she slid the heavy door shut and locked it, her tear-filled eyes reflected in the glass. Despite the hardship of her marriage, the home gave her many happy moments with the staff and J.J..

She turned and made her way into the huge kitchen, back-lit by the sun streaming in the patio door behind her. There were at least a dozen plants she had put on the window ledges over the years to bring some of the nature outside, indoors. She was going to take them, but it would pain her far too much to leave this house with the only other living things in the home. The house would be too dead without them.

As perturbed as she was with James, she pitied him and felt compassion over the utter bondage he was held in with his money and his company. It was his life and unfortunately her son was following in his footsteps. Hopefully, the plants and the life they contained might instill in both of them some sense of the spiritual sustenance derived only from the simple pleasures of life; the beauty of the flowers, nature, the garden, but would they see it? There seemed to be no time in their lives to smell the roses.

Jenny retraced her steps through the various rooms then out to the front door. She thought for sure this would be her final good-bye, but since James had agreed to let her have the furniture, she would have to come back in the morning to meet the moving company and direct them what to take.

Jenny took another look at the home she had lived in for 21 years.

"C'est la vie," she muttered under her breath, as she opened the front door resisting the temptation to slam it. She was too dignified, too self-respecting to react that way. Rather, she walked out, greeted by the glorious sunshine, her head held high, and very quietly, closed the door behind her.

CHAPTER FOURTEEN

Henry parked on 11th Avenue and scooted around the vehicle to the passenger side. He opened the door and held Ivania's hand as she got out of the SUV and stepped onto the street.

"Thank you, Hen-dry."

They were taking in a play at the Globe Theatre, but first decided to enjoy a pasta dinner at Alfredo's. The café was right next to the theatre so it was sort of a one-stop evening of entertainment. After the new city hall was built, the old one became the home for the Globe Theatre situated on the second floor. The main floor had been turned into a small mall consisting of several shops.

As Henry and Ivania walked through the mall on their way to the restaurant, a shadow suddenly streaked in front of Henry catching his attention. He followed it to a window display and was shocked to see Julean's spirit standing beside a roll top desk in the window of an antique shop. He stopped abruptly, jerking Ivania to a halt as well.

"What is it, Hen-dry?"

He led Ivania over to the window, his eyes growing wide. Julean had disappeared however his eyes now studied the piece of furniture in front of him.

"That's some desk Ivania, I've always wanted one like that for my den at home on the farm." Henry checked the time on his wrist watch, "I think we have time, do you mind if we go inside and check it out?"

"No, let's go."

The store owner turned the desk to face the inside of the store so Henry could have a closer look at the table. As Henry studied the desk, the owner rolled the top up and then down several times to show the ease of operation. Henry tried it himself and liked all the compartments at the back of the desk top.

"All my papers and stuff would easily fill all those compartments."

Turning to his date, he asked, "What do you think, Ivania?"

"It's nice, but I prefer a modern oak desk, I have seen too many old things."

"Besides being considered an antique," rebutted the owner, "it is a very fine piece of furniture and built by one of the best manufacturers of furniture prior to the fifties."

The proprietor opened the top right hand drawer and pointed to a brass plate adhered to the inside side of the drawer. Henry leaned forward and read the plaque:

<blockquote>
Manufactured
By
The Kroehl Brothers
1938
Minneapolis, Minnesota
</blockquote>

"Not only were the Kroehl Brothers fine craftsmen, but they were also known for their secret compartments. There is one in nearly every piece of furniture they built, including chairs, beds and even dining room sets."

"Is that so?" Henry replied, his curiosity growing. And before he could ask the owner if this desk had one, the elderly gentleman said, "If you slide your hand into the drawer you will feel a round brass ring; pull on it."

Henry did as he was instructed and a secret door flipped up revealing a compartment behind. Henry felt further and took hold of a brass handle attached to a mahogany wooden box. He pulled it out and opened the lid. It was divided into several compartments lined with black velvet.

"Wow, is this ever neat. That would hold a few of my treasures!" Henry quipped and turned to wink at Ivania. "I'm surprised to hear you say you don't like antique furniture. I've told you before I have always fantasized you as being a foreign spy. A desk like this would be perfect to store secret documents."

"Oh Hen-dry, you have quite an imagination!" Ivania chuckled

"You know, I really like antiques and have several at home. This would fit great in my office if I could get it through a 32-inch wide door opening. It seems to me that this is wider though and even if we turned it on its side, I don't think it would fit, either."

"That's the beauty of Kroehl Brothers' furniture. They constructed it so that, if needed, every piece they made could be taken apart." The owner beamed, having come up with an immediate solution to a potential problem that might cancel the sale.

"We are just off to dinner. When I get home I'll check the space once more and if you could dissemble and reassemble the desk again at my home, we just might have a deal."

Henry pulled out a business card and asked the proprietor to put a hold on the desk until the next day.

During dinner, Ivania asked, "So Hen-dry, does the daily commuting back and forth to the city become tedious and time wasting?"

"Oh, sometimes when I am real tired it can be. But for the most part, I enjoy the ride and it helps me to unwind. And when I reach my spot in the valley, I know it's all worth it. I love the country and the valley, Ivania. I would never want to leave there. It's our home. And I have the art studio there and… I will have to invite you out there some time. The acreage has a beautiful view."

"I don't know if I could take the travel, the lack of conveniences, and… the roads in the winter could be hazardous, no?"

"Yes, they can be. But we have a snow blower and if it's real bad, we just stay home until the weather clears up."

Ivania looked at Henry and rolled her eyes, not so sure it would be something she would want to do.

A quiet silence fell between them as they ate their dinner. They were each absorbed in their own thoughts. While Henry was very attracted to Ivania, he always felt a bit uneasy around her. He felt so transparent, almost as if he were naked under the scrutiny of her penetrating gaze. It was as if she knew his every move and thought. Julean knew him well also, but it was different somehow. With Julean, Henry always felt she used her insight into her husband to give him support and encouragement. With Ivania, her understanding seemed more analytical; information to be used to her advantage somehow. Again, Henry imagined her as a spy and smiled inwardly at the thought.

THE GLOBE THEATRE was founded by Ken and Sue Kramer in 1966. For the most part, their productions varied between light comedy entertainments to more serious social issues. The last three productions Henry had seen were more of the latter and this night's play, dealing with the ethical values of a politician, was the same. The play consisted of just one actor who rambled on and on. Henry found it utterly boring and could not wait until it was over. Ivania must have felt the same way, for suddenly, she initiated a move that sent two sensations immediately throughout Henry's body; arousal and laughter.

Ivania had placed her hand on his knee and gave it an ever so slight squeeze. Ivania wasn't aware of Henry's highly sensitive areas of being ticklish. His doctor also learned that very quickly when Henry went for his annual physical checkups. No sooner had the doctor touched his knee or placed his hand under his arm pit to check his glands, than Henry laughed uncontrollably!

Henry realized that to laugh in a play that was dead serious or at a tender move by his dating companion would be devastating! He flinched instinctively at Ivania's touch, but also quickly thought of a way to keep himself under control. He instantly became the main character in the play, trying to act cool and reserved, but that didn't quite do the trick. He then began quoting scriptural passages to distract his mind, also to no avail. Unable to stand it any longer, Henry quickly but gently put his hand on top of Ivania's, curled his fingers under hers and lifted it to his chest. He gave it a gentle squeeze to reciprocate her gesture and just held it there, suspended, not knowing where to place it because of the arm rest between them. He knew it was an awkward hold and uncomfortable for his partner. He moved her hand back to her side and not wanting her to feel that he was rejecting her affectionate move, he let go of her hand and put his arm around her like any teenager would do. It felt awkward but at least it contained his laughter …but not for long.

Ivania must have sensed Henry's sensitivity to her touch and unbelievably she did it again. He immediately shuffled in his chair and grabbed her hand returning it to her lap. They both started to giggle much to the chagrin of those sitting next to them. Henry had to admit that was the most exciting part of the play

When they arrived at Ivania's home after the play, Henry was once again challenged, but this time with temptation. As they walked to the front door, Ivania stopped just in front of the landing. She turned to Henry, came close to him and put her hands on his shoulders. She looked him in the eyes for a long moment and then drew him close to her and at the same time wrapped her arms around him. He resisted momentarily, then let it happen.

Ivania was the first woman he had kissed since Julean. Their lips met and there was no attempt by either to separate. It was a kiss that carried a message. Not only did Henry feel it was more than a casual kiss or connection, it was clear Ivania wanted to make love to him.

It had been over three years since Henry had made love to Julean, and there were days, and especially nights, when he ached and yearned for his dear wife's warmth and love and closeness. He wanted to make love… but could he with Ivania? Each time he went out with her, he felt that he was betraying Julean! And, in all honesty it was Julean he really ached for. There was no commitment to Ivania on his part; at least not yet. Could he honestly be true to Ivania, or would he be using her for personal gratification?

As he kissed Ivania, the urge and ache zinging through his body was so strong. He recalled the words of his mentor… 'when temptations come along always have a plan ready or you will succumb to your feelings.' Yes, thought Henry, thoughts lead to feelings and feelings lead to actions.

Actions I may regret.

Henry had no plan; the kiss just happened so unexpectedly.

Their lips parted and Ivania simply said, "Come Hen-dry."

She turned and stepped onto the slight elevated landing to the door. Perhaps he could control himself, Henry thought. Would it hurt to go in and have a coffee or a night cap and then be on his way? As Henry almost helplessly followed the seductive figure before him, he suddenly saw a shadow that went up to the top of the storm door that Ivania had just opened. He looked up and there sat Julean on top of the edge of the door!

It couldn't be!?

As he looked again, he stepped forward and simultaneously tripped on the landing. His knees hit the concrete landing and tore through his left pant leg, bruising his knee.

"Oh Ivania, I didn't see the step! What's wrong with me?"

He looked down at his aching knee as he stood up. The pain was quickly driving out the heat that had sizzled through his body a moment ago.

"Here, let me look at it…"

"It's okay Ivania. I think I will just go home and tend to it. I have a big day tomorrow. "

"But come in and I will fix it up," she said, looking coyly at Henry.

He sensed the passion still in her eyes, but his had dissipated enough for him to say, "I think I better go."

Henry stepped forward and kissed Ivania on the cheek. "Thanks for a great evening."

Ivania stared back, clearly disappointed… "Yes, perhaps some other time."

She turned abruptly, went inside and closed the door.

Henry still held the storm door and looked up but there was nothing there except the under eaves partially hiding a star studded sky. He was sure he had seen Julean's spirit. He shook his head and made his way back to the car.

"GOOD MORNING, SON! I hope you don't mind a curious Mom, but I wanted to know how you enjoyed your date last night?"

"It was fine. The play was kind of long and boring. I enjoy the more light-hearted production, especially when there are a group of actors as opposed to just one carrying the play."

"Only one character in the entire play?"

"Yeah, he was good. If the subject matter hadn't been so serious it might have worked better. So, how are you doing?"

"Fine. There is always something. There's a funeral at the church tomorrow and I will be helping out with the lunch and serving and then on Friday I have some other volunteer work to do at the Marion Centre. I often wonder how I had time to work at Sears. My days are so full."

"I can hardly wait for your borscht soup, Mom. It's getting to be that time of the year. I can smell the dill already."

"Yes, I was noticing how all the vegetables are getting ready for harvest in the garden. Try to keep an open noon hour for me in a couple of weeks or so and I will make a big pot."

"That would be great Mom, you know how much I love that soup when made with fresh garden vegetables and dill. In fact, Mom, there is one time you made borscht soup that I still remember to this day. It was just a couple of weeks before Julean and I got married and I remember saying how good it tasted, that it was the best ever."

Oh Henry, Mary thought, that was the day it all started.

How many times have I gone over and over that day in my mind when the Postman delivered Jenny's letter to the door. Oh, how I struggled with that decision to withhold the letter from you and I still do to this very day. The guilt is becoming almost unbearable...

"Mom, are you still there?"

"Oh, I'm sorry. I remember that day, too, when you came home from work saying how much you enjoyed the soup. I think I had let the chicken broth reduce itself more than usual. I had forgotten about it and most of it boiled away. I also added much more dill than usual."

"Well, when you make it this fall, perhaps take a little nap or do whatever you did back then when you simmer the broth and cut a little more dill than usual."

Oh Son, if you only knew what Mrs. Sarsky and I did that day. The pact we made to keep the letters away from both you and Jenny.

Mary just had to change the subject of the soup, it stirred up too many memories that she hoped and prayed would go away.

"And how was your dinner with Ivania?"

"It was great, Mom. Alfredo's makes a good pasta. And, oh yeah, on the way to dinner we stopped at the antique shop in the Old City Mall and looked at a roll top desk. I've decided to buy it. It's a beautiful desk and will just fit into my office den."

"That's good, Son. I know how much you love antique furniture. You already have some lovely pieces and I love sitting in the rocking chair that Julean's Aunt and Uncle gave to you both as a wedding gift."

"Yeah, that was Julean's favourite. She sat and read in that chair all the time. I notice Justin sits in it often, as well. For the longest time, Julean used to put him on her lap and read to him in that chair. I used to think he was getting too big to be sitting on her knee, but neither of them seemed to mind."

"Yes, the boy probably thinks about those times as he sits in the chair."

"Maybe so, I never thought about that. But Justin will really like the desk and all of the compartments. It even has a secret hiding place in one of the drawers. I think I will let Justin store some of his valuables in there."

"Yes, I'm sure he will like that. So… Are you enjoying Ivania's company?" Mary wanted to know and yet hoped she wasn't being too snoopy.

"Yes, I am, Mom. It's different though. She's different than both Julean and Je…"

Henry's words trailed off. Mary hoped that her question didn't stir up too many thoughts of Julean and … Jenny. She was ever on that man's mind.

"You know, Mom, I think I told you about the letter I received from Julean a year after she died from a nurse who was caring for her before she died?"

"Yes, you did, Son…"

"Well, if you recall in the letter she encouraged me to go out with other women and even said that she would lead me to Jenny if that door was open."

"But how, Son? How can she do that now that she is gone?"

"Spiritually, Mom. I know this might sound far-out but Julean's spirit seems to come to me like a shadow. But even more so, I feel her presence. I know it's Julean. It's the same feeling I had when I slept next to her and I knew she was praying even though I never heard her speak a word aloud. There was an aura around her. Her relationship with the blessed Mother was so strong and close, I felt it through her rosary. That is one of the reasons I took it from her the last night before her burial. I carry it with me all the time.

"Anyway, it all started earlier this spring as I walked past the patio doors in the sun room. Suddenly I saw Julean's spirit standing on the deck looking up at the eastern sky. It was almost as if she were encouraging me to come out and do the same."

"And why would that be?" Mary was wondering where this was leading to and hoped that Henry wasn't getting carried away.

"Well, I don't think I have never told you, Mom, but Jenny and I believed that our guardian angels not only kept us together but also that the angel that stands guard over the first star that appears in the eastern sky sends out our love to each other, as well. I know it may sound a bit far fetched, but whenever I've gazed at the star after Jenny first left, I felt her love so strongly. And when Julean came along, this love seemed to wane until eventually I hardly felt it at all when I gazed at the star. Well, as I was saying, Mom, this past spring when Julean's presence led me outdoors onto the deck at twilight time, the first star of the east was visible and it all started again. I couldn't believe how strongly I felt Jenny's love from the star. It was as if she, Jenny, was there beside me! The star's attraction was so strong, it went to the core of my being, just like it used to. I don't know if it was Jenny's spirit, or my guardian angel, or Julean's presence. It's all so confusing, Mom. And now that Ivania has come along, I'm even more in the dark. I'm not sure if Julean is leading me to her or discouraging me or… if it's all just in my head."

Henry checked his watch. "Geez, Mom, it's getting late and I have to get to the gallery. Call me when you make your borscht soup and don't forget to add the extra dill."

"Yes, I will," Mary hesitated, but decided to let it go, "and you have a nice day, Son."

MARY FELT CHILLED and noticed the goose bumps rise on her arms. An eerie, tingle raced up and down her spine. Almost imperceptibly she shook her head. Everything was becoming too much: the letter, the aura of light it yielded, its warmth as if it were alive, and now the star, the presence of angels, Julean's spirit…

Good Lord, what does this all mean?

With Ivania coming into the picture, Mary's confusion only increased! If only she knew Jenny was free and unattached, waiting for her son, the decision to give Henry the letter would be instant.

Oh, Lord… maybe Henry can still find some happiness. He is so lonely. He misses Julean so deeply and…Jenny too.

Oh, help me Jesus.

Chapter Fifteen

I N THE WEEKS that followed, Jenny settled into her new apartment. The antique furniture fit perfectly into the living and dining room except for two chairs. She was going to sell them, but decided to put them into storage in the basement just in case she moved someday and would have room for them. They were too special for her to part with. She had already lost too much in her life and in a way she clung to them much the same as James clung to his wealth and possessions. It was one of the few things left in her life that fed her heart and soul.

She was adjusting to being single, not that it was much different than when she was married to James. She had been alone much of the time then, too, only now it was official. She found herself more relaxed and in control of her life again. And perhaps more than that, a sense of freedom emerged within her. Jenny frequented the libraries often and attended plays and artist led lectures which accompanied art exhibitions. She found herself smiling more often. She was becoming a new Jenny – or rather the old Jenny, the Jenny that was so full of life, who had eyes that sparkled with happiness.

There were moments when she thought about Henry, and the way their lives had parted and the different directions they took, but she never allowed herself to wallow in thoughts of regret or blame. She refused to punish herself any further with thoughts that would keep her from going back to her old self which she loved. She was now free and most of all she intended to stay free.

Her relationship with her mother had never been better. The doctors were amazed to see the immense improvement in her. It was almost as if a miracle had occurred in her life. She was walking again on her own and last week, Jenny and her mother actually went out for dinner and then to a play at the local theatre. Every day they grew closer and more in love. All the secrets were gone, along with the accompanying guilt, fear, and shame. They were both free and enjoyed their new-found relationship to the fullest.

Jenny had just finished lunch and was relaxing in her favourite chair as she continued reading a short story she was enjoying, when the phone rang.

"Hello?"

"Hi, Jenny, it's Millie."

"Oh, hi, Millie." Just as the words tumbled from her mouth, Jenny's heart stopped. Why was Millie phoning?

"Jenny, I have some sad news to tell you...."

Jenny braced herself in the chair "Is it Mom?"

There was a long silence and then, "Yes, Jenny. I'm very sorry to tell you... Your mother just passed away."

Jenny was struck speechless.

"We were so shocked to find her in bed. At first we thought she was asleep. She looked so peaceful and for the last three weeks we've never seen her so full of life. We thought that perhaps some miracle had occurred."

Jenny knew why her mother was in such good spirits; she had received the gift of forgiveness. She had become free to enter fully into life again. She risked facing the truth and the truth had set her free.

After a long silence, Millie asked, "Are you okay, Jenny?"

"Yes, Millie, I'll be okay. I will see you shortly."

On the way to the care home, Jenny couldn't help but feel relieved and thankful that she and her mother had reconciled. That her mother was able to pass on in peace. It would have been so dreadful for Mom to leave her life carrying such an awful unresolved burden to the grave. Jenny was so grateful that at least this one good thing happened in her life. While she was unable to have a relationship with her husband, she was able to finally have one with her mother.

"Thank you, Lord."

The attendants at the care home had left her mother exactly as they had found her, in her bed. One hand was across her chest and the other lay at her side. Her eyes were closed and she almost had a smile on her face. She looked perfectly at peace.

Tears welled in Jenny's eyes. They had been getting along so well lately and Jenny so thoroughly enjoyed visiting her mother. She looked forward to it. Her mother was so witty that most of the time she had Jenny in stitches as she described the goings-on in the care home. Her mimicry of Millie was a theatrical performance in itself.

Jenny went over to her mother and kissed her cheek.

"Good-bye, Mom. I truly love you. Thank you for giving birth to me and being my Mom. I will always treasure you in my heart and you will be forever in my prayers."

Jenny straightened up, then sat on the chair beside her mother. As she gazed at the still figure lying there, Jenny couldn't help but ask the Lord how life could be so harsh. Just getting over a divorce, a son who had disowned her, and now her mother. The one thing that had just started to restore her life and give her such joy, was now also taken away.

"What else have you in store for me, oh Lord?" Jenny felt like Job in the Old Testament. Was she being tested too? Or was there some divine plan to unfold?

Millie walked in and made her way over to Jenny and stood behind her. She placed her hands on Jenny's shoulders.

"Jenny, I am so sorry to see your mom go. I know how much you loved each other and I can only imagine how sorrowful you must feel. Please accept my most sincere sympathy."

Jenny reached back and placed her hand on Millie's.

"Thank you, Millie."

After a long silence, Millie finally said, "What would you like us to do, Jenny?"

"Perhaps, Millie, you could call the nearest funeral home and ask them to take my mother's body there. Mom requested to be cremated so we won't need a plot at a cemetery. Mom has a duplicate copy of her final will and made her wishes known. It's in her keepsake box. I will take it with me. If Mom has requested anything in her will that I need you for, I will let you know."

Millie slipped her hand away from Jenny's and immediately patted it. Without saying a further word, Millie turned and walked out of the room.

As sadness rested on Jenny's spirit in the stillness, once again the sun came to her rescue with its soothing warmth. It was late in the afternoon as the rays of the sun bent around the window frame and streaked across her mother's bed. Jenny looked on as the light gradually worked its way up the blanket and finally rested on her mother's face. It was as if God himself was shining down on her mother, welcoming her into her heavenly home. Jenny gazed intently, trying to carve this sacred moment in her mind. This is a memory she wanted to keep and treasure, just like the letter she received from Henry.

Jenny heard Millie giving the ambulance attendants directions to the room, so Jenny got up then bent down once again and tenderly kissed her mother's cheek warmed by the afternoon sun.

"I love you, Mom. Someday, we will be together again.

Jenny greeted the attendants at the door, then left. She didn't want to stay and see her mother carted away in some bag. She wanted to retain that last image of her mother, greeted by her Lord in all His glory and flying into his waiting arms.

THE NEXT DAY, Jenny was on the phone making funeral arrangements. The funeral mass would be held on Friday morning at 10:00 o'clock at All Saints Church. It was only three blocks away from the care home and would allow those at the care home who wanted to to attend her mother's funeral. Most of Edith's friends had passed away or moved. Jenny really didn't know who else might come.

She placed a death notice in two of the major papers in the city and called James and J.J. again, since neither had returned her message from the previous evening. Jenny also called Matilda to cancel the luncheon date they had in the upcoming week and to invite her to the funeral, as well.

Jenny read her mother's will two and three times, making sure she was carrying out Edith's final requests. Her mother wanted to be cremated with her ashes placed in a bronze container and sealed and embedded in a granite stone next to Ted's grave. Jenny knew her mother had loved her father so much, but had trouble showing it. If only he could have known her as she had been the last few months.

Why does it take almost a lifetime to learn how to love? To give and receive love? What blocks us? Holds us back at the detriment of our closest loved ones? Life is so simple and, yet, we complicate it all so much.

Edith had appointed Jenny the executor of her will and also the sole benefactor of all of her riches and possessions. J.J. was to inherit a generous portion of it as well, but two months ago her mother had stroked it out, leaving everything to Jenny and up to her discretion as to what she wished to do with it thereafter. The change in her will bore her mother's signature and Millie's initial, as a witness. In any case, Jenny would never have to worry again about finances. In spite of James' hoarding, Jenny would inherit a small fortune from her parents and be able to live exactly the way she chose from then on.

Jenny spent the afternoon and evening gathering her mother's belongings from the care home. She had emptied the closet of everything except the keepsake box and one of her mother's favourite purses, which she'd always liked. Tears welled up in Jenny's eyes several times during the afternoon as she sorted things out, taking time not too rush, but to stop and reflect on each item and recall a memory or two related to it. No one entered the room the entire time she was there except for Millie who peeked in to ask if Jenny wanted a cup of tea.

Around eight o'clock, Jenny was done. She left notes on different piles of clothing and to whom they should be given. Little trinkets and souvenirs were left to the various nurses and aides for their kindness. The potted plants were left to Beth in the next room.

Jenny took a final look around and, satisfied that she had attended to everything, she picked up the chest and purse she wanted and left. For the second time in the last two months, she walked out of what had been a home… at least this one was a home filled with love.

Early the next morning, Jenny decided to go out and sit on the bench in the courtyard. It was the closest thing to the gazebo she had enjoyed when she lived at her parents' home and later, James' estate. When she sat there and read, she just imagined herself sitting in her own little world. Soon the story would whisk her away to far off places and adventures and Jenny would forget that she was sitting on a bench, fully exposed to the other tenants.

Around ten, when Jenny returned to her apartment to make herself a cup of tea, she met the mailman.

"Good morning, John."

"Good morning, Mrs. Hamilton."

Jenny wanted to correct him that it was no longer Mrs. but Ms., but didn't want the bother.

"It's a beautiful day."

"Yes, I was just enjoying it out in the courtyard."

John filed through his stack of letters. "Yes, here it is. I thought I saw a letter for you."

Jenny looked puzzled as she took the letter from him. "I wonder who it's from?"

"Well, you will soon know," said John, as he headed over to the wall of mail boxes just inside of the foyer.

Jenny looked at the letter. It was from her mother. Jenny was in a daze as she made her way back to her apartment and sat on the chair next to the sun filled window. There was no return address.

"Oh, that Mom; even in death she's witty. There is no mail service where she went." Jenny smiled as she turned the letter over and slid her little finger into the slight open edge of the envelope, just like she had when she received Henry's letter.

Jenny opened the envelope and pulled out the letter. She laid the envelope on the arm of the chair and, as she unfolded the letter a card fell out and fluttered down onto her lap. It was of a guardian angel walking behind a little girl with blonde hair. They were crossing a rickety old wooden bridge spanning over a deep formidable gorge. On the other side was a path that wound back and forth and disappeared into a soft mist in the far background.

On the bottom edge her mother had written, 'May your guardian angel always watch over you. I love you so much.'

Jenny's eyes filled with tears as she gazed at the beautiful image, perhaps not knowing the special meaning it would have for so many people. Jenny brought the card to her lips and tenderly kissed it. She looked heavenward and whispered, "Thank you, Mom."

Jenny laid the card on the table beside her then read her mother's letter.

> *My dearest Jenny,*
>
> *My last instruction to the care home attendants was that on the day I pass on, they should send this letter off to you. You will note there is no date on the letter, because I don't exactly know when the good Lord is going to come and take me. But when He does, I want you to be the first to know!*
>
> *Jenny, you have no conception of how happy you have made me this past while. Up until we had our heart-to-heart talk, my life was trapped in a veil of guilt, shame and regret. Your forgiveness has set me free. I now know this is the greatest gift one can receive in their lifetime. I'm sure heaven will be a let down. I can't imagine it getting any better than the joy and happiness I have known of late.*
>
> *Truly, the greatest blessing the good Lord gave to me in this lifetime was you, the day you were born. Every mother should be so blessed as to receive a daughter with a golden heart; so understanding, so forgiving, so full of life, so loving. I saw it within you everyday of your life, Jenny. Try as the world might, with all its twist and turns, it could never take away the precious and rare gift of life you were blessed with. You have always been true to your nature, even in your darkest moments*

and deepest yearnings. You are the truest of true hearts.

Oh, my dear Jenny, you are truly special. If ever a person were worthy of love, it is you. It is my deepest, most heartfelt prayer that you find true happiness in your life. And now that I have gone on to be with our Creator, I will use all my motherly influence to have Him bless you with someone special who will cherish and love you as you so deserve.

The enclosed card reminded me of you and your guardian angel whom you love so dearly. May your angel ever be walking behind you, may my spirit now unite with your angel in watching over you, and protecting you.

My love and best wishes go into eternity for you.

Mommy.

Jenny brought the letter towards her, hugging it to her chest. *Oh, Mom, only you could think to do such a special thing.* Jenny's eyes smiled and twinkled through her tears. *I will always love you, too.*

The phone jangled her from her reverie. Jenny took a brief moment to compose herself. She laid the letter beside the card on the lamp table and picked up the phone.

"Hello," said Jenny.

"Hello," said J.J., sounding cold and distant. "I got your message that grandma died."

"Oh, I'm so glad you did, J.J., I was afraid you wouldn't get it and the funeral would go on without you there."

"Well, I won't be there, anyway."

"But, why?"

"Dad and I are at a conference in Los Angeles. There is an important speaker giving a presentation on Thursday evening and Friday. We have been waiting for months to hear him."

"But, J.J., it's your grandma. Surely she takes precedence over a conference."

"Well, what good is it going to do with us being there?" J.J. said defensively, "She's dead, our presence won't—"

"J.J., please don't say anymore. Please, just try to make it to pay your last respects to her, and I would really appreciate having you with me."

J.J. was silent for a long moment. "I know Dad won't be there. He's been looking forward to this conference for too long. And I have, too. I'll see if I can get the right connecting flights on Thursday after one of the talks, anyway. I can't promise."

Jenny listened in silence. How could her son have gone so astray?

"Thank you, J.J.." She heard a click at the other end and then a dial tone. Not once during their conversation did he call her Mom.

Just moments ago, she had been so elated by her mother's letter, then a heartbeat later she was thrust into a world she didn't understand, a world that seemed so full of hate, anger, and bitterness. Jenny shook her head, trying to comprehend a world that was incomprehensible to her nature.

Jenny closed her eyes and looked heavenward, pleading out loud, "Oh, dear Lord, forgive my son, he doesn't know what he is saying and thinking. Oh, please, Mom, if you can reach my son, your grandson, please fill his mind with your light. Fill his heart with peace, forgiveness, understanding and love. Please bring him back to me."

NINE O'CLOCK FRIDAY morning, Jenny walked towards her car, the weight of her inner grief making her strain for each step. But her redrimmed eyes could not detract from her beauty. If it weren't for the black hat that accompanied her stately and elegant black dress, one would have thought that Jenny was going out on a date rather than to her mother's funeral.

What the world couldn't see through Jenny's demeanour was her supreme loneliness. There was no one to talk to, no one there to support her, no husband to lean on, and her son – her only family – nowhere around. The very person she had looked so forward to seeing, who gave her comfort, purpose and joy was now gone. Her daily visits to see her mother; the laughter, teasing, and outings would be no more. This afternoon, her mother's body would be cremated giving finality to it all, reminding her that everything around her, everything she had ever cared for had gone up in smoke.

The black veil hanging from her hat concealed the sorrow in her eyes from the rest of the world. Her utter elegance and radiant beauty, however, easily hid the growing, despairing heaviness in her heart.

As Jenny drove, rain misted the windshield. Thankfully, she had noticed the overcast skies earlier and had thought to bring an umbrella along and put the top up on her convertible. She wondered if the people at the care home who had planned on walking to the church would come if it rained too hard.

Once parked, she opened the door then popped up the umbrella before stepping out and hurrying to the church door. Since Jenny knew this would be a very small funeral, she didn't hire a hearse, limousine, or chauffeur. The funeral home was to bring her mother over in a very simple casket. There would be no pomp or ceremony, only a humble low mass.

When Jenny stepped into the sanctuary there was no one there, just her mother in the casket at the foot of the altar. It looked so lonely and desolate, almost as if her mother hadn't known a soul in the world, as if no one cared. Jenny had so hoped to see J.J. there. Words failed to express her disappointment. Perhaps he would still come. The funeral wouldn't start for another half hour.

Jenny walked down the long centre aisle to the front pew, genuflected, then entered the pew. She knelt and looked up at the casket covered with a white cloth and a bouquet of flowers. Beside the flowers stood an 8 x10 photo of her mother taken about ten years ago before she had fallen ill. Jenny closed her eyes so she could focus on the vision she had of her mother lying in the sun the other day. That was how she wanted to remember her mother.

It felt strange for Jenny to be kneeling in front of an altar in a church. She hadn't been to church for months and even then, it wasn't a Catholic church, but one that was nearest to her at the time. Although her parents were married in a Catholic church and she was baptized in the same one, over the years they had simply stopped going. So often Ted had worked on Sundays and Edith didn't have her own car to drive her and Jenny to church.

Oh dear Jesus, it doesn't seem right to come into the church to have a funeral for Mom. Please forgive us and me for not practicing my faith. I do love you so and you have given so much to us to be thankful for.

Jenny raised her head and gazed at the crucifix behind the altar and then bowed her head again. There were so many things to pray for. For J.J. and her to reconcile… perhaps for her and James to make up, too.

What would happen to her life now? Where was she heading? What should she do? Now that her mom was gone, Jenny was all alone. Most of her friends were married and socialized mainly with other married couples. She had never known any of James' friends, not that she'd ever wanted to.

The door at the back of the church opened, shifting Jenny's thoughts. She turned, hoping it would be J.J., but it was Millie and two other residents from the care home.

At least there would be someone to see Mom off.

The three shuffled down the aisle and moved into the pew on the opposite side, perhaps thinking that family would want to sit next to Jenny. When Jenny smiled at them, Millie came over, shook Jenny's hand and hugged her before returning to the other two ladies.

Just then, Father Kevin emerged from the sacristy, lit the candles beside the altar, then returned to the room from which he'd come. Usually an altar boy did that, but perhaps Father couldn't get anyone, with it being a school day.

The wind picked up, slapping the branches from the tall maple trees beside the church against the stained glass windows. The pounding of the rain on the metal roof echoed inside the hollow of the high-curved ceiling in the church. It muffled the sound of a group of people that had entered the church and made their way to the front.

Jenny's spirits shot up when sliding in beside her was her dear friend Matilda. She was wearing a black coat over top of her white cooking attire. Her beautiful smile warmed Jenny's heart. As the two women hugged, Matilda motioned her eyes to the pew behind. There stood Charles as erectly as he could. Next was Thomas, who had put on a sport jacket over top of his overalls. Beside him was Ramon, wearing a tie around the neck of his usual checkered shirt, and finally, there stood Carlos, beaming with tear-filled, compassionate eyes. They all leaned forward to Jenny and extended their hands in support and sympathy.

Jenny was so overwrought, she began to sob. "Oh, thank you for coming," she softly whispered. They simply nodded.

Off to the right of the altar, Father came out again carrying the Chalice Veil, a cloth covering the chalice and paten. He walked to the altar and set the chalice down, looked up at the few attendants and began the mass.

"In the name of the Father and the Son and the Holy Spirit. Thank you for coming as we celebrate a mass for our sister in Christ, Edith Sarsky…" He read the gospel at the pulpit and spoke briefly about the hereafter, that death is as much a part of life as living. That someday we must all go through the door into eternity and that Edith's death was but a reminder of the only certainty we have on this earth. He had no special words for Edith, as he hadn't known her at all. Jenny had come prepared to say a few words, but didn't feel it necessary under the circumstances.

Suddenly, a bright flash of lightning travelled through the huge, round, stained glass window high above and behind the altar. A prism of colour reflected on the arched ceiling, the pillars shouldering it and the surrounding walls. The kaleidoscope of colours dazzled brightly and for just a brief second, the ominous dimness in the huge church disappeared. A loud clap of thunder immediately followed, shaking the entire church and leaving in its wake dark mysterious shadows throughout.

Almost simultaneously, the rain drummed hard against the stained windows like a million pellets. It was as though all the sins, all the wrongs that Edith had committed were being driven and washed out of her spirit. It was impossible to hear Father say the mass and the Lord's Prayer. Jenny made out the phrase, "Forgive us our trespasses," by reading his lips.

As the time for communion approached the rain abated, and a calm washed over the church. A mellow sun shone through the exquisite windows high above, its light falling gently on the stone tile of the church floor, worn by years of parishioners' footsteps, bringing out their rich warm colour. A shaft of light streaming between two pillars settled over Edith's casket, which seemed to emanate a sense of absolution and forgiveness.

Her mother was finally at rest. Jenny felt totally at peace as she got up to receive Holy Communion. As she passed the casket, she touched it and whispered under her breath, "This one is offered up for you, Mom."

The mass was over in less than half an hour, since there was hardly any homily and no singing. After Mass, Jenny thanked Millie and the other residents for coming, and offered to drive them back to the care home, but they wanted to walk, since the rain had ended. They shook hands and said their good-byes.

Jenny turned to her friends and thanked them for coming.

"Oh, it was like a group of angels had come into the church when I saw you all! Thank you so much for coming!"

"We always enjoyed when your mom came for a visit. We all could see the sparkle in your eyes," said Matti.

"Yes, she loved the garden almost as much as you did," concurred Thomas. "I think the Angel of Thanksgiving reminded her of her late husband."

"You're right Thomas," replied Jenny. "Each time before she left she would pick a flower and put it into the angel's basket in thanksgiving for him."

Carlos was perhaps the only one that had known Edith best of all. He commented on how kind and gracious she was and how much he enjoyed working for both Mom and Dad as gardener on the estate. But it was what he added last that brought a tear into Jenny's eyes, "You better keep checking the rose bushes for a dew drop and yellow butterfly, Miss Jenny. I have a feeling your Mom is going to visit you on this day in the coming years just like mine does on the day she went home."

"I'll be watching, Carlos. Thank you!"

Jenny gave them all a hug and watched them walk down the aisle then disappear through the door. Jenny returned to her pew and sat with her mother.

"Not much of a farewell, was it, Mom? But I was here and people who love and care for us were too, and that's all that really matters." Jenny forced herself to smile. She could hardly believe that neither her son nor her ex-husband had shown up.

"Oh, Mom, I will miss you so much. We were finally coming together and being such close friends. What on earth am I going to do, now? I've never really liked Ottawa. I'm really a small-town girl. I have such good memories of Kelowna and being out in the boat with Dad. He so loved the water, but we have no relatives there and most of your friends wouldn't know me even if they were alive."

Jenny sighed. "Perhaps I should move and make a fresh start. But where should I go, Mom? The only other place I really loved, at least for a short period of time, was Regina. It has been on my mind lately, especially since you gave me Henry's letter. Even though so many years have elapsed, it still makes me feel so good to know that he did not abandon me; that at the time, anyways, he still loved me as deeply as I loved him.

"And then there's Camilla. I think of her so often, too. I'm sure she must be in Ottawa some place. If only I could find her, maybe she and I could become as close as you and I managed to be. It would give me more reason to stay here, but since I haven't heard from her after all these years, chances are I will never see her again. Oh, Mom, I need someone! New friends, a new beginning…"

Jenny looked up and saw light streaming into the stained glass window above the altar as a thought popped into her head.

"What if I did move back to Regina? I wouldn't want to interfere in any way with Henry's family. I did love the city and the park and I remember the old houses near the legislature buildings, how elegant they looked and had so much character."

As she visualized the south end of Regina, her eyes sparkled and brightened. "You know, Mom, perhaps I will call a real estate firm in Regina and see what is available. It wouldn't hurt to at least look into it."

Having made a tentative decision, a strange peace settled over her.

As she bowed her head to say a final prayer for the repose of her mother's soul, the attendants from the funeral home emerged from the sacristy, waiting until she left so that they could return the casket to the funeral home for cremation later that afternoon. She nodded towards them, then motioned with her hand that they could come and take the casket away.

Jenny rose, approached the casket and touched it one more time.

"Bye, Mom. See you in heaven." She turned and walked out of the church.

The sun had chased the clouds off to the east. She took off her hat and let the wind tousle her hair. It gave her a certain sense of freedom and abandon. It reminded her of the time she and Henry ran over the front lawns after the storm when returning home from Balfour Collegiate as if it were yesterday.

"Perhaps, perhaps it just may be the place to finally settle down."

Prompted by the memory she allowed herself to entertain just a moment ago, Jenny felt a sudden spontaneous desire to run barefoot across the lawn. She bent down and slipped off her black pumps. Holding them in one hand and her hat and umbrella in the other, Jenny took off.

"Quickly, hold my hand," bubbled out of her mouth, as she ran freely across the sprawling church lawn towards her car.

Chapter Sixteen

Henry's face stung in the crisp fall air as he stood on the deck outside his home. A cool blanket of frost that covered the valley was invigourating, clean and refreshing. Henry remained motionless, silently breathing it all in. Just beside the Poustinia, a deer rustled out of the bush and licked the frost off dead leaves. And across the meandering stream two coyotes were going into a thick group of bushes; the colour of their fur making them almost unnoticeable. But Henry had trained his eyes to see detail. What most people overlooked, Henry studied and stored in his memory. It was his sketch book that he readily recalled on as he tried to capture the prairie landscape in his paintings.

All of God's creation touched Henry's soul deeply, especially amidst the dawning light of a new day. He keenly watched as the sun slipped up, silently chasing away the shadows. Like a curtain on a stage slowly lifting, each little advance of the morning light yielded a little more of the detail of God's handiwork on a grander scale. It was easier for Henry to grasp the parts than taking it all in at once.

As the light increased, spreading its rays ever broader, Henry muttered, "Yes, it's all about the light. *Spreading God's light!* If we keep the light always ahead of us, the darkness and shadows of life will fall behind as we make our way through the day."

Henry didn't know at the time how prophetic that statement would be. The sermon he and his family were about to hear by Father Engelmann would expand on that very topic; *how to enjoy the gift of each day the Lord gives us.*

Justin was at the roll top desk retrieving some money from the mahogany box. Henry was proud of the fact that his son always put a quarter in the collection basket when the ushers came around after the homely. He was also happy to see how much joy the secret compartment in the desk gave to his son.

"Would you please check to see if Lauren is up, Justin? Tell her we leave in an hour. Breakfast will be ready in twenty minutes."

"Sure, Dad." Justin said as he returned the wooden box to its hiding place and closed the drawer.

Justin sat in the front seat while Lauren lay half asleep in the back as they drove to the city to go to church. Henry pulled out Julean's rosary and gave it to Justin. His son loved the feel of his mother's rosary. He never objected to saying it. Of all the children, perhaps Justin missed Julean the most. He was her last child and Julean had always considered him a gift late in her child bearing years. Many nights Henry would get up and find Julean asleep with Justin in her arms, reluctant to lay him down in his bed. There had always been a special bond between them.

Justin made the sign of the cross and began the rosary saying the first half of each prayer and Henry and Lauren completed it. After Justin said one decade Henry started the next followed by Lauren. By the time they finished saying the rosary, Henry and his family pulled into St. Mary's parking lot. It was packed as usual.

Mary was already seated in the second row, along with Jeremy, Camilla and Josh. Henry peered over his Mom and whispered 'hi' to his son and lovely wife. Josh made his way to Henry and crawled into his grandpa's lap.

Shortly, Father made his entrance from the sacristy, as radiant as ever. He looked up and portrayed a smile that lit up the surrounding altar as if the sun had entered the church.

"Good morning, my brothers and sisters!" Father bellowed.

`"Good morning, Father!" The congregation resounded.

"St. Mary's welcomes all newcomers to the church, as well as those visiting. Let us take a moment to welcome each of them and each other and don't be stingy with the hugs."

After much shuffling and commotion Father began, "In the name of the Father and of the Son and of the Holy Spirit…"

Henry shook his head as he watched his mentor say the mass as if he were saying it for the first time. His passion and love for the holy ritual was so deep that anyone in attendance could not help but feel ever so fortunate that they were there to participate in this beautiful worship of the Lord.

Henry couldn't get over how youthful Father looked and the love and enthusiasm he exhibited. There had never been a time, other than perhaps when Anna died, that he was ever down about a thing. Father lived his life with an attitude of praise and thanksgiving. He was grateful for everything, regardless if it was good, not so good, or a disaster. His faith in the Lord was so deep and strong that he knew there was nothing that God would not turn into good for him. For as long as he could remember, Henry felt the holy aura that surrounded his life-long friend and teacher. The German meaning of his name was perfect: David Engelmann, our *Beloved Angel Man.*

After the gospel was read, Father always asked people to pray that he would speak the words that the Lord wanted him to share with his flock. After being seated, everyone anxiously awaited Father's inspired homily.

As usual, Father gazed out and around to his sheep. His eyes made every effort to touch not only the eyes of each of his people, but their soul as well. Satisfied, he began:

"In Psalm 118: 24 is the very well known scripture, 'This is the day the Lord hath made let us be glad and rejoice in it.' To many of us, this is just a nice phrase that has little meaning or value to our lives. It goes in one ear and out the other without much thought. We usually begin the day the same, not aware of the great wisdom in the psalm.

"My dear friends, if we really understood what this simple passage means and implies, it would change our lives and fill us with unknown peace and happiness.

"You see, in the busyness of our living, we often forget the most important part of our lives and that is the *spiritual side*. We forge through our daily existence day after day without a thought of praise or a prayer to God for the gift of the very day we are living. We take our life for granted, we take each other for granted, we take the beauty of creation around us for granted, we take our guardian angels for granted and unfortunately we take our very Creator for granted.

"It is said that we are what we think and what we think becomes our reality, our life. Our thoughts lead to actions, which plant seeds in our lives and those around us. And as a natural consequence we reap what we have sown. The crops could be good or not so good. The weather and storms of life could cause us to fret and worry, get angry, judgmental of others, resentful and unforgiving and on and on.

"The thoughts we entertain, my friends, are very powerful and often determine the kind of day, if not the kind of life, we are going to live and have."

And then Father said something that got Henry's immediate attention. It was the central theme of his valedictorian speech back in Grade 12.

"As a very close, dear friend, once said, 'to be or not to be, that is the question.' Will our days be filled with joy and peace and be glad for each moment we are alive, or will it be empty, boring, mundane, filled with turmoil and strife? That is the choice before you every minute of your existence from the time you rise to the time you go to bed and for many it even occupies the very time when we should be having a restful sleep.

"How then is it possible to rejoice and be glad each day as the psalmist writes, when our lives are on such an emotional roller coaster of highs and lows?

"Like a broken record, you have heard me say over and over again, that you must begin each day by setting aside a quiet moment in a quiet place to read and meditate upon the words of Jesus. This is the only way to keep ever in the forefront of your daily existence the spiritual side of your life as well as the only true path that leads to peace, joy and fulfillment in this world and leads us safely into the next.

"Is it not just plain common sense my brothers and sisters to do this?

If someone promised you that if you got up each morning at 6 am and read his book for a half an hour that you would have a gloriously happy day, would you not do it?

"Jesus promises you exactly that!

"Jesus knows all about us and our self-centred nature and the many temptations we fall into daily. Jesus did not only come to die for our sins out of His love for us, but for three years prior to His death He taught us how to live so that we could enjoy each day and be glad in it as the Psalm suggests.

"You see, as we read the Holy Bible we find for the most part His teachings and life lessons revolve around the two greatest commandments He gave us: to love the Lord our God with your whole heart, with all your soul, with all your mind and with all your strength. The second is to love your neighbour as yourself.

"Now, if we meet with Him every morning He will instruct us how to fulfill these two commandments which is the secret to living peacefully and fruitfully in today's world. If you do this faithfully, my brothers and sisters, I will guarantee that you will truly come to know the meaning of the Psalm, 'This is the day the Lord hath made, let us be glad and rejoice in it.'"

Father stopped and once again swept his penetrating gaze at each parishioner allowing the *truths* to sink in. Satisfied, he continued:

"You see my friends, His *words* are alive. The Holy Bible is not just an ordinary book, but filled with the inspired *words* of God. The *words* have transformational power that enter your mind and soul and change your heart.

You will come to know Him and to know Him is to love Him; and to love Him is to trust Him and to have faith in Him.

"It is no different than the way you met and developed a relationship with your spouse. You did not just meet on the street and say, 'Let's see Father Engelmann and get married.' No…you dated and spent time together and through your courtship you got to know each other and developed faith and trust in one another. Your love deepened and eventually you made the choice to spend the rest of your lives with each other.

"It is the same, but even more powerful with Jesus. Once He enters your life, the old is pushed out and the new comes in. His light replaces the darkness and you will increasingly be ever more fully alive in the moment to love and serve our Lord and neighbour. Ever so gently we are fulfilling Jesus' two commandments and entering into God's loving light, just as our guardian angels who constantly see His face. Some mornings His presence in your quiet times will be so filled with His loving light, your heart will overflow in praise. Truly you will say and mean from the bottom of your heart, "This is the day the Lord hath made, I shall be glad and rejoice in it!

"You see, my friends, when you fill your mind in the morning with the "*light*" of God's words contained in the Bible, you are preparing yourself to live your day out with Jesus in your heart. Imagine being so filled with gratitude and thanksgiving to God for the gift of this day, that you praise Him in every situation and encounter. Just like Jesus, we make every moment count and become certain that it will not be lost.

"Every thought, word and deed you carry out will have a spiritual side. Each and every moment of the day you will be living and acting in the presence of Jesus who invites you continuously to live in and through Him to love others. Moment by moment, as we yield our will to Him, we are fulfilling His purpose to bring us all into His kingdom.

"Let us look for examples how a Christian steps out into the day and journeys hand and hand with Jesus. He does not require great actions from us, but just consistently giving small ones. What are some small acts of charity that have a huge, if not profound affect, not only on others but ourselves?

"Let us begin with something that you should put on as soon as you jump out of bed; a smile! Never is the saying, 'a picture is worth a thousand words' more true than a friendly welcoming smile on your face to all you meet. It not only transmits peace, love and warmth, but reveals the kind of spirit that resides within you; a cheerful heart. And this is true, no? If we fill up with Jesus we are glad and joyful for the day and reflect it to others with a smile. And as a bonus, a smile takes less energy and uses fewer muscles than a grumpy frown.

"The other day, while a parishioner was driving me back to the rectory he stopped at a gas station and while there I visited the washroom. Many times on the walls of a men's washroom things are written which are not only inappropriate to repeat, but shocking to read! However, this day I was pleasantly surprised to see taped to the wall a poem that was simply titled:

SMILING IS CONTAGIOUS

"When I left the washroom I spoke to the manager and commended him on putting such a beautiful poem on the wall and asked him if he had an extra copy. Without hesitation he reached below the counter and gave me one.

"'You're not the first one to ask and you won't be the last. I've given out more copies of that poem than I sell candy bars,'" he told me. I told him that the reason his sales were higher was because the words in the poem were sweeter than any chocolate.

"So now that I have your interest, I can see by the twinkle in everyone's eyes they want to hear what I read in a men's washroom of a service station."

Father lifted the Bible and took hold of a page of paper and then began to read the poem.

SMILING IS CONTAGIOUS

You catch it like the flu,
When someone smiled at me today,
I started smiling too!
I passed around the corner,
And someone saw my grin.
When he smiled I realized,
I'd passed it onto him.

I thought about that smile,
Then I realized its worth,
A single smile,
Just like mine,
Could travel around the earth.

So, if you feel a smile begin,
Don't leave it undetected,
Let's start an epidemic quick
And get the world infected!

"See my friends," Father said, as he gazed out at the congregation, "Just by reading, how the power of smile can have a global affect, I can see already how all of you are smiling! And if I stare long enough you will even laugh."

Father stopped and pointed his finger at several parishioners laughing. "Ah, I hear some more giggling over here!" and as Father pointed here and there, the entire congregation began laughing along!

"See the power of just a smile and the good feelings it sweeps through us?! A smile can cheer someone up, make someone's day, open up doors to sharing and trust and puts a huge smile on the Lord's face as well.

"Closely related to a smile is kindness. When one is kind it brings a smile to others. It lifts the heart of both the giver and receiver. Not only do you enjoy the moment of the day but so too is the recipient happy and glad. And isn't kindness another manifestation of Jesus' love? Did He not say, 'be kind and tenderhearted towards one another?'

"Kindness, my friends, is what the world is so much in need of. A kind remark, an act of kindness, taking time to listen, encouraging someone, being courteous and polite, giving support, visiting the sick or shut-ins and being generous. There are countless ways to let others know we care.

"When you leave your quiet time with the Lord, occupy your mind on how you can be kindlier than the day before. And isn't it better to focus on how you can shower others with blessings than spend those precious moments of life worrying or fretting?

"I am often reminded about the life of St. Therese, also known as '*the little flower*.' She only lived to the age of 24, yet she is the most revered saint in modern times. She lived each day simply and with unshakeable confidence in God. She has touched the hearts of countless millions by her spirituality of doing the ordinary with extraordinary love. Small acts of kindness, when done out of love, become great deeds.

"As St. Paul said in Corinthians 13:1-13, 'love is patient and kind, it is not jealous or conceited or proud. It does not keep score of wrongs or delight in another's trials.'

"Trust me, my friends, if you fill up each day with the Lord's words and obey and follow His teachings, you will be blessed with a beautiful day and a saintly life. It's just that simple! He laid out the map for you to follow perfectly! The Bible covers every aspect of life and applies to all situations!

"Yes, there are times when it is difficult to be kind to a person who is rude. But that is precisely the time we ask Jesus to give us the strength and grace to love this person the way He does. Stay in the light and reflect back kindness, otherwise we give power to the darkness. In this way we plant the seeds of faith. *That's our purpose, my friends, to ever be beacons of light and be workers for God to bring all of His children into the kingdom of heaven.*

"I would be remiss if I did not mention very briefly two of the main culprits that steal away from the two virtues I have just talked about. They sneak up on us so subtly that if we open the door to either or both they immediately have a strong foothold on our minds.

"So what should we guard ourselves against that prevents us from smiling and being kind and being glad and enjoying the day the Lord hath made?

Judging others.

Jesus said, 'judge not lest ye be judged.' Did you know that as soon as we judge others, it is impossible to be kind to them? Judgment immediately steals away the love that could be present in the moment. If we dwell on resentment or anger and look for the flaws or bad in others, what is occupying your mind? Can you not see that the moment you do this you are seeing in others a refection of what is in your own heart?

"I remember my father telling me when I was a young lad that when you point your finger at someone, notice that the other three are pointing back at you."

And as Father spoke these words, he demonstrated with his hand. Henry still had not forgotten that lesson from Mr. Engelmann out back of the store sitting on the old grey crates in his school of life.

Father continued, "But the moment we shift our thoughts to focus on the good in others then once again we enter the *light* that Jesus wants us to be in.

"Remember, we are what we think. If we entertain the negative, our thoughts quickly expand like wildfire and soon we find ourselves upset, hurt, resentful and unforgiving. If we stay on the positive and love and accept others, our minds expand in the same way, but only now it fosters growth and acceptance and, most important, we stay in the *light*!

"The blind cannot lead the blind lest both fall in the ditch. We must be the beacons of *light*. Just like flowers grow in the sunshine, others will too if we accept them where they are, and through Jesus' *light* in us, we love them to bits!

"Closely related to 'judging others' brings us to perhaps one of the most crucial of all of Jesus' teachings and that is to foster a forgiving heart. Unforgiveness steals joy and happiness out of our heart instantly. It locks both the hurt person and the one who caused the injury into a stalemate of anger and resentment for hours, days and then years. It sucks the life out of us and if we do not obey Jesus' command to forgive, then He cannot forgive us.

"My friends, it is impossible to say, 'This is the day the Lord hath made and I shall be glad and rejoice in it,' when a spirit of unforgiveness occupies our hearts!

"*Impossible!*

"It is in this arena of life that we need Jesus' help. As we come to Him with a sincere heart, he will give us the grace and strength to be compassionate and merciful and to overcome and forgive any injury.

"*We need Jesus to do this.*

"In all the years of my life I have known of no other way. We need a power greater than ourselves. We forgive not only to be free, but because we want to be at one with our Lord. We know the great benefit of remaining in His *light! Just as the air we breath is necessary for our existence, so too it is critical to have Jesus in your heart.*

"It is clear what He said, '*I am the way, the truth and life.*'

And in John 10:10, the Lord says. "I am come that they might have life, and that they might have it more abundantly."

"And so, my friends, this is the secret of how we can have good days, today, tomorrow and the next and the next. Come to Jesus daily and learn from Him. Fill your mind with Jesus, fill your heart with Him, and soon energy, vitality, exuberance, joy and praise will well up within you. Can you not see the great benefits by placing your hand in His every day and saying 'Yes, Jesus, I am here to do Your will.'"

Father stopped for but a moment and gazed out amongst his beloved congregation. And with a smile that melted one's heart, he softly ended his homily by saying, "If you do this my friends, you will truly say each day for the rest of your lives what the Psalmist wrote so many years ago;

"*This is the day the Lord hath made and I shall be glad and rejoice in it!*"

Father returned to the altar and continued the mass. When it came to the part before Holy Communion where Jesus said to the Apostles, "Peace I leave with you, my peace I give to you…" Father stopped and gazed out at the parishioners and invited everyone to extend peace and good will to their brothers and sisters in Christ. It was visibly noticeable that morning more smiles and hugs and signs of kindness filled the church.

"Great sermon, Father," Henry said, as he shook Father's hand on the way out of the church. "Are you coming to Mom's for dinner?"

"Yes, I so look forward to Mary's delicious cooking and being with all of you."

Just then, Mary, along with Jeremy and Camilla came out.

"Oh, Father, your homily was just what I needed. I have neglected my quiet time for the past week and was wondering why things haven't been going the way they should," said Camilla, her blue eyes sparkling in the light.

"We cannot be reminded of that often enough, Father," concurred Mary.

"So, what do you call a bunch of rabbits walking backwards in a straight row, Father?" chimed in Justin.

Father thought for a moment and shrugged his shoulders, "I'm afraid you will have to tell me, Justin."

"You should know this one; it's a receding hare line!"

Everyone laughed.

"Well, let's go gang, we are holding up the traffic. Are you coming to Camilla's for breakfast, Mom?"

"Yes, Jeremy said he would drive me home afterwards and I so want to see their backyard."

"There still may be the odd butterfly left, too, Mom. I just love the way they flit about in the yard. It's like seeing angels everywhere!"

Henry gazed at his daughter-in-law, clearly entranced by her features, and the very things she loved reflected Jenny's love as well. Angels, butterflies, her personality and looks…

He shook his head as he and the children made it back to the car, filled with the wonder of it all.

CHAPTER SEVENTEEN

FIRST THING MONDAY morning, Jenny made two phone calls. The first was to Remax Real-Estate in Regina. She told them to look for a bungalow in the south end large enough to accommodate all of her antique furniture and a large backyard.

The second call was to the welfare agency to determine what action she could take to find Camilla. Jenny was hopeful as the laws had changed since the fifties and information had become much more open and available.

Jenny was instructed to write a formal letter indicating her desire to find her daughter and to agree that she was open to be contacted by either the adoptive parents or the child. Once they received her permission letter, the agency would contact the adoptive parents to determine if they wished to be contacted or if the birth parent could contact the daughter directly. Depending on how either of these two inquiries turned out would determine whether Jenny would stay in Ottawa or move to Regina.

Jenny still debated in her mind if moving to Regina was the wisest move to make. It would bring her to a small city that she liked and had fond memories of, but Jenny worried about meeting Henry. She was adamant that she did not want to interfere in his life or marriage.

In regards to Camilla, Jenny assumed that since she gave up the child in Ottawa, in all probability she and her parents would still be in the city. If that turned out to be the case, then she would abort her plan to move to Regina and stay in Ottawa.

Regina Remax faxed information of several properties to their affiliate company in Ottawa and they in turn couriered the information to Jenny. Of the five possible listings for her consideration, one stood out over the others. It was a spacious three-bedroom bungalow on Hill Avenue. The exterior appealed to Jenny right off the bat. It was completely finished in warm, earth coloured fieldstone with steep roofs. She loved how the roof curved at the eaves. It looked so quaint, rustic and inviting. The interior had a spacious layout. The master bedroom was huge and could easily accommodate all of her en suite antique chairs and writing desk. The second bedroom could be left as a guest room and the third and smallest was already turned into a laundry room, which was just perfect.

The living room and dining room were also of good size and basically open to each other, separated only by an archway and pillar at each end. Jenny saw all of her antique furniture fitting easily into the space. She loved the stone fireplace at the end of the living room snuggled between bookshelves on either side. She could hardly wait to be reading a book by the open fire.

What sold Jenny more than anything, however, was the huge front and backyards brimming with flowers and trees. The landscaping was not perfect, but the yard had potential. She visualized a gazebo in the far corner of the backyard and a winding paving stone path leading up to it. Jenny was excited about it and hoped and prayed that the home would not be sold until she made a final decision to move or not.

A week passed and then another and Jenny still had not heard from the agency. She called at the end of the second week, but the lady she was dealing with said they had not heard from the adoptive parents. They could tell Jenny no more. Jenny worried if she didn't find out soon, the home she was interested in in Regina might be sold.

"Oh, dear guardian angel please help me. Please touch the adoptive parent's hearts and let me become part of their lives and family. I have always felt that Camilla was not only an answer to their prayer but that somehow we would one day be reunited."

Incredibly, the following Monday morning Jenny received the call that would be an answer to her deepest most heartfelt prayer.

"Ms. Hamilton, I have good news for you. We have received a call from the adoptive parents and they, or rather he, has agreed for you to contact him in regards to your daughter, Camilla."

A rush of emotion that Jenny had buried within her from the day she gave birth to her daughter and accumulated over the years surged through her with such magnitude Jenny dropped the phone and collapsed on the chair by the phone. Tears immediately filled her eyes. She was speechless.

"Ms. Hamilton? Ms. Hamilton?" Jenny heard from the receiver lying on the floor. It took her a moment to regain her composure and come back to the reality of the moment. Jenny bent down and picked up the phone.

"Yes, I'm so sorry. It's…it's just that I have waited and dreamed of this moment for so long…" Jenny couldn't speak any further, she just held the phone and cried.

"I can call back a little later if you like," said Mrs. Blake.

"No, just give me a moment, I wi…I will be fine." Jenny breathed deeply, slowly gaining control. But she heard Mrs. Blake sniffle and that made Jenny cry all the more. They laughed through their tears.

"Oh, Mrs. Blake, I'm just so elated with this news. In what part of the city are they living?"

"They don't live here anymore, they moved years ago and retired in Victoria, British Columbia. We had a nice long talk when Mr. Breckhart, your daughter's father through adoption of course, called and explained how they finally settled on the West Coast. When the Breckhart's adopted Camilla, Mr. Breckhart was employed with Eaton's here in Ottawa. In the late sixties he was transferred to Saskatoon and a few years later he was transferred to manage the Eaton's store in Regina where he worked until his retirement in 1981. They then moved to Victoria."

Jenny couldn't believe they had moved to Saskatchewan and to Regina of all places!

"So, they are all living in Victoria?"

"No, Mrs. Breckhart passed away a year ago and Camilla is married and lives in… Well, I'm getting ahead of myself. Mr. Breckhart should really be giving you these details. It is still up to him how far this matter goes. I feel confident though that he is prepared to tell you everything he knows from the conversations I have had with him."

"So, what is the next step?"

"Mr. Breckhart gave me permission to give you his telephone number. If you decide to still go ahead with this you can call him to discuss this or arrange to meet him."

Jenny could not believe this was finally happening. She was elated! She felt like she was floating. How it happened so quickly! It was unfortunate Mrs. Breckhart was gone. Jenny would have loved to have met the woman that had taken her place all those years.

"Oh that's wonderful, Mrs. Blake. Just give me a moment while I get a pen. Okay, what is the number?"

Mrs. Blake gave her the number.

"I was so surprised to hear from him last Friday morning since he hadn't responded to the letter we sent over two weeks ago. We thought for sure that he wouldn't answer as a lot of adoptive parents choose not to. But lo and behold, the call came just when we were giving up hope! Anyway, I told him that I would be calling you today, and that he could expect to hear from you in the very near future."

Jenny repeated the number back to her.

"Yes, that's correct. Well, Ms. Hamilton, I wish you all the best. I know from your file you have waited for this moment for a long time. I hope everything works out to your heart's desire."

"Oh, thank you, Mrs. Blake. I hope it will, too. To meet my daughter in person has been a dream of mine for almost thirty years. I still can't believe that it is about to come true. Thank you, again."

Jenny took a deep breath and rested her head against the back of the chair. She was still so excited. Her heart threatened to burst through her chest, her hands were sweaty and her entire face was flushed and damp with perspiration. She picked up the paper she had written the telephone number on, read it and then waved the paper in front of her face to cool down.

"Oh, thank you dear guardian angel, for helping bring my little wildflower back to me!"

She wanted to dial the number right away, but a million thoughts raced through her mind. What should she say? How should she start? How would she introduce herself? Would Camilla's father like her? What if he changed his mind after they spoke? Jenny had forgotten to ask Mrs. Blake if Camilla even knew she had been adopted, though based on their conversation, it sounded like she didn't. She hoped it hadn't upset Camilla's father to receive the news that her biological mother was looking for her.

Jenny couldn't sit still. She wanted to phone right away but she was too excited. Perhaps she would go down to the courtyard for some fresh air and think more about what to say.

The air felt good as Jenny walked out the door. The smell of fall was in the air. Soon the leaves would begin to change. She loved the large maple leaves when they turned to their golden yellow colour and fluttered to the ground. She recalled saving so many as a child and pressing them between books.

Jenny sat down and recalled the morning Camilla was born in the hospital. Her only memory of her little baby was dangling from the doctor's hand and squealing for her mother. Jenny would have given anything to hold her for just a moment. To touch her, to smell her, to cradle her in her arms and count her fingers and toes. But it was not meant to be…

Within minutes, a nurse wrapped the infant in a white blanket and scurried out of the delivery room to the waiting arms of the adoptive parents. That was the last she saw of the precious infant that she had carried in her womb for all those months. The separation from her baby pained her for days on end. Jenny could feel the ache in her breasts now as she recalled how she yearned to nurse her newborn as nature had intended.

It was nature that had come to her rescue, as it was doing now. God's creations had always been Jenny's way for re-connecting to her herself and her spirit. Perhaps that is why she decided to come outside and feel the sun on her face and smell the fragrance of the flowers. Slowly Jenny calmed and peace began to gently sweep within her being. She was returning to the now of life. Memories are good but it's in the present that we move forward. There were many days, months and years that were filled with separation but from now on a new beginning was about to start. A beginning that would involve her and her daughter, and Jenny was determined to make the best of every moment of what was to come.

Jenny tilted her face toward her friend and was soothed by the warmth of the sun's rays. Accompanying this quiescence a thought emerged that gave Jenny further comfort. It had back then and was now resurfacing to hearten and refresh her once more. There was a reason for having given birth to Camilla. Her guardian angel had protected her from the memory of the rape itself but had not spared her the pregnancy. It may have been the answer to the prayers of Camilla's adoptive parents, but Jenny sensed there was something more…something that had to do with her first love as well. *What is it that is yet to unfold?*

Jenny pushed herself off the seat and made her way back inside the apartment. She went to the kitchen for a glass of water. She bit her lip, took a few sips and headed back to the phone. Her heart raced as she carefully dialed the number to Camilla's adoptive father. The phone rang three times before a male voice answered.

"Hello? The Breckhart residence."

"G-good morning." Jenny's heart leapt into her throat. "Is this Mr. Breckhart?"

"This is he. Who is calling?"

"Mr. Br-Breckhart… This…this is Marjorie Hamilton, I-I'm—"

"Yes, Marjorie, I know who you are. I was told you might call. It is so good to hear from you."

Jenny relaxed. She sensed a kindness in his voice and nature. She intuitively knew her daughter had been raised by good parents. They spoke for almost a half-hour. Much of what Mr. Breckhart said about his wife and how they eventually ended up in Victoria, Jenny already knew from her conversation with Mrs. Blake, but Jenny enjoyed hearing it from him and loved hearing his jolly voice.

When the conversation lulled, Jenny finally asked, "So, Mr. Breckhart, is Camilla still living at home or does she have her own place in Victoria?"

"She lives on the prairies. Cold, cold Saskatchewan! I keep telling her that she and her family should move to the coast. Much better weather here, but they are happy where they are."

"So, she is married?"

"Yes. When I transferred to Regina she met a young man in the early 80's and within two months they got married. Love at first sight, as the saying goes. They have one wonderful son a bit over two years of age."

Jenny couldn't believe her ears. Camilla living in Regina? Maybe that's another reason why she had felt drawn to move there. How could this be!

"Marjorie, I should confide in you; Valerie, my wife, and I never did tell Camilla that she was adopted. Perhaps we should have, but the thinking at that time was to let sleeping dogs lie. Why create a problem when we were all so happy?" He paused. "We felt that not telling her would be for the best. That it might put too much pressure on her, create needless problems… and we have always loved her so much, as if she were our very own. We didn't want to tell her we really were not her real parents, if you know what I mean?"

"Yes," Jenny said, then unthinkingly added, "and that her mother gave her away…"

"Well, that didn't really occur to us," Mr. Breckhart corrected. "You were so young…"

Jenny's mind wandered, no longer listening to words that were meant to be consoling. No words could ever console the months and years of regret and sorrow she suffered for giving away her baby, her own flesh and blood, never to hear from her again. Thankfully, she had been given a second chance.

"If you like, I will call Camilla and explain everything. In fact, Valerie was going to before she died. She felt that Camilla had a right to know that we were not the birth parents. But unfortunately, Valerie passed on unexpectedly and I just never had the heart to tell her… until now.

"To be honest, I never thought about Camilla's birth mother or had any notion of your desire to locate your daughter until I received a letter from a Mrs. Blake a few weeks back. After I got thinking about it, I suddenly realized why Valerie wanted to reveal to Camilla that she was adopted and that if she knew, maybe she would want to search out her real mother. Well, now knowing that you, too, had the same goal… well, I immediately agreed to receive your call. Funny how things turn ou—"

"I was just wondering, Mr. Breckhart, if it would be better for Camilla to learn of this in person rather than by phone?"

"See, women are better at this than men. Funny, I was just visiting with them in Regina this past summer… but I am planning a trip to Regina for an Eaton's staff reunion in two weeks again. We could leave it until then?"

"Yes, Camilla may be more receptive that way. It will likely be upsetting for her. Please let me think on it for a few days. I might have some suggestions as to how we might tell her. In any case, would you tell me her married name and the name of their son? And, my grandson, too!"

"Yes, I can do that. I know that you will not try and contact her before I speak to her and explain our reasons—"

"Of course, Mr. Breckhart, you can be assured I will not approach Camilla until I get the go ahead from you. In fact, we may even want to leave it up to her."

What came next, however, Jenny could never have been prepared for.

"Her married name is Pederson. Her husband's name is Jeremy."

Pederson? No, couldn't be! Camilla married to a Jeremy Pederson? Mr. Breckhart also named their son, but Jenny no longer heard.

"Are you still there, Marjorie?"

"Yes, yes, Mr. Breckhart, it's just the shock of it all. I know of a Pederson in Regina. Would Jeremy be related to Henry Pederson?"

"Why, yes!" exclaimed Mr. Breckhart. "Henry is Jeremy's father, that is, Camilla's father-in-law. He owns that fine gallery, café and gift shop in Regina. Do you know Henry? He's quite a famous artist."

Jenny was flabbergasted and, again, speechless. Her deep-rooted longing for Henry over all the years and her deepest wish that he had been the father of her child indirectly had come true! Over and over she had prayed to her guardian angel that Henry would be the father. Could her heart's desire have somehow been infused within her unborn child? Could Camilla in some miraculous way have been led to return to her mother's first love?

Henry Pederson, my daughter's father-in-law? Unbelievable!

"Perhaps this is all too much for you, Marjorie. Would you like to take some time to think on this and call back?

"Sorry, Mr. Breckhart. I'll-I'll be fine."

"So…you know Henry Pederson, do you?"

"Yes, I do, Mr. Breckhart."

"Please call me Stanley as my wife used to. We are too old for this kind of formality and besides I miss not having Valerie around to call me by name."

Once again, thanks to Mr. Breckhart, Jenny relaxed. She wondered if she could ask him to call her Jenny as well but it might get too confusing.

"Thank you, Stanley, and yes, I do know Henry. Oh, this is getting quite complicated—"

"What do you mean? Good Lord, Henry wasn't the father?"

"No, no, he wasn't."

Stan sighed.

Jenny wasn't prepared for this and didn't know if she should tell Stan all the circumstances around this.

"No, Stan, Henry was a close friend I knew years and years ago. Over 30 years, in fact. He probably no longer remembers me. Well, Stan or Stanley, before we proceed with this, can I call you back in a week or so?"

"Of course, Marjorie, this is a big decision for you and… it is for me, too. I wish Valerie were here, she would be able to handle all this far better than me. But, Camilla is a very understanding girl. I'm certain she will be able to deal with this entire matter just fine and perhaps she already senses in her heart that her real parents are still out there. Her strong desire to work with unwed mothers makes me think that."

And after a pause, Stan said, "I've lived long enough to know that somehow life can never carry a secret forever."

Jenny had difficulty keeping up with the conversation, as Stan's last words reverberated through her mind.

Keeping a secret. Yes, secrets can never be kept, forever.

She thought of Henry's letter, of her mother revealing it to her, of Camilla, her love for Henry.

But then, perhaps some secrets were meant to die in one's heart.

"It was so nice to talk with you, Stan. I just know you and Mrs.…. Valerie were so good for Camilla. This has been quite a day for both of us. I will call within two weeks, Stan, before you leave for your reunion."

"It was good to hear from you too, Marjorie. Valerie and I talked so many times about you. We loved the name you selected for Camilla. It was always a reminder of the special gift you gave to us. Valerie and I could not have children and so we considered it such a blessing when we heard a baby was coming up for adoption. You were in our prayers every day. We know how difficult it must have been for you and carrying it in your heart all these years."

Tears welled up in Jenny's eyes. The truth of Stan's words opened so many sad memories, but it was all about to change for the better.

After a long pause, Jenny said, "It makes me very happy it was you and Valerie. I, too, thought so many times about the home I placed Camilla in. Thank you, again. Good-bye for now."

"Good-bye, Marjorie."

Jenny collapsed back in her chair and let the receiver slip out of her hand onto its cradle. Finally, finding Camilla and learning that she was in Regina and… then learning that Henry was Camilla's father-in-law was all too much for her to fathom at once. There was no doubt in her mind now: she would move to Regina as soon as she could.

However, it does complicate things…

She sat in awe at the way everything had turned out. Only a few months ago, she never would have entertained the idea of moving to Regina, and now…it was becoming a reality.

Jenny recalled a scripture, Isaiah 55:9, "As the heavens are higher than the earth, so are my ways higher than your ways, and my thoughts than your thoughts."

"Yes, dear Lord, Your ways and Your thoughts certainly are!" Jenny concurred.

Chapter Eighteen

"Hi Matti, it's Jen. Do I ever have some thrilling news to tell you! You better sit down!"

"If I sit I might fall over. Better I be standing so I can shake off whatever you're fixin' to share with me. What is it, Jen?"

"I'm moving to Regina!"

"Oh Jenny, that's sad news! Why you sounding so happy? Say it isn't so."

"Oh Matti, we will still get together and we can phone each other every Sunday night or even more. Since Mom died, I have decided to make some changes in my life. I have always liked small cities and even though I lived there for a little over two months before we moved to Ottawa I enjoyed our stay there so much it keeps drawing me back."

"Good Lord, Jen what could possibly have been so powerful in those two months that wants you to go back to Regina? Why, you be so young at the time, surely you would forget most of it. Come clean, Jen, I just feels there is more to this move than you're letting on."

A silence fell between them…

"Well what in heavens name is it?"

"I can't get over how you know me, Matti. My friend Tammy was the same way, too; she always knew when I was keeping something from her. Oh Matti, I am so happy we are friends. And yes, there is another reason why I'm moving back there.

"Do you recall that Sunday evening when my Mom was over for dinner while I was still pregnant with J.J.?"

"No one can forget that evening. Seemed like an explosion happened at the dinner table. Charles and me just about jumped out of our skin."

"Did you know what it was all about?"

"Yes, Jenny, the conversation was so loud I was afraid the entire neighbourhood from miles around would be waking up."

"Then you know it had to do with a previous baby girl I had?"

"Yes, Jenny, and it seems to me that it occurred under undesirable circumstances. Oh, Jenny, I be feeling so sorry for you. And that man of yours, not givin' you one ounce of understandin'. Why he went on and on like a roaring lion. Charles had to hold me back in the kitchen lest I smack a frying pan over that inconsiderate beast."

"Well, it's true. I was raped when we were in Regina for those two months, but I only found out that I was pregnant after we had moved to Ottawa. At first I thought it was all so awful, Matti, but I decided to deliver the baby and give it up for adoption. Even though I never knew the father, I learned to love the infant growing in my womb and there was no way I would ever have an abortion. Anyway, Matti, for years I wanted to know what happened to my little wildflower and I spoke yesterday with the adoption father and he has agreed to let Camilla, my daughter, know that she was adopted and to contact me. But here is the best news…"

"Oh, Jen, I don't want to say this but I be betting that your daughter is in Regina and that's why you be leaving!"

Jenny couldn't believe Matti's perception. It was a good thing she was sitting down!

"Matti! I can't believe how you just see into situations. Goose bumps are forming on my skin. But that's exactly right. Camilla lives in Regina and, not only that… well, there is more to tell, but I will share it with you some other time. I have to meet with the real-estate office and close the house purchase I made. And…and," Jenny added, her voice overflowing with excitement, "I have so many arrangements to make for moving and giving notice to my landlord and… and I have to call the school board and let them know what is happening! I hope they let me resign with such short notice like this. I will stay until they get a replacement but there are so many teachers looking for work in the city I don't think they will have trouble finding someone. Oh, Matti, I am so excited… I have to pee!"

"I feel the same and wouldn't you know it Charles be in the toilet just this minute. Happen all the time. I have to re-regulate my cycles so they don't coincide with that man's."

Jenny chuckled. "So if everything works out, Matti, I hope to leave by the end of the month. I am going to drive and enjoy the scenery. I hope the weather isn't too cold as I love it when the roof of the car is down and my hair is blowing in the wind."

"You best wear your seat belt so that delicate little body of yours don't fly off in the wind."

"Oh, Matti, I will miss you dearly! I love our lunches every week and our outings, but I am so excited to move there. I just know everything will all work out so well. And I will call you as soon as I am settled there."

"I just can't stop the tears from rolling down my cheeks, Jen. The only good thing is that Charles be out of the washroom as I can't hold on for another minute. I love you, Jen, and I wish you all the happiness in the world. That child of yours is going to be in for one big surprise to find out that her mother be an angel!"

"Oh, Matti, I love you and will miss you so much, too!"

A FEW DAYS later, Jenny decided she would fly to Victoria to meet Mr. Breckhart in person. That way she would learn all about Camilla, see pictures of everyone, put faces to all the names. She had also decided to leave it up to Camilla to contact her once she learned of her adoption.

Jenny also wondered about Henry and his wife. She knew she may very well run into Henry; Regina was a small city, after all. She even wondered if it would be beyond the realm of possibility to become friends with Henry after all these years? Jenny imagined his wife would be a wonderful woman…

Would she be interfering in their lives and marriage?

Perhaps it would be best for her to talk to Camilla in private. Jenny didn't want to have happen to Henry and his wife what had happened with her and James and the bookstore dealer.

At the end of the week, Jenny called Stan to ask if she could come to visit him. After several rings, Jenny was startled by a woman's voice.

"Oh, hello. Is Stan Breckhart in, please?'"

After a long pause, the woman answered, "He's not here at the moment." There was another long pause. "This is his daughter, Camilla. Can I be of some help?"

Jenny's heart almost stopped. She was talking to her daughter!

"Are you there Ms…?"

"Yes. I'm sorry. Do you know when he might be home? I've been in contact with him lately about a very important matter and it's quite urgent that I speak with him as soon as possible." Jenny realized she was saying too much, but her mind was reeling at the sound of Camilla's voice on the other end of the phone.

Again, Camilla didn't answer right away. Jenny realized she was gripping the phone so tightly her knuckles were turning white. Finally, Camilla softly spoke.

"Actually, I'm sorry to tell you, my father passed away suddenly several days ago."

The blood drained from Jenny's face as her legs gave out beneath her. She slid to floor, as the enormity of the news hit home.

"Hello?" Camilla inquired, "Are you still there?"

"Yes. I'm here. I'm sorry. I'm just so shocked by your news. I am so sorry for your loss… I… I didn't really know your father… I had just called Mr. Breckhart less than a week ago about a certain matter. But… it is no longer important under the circumstances." Jenny didn't want to hang up, nor did she know how to handle this unexpected situation! She longed to hear more of her daughter's voice. She wanted to scream into the phone, *It's your mother! You're talking to your real mother!*

"When will the funeral be? Or, has it taken place?"

"It's tomorrow morning at 10:00 o'clock. The funeral services will be held… just give me a minute while I find the address of the church…"

Jenny knew she couldn't attend, but just to hear Camilla's voice was such a joy… anything to prolong it.

"Yes, it's at the corner of Blanshard and View Streets, St. Andrews Cathedral, if you want to attend. I know Dad would so appreciate having all his friends there. Who did you say is calling?"

Jenny paused for a moment, then feeling it safe enough to give out her identity, she said. "It's Mrs. Hamilton…" Jenny didn't want to say her first name, but now she wished she had. Mrs. Hamilton sounded so formal and the name "Jenny" wouldn't mean anything to her daughter…

"Well, Mrs. Hamilton, it was a pleasure to talk to you. Perhaps we will meet at the funeral."

"I'm afraid that will be impossible. I'm calling from Ottawa and it would be difficult to get a flight now on such short notice."

"Oh, that's too bad," said Camilla. "Please keep Dad in your prayers, then. Perhaps we will meet some day?"

"Yes, I certainly hope we will, Camilla." Tears tumbled from her eyes as she spoke her daughter's name.

"Good-bye, Mrs. Hamilton."

Jenny struggled for enough control to answer, "Good-bye, Camilla."

Camilla! Camilla! Camilla! Camilla! The name ricocheted through Jenny's mind. A rush swept over her. A long-suppressed bond resurfaced and filled Jenny with a joy she had lost since giving birth to her daughter. Mr. Breckhart's death was furthest from her thoughts as the melody and soft tone of Camilla's voice sang through her mind. She relived every moment of their conversation, trying to put a face to the words.

What did Camilla look like? What colour was her hair, her eyes? How tall was she? Jenny just knew she would be able to recognize her daughter in an instant.

Jenny sat down, her mind swirling and going over the conversation much like she did after talking to Stanley last week. Did Stan tell Camilla that she was adopted? Probably not. If he had he would have given her name to Camilla and she would have reacted differently when they just spoke.

What should I do now?

How is she going to break this all to Camilla? Should she work through the agency? What if Camilla doesn't want to have anything to do with her?

Should she re-think going to Regina?

SOMETHING ABOUT THAT woman's voice tugged at Camilla's heart. It was so soothing and somehow familiar, as if she had known her all her life. Camilla searched her memory.

I've never heard Dad or Mom ever mention that name, yet there is just something…

She listened to the dial tone for a brief moment longer and then hung up the phone. As she did so, her eyes rested on the telephone pad beside the phone.

Her father had drawn a circle around the last two words and retraced several times, making it difficult to tell if her name had an 's' in it or not.

"Camilla… mother, or is it, Camilla's mother. What on earth does this mean?" Camilla muttered. Hamilton was the name of the lady she'd just spoken to. Was it connected to that woman's name, or was it something separate?

Camilla tore the page off the note pad and stared at it for the longest moment, then slipped the note into her purse.

CHAPTER NINETEEN

BRRRRR, IT SURE be getting cold out here, Thomas. 'Spect winter be just around the corner. I don't think Miss Jenny will be able to drive her convertible with the top down on her way to Regina."

"When did she leave, Matti?"

"Just over two weeks ago around the first week of October. She said at the time the forecast looked good and no snow in Saskatchewan so far. I pray to the Lord to hold off on them pretty snowflakes until December. So far so good."

"That's for sure, Matti. I'm glad we were able to move Mr. Hamilton's furniture back into the main house before the snow fell. By the way, how is he doing? Last time I heard, he had some serious medical condition."

"From what I be hearing, he was concerned that it may be the same condition that his father died of."

"Prostate cancer?"

"Yep, that be it alright, Thomas. I overheard Mr. Hamilton and his son talking that he should get it checked into real quick. I think that's why he wants the estate cleaned up just in case he needs to come back here to recuperate and rest after the operation."

"Yes, if it is malignant it is best to catch it at an early stage if possible."

"He be talking of freezing himself if it gets worse. He don't want to end up six feet under like his daddy, that for sure. I never heard of such a thin', freezing your body and then bringing you back when the doctors have found a cure. Good Lord, he be rich enough to live forever!"

"I've read about that, Matti. At the moment one dies, they freeze the body and when a cure is discovered, it's as you said - the doctors bring the body back to life, if they can thaw the person out quick enough."

"But if you're dead, how can they bring you back? Lazarus, be the only man who I know was. He be dead for four days when Jesus came along and said, 'Brother, you wake up and be comin' out now, hear me.' And sure enough, he walked out of the cave he was buried in. But one thin' I know for sure, the good Lord is not going to bring Mr. Hamilton back! No way, Thomas. When he gone, good riddance!"

Thomas chuckled. "Well, they say it can be done…"

"In my humble opinion, Thomas, such a thing be preposterous! And another thin', that man don't need freezing, he be cold enough already. I 'spect not even the devil's house can thaw him out. I think that man be wasting his money."

"Now, Matti, we have to think kindly of Mr. Hamilton."

"I just keep slipping back to my old way of thinking every time his name pops into my head. What on earth a man want to freeze himself for anyway? When your time is up, it's time to go home. Maybe that be the problem - he knows which home he be heading to and it ain't the one up there!" Matti pointed to the heavens.

Thomas chuckled again and shook his head slightly, "People who live for the world are afraid of death, Matti. And further, when you strive all your life to make wealth and possessions your God, you don't want to leave it. He's a poor man, really; he lacks a close relationship with Jesus"

"The good Lord is not the only one he has a poor relationship with. How he could divorce that sweet wife of his is beyond my understanding, even more so than this freezing nonsense."

"Yes, it was sad to see Miss Jenny leave the estate."

"Well, he sent me over to clean it and make sure it be spotless. I just hate to clean that modern furniture after dusting Miss Jenny's antiques for all those years. Why, it was such a pleasure dusting that nice, rich warm furniture. Each piece had so much character, I be expecting them to speak to me. Makes me feel colder by the minute to go in and be cleaning that modern furniture of Mr. Hamilton's. It's like the winter has come on the inside before it's actually arrived!"

"Everyone has different tastes, Matti. That's what makes the world go around."

"See, there you go again, just accepting things the way they be, just like Miss Jenny, and not making a big fuss over it. I know we be talking about this many times before, brother Thomas, that Miss Jenny's way is best for all concerned, including herself. How she be loving that man when he be so cold and cunning and cruel is beyond my understanding and acceptance of another of God's creatures. Where I would be yelling and screaming and using my rolling pin, she showed kindness.

I be upset and she be calm. I be filled with hate, and she be filled with patience and forgiveness. I know full well I allow that man's shortcomings to control how I feels, but Thomas, try as I might, I can't accept the terrible things he did and said to that poor sweet thing. And now he found a way to divorce her and drive her away. Even turned that boy of hers against her. Good Lord, my blood just boils thinking on it all! What am I missin', brother Thomas?"

"Well Matti, the secret to Miss Jenny's life is that she allows her heart to lead rather than her mind. She chooses to accept Mr. Hamilton as a person, not his behaviour or obnoxious actions, but the person that the good Lord made. She understands his true self and that it is covered over by things in that man's life that have brought him to be the way he is to this point in his life."

"But to most, and especially to me, he be sooo unacceptable."

"According to your judgments of him, that may be so. But if you stay stuck on your rulings, Matti, the only way you will like Mr. Hamilton is when he reforms and changes to be the way you want him to be and then you will like him."

"Yes, Thomas, isn't that fair? If I be treating him kindly then I 'spect him to do the same. If not, it's just too upsetting to continue, or too discouraging to keep trying."

"There is an old saying Matti, if you want to change someone then you must first choose to change yourself. You have to become aware of your automatic judgments and choose to react to him in a different way. Right now you are allowing yourself to be controlled by what he says or does that you find intolerable.

"You see, Matti, we are the way we are at any given moment by things that have happened in our past. We may not understand why Mr. Hamilton is the way he is, and it's really not necessary that we do even though it might help to be more accepting of him; but to do that is to simply make another judgment."

"You be talking in circles, Thomas, surely if I could understand what makes that man be the way he is, it might help me to accept him more. Isn't that the truth? Come down to my level of communicating, brother. Something ain't right."

"There is another old Indian proverb that says 'if we were to walk in another man's moccasins for a day, we could understand and accept him."

"That's what I be saying, Thomas. But you seem to say we can accept others regardless that we know what makes them other tick or not."

"Yes, Matti, that is Miss Jenny's secret. Let me give you an example of what I witnessed the other day.

"I was in the grocery store picking up some things for the missus and a three year old child was clearly out of control. Why he was running around, up and down the aisles, throwing things off the shelves onto the floor and being very mischievous. Usually I am a pretty accepting person, Matti, but seeing the mother standing there doing nothing while the owner's property was being destroyed and the patrons were having to witness that... well, it tested my patience.

"Just as thoughts of annoyance and criticism entered my mind, which would have generated ill will and anger towards the mother for not disciplining her child, the cashier came over to me as if reading my mind and whispered, 'Her husband had a heart attack and died this morning,' and then she made her way over to the child and enticed him to help pick up the boxes and cans.

"Immediately, Matti, there was a shift in my thinking about the situation, especially the mother. I understood and accepted her actions because I was more aware of what brought her to this point—"

"See there, now I follow you, Thomas. That makes sense and just reinforces what I be saying."

"But here is the thing Matti, we don't have to see what is going on inside others for us to be accepting and kind because most times we never will! We must choose to take full responsibility for our behaviour and how we feel. We choose to accept others unconditionally and respond to them as we would like to be responded to, regardless. That is the only way others will change. That is the only way we can find peace and joy within our own lives.

"When I saw that child misbehave, rather than get judgmental ,had I simply gone over and done what the kindly cashier did, I would have remained at peace and brought love into the situation and be an example like the cashier was.

"You see, Matti, Miss Jenny has learned to see things as they really are. She does not look at the specific act and get stuck there. She sees it, but goes through it to accept and love the person behind the act. Like I said, she does not allow her mind to be judgmental and get all entangled in the situation, but rather she leads from the heart. She remains calm and centred both from within and without. And that is the key, Matti, she always chooses acceptance, peace and love; she gives without expecting anything in return. It is her example and dignified behaviour that will help Mr. Hamilton one day to see himself as he truly is inside.

One day he will see the golden mirror of love Miss Jenny reflected to him. I have said it before Matti, one day he will fall to his knees and be thankful."

Matti shook her head and softly muttered, "My, my..." She marvelled at the wisdom Thomas displayed. He encouraged her to want to be a more accepting person, too.

"You know Matti, Miss Jenny just accepts things and makes the best of it. What is the point to get upset over things you can't change? I will never forget a real good example of this. One day this past summer before Miss Jenny left the estate the sun was out and Miss Jenny seemed to dance down the path raising her hands in joy chasing the butterflies. The sun seemed to ooze out of her cheerful face.

"A day later it was raining and once again I saw Miss Jenny dancing down the path, praising the heavens for the freshness of the rain. Her face was glistening as if the sun were out, same as the day before. She just accepts what is, plain and simple. She didn't need to know or understand what warm front or cold front was causing the weather to change and why it was the way it is, she just took it as it came and enjoyed it or made the best of it."

"I understand now what you be meaning, brother Thomas. Knowing why a person be the way he or she is may help in our acceptance of them, but if we wait for that, things never may get better and we just continue to be miserable in our relationships. I see, it is best to be like Miss Jenny and love people the way they are. That be a far better way to help them than criticizing them. And as you be saying over and over, 'the blind cannot lead the blind, or else they be both falling in the ditch!

"I can see it, brother, but oh, my dear sweet Jesus, gonna have to help me. I needs such an overhaul in my thinking!"

Thomas laughed. "We all do, Matti. Love, acceptance, leading by example, taking full responsibility for our lives and happiness is the secret to Miss Jenny's peace and ours as well."

"And I know where she got the strength and wisdom from to be that way. Everyday she be here she be communicating with the good Lord in that garden of hers. She just glowed every time she came back into the house."

"Can't argue with you on that, Matti. I've seen it all the time, too when she was out in the garden. Some days it was harder to tell which gave off more light and brightness; the sun or Miss Jenny!"

"It's all true, brother, she be an amazing woman. If we could choose to live like her, the happier the world would be and we would be planting the seeds in those we meet and touch, each day to pass it on."

"Relationships dominate our lives for the most part, Matti. How we get along with others determines to a large degree our happiness and wellbeing from day-to-day as we journey through life. The sooner we see that love is the real power to living, the sooner we will have inner peace and great relationships. And I must add, as you just said about Jenny's ability to live this way, first and foremost we have to develop a relationship with Jesus and He will give us the grace and strength to follow His example of how to love others."

"Amen, brother!"

"You know, Matti I used to worry about all the starving people in the world and that I couldn't do enough to help them or about all the wars and persecution that is going on as well. Matti, it came to me one day that all this fretting and worrying, no matter how hard I did it, it wasn't going to change things or do one bit of good, except give me an ulcer.

"No, Matti, I do and give what I can and then turn it over to the Lord in prayer. And then I go about my business of being the best I can be. For I know, Matti, as I touch one person and then another and they do so in turn, eventually it will sweep across the planet and in time there will be world peace, there will be enough food for all.

"What the world needs now more than ever, is love sweet love."

"Amen, I have to say again! Oh Thomas you fill my insides with such good feelings that I go in this minute and polish Mr. Hamilton's furniture with such love and care, why they be turning in my mind as being the same as Miss Jenny's antique furniture. Why I feel the chill in the air inside warming up already, brother Thomas. I 'spect I won't be needing to wear my overcoat after all!"

CHAPTER TWENTY

"Hey, Hank ol' buddy, how ya doin? How's the weather in cold Saskatchewan?"

"Eddy! Geez, never would have thought that would be you phoning. Figured for sure you would be sailing the seven seas with that new yacht of yours. Great to hear from you. Yeah, the winter was cold but seems like spring is coming early this year. So how has life been treating you?"

"Never better, ol' buddy. Just called to let you know I got hitched last night. Coreena and me tied the knot!"

"That's great, Eddy! Congratulations! I was kinda expecting this. From past conversations with you it sounded like you liked more than her cooking!"

"Yeah, I hired a preacher to come on board the yacht and we sailed out into the middle of the Caribbean and proposed right then and there. I told her we would never go back to land unless she married me. She finally agreed, but said she wants a church wedding. So who better to do the job than the Padre?"

"You mean Father Engelmann!?"

"Who else, Hank? Thought me and the Missus would fly to Regina towards the end of July or first week of August and get hitched again. I think we should be able to make the arrangements by then. No big wedding, just Mom. Dad's gone and so just a few relatives and friends of mine. Coreena wants her sister from Ottawa to come, too."

"Geez, Eddy, that's great! It just so happens that I am meeting with the Archbishop next month to talk about plans for a 25th anniversary for Father Engelmann in the priesthood. We are scheduling it for the last Sunday in July, about the same time as you want to come home. Say, listen Eddy! It would be great if we combined your wedding with the anniversary. Father could marry you and Coreena at the 9 o'clock Mass and then we could have the surprise Mass for him at the 12 o'clock one. There's a reception in the hall after where we could all get together at the same time."

"Hey man, you must be reading my mind or something! That's the exact weekend me and the wife had in mind. I already phoned a few people asking if that weekend would work. Isn't that a coincidence or… is it? The Padre always did try to get me back into the church. That would make a great anniversary present for him to have converted, 'Eddy the sinner!'"

Henry laughed, "Yeah, Eddy, his greatest triumph!"

"Yeah, and maybe the next day we could have dinner at your café."

"Sounds great, Eddy! I'm really excited to meet your wife."

"She's a good two feet taller than me. Have to say I enjoy the view, if you get my drift. She's a great gal, has a heart of gold, knows how to cook, how to sail and makes me feel like a tall man."

Henry chuckled once more, "That's wonderful Eddy. I can't wait to meet her. And you say her sister is coming, too?"

"Yeah, she can get a few days off and apparently the two girls haven't seen each other in years. I've never seen Coreena happier than to talk to Matilda and tell her of the news that we got married. But they seemed to be even happier when Coreena told her we would be sending her a ticket to come to the church wedding in Regina."

"That's great, Eddy. Say, didn't you tell me a long time ago that she worked on an estate for a man named Hamilton?"

"Yeah, apparently he's a real mean bugger. Damn hard to work for."

"Geez, I wonder if it's the same Hamilton I once talked to a long, long time ago…?"

"What's that, Hank?"

"Oh nothing, Eddy. It couldn't possibly be the same guy. So, tell me man, how are you enjoying your retirement? You're the only one I know who has retired before his 40th birthday!"

"Never better. I'm tanned almost as dark as Coreena. I'm thankful for every day and enjoy life to the fullest, ol' buddy. Take it from me, sell the business, come to Jamaica and learn to smell the roses. You work way too hard, Hank. *Time goes fast.*

"From morning to night, I enjoy my life. And I'm surprised on how little I really need. Most people work and work and never use up what they have amassed and before they know it, they are old and gone and never really appreciated what they had strived for, for all those years and years. The good life is right under their noses and they can't see it…or choose not to see it."

"Geez, Eddy, you're becoming a philosopher in your young age."

"You don't need to be a brain surgeon to know how to enjoy life.

Most things that give me a kick are free. The beauty of the ocean, the flowers, the star studded night sky while I'm slowly drifting on the boat, good friends, the daily sunset and sunrise, walking hand in hand with my wife on the beach, a simple flavourful meal, a siesta in the afternoon, sailing my boat whenever I can and a restful sleep. And you know Hank, this would make the Padre a happy camper, I'm beginning to see the Boss upstairs' hand in it all, you know what I'm sayin'?"

"I know exactly what you're saying, Eddy, and it makes a lot of sense. I think I better take a retreat and reassess where I'm heading."

"And I'd do it sooner than later. And, by the way, did Pete ever phone you?"

"Pete? ... Oh, your friend Pete...the guy that took Jenny to..."

"Yeah, that Pete. I don't want to stir things up, but I talked to him a few times since that pool game we had at the Royal and he was still hung up on his dreams and wanting to make things better with the blonde chick. I told you you didn't know how to get a hold of her either. I gave him your phone number and told him to talk to you directly, but I guess he must have chickened out."

"No, he never called and I must say, Jenny has been on my mind a lot lately, too. And I do remember us talking about Pete and what happened that night at the Royal and...I have to agree with Pete... I still think that Jenny just might have gotten pregnant that night..."

There was a silence between the two men and finally Eddy spoke, "Maybe there is something to all this. Anyway, I have invited Pete, Bud and John to come to the wedding. I hope that's alright with you?"

"Yeah, it is Eddy. I've made friends with both Bud and John as you know. It's amazing how Bud bought my old house in Whitmore Park and that he is an artist, as well. The only one I haven't met face to face since that night is Pete. It may be interesting to meet him. Just maybe we can make some sense of all this."

"He's a good guy, Hank. I think I told you he turned into a preacher, as well. He's got a good heart. Well, okay ol' buddy, the wife's waiting outside for me. The sea is calm today with just a little warm breeze to fill the sails. Wish you could be here to enjoy a bottle of Jamaican beer on the high seas. See ya, Hank."

"Yeah, see you Eddy and give my best to the Missus!"

"PETE,...PETER WAKE UP ...wake up!" Angie shook her husband's shoulder in the darkness. She rolled over and flicked on the night lamp and turned back to her husband who was finally breaking free of the nightmare that had plagued him for years. Perspiration beaded on his forehead. He rolled over to face his loving wife.

"I'm sorry, honey, for waking you. The nightmares seem to be getting worse. I know there's a reason for it and I wish God would let me know what it is."

"Perhaps when we go to Regina for Eddy's wedding you can talk to the man that was with the girl that night. Henry or Hank…wasn't that the name that Eddy gave you?"

"Yes, but Eddy told me that when he asked Hank for the girl's phone number he said he didn't have it. And by the way, Eddy told me the name of the girl was Jenny. Anyway, Eddy thought that Hank might have known the number, but didn't want to give it to me to protect her."

"Perhaps he will be more willing to talk to you in person. You have to take a chance, Peter. Somehow I feel it's meant for you and him to meet. Maybe, the same thing will happen between you and Hank that happened between him and Eddy. Eddy is still amazed how they became such good friends over the years when initially they disliked each other. And for Eddy to even end up being Hank's best man at his wedding is the workings of the Lord. I firmly believe that God has a plan, I just feel it, Peter."

"I know you're right, Angie, and I am blessed that you are so understanding of all this. At least I am able to talk it out and not have to hide it from you."

Angie put her hand on her husband's shoulder once more and gently rubbed it, her eyes filled with compassion, understanding and forgiveness. How many nights had she heard her beloved moaning and crying over that eventful night when he and his friends took that girl to the park and raped her. Peter was so sure that the girl had conceived his child that fateful moment, but was never able to find out for sure.

"Is your dream still the same, Peter?"

Peter nodded, "Yes, Jenny gives birth to a blonde little girl… and lately I have seen the girl's eyes and they're blue. And there's another thing…when I talked to Eddy awhile back after he spoke with Hank about getting Jenny's contact information, Hank had asked Eddy if the child's name is revealed in the dreams I have. I am sure Jenny mouths the name, *Camilla,* but I'm not certain. And just when Jenny does call the girl by name… I wake up."

"Did Hank tell Eddy the name he thinks it might be…?"

Peter turned and gazed long and hard into his wives eyes, "Hank asked Eddy to ask me if the little girls name is *Camilla.*"

"Could it be possible that the connection is so strong to this event that even the name of the baby is coming to the fore?"

Angie rolled over and flicked off the light, but sleep didn't come. She was more concerned over the prognosis Peter received from the family doctor six months ago. A tumour had developed beside his kidney and the lab results showed that it was malignant.

Her heart went out to her husband. He was such a kindly man, such a wonderful pastor and everyone loved him. And yet, somewhere out there was a woman who may have very well given birth to Peter's child, as his reoccurring dreams hinted at.

Angie rolled over and placed her hand on Peter's shoulder once more, ever so tenderly and prayed:

Oh dear Lord, my husband's heart cries out for forgiveness. Daily he prays that he finds this Jenny to correct the wrong he has committed. Please help him, Jesus.

It was so hard on the both of us today when the doctor told us that his cancer has returned and is spreading. The only way to stop this disease is for Peter to find Jenny and receive her forgiveness. His guilt has plagued him for far too long. He is so hard on himself, Lord. *I feel the self destructive force he has created within himself to…to punish himself.*

Please let him live long enough to reconcile his past. It is the only way he will ever find peace, or die in peace…or if it is in Your will, Oh Lord, his only chance to be cured.

Oh Lord, please help him before it is too late for him and for Jenny.

Chapter Twenty-One

As Henry sat in the receptionist area waiting to meet with the Archbishop, his mind reeled back to the Sunday evening when Mr. Engelmann told him and his parents that he was going into the seminary to become a priest. What a perfect choice the Lord had led him to. For months after Anna's death, Mr. Engelmann struggled with the decision to sell the grocery store. It had been his life. It was what he and Anna had done ever since they had come to Canada from the old country.

What Henry and most people in the neighbourhood realized however, was that selling groceries was not the Engelmann's main purpose. Their primary mission and goal was in serving their fellow man. They were truly examples of living out the principles and values of the Bible.

Mr. Engelmann's decision to become a priest was not only a perfect decision, but a natural transition into a new career which would more aptly identify what Mr. Engelmann was already doing. He had been a shepherd to his neighbourhood and as a priest he had become a shepherd to a larger flock…the parishioners of a church.

When Mr. Engelmann was assigned to St. Mary's Church after he was ordained, he and Father Connelly made a perfect pair. Henry chuckled as he recalled how they had both performed he and Julean's wedding ceremony almost in perfect unison. Father Connelly's Irish accent had gone high against Mr. Engelmann's lower Austrian one. The combination was melodic and spellbinding.

When Father Connelly died, Father Engelmann had at first seemed so lost, but he soon reached out to the people in a way they had never seen before. It was almost as if Father Connelly's spirit had united with Father Engelmann's. He became tireless and for years after, ran the entire church himself. His homilies became more and more powerful. He was totally and completely spirit filled. His face always exhibited a smile, so kindly, that it was holy. The people flocked around him as if he were the Pope.

The amazing thing was that he never seemed to age. In fact, the older he got, the younger he looked. His appearance and energy reflected that of a man in his sixties and yet most people realized that he must be well into his eighties if not more. Was his secret to the fountain of youth his detachment from the pursuit of worldly possessions and his total commitment to serving the Lord? Father Engelmann had achieved what most people failed to achieve: to become Christ-centred; not self-centred.

"Mr. Pederson," said the receptionist, breaking into his thoughts, "the Archbishop will see you now."

"Oh, thank you, Diane."

Archbishop O'Neil greeted Henry at the door, wearing a long black cassock. The close-fitting vestment accentuated his tall, rather lean frame. He wore rimless, round glasses which fell towards the end of his rather long nose. His sparse white hair was combed from one side to the other looking flat and unnatural in its bid to conceal his baldness. He wore a broad smile and extended his hand as Henry walked through the open doorway.

"So nice to see you, Henry, sorry to keep you waiting, I had an urgent call."

"Not a problem, Your Holiness, it gave me a little time to reflect on things."

"Well, we all need time to do that. Come, sit down."

There were two chairs in front of his large oak desk. Instead of seating himself in the chair behind the desk, he sat in one of the chairs in front and motioned for Henry to sit down next to him.

"So, tell me, how is the art gallery doing?"

"We're as busy as ever, the café continues to do very well, too. With spring coming so early customers want us to open the patio already."

"It was a long hard winter and many people I'm sure developed cabin fever."

"Yes, March came in like a lion and out like a lamb and most of April has been so mild that most of the snow is gone. Anyway it's the middle of May and the weather continues to be so nice that we are thinking of opening the deck this weekend."

"Well, you certainly have created something which the city is proud of and gives so much joy to all of us."

"Thank you, Your Holiness."

"Please call me, John, Henry, it always makes me feel a little uncomfortable to be referred to as, *your holiness*. It's quite a title to live up to."

Henry smiled.

"And how is the art coming along? Are you working on any new paintings?"

"As a matter of fact I am, John. I have two commissions which I should have completed a little while ago. One is a valley scene and the other a prairie sunset landscape."

"You do such beautiful work, Henry. The Lord has certainly blessed you with a gift. Like your shop, your paintings give us so much aesthetic pleasure. It's amazing how when I look at your work, you are able to capture the prairies in such a way that it makes one stop and look at what we see all the time and, yet, the composition, the colours, the light…well, you make what seems ordinary, extraordinary."

Warmth rushed to Henry's face at the Archbishop's comments.

"Thank you again, John. I appreciate your kind words very much."

The Archbishop smiled revealing his protruding front teeth. Perhaps braces when he was young would have straightened them, yet, the apparent flaw added to his friendly, approachable character.

"Well, John, as you know, Father Engelmann is celebrating his 25th anniversary as a priest."

"Yes, how the time does pass. I've tried to get him to retire, but he just refuses. He is in such good health and he seems to thrive on it. Frankly, I don't even see him as old, and almost forget the fact that he should be retired!" The Archbishop chuckled and his eyes twinkled.

"Yes, I know what you mean. I was thinking about that as I sat in the reception room. He doesn't celebrate his birthday and he's never told me his age. Do you know how old he is?"

"I do, Henry, but I know he doesn't like to reveal his age. He simply says that he is as old as he thinks and that at the present time he thinks that he is still in his youth for the Lord. I think that's how he wants to be perceived by the parishioners not as a number that may portray him as old, but as a man that is still ready and raring to serve his parishioners."

"Yeah, see that's just another example of the remarkable man he is. In fact, John, I consider him a saint."

"Yes, Henry, I would have to agree with you. In all the years of my priesthood and work in the dioceses, he has been a beacon of light for me and to all those whom he touches with his love for Christ! A very holy man, indeed!"

"I swear that when he comes out to the acreage to do his mini-re-treats in the prayer house at the bottom of the valley, at night it seems to just glow."

"Yes, David told me how much he enjoys the prayer house, or rather the Poustinia."

"Oh, you know of that do you?"

"Yes, a few years back when I was visiting Madonna House I used one for a day. That's all my time allowed, but it is a beautiful holy place. I can see why David enjoys his time there. And he tells me it's beside a pond fed by the valley creek."

"Yes, it's a very peaceful and beautiful setting. Unfortunately I haven't made much use of it myself."

"Well, we must make time for the really important things in life." The Archbishop winked at Henry.

"So, I understand," continued the Archbishop, "that the members of the parish council would like to do something special to honour and recognize Father."

"Yes, John," Henry replied, beginning to feel a little more comfortable with the first name. "We are planning a surprise party for Father after the twelve o'clock mass on the last Sunday of July, and were hoping that you could attend and if you would be so kind as to celebrate the Mass in his honour."

"It is I who would be honoured to do so, Henry. How do you plan to keep it from him?"

"We thought we could let him come in, assuming he is going to say Mass and perhaps once he starts you could come in from the entrance to the church with some of the other priests who would like to participate?"

"That sounds wonderful. It certainly will be a pleasant surprise for David. I'm excited already just thinking about it."

"Yes, we are all excited about it, too. And there has been another development. Eddy Zeigler who was my best man when Julean and I married has also wed a girl in Jamaica. He called a couple of weeks ago and I think he has already contacted Father Engelmann to see if he and his wife could re-enact their vows in the church and invite their friends. This is going to happen at the nine o'clock Mass and will also act as a diversion from his planned anniversary."

"Yes, it certainly will."

"Eddy and most of his friends also know Father, so they will join in on the party after the twelve o'clock Mass. It should be fun."

The Archbishop paused for a moment, stroking his sharp chin and looking into Henry's eyes he asked, "Is there anything else I can do?"

"Well, if you could stay for a while after Mass and join the party that would be great."

"I would be more than delighted to do so, Henry."

"Well, that's just great, John. The parish council will be so pleased to hear that you will be there."

"It really is my pleasure, Henry."

"Well, I know you are a busy man and I appreciate your taking the time to see me."

"Not at all, it's always nice to see you and members of the parish council, you all do such good work. Priests would not be able to run the church without your help and assistance."

As Henry stood, the Archbishop did the same and extended his hand, once again.

"It was so nice seeing you again, Henry. Thank you for coming."

"Thank you for seeing me."

ON HIS WAY home to the farm, Henry went to Lumsden to pick up his mail at the post office. He was glad to receive a letter from Gary. He had written Gary just after Christmas to see if he could make it home for Father's anniversary. Henry couldn't wait to get home and read to see if his friend could come.

Henry made himself a cup of tea and took it and the letter out to the deck. The sun was still high and a warm breeze filled the air. He knew if Julean were there she would have been out for most of the day. She loved the outdoors and the valley view.

Henry sat down, rested the cup on the table beside him and opened the letter. "Oh good!" he exclaimed, Gary would be coming home. His friend Alice would be staying as she had decided to join Mother Theresa's Sisters of Charity. Henry was also surprised to read that John McBryne was there working in the centre as well and that they had become good friends. Once again, Henry marvelled at how God worked to heal the relationships in our lives and draw us to Him.

As Henry laid the letter down on the table beside him he felt moved by Gary's continuous plea for the western world to help their brothers and sisters abroad. So many of us, he thought are blessed with so much and yet we fail to think of those who are suffering and starving, and those without medical attention, water, or even the basic essentials of life.. We fail to realize, and for the most part aren't even aware, that it is our responsibility to reach out to others. We are stewards of all of God's bounty and are asked to use it for the benefit of others and not just ourselves.

Henry knew that he gave of his money, but what of his time? What could he do to help Gary? *How could he make others including himself more aware of our brothers and sisters both abroad and at home who are in such need of help?*

CHAPTER TWENTY-TWO

E VEN AFTER SO many years had passed, Jenny still celebrated her daughter's birthday on May 24. She had just finished putting the icing on the cake she had baked earlier that morning and put her usual single candle in the centre of the cake. It was her intention that when they were finally united she would put the exact number of candles on the cake.

Today, Jenny was not only celebrating Camilla's 30th birthday, she was also celebrating that her daughter was somewhere here in the very same city more than likely celebrating with her family! It would be so easy to pick up the phone and call Henry at the gallery and ask for Camilla's phone number. The very thought of speaking to her wild-flower and wishing her a happy birthday sent an overwhelming surge of excitement through Jenny's body.

Jenny had already checked the phone book for a listing under Jeremy and/or Camilla Pederson, but it wasn't there. If she knew their address, she would have already driven by to see their home with the hopes she would be outside and the chance she would see her daughter at long last. Stan had told Jenny Camilla was married and had a small child, a boy. Oh, how Jenny would love to meet and hold her grandson!

Just as Jenny was thinking on these things the phone rang.

"Hello."

"Hi Jen, this be Matti."

"Oh Matti, it's so good to hear from you! I was just celebrating my daughter's 30th birthday!"

"What? She be there with you?"

"No, Matti, I am still pretending she is. I made a cake and was about to blow out the candle and sing her happy birthday."

"Jenny, why I would have thought you'd be in touch with that girl of yours by now. This ain't no good, Jen. It's not fair to her or to you to be separated by this any longer. What's the hold up?"

"When I initially contacted Mr. Breckhart, Camilla's adoptive father last fall, he was planning on going to Regina for a staff re-union where he worked before his retirement. At that time he was going to speak to Camilla and explain that she was adopted and that her biological mother was looking for her.'

"Well, did he tell Camilla?"

"Would you believe it, Matti when I called him a week or so later to discuss how best to tell Camilla, I learned he had died—"

"Good Lord…"

"And guess who answered the phone? Camilla! I was so shocked over learning of Mr. Breckhart's death and then talking to my daughter, I didn't know what to do!"

"Did you tell her you was her mama?"

"No. It would have been too much of a shock for her. And with her father just passing away…that would not have been a good time to break the news of her adoption to her."

"I see what you mean."

"It's all so anxiety provoking, Matti. I'm just so worried about disrupting their lives. If only her adoptive parents had explained it to her, but I don't know if her father had a chance to tell her before he died! Just think, Matti, if you got a call out of the blue by someone saying that your parents were not your real parents and that I am your real mother. You would think this to be some kind of a crank call. And even if I could convince her, just think how upsetting it might be. She might end up hating her adoptive parents for not being truthful with her and me as well for giving her up. The girl might feel in limbo not knowing who she is, who she belongs to…Oh, Matti, don't you see how upsetting this all could be? It has to be handled just right."

"I see your point, Jen, but how on earth are you going to tell the woman? She has to know at some time!"

"Well, right now I am still getting settled here in my new home. I have so much to do and know I'm going to be busy for the next few months. I have so many plans for the front and backyard that I have already started. I thought I would wait until fall when I'm better established here and then call the Social Welfare agency in Ottawa to see how this situation can best be approached."

"Well, I would do it sooner than later, Jen. You have wasted enough time over the years living apart. I'm sure the good Lord will light the way for a reunion that be filled and blessed with joy."

"I suppose you're right, Matti."

"Well, another reason I be calling besides how much I enjoy talking with you was to let you know my sister, Coreena, done married that man she's been seeing for years."

"Yes, I recall you telling me that she was going out with a man named Eddy Zeigler."

"You got one good memory, child, that be the same man alright. Coreena be head over heels in love with all five feet one inch of him. She says he be the kindest man she ever knew…"

Jenny wondered if it was the same Eddy whose friends it was that took her to the park that night? Eddy was short too…but he wasn't very nice…

"They called to let me know that they got married on Eddy's yacht, but Coreena wants to be married in the church and so they decided to come back to Regina where Eddy lives and be married again. Now here's the best part, Jen, and I hope you be sitting down…they sent me a ticket to come there for the wedding!"

"No way!?"

"Yes, ma'am, I'll be there the last week of July and staying in what I hear is a pretty ritzy hotel…the Hotel Saskatchewan!"

"That's unbelievable, Matti. Oh, that's wonderful news! Now I really will have to get things into high gear and have my home and yard all finished before you get here."

"Yes, I be looking forward to see your new home, Jen, but I won't be staying long. Only three days, that's all Mr. Hamilton gave me off. He is moving back into the estate. I already spent several days there cleaning everything spic and span from top to bottom, including his modern furniture."

"So, James is moving back? That's a surprise. Is J.J. moving back too?"

"No," Matti hesitated, "I guess they never told you I jus' learned the other week myself that J.J. got married to that young girlfriend of his. Apparently she gave birth to his baby boy last fall and just after Christmas the two young one's got married."

Jenny was flabbergasted. She had seen so little of James and her son the last few years that she really didn't know what was going on in their lives. But for J.J. to marry and not let her know stabbed at Jenny's heart.

"Sorry to be telling you about this, Jen. But thought you best know if you didn't already."

"No, I didn't know," Jenny said, slowly still trying to grasp the news. "I met Nora for the first time just the other night when J.J. brought her to dinner. She's a pretty young thing and the baby was crawling around and getting into everything."

"Oh, Matti, it breaks my heart to learn of this in this way. How old is the boy and what did Nora and J.J. name him?"

"Mr. Hamilton's mother was there as well and I believe I overheard her say how well co-coordinated James the 3rd be for being only seven months old."

"They named him James, too!?"

"No, they named him James three!" Matti joked, but then realized Jenny wasn't laughing. "Yes, Jenny. I guess they love the name and want to be sure it goes on forever."

Once again Jenny fell silent, still trying to absorb the shock that her son was married and had a child already and that she was never told.

She was just thinking how good it would be to hold Camilla's son, and now J.J. had a son, too! It just seems so cruel that she has two grandchildren and hasn't seen either of them!

"Oh, Jen I'm sorry to be the one to have to tell you all this. I can feel how you be hurting through the phone. Maybe I should have waited until I got there so I could tell you in a more gentle way and give you a hug at the same time."

"No, I'm fine, Matti. It is a little hard to take in all at once…Oh, Matti, I don't know what to say… but it will be good to see you."

Jenny wiped away a tear and continued, "Now, you said you were coming the last week of July?"

"Yes, Friday, July 24th, and my younger sister, Coreena be marrying the man of her dreams at St. Mary's church in Regina at nine o'clock in the morning and on the Sabbath Day to boot! Sunday, July 26."

"Oh my gosh, Matti, did you say St. Mary's church?"

"Yes, I did. And it says right here in my notes that it be located on the corner of 13th Avenue and Winnipeg street. Besides them getting married, there is also the parish priest's 25th anniversary going on that day, too. Since Eddy knows him, they plan to join the party in the afternoon and then the next day they are holding a small reception at a friend of Eddy's who owns a café and art gallery."

The blood was draining from Jenny's face.

"Matti, would the name of the café be Henry's and the art gallery, The Pederson Art Gallery?"

"Now, Jenny, you be reading my piece of paper in front of me before I even be telling you!?"

"Oh, Matti, I know Henry!" Jenny didn't want to say she knew Eddy in case it was the same one that along with his friends attacked Henry and her.

This was unbelievable!

"I met him the summer my parents moved from Vancouver to Regina way back in 1956. We only stayed for two months before moving again to Ottawa. But Henry and I became very close that summer."

Something just didn't sit right with Matti and she thought she would just say it straight out. "Now a lot has been going down for you today, Jen, but I needs to ask you and if you want to tell me it's none of my business, go right ahead… Is Henry the father to Camilla?"

"No, Matti, I really was raped. One night Henry and I went to a movie and as we were walking home after the show, some boys attacked us and three of them took me to the park and that's where and when it happened. I didn't even know it did. I fell unconscious when they dragged me out of the car and when I came to, Henry and some people found me. It's amazing Matti, but I think my guardian angel erased the memory of that awful event from my mind. I was totally surprised to learn that I was carrying the child of one of those boys a few months later after we moved to Ottawa. I have always felt there was a reason why my angel saved me from the trauma of that night but still allowed the pregnancy to take place. I feel it has something to do with my coming back here."

"Back to the scene of the crime, you mean?"

"Well, not exactly. You see, Matti, there have only been two men in my life: one was James and the other was—"

"Henry!… Right!"

"Right, Matti! You are just too perceptive. You see through me as easy as looking through glass. Am I that transparent?"

"The thing is Jen, you're always in the light. It's easy to see where your heart is. Trouble be, most people live in the dark and that's why many relationships be cautious, suspicious and filled with mistrust. It's hard to see where they be at or what they up to. With you, it be the same as if I be talking to my angel."

"Oh, Matti…well, let's hope our relationship is always open and honest. That's the way I want it to be."

"And me too, Jen, and now that you opened that door so kindly for me, I would just love to walk right in. So, tell me all about this dream boy or should I say, this dream man, that still has a home in your heart."

"I know this may sound juvenile, but the morning we met in a grocery store something magical if not spiritual happened when we gazed into each others eyes. I fell instantly in love with him and so did he with me. And in the two months that followed, our love for each other just deepened. After we moved to Ottawa, Henry and I wrote to each other, but something happened to our letters... I... I don't want to get into it, but as a result we both met other partners and got married."

"But the love you had for him never went away...?"

Tears surfaced in Jenny's eyes.

"Yes, Matti, I really still do love him, but he's married and here's another big reason why I am so worried about approaching Camilla—"

"Oh my good Lord, Jenny, this be getting better than the TV series, the Young and Restless! You've got me on pins and needles now. I am listening to your heart speak, not your mind, and it gives me tingles throughout my body."

Jenny chuckled through her tears. "I needed that, Matti. It really is an almost unbelievable story."

Jenny took a deep breath and then went on, "When I spoke to Stan, the father who adopted Camilla, I nearly died when he told me who Camilla married."

"Surely, not Henry!?"

"No, but you're close, Matti. She married his son, Jeremy. They already have a young son. Do you see now why I am so nervous to contact Camilla? I don't want to get mixed up with the family for fear of what might happen again."

"This be an incredible story, Jen. What more is there possible to tell?"

"Well, I told you before why J.J. hardly speaks to me, right?"

"Besides that husband of yours taking him away you did mention that J.J. blames you for the divorce. That he saw a bookstore owner giving you a farewell kiss on the cheek and he thought you was doing something more serious with the man."

"That's right, Matti. J.J. accused me of being unfaithful and breaking up our home. He would never listen to me or my side of the story. I would hate for this to happen again in the Pederson family."

"You mean, Henry might get interested in you again and your daughter, Camilla be like J.J. blaming you for a possible breakup between Henry and his wife?"

"I know it all sounds so silly, Matti. Henry probably isn't interested in me in the least anymore, but I'm just so afraid of the possibility that it paralyzes me to make a decision. I think that's why I am putting it off to the fall. I've already lost my son, so it seems and now to lose a daughter would be devastating. Just telling Camilla she's adopted will cause enough grief. I certainly don't want to add more. In a way I now wish I didn't know that Camilla married Henry's son. It just makes me so nervous."

"Well, Jen, I now done heard everything. That is some tale. That would make one great story. People would hardly be able to put the book down. No ma'am, that be one amazing tale. For once I don't know what to say or what to do or what to tell you."

"You have no idea how long and hard I struggled with the decision whether I should still come to Regina. But something inside kept urging me on and so, for better or worse, here I am and so far things are going so well."

"See there now, you done right, Jen. It's good to be with your daughter and catch up on all you missed. That social welfare worker lady you keep mentioning will help you with all this. She'll know what to do, that for sure."

There was a long silence. If Matti knew how her new brother-in-law, Eddy Zeigler fit into all this she would be incredibly upset, Jenny thought. Jenny wondered if it was possible that Eddy and Henry became friends over the years? There was no love between them when she had left for Ottawa.

"My gosh, we've been talking for a long time. But I'm so happy to hear that you will be coming. This gives me all the more motivation to get my yard done. I already put in the paving stones in the backyard, which will lead up to a gazebo at the very back by the fence and I've already given the plans for the gazebo to a carpenter to study. They were the same plans that James had given the carpenters in Ottawa to build the gazebo on the estate. This will be a smaller version, of course. I have a wildflower patch planned near there and the only thing that will be missing is my Angel of Thanksgiving. I plan to write James and ask if he will send it to me. Oh, I hope and pray he does."

"Well, it don't belong to him! It belongs to you. It was a gift not only from us, but the way I understand it, it was even commissioned by your papa before he died. Wasn't that so?" "That's exactly right, Matti. But how it came to me by way of Thomas and the rest of you is incredible."

"It seems to me that everything surrounding you is unbelievable. All that has happened to you, and still you remain so calm and peaceful."

"Oh, I hope I can attract the Monarchs this spring. I had a landscape gardener look for some milkweed plants to put in the backyard before the winter came last fall, but he couldn't find any. He did manage to plant some mature Lilac trees though in front and back of the house. I just don't want to wait years for things to grow. If I spend a little more on mature plants, trees and flowers I can start enjoying them all right away. I can hardly wait for June when the Lilacs bloom…I love the fragrance so much."

"So what will attract the Monarchs then if your gardener couldn't get any milkweed plants? Have you some other flowers that will attract them?"

"Matti, you're not going to believe this, but I found some a week ago when I went to the nursery at the south end of Regina. It's a good thing I recognized them as they were identified by their Latin name. Funny thing though, the lady that served me said that I must have some kind of a double as she sold several milkweed plants to a younger lady a year ago who also loved butterflies and wanted to attract them. And what she said next sort of took me back…"

"What did she say?"

"She said, the woman was as beautiful as a wildflower! It was kinda eerie as I always thought of Camilla as being my wildflower…"

"Yes, you be saying many times that little child of yours be a wild-flower…now, ain't that something?"

After a brief silence, Jenny shrugged and continued, Oh Matti, I am so glad spring is here. By fall or sooner everything will be done. It will look like a miniature Greystone Manor Estate garden!"

"Oh yes, Jen, I'm sure it will be all of that and more. Thomas said many times, your knack for gardening is just as good as his. And tell me, did all your lovely antique furniture fit into your new home?"

"Perfectly, Matti. It almost seems as if the home were especially made for every single piece. The dining room is even big enough for the tea wagon and wait until you see the bedroom. The writing desk fits so nice by the bay window and the two Victorian chairs fit into the corner as if they were made for that space. I'm so glad I bought the antique bedroom set three years ago. James would never have allowed it had he lived at home. Amazingly, James never even saw the set in all that time."

And before Matti could get a word in edge wise, Jenny rambled on, "Everything is just fitting so well here. I've even met one of my neigh-bours next door. She's very nice, and after learning of my love of art, she suggested I volunteer at the MacKenzie Art Gallery, so that's what I did. I have already made several friends there, and Matti, the driving here is nothing compared to Ottawa! I'm downtown in ten minutes or less, five minutes to the public gallery and there are two shopping malls in the south end that are so easy and quick to get to as well! The only downside to this move that I can see is the winter driving, especially when it melts and freezes, but it was like that in Ottawa at times, too. All in all, Matti, I am so glad I moved!"

"I be so happy for you, Jen! I just can see your sparkling blue eyes, filled with the Lord's blessings, shine even more brightly if that's at all possible. Like I said, I never did know anyone who can be happy and content in most, if not all situations. You truly be an earthly angel."

"Oh, my friend Tammy used to think that too, Matti. But the truth is we all are, and if not, we're supposed to be. The purpose of angels is not only to protect us, but to help us shine and bring us closer to Jesus and each other."

"See, just the way you talk and think Jen, be such an example to me. I am one to get fired up quick when things don't sit right with me."

"You still can, Matti, as long as it doesn't control you. You must always be the boss of your mind because if you're not, feelings can get stirred up very quickly causing us to say and do things we may regret. At times we can get upset so much that we are in a state of turmoil sometimes for days on end."

"I think you and Thomas would make a good pair. He be thinking that way all the time, too. "Take it easy, Matti," he say time and again. "You are in control of how you feel. You don't have to allow circumstances and the weaknesses or shortcomings of others to control you." It makes sense, just it be so difficult for me to put into action, but I keep trying."

"When that happens to me, Matti, I discuss things over with my guardian angel and tell her to put thoughts into my mind right away that will bring healing and love into what's troubling me."

"Now you see, that be what Thomas says. Or he asks, 'how would Jesus want me to react or look for the good in others so as to diffuse the situation and remain in peace?"

"At times it's difficult, but it can be done. It's a moment to moment choice we make. We can allow ourselves to get upset or choose to remain calm and at peace. Otherwise not only is the situation upsetting, but our thoughts about it can prolong the upset for hours if not days. If we are diligent and think carefully before we speak or react and ask for strength from above or from our angel it can be done."

"And you be a living example of that! Just being your friend has helped me reassess the way I look at things and helps me to break out of my bad habits. You be one of my greatest blessings. You be a beacon,

Jen, like a lighthouse full of light to guide those around you just like a lighthouse be guiding a ship in the dark and going through stormy waters."

"Oh, Mattie, that's a good way to describe it and so kind of you to say. And before you go, would you please try to get J.J. and Nora's phone number for me? I would like to give them a call and wish them well."

"For sure, Jen. I'll get the number and call you back real quick."

CHAPTER TWENTY-THREE

J EREMY STOOD AT the kitchen window and gazed out to the backyard at Camilla sitting in her new gazebo. It was finished just in time for her birthday!

Neither he nor Camilla could believe that the carpenter had the exact plans of the gazebo that Camilla had seen in her dreams. No sooner had she started to describe the gazebo she wanted built than the carpenter went to his truck and brought back a set of plans that another lady across the city wanted built that summer as well. It was amazing!

Jeremy studied Camilla more closely. She was writing in her journal when he noticed her chest heaving; she was crying. Jeremy went outside and made his way over to his wife and sat down beside her. He put his arm around Camilla and softly asked, "What's troubling you, honey? It's your birthday, shouldn't you be happy?"

Camilla couldn't answer and sobbed all the more. She opened the journal she was writing in and showed it to her husband. He lowered his eyes and read:

May, 24, 1987

Today is my 30th birthday and I don't know who I belong to!

"What do you mean you don't know who you belong to…?"

"Oh Jeremy, this may sound so silly, but for as long as I can remember, I have always felt that my Mom and Dad were not really my parents."

"Oh, Camilla, what on earth got you thinking that? I met your parents and they love you to bits. I have to admit there's not much of a family resemblance, but Stan and Valerie were your mom and dad. They would have told you if they weren't.?

"Not necessarily. Two years ago when I took the job at the Balfour Tutorial School for unwed mothers I counseled a girl who had similar feelings to mine. She said for as long as she could remember she felt that she was adopted and sure enough, when she was eighteen, she found out through her aunt that she was! She was so upset with her adoptive parents for not being truthful with her. I spent months trying to help her understand her adoptive parent's position and the many reasons why they withheld that from her."

"Why on earth would you feel that you're adopted, Camilla?"

"Well, for one thing, just as you just said, my appearance is so drastically different from them and… I guess it is just a feeling that I have that I can't explain. But it was when Dad died that I really got to thinking. I never told you this, but when we were in Victoria, the day before the funeral, a lady phoned and asked for Dad. I told her Dad had passed away. She identified herself as Mrs. Hamilton. When I asked her what it was about she said under the circumstances it didn't matter any more."

Jeremy looked at his troubled wife, "So?"

"Oh Jeremy, I had the strangest feeling that I knew that woman all of my life. There seemed to be an energy or connection between us that is hard to explain. It was almost spiritual and I can't seem to shake it from my mind. And what is even more, after I spoke with her and hung up I noticed a name on the pad of paper that my Dad had written down…"

Camilla opened her journal and took out a small piece of paper that was hidden between two pages and showed it to Jeremy. Once again he lowered his eyes and read:

"Does it look like it reads Camilla mother or Camilla's mother?"

"It's hard to tell the way your dad put a double circle around your name. But that doesn't mean that this woman is your mother if that's what you're getting at."

Jeremy gazed at his wife and studied her long and hard, "Is that what you think, Camilla, that Marjorie Hamilton is your mother?"

"I don't know, Jeremy… I feel so guilty for thinking that my Mom and Dad aren't my real parents, but I can't help it…"

Camilla broke down again and began sobbing. And before Jeremiah could offer some comforting words, Camilla blurted out between sobs, "And I think the girl that I remind your Dad of is connected to this somehow, too!"

"Camilla, now that's silly. How could this be possibly connected to some girlfriend that Dad had when he was fifteen? Why that was…30 years ago…"

"See, exactly my age…and, and the girl moved to Ottawa. Don't you see, Jeremy? And remember what your grandmother said, that the girl moved away just two weeks after school started and your dad never heard from her again."

"Look, Camilla. I know my Dad and the way he's raised us. He would never have sex before he got married and for you to jump to some conclusion that his girlfriend is connected to this Marjorie Hamilton and that…that Dad made her pregnant before she left for Ottawa is absolutely preposterous!"

"I agree with you, Jeremiah, but I have this gnawing feeling in my stomach that I can't shake…"

"Look, when I go to work today, I'll ask Dad what the name of his girlfriend back then was. Let's see what he says."

Jeremy hugged Camilla close. "Honey, please stop this and enjoy your day! It's your birthday, for Pete's sake! Look, I'll be home around five, and then we'll head out for dinner to the Diplomat. Enjoy this beautiful day and don't upset yourself, sweetie."

Camilla put her arms around Jeremy, "I hope I am not upsetting you, Jeremiah… It's your birthday today, too."

"See, honey, just another coincidence, right?"

THE FIRST THING Camilla asked Jeremy as he came into the door was, "Did you ask your father what his girlfriend's name was?"

"Oh, geez honey, it was so busy, I forgot. But listen, Grandma knows. When we drop off Joshua at her place on the way to the restaurant we can ask her."

"All the way to Mary Pederson's home, not a word was spoken between Jeremy and Camilla. Even Joshua, perhaps sensing something between his parents, remained silent until they parked just outside of the house.

"I see Nana at the door. Let me out!"

"Just hold your horses, Josh."

Jeremy opened the door and Joshua scrambled out and ran up the stairs to Mary's open arms. Both Jeremy and Camilla got out and approached Mary.

"Thank you so much for watching Josh for us. We shouldn't be more than two hours."

"Oh don't rush, I love to watch Joshua and happy birthday again,

Camilla and to you, too, Jeremy! It's quite a thing for the both of you to celebrate your birthdays on the same day. Did you have a nice day?"

"Yes, it was fine. I didn't eat all day and so my stomach is growling."

"Yeah, I'm hungry too, so we better go." And just as Jeremy turned he asked the big question that was burning in both his and Camilla's mind, "Say, Grandma, Camilla and I were wondering what Dad's girl-friend's name was when he was fifteen? You know the one you said moved to Ottawa and never heard from her again?"

Mary wrinkled her brow and gazed at them, a puzzled look growing on her face. "Her name was Jennifer, but most of the time I believe Henry called her Jenny. Why do you ask?"

"Oh, we were just curious. You know, it's kinda cute Dad having a girlfriend back then. We always think of him as having known our Mom forever. See ya in a couple of hours, Grandma."

Jeremy took Camilla's hand and almost floated to the Jeep. Relief clearly evident in their step and demeanour.

Chapter Twenty-Four

A LTHOUGH JAMES HAD intended to move back to the estate after Jenny left, business commitments hadn't allow him the time to do so. He had a serious stomach ailment at the time which turned out to be an ulcer and not prostate cancer that had killed his father. Over the winter however, the ulcer got worse and the doctors ordered him to rest for a month or longer. Rather than stay in his condo he elected to convalesce at the estate for the remainder month of June.

Rising from the patio chair where he had been resting, he walked down the winding path of the grounds. Jenny had made that same journey so many times over the years she lived on the estate, and he could never understand what drew her back down the same walkway time and again. He considered it boring and a waste of time. But, he was stuck on the estate for at least another week and was tired of sitting.

As he made his way down the path, James had to admit that the grounds were beautiful. The closer he got to the gazebo, the more the immense spray of different flowers teased his vision. Even his hard nose had to twitch, tantalized by the growing aroma. James was not used to such a natural fragrance. It both weakened and strengthened him at the same time. He was relieved to see the chair inside the gazebo. He shuffled towards it as quickly as he could and sat down.

Letting out a long sigh, his eyes were instantly captivated by the dazzling, brilliant colour of the wildflower patch. While it overwhelmed James, it bothered his sense of order and precision. There was no rhythm or reason to it, just a scatter of flowers, all so different and, yet, so compatible.

If only people of the world could live in such harmony.

As quickly as the thought popped into his head, James rejected the notion as preposterous and impossible. He chastised himself for even entertaining such a ridiculous prospect.

Some of the flowers near one side of the patch appeared more radiant than the others. James' gaze rested upon them for a moment and then followed the source of light to a statue of an angel with a glowing aura shimmering around it. James became transfixed by the image before him. It truly was a beautiful angel and the bouquet of flowers lying in the angel's basket seemed almost more glorious and emanated even greater radiance. James rose and walked over to it to study the angel more closely.

As he approached this extraordinary vision, Thomas walked down the stone-paved lane. They reached the statue at the same time and stood silently before the heavenly sight.

James's voice broke the silence. "Where did this statue come from, Thomas? I haven't been aware of it before."

"This is a gift that we gave to Mrs. Hamilton. Me and the other workers. She called it the 'Angel of Thanksgiving.' Everyday when she was here she would place flowers in the basket giving thanks to someone or for something."

James was stunned by this revelation. Had he known the staff was doing this he would not have allowed it. He vehemently despised patronage or association between themselves and the workers. His perturbed feelings, however were calmed by the freshly cut, glimmering bouquet of flowers in the basket.

"I assume you are continuing Mrs. Hamilton's practice of placing new flowers in the basket daily?" James asked in an unsettling tone.

Thomas hesitated for a moment. "No, Mr. Hamilton. I am not. These flowers were placed there by Mrs. Hamilton herself on the day she left the estate."

"That's preposterous! Marjorie left last fall. At best cut flowers will last two weeks but to survive over the winter is ridiculous. These flowers look as though they were cut this morning. Someone is playing you for a fool, Thomas. You or someone else must be replenishing them and…watering and tending to them somehow…?"

"I assure you, Mr. Hamilton, neither I nor Ramon have touched or placed any new flowers into this basket. These are the very ones that Mrs. Hamilton placed in here the day before she left the estate. I saw her put them in and the truth of the matter is, I have not touched them or watered them in all that time. It's astonishing, isn't it?"

James was flabbergasted. "Are you certain that neither you nor anyone else has cared for these flowers since last fall!?"

"Yes, sir. That is the case."

"Were you speaking to Mrs. Hamilton that morning when she placed the flowers in the basket?"

"Yes, sir—"

"Did she say what they were in thanksgiving for?"

A quiet silence descended upon them. Even the robin resting in the tree above held its breath waiting for Thomas to answer.

"Yes, she did, Mr. Hamilton." Thomas turned from the angel and gazed at his employer. "They were meant for you, sir. She wanted to thank you for giving her such a beautiful garden while she lived here." And, after a brief reflection, tears welling in his eyes, he added, "It was a gift of love and thanksgiving for you. I believe that is what has sustained these flowers, Mr. Hamilton."

It was as if a bolt of lightning came out of a cloudless sky and struck James to the core, cracking through his hard exterior. He began backing away from Thomas and the Angel of Thanksgiving, on his face a look of horror and disbelief. How could Jenny have given him a gift of love and thanksgiving after what he did to her?

Suddenly, James stopped staggering and, like a statue himself, seemed to begin to break apart, piece by piece, as the realization of what Jenny had done overwhelmed his heart and soul. As tears filled his eyes, he made no move to stop them. He stood exposed, his guard down, his defensiveness gone, weeping uncontrollably before the angel and his grounds-keeper. His old self crumbled while his heart softly strengthened by the touch of love. He was so awestruck by Jenny's act, despite his actions towards her that he remained speechless and unable to move. He wanted to reject it all and gain control, but was defenceless to do so.

Out of the corner of his eye, he saw tears streaming down Thomas' cheeks, as well. Feelings of embarrassment and shame crawled their way from James' rubbery legs to the top of his head. He couldn't stop his crying or his lips and chin from quivering. Instead of appreciating and accepting the miraculous sight and gift before him, he began to imagine what he must look like in such a weakened state before one of his subordinates. And suddenly, James remembered that it wasn't he who treated Jenny badly, it was she who had betrayed him! It was Jenny who he reviled! The thought of receiving love from a woman who caused him such revulsion pushed its way through the brief moment of ecstasy he had enjoyed.

Old thoughts and feelings joined forces to fill James' mind with ideas he knew and understood and was comfortable with. He could not accept a gift from the woman who was impure, touched by others… and raped. The thought that he had actually made love to her sent him mentally spewing vulgarities.

Thomas, being a man of peace, stepped back as he sensed anger, hostility and hatred filling James, even though a word had not yet been spoken. As Thomas' eyes shifted from James back to the Angel of Thanksgiving, he saw the flowers squirming and twisting, as if in pain. Little did he know that for each thought of hatred towards Jenny that entered James' mind, one of the beautiful wildflowers in the basket began to die. Before their very eyes, the magnificent bouquet that had shimmered with such light for months on end began to dim, shrivel and dry. Within seconds, the flowers were completely dead, so brittle and devoid of life, they cracked apart and became dust. The gentle breeze flowing through the garden lifted the remains and scattered them about until the basket was left empty except for the odd trace and fragment of a dried petal or stem.

And as the power and wonder of the vision abated, James' old strength increased. Control was back and his old senses restored.

"Thomas!" James bellowed, ignoring Thomas' startled expression. "I want this damn thing taken away. Get it out of my sight. I don't want to see it anywhere on the grounds."

"Y-yes, sir."

James turned abruptly from the angel. "And these wildflowers, roto-till them up. They lack order and look so wild and haphazard. What are those flowers in front of the house, Thomas?"

"You mean the petunias and marigolds?"

"Yes, those are the ones. They are neat and in nice straight rows and easily identifiable. Plant them here, instead."

Thomas could barely agree to the order. The life of the garden would be taken away. He gazed at his employer making certain he heard him correctly then slowly hung his head.

"Yes, sir."

As James stormed back to the house he began swatting the butter-flies away and spewing curses at them. Just before he entered through the patio doors he turned and bellowed at Thomas.

"And get rid of these damn butterflies! Spray them, do what you have to and pull up all those stinky milkweed plants. I should never have allowed Marjorie to grow them."

Thomas didn't answer. He was devastated by the order. It would be like killing family.

Later in the morning, Thomas and Ramon moved the Angel of Thanksgiving into the tool shed. Thomas fought to control the tears and sorrow as he saw the beloved statue amongst the tools, hoses, dirty boxes and gasoline cans.

"Why do we have to place the angel in here?" asked Ramon.

"It's sad, Ramon. *Mr. Hamilton's nature is still not yet open to receive acts of love. Perhaps someday when more tears flow from his heart, he will see.*"

As they turned to leave the shed, they both noticed the nimbus of light coming from the angel. And strangely, instead of the oily and gasoline smell, a sweet fragrance filled the air. Their spirits lifted as they looked at one another then both bowed their heads in prayer towards the shimmering statue.

"Remind me to pick some flowers and place them in the basket, Ramon. Mr. Hamilton needs our mistress' continuing prayers."

To remove the Angel of Thanksgiving from the grounds was one thing, but to roto-till the wildflower patch was something Thomas could not bring himself to do. It had been such a source of joy and beauty not only for Miss. Jenny, but for them, as well.

"Ramon, my heart cannot bear to do this task. Would you please till the flowers?"

Thomas turned and quickly walked away as he heard the tiller fire up. Each time he heard the motor bear down into the lavish thick garden, stabs of pain doubled him over.

By late afternoon the area around the gazebo looked dead and barren. All the beauty, grace, charm, and radiance of colour which gave the grounds its ethereal atmosphere had been replaced by the cold, hellish world James lived in. He smiled from his second floor bedroom window as he saw Ramon uproot and destroy the last memories of his soiled ex-wife.

The next day, however, as James made his way back to the gazebo, new wildflowers had already poked their way through the dark rich soil. By mid-afternoon, the dirt was covered with an unbelievable spray of dazzling flowers.

As James stood there in a daze, Thomas arrived and was also taken aback by the scene. He instantly knew it was his mistress' love, her gift to James and her heavenly haven that could not be destroyed.

James was once again struck speechless. His face reddened as anger overtook him. He stormed back to the house and within an hour was dressed and out the front door, determined never to set foot on the estate again. *Destiny, however, had different plans. James would be back much sooner than he thought...*

CHAPTER TWENTY-FIVE

I T WAS JULY 6, and if Julean were alive she would have braced herself for a night of restless sleep. During all the years of her marriage to Henry, his dreams of his teenage sweetheart manifested the most on this day. Julean had come to learn much of Henry and Jenny's relationship through her dear husband's dreams. July 6 was the day they had met and fell into a deep, everlasting love that stood the test of time.

Just as it happened every year, Henry's dreams of Jenny that night were more vivid than ever. It was as if he were reliving for the first time how powerfully he was stirred when he saw Jenny Sarsky walk past his house on her way to Mr. Engelmann's store. In his dream, he followed her to the store where they had first met and the moment he gazed into her eyes he was completely smitten all over again. It was love at first sight; the yearning in his heart for Jenny was as strong now as it had been then.

How many times had he dreamt that dream and played that scene out in his mind over the years? What was it that had such a power to keep this love so alive for all those years? He recalled to this day something being caught in his eyes when their gazes were locked into one another…what was it that had such an electrifying surge of energy?

Just last year he had slipped into a similar reverie when he was being interviewed by Brenda, the journalist from the Leader Post Sun. He was still amazed how quickly he was drawn back to that summer and the effort he had to exert to pull himself back to the moment.

In just two short months in 1956 a love was sown that has lasted to the present day. Henry turned over and recalled the phrase that Jenny so often said, "Quickly, hold my hand." Instinctively he squeezed his hand tightening his grip around Julean's rosary.

"Oh, honey, I'm sorry. He brought the rosary to his lips. If she had not encouraged him to seek Jenny or another out he would be guilt ridden for days.

Henry decided to get up and enjoy the day at home. When he spoke with Ivania yesterday he was glad that she had a seminar and had to cancel their date for this evening.

He couldn't wait for nightfall. He wanted to gaze at the star of the east…

IN THE SAME way she celebrated Camilla's birthday each year, so too Jenny still thought of Henry and their anniversary as well. Now that she and James were divorced, she no longer felt pangs of guilt for thinking on these thoughts. However, she knew they were just memories, consoling perhaps, but just memories that held no promise.

Yet, there was something that kept drawing her back to that memorable summer that was filled with such promise for a life of bliss together. She reached up and gently took hold of the pewter angel hanging on the end of her necklace. What if she and Henry had received each other's letters back then, how would her life have been so different? Would they have married and had children? Would they be living in Regina or on his acreage…?

"Oh, Jen, don't torture yourself so. Henry is married and has a beautiful family. What was done was done."

Try as she might, Jenny just couldn't push her first love out of her mind. Being so alone without any family support except for friends, Jenny found thoughts of Henry uplifting and comforting. It was the one time she allowed the past to steal away the precious moments of the present.

Jenny took her diary out to the backyard. It was coming along so beautifully. The landscaper and his help were doing such a lovely job and each day fulfilling her dreams of what the yard might look like. Many days, she too, worked side by side with the landscaper both in the designing and planting of flowers and plants.

The carpenters had built the platform for the gazebo so that Jenny could plant all the wildflowers. She even left a spot where the Angel of Thanksgiving would go in anticipation that James would ship it to her. The carpenters promised to finish the gazebo that fall. In the meantime Jenny had set a wooden lawn chair beside a cedar table on the platform so she could still use the partially constructed gazebo until the rest of it was built.

Jenny strolled down the winding stone path, her feet crunching the thyme between the stones giving off its intoxicating aroma. It joined the fragrance released by the other flowers and then as she got close to the gazebo platform the scent of her beloved wildflowers kicked in.

By the time she sat on the wooden arm chair she was dizzy from the overwhelming dazzling colours of the different flowers and the unique perfume each gave off.

She was so happy the milkweed plants had attracted the Monarch butterflies so quickly. The landscaper was surprised to see so many. In all the years of landscaping in the city he had never seen such a multitude of them. He attributed it to the array of flowers and wildflowers. The yard was literally bursting with so much colour that the butterflies couldn't help but notice as they flew overhead and wanted to spend the summer there.

Jenny liked that analysis and yet she felt there was something else. She had a special bond with the Monarchs and often thought that amongst all of the ones in her yard there was one for each of her loved one's. It would only be a matter of time for her to recognize Tammy, her dad and mom. Jenny would know when one sat on her hand which it was, just like Carlos knew when one came in his mother's spirit each year.

Henry's letter fell on her lap as she opened her diary. She read it and then reread it. She could feel his love so strong and deep. Hers was the same for him. A tear fell on the letter as she turned to the inside back of the front cover and got the key out of a little paper pocket and opened up the back half of her diary. The part where she had written so many private thoughts over the years since she was fifteen.

She unlocked it and paged through to where she had penned a prayer of hope and love inspired by the closing sentence of the last letter she'd written to Henry, the one that contained the pewter angel. "Even though we are far apart, you are forever in my heart."

Jenny was still in awe that Henry would close the letter to her, not only with the identical pewter angel inside, but also with this very sentence as well! The only explanation Jenny could think of was that it was their guardian angels who had prompted such a miracle to occur.

A tear fell on the page beside the stain of other ones that had fallen over the years as she softly whispered the poem once more.

> *The star of the east we both can see,*
> *its bright rays your warmth caressing me.*
> *I long for evening on this special day,*
> *for the star of the east to gleam my way,*
> *to fill my heart through our star*
> *with all your love, though from afar.*

Jenny ran a finger over the words and smiled. How true the poem was. Each time she gazed at the star in the eastern sky, she felt enveloped by its shimmering rays as if Henry were there, holding her hand. And then the warm love from the star began to fade and Jenny now knew why. It was when he had met Julean and got married. Tammy had found out from a conversation she had with Henry's mother that he had gotten married at that time. What puzzled Jenny though was why was she feeling the love return? For the past few months when she gazed at the star that same warm feeling was coming back and growing stronger each time.

Jenny gazed at the poem she had added exactly a year later to the one she just read. It was 1959, three years to the day that they had met in Mr. Engelmann's store. The yearning and longing for her first love was so strong that she just had to share that magic moment with her diary:

> I'll always remember the day we met,
> Into your arms I was easily swept.
> 'Twas your eyes drew me, clear and bright,
> Into the depth of your heart with pure delight.
> Oh, dear, sweet Henry on our anniversary day
> I send an angel just to say
> I'll love you forever, come what may.

Amazingly, that same yearning and longing for Henry was still the same. She could very well have written that same poem just now.

Jenny recalled how beautiful that day was as she sat in the garden of her parent's estate. Just as she had finished writing the poem, Carlos came by. He was not only an incredible gardener but became such a dear friend. Besides, Tammy, he was perhaps the only other person who could see into her heart.

When she spoke of Camilla that morning, he knew instantly that Camilla was her daughter. He knew too, that she missed and loved Henry. He was so insightful and his words so heartfelt she found herself opening up to him as easily as if he had been a life long friend. Jenny would never forget that as they spoke a blue butterfly had landed on her arm and the words he spoke, "A beautiful butterfly sometimes appears following the departure of a loved one. It is an expression of love and comfort to the one who remains behind."

His words were so soothing, sincere and described perfectly what she was feeling and thinking. She, too, thought the butterfly was a gift to comfort her and that there was a spiritual side to nature and its creatures, especially butterflies. She had felt silly at the time sharing that with Carlos but he quickly confirmed the possibility with such faith and sharing that she never questioned her belief in butterflies, and how they come at times in disguise as angels, again.

"Oh, no, Senorita Jenny, butterflies remind us of the beauty of love and our loved ones." Carlos had said, and later he confirmed that the blue butterfly resting on her hand was a gift of love from her loved one and that he could see in her eyes how deeply her love was for Henry.

She missed Carlos and wished he were there now, walking up the stone paved lane coming to her to stop and chat for a moment or two. Tears surfaced as she thought of those memorable times in the estate garden.

She thought when she wed James that she would never be able to recapture the beauty of her parent's garden and the work Carlos had done to make it so beautiful. But Carlos had tried to console her, that the estate she was going to the gardener there would surely fill her heart with just as much beauty.

As usual, the insightful gardener was right. Thomas was an amazing gardener, too and had created for her a haven that assuaged her heart time and again during those lonely and difficult years in Greystone Manor. Thomas became a dear friend too, just like Carlos. His heart was filled with beauty as well, and was just as insightful and sensitive to others. Jenny concluded that it just couldn't be any other way for both men to be so. It was just a natural by-product of being immersed day in and day out in God's creations.

Jenny raised her chin upwards so the sun could catch her entire face. She loved the warmth her friend always gave to her. From previous habit on the estate, Jenny pushed her feet against the floor of the gazebo thinking she was on a swing. It jarred her and she opened her eyes only to see the glistening wildflowers and the butterflies flitting about them, touching each flower as if kissing its petals.

It was such a beautiful day and the garden looked so beautiful. If only James would send her the Angel of Thanksgiving, the garden would be complete and perfect. She missed the peace and memories it gave to her of her father.

She allowed her gaze to return to the diary and read the poems again. She knew by doing so she was torturing herself but couldn't help it. The yearning and longing was so deep in her heart. Jenny could hardly wait for evening to gaze at the star of the east and feel the warmth of the rays.

Just then a blue butterfly landed on her hand. Blue always reminded her of Henry as blue was his favourite colour. Sunlight glowed through its gossamer wings. As Jenny studied and admired the depths of its colours she knew if Carlos were here he would say the butterfly was sent from Henry as a message of love on the wings of a butterfly.

"Oh, thank you, Henry," Jenny whispered, wanting so deeply to believe in the possibility.

"Yes, Carlos you are so right. *She could feel the comfort and message of love.*"

PERHAPS IT WAS the coolness of the evening or the warmth of the stars rays sneaking through the tall fir trees that woke Jenny. The first thing she noticed was the first star of the east shining directly on her. She must have fallen asleep earlier that afternoon. Her diary still lay open on her lap. It was too dark to read the poems not that she needed the light anyway. She knew every word by heart.

She rested her head once again on the back of the high lawn chair and gazed at the star feeling its shimmering rays as if Henry were there placing his arms around her. She couldn't get over how strong she felt Henry's love. Could it be possible that he was sending out his love to her? She knew Henry's heart, he would never do anything to hurt his wife...what was happening, she wondered?

She recalled the night when Tammy told her about making a wish on a shooting star. She believed that if you made a wish as soon as you saw a star streak across the sky, the star's dust would settle in your heart and your wish would come true. It did for Tammy. She wished that Robbie would come back to her and that they would get married, and they did.

She had shared her deepest wish with Tammy that night too when they revealed their hearts desire to one another. She had always prayed to her guardian angel that she wanted to look into Henry's green eyes and kiss his warm, tender lips. It was denied to her the day she left Regina with her father to fly to Ottawa.

Henry had come to see her off and her heart fluttered with joy. She ran into his waiting arms and just as they were about to kiss and gaze into each other's eyes, her mother grabbed her arm and tore her from Henry's embrace. She pleaded to her mother to let go but she was unrelenting and dragged her to the taxi. Jenny had never got over that longing desire to kiss her sweetheart, and it was something she wished for to this very day.

Well, at least she had received some closure to it all by finally receiving Henry's letter. It was so good of her Mom to give it to her. They had kept their promise to one another to write, and it seemed that their love was still so real and alive.

Jenny gazed into the evening sky. The star of the east was no longer visible as more and more stars budded in the growing night. She wondered if her wish would ever come true. She had made her wish on a shooting star. It was the night she and James had visited Tammy and Chloe in her parent's basement suite. After James brought her home she went out to the patio and gazed into the sky, and saw a shooting star streak across the sky. And she had made her wish. She felt so hopeful at the time, as the star dust settled in her heart, but nothing ever came of it.

Tammy said that it sometimes takes a long time for a wish to be answered. In fact, she had even forgotten about hers until one evening when she saw the sky filled with a bunch of shooting stars. It was such a festive, spectacular array of dazzling colour. It reminded her of the wish she had made and moments after, Robbie called. The rest was history.

Jenny wondered, if she saw a kaleidoscope of shooting stars in the sky *would it mean that her wish just might be coming true?*

Chapter Twenty-Six

MARY HAD BEEN cleaning out the bedroom closet for an hour when she thought she heard the telephone ring. She laid the dress down, which she was considering giving away, and ran to the kitchen to answer it.

"Hello?"

"Good morning, Mom, were you out in the garden? I was ready to hang up. It rang at least eight times."

"Oh, I was in the bedroom sorting out the closet, deciding what to give to the Salvation Army. I thought the phone was ringing, but I guess I was too deep in thought."

"Well, I'm glad you caught it in time. Have you started lunch, yet?"

"No, not yet, but I can make a lunch soon enough, it's still early."

"Are you sure, Mom? I don't want you to go to any trouble."

"Oh no, it's no problem, at all. You know how much I enjoy having you come home."

"Okay, then, I'll be by around noon."

"Yes, I'll look forward to seeing you, then. Bye."

Mary returned to cleaning out the closet for another hour before stopping to prepare lunch for her and Henry.

The thought of Henry coming for lunch made her look up towards the top shelf of the closet before she closed the door. She stepped back and raised herself up on her tiptoes. Even though it sat at the very back of the shelf, the shimmering light surrounding her treasure chest was clearly visible. Mary knew the unexplainable light was from Jenny's letter. A chill swept through her as a constant reminder of the decision she'd made many years ago.

She stepped forward with the intent of bringing the chest down, but then decided not to. It still bothered her that she kept it from Henry and that she hadn't kept her agreement with Mrs. Sarsky to destroy the letter.

Mary looked into the dresser mirror. She recalled vividly that day she decided to keep the letter from Henry and store it in her treasure box. She remembered looking into the mirror hoping to see in her eyes that she had made the correct decision. But, like back then, the reflection before her only confirmed that what she and Mrs. Sarsky had agreed to do was wrong. No one, not even the love of a mother has the right to decide the fate of their child.

Henry had a right to know and a right to decide his own future, but so many circumstances at the time all seemed to work against doing the right thing: Henry and Julean were getting married in less than two weeks, Jenny too, was engaged and soon to be married, the pact she made with Mrs. Sarsky, and Henry had seemed to have forgotten about Jenny and had moved on with his new love. The uproar and trouble and turmoil it would have caused for all concerned would have been too formidable.

It all made so much sense then, what she and Mrs. Sarsky had done, and yet, a brief glance into the mirror was all it took to convict her, again. Immediately stirring up the guilt she'd felt all these years. Not even a Novena to Saint Therese could absolve her of her wrongdoing. She had prayed to her patron Saint, over and over again, but all to no avail. Finally Mary accepted the fact that neither a Saint nor God could absolve her for what she had done. She'd made the wrong decision and peace would elude her until she corrected it.

As Mary shuffled her way to the kitchen, she unlocked the front door in anticipation of Henry's arrival. She, like Henry, tried to revive the good old days when Henry lived at home and he would burst through the front door hardly able to contain himself from devouring the meal she always had prepared for him. Oh, how she missed those days, those precious days.

Mary opened the cupboard and took out some vegetables, deciding to make Henry his favourite meal. She carried the vegetables over to the sink, took out a knife, and began peeling the potatoes, reciting Hail Mary's as she did so. When she started peeling the onions, tears welled up in her eyes, but it wasn't because of the sting from the onions, rather it was the sting of guilt that she just couldn't seem to shake herself loose of.

THE GALLERY HAD been bustling all morning. Henry spent most of it with a couple just starting their art collection. They decided to take two of his works home on approval for a day or two. They liked both paintings, but could only afford one. "On approval" would allow them to see how the paintings looked in their home so they could decide which painting they like best. Most times, the customer ended up keeping both.

Justin had been busy as well helping the framer assemble some of the framing orders. Both the framer and Henry were impressed with Justin's skill for his age. Henry hadn't had a chance to tell Justin about his plans to see Mom for lunch and hoped he could help look after the shop till he got back.

Finally, the last customer left and Henry told Justin he was going to Mom's for lunch.

"Not a problem, Dad. I can have my lunch in the back. I don't need to go to the café. Besides, there is an article I want to read in the framing magazine that came yesterday, about cutting V grooves."

"Well, I hope you get time to read it. If it's anything like this morning you may have to put it off for another day. How are you and Doug coming along with Lydia's paintings? Have you started to frame them for the upcoming exhibition next month?"

"Yeah, I have assembled two of the small ones, still another 18 or so to go. Doug will have to do all the large pieces, but don't worry, Dad; we'll have them all done in time."

"I know you will, Justin, and I know they will look great, as usual."

Justin smiled then headed into the back of the gallery and the fitting room. Henry followed to retrieve his jacket.

"We'll see you in an hour and half. I have a meeting with the accountant at one-forty-five, so I should be back by one-thirty. If it gets too busy call Doug to help and Lauren too, if she's not busy in the café."

"Have a nice lunch, Dad, and say hello to grandma for me."

"I will for sure."

"Hi, Mom," Henry shouted as he let himself in the front door. The pungent smell of fried potatoes and onions hit his nostrils and stirred his appetite.

"I'm in the kitchen."

"Where else would you be," Henry chuckled as he entered the kitchen. As usual, his mother had her hands in the sink.

She turned to him. "Hi, son, I'm so glad to see you."

Henry stared at his mother standing there at the sink, the light streaming in from the window casting soft shadows on her face.

"I've just got to paint a picture of you standing at the sink, Mom, and the way the light brings out your features."

Henry remained speechless for a few more moments, trying to burn the image of her standing there into his mind's eye. She ducked bashfully away. Her soft kindly face contained such a quiet strength. Henry hoped someday he would be able to capture that in a portrait of her. He knew it came from her faith.

Henry walked over to Mary and kissed her cheek.

"I made some fresh orange juice, care for a glass?"

"Yes, a nice cold drink would be great, Mom."

Mary dried her hands on a dish towel then turned to the fridge.

"Was the gallery busy, today?"

"It sure was. I spent most of the morning with a young couple who ended up taking two of my paintings home. I know they will keep one of them for sure, if not both."

"I'm sure they will, Henry."

"Thanks, Mom. Man does it ever smell good in here. I can hardly wait for lunch. I should send our chef from the cafe over to take a few lessons from you."

"Oh, I'm sure I could learn a thing or two from him. Well, just sit down. It will only be a few more minutes."

Mary went to the stove and turned over the potatoes and onions in the frying pan, the golden brown colour looked so tantalizing that Henry couldn't resist taking one of the crusted potatoes before sitting at the table.

Henry studied his mother working at the stove. She was shrinking and hunched over a bit more. She was diagnosed with osteoarthritis a few years ago, but never complained of the pain. Her hair had a little more grey in it. The light from the window above the sink also revealed the deepening wrinkles in her face, all signs that time was moving on. But while she was nearing 70, she was still in very good health. Each day, however, brought them closer to the day that one of them would leave this earth. And, as the days passed, Henry became more conscious that time was slowly but surely running out.

"Your son and his lovely wife, Camilla, and Joshua were over for a visit, Tuesday evening," Mary said, as she stirred the potatoes.

"Yeah, Jeremy told me they were coming over. I'm sure glad they are keeping in touch with you. Since Julean passed away, we don't get together as often as we used to."

"Well, you know how it is. Working every day and raising a family is a big responsibility, and their son is quite a handful. I don't know how that lady does it, working and looking after the boy."

"She is a very capable woman, that's for sure. She loves her job at the Tutorial school."

"Oh yes, she would be so good with the girls, so understanding. She always speaks so caringly of them as if they were her daughters."

"Yeah, she is a great girl alright, Jeremy married a gem for sure and it's made him so responsible."

Henry turned to his mother and almost hesitatingly said, "I still can't get over how much she looks like Jenny. I know we have spoken of this before, Mom, but when I see her I almost get the urge to call her Jenny."

"Yes, she certainly does have very similar features to that young girl, Jenny. But these things happen, I know in my lifetime people have come up to me as well confusing me for someone else. I heard once that we all have a look alike somewhere on this earth."

"Yeah, I've heard that, too, and it has happened to me as well."

Henry shook his head and then asked, "So, how was your morning, Mom?"

"Oh, fine. I spent most of it cleaning out the closet. It was so packed, I decided to give away some of my clothes."

Thoughts of the letter immediately popped to mind with the mere mention of the closet. Mary quickly returned to the stove and picked up the pan and brought the fried vegetables over to Henry. He scooped some creamy cucumber salad on his plate as well as a slice of home-made bread he'd just finished buttering. He then eagerly took the plate from his mother and emptied well over half of it onto his plate. Mary looked on in delight.

She turned back to the fridge and took out a plate of cold cuts and set them on the table as well. He was already nibbling away at the potatoes before she sat down, he couldn't help himself.

"Why don't you say grace, today, Henry?"

Henry crossed himself, "Dear Lord, we thank you for this food and each other. Thank you for Mom and the wonderful meals she always prepares. Bless our conversation. Amen."

"Amen," said Mary and continued, "so, is everything set for Father's 25th anniversary celebration?"

"Yeah, it's coming up fast and only two Sundays away. We still have so many pictures and memorabilia to hang up and display. I'm amazed at all of the baptisms and marriages and funerals he's performed over the years. I hope we can keep his surprise party at the church hall secret from him."

"That may be difficult. He is so alert and attuned to everything, it will be a challenge to hide this from him for sure, son."

"Yes, and he indicates no sign that he will be retiring any time soon.

When I asked a couple of Sundays ago he said he still feels healthy and there are so many needs to fill."

"I wonder how Father Knuka is working out?"

"I think he's been a big help to Father, but he did say Father Knuka needs a little more experience before taking over such a large church. It's very difficult for one person to do it especially when starting out. There is such a shortage of priests that Father feels he just has to stay on a little while longer or until Father Knuka gets some help.

"And he keeps saying, he feels young and is still raring to go, and ready to do God's work." Henry swallowed his food and continued, "The next two weeks are going to be hectic. Gary's coming in this week and staying until after the anniversary. It sure will be good to see him. Next week will be hectic, too, with Eddy and his wife flying in from Jamaica. It's going to be great to see them all."

"Gary hasn't been home for almost two years. The last time was for his dad's funeral."

"Yes, that's right, Mom. I guess his friend Jane has joined the Sisters of Charity…I wonder if Gary will become a priest now?"

"Well, he seems to be called in that direction, for sure."

"I think Father Engelmann wants him to talk about his work in India at all three masses this Sunday. I'm looking forward to what he will have to say."

"Yes, that will be interesting to learn more of what he is doing there."

"I was wondering Mom, could I invite him to Sunday dinner? Father Engelmann can't make it this Sunday and I thought Gary might enjoy one of your fine home cooked meals."

"Yes, that would be fine. I would love to have Gary here."

"That's great, Mom. Every now and then I wish Gary still lived here. We used to have some good talks. Come to think of it, I really have never met anyone since that I could open up to like Gary. Eddy and Red were friends too, but the relationship I had with Gary was special."

"I understand what you mean, son. I've had one or two friends like that in my lifetime as well. They are definitely people we treasure and are a blessing in our lives."

Once, again Mary sensed Henry's loneliness…

"So, you say Eddy and his new wife are coming next week and I understand they will be renewing their vows?"

"Yeah, I'm not exactly sure how Father is going to fit it into the 9:00 o'clock mass. I know Father is sure excited about it. There is a special connection between Eddy and Father. Whenever Eddy used to come in for a pack of smokes into the store I could tell Mr. Engelmann appreciated Eddy's honesty as to who the smokes were for and his brashness. I must admit it appealed to me, too. Yeah, his cocky forwardness backed by a quiet confidence…this is me, take me or leave me, it's your choice. Eddy wore no masks."

"Authentic is a word that I will always remember from your grade twelve valedictorian speech. Your exterior should reflect your interior."

"That's a good way to put it, Mom."

"And the Archbishop, is still going to make it to Father's anniversary?"

"Yes, I spoke with him last week and he's as excited about it all as we are. Man, will Father Engelmann be surprised when the Bishop comes in from the back of the church and walks down the aisle with his entourage."

As Henry gobbled down the rest of his food, Mary struggled with her conscience whether or not to tell Henry of Jenny's letter. Since he walked in the door, the compulsion to do so was so powerful. Both the pain of guilt and a building anxiety was growing on her face.

She didn't notice her son staring at her.

"Are you okay Mom? I've finished my entire meal and you haven't even started on yours."

Mary shook her head. "Oh, I'm sorry, I was just thinking of how you and Ivania are doing and didn't know if I should ask?"

"You can ask anytime, you have known my life story right from the start and I never mind sharing with you what's going on. I still recall the fun we had when I was in grade twelve and had plans to visit Jenny. Do you recall that, Mom?"

"Yes, I'll never forget that Henry. Oh, I was so nervous every time I took a peek inside your drawer to see what you were up to and if you were still going to seek your girlfriend out."

Mary reached over and patted Henry's hand relieved that he didn't sense her real thoughts over her growing anxiety.

"I'm glad that we can be so open with each other." No sooner had the words left her mouth than the feeling of deceit swept through her with an alarming force.

Oh Lord, help me.

"Well, Mom, Ivania and I are doing well. She has been off to Toronto several times this spring taking a course that the company sent her on. She left again last week and will be back just in time to attend Father's anniversary party with me. She's so different from Julean, but I am getting used to her ways and we seem to have a good relationship. I think she wants a closer one, but I just don't feel ready yet. I still think so much on Julean and …Henry was going to say Jenny, but didn't want to upset his mother.

Mary however immediately knew what Henry's thoughts were. Jenny was always just below the surface of his mind.

"Geez, mom!" Henry exclaimed, as he looked at his watch. "It's almost one-thirty. Where did the time go? I've got a meeting with my accountant in 15 minutes. I hate to rush off like this."

Mary felt some measure of relief as she almost was going to push herself into telling all to her son.

She and Henry rose at the same time.

"That was sure a good lunch, Mom. You're the best cook in the world."

"Flattery will get you everywhere, son."

"I mean it with all my heart."

Henry kissed her cheek. "I love you, Mom. Thanks again for the lovely meal and visit."

Mary returned to the kitchen table and sat down. She was in no hurry to clear the table. She stared at her untouched meal. Her heart felt heavy over the loneliness Henry was feeling. She could see it in his eyes. Ivania may be good for him and might perhaps appease his loneliness since Julean's parting, but neither Ivania, nor any other woman would ever be able to replace Jenny. Not even his dear sweet wife, Julean could erase the memories that Henry held in his heart for his first love.

There was never any closure with Jenny for one thing, but even more, there was a spiritual connection between those two that she saw from the very first day they met. To this day Mary recalled her son coming home for lunch and not eating a mouthful of food, and then when Jenny came to call on Henry to take her to Balfour High School she saw then the look of love in her son's eyes that never went away.

Perhaps it is as they say, *theirs was a match made in heaven.* So deep and strong that nothing would ever be able to separate the love they had and still have for one another.

Mary wondered, as she sat there in the kitchen, if by keeping the letter from Henry that she and her son were being kept prisoners by the past. The fateful decision she had made that day in 1962, in the hopes that Henry would get on with his life with Julean, had it really only kept him a prisoner of his past?

And like Henry, had she too been imprisoned in the past over the decision she had made?

"Yes," Mary muttered, "it was a fateful decision I made, but one that can still be changed."

It was just a matter of time now before it all would come to the fore, regardless of what she wanted. Mary was losing the battle within her. Every day the struggle was becoming too great. The truth can never be held in the recesses of darkness. The truth will always win out in the end and along with its light…*bring freedom.*

CHAPTER TWENTY-SEVEN

IT IS WONDERFUL to have you home, Gary, and good of you to say a few words to the parishioners. It's important that they should know the wonderful work that their neighbour is now doing in the missionary field."

"Well, we all can do God's work whether we are there or here, Father."

"Yes, very true, and very well spoken."

"If you want to sit in the front pew, after the gospel reading I will let the parishioners know that in place of the homely they will hear you speak. It will be a welcome relief for them not to have to listen to me this Sunday."

"I'm not so sure about that, Father. The people love your sermons. They come from the heart and are inspired."

"Thank you, Gary, but the Holy Spirit gets all the credit. On my own I could do very little to move hearts."

Right after Father read the gospel he introduced Gary.

"My dear brothers and sisters, in Christ, we are very fortunate this morning to have Gary Franklin to speak to us today. As many of you know he is from our neighbourhood, and he's here to speak to us on the missionary work he is doing in India. I'm sure what he has to say will enlighten us and be informing of what goes on in the third world and how we can help and be of service."

The congregation clapped as Gary made his way up to the podium. He was carrying Anna's bible in his hand. The bible that Anna had given to Henry, who in turn had given it to his friend.

Gary set the bible down and adjusted the microphone to his height.

"Thank you Father for giving me this opportunity to share some of my thoughts and experiences." And turning back to the congregation he started the same way Father did, "My dear brothers and sisters in Christ, …"

Gary had not spoken for more than five minutes when Henry

noticed and felt a deep peace in his friend. Where he would have been nervous and concerned about the approval of others, Gary showed no fear or being uncomfortable in any way. He was simply Gary through and through much like Eddy would be and yet, with Gary, his presence and words were more like that of Father Engelmann. They both possessed an invisible power, and yet its effects were visible. They were beacons of Jesus' *light* that instilled hope and faith in others. Just the way their words, coated with caring and love, flowed from their mouths captivated your attention and heart at the same time.

When Gary picked up Anna's bible, Henry's reverie was broken and he listened more attentively.

"This is Anna Engelmann's bible who as many of you know was Father Engelmann's wife before he became a priest. When she passed away she gave it to my good friend, Henry Pederson, who in turn so generously gave it me when I decided to go overseas and do missionary work. I would like to read what Henry has written in it:

Gary

I want you to have this. Mrs. Engelmann loved you as much as she did me and considered you her son, too. May this Bible be a reminder of that love for you and know her spirit and guidance and protection will constantly be with you in your work for God. You're my very best friend, Gary, and I love you...

I'm so proud to be your friend and brother in Christ.

Henry June 29, 1960

Gary didn't read the last sentence. He stopped, gazed directly at Henry and said with tears coming to his eyes, "I love you too, Henry for being my friend and giving me something that I know you cherished as well. You have no idea how the familiarity of this Bible helped me to overcome fear and aloneness in a strange land. But more so, if you had not given me this treasure I would have forgotten the loving spirit of Anna Engelmann and the encouragement and love she gave me when I worked in the store. It reminded me constantly of her faith and belief in the power of the Bible. It was the foundation upon which my faith grew. The words in here," and Gary lifted the Bible, "are truly living. On more than on several occasions Alice and I experienced the protection of this belief."

Gary went on to share two incidents. The first was when they were doing work in the Amazon rain forest and were attacked by several men with raised and swinging machetes. Just as one was about to strike him, he raised Anna's Bible and saw the large metal knife shatter like an icicle hit by a baseball bat.

The other incident he spoke of was just over a year ago when he and Alice were on a bus in India. A group of young men tried to take Alice. Once again Gary raised the Bible causing the group to be momentarily paralyzed. Two fled and the other two fell to their knees and begged for forgiveness. Two of the young men are now workers trying to reform street gangs.

Gary went on to speak of the poverty and need for medical help for so many people. What he considered even more so was the charity of the kind that helped them to live on their own like we do.

"We need people, leaders and companies that do not go there to exploit the land and their resources and use the cheap labour to their advantage. We need people of faith and integrity who come for the purpose of developing the country and teaching these people to take over themselves. We need to learn the truth of honestly serving our fellow man."

Of all the things his friend spoke of, the one thing that resonated in Henry's heart was the need for someone to travel the western world and keep ever in the forefront the needs of the poor not only abroad but in our own backyard.

Henry couldn't wait to talk more of that with Gary when they had dinner that evening.

"It's so nice to see you, Gary, welcome home."

"It's nice to be home, too, Mrs. Pederson," Gary replied as he stepped forward into Mary's open arms and embraced her.

"You haven't changed much. A little thinner and leaner, I suppose."

"Food and cooking is a little different there, and we do fast for a day or two most weeks."

"Well, come in and sit down with Henry in the living room, dinner is just about ready. Hope you like Chicken Parmesan and rice?"

"From the many times I ate here in grade school, I liked everything you made, Mrs. Pederson."

"Henry, I made some punch and put it into the fridge to cool. Please get some for you and Gary."

"Sure, Mom."

"It's sure good to see you, Gary," Henry said as he handed the drink to Gary and sat down. "So how long can you stay?"

"About two weeks. The Sunday after next, John McBryne and I are flying back to India. And Mom would like some help to paint the outside of the house. So, the time will go pretty quickly."

"How is John doing, by the way? I was sure surprised when I heard that he ended up working with you."

"He's doing great. I've never seen anyone so on fire for Jesus. He's great with the kids on the street, too. They all love it when he picks them up and tosses them even higher and catches them."

"Yeah, he sure is tall, close to seven feet, I would say. So, do you still like doing what you're doing? Does the poverty get you down?"

"There's unbelievable poverty there, Hank. So many families living on the street with just a piece of plastic supported by four sticks. I sometimes see families of four or five huddled together to keep warm."

"Supper's ready, boys," Mary said from the kitchen. "Bring your glasses and you can continue your conversation at the table."

After grace and they each helped themselves to the delicious dinner, the three continued their conversation. Most of the discussion centred around Gary's life not only in India, but other places that he and Alice had served as missionaries.

The one thing Gary had mentioned in his talk at the church that morning, he brought up again. "You know, Hank, we need people to travel around and talk about the needs of people not only in our own cities and towns, but also of the third world. For most of us, we get so caught up in our work and daily affairs that we never or rarely think about how others are living and what we can do for them. So many of us have more than we need and keep striving for more. Awareness of the problems and the needs of others is so important."

"You mentioned that this morning and I agree with you. We get so caught up in our own world that we rarely give it much thought. I remember a few years ago when Mother Theresa toured the United States and spoke at Thomas Aquinas College. Even though I was watching TV and not present there, which I would have loved to be, I could feel her holiness and knew that a saintly person was speaking."

"She is very holy, Hank, yet very demanding. She constantly encourages us to love until it hurts. Jesus loved until he gave Himself on the cross for us and she expects us to do the same."

"What she was getting at in her address to the College that day was not so much for an appeal for donations or for giving to the Third World, but rather to point out that the poverty in North America that was prevalent, was spiritual poverty. All too many of us live in man's world and not in God's. We are so focused on accumulating wealth and possessions that materialism has become our God. I still remember her encouraging the world to turn back to Jesus, to be the light that He was, to share the truth that He professed, and to exhibit the joy that comes with living for Jesus."

"She's big on family, Hank. Loving starts in the home and spreads out from there. I recall you telling me once how your dad started to say the rosary by being influenced by Bishop Sheen on TV. See? There's an example of what Mother Theresa believes. Not only that the family that prays together stays together but that it will spread beyond the home and reach others. This is what she professes constantly, that we must all be the light of Jesus to save the world."

"It all makes sense, if we are spiritually dead it reflects in the way we live and is usually for ourselves and personal gain. If we are spiritually alive and filled with the light of Jesus it will only follow that we will give of our resources and time to others."

"That's it exactly, Hank. If we all started to develop a closer relationship to Jesus, wow, the ripple affect would be mind boggling. Mother Theresa is such an example of faith. She places her trust in God completely. Often we are running low on food or medical supplies or just about anything. She just shoos us away when we come and fret about it. All she says is we are doing God's work and through His divine providence all our needs will be met just like He meets the needs of the flowers and birds in the sky.

"And sure enough Hank, the very next day and at times within the hour whatever we needed comes to the door without us even asking for it. Miracle after miracle like this happens. It's mind boggling and yet so faith building."

"Which just shows how important we are to each other by the way we choose to live." Mary finally chimed in. Both Henry and Gary turned to her almost as if they had forgotten that she was at the table.

After Mary's famous lemon meringue pie for desert and some tea, Henry decided to walk Gary home. It sort of reminded both of them walking home after school or going to a movie. As the men walked in silence, Henry was wondering in what direction his friend's life was going.

"So Gary, are you still thinking about going into the priesthood?"

"Yeah, I might. I love what I am doing now. When I first saw people laying in the gutter covered with filth and worms they seemed so repulsive. The sight and smell more than once made me throw up and yet, with prayer and developing a closer relationship with Jesus you receive the grace to love and accept anyone in any condition. Now when I see a person dying my heart just goes out to them and I want to love them in their dying moments. To make them aware of the love of Jesus and die in peace."

"That's really something, Gary. You have been given a special gift. I don't know if I could do that. It takes a special kind of person to be able to look beyond someone's physical state."

"That may be, but as you draw close to Jesus, you would be amazed at what you can do. When I get back I am going to be sent to work with lepers. It's such a horrible condition, Hank, to see entire parts of them eaten away…… But, enough of this talk of death and illness… what about you, how are you doing?"

Henry remained silent as the men turned into Gary's yard and sat on the front steps."

"I'm doing okay. I still miss Julean a lot. Things aren't the same when a mother and a wife die. I try my best but it's just not the same."

"I understand what you mean. Now that Alice has entered the Sisters of Charity Order I sure miss her too. We were like two peas in a pod for the longest time. So, has anyone else come into your life?"

"Yeah, actually a lady that came into the café and gallery while Julean was still alive has become a close friend of mine. I think she wants a closer relationship, but I'm just not ready and…" Henry's words trailed off.

As if sensing Henry's thoughts, Gary asked a question that surprised him.

"Whatever happened to Jenny, Hank? She left for Ottawa, I think it was, and for the longest time I prayed that you two would get together again. Whatever happened there?"

"Funny you should ask, I was just thinking about her as I spoke of Ivania, the lady I was just telling you about. It's the strangest thing, even though Jenny left way back in grade nine and even though I never received a letter from her or heard from her again, I could never shake her from my mind or my heart. It's like I have loved and been married to both Julean and Jenny all my life until now. Julean sensed it right from the start and amazingly accepted it."

Gary didn't answer right away. "That's really something, Hank. There must be a reason for this. Do you think Jenny is still around or married?"

"I haven't got a clue Gary. Lately however, I must say that I sense her presence more like I used to."

"What do you mean?"

"Well, this might sound a little far out, but when Jenny and I went together we believed very strongly in our guardian angels and that they would always keep us together and protect us. And whenever we were apart and looked at the first star of east at night we believed that the angel guarding that star sent out our love to each other. And I must say that lately when I look at that star I am beginning to feel that love again like I used to."

"Wow, that is far out, Hank. Maybe that's a sign you will meet up with her again. I only remember her from a couple of times when we walked to and from Balfour. She sure reminded me of Grace Kelly."

"Yeah, she was pretty alright, and yeah, maybe this star thing is some sort of sign, but yet, I do feel attracted to Ivania. I guess I'll just go along and see what happens"

"When I'm confused about something, I always turn it over to God and pray about it. I just leave it up to Him and trust that it will all turn out for the good."

"Amen, Gary. That's what Father Engelmann would say. Well, we have a big week coming up; Eddy's getting married at the nine o'clock mass, Father Engelmann's surprise at the 12 o'clock mass, and then the party afterwards. Are you going to come to Eddy's wedding?"

"No, I don't really know Eddy but it sounds like he and his bride are coming to Father Engelmann's party as well in the hall, right?"

"Yup, that's right."

With that, Henry slapped his knees and got up followed by Gary. The two men stared at one another as a soft sheen grew in both their eyes. Recalling their usual farewell greeting from long ago they each raised a hand and slapped them together into the star studded sky.

As soon as Henry and Gary left, Mary felt compelled to go to the bedroom closet and get Jenny's letter. She returned to the kitchen, set the letter on the table and made herself a cup of tea. Mary knew she had to do something. The compulsion to give it to Henry was growing stronger by the day.

She stared at the letter before her as she held the cup of tea in both hands, supported by her elbows resting on the kitchen table. The scene in her mind's eye of herself sitting there was the same as the day she had received the letter. She had sat in the same chair at that very same table gazing at this very letter when it was delivered to her. How hard she had struggled with the decision whether she should give the letter to her son then and here she was 24 years later still struggling with the same decision.

Unbelievable!

She blew over the cup's surface cooling the liquid and trying to cool the thoughts simmering through her mind. The warmth of the tea cup felt good as she hugged it in her hands, but it failed to soothe her spirit.

Almost imperceptibly she shook her head. Why didn't she think of this before? The burden of carrying the secret and of her deed was becoming too much for her to bear alone. The thought came into her mind to see Father Engelmann about this matter. She had thought to talk to him and Bill over the years, but felt they couldn't really do anything since the decision was made and she didn't want to put an unnecessary burden on them. But increasingly she felt the decision was wrong and needed to be corrected. Just looking at the letter before her, the aura of light it yielded and its warmth as if it were alive…it was almost as if it were pleading with her to do the right thing.

Yes, as soon as Father's anniversary is over she would see him and confess all.

If anyone can help me, David will.

Chapter Twenty-Eight

"HI JEN! I be here in Regina! The room is big and spacious and most elegant. It's like a small house, Jenny. There be a living room, a powder room, a huge bedroom and a toilet room almost half the size of the bedroom I had on the estate. I'm only here for three days, by the time I find my way around here, why, it be time to go home!"

Jenny was laughing so hard she hardly heard all of what Matti was saying.

"That's wonderful Matti, you need to be treated like this."

"Honestly, Jen, now this be the gospel truth, I feels like Queen Elizabeth herself. They tell me that this be the place they hang out when they come to the Regina. And same goes for prime ministers and other dignitaries. Spect people get me confused when I walk in the lobby and think I'm Ella Fitzgerald. Wouldn't that be something, Jen, someone asking for my autograph? Whooeeey!"

Jenny had to get a Kleenex and dry her eyes. She hadn't had such a good belly laugh in a long time.

"I'm so happy for you, Matti, how was your flight?"

"It be smooth as silk. This be my third time up in the air. Second time I thought the plane would break apart it was so bumpy, but today, no ma'am, the ride was perfect. When we land I be looking for Eddy and Coreena and they be nowhere to be found. Then I see a man dressed in a black suit and bow tie holding a sign with my name on it:

MATILDA

Now I wonder about this…is he looking for me? He must have had the same thought cause as soon as he seen me he come right over and ask, "Good afternoon, ma'am, would you be Matilda Belafonte?"

"That be me, I told him and then he explained that Eddy and Coreena were detained at the church and he came to get me and escort me to the hotel. Jenny, he took the suitcase out of my hand and led me to his car. Whooeeey, it be twice as big as an ordinary car, even longer than Mr. Hamilton's! The chauffeur open the door and I get in as dainty like I can with the body the good Lord gave me and sat down. Jen, I swear I never seen such a big interior in all my days. Why six more Matilda's would have easily fit in that vehicle!

"Now, here's the thing. I expect to enjoy this ride for at least an hour as is normal in Ottawa but in six or seven minutes my ride in this fine car be over. I didn't even get a chance to stretch my legs out. I wanted to tell him to go back cause I forgot something just to prolong this most enjoyable trip.

"I wondered if this be how Mr. Hamilton feels? He must ride in something like this all the time. I sure hope he don't take his vehicle for granted. Well, Jen, I done run out of steam. I be sitting for a spell just to catch my breath!"

"I'm sure you need to, Matti. This has been such a nice trip for you so far and the best is yet to come."

"I want to see my sister so bad I have to pee. This will only be the second time in twenty years I have seen my sister. Last time Eddy paid for her trip to come and see me was four years ago at Christmas. Do you remember when Eddy paid for her trip that time too?"

"Yes, I do remember meeting Coreena, such a lovely lady."

"Besides Coreena and you being my friend that's all the family I have. Most of my relatives along with Mom and Dad where killed when a hurricane struck the island."

"I'm so sorry to hear that, Matti. It must have been so lonely for you at times."

"I was until you came to the estate and after that it seemed as if family moved in. Why you made me feel so at home even though it should have been the other way around. Well now, enough about me, how you be doing Jen? I can't wait to come and see you and your new home!"

"Matti, you won't believe this, but between the work that we did last fall before winter came and this spring, both the front and backyards are almost done. It looks beautiful and the entire neighbourhood just raves about how nice it looks. The carpenters are just about finished building the gazebo in the backyard and guess what!?"

"I can't be guessing what comes into your pretty life, Jenny. Please tell me."

"Do you recall earlier this spring I asked you if you thought James would send me the Angel of Thanksgiving?" Jenny didn't wait for Matti's answer, "well, he did! I sent him a short letter requesting it towards the end of May and low and behold in mid July a mover called to inform me that they had a delivery to make. It was the Angel of Thanksgiving! It was well packed in a wooden crate and two days later I received a short note from James. It was only one sentence long but I treasure it. It said:

Marjorie,

I sent the statue you asked to be returned. Hope it arrives in one piece.

James.

"Wasn't that thoughtful of him, Matti? To actually take the time to write a note and express concern that it came safely."

"It must have broke the poor man's arm to write all those kindly words," Matti said, with a tone of sarcasm.

Jenny ignored it, however and went on excitedly, "Before the statue came while the wildflowers looked beautiful enough on their own, it was if they were as excited as I was when the statue was placed just behind them. The very next day, they turned their faces and leaned towards the angel. That very same morning I placed a handful of white and yellow daisies, bright poppies, and white foxglove in the angel's basket to thank James for relinquishing it without too much ado. I can't wait for you to see the statue and the yard and flowers, Matti."

"I be here for just three days. Later today, Eddy is having a small dinner party for all of us here at the hotel. There be me, Eddy and Coreena, Eddy's mom, some relatives and his high school friends. Tomorrow is the wedding and then right after the last church service is a party for the priest in the hall which we all be going to, too. And on Monday, we be having a lunch at Henry's café and then later in the afternoon I be flying back to Ottawa. So the only time I can come is Sunday afternoon. I will attend the anniversary party for a spell and then sneak away to your place. I have the address and everything. I should be there around three. Does that work for you, Jen?"

"Yes, that will be fine and I will prepare a special Jamaican dinner for us."

"I can't wait to taste it, Jen, and I look so forward to seeing you and your beautiful home and garden."

"Can't wait to see you either, Matti."

"HEY, HANK, HOW ya doing, man?'

"Great, Eddy. How did the rehearsal go at the church this afternoon?"

"Nothin' to it. This is the second time around. Didn't hurt one bit. Coreena wanted her sister, Matilda to stand beside her and so I asked Pete to do the same for me. The Padre went through what we had to do, when we're suppose to come up to the altar, what we're suppose to say and when it's okay for me to kiss the bride. I told him that would be the best part of the mass."

Henry laughed. Eddy, would always be, Eddy. Saying it like it is.

"That's great, Eddy, sounds like you have everything under control?"

"Yup, everything's cool, ol' buddy. Was just wondering if you could make it to the hotel for dinner with me and the gang. Would love to have you here, and if you have a lady friend she'd be more than welcome."

"Thanks Eddy, but my friend Gary is home for this anniversary event, too and he invited me over to his place for dinner. We're thinking of going to a movie later on. He's going back in another week and I guess doesn't go out much in India."

"Yeah, I think he and John came home on the same plane a week ago. Funny how things work out, Hank. Who would have thought that John would be doing missionary work and finding his way to India to work for Mother Theresa. Then again who would have thought I would end up sailing a yacht in Jamaica and end up marrying an island gal!"

"That's life, Eddy, one never knows what is just around the corner."

"You can say that again." Eddy was silent for a minute and spoke with a tone of caution in his voice, "Say, listen, Hank, ol' buddy, Pete is kinda anxious to talk to you about Jenny. I hope you don't mind. I guess he's having some real doosie dreams about what happened way back when."

"Actually Eddy, I'm looking forward to meeting Pete. I only met him briefly and not under the best of circumstances and if the truth be known, Jenny has been on my mind a lot lately as well."

"That's cool, Hank, I appreciate you saying that. Pete and the guys, including me did some foolish things back then, but we seemed to turn out okay, you know what I'm saying? And Pete especially, Hank, turned out to be one good guy. Never would have thought he'd be a preacher. But like you said, one never knows what's just around the corner."

"Amen, brother!" Henry chuckled. "Well, I'm very glad you're here, Eddy, and I am really looking forward to meeting your wife, Coreena. So, I guess we'll see you at the nine o'clock mass then. Are you going to come to the twelve o'clock one too?"

"Wouldn't miss it. I came home as much for that as for my wedding. The Padre is one cool guy, Hank. He's one rare breed who only comes along once in a life time."

"Amen, again brother. Well, we'll see you in the morning. Don't chicken out and not show up."

"Oh, I'll be there alright, it's Coreena, I'm worried about. Hope she don't change her mind, ha ha."

"See ya Eddy."

"See ya, ol', buddy."

CHAPTER TWENTY-NINE

F OR THE PAST three Sundays, Father Knuka purposefully switched masses with Father Engelmann. One Sunday, he would say the nine and ten o'clock mass and let Father do the twelve o'clock one. The next, he would say the ten and twelve o'clock Masses. That way, all the parishioners would know of the secret party for Father. They also decided to take a chance and put a small ad in the newspaper to let others who knew Father outside of the parish to come for the event as well. There wasn't much of a risk, because Father much preferred to spend what little free time he had, reading the Bible rather than the newspaper.

The parishioners were getting so excited they could hardly wait for the party. For the last few weeks, when either Henry or Mary were speaking to Father either over Sunday dinner or when they called each other, they were careful not to share with Father what they had planned, and pretended as if nothing out of the ordinary were going to happen.

Father knew that Sunday would be his 25th anniversary in the priesthood and insisted on being present at all three masses to thank the people and share his anniversary with them. He was especially eager to say the nine o'clock mass because during the celebration he would also be joining in wedlock his life long friend, Eddy Ziegler and his bride, Coreena.

Henry arrived about ten minutes before nine and made his way down the aisle towards the altar. White ribbons adhered to the side of the first two pews on either side. He spotted Eddy in the front pew to the right with his bride and entourage. Relatives and friends occupied the other pews. Henry genuflected and slid in the pew right behind Eddy and patted his shoulder.

Eddy turned to see his friend. "Hey, Hank, nice to see ya, ol' buddy." And then Eddy turned around in the pew, "I'd like you to meet the girl of my dreams, Coreena!"

Henry extended his hand to his bright smiling wife or fiancé, as

Henry wasn't sure if the first marriage ceremony on Eddy's yacht was legal or not. "I'm very pleased to meet you, Coreena"

"Pleasure be all mine, Hank. Eddy speaks almost every day about you, seems like I know all about you…kinda scary, huh?"

Henry smiled, and within the few remaining moments they chatted before Father made his entrance, Henry could see why Eddy was head over heels in love with Coreena. She was a very attractive, charming, down to earth lady with a radiant smile that revealed brilliant white teeth and twinkling eyes that could compete with any star in the sky and easily win.

Shortly into the Mass, Father asked Eddy, Coreena and their two attendants to come forward. Henry smiled as the couple made their way to the altar. Coreena was a good two heads taller than Eddy. His pompadour was still the same only higher; perhaps an attempt to reach up to Coreena in any way he could. It made Henry's heart feel good to see his friend beaming and his eyes sparkling with joy. Eddy never allowed his wealth to interfere with enjoying and having fun in life. He knew when he had more than enough and set about enjoying it.

It was easy to see that Coreena and Matilda were sisters. They had similar features, but it was obvious that Matilda enjoyed her cooking more than her younger sister.

Standing next to Eddy was Pete. Henry would never have recognized him as one of the guys who attacked him and Jenny the summer before starting high school. Funny, as much as Henry had hated those guys, strangely enough he now felt no animosity towards Bud or John, or even to Pete who claimed he was the one to have raped Jenny that night. Henry thought he should be angry and yet found himself compassionate and forgiving towards them all. He suddenly realized he was passing his fingers over one bead and other of Julean's rosary in his pocket. He wondered if Julean's spirit was helping him to accept someone he loathed in the same way he forgave John.

Thoughts of understanding entered Henry's mind that the boys were young and immature. They had been drinking that night and perhaps would not have done what they did, had they been in full command of their senses. As he turned to the other side of the aisle, he saw John, and Bud and his wife. He had come to know them and they were really nice guys. And from what Eddy had told him about Pete committing his life to God, Henry found that he would be very remiss if he did not forgive and try to heal the past with him, too.

Henry was so engrossed in his thoughts that he missed the entire marriage ceremony. He snapped out of his reverie just as Father said, "And I now pronounce you, Man and Wife. You may kiss the bride Eddy." Eddy raised himself on his tiptoes while Coreena bent down and their lips met to the standing ovation of the parishioners.

After mass Henry met all of the attendants and said he would like to chat with them more at the anniversary party in the hall and excused himself.

Henry chuckled at Father's comment that the attendance was less than usual. That Father, Henry thought, he's on the trail to discovering that something's amiss, but he still wasn't aware yet that most people were coming to the twelve o'clock service today.

He was glad that Jeremy was picking up Mom. Allison came home for Father's anniversary and was bringing Justin and Lauren. So everything was under control except for scooting across town to get Ivania.

It was almost fifteen minutes before noon when Henry and Ivania parked in the reserved space for Father Engelmann in the church lot. Fortunately Henry was one of the few who knew Father didn't own a car. Otherwise, the lot was full and so were the streets. Cars lined both sides for several blocks.

"My goodness, Hen-dry, this is quite a turnout for Father Engelmann."

"I expected a good turnout, but not this big. I'm glad the first rows on either side were reserved for the parish council members or we might have had to stand outside."

As they made their way to the church, still more people were streaming in.

When Henry and Ivania got inside he couldn't believe it. The church, which held over 700 people, was packed. Well wishers had come from all over.

As they walked into the vestibule, he was greeted by one of the senior ushers.

"Hi, Henry, I have never in all my years of ushering seen such a large attendance. If this keeps up, people will have to stand outside."

The huge vestibule was already half-full and people were still coming in.

"Yes, I never anticipated such a gathering. All we can do is leave the church doors open and turn up the volume in the back area. Does Father suspect anything, yet?"

"No, he hasn't come out of the sacristy, yet. Father Knuka said he would try to keep him busy back there and pretend he was ill if he had to."

Henry smiled at all the planning and participation of everyone involved just to see this happen.

Just before Henry and Ivania turned to go back into the vestibule, three black limousines approached the front of the church. One was the Archbishop's car, and Henry surmised the other two held the priests who had wanted to attend. Henry told the usher to keep a pathway open for the Archbishop and the other priests down the aisle. With that, Henry and Ivania made their way through the gathering crowd and walked down the long aisle to the altar. About mid-way he passed Eddy and his wife and her sister. Henry patted him on the back as he passed. Henry heard him say, "about time you showed up ol' buddy."

Henry was both excited and nervous; he could hardly contain himself. He couldn't wait for the big surprise awaiting Father, and yet it made him feel nervous coming in with Ivania in front of his family. Almost as if he were cheating on their mother. Mary was already seated in the second pew. Henry patted her on the back as he passed her and winked at Camilla and Jeremy. He nodded to his children seated next to Mary and then motioned for Ivania to go into the front pew.

"Have you ever seen anything like this?" One of the other members said to Henry as he knelt. Henry shook his head.

No sooner had Henry sat down, than the door to the sacristy opened. Four altar boys emerged followed by Father Engelmann, totally unaware of the packed church. As soon as the parishioners noticed Father, a hush swept over the church as everyone tried to hold on to the surprise and at the same time wanting to see Father's reaction to it all. Father followed the altar boys to the front of the altar. They all bowed their heads.

The altar boys then separated and stood on either side of the altar. Father walked up the two steps, made his way around the other side of the altar then faced the congregation. He still was oblivious to the packed church. Everyone held their breath waiting for him to notice.

Father opened the red book on the altar, raised both of his arms as a sign of welcome to his flock. He was about to greet all those present when he stopped and stared ever so intently down the centre aisle of the church. He looked as though he were seeing an apparition. His arms slowly lowered…sounds of shuffling and chuckles and laughter erupted here and there throughout the church. Tears filled the eyes of many parishioners as Father recognized the Archbishop and the entourage of priests walking down the aisle towards the altar.

"Jesus, Mary, und Joseph…Ach mein lieber Gott" Father said, into the microphone attached to his white vestment. Finally, Father understood what was going on. He raised his arms, again, bringing his hands to either side of his head in total shock and surprise. The ovation and roar of the congregation that followed was deafening. It was as if a dam broke as the parishioners clapped and cheered. They watched as their shepherd was hugged by the Archbishop and the priests behind the altar. There wasn't a dry eye in the church.

Father was then led to a chair beside the lectern, where normally the Archbishop would sit. But, today, Father Engelmann was being honoured. He would sit and watch as the Archbishop performed mass celebrating his 25 years as a priest. Father sat down, his eyes filled with tears. He shook his head as he looked at the Archbishop and then to his flock, his expression carrying unmistakable heartfelt gratitude to all those present.

After several more minutes of cheering and clapping, the congregation settled down and Archbishop O'Neil began mass. Instead of a homily after the gospels were read, first the Archbishop and then priests who were friends of Father Engelmann, spoke of their relationship with him. Although some reference to scriptures were made, reference was made in such a way as to recognize the saintliness of Father and at the same time roast him in a tender loving way. In the end it was a fervent outpouring of love for a man who had tirelessly given and continued to give his life to his Lord and serve his fellow man.

Following the presentations by the Archbishop and all of the priests who had spoken, Father Engelmann stepped up to the lectern. He was so emotional that he could hardly speak. Many of the parishioners cried loudly in empathy. When he finally did regain some composure, his voice trembled and threatened to break.

"Thank you…" Father nodded, struggling for control. "From the bottom of my heart … thank you." He turned to Archbishop O'Neil and shook his head. "When I saw you and my brothers in Christ coming down the aisle I thought I had died and gone to heaven."

The Archbishop's laughter was instantly extended as the parishioners joined in and clapping swept throughout the church. Gazing at Father Knuka he raised his hand and shook his finger at him. "How well you pretended to be sick so I would say the mass…that was performed with such skill I was ready to call for an ambulance. My, my what a pleasant surprise."

Laughter erupted again as Father Knuka held his stomach and feigned to be ill again.

Turning to the congregation Father Engelmann raised both arms and continued, "And you, my brothers and sisters in Christ, have made my life complete. The Lord has blessed me richly with so many friends. When my Anna went to be with the Lord, I thought for sure I could not live without her, but then so many of you in the neighbourhood came to my rescue with your love and support and helped me fill my days. And then the Archbishop allowing me to enter the priesthood and being assigned to St. Mary's Church was such a blessing that at that time, too, I thought I had died and gone to heaven."

Laughter and clapping once again swept amongst the congregation.

"You are my family and I love you all. Everyday I thank the Lord for the privilege of being allowed to serve you."

Tears gathered in Father's eyes and once again he found it hard to go on. He tried to speak more, but words had left him. The parishioners stood and clapped enthusiastically as Father returned to his seat. The air was charged with love to overflowing.

After communion, Margaret Tearhorst sang a solo in Father's honour, his favourite song, 'Amazing Grace.'

She stood just to the side of the altar and as she sang there wasn't another sound in the church, just a melody of purity, like a pristine stream of flowing spring water. The words were sung so softly, with such serenity and velvetiness, they were as though precious pebbles, smoothed and polished by years of rolling in the gentle ripples of a stream's melody. And, when the last word of the song flowed out of Margaret's quivering vocal chords, a silence filled with God's wonder, spread throughout the church. A silence so utterly quiet and still, that had a pin dropped at that moment, it would have made a thunderous echo. The congregation was caught in the spell of God's creation...how a human being could possess such an incredible voice.

It was some time before the Archbishop dared stand and continue with mass. Every and any sound which followed Margaret's singing would desecrate the lingering memory.

After almost two hours of worship, talk, and sweet singing, the organ fired up and sounded out the 'Battle Hymn of the Republic' and 'O When the Saints Go Marching In,' so apt and true of Father Engelmann.

There sure was a lot of hooting and singing and clapping and dancing, and Henry thought for certain that the roof of the church would lift off.

CHAPTER THIRTY

WHEN THEY GOT to the hall there was another surprise. The hall was decorated with streamers and balloons. On the far back wall hung huge block letters:

HAPPY 25TH ANNIVERSARY FATHER ENGELMANN

Pictures of Father being ordained, of his wife Anna, of Confirmation, Baptisms, births, weddings, funerals and snapshots of his visits to the many families of the church taken over the years adorned the walls.

Members from other churches and denominations were there, too. Father had worked hard to break down walls of indifference between the Protestant and Catholic faith. Father was a firm believer in bringing together all of God's children.

Off to the right, Henry saw John McBryne approach Gary. John was always easy to spot as he towered two heads over most people. Gary's head buried in John's chest as the two embraced. Henry marvelled how a man he hated so much had turned out to be a friend, and how through his dear wife's death came such good. Who would have thought a man so immersed in drugs and a life so filled with turmoil and problems could have such a dramatic turnaround and end up serving God like Gary!

But perhaps his biggest enjoyment was seeing the many professional people there who had helped Father Engelmann in some way or other over the years. One of those was Johnny Balfour, the young lawyer who so skilfully handled the sale of his store. His hair was no longer black and slick, but grey mixed with pure white hair.

"And so, Father, what investments did you make with the money you got from the sale of your store? At that time $75,000 was a lot of money. With the brokers we had represent you, you could easily have turned that into well over a million over the years and perhaps more."

"Well, Mr. Balfour, I made two investments; I gave Henry $10,000 to go to university and the rest I invested in the poor. Every year the Lord pays me a huge dividend. I know I will never leave this earth broke."

They all laughed. To look around and see all of the people who so loved and revered him, one couldn't deny that Father Engelmann was truly the wealthiest man of all of them there.

As Henry watched Johnny Balfour and Father Engelmann discuss the immigrant families in the east end, Henry couldn't help but think about the contrast between how each lived their lives. Johnny spent much of his time striving for money, power, status, prestige and acceptance from man. Father, on the other hand, was free of all attachments. He gave away all of his money and strove daily for humility and acceptance from God. His only goal was to serve his Master and his fellow man. Two different value systems. Two totally different commitments to life.

Henry knew only too well that he had been struggling with that issue for years and was still no further ahead. It was at times like this when he was around Father Engelmann and bathed in his love and acceptance that he reassessed his own direction in life.

The clock is ticking down on your life mission so don't delay another day.

"That was a wonderful service, Hen-dry, it touched me so much. I think my mascara ran."

Henry looked at his attractive date and raised his hand to her left eye and wiped away a little black run.

"It's okay, Ivania, I teared up a bit myself." He put his arm around her and pulled her in. He liked this side of Ivania as opposed to her cool, intellectual business stature.

Just then, Henry felt a sharp slap on his shoulder, jostling him off balance and snapping him out of thoughts. He turned to see the grinning face of Eddy Zeigler and his radiant bride, Coreena.

"Hey, Hank, ol' buddy, gimme five."

Henry stepped back enough to slap Eddy's hand and then embraced his friend in a tight hug.

"Eddy, it's so good to see you and I couldn't be happier for you and Coreena." Henry turned to Ivania and then introduced her to Eddy and his wife.

"I'm pleased to meet you and congratulations! I understand you got married this morning."

"Yeah, me and the little one tied the knot," quipped Eddy as he turned to Coreena, his nose brushing her well-endowed bosoms.

"It's so nice to meet you too, Ivania. I sure enjoyed the surprise for Father at the twelve o'clock mass. It's so nice for him to be so loved by his parishioners."

"Yes, I was just saying to Hen-dry, it's not often something brings me to tears, but this morning's mass was very touching."

"So, when are the two of you tying the knot?" Eddy quipped again, but with a more serious tone. Henry kinda looked at Ivania and was going to reply when Eddy pushed the matter even further.

"You can take your honeymoon in Jamaica, I'll show you how to sail, you can eat free at Coreena's restaurant, best food on the island, and I know just the most romantic spot."

Henry was turning red, not sure how to reply and as usual Ivania knew just what to say both to Eddy and to Henry.

"That sounds wonderful, Eddy. As soon as Henry and I get over the memories of the previous loves in our lives we will surely take you up on your exciting offer!"

Father Engelmann came over and hugged Henry and Ivania, then did the same to Eddy and his wife.

"That was some surprise, Henry! I thought for sure my heart would jump out of my chest. And to keep it secret from me for over a month is wonderful. Not too much slips by me, maybe it is time to retire."

"I don't want to hear that, Father, we need you as long as you will put up with us."

"And you Eddy, how wonderful it is for you to come not only to be married in the church, but to come to this party."

"As soon as ma wrote and told me of the anniversary party, I thought I would have to pay my respects to the man who sold me smokes stunting my growth!"

Father poked at Eddy, "Do you still smoke Black Cat?"

"Na, I don't think they make them anymore, I switched to Export A a few years back and I'm still on them."

"I'm trying to get him to quit," chimed in Coreena.

"She just might be able to. She's a pretty persuasive gal." Eddy looked up at his beautiful bride and winked.

"Hey, Jeremy, come-on over. I want you to meet someone."

Jeremy and Camilla made their way through the crowd and stood next to Father. "Eddy and Coreena, I would like you to meet my son, Jeremy and his wife, Camilla." And then turning back to the newly wed couple said, "Father just married them this morning at the nine o'clock mass."

"That's great, congratulations!" Jeremy and Camilla almost said in unison.

Eddy gazed perhaps a little longer than he should have at Camilla. A memory of long ago twigged at his memory. It was like seeing a ghost in his past. Camilla felt his stare and grew uncomfortable. Eddy reached for his cigarettes.

"Oh, Eddy, I don't think it be best to smoke in here, it's already getting stuffy," said Coreena.

"Yeah, you're right." Then turning back to Camilla, Eddy continued, "Sorry for staring, Camilla, it's just that you seem to remind me of someone long ago…"

Camilla looked at Henry and back to Eddy. "Yes, I seem to do that to a lot of people. I must have a double or twin out there!"

"So, what is it like working for your Pop?" Eddy asked Jeremy.

As Jeremy proceeded to tell Eddy, Camilla was no longer listening to her husband as she felt the stare of another man just ten feet away.

She turned to him abruptly catching him off guard. A strange eerie feeling swept through her. She felt it surge throughout her body. Neither she, nor he, could turn away as if locked into each other's gaze. It was not the kind of look that Camilla frequently felt of men wanting to flirt with her. This stare carried something powerful; something that touched her to the core of her being.

"Honey, Coreena asked you a question…"

"Oh…oh, I'm sorry, my mind drifted for a second, I'm so sorry, Coreena. What was that you asked?"

"Oh, don't you worry none about that, Camilla, my mind be driftin' all the time. What I asked if you be a stay at home Mom or do you do some outside work…?"

"I think you be staring at the same lady I was, Peter…good Lord, you look as if you be seeing a ghost or someting."

"Yes, Matilda, that young lady next to Father looks so familiar—"

"I was just thinking the same thing…I wonder what that lady's name be? I just have to know."

Matti turned to a nearby parishioner and asked, "Excuse me, but do you know who that blonde girl be standing with Father Engelmann?"

"Yes, that's Henry's daughter-in-law, Camilla and beside her is of course, her husband, Jeremy and you must know Henry. Everybody knows him…"

"Did you say her name is, Camilla?" interjected Peter, the blood draining from his face.

"Yes, Camilla Pederson…"

"My sweet Lord, my Mistress be in for one huge surprise when I tells her who I did see…my, my, my…she be as pretty as an angel!"

"Why don't you go over and talk to Henry, and ask if she is the one, Peter?" said his wife Angie.

"Yes, I am certain she is the one I keep dreaming about and her name…"

"Did you say you be dreaming of that heavenly thing?"

Peter stared at Matti for a long moment and nodded, his eyes reddening.

Just then, the loudspeaker came on, "Attention everybody, we have some announcements to make, some speeches to give and gifts to present to Father Engelmann. Would Father please come up to the stage? And I can't seem to see where Wilma is…if you could come up at this time as well."

Matilda checked her watch, "Oh, good Lord, it's past 3 o'clock, I best be going. I have a friend I just have to see. It was so nice meeting you Peter and you Angie."

"It was a pleasure meeting and chatting with you, too, Matilda."

"I must say I am glad to know you be a preacher man. Just from the short time I talk with you last night and today, I feel you have a good heart."

"Why thank you, Matilda."

Matilda shook both of their hands and worked her way to the door looking for a telephone to call a taxi to take her to Jenny's new home.

HENRY LEANED TOWARDS Ivania who was listening to the master of ceremonies on stage and whispered, "I need to go to the washroom, I'll be back in a few minutes."

Ivania, nodded and turned back to the stage. Father was just climbing the steps…

As HENRY MADE his way through the crowd someone grabbed his arm.

"Hi Hank, I'm Pete, I met you this morning at the wedding ceremony."

"Yeah, sure, Eddy's best man."

Henry extended his hand and the two men shook hands for the second time that day.

Pete turned to his wife, Angie, "Would you excuse us, I need to talk to Hank about something?"

"Yes, you go right ahead."

"I was just heading to the washroom, let's head back there, I think it will be a little quieter too."

When they got to the back of the hall, Henry turned to Pete and said, "I think I know what you want to talk to me about. Eddy was telling me that you have some dreams of that night when Jenny and me met up with you guys coming home from a show."

"Yeah, that's right, Hank. But first I want to apologize from the bottom of my heart for what me and the guys did that night. I am so ashamed of myself and believe me, I know feeling guilty can't make up for what I did, but I have suffered almost everyday since then. So first, before we even begin to talk, I need to ask for your forgiveness."

Wearing his heart on his shirt sleeve, as usual and the sincerity in which Peter asked for pardon touched Henry. His eyes watered up as he nodded his head. Henry extended his hand and the men for the third time shook hands.

"You know, Hank, I couldn't keep my eyes off your daughter-in-law. I'd swear she is the girl in my dreams. I don't recall everything that happened that night. We were all pretty well inebriated, but I keep having the feeling that I fathered a child with Jenny that night. It didn't seem like I had time, yet the feeling I have is so overwhelming that it must have happened. Anyway, Camilla looks just like the girl that Jenny in my dreams gives birth to. She is younger in my dreams, but it is the same girl, I swear."

"I came to the same conclusion, Pete. When Jenny moved away two weeks after school started that summer or rather fall, I wrote a ton of letters to her, but never heard from her again. I too always felt that Jenny got pregnant that night. In fact, I had a stomach ache almost every morning until the spring of the following year when one morning I ran to the washroom at school and threw up. After that it went away. And when I do my calculations from the night that we came across you guys to that spring was around nine months. The weird thing is, Camilla was born that same spring, May 24, 1957. So, you can see why I have the same feeling about Camilla."

"My God, Hank, then she is the one! She's Jenny's daughter! Did you confront her about it?"

"That's the thing, Pete. She is not Jenny's daughter. I met her real parents when Camilla married my son, Jeremy. Even though I know that, I still can't get over how much she looks like Jenny; the blue eyes, oval face, blonde hair and even her personality is exactly like Jenny's."

"What do her parents look like?" Pete wanted to know.

"Here's where this whole thing gets very weird. Camilla's parents don't look at all like her. It looks like she came from a different family! I shake my head every time I look at her and imagine her parents. It seems impossible, but what can you say? Camilla claims that Stan and Valerie Breckhart are her parents."

"But Hank, there must be some mistake, she has to be."

Henry just shook his head and shrugged his shoulders, "I'm afraid not, Pete."

"Well, would you know where I could find Jenny? I so much want to apologize to her as well for that night. Please Hank, if you know, tell me."

Once again Henry shook his head from side to side, "Honest, Peter, I don't have a clue where she is."

Pete turned towards the crowd with searching eyes. Henry followed his gaze and wouldn't you know it almost at the same time the men's stare fell on Camilla *she in turn was staring back at them.*

CHAPTER THIRTY-ONE

As the taxi slowed looking for the correct address, Matilda knew immediately which was Jenny's house. Oh my good Lord, would Thomas love to see this!"

Matilda wasn't a gardener, but over the years Thomas had named the flowers he planted and the reason for their location so many times that she could name almost any flower. What Matilda saw before her was the skill and vision of a landscape artist that knew what flowers to place where and when and in order according to the size they grew. Not one flower was hidden from view by another. The design was masterful and Matilda knew in her heart the angel that touched the yard with her magic wand was Jenny. Jenny's love of nature was written all over the yard. She had learned from Thomas, the best there was, and she learned the trade so well that she may very well have surpassed her master.

"That's the house there, ma'am. The one with the beautiful flowers," said the taxi driver.

"I spect it was as soon as I saw it half a block away. Now ain't that something!"

"It sure is, ma'am."

Matti paid the cab driver and stepped onto the sidewalk. The curved paving stone walkway lined with dusty millers and chamomile leading to the elegant bungalow was very inviting. The house was so elegant and quaint it reminded Matti of a fairyland home. She loved the steep roof and the way it curved when it came down to the eaves. The separate stone walled entrance was rustic with its curved top entrance door. And the stone chimney on the end of the house partially hidden by towering fir trees must have such a beautiful fireplace inside. Matti could hardly wait to see the interior and how Jenny's beautiful antiques were situated and arranged. She could only imagine it would all be so beautiful. Goosebumps raced up and down her spine just thinking of it.

But the landscaping was what took her breath away! The combination of herbs, plants and flowers sent up clouds of scent filling the air with an intoxicating aroma. Matti's senses could hardly take it all in!

She loved how the two huge pyramidal cedars stood like sentinels on either side of the front entrance and how the front of the house was hugged with globe cedars and different species of juniper that grew at different heights and yielded different shades of green. And there was more! Wrapping around the house and lining the sides were more junipers along with elders, dogwoods, lilacs and spirea for colour and variety.

It was the perennials against the backdrop of greens in front of the house that overtook Matti. A dazzling mixture of irises with their sword-shaped leaves and showy flowers intermingled with the peonies and hydrangeas. Beautiful clusters of white, pink and blue flowers, danced beside the large showy red and yellow peonies, each trying to outdo the other for attention.

And if that wasn't all enough, further interspersed were tiger lilies and spikes. Matti marvelled at all the different colours, heights, and complimentary arrangements!

"Why it be like a musical scale keeping the eye singing and dancing endlessly along." Matti blurted with amazement. The floral landscape exhibited the skills of a highly trained professional, yet Matti knew that her Jenny did this out of sheer instinct and her love of gardening.

Jenny came to the front entrance and saw Matti standing there in awe. She ran out to her friend and hugged her, "Oh Matti it's so good to see you! I couldn't wait for you to get here."

"And I couldn't wait either Jenny. Oh my, your home is so beautiful and the landscaping be taking my breath away! If Thomas was standing here, Jen, he would marvel at this incredible display of God's creation as if they be singing songs of praise. Why he would say, 'Miss Jenny, the trees, cedars, and flowers all grow and meld together like a magnificent orchestra, each species complementing and enhancing the other yielding a spectacular performance of visual and auditory beauty.'"

"Why Matti, that's beautiful what you just said."

"I hear brother Thomas say that many times when he look at the beauty of God's creation at the estate. The good Lord, help me to remember them beautiful words for this very occasion, Jen."

"Oh Matti, you're wonderful. Come, let's go inside."

Jen took Matti by the hand and led her inside. The interior was even more beautiful than Matti had imagined. Words failed to come to her mind to describe the exquisiteness of it all. Matti just shook her head, tears filling her eyes.

"This be the closest to heaven I been in a long while, Jenny. It's just all so beautiful and elegant."

"Can I get you something to drink, Matti? And I can hardly wait to hear how your sister's wedding went and …"

"Oh, Jen, the wedding went fine, but you best sit down as I have some wonderful news to tell you."

Jenny couldn't wait to sit, her eyes pleading with Matti to tell her the news and hoped it would be about Henry and her daughter, Camilla.

"Jen, the moment I see this blonde haired, blue eyed young lady, I knows right then it be your Camilla. At first I thought it be you at the party. She be the spittin' image of you, Jen. I couldn't believe my eyes. I was mesmerized and couldn't keep my eyes off her. Her smile, her twinkling eyes and expression be the same as yours. It be like she was raised by you all her life!"

Tears filled Jenny's eyes, emotion sweeping through her at lightening speed. She couldn't speak and hoped Matti would continue.

"And that man of hers is such a handsome tall young man. The two could pass for just stepping out of the movies, if you know what I mean. And the way they looked at each other every now and then, why I could tell how much they loved each other. She be one happy woman, Jen. I could tell that for sure."

Matti reached over to Jen, and took her hand. "I'd find a way to break the news to her, Jen. She be your daughter no doubt about it. You could be enjoying such a fine relationship with that pretty young thing and her man."

Jenny nodded in agreement and then she dared to ask, "Did you see Henry, Matti?"

"Yes, I did. He be one handsome man, too, Jen. His shinny head showing through some grey hair and his beard turning a bit white. He look distinguished that for sure."

"And, and…did you see his wife?' Jenny wanted to know and yet held her breath…

"Yes, she be standing beside her man, Jen. The two of them make a fine couple, too. She look to be younger than him, but she be an attractive lady. The two of them stood next to Camilla and her husband."

"Did you talk to him and his wife?" Jenny wanted to know.

"No, I just met him at the wedding ceremony in the morning. Just shook his hand as he went down the line. I wanted to talk to him at the party after church today, but it was too crowded and people coming up to him all the time."

"Oh Matti, this makes it all so difficult. How can I come into their family knowing of the past relationship I had with Henry?"

"I know you still love the man, Jen, and that make it difficult, that for sure. But like you said before, perhaps talk all of this over with the social worker. I'm sure she be helping you some."

Jenny took out a tissue from her sweater pocket and wiped her eyes. "Yes, I'm sure Miss Blake will help me figure something out. Come, Matti, let me show you the backyard and then I'll start dinner and we can chat some more."

Jenny took Matti's hand and led her to the back patio doors.

The two ladies had no sooner stepped onto the elevated cedar deck than Matti started to ooh and aah once more.

"This be like stepping into paradise. I can't believe it could be any more beautiful."

"The gazebo at the back is almost finished. I had the carpenters build it in the far corner so the sunshine coming through the high fir trees later in the day falls on the gazebo."

"It's doing exactly that right now. The sun is resting on the swing just like it did at the estate. I can just see you sitting there, Jen, as radiant and pretty as ever. And I like the high fence covered with the different flowering vines. The morning glory and rose are my favourites, too. Oh, Jen it's all so beautiful."

Matti and Jenny stepped off the deck in unison onto the paving stone path leading all the way back to the gazebo. As they strolled along, Matti could see that the same love and attention to detail was exhibited in the backyard as was in the front.

Soft rolling mounds of earth filled the yard on the west side of the walk. Different sized rocks were strategically placed and then interspersed with herbs, perennials of different heights, and roses to form an ever-changing tapestry of fragrance, colour and texture.

On the east side, Jenny saved a small area of lawn halfway to the gazebo for a pair of iron chairs with matching round table where she could sit and view her organic festival and perhaps visit with a friend. Surrounding that island of green was a woodland of shrubbery, lilac and other flowering trees, which accentuated the area with a cozy feeling of privacy.

But even here the eye had to wander down to the base of the trees to the profusion of foreground flowers. Candytuft, golden alyssum, heather, thyme, coral-bells, crested iris and violas sang for attention as they bordered the lawn.

"Oh, Jenny, it be like strolling through a sea of dazzling colour, with wave after dizzying wave of intoxicating natural fragrance. I soon gets drunk!"

The girls laughed. Jen wrapped her arm around Matti and continued their walk.

When they reached the backyard Matti stopped and held her breath. It was the meadow of wildflowers surrounding the Angel of Thanksgiving that touched Matti's heart. It was even more beautiful than on the estate. Matti could clearly see how the freedom, disorderly and ever-changing tapestry of these woodland delights sang a constant song of peace to Jenny's spirit.

"Jen, I be so happy for you. And I have to say, it was good of Mr. Hamilton to send you the Angel of Thanksgiving. Just look at it. The angel almost seems to be smiling, it so happy to be here!"

AFTER A LOVELY candlelight dinner in the living room and telling Jenny once again about the day, Jenny out of curiosity asked. "So what were Eddy's friends like, Matti?"

"They all be fine gentleman as far as I could make out, Jen. Seems to me they be friends for as long as they can remember. The one I spoke to the most was Pete. He be a preacher man living in Calgary. He's a fine man and has a good wife that stands beside him. You know, come to think of it, he be as interested as I was to know who the blonde-haired blued-eyed girl was. When someone told us that was Henry's daughter-in-law, Pete looked real surprised almost as if he be knowing who she was. And come to think of it, Jen, his wife suggested he talk to Henry about Camilla and then he said something real strange…"

"What did he say, Matti?"

"He say that he dreams of her all the time…it's just the way he say though, his eyes were filling with tears and seemed to be troubled over it. I wanted to talk to him about it but then the speeches started and I wanted to get here and so I said goodbye and left. He be connected to that girl somehow, Jen, I just know it."

Pete, the name triggered a far off memory. She was sure that was the boy who took her to the park. She had so many nightmares of that evening. Flashbacks of that night momentarily ricocheted through her mind, "Let's take her to the park, John. Move over, Bud. Come-on Pete help me get her into the car…no, no, please…"

"You be okay, Jen? You look as if you be seeing a ghost or something."

Jenny shook her head. She didn't want to change Matti's opinion of

Eddy's friends and she wasn't a hundred percent sure it was really them."

"I'm fine, Matti. What did you say the names of Eddy's friends were beside, Pete?"

"There be Bud and John. Now that John be one tall man. It's like looking up an oak tree. Tall and thin. They all seem like fine men as I said before. I spent most of the time talking with Peter. I enjoyed the company of him and his wife very much."

Those were the names of the very boys that took her to the park that night, Jen was positive. Perhaps, it was Peter who fathered Camilla… maybe his heart is searching for his little girl as well.

An eerier feeling crept down her spine.

"So, what's up for tomorrow, Matti?"

"Well, Eddy be taking us all out to dinner at Henry's café. I think I told you about that. Only thing my plane be flying to Ottawa at 3:30 and the lunch be at 1:30 which doesn't give me much time. So, I plan to go over earlier and take it all in. The airport is not that big and so if I be there 30 minutes before it take off I'm sure they won't be leaving without me if they know what's good for them."

Jenny chuckled. "Yes, if you get there before 3:00 I'm sure you'll still get on, but I wouldn't leave it much later."

"Well, Jen, I sure be happy for you with your beautiful home, yard and all. And you say you making friends and fitting into the community some?"

"Yes, it's been all so hectic, but yes, I am fitting in and making new friends. I must slow down on the volunteer work I'm doing though and get rested. I'm feeling exhausted."

"Yes, you be taking it easy, you sure done a heap of work in the last few months."

After a delicious dessert of white cheesecake covered with fresh strawberries, Jenny drove Matti back to the hotel. Jenny got out of the car along with Matti and made her way over to her beloved friend.

"Oh, Matti, it was so nice to see you, I wish we lived closer."

"Yes, that be my thoughts too, Jen. Now you figure a way to get back to that daughter of yours as soon as you can.'

Jenny nodded, tears already filling her eyes. She stepped forward and the two girls embraced for the longest time.

"I love you, Jen and I be so happy for you and all the good things coming your way. May the sweet Jesus fill your heart with peace and love."

"I love you too, Matti and phone me as soon as you get home."

"I be doing that very thing first thing tomorrow night."

CHAPTER THIRTY-TWO

LESS ME FATHER for I have sinned. Although I have been to confession many times over the years, there is one deed that I have never confessed. It's been a sin that was planted in my heart in August of 1962 and has grown to the point that I can no longer hide its tentacles. The good Lord has planted in our hearts the need to bring to light things that need healing…I now realize that it is the only way I shall find peace.

"Father, I know you know who this is. It is me Mary."

"Yes, Mary, please share with me and the Lord what troubles you so deeply? I feel your sorrow and my heart reaches out to you…"

"So many times, David, I have wanted to share this with you or Bill, but the situation seemed so hopeless and needless. What could either of you do? It would just cause more trouble and turmoil and worry and to what end? The heartbreak for all concerned would have been too great and so I kept it to myself. But now the guilt of my deed surfaces daily and in my sleep. I can no longer carry this secret any longer…Oh Father…"

Mary began to cry.

Slowly, as Mary's weeping subsided and Father sensed her composure restoring he gently went on. "Share with me the burden you have carried alone for so long, Mary. What is it that lies so deep and heavy in your heart?"

"Father, just before Henry married Julean in 1962, a special delivery letter came to our doorstep for Henry. It was from Jenny. After all those years, David, the letter Henry had ached for since his teenage girlfriend left Regina in 1956 came." Mary's voice caught…

"But…but, David, Henry was to marry Julean in less than 2 weeks. I was so torn. I didn't know what to do…Oh David…" was all Mary could say as once more she broke down.

Father Engelmann wanted to go out and console his dearest friend, but there were others waiting to go to confession. Mary's confession stabbed at his heart too. He knew all through high school of Henry's heartbreak and how he longed for a letter from Jenny. It would have been like receiving a gift from God Himself. Father could still see in his mind's eye the sadness in the boy's eyes for days, months and years. And the box of letters they had sent and how Henry longed for an answer to his multitude of letters. The most incredible and unfortunate thing of all this was that Henry never got over it. His heart continued to long for his loved one not only at the time but over the years into his married life, and even until today!

Father shook his head in the darkness of the booth. So often in this confessional he had heard this same or similar matter come up time and again. He recalled that day when Julean wanted to know Jenny's address and how adamant she was to find Henry's former sweetheart and her willingness to even share Henry with his first love. And how Henry as well not only in the confessional, but over the years struggled with his feelings for Jenny. And now, Mary! It's incredible that she too was involved with this struggle, he thought. I feel her guilt and upset so deeply.

Mary broke into Father's thoughts, "I thought for sure when he and Julean married that his heart had mended, but it didn't, David. Even she knew, that with all her love, it could not appease the ache that Henry held so dear and steadfastly in his heart for his Jenny."

"Yes, I see your dilemma, Mary. Jenny did respond, but at a time that would have caused a great upheaval…the decision was so great …"

"Yes, but what made the decision even greater was that Jenny had not written it at that time or even a few weeks or a month or two prior to sending it…it was a letter she had sent back in 1956, just before Christmas! I could not believe the date the envelope was stamped! How could a letter after all those years suddenly be mailed? How did I know that Jenny still felt the same about Henry six years after she had written this letter? It was all so mysterious how it just arrived at our doorstep out of the blue like that. And the timing couldn't have been worse…my only consolation was a pact I made with Jenny's mother to destroy the letter."

"What do you mean a pact…and with Jenny's mother!?"

"Yes, that very same day the letter was delivered by a postman to our door, I received a call that same afternoon from Mrs Sarsky!"

"Incredibly, she too had received a letter for Jenny from Henry that same day. She too was struggling whether she should give Jenny the letter as she was getting married as well. When I told Mrs. Sarsky it was all too late now that Henry was getting married in ten days, Mrs. Sarsky felt relieved and we both decided to make a pact not to reveal the letters to our children.

"Oh, Father, how that decision has haunted me. Although we had agreed to destroy the letters I could not do it. I still have the letter in my hope chest in the closet."

Mary paused… "The letter seems to beckon me to give it to Henry. It emits such a strange warm light, David, as if it has life…I don't know what to do. Jenny is married and probably has a family, and now Henry is once again moving on with his life with, Ivania…can you see the dilemma I face, David?"

"Das ist unglaublich…unbelievable…" muttered Father. He was speechless. He was amazed over this entire matter and how it has involved so many lives. And the light Mary speaks of surrounding the letter…what could that possible be? Is it supernatural and of what origin?

Life with its entanglements and twists and turns.

Ach, miene leiber Gott!

"Mary, I can understand your dilemma. I have noticed Henry, for the first time, coming out of his despair now that Ivania has come into his life. It would complicate things and perhaps throw his life into a spin of regret of what could have been. Yet, it has always been my philosophy to be open and truthful in our relationships. It is as you said, Mary, *the heart and soul yearn for truth and light. Yes, our Maker has built this into us.* That's why we have these feelings and a conscience that tells us to do the right thing. I know how difficult this will be, but Henry is a compassionate, sensible young man and will understand the reasons for your decision. This has gone on for far too long, trust in the Lord and don't lean upon your understanding. Remember, *God turns all things into good for those that trust Him.*"

Mary felt a warm peace as she left the confessional.

When she got home, Mary went directly to her bedroom and opened up the chest which was still on the dresser from the other day. She knew what she had to do. Mary retrieved the letter from the chest and laid it on the dresser. She picked up the picture of St. Therese on her dresser and turned it over. On the back was the Novena she said to St Therese so many times before, but this time the prayer would be different.

Mary looked up and saw her reflection in the mirror and began to recite the prayer. She still had it memorized so the words came back to her effortlessly…

"St. Therese, the little flower, please pick me a rose from the heavenly garden and send it to me with a message of love. Ask God to grant me the favour, I thee implore, and tell Him I will love Him each day more and more."

Dear St. Therese, help me in my prayer request to correct the wrong. Help me to tell Henry the truth, the whole truth and nothing but the truth, so help me God and that Henry receive this truth with understanding and is forgiving of me."

Mary had just begun to say the five Our Father's as part of the Novena when she could barely believe the transformation in the mirror before her. The look of guilt and shame she saw in her eyes for so many years dissolved before her. Her eyes cleared and whitened as a redemptive peace emanated from deep within. The lilac fragrance emanating from the letter sweetened the air and soothed Mary as she returned to the kitchen and placed the letter on the table.

After making a cup of tea she sat down as if to relive the day the letter had arrived. This is where the decision was made to the day and now this is where the decision to end this matter once and for all will also be made.

Mary sipped her tea and thought about the contents of the letter. She recalled the events leading up to her knowledge of weighted object inside. Shortly after Bill died, Henry came for a visit and found her in the bedroom putting Bill's death certificate inside the treasure chest. The chest was open and she had removed Jenny's letter at that time and placed it on the dresser. It made her so nervous when he picked it up and held the letter in his hand. Mary knew he felt Jenny's love by the expression on his face. But she snatched it away before he was certain and that is when the object flew inside and a tiny part of it pierced the end of the envelope as if to go to Henry. She saw the metal catch the bedroom light and Henry did too, but Mary shooed him off to the kitchen.

That would have been the time to give it to him and this entire matter would be over with. But no matter, soon it will be.

It was well over a year later when she was going through the chest again that she noticed the glint of a tiny silver metal protruding from the envelope. It not only caught her attention, but this time also her curiosity. She pulled out the metal object from its paper chamber and was so surprised to see a pewter angel with a beautiful inscription on the bottom, "Watch over my beloved."

"Yes," Mary said as she returned to the present moment, this is truly an angelic letter with its own destiny in mind. Mary could almost see the metal wings fluttering inside trying to deliver its heartfelt letter to its loved one.

Mary gazed at the letter. She noted the bobby pin she had slipped over the opening that was made when she retrieved the angel from the envelope. She wondered if she should tape the slit shut, but thought the bobby pin looked secure and decided to leave it.

Mary got up, picked up the envelope and before any doubt could enter her mind she picked up the phone and called the gallery.

"Pederson Art Gallery."

"Hi Henry, I'm glad you answered the phone."

"Hi, Mom. It's nice to hear from you! What's up?"

"I thought I'd call and invite you over for lunch next Tuesday or Wednesday. The garden vegetables are just about all ready to harvest and I know how much you like borscht soup. Are you free one of those days?"

Henry checked the calendar, "Yeah, Wednesday will work fine, Mom."

"Good." And to make sure she would follow through, she committed herself, "There is something I want to show you and give to you that I should have a long time ago."

"Oh? What is that, Mom? What do you have for me?"

Mary looked at the glowing letter long and hard and then placed it in her apron pocket. She could feel the warmth of the love in the letter instantly against her thigh.

"It will wait till then, but you remember the borscht I made for you before you and Julean got married?"

"I'll never forget the borscht that day, Mom, it was something else."

"Well, I want you to know, Henry, when you come next Wednesday, you will taste the best borscht you have ever eaten. Even better than that day. I want it to be a reminder of how much I love you, son!"

Henry was taken back by the fervour in his mom's voice…

"I can hardly wait, Mom, and I love you with my whole heart, too!"

Mary beamed as she hung up the phone. A peace that swept through her now made her feel so light she thought she would fly any moment just like the pewter angel inside the pink envelope.

Suddenly the door bell rang. As she made her way to the front door she saw her neighbour standing just outside the screen door.

"Well, good morning, Rose, it's so nice to see you."

"Hi Mary, My husband, Tom, sent me a dozen roses this morning as it's our twelfth anniversary today!"

"Congratulations, Rose, and what a beautiful gift from Tom."

"Yes, since we got married he has sent me a rose or roses for the number of years we have been married. He always says a rose for my Rose. Sweet, huh?'

"Yes, it is Rose, very thoughtful, indeed."

"When I opened the bouquet the florist delivered I noticed they had sent an extra white rose. I noticed it immediately because it was amongst the other red roses. I counted them and sure enough it was an extra one beside the twelve that were there. Immediately a thought came to me that I should bring it to you. So here it is? Are you celebrating some kind of anniversary today too?"

Tears surfaced instantly in Mary's eyes as she held the beautiful white rose. She recalled how the Novena to St Therese got started was when a Jesuit prayed to the saint to grant him a favour. He also prayed that she send him a freshly plucked rose as a sign that his prayer had been heard. On the third day of the Novena someone sought the priest out and presented him with the rose.

"Oh Rose, that is so lovely. You have no idea what this means to me. In a way I am celebrating an anniversary. Twenty four years ago to this day, I made a decision which I thought was for the best. Time however proved me wrong and that choice has held me captive since that time, until today. Today, I chose to rectify that decision. This is a gift from "The Little Flower" as a sign my prayer has been answered."

CHAPTER THIRTY-THREE

THE SUNDAY FOLLOWING Father Engelmann's anniversary something happened at the ten o'clock mass that many called a miracle. It was both powerful and life changing not only for those present in the congregation, but also for Father Engelmann. A seed of change was planted in Father's heart that would have him begin to consider something that most parishioners thought would never happen nor hoped would ever happen; retirement.

Father's youthful enthusiasm, his health, his looks, his burning passion for the Lord was always like someone who was just born again and would go on forever! But this morning, God, revealed that none of us is indispensable and even God's most devoted disciple has his day under the sun. If fact, Father often spoke that he was replaceable. That he was simply a man of God through which He could work. He was simply a vessel to be used by the good Lord for His purposes.

Usually, either Father Engelmann or Father Knuka said the mass. They developed a rotating schedule which gave a clue as who would be at which mass each Sunday. As expected, Father came out of the sacristy to say this morning's service but what wasn't expected was Father Knuka's presence when it came time to read the Gospel for that particular Sunday. Usually a parishioner would do the first and second epistle readings and then Father would get up, come to the podium and read the Gospel.

The congregation was both surprised and perhaps disappointed when Father Knuka went to the pulpit to read the Gospel.

Would he be giving this morning's homily?

Henry could feel an uneasiness sweep through the church. He knew deep down the parishioners much preferred Father Engelmann's homilies over Father Knuka's. But they were all in for a big surprise. For that morning something so miraculous happened that the words uttered by Father Knuka touched their hearts and souls just every bit as good as Father Engelmann's, if not more, right from the beginning of his homily to the very end.

"My dear brothers and sisters in Christ. I asked Father Engelmann if he would allow me to do this morning's homily and if he would be present while I did so. I never explained to Father why I wished to do this and in his usual kind accepting manner simply nodded as if to say, 'as you wish.'"

Father Knuka moved the Holy Bible aside exposing the usual notes he read. Over the years parishioners noted that there were usually four to six pages and many times wished it was the former.

A clue that this morning's homily would be different was the way Father Knuka looked out to the congregation and in a manner that was similar to how Father Engelmann tried to make eye contact with all those present. In Father Knuka's effort to do so, his survey of the people grew longer than usual and began to create uneasiness amongst those present. Even Father Engelmann raised an eyebrow towards his fellow colleague. Finally, he spoke. "Before I came to St. Mary's church four years ago I prided myself in my homilies. I read scripture daily and was pleased with the way I explained it to the people. In a sense, I revelled in my superior insight into the teachings of God.

"And then, to my good fortune, the Archbishop transferred me to this parish to assist Father Engelmann. When I heard Father's first homily I was not only impressed, but moved. Every now and then, I too had a singularly good homily, and I thought this was one of those times for Father Engelmann. But I was wrong. His next homily was equally profound, and so was the next, and then the next after that.

"In fact I was so touched by his homilies, I would come into the sacristy and open the door slightly and listen. Surely he had to have an occasional miss, but it never happened. Each homily touched and moved me even more so than the congregation. I was amazed how the Holy Spirit moved through him. His homily at the nine o'clock mass was at times almost completely different than at the twelve o'clock mass. It was as if he were speaking words to members of the congregation that they needed to hear in a different or new way!

"In sharing the same house with Father, I came to see what faith was really all about. Whether Father was saying the mass, giving a homily or just living his everyday life, I noticed in Father a complete submission to Jesus. Father has given his will completely over to the Lord. He is will-less, real, authentic, and gives all glory and praise to God. There is no self pride in Father Engelmann, but rather a sincere humble man that has complete trust and faith in Jesus.

"What Father Engelmann has taught me my friends is that in the same way Jesus was obedient to God the Father even unto death on the cross, so too, is Father Engelmann obedient to Jesus and through Him to the Father. "When I see Father stand here Sunday after Sunday and witness how his faith touches your hearts, I see what it is that I lack. While my relationship with Jesus and God is from the head, Father's relationship is from all his mind, all his heart, all his soul and all his strength. His relationship has grown so close to God that he fulfills Jesus' two great commandments perfectly.

"My dear friends, I see little value for me to stand in front of you Sunday after Sunday and spout an intellectual analysis of scripture that carries no real faith. You see, we all have a spiritual side that recognizes a true spirit when it is touched by it. The love that is within the core of each of us is moved by the *light* of real faith and true love. It can't help, but to touch our heart.

"This is the lesson I learned from my dear brother in Christ. He has made the journey from the head to the heart many years ago and it is my sincere desire to make that same trip now.

"And so, my brothers and sisters in Christ, as Father Engelmann would say, I stand before you naked today. I am a proud man, but I want to be humble. I want to be authentic and true to God and to you. I want to submit myself completely to Jesus. I want to trust Him with all my heart and exude a burning faith that lights a fire within you as well. I am of no value to myself or you if I don't reflect the real Jesus within my heart."

With that Father Knuka tore up his notes.

"I stand before you now and wait for the Holy Spirit to come into my heart as he does with Father Engelmann Sunday after Sunday to give you inspired homilies. The Holy Spirit entered the hearts of the apostles as well at Pentecost and look how this small group became the spark that changed the lives of mankind. This is my hearts desire, and if I don't receive this gift of faith today, I will come Sunday after Sunday and stand before you until the Lord touches my heart.

"I ask all of you to please bow your heads and pray for me that I may follow in the footsteps of Father Engelmann. For then I will be ready to touch your spirit as a true shepherd of God that is really ready to lead and guide his flock."

What the people were about to witness was a revelation that equalled where most of them were at in their relationship with Jesus as well. Through Father Knuka's honesty and exposure of his heart before them, they saw into their own hearts and saw what they needed to do to be authentic Christians too. They realized there is a huge difference between a superficial faith, a showy self-righteous faith that the Pharisees exhibited, a self-centred faith mainly concerned with one's own needs, a going through-the-motions type of faith by mainly attending church on Sundays and *a faith that is based on a deep personal relationship with Christ. A relationship in which one's exterior life is at one with one's interior.*

Henry's heart went out to Father as he stood there waiting for something to happen. But what? Tears surfaced and sat on the edge of his eyelids as he empathized with Father. Before him was a man who desired to come and commit himself to Jesus. Henry had often thought of that too, but never followed through at this level and would he even have the courage to do what Father was doing?

Father was showing to Henry and to all of them how a real, authentic relationship is formed. Coming to Jesus with a sincere desire to know Him, to love Him and to serve Him.

What a powerful blessing it was to those present to witness such a transformation taking place before them. It was the perfect example of what must happen in their hearts as well. There, before them were two priests; the one fully alive in Christ and the other desiring that life as well and exhibiting a leap of faith to do so.

Father Knuka was now trusting the Lord with all his heart and no longer leaning on his own understanding!

The scripture Henry had heard and read so often gained new meaning:

'Ask and you shall receive, seek and you shall find, knock and the door shall be open unto you!'

Father Knuka remained standing there, his head bowed. Father Engelmann's head was bowed as well, his lips moving. If a pin dropped at that moment it would crash to the floor like an explosion. An expectancy was growing. Henry could feel his prayers joining with other parishioners, a power was building.

Henry looked up and looked from side to side. Every head was bowed, shrouded in a prayerful hush. Just the odd hand moving silently up to wipe away a tear from their eyes.

The silence grew as Father waited; as the people waited, not sure for what it was. Nothing was coming forth and an uneasy nervousness began to steal away the expectancy of faith.

Over five minutes had elapsed and then six…how long could this go on? Henry wondered. Would Father Engelmann get up and rescue,

Father? No, Father Engelmann would not do that. His faith in God was so strong that he knew his Lord would come. And then...

Father Knuka raised his head and a strange sound came from his lips. He began to babble words that made no sense and then he sang songs in those same words. It seemed like gibberish or another language, yet the melody was incredibly appealing.

Slowly the people began to understand what was happening. God had rewarded Father Knuka's trust and faithfulness.

In front of his congregation, Father Knuka was given the gift of tongues and was filled with the power of the Holy Spirit.

Henry recalled reading about that in Corinthians 12:4-11. Spiritual gifts are given by the Holy Spirit to believers enabling them to edify others and honour the Lord. Henry had always believed that Father Engelmann had received the word of wisdom through the Spirit because of his extraordinary ability to understand God's word and His will and his ability to skilfully apply that understanding to life.

After going on like that for well over five minutes, Father Knuka went on to give the most powerful sermon the parishioners had ever heard about trusting in the Lord. The part that stuck in Henry's mind and heart the most was when Father spoke of coming to Jesus in childlike faith. Father used the analogy of a child standing on a ladder looking down on his father with open arms saying, "Trust me, son, jump!" It was exactly what Father did that day. He took a leap of faith and jumped ever so beautifully into Jesus' waiting arms for all to see!

When Father Knuka finished his homily he stepped down from the pulpit and was greeted with open arms by Father Engelmann. Both men had tears flowing down their cheeks. The congregation stood and clapped their hands; many with tears filling their eyes as well.

That day was a Sunday that will forever be burned in Henry's memory and he knew it would be in the minds and hearts of every parishioner fortunate enough to have been in attendance. The power of God was clearly demonstrated, but perhaps just as important it made the entire congregation look into their own hearts as well, to see how far short they were from really being committed to Jesus and entering fully into His light.

It showed Henry once more how God's divine providence constantly works through us and others to draw us back to Him. When we say, *yes*, thought Henry, like Father Knuka did today, we, too, will become faithful workers in the harvest.

One day, I will make that leap of faith.

CHAPTER THIRTY-FOUR

JENNY WATCHED FROM the kitchen window as the two carpenters packed up their tools and then stood there admiring the cedar gazebo they had just finished building.

The carpenters were highly recommended and worth waiting for. The gazebo looked so beautiful, she could hardly wait to sit in the swing that hung from the rafters, just like the one at the estate.

Jenny went to the back patio door and shouted, "Mr. Carson, if you'd like, I can pay you now."

"That would be nice, we were just coming there to give you the invoice."

"I'm very pleased with the job you both did and it went up so fast."

"It's because we built one exactly like that earlier this spring across town in the new north-west area. Apparently she had been dreaming of this gazebo for years and when she started to describe it to me, I could see right off it was just like the plans you gave me to study. When I showed her the picture she nearly keeled over. It was exactly the same as the one in her dreams."

"Really...? Jenny said, her eyes widening. And then she dared to ask, "Would her name be...Camilla Pederson?"

"Why yes, and I was just going to say, she sure looks a lot like you—"

"You can say that again," interjected the other carpenter. "She's the spittin' image of you, ma'am. You two could easily pass for sisters...you don't seem old enough for her to be your daughter."

Jenny was flabbergasted and didn't know what to say...

"Someone else told me that a few weeks ago. I am looking forward to meeting her some day."

"You better be sitting down when you do, she could almost pass for your twin."

"Her yard is much like yours, too," said Mr. Carson. Not quite as many wildflowers and butterflies, but close. Seems to me you both not only look alike, but seem to think alike and have similar tastes."

A surge of wonder soared through Jenny. This was beyond coincidental…

Jenny looked at the invoice. "Just give me a minute, Mr. Carson, I'll write out a cheque and then it's all looked after."

"I'd appreciate that, Ms. Hamilton. I'm not much good at bookkeeping and sending out invoices."

Jenny returned in a few minutes and gave the carpenter the cheque and the two men left out the back gate next to the garage.

"Oh, I just have to meet Camilla. I was so excited when Matilda described Camilla to me and now two more opinions were expressed confirming even more than what Matti had told me."

Jenny could hardly wait to speak with Mrs. Blake, the social worker in Ottawa. Jenny had called a few days ago, but rather than take her holidays during the summer, Miss Blake took her holidays for the month of September.

Well, I've waited this long to reconcile with my daughter, thought Jenny, another few weeks won't matter. *I just hope she has some workable suggestions on how to relate with Camilla so that I don't interfere in any way with Henry and his family."*

Jenny seemed as if she was on a cloud as she strolled to the backyard to have a closer look at the gazebo.

"Oh, it's so beautiful!" Jenny exclaimed.

She went inside and sat on the swing. It was perfect. Her feet just dangled a couple inches off the floor so she could swing unimpeded. She closed her eyes and imagined Camilla and her swinging side by side. Oh, it would be so much fun!

Jenny left her haven and looked around at the backyard. It could use just two or three more pyramidal cedars to hide more of the fence and then it would be complete.. The yard for the most part was as she had envisioned it.

Jenny tossed her hands up in the air trying to entice the remaining few butterflies that hadn't left for their long trek back to Mexico. She loved it when they landed on her hand. She was thankful that so many were attracted to her yard since that spring.

Perhaps she will drive to the nursery to see if they had any more milkweed plants to place behind the gazebo now that it was built. She loved the butterflies and how they flitted about like angels. Jenny was certain that she received several messages of love through them from Tammy and her mom and dad over the summer.

"Oh, Tammy, I wish you were here. I miss our talks so much. I know you would be able to help me to decide how to approach Camilla and the Pederson family. And that reminds me, I have to call Chloe and see how she is doing. She is so much like you, Tammy, so dedicated to saving baby's lives. It's all so unbelievable what's happening because of these silly laws allowing mother's to kill the precious gift of a child within their womb. And for doctors, who strive daily to heal the sick and save lives, that they could actually perform one abortion after the other is incomprehensible!

Just then the phone rang.

"Hello."

"Hi Jenny, it's Joan. Did your company come?"

"Yes, my friend Matilda only had three days including flying time so it was a short but very sweet visit. However, we did have a chance to enjoy Sunday dinner together, so that was nice, and we had a nice chat."

"That's good. Have you got time to come over for coffee or tea?"

"I was just thinking of going to the nursery, but I can swing by that way first. You live on Smith Street near College Avenue?"

"That's right. The two storey white house with the attached garage. And since Smith Street is a one way street heading south, it's best to go down Albert Street to 14th Avenue, turn right and then right again on Smith. The Pederson Gallery is on that corner, you can't miss it. "

"Yes, I remember, I'll see you in about twenty minutes. Bye."

Jenny knew only too well where the gallery was. On several occasions she had driven by and always ached to go inside. She had heard so many exciting things about Henry's shop and how beautiful it was. On two occasions she turned down an invitation from lady friends to have lunch in the café and then browse through the many different shops in the complex. Jenny was perturbed with herself for doing this, but she was adamant not to cause a problem or interfere with the Pederson family in any way.

Jenny was going to put the top of her convertible down, but it looked like it might rain and so decided against it. She couldn't get over how quickly she could navigate from one part of the city to the other as compared to Ottawa. In no time she was at 14th Avenue and turned east towards Smith Street. Since 14th Ave. was a one way street, cars traveled in two lanes. To her left was a red SUV. Jenny's car and the SUV came to the stop sign at the corner of 14th and Smith at the same time. Jenny knew Henry drove a red SUV Escalade as she had spied on him before. Her heart began to race as she wondered if it was him stopped beside her.

She gazed into the vehicle and her heart stopped. It was him! Subconsciously she prayed to her guardian angel that he would turn her way. Henry's gaze however, remained fixed straight ahead.

Suddenly, Henry leaned forward as if something caught his attention. There before him in front of the car was, Julean. He couldn't believe what he was seeing. She was like a shadow, transparent somehow, but glowing.

She stared at him, smiled and then walked towards the car stopped at the corner beside his. She walked around to the passenger side and passed through the closed door and sat beside the driver. Henry still didn't notice that the driver was Jenny. Julean leaned towards Jenny's face which was fixed on Henry's gaze. The reflection of the overhead trees on Jenny's car window partially obscured Jenny's face.

His focus was now on both girls.

He edged forward ever so slightly to rid himself of the reflection so he could see with more clarity. He stared more intently, but a car that came up behind them moments ago began to honk his horn startling Henry and snapping at his concentration. For but a flashing second a warm feeling singed through him as his eyes locked on Jenny's reddened and flushed face. *At that moment Julean disappeared.* He moved his head from side to side desperately trying to rid the annoying reflection and get a better and clearer view. A memory of long ago began to surface carrying with it the same spiritual unforgettable energy he felt that day when he had met Jenny…but neither the reflection nor the dust spotted window wouldn't go away. He moved this way and that…

The car behind now honked more vigourously. There was anger in the sound. And now the car behind Jenny honked as well. Julean was no longer there…he had to get a better look.

"Geez stop the honking," he muttered.

If only she would turn down her window and get rid of that damn reflection!

More honking…Henry crept forward, the reflection was moving away offering a clearer view, but just then another honk spurred Jenny forward giving Henry one final split second glance of the woman before she turned right onto Smith Street and sped off. …It couldn't' be Jenny…could it? Or, was it Camilla…?

Jenny was shaking, she was so excited. My gosh, what was she doing? Here she wants to avoid Henry and there she was praying he would see her. Oh, it would have been so easy to turn down the window and call out to him, but she only did so in her mind. She smiled feeling like a teenager spying on a boy she had a crush on. But this was no crush; it had gone beyond that along time ago.

Jenny shook her head; this was the closest she had been to Henry in thirty years. It was such a critical moment, one that could have brought them together, but the moment passed them both by, lost and forgotten in the past, only to be relived as a fantasy, at least in Jenny's mind.

Jenny drove slowly towards Joan's place reliving the moment and giving her heart a chance to settle down. Jenny turned towards the passenger side…it had felt as if someone had been in the car with her at the same time she stared at Henry. Almost as if a close friend had been sitting beside her urging her to call out to… "Oh, it all happened so fast it's probably my imagination getting the best of me," Jenny muttered.

"Hi, Jen, come on in. I'm just loading the dryer with wash, please make yourself at home. There are some old magazines piled up next to the bookcase that I'm clearing out. You're welcome to any if you don't mind outdated issues."

"No, I don't, Joan, I'll have a look through them, you go ahead and finish what you're doing."

Jenny entered the home of her new friend who she had met at the MacKenzie Art Gallery. They were both volunteers and instantly hit it off. The painting hanging above the chesterfield looked like one of the group of seven. It looked like an A.Y. Jackson. Jenny also recognized another one hanging in the living room. She thought it was a Casson but was not certain. She remembered seeing it on the poster rack in the gift shop. Jenny sat down on a rocking chair near the book case and began to scan through the stack of magazines on the footstool. She almost lost her breath when she saw a photo of Henry on the front cover of the Leader Post Sun magazine. It was last year's magazine. The headline read, 'Henry Pederson, a Man Always Looking for a New Challenge.'

If his name hadn't appeared on the headline, she might have missed it. The eyes and mouth were the same, how could she forget. She'd looked into them so many times during that short summer and kissed his soft lips. She could almost feel him there as she was lost in time. She'd just turned to the page where the article began when her friend returned.

"Did you find something you might enjoy, Jen?"

"Yes, as a matter of fact I did. May I borrow this magazine, there is an article in here I would like to read?"

"For sure, actually that's an old one; you can just keep it and throw it away when you're done."

I would never throw this magazine away!

"I see you like the work of the group of seven, Joan. Is that a Casson in the dining room? I wasn't sure."

"Yes, it's called Country Road. I love the bright fall colours. I have a print of another one of his in the kitchen called the Blue Heron. I think that one is my favourite. Why don't we go there and sit down and I'll make us some tea?"

"Oh, I love this one, too, Joan." Jenny said as she studied the small Casson."

"We have some in the hallway and the family room of the other artists as well. They are all prints but Steve and I enjoy them. We have a very small original oil of A.Y. Jackson in the bedroom and I'm afraid that is the extent of our collection. So how are you enjoying Regina?" Joan asked as the ladies sat at the kitchen table.

"I love it, Joan. I have settled in and the yard is all fixed up and I'm making so many friends already."

"That's good, I was …oh my, that's a lovely pewter angel hanging from your necklace!"

Joan reached across the table and took hold of it. "What a lovely inscription."

"Yes, it is isn't it? It's a gift from a very special friend a long time ago."

Joan looked into Jenny's eyes before letting go and continuing, "As I was saying the girls and I were wondering if you would like to join our Bridge Club? We meet in different homes once a week. It's a lot of fun."

"I think for now, I have my hands full. Last week I joined the Catholic Women's League at the church I attend and also do some volunteer work which keeps me pretty busy. In fact, I might have to slow down a bit, I am feeling so exhausted lately…I guess with the yard and all."

"Well, if you change your mind we'd love to have you join the club."

"Thanks, Joan, I must say I love helping out at the MacKenzie Art Gallery. I am learning at little more about art all the time. I'm beginning to really like some of the pottery and am even able to recognize some of the artists who've created certain pieces."

If the truth be known, Jenny's motive for volunteering at the MacKenzie was to familiarize herself more with the world of art. If she couldn't be with Henry, then at least she could live vicariously in his world and be a part of his life and career. She wondered if she should inquire about the Pederson gallery and see if her friend knew more about Henry and his family, but thought better of it.

The ladies chatted for over an hour. Jenny had to admit however, that she had impolitely tuned out Joan several times during their conversation. Jenny could hardly wait to get home and read the article in the Sunday Sun.

After picking up some more milkweed plants at the nursery, Jenny went home and immediately set out to read the article about Henry.

She read and reread the interview that he had with a Sun reporter. It said that Henry was married and had four children. The article confirmed her firm belief that Henry would be a successful entrepreneur and artist, some day. She studied his features in the photo on the front page. Jenny was elated to finally have a picture of him.

His hair was thinning on top, almost bald, but his beard and mustache made him look distinguished and distracted from his receding hair line. He looked so handsome in his sports jacket and oh, so professional. At one point Jenny decided she would cut out the photo and frame it, but quickly thought better of it. She was already allowing herself to live in the unreality of a relationship that never was and could never be.

Try as she might, she could not stop reading the magazine or Henry's letter that her mother had given to her. It only made her think all the more about her first love. How would Henry react to this or that? What were his favourite foods? And when she took a walk in the neighbourhood she would walk on the inside as Henry had always walked on the outside to protect her.

Memory after memory crossed the screen of her mind of that memorable summer. And, when she caught herself in her reveries and realized that such wishful thinking was all for naught she was so disappointed that she actually became sick. Perhaps moving to Regina was not such a good idea.

Finally, she placed Henry's letter in her mother's hope chest in the bedroom closet. She also saw another large brown envelope there that was still sealed. She had written on the outside what precious contents were inside:

Love notes from my first love.

Jenny recalled sealing all the notes that Henry had written to her and hid behind the fence gate post. She knew she should have torn them all up years ago, but could never bring herself to do it.

She was going to open the envelope and read the notes, but she had already spent too much time thinking on the past.

She returned to the living room and stored the worn and tattered magazine into the drawer of the round table next to her chair. It was the same drawer that housed the secret compartment where she hid and kept her diary. It was a dangerous link to the past to which she could so easily succumb to live in. She knew she should discard the magazine and move forward, but all she could bring herself to do was to turn the magazine over, so the photo of Henry would be face down in the drawer. It was the only compromise she was willing to make.

Many days Jenny's heart ached so strongly for the love of her youth she would call the gallery just to hear his voice, "Pederson Gallery, how may I help you?" then she'd say she had the wrong number.

CHAPTER THIRTY-FIVE

THE PHONE RANG at least eight times and Henry was about to hang up when Mary answered.

"Hello," Mary said, catching her breath.

"Hi, Mom, were you outside?"

"Yes, just bringing in some fresh vegetables from the garden."

"So, are we still on for Wednesday lunch? I can hardly wait to taste the Borscht soup. You said it would be the best I have ever tasted. Last year's was pretty good, Mom. It will be hard to beat!"

"Yes, Henry, I'll do my best. Hopefully it will help you to always think kindly of me. And I will bake some fresh bread for you, too!"

"Wow, Mom, you're really going all out. And believe me, Mom, soup or no soup, I will always think of you as the best Mom in the world!"

"Well, let's see."

"And, Mom, for the life of me, I can't think what it is you want to tell me and show me. Can you give me a clue, Mom?"

Mary looked down at the pink envelope in her apron pocket and patted it. She carried it with her every day since deciding to give it to Henry. The lilac scent soothed her.

"You will know all about it soon enough, son. If you can spare the time try to book off two hours."

"Will it take that long!?"

"Perhaps even longer."

"Now you really have me curious. Okay, Mom, I love you and I'll see you the day after tomorrow. We are starting to hang a new exhibition and should have most of it done by tomorrow. So with that out of the way I should have lots of time for us to spend together."

"That will be just fine, Henry. Take care and I love you, too."

Henry hung up the phone and went to the fitting room. Shelly was just taking some pottery out of a box.

The decision to hire Shelly after Allison left for College was a good one. She not only was a good sales associate, but she also brought a little flair to the gallery.

Still in her early twenties, she was quiet and reserved. She had long brown hair and wore it in many different styles, but usually up in a bun. She walked very erect and together with her soft demeanour possessed an air of elegance. Her clothes were another thing. Everyday she wore something different and on the edge, definitely artsy. She was a very steady worker, but relished her private time.

When five-thirty came, she'd get on her bicycle and pedal off down the street. Her erect posture on the bike and air of sophistication reminded Henry of Mary Poppins.

"Well, Shelly, we'd better finish setting up the rest of the exhibition. Doug has all of Lydia's paintings framed and ready."

"I've started to put the pottery on display, Anne brought it in this morning. Is her work ever beautiful," commented Shelly, as she opened another box of Anne's pottery. "Each piece is so unique. I'm in love with one of her teapots that has an extra long spout and handle. It is so different."

"Yes, I noticed it earlier this morning. I'm certain it will be one of the first to sell."

Justin emerged from the frame shop in the lower level carrying a framed watercolour in each hand.

"Well, Dad, Doug just finished these and asked me to start taking them up to the second level. I'm going to help him hang the paintings. We might finish today."

"That sounds good. We still have to price everything and print out titles for all the paintings. Some of Lydia's followers want to preview her work tomorrow afternoon prior to the opening."

"Let's get a move on, then," said Shelly, as she picked up several pieces of pottery to take up to the second floor as well.

From the day Henry opened the Gallery, his philosophy had always been, 'art is for all.' It was his goal that both beginning and experienced art collectors would feel equally at home in his gallery.

Henry liked to exhibit three-dimensional pottery or sculptures along with two-dimensional paintings during exhibitions. It made for a more interesting exhibit and drew a larger crowd. Furthermore, the abundance of natural light flooding the gallery through all the windows displayed the pottery, fused glass and raku pieces so well.

They finished hanging all the paintings shortly after six. As always, Doug had done such a nice job in selecting mouldings and mats that presented the paintings at their absolute best.

"Well, Henry," said Shelly, "I really have to go. Our dinner is around six and I'm a little late now."

"Sure, you go ahead. Please prepare the title cards for each painting in the morning. The list of titles and sizes are on the table in the fitting room. Doug is figuring out the frame cost for each painting and I'll add the gallery prices to the watercolours."

"As soon as you give me the final price of each piece I'll finish the title cards and stick them beside each painting."

"Excellent, Shelly, see you in the morning."

Henry turned towards Justin. "Why don't you grab a Coke and make yourself a sandwich in the kitchen. I'd like to go up and check everything over once more before we head home."

"Sounds good, Dad."

Henry made his to the second level and reviewed all the pottery and paintings. He was glad they had left, he didn't like hurrying an exhibition. Both artists had worked hard to get their pieces ready and he wanted to make sure they were hung right and displayed to their best.

Henry walked through the rooms several times studying the art, their shape and colour, then made some minimal changes. It took over an hour before he was finally satisfied that the paintings and pottery were in their best position and light. The show was almost ready for exhibition.

Henry wandered through all three rooms again. Satisfied with the flow and balance and that everything was well displayed, he relaxed.

As he gazed at the show, his mind turned philosophical. There is something about art that emits a peace of its own.

"Aesthetic sustenance for the spirit – food for the soul," he would always tell his customers. "We need art in our lives. It provides a respite from the hustle and bustle of daily living. It gives us pleasure, a sense of awe and wonder and peace. It makes us aware of and appreciate the world around us.

"What artists do is give us a part of themselves, their vision and the gift of creativity God has given them. They make us stop and look at ordinary moments in time by making them special."

Fatigue settled in. His legs were not as strong as they once were. Standing up and walking around all day was beginning to take their toll. He looked around one final time, then pivoting on his heel, starting with the storage room, he began turning the lights off one by one until all was still and dark except for a night light in the front room.

He instantly felt at peace. He was surrounded by art – the world he loved and was fortunate enough to work in.

His heart's only desire now was to have someone to share his passion with.

The thought made him think about the lady who was driving that car he pulled up to the other day. At first it looked like Camilla but it couldn't have been. It wasn't her car for one thing and the feeling he had when their gazes met for that split second was so strong and memorable…the encounter still tugged at his memory…and heart. What was Julean trying to tell him or show him?

And why don't I have that kind of feeling when I am with Ivania? Surely a stranger in another car shouldn't have generated that kind of feeling. But then was it a stranger? It was so difficult to get a clear view…

Perhaps it was someone that he knew only too well.

THE NEXT MORNING Henry was on the phone calling his mom when Justin came in.

"Geez, Dad, eight of Lydia's paintings sold already and the exhibition hasn't even opened yet."

Henry covered the phone, "Yeah, I noticed. I'm just trying to get Mom and let her know I'll be there in half an hour."

Henry let the phone ring until it cut itself off and then hung up.

"She's either in the bedroom getting ready for me and can't hear the phone or she's out getting in some fresh dill. She knows how much I love the flavour and aroma of fresh dill."

The mere thought of the dill tantalized his nostrils. He could hardly wait to taste it. Yet, he wished she had answered the phone.

"I like Grandma's soup, too, Dad. Can I come along?"

"No, Shelly has some errands to run over the noon hour so you may be needed to watch the gallery and Mom has something she wants to talk to me about so maybe next time. In fact, I'll bring some back for you."

Henry grabbed his sports jacket and hurried to the parking lot.

CHAPTER THIRTY-SIX

Hi Henry," patrons called as Henry passed through the café.

"Good afternoon, Frank. Nora," Henry nodded to his customers each in turn as he hurried through, not wanting to stop.

"Great day!"

"Yeah, it sure is," Henry replied. "Enjoy your lunch."

Henry loved the camaraderie of his business the most. He knew many of his customers by name, and they were like one big family to him. It was a beautiful fall day. The ascending sun had burnt off the morning chill bringing warmer temperatures with it. The slight breeze felt good against his face and slowly worked its way through his jacket and shirt. The sky was clear except for a jet taking off from the airport. A long white trail of vapour followed the jet as it rose upward then banked towards the west.

Henry hopped into his SUV, pulled out of the parking lot, and headed east towards Broder Street. He wished his Mom had answered the phone so she knew for sure he was coming. It always bothered Henry when his mother didn't answer the phone. The building noon-hour traffic only added to his tension.

When he pulled up to the front of his parents' house, the curtains were drawn open which was a good sign. His mother usually closed them at night and opened them again first thing in the morning.

He stepped out of his car and walked up the walkway and climbed the three front steps as he had done a million times before. The screen door wasn't locked, but creaked open with effort. It needed oiling. Henry rapped on the inside door then turned the knob. It was locked. She always had the door unlocked for him, but then maybe she had forgotten that he was coming today.

Henry knocked louder. He pressed the doorbell longer than he normally would just in case she was in the bedroom or bathroom or something and couldn't hear him. She still didn't come to the door. He put his ear to the door and heard music.

"The radio is on and that's why she can't hear me." He knocked harder and when she still didn't answer, he reached into his pocket for the house key.

Henry opened the door and shouted, "I'm home, Mom!"

Willy Nelson crooned from the radio in the kitchen. Instead of the dill he expected to smell, the air smelled like something had burnt. His gut knotted. For one, his mother had never burned anything in her life, and two, his mother had always greeted him by now.

Something was wrong.

A hot flush of panic gripped Henry. His heart pounded and his body tensed preparing itself for…

"Mom, I'm home," he called out, not wanting to startle her as he neared the kitchen doorway.

"Mom?" he yelled again just before he entered the kitchen fully expecting to see her standing at the sink as usual, but instead his eyes dropped to the floor in front of the sink where his mother lay, her legs slightly bent and apart, her right arm up over and behind her head, a paring knife still in her hand. Her eyes were open, staring straight up towards the ceiling. They were motionless and, yet, Henry expected them to turn and look towards him. But they were cold, vacant and deathly still. Her other arm lay across her chest and the elbow was tight against the cupboard door below the sink. She must have collapsed and just fell straight down.

Henry stood there in a state of shock. He was compelled to go over and feel her pulse or to listen for a heartbeat, but he couldn't move. He knew she was gone. He did everything in his power to ward off the flood of feelings and thoughts rushing to his mind. He wasn't ready to deal with what he knew was at hand.

Carrots and beets lay on the counter. The carrots were clearly drying out and beginning to warp. A few strands of dill lay towards the back of the counter and onion peels lay in a neat pile along with some carrot peelings as if ready to be picked up and thrown into the garbage. On the stove was the heavy aluminum pot his mom had used forever. The pot was completely black around the bottom nearest the electrical element. The knob was on simmer.

He walked over to the stove and turned off the knob. If there had been anything inside the pot it was nothing but black soot now. Henry reached up to the high window above the sink and opened it. He turned off the radio on the corner shelf and was overtaken by the deadly, still silence. How lonely Mom must have been some days all alone in the house.

He pushed the kitchen table further away to make more room to kneel down beside his mother. As he lowered himself he reached for the hand that rested on her chest and felt for a pulse. It was so stiff and cold he couldn't move it.

"Oh, Mom, I love you so much."

He bent over and kissed her cheek. It too was cold and had lost its softness. Henry sat back on his heels and looked at Mary. Her brown eyes, looked hazel in the light. It bothered him to see her stare straight ahead looking shocked; more likely frightened. So different from the warm, kind, loving look he was used to seeing.

Henry pushed her eyelids closed, hiding the windows to her soul and freezing in time her last thought and view of her beloved kitchen.

"There...," Henry said, as he sat back again on his haunches. "You look asleep now...and peaceful."

His mother had such a kindly face. Her hair had changed from dark brown to a mousy grey as white strands infiltrated over the years. She looked older, but still very pretty. There was such a special bond between him and his mom. They knew each other beyond the head level. They sensed what each other was feeling and somehow were always there ready to help and support. She knew him inside out and loved him as only a mother can love her child.

As he sat there on his haunches, he became aware of a faint lilac fragrance that seemed to overpower the burnt vegetable odour from the pot that filled the air. It reminded him of Jenny. She was gone too, yet the sweetness of the smell soothed him.

Where on earth could it be coming from?

His knees were getting sore and his legs falling asleep. He tried to pull the arm behind her head down, but it was too stiff and he couldn't bring himself to force it down onto her chest.

He reached for a kitchen chair behind him and pulled himself up and onto it. The blood flowed freely again and his legs tingled.

"You were making my favourite soup especially for me, weren't you?" Henry said almost expecting his mother to answer.

"You loved to watch me eat and enjoy the food you prepared. I think at times I even ate more than I should have thinking it might make you happier." Henry smiled at the thought.

"This was your favourite room, Mom. I loved to come home and smell your cooking and see you stand there with your apron on. I could always depend upon it. You never failed, never once, except perhaps today, but I knew someday it would happen, not because of anything of your accord, but because our Lord wanted you and maybe some of your good cooking, too," Henry added, as he looked heavenward and smiled.

He returned his gaze to his mother. "In a way, Mom, I'm happy you passed away in your kitchen. This is where your heart was. This is where you greeted Dad and me. This is where we usually talked and shared our concerns around your kitchen table. It's good that this is where you left your heart behind."

Just as Henry was about to straighten Mary's apron which had flipped upwards when she fell, the phone shrilled startling Henry out of his wits. He looked up at the kitchen clock as the phone rang the second time, 1:30 p.m. He got up and answered the phone on the wall.

"Hello?"

"Hi, Dad, it's Justin. How's grandma?"

Henry didn't know what to say. For the first time, tears welled up in his eyes. "Not good, son. She's passed away."

There was a long silence as they listened to each other breath over the phone.

Finally, Justin said, "I'm really sorry, Dad. Is there anything I can do? Do you want Jeremy and me to come…?"

"No, son" Henry paused to regain his composure. "I have to send for an ambulance and phone her doctor. I'm not sure what I have to do just yet."

"Was she in her bed?"

"No, I found her in the kitchen. She was lying on the floor."

"Geez…"

"Just look after the gallery. You and Shelly will have to look after the show opening. I'll get there as soon as I can."

"Yeah, sure, Dad. Don't worry about a thing. We'll look after everything, here."

"Thanks, son. Good-bye"

"Bye, Dad."

Henry hung up the phone then grabbed the phone book from the shelf beside it and returned to his chair. Then he remembered that she had written her doctor's number on a list beside the phone. He stood and walked over to the phone again.

Henry dialed Dr. Morgan's office number. He told them about his mother and they promised to make arrangements for a coroner to examine her and declare her dead. Once that was done, in the presence of a police officer, he was told, then he could contact a funeral home.

Henry hung up the phone and collapsed into the chair nearest him.

He felt numb and helpless, the complete opposite of what he usually felt.

As he waited for the coroner, he began to wonder when she passed away. It must have been shortly after they spoke on Monday. She is all dressed, has her apron on, so it definitely was during the day some time. He further reasoned she passed away in the morning rather than the evening since the stove was on simmer and it also appeared that she had just started preparing the vegetables from the garden.

"She probably had a heart attack soon after she came in from getting vegetables from the garden."

He got up and surveyed the counter. Soil still clung to the dried out carrots and beets, another clue that she died shortly after coming in from the backyard. He was glad she had a last look at the garden. It had given her much joy, too.

He went into the living room in search of her rosary and found the crystal beads that Dad had given her in a table drawer. He wondered if she had said her daily rosary before she died.

Back in the kitchen, Henry sat on the chair nearest his mom, bent over and rested his elbows on his knees.

"In the name of the Father and the Son and the Holy Spirit," said Henry, as he crossed himself with the cross at the end of the rosary, kissed it and began to say the rosary for his mother. The one she wouldn't be saying, today. The beads sparkled as he slowly fed them through his fingers.

It was difficult to concentrate on the prayers alone as flashes of precious memories of his mother passed through his mind between almost every word. He made no attempt to focus on the words of the prayers alone. This was a rosary in dedication to his mother and for his mother. The prayers and the loving memories Henry held in his heart were one and the same.

As his thumb and forefinger worked their way around the beads, tears fell down from his drooped head onto his hands. The tears rolled along his fingers onto his mother's beads and cascaded down towards the dangling cross, finally dripping from the end of the crucifix onto the floor beside her. All Henry could think about now was how much he loved her and how dearly he would miss her.

Just as he was again becoming aware of the faint odour of lilacs drifting up from his mother, he heard talking and someone coming up the front steps. With the back of his hand he wiped the tears still in his eyes, then he bunched up the rosary and put it into his pocket as he stood up to get the front door. A man in a dark suit and a police officer stood on the other side of the screen door.

"Good afternoon," the man said as Henry opened the door. "You must be Mr. Pederson?"

"Yes."

"I'm Doctor Freedman, and this is Officer Stafford. We got a call from Dr. Morgan's office. I understand your mother passed away?"

"Yes, please come in, she is in the kitchen." Henry walked into the kitchen and stepped aside allowing the doctor to view the body. The coroner went over to the body and knelt down, placing his bag on the floor beside him. He raised one eyelid and then closed it. He felt her wrist and raised it, not to take her pulse, but more so to determine how stiff she was.

Still staring at his mother, the doctor finally spoke. "It appears she had a heart attack and died on the spot. She has been gone for well over a day; we will be able to tell more accurately as to the exact time of death at the hospital."

The doctor took out a form and placed it on the kitchen table then asked about Henry's mother's name and other vital statistics.

"Well, that will be all for now, Mr. Pederson, you are free to call an ambulance or funeral home to come and get your mother."

Dr. Freedman extended his hand to Henry with a look of sympathy on his face and nodded. The police officer who had stood in the doorway the entire time now also approached Henry and extended his hand. They shook hands, just a brief glance; no exchange of words. The bang of the screen door announced their final departure.

Henry walked over to the kitchen table and looked up Speer's Funeral Home in the phone book. They informed him they would be over immediately.

He returned to his mother's side, knelt down, and put his hand over hers. It was very cold and seemed bluer than when he first saw her. All the warmth was gone from her skin, but not from the memories Henry steadfastly now held onto. He needed the support of memories and the strength they would give him to do what he had to do. Yet, at the same time, Henry shut down the feelings associated with those memories, at least for now to prevent him from completely breaking down.

He stood up and tried to visualize what the attendants would do when they came in and how they would remove the body. Henry pushed the kitchen table even further away to give the attendants as much room as possible.

He recalled the time he had witnessed the removal of Anna's body.

How the attendants had entered the bedroom, unzipped a green vinyl bag, and laid Anna in it. It was a very cold scene and one which he still recalled from time to time.

A vehicle pulled up out front and two men got out. The attendants did pretty much what he'd seen the attendants who had taken Anna had done: they pulled out a stretcher and a vinyl green bag from the back of the ambulance.

As the two men climbed up the stairs, Henry held the door open for them.

"She is in the kitchen," Henry directed from the rear then followed them. The attendants laid the stretcher beside his mother and unrolled the green bag on top of it. It was already unzipped. Henry recalled how the attendants placed Anna's body into the bag and decided he didn't want to carry the memory of his mother being placed in it.

"I'm just going to step out back while you get Mom ready. Thanks for coming so quickly"

The attendant at the head of the stretcher looked up and nodded. They were just getting ready to lift her onto the open bag on the stretcher when Henry turned and walked out to the back door landing.

He looked up at the bag of clothes pins in a white cotton bag hanging from a clothes line. He remembered his mother hanging out the clothes and how she loved the fresh smell of clothes drying this way rather than in the electric dryer in the basement. He smiled as he thought about how stiff the clothes hanging outside would get late in the fall when the weather cooled and how clothes such as long underwear or nightgowns would keep their shape when removed from the line then collapse as they warmed inside the house. He loved to watch this happen and just loved the fresh, clean smell of the clothes.

His eyes wandered down to the garden. She loved her garden and spent so much of her life out there. He visualized her working in the garden as he'd seen her do so many times growing up. The very first row of her garden was always a row of annuals; she loved the beauty they gave off and was a reflection of the love she had for her garden. She always said that this row of flowers was meant to offer a bouquet to the garden for the food and nutrients it gave to them every summer.

What a beautiful offering. So typical of Mom's sensitivity to everything around her.

All the rows were devoid of weeds and very neat and straight. The tomatoes and peas were near the fence and each plant had a stick for the vegetable to climb up on, a practice she had learned from Mrs. Goronic next door. Henry looked over into her yard.

Mrs. Goronic had died many years ago and the house was purchased by a young couple. Half of her yard was now lawn and the other half garden, but not at all the way Mrs. Goronic had it. There were so many weeds it was hard to discern what vegetables were there. Oh, how she would weed her garden. He remembered only too well carrying out the weeds she pulled to the back lane for her and the nickel she'd paid him for doing so.

He smiled. Those were the days, so many memories. And that's all they were. Just memories.

"Mr. Pederson."

Henry turned to see one of the ambulance attendants standing at the back door.

"We have your mother in the van and will take her to Speer's Funeral Home now."

"Yes, thank you."

"Is there anything else we can do?"

"No, that will be fine."

The man turned and walked back into the kitchen. Henry followed.

Henry looked down at the floor where his mom had lain. He pictured her lying there. So many times he'd wanted to visit more, call more, but he was always to busy with matters he considered more important and he had never made the time. Now it was too late, time had run its course. There would be no more of those precious moments to visit and chat and just sit with each other.

He had taken for granted a treasure he foolishly assumed would be with him, forever.

He met the attendant's gaze, as he looked up. "Is everything okay?"

"Yes, thank you." Henry nodded.

He extended his hand to Henry. "I'm sorry about your mom."

"Thank you," Henry said, fighting to control the tears working their way to the surface.

Henry felt a little uncomfortable with the considerate thoughts of a person who'd never known either him or his mom. Like the exchange with the police officer before, Henry and the attendant shared a brief glance before he turned and left, the screen door banging shut behind him.

Henry stood in the kitchen momentarily then walked to the front door and watched the ambulance pull away, carrying his mom. She would never come back to her home again. Henry would never have thought that when he arose this morning he would be confronted with such a scene as this. He never realized death was so near.

But, as the Lord sayeth; *man knowest neither the time nor the hour when He will call.*

CHAPTER THIRTY-SEVEN

RATHER THAN RETURN to the gallery, Henry decided to drive straight home. He needed to be alone for awhile. He didn't want to be around people and put up a cheerful front when his heart felt so heavy. Neither did he want to put others in the uncomfortable position of trying to cheer him up or of deciding what to say.

It was a beautiful hot, sunny afternoon, he'd sooner let nature do its healing work. He turned off the highway onto the shortcut back road. Heat waves shimmered over the country lane blurring a cluster of three granaries in the distance.

Henry loosened his shirt collar button and opened the roof hatch to his SUV. He pushed a button on the side of his door and the window next to him slid down. The warm air gushed through the vehicle as he sped down the soft, dirt road. It reminded him of riding his bike when he was young. Just like then, the breeze felt good against his face, it soothed him, cleared his mind, and dried the dampness clinging to his body, the harvest-time air filling his lungs. The golden tips of the tall wheat swayed and rippled like a sea of waves under the vast prairie sky. It felt as though he were in a boat, travelling in the middle of the ocean.

Almost without thinking, he slowed down and pulled over to the side of the road. He needed to just stop racing, stop time, even for just a moment. He wanted to see and feel and smell the sight before him; to let it comfort him, his life on the farm, his roots, his heritage, his parents who were no more.

He turned off the SUV and opened all the other windows, the noise of traffic barely reaching him from the highway. Bees droned around the wildflowers on the edge of the road. The meadowlark resting on the telephone lines overhead warbled to the steady hum from the cables. But it was the sound of the combine working in the field, that he wanted to hear. He bent towards the open window and strained to listen. The wind faintly carried its soothing sound towards him.

As he watched the combine cut precisely into the field of waving wheat, his mind cut deeply into the past recalling memory after memory.

The hot sun beat down on his elbow resting on the ledge of the open window. There was not a cloud in the sky, but he knew that could quickly change. Clouds and storms could rush in with very little warning on the prairies. Henry had been on the prairies long enough to know that there was always a race to get the crop off. Farmers waged a constant battle against the elements. Too much rain or too little. Hail could cut down a bumper crop just days before the harvest quicker than a hundred combines combined. Drought, early snow, late snow, low prices, high prices – there was always something.

The combine turned and approached Henry. The farmer inside the cab waved to him. Its churning sound became more audible, somehow more melodious than the trills of the meadowlark it was drowning out. He loved to watch the hungry machine gobble up the wheat. Reap what the farmers had toiled and worked for all spring and summer long.

The smell of freshly cut wheat grew stronger. The wind whispered through the ripened wheat which intermingled with the chaff swirling out from the fan behind the huge machine. He took a long breath of air, trying to drink in the harvest aroma of dust and cut straw. For him it possessed the essence of the good earth, the making of bread for all mankind.

It made him think of the homemade bread his mom baked every week. What an appetizingly powerful aroma. The smell had greeted him before he opened the door when he arrived home from school. The sight of his mother bringing out another loaf of baked bread from the oven in his mind's eye, caused his eyes to widen in anticipation. He could hardly wait to get inside and devour it with melting butter filling its air pockets while it was still hot and steaming. He wondered if the farmer in the combine thought about the utter joy his harvest eventually brought to families?

A sudden breeze rushed through the windows carrying away the delicious aroma that clung to his memories. It hit him that he would never again smell baked bread in their home.

He pushed his mind back to the harvest scene before him, but it agitated him as well. The yearly passing of another harvest; a steady reminder of the passage of time and his own impending harvest. That one day, he, too, would be cut down and judged for what he had reaped. The dust stirring into the air from mother earth was more than a prairie harvest, but a clear reminder that it was from dust he had come and to dust he would return. And that he, just like his mother and dad and their parents before them, would become a part of the ever growing prairie wind.

It suddenly dawned on him that the scene before him was not just a combine reaping wheat, but contained within itself the roots which bound them to the past, the toil of those who'd gone before, that their memory was here, ever present, that they were a part of what made this land. Like soldiers in a war they fought against the elements. The sweat, the toil, the pulling together…the good times and hard ones. Each year, more virgin land was broken, each year brought a new crop and a new hope that that year's crop would be bigger and better. Each year the battle waged and each year the victory over the land and perils coming from the sky was won.

"Ah," Henry muttered, "This truly is what the spirit of a prairie harvest is all about. Thank you Mom and Dad," he whispered. "Thank you Grandma and Grandpa and to you…my great-grandparents, thank you, too."

Henry knew his children would never fully appreciate or understand what the pioneers had done for them. His mother's passing was the end of an era for him and, yet, he felt compelled to keep this legacy alive.

"Oh, Lord, paint words so vividly and strong in my mind that I can pass along to my children what I am feeling and thinking now. Make my paintings always capture the spirit of the prairies." Yes, this was the passing of another era in the fleeting passage of time…yet these were their roots; planted much deeper than the seeds of the wheat still swaying before him. "And, our roots should sway and dance in the wheat, the grass, the wind, the land and the sky, forever. They should never be forgotten; for we are all one, under the prairie sun," he almost sang as his spirits lifted.

Tears welled up in Henry's eyes as one visual memory after another of his parents and ancestors projected on the screen of his mind. He felt their presence; the spirit of the prairies was in his bones, his heart, and in his soul. He knew he was not alone; he felt encouraged and supported and refreshed by this spirit. Somehow it gave him the courage and strength to go on.

The combine had turned again and was now heading away from him towards the descending sun in the west. The dust and straw spewing out from behind almost hid the entire burning silhouette of the combine. Its sound was receding, no longer audible; just like the memories disappearing in his mind.

He wiped the spilled tears from his cheeks with the back of his hand. He listened once more for the soothing trill of the meadowlark, but it was gone. He revved up the SUV and headed down the dusty road towards home, much slower than usual, savouring the lingering memories which were already fading as quickly as another day on the prairies.

After a late light dinner, most of which he left on the plate, Henry phoned Jeremy who had been shocked to learn of the news from Justin earlier. Henry was glad that Justin and Lauren were spending the night with Camilla and Jeremy. Henry hesitated to call Allison, and as he had expected she seemed to take it hardest of all. She and Grandma were very close.

Henry also called Ivania who was shocked by the news. They canceled the movie and dinner date they had planned on going to Friday. Ivania said she would be at the Speer's funeral service and asked if there was anything she could do. Henry simply said that it would be good of her to come to the prayers.

Then he called Father Engelmann to make funeral arrangements for next Monday morning. Father said he would also do Mass for Mary the following morning at eight.

Henry wanted to talk further, but feelings of mourning were settling in. Fresh tears welled up in his eyes. He wanted to say to Father that they would not be meeting at Mom's this Sunday evening for dinner like they usually did and that they wouldn't have her special borscht soup this fall; but he just couldn't talk anymore.

After Henry promised he would be at the mass, he hung up and headed to bed.

A few minutes past nine, he turned out the bedside light. The soft light of the setting sun cast a glow in the room yet it could not calm his racing mind. He tossed and turned as he thought of all the funeral arrangements he had to make in the morning; put a death notice in the paper, lunch after the funeral at the hall. He didn't have to concern himself with the cemetery plot or casket as that was already looked after.

And then it came to him, he was so overtaken by his mom's death he had forgotten about what she wanted to tell and show him. He thought back to the time he entered the house until he left and he didn't notice anything there for him. The table was empty, no plates or cutlery... *nothing!*

Where would Mom have put what she wanted to show me?

His eyes were heavy. He felt so lonely with Julean gone and now his mom. Every breath, every moment a person lives brings them closer to their inevitable death. One by one people part ways and as each one leaves a void is created in the hearts of those left behind that no one else can fill.

Finally, as Henry began to drift off he faintly smelled the lilacs coming from his mother's body that morning. He didn't feel his eyelids push out warm tears as they closed and he began to dream.

He saw Jenny, her golden hair glistening in the light as she stood at the screen door at their house. She was calling on him to take her to Balfour Collegiate to register for grade nine. Henry's mom and Jenny were chatting as he came down the hallway. She had commented on the smell of fried onions and potatoes in the air. How they were her favourites, too. Somehow the dream comforted him and he settled into a deeper sleep.

In the morning, just before he woke, his dream of Jenny continued. Jenny was leaving…she was going away; it was storming, there was lightning and thunder. He felt as if he were being torn apart, losing all control and then…he felt the touch of an angel behind him. His mother put her arm over his shoulder soothing his troubled heart. She was always there.

But who would be there now?

CHAPTER THIRTY-EIGHT

CAMILLA TOSSED AND turned and finally decided to get up. Not only was she filled with such sorrow over the death of Grandma Pederson, but the dreams she was having were so troublesome to her spirit. Besides her usual dream of a stork flying in the sky delivering a baby to a lady sitting in a gazebo surrounded by wildflowers, ever since she saw that man staring at her at Father Engelmann's anniversary party, he was in her dreams as well.

In the dream, the man is gazing into the sky with his arms outstretched upwards as if waiting to receive something from the heavens. Although the stork does not appear in that dream, it almost seems as if he is waiting for the stork to deliver the baby to him as well.

Oh, what does it all mean? And why is it about that man that draws me to him?

Camilla quietly got out of bed, made her way into the kitchen and plugged in the kettle to make a cup of tea. Her journal was on the shelf above a small desk at the end of the kitchen counter. She retrieved it and sat down at the kitchen table.

She opened the journal to her last entry. It was dated Sunday, 9, 1987, the day of Father's anniversary. She remembered writing the following entry that same evening after she and Jeremy got home:

I saw a man at the party for Father Engelmann today. I felt him staring at me. When our gazes met, I felt so strange, as if I knew the man from another place and time. Neither he nor I could look away for several moments. For the first time in my life I saw features in the man that reminded me of myself. His eyes and the shape of his mouth had such a familiarity. And when I look in the mirror I see those same features in myself. I know that this is just a coincidence and yet for as long as I can remember I never had that same feeling of familiarity when I looked at my own mom and dad!

The black lady he was talking to, also stared at me for longer than is usual as well. It felt as if she knew me and was surprised to see me. She kept shaking her head. I saw her talk to someone near by and they both stared at me. It looked like he was telling the lady who I was. I don't recall ever seeing her before though. Who is that lady? She might be related to Eddy's wife Coreena, whom I met. I should have asked her if that lady was.

And later, Henry and that man were talking to one another for the longest time and then they both started to stare at me, too!

Am I just imagining all this, or are all these people connected to me in some way?

Camilla opened the journal that was marked with a white piece of paper sticking up. She pulled it out and stared at the name for the umpteenth time.

Marjorie Hamilton
Camilla's mother

She was certain, it read Camilla's mother. Could there possibly be something to this? The same feeling she had towards that man at Father Engelmann's party, she felt that day she spoke to Mrs. Hamilton.

And Jeremy's father, the way he keeps looking at me as if he knows something I don't…

Jeremy came into the kitchen, startling Camilla. He went over to the counter and pulled out the plug. Camilla hadn't even noticed or was aware the water had been boiling away.

"Did you want some tea, honey?"

"Yes, but it's okay. I'm sorry if I woke you up."

Jeremy sat down opposite Camilla, at the table.

"No, I heard you get up, I couldn't sleep either. I was thinking of Grandma and how much we all are going to miss her. I was wondering how to best tell Joshua when he gets up this morning."

"I was thinking about that, too. It's going to be so hard on him. They were so close."

"Dad will be taking it pretty hard, too. He loved his mom so much. He would never let anything interfere with Sunday dinners with her and Father. He will seem so lost…I don't think he will ever get used to that."

"I saw the close relationship they had, Jeremy, it was very special."

The kitchen fell silent. Jeremy could tell something more than the death of Grandma was bothering his wife.

"Were you writing something in your journal?"

"Yes, I just read over what I wrote about the man I saw at Father's anniversary party. Remember I asked you if you knew him and you said no."

"Oh, yeah, I saw him again at the café when Eddy and his wife Coreena had their reception and lunch. He was Eddy's best man. His name is Peter and his wife was Angie, I think. Can't remember their last name."

"Did you speak with him?" Camilla was anxious to know.

"Actually, it was he and his wife who approached me and wanted to know about us. How long we were married and if we were both from Regina and several other questions that I can't really remember. It was Peter who seemed especially interested in you and commented how beautiful you were and his wife concurred. So why are you writing about him?

Camilla shrugged her shoulders, "I don't know for sure... I feel I know him from some place...do you think he looks anything like me...?"

Jeremy turned to his dear wife and gave her a strange look, "Oh, oh we're not going there again are we? Surely you don't think he's your father...? First, Dad and now Peter?"

Tears surfaced and Camilla just shook her head. "Don't you see, Jeremy, I want to know who I am! I just get these messages lately that I just can't seem to shake. I know it's silly for me to think of all these possibilities, but...but, I can't help it."

Jeremy reached out to Camilla and took her hand, "I'm sorry, honey, I just don't know where this is all going. I just think, Stanley and Valerie are your birth parents and you may be going through all this torture and turmoil for nothing."

"Oh, Jeremy, I'm sorry..."

Camilla looked at her husband, tears filling her eyes. She shrugged her shoulders and shook her head from side to side... "I can't help it honey...I feel like I'm in limbo somewhere."

Camilla broke loose of Jeremy's hand, got up and hurried back to the bedroom.

Jeremy sat there in shock, not knowing what to do.

CHAPTER THIRTY-NINE

Shortly after seven, Henry drove to the city. It would be a busy day. His first stop was to attend the mass Father was saying for Mom. Henry didn't know any of the handful of parishioners that were present during a weekday service.

Immediately following the mass, Henry went to the funeral home and made arrangements. He selected a memorial card with the verse that captured his mom's nature. Since he still had her rosary in his pocket, he left it with the director to put in her hands. He would have to stop by the house to pick up another dress for her and return it in the afternoon. He wondered what they did with the dress, apron and shoes she was wearing, not that it really mattered.

Henry decided to stop by the gallery before going to his mom's place for the change of clothes. News had spread fast and all the staff expressed their condolences to him as soon as he arrived. The opening of the exhibition had gone well the day before. A large crowd turned out and several more paintings sold and over half of the pottery.

Henry had coffee with Jeremy and Justin to discuss the funeral arrangements and what scriptures they would want read, and who in the family would read them. He told Justin to come home with Lauren as he wouldn't be back. After he dropped his mom's clothes off at Speer's he headed home to clean up a little before Allison came home and prepare for other relatives that would maybe drop in.

When Henry arrived at his mother's place, he felt lost, as if he were in the wrong house. It seemed so quiet, its life was gone. He walked into the kitchen and looked down on the floor where he found his mom the day before. He quickly pushed that scene out of his mind and visualized her in front of the sink like he usually saw her.

"Good morning, Mom," he whispered under his breath, fully believing that her spirit was in the home with him.

He went to the bedroom to see what dress he should find for her to wear. She especially liked her navy dress with the crocheted white collar that she wore for Sunday Mass. The blue looked so nice with her greying hair. When he opened the bedroom closet, it was the first dress he saw. He picked up her black pumps directly below even though he wasn't sure if they were necessary as the person's legs and feet are hidden under the lid of the coffin. Her cosmetic bag lay on the dresser and he thought it might be a good idea to take that as well in case they wanted to put some rouge or lipstick on. He placed all the articles in an empty Sears shopping bag that was in the closet. He looked up into the mirror and wondered how many times his Mom did the same.

Looking at his reflection he saw a beautiful white rose in a clear glass vase. He hadn't noticed it till now. A card was propped up against the stem of the vase. It was a photo of St. Therese and on the back was a Novena to her. Mom had read all about the saint she had prayed to so often for favours.

I wonder what Mom was praying for this time?

He whispered the words of the little prayer to himself as his eyes noted his mother's treasure chest at the end of the dresser.

My gosh, he hadn't seen that in years. He looked into the mirror and saw himself trying to think when the last time was. He saw the light go on in his eyes. Yes, it was shortly after Dad died and when he came over he found his mom in the bedroom sitting on the edge of the bed holding Dad's death certificate. She looked so sad and alone his heart went out to her.

He recalled looking at what was in the treasure chest and picked up a pink envelope. It seemed to upset mom and she snatched it away. And…and come to think of it, it gave off a lilac scent just like the sent he smelled the other day when he prayed over her body.

An eerie feeling crawled up his back and he felt the hair on the back of his neck rise.

He stepped over to the chest and tried to open it, but it was locked. He looked on the dresser for the key. He opened the top drawer, but it wasn't in there either. He looked at his watch and decided to check it out when he came back to clean things out.

Henry walked out into the hallway and as he passed his old bedroom he decided to look in. It hadn't changed in all the years since he left. His old desk and chair were still there. Pictures and memorabilia on the walls along with a shelf his dad had made to set all the trophies on that he won at school. He set the shopping bag down and walked into his room and sat down at his desk. How many times had he sat there doing his homework, when the aroma of his mother's cooking drifted in, disrupting his concentration?

Absently, he pulled open the bottom drawer and there they were after all those years – the little notes that Jenny had written to him and hidden behind the front gate post of her fence held by an elastic band. He picked them out and laid them on the desk in front of him. One by one he read them recalling the memories, smiling and even chuckling to himself over some of the thoughts:

> 'Oh, Henry, if you were a chocolate bar, you would be the only one I would ever want.'

He wondered what ever happened to Jenny. All those letters he wrote to her and not one response.

Henry recalled the first letter he wrote to her, his very first love letter to a girl. He tried to remember its contents as his mind traveled way back in time. He recalled it was short, but couldn't remember exactly what he wrote, only that each word was filled with a deep love which he still felt.

He replaced the notes in the bottom drawer and closed it. He was about to get up then hesitated and pulled open the top drawer and took out a fresh sheet of paper. He reached into the inside pocket of his sports jacket for his fountain pen. Henry needed to do one more thing; he knew if he didn't do it now his thoughts would be lost in the busyness of life.

A heart overflowing with memories and gratitude yearned to express itself.

He wrote his final love letter to his very, very first love…ever!

THE VIEWING ROOM was dim except for a soft light shining down on his mother. Only part of her profile in the casket was visible to Henry and Allison as they entered the room, both a little tense and nervous. They had always seen her alive and well, and now the thought of seeing her dead, filled them with sadness, regret and apprehension.

As they neared, however, Henry began to feel better. She looked as if she were asleep, so peaceful. Her skin looked soft and pale, even though he detected a bit of rouge. She was wearing her blue Sunday dress and her rosary was intertwined in her hands and fingers. She still looked beautiful, but her features slightly altered as the skin no longer had a life force to support it. He and Allison said a prayer and then silently stood there, each in their own thoughts.

Finally, Henry made the sign of the cross over his mother's forehead then went to the front pew in the chapel where Ivania was already seated. Allison remained for a few minutes longer, then followed. Lauren, Jeremy and Camilla, Joshua, Justin and a few relatives and friends were already seated, waiting for the evening prayer service to begin.

It was a small gathering since most of Mary's friends had passed away. Most of the relatives were gone as well or too sickly to attend the service. A few of the distant cousins and several nieces and nephews were present, as well as Mary's neighbours.

Father Engelmann approached the pews and shook hands with all the family and many of the people present before he said mass. He seemed like the Pope passing amongst his flock.

Father returned to the altar and began the mass. Justin read the first reading while stopping several times to regain his composure. Camilla, looking radiant as always, did the second reading. She appeared as an angel before them. Henry had great difficulty paying attention to the words of scripture she read. Every time he saw Camilla, he saw Jenny.

Camilla finished reading and returned to her pew. Henry was captivated by her sparkling eyes and buoyant manner. Henry had never forgotten what Mr. Engelmann had said as Jenny hopped out of his store one afternoon a lifetime ago, "*A happy heart makes a cheerful face.*"

As soon as Camilla was seated, Father rose and read the Gospel and then spoke of his relationship with Mary. He shared the family relationship he had with her, how much he loved her, how good her cooking was, and more importantly, her loving heart. She was always so happy for others when good things happened to them. He told how they danced like two children doing "Ring Around the Rosy" when he'd sold the store.

When the mass was over, Father opened the floor to anyone wishing to speak. Each of the children got up and said a few words recalling special memories and stories they had of their grandma's kindness and generosity and understanding. Henry was going to speak, but decided not to, he was feeling too melancholy. He just remained silent and passive, holding Ivania's hand, looking on with pride and love at his family, which now would be missing a member and no longer seemed complete.

When the mother dies the heart of the family is weakened. It is when the father dies as well. But there just seems to be the special bond a child has with their mother that is forever. A mother is the one God has chosen to give the precious gift of life and birth to. And somehow that gift from both mother and God is never forgotten.

In the end we all desire to come home to our earthly and Heavenly creator.

Everyone chatted and mingled with each other for a half hour after the service and then went home. The following day the funeral would take place at St. Mary's Church and would be another difficult day. Henry's family went home with him to the acreage. After Justin went to bed Henry reminisced for awhile over a cup of tea with the girls and shortly thereafter, they all retired.

HENRY WOKE A few minutes before six with the bright sunlight flooding into his bedroom through the east window. From his vantage point the sky was swept clear of all clouds. It was a gorgeous fall day. His mother loved the sun and it was only fitting that it would shine down on her.

Allison was already up, sitting in the sun room reading her Bible. Henry made a cup of tea and joined her.

"How are you feeling, Dad?"

"A little more rested, actually I slept better last night than the night before. You're up bright and early."

"Just following a practice I learned from you," Allison replied with a smile.

"It's a good way to start the day. I've being doing it for almost thirty years. Whenever I'm rushed in the morning and skip being quiet with the Lord, I always regret it. It's impossible to go out into the world without being charged, focused and knowing what your purpose in life really is."

Allison nodded. They chatted for awhile, recalling the times grandma was out at the farm and the good chats and walks down into the valley they had. She remembered so many images of grandma sitting on a chair with her elbows on her knees saying the rosary. The sun was streaking in through the windows casting such a beautiful aura of light around her. There were a few times, too I caught her up at the barn sitting on a water pail doing the same thing with the horses roaming around her.

"Yeah, she loved the farm. I think both Mom and Dad regretted having moved into the city. They often said it just wasn't the same and missed their relatives and neighbours.

Soon Lauren and then Justin appeared on the scene. As they talked,

Henry began breakfast. He was happy that his children were close and got along so well. They seemed to bond even more after Julean died.

He recalled only too well when he was counseling parents how misunderstandings, carelessly chosen words or foolish actions could cause rifts and feelings of unforgiveness that could linger at times for years and years. Many times Henry found members of a family could be more forgiving to strangers than to each other. Perhaps because of the close ties in a family, when one hurts the other the pain goes deeper and lasts longer.

Henry remembered how it took his mom years to forgive his father for his unfaithfulness to her. He hoped and prayed that his family would continue to get along so well.

Perhaps too, it was Father Engelmann's encouragement to them all to start every day with the Lord and listen to His command to love, to quickly close the door to any injury or harbouring of ill will and to *never* allow it to take a *foothold* as it would often become a *stronghold*.

After eating breakfast and chatting some more, everyone got dressed and ready for Grandma's funeral. Henry and his family arrived at Speer's Funeral Home shortly after nine. After a brief exchange of hugs and meeting the other pallbearers in addition to Henry's two sons, they all piled into the limousines and followed the hearse to St. Mary's.

As they stepped out of the limousines in front of the church, Henry recognized a few of the relatives. He thought it funny in a way how they never seemed to get together unless there was a marriage or death in the family. Everyone was so busy in their own lives and their little world that there never seemed time for anyone else. A lot of the other people in attendance were acquaintances of Henry's who had come out in support and respect for his loss, even though they'd never known his mom.

Ivania was there too, however at this service she sat apart from the family with the rest of the people. Henry was happy to see her there.

The funeral on the whole went smoothly. Who would have thought, though, that Father Engelmann would be officiating at the mass for his mother? He was much older and had outlived most of his friends so far.

His talk centred on Mary's perfect acceptance of her role as loving mother. She was the heart and soul of her family and he was so glad to have been a part of it.

Jeremy and Allison did Bible readings. Margaret at the start, after communion and at the end of the mass sang solos which brought everyone to tears.

Again, Henry decided not to speak. He couldn't bring himself to read the letter he wrote the other day in his old bedroom. If he read it, he somehow felt it would only draw sympathy and attention to himself from those in attendance. He decided he would say it in private, just between him and his mom. He would wait and say his parting words, his last farewell to his mother at her grave site, when the two of them had a moment alone.

Chapter Forty

J AMES DICKSON HAD looked after the Memorial Garden Cemetery for almost forty years. His co-workers called him Rip, short for 'Rest In Peace.' He was the chief grounds-keeper for the cemetery. It was his job to put down the sod, trim and cut the grass, plant flowers and in general make the grounds look beautiful and serene, conveying the atmosphere that everyone there was in fact well looked after and 'resting in peace'.

Rip was an only child, his parents had long preceded him and over the years the deceased members of the cemetery had become his family. Tending to the cemetery was more than just a job, it became his mission in life to serve and honour the dead by making their final home as beautiful as possible.

Over the years Rip had come to know the remaining living members of the various families as well, when they visited the respective grave sites. He got to know their habits, the days they would visit and anniversary dates so well, that he went out of his way to plant a flower or lay a bouquet at the grave site in anticipation of them coming. He derived such joy and pleasure seeing how his efforts lifted their spirits and alleviated some of the grief they still carried. Rip served both the living and the dead and he took his purpose in life *deadly* serious.

He was just pruning and turning the soil around a row of petunias and irises along the front of a 10-foot long, 4-foot high continuous tomb stone. An entire family of six had died in a house fire over a year ago and relatives decided to put one huge tombstone in, rather than individual ones to convey the idea of a family being together.

Just as he finished tending to the plants, the slamming of car doors drew his attention. He stood and saw Henry's family and a few other mourners, walking towards the grave site prepared for the deceased just on the other side of tombstone where he was standing.

A priest and six pallbearers, carrying the casket, led the way. Rather than head back to the shed, Rip decided to just sit down behind the large tombstone and wait until the funeral was over. It looked like a small funeral party and probably wouldn't take all that long. He enjoyed listening to a funeral service; it helped him gain some background for the newest member of his family. Besides, his bones had been aching lately, and a little rest would do him good.

Father stood at the edge of the open grave, while the pallbearers set the casket down. Everyone else gathered around the casket to join in the prayers and say their final farewell. After everyone was settled, Father bowed his head and began the graveside prayers. He didn't speak anymore about Mary and her life, rather he said a private prayer to himself and ended up by saying out loud, "We will miss you dearly, Mary." Finally, he blessed the grave and put ashes on top of the casket.

When the burial service was over, several people approached Henry to express their condolences then headed back to the church hall for a lunch and social gathering. His children as well, came to him and they hugged as they gazed for the last time at their grandma. Henry told them to go back to the hall and wait for him there as he wanted to stay behind for a little bit. Henry asked one of the chauffeurs to return for him in about half an hour. He watched as they all piled into the car and drove away. He then walked over to the edge of the grave and stood in front of his mother's casket, almost in the same spot that Father Engelmann had stood just minutes earlier.

Rip, assuming everyone had left, got up to resume his work. He was surprised to see Henry standing all alone at the edge of the open grave in front of the casket, his back towards him, not more than three feet away. Not wanting to disturb or frighten Henry, Rip quietly sat down again out of view behind the tombstone.

Henry reached inside his breast jacket pocket and pulled out the letter he had written to his mom. Thinking he was all alone, he unfolded the letter and began reading it to her.

"Perhaps when I was writing this letter to you in my old room, Mom, you were standing over my shoulder and already knew what was in my heart, but I need to read this to you now, to get it out...and...well...

Dear Mom,

What words can a son say to his mother that would express his gratitude for giving me life, for giving me the joy of knowing you, being loved by you, being served by you and for all the sacrifices you have made over the years, for all the days of my life...

Henry stopped, as he walked over to the side of the casket, knelt down beside it, and released the clasp which held the lid of the casket closed. He opened the casket and the sun chased out the inner darkness, enveloping his mother with warmth. Her face glistened, as the light danced off the stillness of her features.

"There, I am so glad it was sunny, today. Oh, how I wish I could package the sun and enclose it with you."

He stood up, again, and spoke in a tone of sadness and joy. Sadness, because she was gone and there would be no more visits, no more Sunday evenings, no more chats and laughter like bursts of sunshine around the dinner table. Her smiles, the twinkle in her eyes, her mannerisms, all would now be memories.

And yet, Henry felt joy and gratitude. How fortunate that he had been blessed with a mother like her, the care and tenderness she always exhibited, her example of faith, her life of integrity, her grace and elegance. She had always been there, always so ready to give, to guide and to help.

Henry started to read the letter again, but his hands immediately dropped to his sides, the right hand still holding the letter. Some of the thoughts he just expressed were in the letter, he didn't need to read it, and she knew what it contained. So he spoke from the heart, expressing each thought as it came to him.

Going back in time, from his earliest memories, starting at elementary school and how this was the beginning of them being separated from each other and how it continued over the years. How she had instilled values, discipline and responsibility, gradually letting go, giving him more freedom to be more independent into the teenage years, then getting married and leaving home until now…their final separation.

Yet within his growing independence, rather than grow apart as often happens in families, their bond and friendship just grew and deepened. She so enjoyed being a part of his life and participating in it. It made Henry reflect on talks they had when he started dating. First with Jenny and then with Julean his mom just loved to hear about his feelings and about how his date went. She showed interest without embarrassing him or stopping him from talking.

Henry shifted as he recalled how many times he held back, and now he wished he hadn't, he denied her joy. He realized now that his feelings were not really so special; that she, too, had been a young girl once. She, too, had similar feelings. Henry wished he knew her private thoughts – how she was when she was a little girl, about her teenage years and her boyfriends before dad, how her relationships were with her parents, her likes and dislikes.

"Why is it we wait so long to have these talks?" Henry now questioned. "As I see you pass into eternity, everything about you is uppermost in my mind and I now regret, not taking the time to talk to you more about your life and what was important to you.

"Yet, I do know you, at least what I feel are the important parts. I know you had a very good heart, a very kind and caring heart, so insightful and sensitive. You never went to school beyond grade 10, and yet your instinct, empathy and understanding would have made a seasoned psychiatrist look like an apprentice.

"I was always amazed how you knew me through and through. I couldn't hide anything from you." Henry smiled at the thought of her discovering his plan to seek out Jenny after grade twelve.

"I am who I am, today, because of you. I know what is important, today, because of you, as well, especially by the example of your faith, how you believed in God. Yours was a simple accepting faith, nothing complicated. You never made believing in God difficult like I do so many times, questioning this and that, always going around in a circle, trying to be so smart and lofty. And, as soon as a problem comes along, I run to Him like a child to his mother with a bruised knee, seeking comfort and help.

"I remember to this day how when you and dad had your troubles, you placed your entire faith and belief in God that He would restore your relationship with each other and He did, and that will forever be in my heart."

Henry shifted again to catch some shade from the elm which had moved with the sun.

"So, here we are. You have finished your role as a mother, you have raised your family as best you knew how, you have been a very good mother and a faithful wife and now you are laid to rest. I will miss you, Mom. I will miss you more than anything. I know that a part of me is going down this grave with you, today.

"How quickly life goes by. The cycle of life goes on and doesn't stop for any man and yet I wish I could stop time for a moment and have everyone and everything pay tribute to you. For the whole world to be silent for just one minute and give recognition for your existence, that you were here and what you have done, the seeds of love you have planted and given so freely, the lifestyle you lived for us to emulate, we should honour you, bless you, praise you and thank you for everything."

Henry didn't know how to say any more deeply how much she meant to him, to Dad, to the kids, to Father, and how dearly, how very dearly they all loved her.

Henry regretted not telling her that more often, giving her more hugs, saying more words of appreciation and that he was sorry for all those times he took her for granted, perhaps all those times when she needed a kindly word, when she needed some care and kindness like she always was ready to give to others.

"Regardless of how tired you were." Henry muttered. "Yes, we should take more time to let each other know how deeply we appreciate each other, how much we love each other and care for each other and need each other.

Why does it take the death of loved one to make us realize what we have failed to do?"

A WATERFALL OF tears flowed from Rip's eyes as he listened intently and was smitten by Henry's words. In so many ways it brought back memories of the relationship he had with his mother, as well. There was one memory that he'd tried to suppress over the years, but every now and then when his guard was down – like now, for example – it would come to the fore. He didn't approve of his mother remarrying after his father died and had never accepted his step-father and was always cold and distant towards him. He knew it hurt his mother, but he ignored his mother's feelings until the day she died.

Henry's words, stirred Rip's feelings of regret. His guilt and shame now faced him head on and more tears of sorrow flowed from deep within.

The dappled shadows of the elm's leaves fell on the casket as flickering light. It reminded Henry of the light streaming in from his mother's kitchen window. How she loved the sun warming her face as she stood in front of the sink, her fingers playing with the water. Often Henry would catch her with her eyes closed and her face titled towards the rays of light as if in prayer.

It's ironic that she would die on the day she was making his favourite soup. He could smell it now with extra dill in it, as if he were in the kitchen. To him, its fragrance was more aromatic, more unforgettable, more lasting, than the most expensive French perfume that money could buy. In a way, it was her last gift to him. He had so been looking forward to their Wednesday lunch together.

Henry looked at the letter again almost checking to see if he had forgotten to express anything. His eyes brightened as he thought about what he would most miss about his mother. He raised his eyes from the page and looked lovingly at his mother closed eyes.

"You were always there for me as my very best friend. Your smiles like sunshine, ready to chat in a world that seemed to never sit still. There was no hurry in your home. Everyone who sat at your table got your full attention. You made it a safe haven of joy and peace and whenever I left, I left with a happy heart and for the better. You made me feel welcome, that I was lovable and good, that I always had a home to come home to…"

Henry couldn't go on. He was spent and had exhausted himself. Tears spilled out and rolled down his cheeks as the full realization that it would all be a memory hit him – the home he once knew and loved would never be the same, again. He wept as he fell silent and watched as the shade crept further up the casket ready to steal away the last ray of sun from his mother's angelic face.

Rip could no longer hear Henry and thought that perhaps he left. He crawled on all fours to the edge of the tombstone and peeked around the granite corner. He was awestruck by what he saw. The lid of the casket lay open and Henry still stood there holding the letter he had just read. He seemed to be in a deep state of contemplation or prayer unaware of the beautiful butterflies flitting all about him. For years Rip was well aware of the significance of butterflies in the cemetery. To him they served as angelic messengers or the spirits of the deceased loved ones themselves coming to comfort those left behind.

Henry blinked, bringing himself out of his ruminations and folded the letter, then bent over and tucked it between his mother's arm and her chest. He looked at his mother one last time.

A vision of perfect peace.

"Take my words of love wrapped in the sunshine with you into eternity, mom."

The grounds-keeper stared intently, as Henry closed the lid of the casket and secured the clasp once again. Henry stood erect, patted the lid, and walked away.

Rip was dazed by what he had just witnessed. In all the years as chief landscaper and caretaker for the cemetery, he had never witnessed such a poignant scene. He hoped that the grieving man had seen the beautiful yellow butterfly that had landed on top of the closed casket. He got up, brushed off the soil from his hands and the knees of his work trousers. He made his way to the other end of the cemetery where his mother lay at rest. He wanted to thank her, now, as well, and to ask for forgiveness for all the times he had hurt or disappointed her. He really had liked his step-father, but his stubbornness and pride had gotten in the way. He wanted to set the record straight.

In the week that followed, Rip's heart, heavy from caring for his increasing family in the cemetery, finally gave out. Someone else would take over his duties and make certain that *Rip could 'Rest in Peace.'*

HENRY MEANDERED THROUGH the cemetery towards the lane where the driver would come to pick him up.

"Please, Lord," Henry muttered as he strolled along, "Help me never to forget my mother's greatest lesson, *to always take time for family, to love and to serve.* Help me to pass on to my children the example you were to me."

Perspiration rolled down Henry's back as he strolled under the hot sun. The leaves in the large elm trees were motionless, not even a slight whisper of a breeze, unusual for the prairies. Absently, Henry wandered into the shade of the trees, one of those rare times he sought respite from the sun. The silence of the cemetery was unceremoniously broken by the honking of hundreds of Canadian geese heading south.

It made Henry think of his own mortality. How quickly the years go by. How we are born into a family, have our childhood, and soon leave to raise our own family and all too soon our parents die and then it's our turn.

Just one continuous ongoing cycle.

At the end of the day *it's all about love, isn't it?* How many people lying here are remembered for how much they have loved? How would he be remembered? Perhaps for his accomplishments, his paintings, his business, the houses he had transformed. But that would only be for awhile; he knew it wouldn't last.

"No," Henry whispered to his silent listeners who knew the full truth albeit for some too late. *"If our worth comes from what we have accumulated and amassed, we have failed.* Many of our struggles at the expense of family and friends and others have been in vain. You are right, Mom, you always told me I was too busy, to take more time for family, to smell the roses and serve my Lord."

Pangs of guilt hit Henry's stomach as he thought about his life. He was a good family man and much of what he did was in service for others, but he busied himself too much. When Julean was alive he was more focused on life. Since her death, perhaps out of loneliness, he had immersed himself more into the material world, overextending himself more than he needed to. His mother's death was a wake up call to get back on track and not take for granted what really mattered in life. All his projects, his paintings brought him satisfaction and a sense of security, but not true success.

Father Engelmann was a prime example of one who had gained true happiness and success. He was free of attachments. He pursued truth not illusions, things which are here today and gone tomorrow. His worth came from being a child of God, one who obeyed the commandments of Christ to love and serve his fellow man. And like Father Engelmann, his mother had lived a life of love, too. She saw the world around her through the eyes of love and this is what Henry knew deep in his heart that he would always remember her for.

The crackle of gravel beneath the tires of the limousine winding down the lane severed his thoughts. He waved to the chauffeur. As he weaved among the tombstones something looked and felt strangely familiar to him. His eyes immediately dropped to the large inscription below his name and date, larger than life, larger than his own name:

JACOB STEVENS

1873 - 1946

ETERNALLY I ASK FOR FORGIVENESS

Henry stopped briefly to thank Mr. Stevens, once again, for the part his words played in helping to heal the family. Fresh tears surfaced as he recalled the day he forgave his dad and how his mother, too, had been affected by this complete stranger.

"Thank you, Mr. Stevens, and if it were up to me to grant you peace, I forgive you completely for whatever during your life lay so heavily on your heart."

Henry turned and made his way to the limousine, whispering a prayer:

"Help me Lord, to live each day as if it were my last, to pursue more of what really matters in life, what is important, everlasting and to truly follow in Mom's and Father Engelmann' footsteps who are such great examples of how to emulate Your love filled ways and truths."

CHAPTER FORTY-ONE

OVER THE COURSE of the summer and into the fall, Jenny began feeling more and more fatigued. She also noticed an intermittent pain in her side that didn't want to go away. She attributed it to all the work she had been doing in and around the house, as well as her volunteer work. She enjoyed everything she did so much she was reluctant to give any of it up. But when she started cancelling luncheon engagements because she was just too tired to attend them, she decided to go to the doctor.

One of Jenny's friends had recommended Dr. Kreake. He was very amicable, in his early fifties or so, a good head taller than she and had black wavy hair. The tufts of grey growing out the sides of his temples only accentuated his distinguished appearance. He took her history and listened as she related the feelings of fatigue and the pain that came and went in her side. He couldn't detect anything out of the ordinary after feeling Jenny's abdominal area.

"You look fine to me, Ms. Hamilton, however, I would like to run some blood tests and take an X-ray of your chest and abdomen. Since the pain is on the left side, it rules out kidney stones, gall stones or anything to do with the major organs as they are on the right side. But we'd better check anyway. I can't really prescribe any medication or supplements until I look at the blood test results."

Dr. Kreake filled out the proper requisitions while explaining the protocols for the various tests. Jenny decided to have the tests completed the following day, since the blood test required her to be fasting for 24 hours. On her way out, Jenny scheduled a follow-up appointment in two weeks.

BARELY A WEEK had gone by after Jenny's blood tests and X-ray were done when the doctor's office called and asked her to come in around three that afternoon.

As Jenny hung up the phone, she wondered why they had called her in early. Clearly they had found something. A pain hit, then, much stronger than before. She almost doubled over. She sat in the chair by the phone unable to move for well over three minutes until the pain subsided and gradually went away. When she got up to head to her bedroom for a nap, the pain returned. Once again she doubled over and thrust her hands to her side. She hoped Dr. Kreake would be able to tell her what was going on.

She tried to rest, but couldn't sleep. She was growing more and more worried about her health. She was settling in so nicely, had good friends and loved Regina. Perhaps, the only thing in her life that needed healing had to do with family, the estranged relationship with J.J.. He was still so cold towards her. Fortunately his new wife, Nora, was pleasant and talked to Jenny when she phoned.

It saddened Jenny that she had to learn from Matti that Nora had given birth to a son and that shortly after J.J. and Nora got married. Jenny would give anything to see her little grandchild and hold him in her arms.

"Oh, Lord," Jenny called out in the stillness of her bedroom. "Please heal our relationship. Bring peace into this family and please heal me of this awful pain." At that precise moment the pain returned and lasted much longer.

JENNY ARRIVED AT her appointment ten minutes early.

Five minutes after she sat down amongst the four other people in the waiting room, a young lady exited the examining room and Jenny wondered who would be next. To her surprise, the receptionist called her name.

One of the men glared at her as she stood and followed the receptionist inside. Dr. Kreake was standing behind his desk when she walked in. She studied his eyes and instantly she knew just like the time she would learn of her rape and pregnancy that this was serious.

"Please sit down, Ms. Hamilton."

"Please, doctor, call me Jenny, I much prefer it."

"Certainly…Jenny."

Jenny chose a chair by the desk in the examination room, as Dr. Kreake sat down and opened the file in front of him. His dark eyes lost their sparkle as his expression turned even grimmer.

"Your test results came back, Jenny, and I'm afraid they don't look good."

Jenny's heart began to race. She pressed her hands against her thighs to control her trembling legs. "What is it, doctor?"

"Well, the blood samples show irregularities, however it's the X-rays. Jenny, you have a tumour in the colon. That's probably why you are experiencing pain in your side."

"Oh my God. Is it…?" Jenny couldn't say the word.

"At this point, I don't know how serious it is Ms…I mean, Jenny… but I would like to admit you to the hospital, right away. I want to have more tests done, an ultrasound and even operate, tomorrow, if I can schedule a surgeon."

Jenny was stunned, how could this be happening? It must be a dream. Yet the pain in her side, especially that morning clearly indicated that something was very wrong.

"Are you sure? Are you serious that I be admitted, today?"

"Yes, Jenny, I am dead serious. I wish you would have come to me sooner. Early diagnosis is still the best treatment for cancer, should your tumour be malignant," Dr. Kreake quickly added.

The word cancer sent shivers through Jenny's entire body. She had always been so healthy. She ate a lot of raw vegetables, exercised at least three times a week.

"This can't be happening to me," Jenny murmured.

"I know this is a shock, Jenny, but cancer can strike anyone and at any time. I hope and pray it isn't, but we can't be sure until we operate, remove it and biopsy it. I'm sorry I have to be so blunt, but I can't stress enough how each moment from now on is important. We must admit you right away."

Despair pushed Jenny into a state of shock. She saw Dr. Kreake's lips move, he was saying something, but she was as good as deaf. She thought about her mother dying and perhaps now she would soon follow.

"Jenny…Jenny, are you okay?" Dr. Kreake asked as he rounded his desk, watching her.

Jenny saw him coming, but didn't know why. The room started to spin, the white coat reached out to her and in the next instant…she was in her garden pruning the geraniums. Of all the flowers in her garden, she liked the geraniums the best. It was the flower patch with its beautiful array of flowers that brought her healing, though. She would put daisies into the Angel of Thanksgiving's basket and also….

JENNY'S EYES FLUTTERED open to see the white coat standing over her.

"Jenny, Jenny. Everything is okay."

Jenny looked into Dr. Kreake's eyes, but still wasn't entirely sure where she was.

"What happened?"

You're in Dr. Kreake's office, you're fine. You just fainted. I guess the shock of going into the hospital and possibly having an operation tomorrow was just a little too much for you to take in all at once. Perhaps I should have eased into it, but this is urgent, Jenny, and I don't want to waste any time."

"I…I understand, doctor, actually I have a habit of doing this" Jenny said, as she forced a smile and tried to sit up.

Dr. Kreake held her arm as she swung her legs down off the table so they dangled there unable to reach the floor.

"You have had fainting spells before?"

"Well, when I learned I was pregnant, but that was so long ago."

The doctor studied her for a long moment, "Are you okay now? Can you sit by yourself?"

"Yes, yes, I am fine. I guess I was overwhelmed by it all."

"Of course, Jenny, it's very understandable."

The nurse popped her head into the office, again. "Is everything okay? Do you need my help?"

"No, I think everything is fine now, thanks, Irene."

Irene nodded and closed the door.

"Are you driving, Jenny?"

"Yes, I am. My car is parked just down the street."

"Do you think you are well enough to drive?"

"Yes, I think so."

"I can get someone to drive you home."

"No, I am fine, now. I would like to go home and get a few things, though, my books and so on."

"I understand, but may I suggest you leave your car at home and take a cab to the hospital."

"Yes, that's a good idea. How long do you think I would be in the hospital for?"

"Well, a few days for certain."

Jenny slowly slipped off the examination table until her feet touched the floor. She felt a bit woozy, but took a deep breath and the world stabilized. She noticed the overturned chair near the door.

"Did I faint way over here?"

"Well, not quite, I pushed you over there in the chair so I could call Irene to help me lift you onto the table."

"Oh my!" Jenny chuckled.

"I'm a bit reluctant to let you go and drive home. Are you sure you are all right to do so?"

"Yes, I'm sure, doctor. If at any time I think I might be a risk to anyone, I assure you I will pull over and call a cab."

"Well, perhaps sit out in the waiting room for awhile and read a magazine until you catch your breath and this whole matter sinks in a little more."

"Oh, I assure you, it's sunk in."

"Well, Jenny, take a cab to the emergency entrance, it's quicker there than the admitting desk in the front lobby. I will tell them you are on your way and to admit you at once. I will do everything I can to get you a private room."

Jenny looked at Dr. Kreake. "Thank you for your care and attention and concern, doctor." She reached out her hand and he shook it. He watched her exit and knew it was probably one of the last times he would see her flowing wheat-coloured hair.

Jenny parked the car in front of her home and even before she stepped out her spirits perked up. She was surrounded by her flowers and plants, things she loved and gave her sustenance. It was almost as if she had taken a tranquilizer; the sweet natural aroma of the roses next to the front steps soothed and relaxed her.

"Hi, Jenny," called Mabel from next door.

"Hi, Mabel," said Jenny. "I'm glad to see you. Can you come over for a minute?"

"Sure."

Jenny stood at the landing to the front door and waited for her neighbour.

"Well, you look very nice, Jenny."

"Thanks, Mabel. I have to ask a favour of you."

"Oh? What's the matter?"

"Well, Mabel, I'm just home from a doctor's appointment and they discovered a tumour in my colon and I need to go into the hospital, right away." Jenny took a deep breath. She knew her pasted-on smile wouldn't pass as cheery. "He would like to have a surgeon perform surgery tomorrow, to remove the tumour."

"Oh no, Jenny." Mabel stepped on the landing and reached out her arms. Jenny leaned into Mabel's warm embrace.

"Oh, what can I do, Jenny? Is there anything...?"

"Yes, there is." Jenny pulled slightly away from Mabel. "I don't know how long I will be in the hospital, but I would sure appreciate it if you would look after the lawn and the flowers."

"Oh, certainly, Jenny."

"There are several plants in the house, as well, that will need watering."

"No bother at all, Jenny, don't worry about a thing. I just love being around your flowers. They all look so healthy and beautiful."

"Could you come in for a minute now? I will give you a key and the code for the security system. You will have to activate it each time you come and go. I'll show you where the plants are, as they're scattered through-out the house."

"We have a similar system at our house." Mabel said as she looked at the security system. "Can I help you get ready? How are you going to get to the hospital?"

"Oh, I thought I would take a cab."

"Oh no, Jenny, I will take you. Please let me."

"Are you sure?"

"Positive. I wouldn't think of you taking a cab."

"Oh, Mabel, that's so kind of you. I would rather go with you than a cab driver. You can take my car and perhaps drive it into the garage at the back."

"Oh, for sure, Jenny."

Jenny walked Mabel through the various rooms and showed her where all the plants were. When they stopped in the kitchen, Jenny wrote down the code for the security system on a slip of paper and handed it to Mabel. She then slipped one of the house keys from her key ring and handed it to Mabel, as well.

Just as Mabel took the key, a sharp pain stabbed at Jenny's side, immediately doubling her over. Mabel reached out for her.

"Are you okay?"

Jenny couldn't speak for a moment. She tried hard to straighten to relieve her neighbour's concern, but the pain was too strong. Mabel wrapped her arms more around Jenny not knowing how else to help. Slowly the pain subsided and Jenny breathed deeply once more. Mabel's arms slid off Jenny's shoulders as she raised her chest enough to gaze at Mabel who seemed to be in a state of shock.

"It's gone now. It's almost like a labour pain," Jenny said as she winked at the same time. "I wish I were pregnant, though. Well, I better get ready. I'll be fine." Jenny said, again trying to reassure Mabel.

Mabel studied Jenny for a long moment. "Okay, Jenny, I'll go now.

When you get your things ready, just come out and I'll take you to the hospital. Which one are you going to?"

"Oh my gosh, I forgot to ask Dr. Kreake. He probably told me, but I was in shock I didn't hear everything. I will phone the office and find out."

"Okay, Jenny. I will go home, now, and wait for you."

As soon as Mabel left, Jenny began unzipping her dress at the back. As she did so, a pain pierced her left side. Once again Jenny crouched over, but the pain was so excruciating, she yelled out in agony.

"Oh, dear Lord, please help me." Jenny began to cry.

As the pain dissipated, again, she slowly straightened up. She lifted her dress up as high as she could to give her a little more leeway to reach her back zipper. Finally, she managed to get her dress off. She walked into her bedroom carrying her dress and sat down on the edge of the bed. She took a deep breath and let it out.

"Oh my, that was an ordeal."

Jenny was exhausted and extremely worried. The stress induced by the pain in her side and the news of possible cancer had taken the wind out of her. A new weariness wriggled inside her stomach right next to the tumour.

Just when things seemed to moving forward so well. Mrs. Blake would be back next week from holidays and I was looking forward to discussing how to re-unite with Camilla...

"Now this," she sighed, slouching her shoulders even more.

"Must get ready." She slid off the bed and carefully stood, making every effort not to awaken the pain again, then inched her way to the closet. She decided on a pair of slacks and a blouse that buttoned up the front, something that she could get on and off with as little effort as possible.

Jenny changed, packed her cosmetic case, two books, her robe, pajamas, underwear and slippers. If she discovered she needed anything else she would ask Mabel to bring it to her.

After she placed her things by the front door, she returned to the kitchen and was about to pick up the phone when it rang.

"Hello?"

"Oh, Ms. Hamilton. This is Irene from Dr. Kreake's office. You got home okay, I guess."

"Yes, I did fine, Irene. I was just about to phone you."

"I bet you want to know which hospital you should go to."

"That's exactly why I was about to call you."

"Well, it's the General Hospital. Do you know how to get there?"

"No, but my neighbour is going to drive me and I'm sure she knows where it is."

"That's good. You will need to go to the emergency entrance off 15th Avenue. I'm sure you will find it."

"I'm sure we will, Irene, thank you for calling."

"All the best, Ms. Hamilton."

"Thanks, Irene."

Jenny hung up and walked over to the sink. She looked out the kitchen window to the gazebo; her private little sanctuary which had provided her with so much solace. She hadn't sat out there for over a week.

"Oh, I must do so before I leave. I'll just take a minute."

Jenny walked out to the deck. Rays of sun peeked in between the two large fir trees and shone on the gazebo just as she had planned. It looked like some holy shrine with the Angel of Thanksgiving standing watch just off to the side. Jenny marvelled at how the yard had changed since she began working on it. She stepped off the deck and strolled along the winding stone path.

"Oh, what will the future hold for me, now?"

Jenny stopped several times to pinch off flowers, which had bloomed and were wilting. She knew that more would take their place.

Finally, she made it to her retreat. The cedar aroma of the new wood pleased her sense of smell and momentarily overpowered the fragrance drifting off the herbs and wildflowers. She entered the gazebo and sat down nearest the opening that faced the sun.

Softly, her eyes closed and her head, like a flower, tilted towards the light. The sun shone brightly upon her luminous skin smoothing out the furrows of worry as the rays gently danced off her features. The sun was her comforter, her consoler, her friend. The warmth assuaged Jenny and for the first time that day instilled within her a peace. She gently swung back and forth under the clear prairie sky.

Time stood still. She let her mind go blank, and drifted with the motion of the swing – back and forth, back and forth. Thoughts which had the potential of disturbing her peace came and went. In one moment she pictured her mother, wishing she were here. And J.J., should she phone him? Would this all turn out to be nothing? Perhaps she'd wait. She would put off calling Mrs. Blake, too, until she knew her future better.

And then the little *Guardian Angel Prayer* came into her mind chasing out all the other thoughts. *Oh angel of God, my guardian dear, to whom His love commits me here. Ever this day be at my side to light and guard, to rule and guide...Oh, please dear angel help me...*

Jenny heard the soft flutter of wings. So often at the estate and just like now as she sat in her haven, it was as if a hummingbird were hovering over her. She took it as a sign that her guardian and protector was ever so close to comfort her. Jenny reached up and took hold of the pewter angel hanging on the chain around her neck. She thought of the inscription written on it. *Watch over my beloved.*

Instantly, she felt Henry's warmth and love.

She opened her eyes and there it was – her Angel of Thanksgiving, smiling, reassuring her all would be well. She held that vision in her heart as she rose and made her way to the wildflowers. Carefully she bent over and snapped off several yellow daisies, a couple of blue delphiniums, a bunch of bright red poppies and a handful of pink, blue and mauve Canterbury bells that should have stopped blooming a month or so ago and placed them in the angel's basket.

"It has always been my heart's desire to see my daughter and Henry, my first love again."

"Thank you for the miracle!"

Just as she bowed her head in prayer and thanksgiving, Mabel called her name.

"Jenny, are you back there?"

"Oh, yes, here I am, Mabel, back here. I wanted to see my gazebo one more time. The carpenters did such a fine job, didn't they?"

"Is it ever beautiful, Jenny," Mabel's eyes brightened as she walked up the winding path. "This entire backyard is beautiful! I've never seen such a wonderful array of flowers and everything so well arranged."

"Thank you, Mabel, I do love flowers and gardening. Besides reading, it's my main love. Well, are you ready to go?"

"Yes, if you are."

"Okay, I'll get my suitcases and meet you out front."

"Oh, let me help you with the luggage, Jen."

They both walked back towards the house. Jenny locked the back door and then followed Mabel to the front door. Mabel picked up both suit cases and headed out.

"See you at the car, Jen."

"Thank you, Mabel."

Jenny slowly surveyed the living room and looked at each of her antiques. Everything looked so nice and complimented each other.

Reluctantly she turned, activated the alarm system, and walked out.

Mabel had already started the car and lowered the roof because she knew from past rides how much Jenny liked the feeling of freedom it gave to her.

Jenny strolled down the winding stone path to the car. Before Jenny got in, she turned and tried to soak up as much spiritual sustenance as she could from her flowers. The fragrance of herbs amongst other flowers at the base of the tree next to her tantalized her nostrils. She bent over and snapped off a twig of rosemary and mint and brought them to her nose. She took a deep breath and smiled.

"See you soon," she whispered.

"What a great day to ride in a convertible! Thanks for putting the top down," Jenny exclaimed, as she lowered herself onto the seat and buckled her belt.

Jenny's hair flew back and tossed about as Mabel sped up Hill Avenue to Albert Street, turned left and headed north. At 14th Avenue, Mabel turned right.

Jenny's heart began to race as they approached Henry's Café and the Pederson Art Gallery on the corner of 14th and Smith.

"Have you been into Henry's, yet?" Mabel asked, as she stopped for a stop sign on the corner.

"No, I haven't, yet."

"Oh, you must go there. There's nothing like it in the city or anywhere for that matter. Henry sure did a nice job with that old building, such a unique addition to the city. I take all my out-of-town guests there."

Jenny listened in silence, as she intently stared at the Gallery on the corner. "Yes, it has such appealing heritage architecture, and I love the blue exterior." Jenny finally said, as they drove by.

"Well, as soon as you get out of the hospital we must go there for lunch, it will be my special treat."

Jenny didn't answer. So many times she'd wanted to go into the store, but was afraid she might see Henry. Her heart ached just thinking on it.

"I guess going to Henry's is the last thing on your mind though isn't it, Jen?" said Mabel.

"Oh, I'm sorry, Mabel. Yes, Henry's sounds so nice, I've heard so much about it, perhaps when I get out…" Jenny didn't finish. She didn't want to make a promise she might not be able to keep. To visit Henry's and to see Henry was a wish deep in her heart. Jenny slowly turned her head keeping her gaze steady on the gallery and café as they sped by. So close, yet so painfully separated.

Mabel was commenting on the landscaping around the gallery, how it contained a few of the Junipers and cedars similar to Jenny's front yard, but Jenny didn't hear her neighbour anymore. Instead, she drifted back to those warm summer days she'd had with Henry, his hand in hers. It seemed like yesterday. And yet, it happened thousands of yesterdays, ago.

As Henry stepped out of the café into the sunlight, he noticed the blue BMW convertible making its way down 14th Avenue.

A great day to own a convertible.

He wished he were in the driver's seat. He had planned to go clean out his mother's place, but it was getting too late in the day.

"Yeah," he muttered, "I'll go over first thing tomorrow morning. *God only knows what I will discover there.*"

CHAPTER FORTY-TWO

"GOOD MORNING, DR. Kreake," said Jenny, as he walked into her hospital room.

"I'm just making my morning rounds before going back to the office."

"You sure must have long days."

"Yes, just ask my wife. She thinks I'm a stranger half the time."

"Well, we certainly don't want that. Family should be first, you know."

"Yes, I know. So, how are you? You seem to be in good spirits."

"Well, it all depends on you, doctor. What's the scoop?"

"Well, two other specialists looked at the X-rays and they too feel that we should remove the tumour as soon as possible and have a biopsy done. I have you booked in for surgery at 2:30, this afternoon."

"You were serious, yesterday, weren't you?"

"Yes, Jenny. The sooner we get that thing out of there the better. And once we do, we will know for sure what we are dealing with. Are you okay with all this?"

"To be honest, I'm scared as a rabbit about to be ripped open by a wolf."

"I assure you, we are not wolves, but I can appreciate your analogy. Surgery is scary, but if it's any consolation, the surgeon who will operate is the best in Saskatchewan. In fact, he travels to Toronto several times a year and does surgery there, as well. He uses some different techniques which have produced incredible healing results. He is training other doctors with his new procedures. You are in very capable hands, Jenny."

"That does make me feel better."

"Would you like a sedative to keep you relaxed?"

"No, I'm fine. It's begun to sink in, now, and I feel a little more prepared than I was, yesterday. I must have been some concern for you."

"A little, I must admit. You are the first patient to have a fainting spell in my office."

Jenny giggled.

"Well, Jenny, I better finish my rounds. I will see you later this evening after your operation."

"My gosh, you do have a long day. You really don't have to, you know."

"I know, Jenny, but I am concerned about you and I wouldn't be able to relax at home if I didn't see you first, and make sure you are okay."

Unbidden tears pooled in her eyes. "Dr. Kreake that's the nicest thing anyone has said to me in a long time. Thank you."

Dr. Kreake patted Jenny's hand. "Try to have a little rest, everything will be just fine. See you, tonight."

"MARJORIE? MARJORIE HAMILTON." A kind, sing-songy voice reached through the grogginess.

"Marjorie, you're in the recovery room, I'm, Elsie, the nurse on duty."

It took a few seconds for Jenny's eyes to open and for her to orient herself.

Elsie moved closer to Jenny's bedside. "You're okay, Marjorie. You're in the hospital recovery room."

"What…what did you say…?"

"You're out of surgery, Marjorie. You're in the recovery room."

Jenny raised her arm to put it under her head until pain from the incision stabbed at her side.

"Oow!"

"Does it hurt, Marjorie?"

"Yes, it's very sore."

"Just a minute and I will increase the medication in this IV, you will soon feel better. Try to stay awake, now. Would you like some water?"

"Yes, please. My mouth feels so dry."

Elsie reached for a glass of water that had a flexible straw. She adjusted the straw and inserted it into Jenny's mouth.

"Oh, that feels and tastes so good. So, how did the operation go?"

"You will have to ask the, doctor. I don't have any details. I just know that you experienced no complications associated with the procedure, at all."

"What time is it, Elsie?"

"It's 15 minutes to six. Your operation took one hour and thirty minutes. And you have been in the recovery room for just over an hour and a half."

"I see," said Jenny.

"We will keep you on fluids for another hour or so and then maybe you might feel like a piece of toast and hot soup."

"That sounds nice. Surprisingly, I do feel hungry."

"That's common after coming out of surgery. But we will wait until you are well awake. How are you feeling, now, is the medication taking effect?"

"I think so." Jenny tried to raise her arm cautiously and was surprised that she could almost raise it to the back of her head. "Yes, yes. Much better."

"That's good. Well, you just relax while I see how John over here is doing." Jenny tried to look over towards him, but couldn't raise her head high enough.

Fifteen minutes later, Dr. Kreake walked in.

"Well, how is Jenny doing?"

Jenny turned her head towards the door. "Oh, hi, Dr. Kreake. I'm awake."

"That's good. They will move you out of here very shortly and back into your room."

"Well, how did the operation go, doctor? Do you know what they found?"

"Yes, they found a tumour, all right, the size of a large lemon."

"Oh dear, no wonder I was in pain. Was it malignant?" Jenny asked nervously, looking directly into Dr. Kreake's eyes.

"We are not sure."

Jenny knew from his tone that that wasn't quite the truth.

"The tumour was sent to the lab. We should know, tomorrow."

"You're not keeping anything secret from me, are you?"

"Well, Jenny, we feel the tumour was malignant, but the lab will confirm our diagnosis."

"Thank you, Doctor, I feel better knowing, than having to wait another day. But, I'll tell you one thing, I'm a heck of a fighter. It won't be easy for that disease to take me down. I'm already expecting a miracle."

"That's the spirit, Jenny. A positive attitude is very important. We have some very good medication these days."

"Will I need chemotherapy and radiation?"

"I don't know just yet, Jenny, the next day or so will determine what treatment will be best. There are different forms of cancer and each requires a different approach. And really, Jenny, we are putting the cart before the horse. Let's see where we are with all this. The nurse will take you to your room in a few minutes, try to get some rest and I will see you, tomorrow."

"Thank you so much for coming."

"You're welcome, Jenny, take care."

As he walked out the door, Jenny blurted out, "And thank your wife, too!"

Once again Dr. Kreake didn't look back. He just waved a hand into the air then disappeared down the hall.

Elsie overheard the conversation and came over to comfort Jenny.

"So, now I have cancer. I just hate that word. What else can possibly happen to me?"

Jenny turned her eyes towards the ceiling, "Lord, I feel more like Job every day. I so wish mom were here, but then, I suppose you are, aren't you?"

Jenny didn't know if she was talking to Elsie or to God. But Elsie didn't discourage her.

Jenny thought about her guardian angel, and the card her mom had sent to her the day after she died…

"Your guardian angel will watch over you and protect you."

And suddenly Jenny also remembered another angel. She reached up to her chest with her right hand and clutched the pewter angel. Henry had requested that she wear it always as a memory of his love and that it would always protect her. And she had kept her promise to him. She lifted the angel at the end of the chain and read the inscription:

'Watch Over My Beloved.'

"Yes, I will have no fear. Besides my own guardian angel I have two other angels watching over me and both are from my first loves."

Elsie watched the metal angel glisten in Jenny's fingers and smiled. She was glad she had put the necklace back around her neck after the surgery. "What a lovely thought to have coming out of an anaesthetic."

Jenny kissed the angel and brought her hand back down to her chest. The angel gave off soothing, healing warmth, almost as if her beloved sun were in the room. A peace washed over her as the residual traces of the anaesthetic lulled her back to sleep.

Or, was it her guardian angel, cradling her tenderly in her arms, preparing her dear sweet Jenny for what was yet to come?

CHAPTER FORTY-THREE

H IS MOTHER HAD passed away over two weeks ago and Henry still hadn't cleared the house of his mother's belongings. He had put off the responsibility for days and he just couldn't put it off any longer, as the house was scheduled to go on the market in another week.

On the way over, Henry stopped off at the funeral home to pay the funeral expenses. After he paid the bill he asked if they still had the clothes that his mother was wearing when the ambulance attendants had picked her up. When he had brought the clothes that his mother was going to wear he had forgotten to pick up what she had been wearing.

The receptionist went into an adjoining administrator's office and almost immediately the assistant manager came out and said he would check. A few minutes later he returned to inform Henry of the unfortunate news, "I'm so sorry Mr. Pederson, since you or no one came to pick them up the staff discarded them a week ago. Was it something important she had on?"

"No, well, yes, not her dress, but the apron she had on over it was what I was more interested in. It was her favourite, the one she wore most often. It was more for nostalgic purposes than for anything else."

"We apologize, Mr. Pederson, is there anything we can do?"

"No, that's fine and thank you for carrying out the funeral in such a caring way and all the extras you and the staff have done. Much appreciated!"

Henry shook hands with the assistant manager and left.

IT WAS EERIE entering the house now devoid of life and sound, the smell of something cooking in the air, and perhaps most of all, it was eerie to have his mother no longer greeting him from the kitchen. Suddenly, Henry realized how even this simple act of her standing there was so important. If he could turn back time he would never again take for granted her presence at that doorway. How foolishly he had discarded such precious moments of welcome, believing they would go on forever.

Henry slowly walked down the hallway to his mother's haven still fully expecting her to come out. At the doorway he stopped and peeked in, his gaze dropping immediately to the floor then back to the sink. He tried to visualize her standing at the sink like he had seen her a thousand times before. Despite his vivid imagination, he was unable to conjure up any image to fill the emptiness he felt at that moment.

She really was gone.

Things were as he had left them. The scorched pot was still on the stove and a faint odour of burnt vegetables still lingered in the air. Flies buzzed and danced and beat against the kitchen window. When his mom was alive there were never any flies in the house. How easily pests can gain their freedom in the wake of death. Henry opened the window in front of the sink inviting the breeze outside to chase out the stale air. He reached for the radio on the shelf, but stopped his hand in mid-air. He didn't want to be distracted from his memories.

All too soon the house would be sold and a new family would begin their life here and make it their home. But, for the moment, it was still his parents' home, and his home, and he wanted to remember and take as much of it with him as he could.

He decided to start in his parents' room.

He turned on the light and smiled at the king-sized bed. It was way too big for such a small room. But it certainly was a far sight better than those two twin beds.

The door to the closet was partially open. He opened it all the way and stared at the tightly packed row of clothes. On the top shelf, he noted only a few things, and decided to start there and work his way down. He took down several hats and sweaters and then another box which was on the far left of the shelf. It was the hat box which contained his mother's red hat – the one she wore for the first time, the day he gave his valedictorian speech in grade twelve.

"You looked great that day, Mom," Henry muttered. As Henry reached up one last time, he wondered how on earth his mother had ever been able to reach up there. The shelf was so high and she was so much shorter than him.

Next, he took out the clothes and piled them onto the huge bed, fully emptying the closet except for shoes, slippers and shoe boxes on the floor. He would sort out those things later. As he stepped backwards out of the closet his eye caught the white rose almost glowing next to his mother's treasure chest sitting on the dresser. He stepped over to the dresser and looked at the rose. The water had evaporated long ago leaving a white mineral deposit on the inside of the vase. Amazingly however, the rose appeared as fresh as the day he saw it when his mother passed away. He picked it up and smelled it. Its scent still sweet as ever. He replaced the flower and looked at the chest. He was going to check it out last time he was here. He had seen his mother put many things into it over the years and often she said it contained treasures of the heart. He recalled once again that the last memory he had of the box was when his mom had put his dad's death certificate in there.

Henry remembered too, that the chest was locked.

"I wonder what treasures of the heart Mom has locked inside?" He muttered, as he began to survey the top of the dresser in search of the key.

The small jewellery box resting on the other end of the dresser caught his eye. He lifted the lid and stirred his finger around the jewellery inside. At first he missed seeing the key as it had worked its way to the bottom and was covered by rings, earrings and two gold chains. Henry picked up the box and emptied its contents on top of the white crocheted runner on the dresser. The very last thing to fall on the heap of sparkling jewellery was the tiny bronze key.

"Aha!" Henry said, as a feeling of discovery surged through him. He picked up the key, inserted it into the keyhole and the latch sprung open.

He felt like an intruder. These were his mother's private articles and he was about to enter her world, her private thoughts and see things which she considered to be precious memorabilia. Henry raised the lid and slowly removed the contents, giving each one consideration and thought, trying to recount or relive what his mother was thinking as she placed them inside.

The third item following his father's death certificate and insurance policy was a folded letter. He recognized it as the letter he'd left to his mother about aborting his plan to go to Ottawa. Many times since then Henry wondered what would have happened had he carried out his plan. Would he have found Jenny? How different things might be now.

But he had found a new love who had restored his life.

He began to think on Julean and how quickly she stole his heart, and he fell in love again.

Henry smiled as he re-read the letter and the precious time they shared each trying to outwit the other. The tear stain in the bottom left corner of the letter drew his attention.

"Mom's trademark," he chuckled. He rubbed the stain with his fore-finger, then brushed the tear rolling down his cheek with the back of his hand. He folded the letter and placed it on the dresser then continued sifting through the rest of the items.

He noticed Julean's remembrance card in the box. He hadn't read it for a long time. He picked it up and gazed at his lovely wife's picture on the front of the card and was immediately overcome by the sorrow of her absence. He opened the card and read the comments that he and his children had written. He smiled at Justin's comment that he wanted his mommy to come and tuck him in each night, and that she could take the teddy bear he gave her at the hospital to heaven.

The verses he wrote he still felt so deeply:

That life would go on without her, but nothing would be the same. How sad are the tears that love her, how silent are the tears that fall…

Henry couldn't read anymore. He wiped the tears away with the back of his hand and peered inside the chest. He took out more items one by one and finally reached in for the last item. It looked like the death certificate of some relative. It was difficult to read as both the writing and colour of the yellow paper had faded:

The Death Certificate
Of
Louise Wagner
1863 - 1945

Henry thought for a moment. Grandma, his mother's mother. He was only six when she died and he had very few memories of her.

And then it came to him that the item he was really looking for was the pink envelope. He still recalled holding it in this room when his dad died and the warmth it gave off.

Mom sure didn't want me to see that letter. I wonder where it went?

As he thought still further on it, he remembered that the envelope had given off a lilac odour…such a familiar fragrance. That was Jenny's favourite flower. She liked the smell so much she used that scent for her perfume as well. But there was something else…

Henry raised his head and peered at the reflection of himself think-ing, and then it came to him as if from his image inside of the mirror…

I smelled that fragrance the other day when praying over Mom! But Mom never put on perfume as Dad had been scent sensitive to the odour of any perfume.

I wonder...

Henry turned as if led and walked out of the room and back to the kitchen.

Could Mom have had that letter with her the day she died? Could that have been what I was smelling. Could that have been what Mom wanted to talk to me about and give to me!

But, but...she must have had it in her apron pocket...*which was thrown away at the funeral home!*

And just as despair began to wash over him he saw a shadow move towards the phone on the wall. There was Julean her hand reaching to the phone.

It RANG!

Henry was nearly startled out of his wits! It rang again. Julean smiled and disappeared as he reached out to her. His hand pierced the air landing on the telephone receiver!

He picked it up half way through its third ring...

"Hello, is this Mr. Pederson.?"

"Yes, it is."

"I'm Scott Allan and I work at Speer's Funeral Home. I called your gallery and they said that you could be reached at this number."

"Okay, that's fine...what's this about?"

"Mr. Manser, the assistant manager talked to me about fifteen minutes ago to check if any of your mom's belongings were here, I told him they weren't. When I spoke with him later he said that you were really interested in the apron your mom was wearing and that it was unfortunate that the clothes had been discarded."

An eerie feeling started crawling up Henry's spine, he knew something supernatural was going on.

"Go on, Scott."

"Well, this may be hard to believe, but when we lifted your mom off the floor she was so stiff and light it was easy to transfer her to the bag on the stretcher. But as we did so something quite unbelievable happened.

"While she was six inches off the floor it seemed as if her apron was being untied and it simply slipped off her and fell to the floor. Both Ron and me saw it. In fact Ron even commented out loud on it, 'Did you see what I just saw?'

"We see a lot of things in this business, but that one was kinda scary. When we were driving back to the funeral home Ron and I talked about it, and thought that perhaps we should have told you what happened, but then we didn't want to frighten you. The main thing was that the apron was left there. When I picked it up to put it on the chair I felt a letter inside the pocket. And I have to tell you, the letter sure felt warm.

"We thought for sure you would see it on the chair. Anyway, if the apron hadn't slipped off your mom, it just may very well have been discarded along with the rest of her things."

"Thanks for phoning Scott…"

Henry hung up the phone, certain that both his guardian angel and Julean's spirit must be having a good laugh over this!

"Unbelievable," he muttered as he turned to the kitchen table. All the chairs had been pushed under the table hiding the seats. He pulled one back out and then a second…*there was his mom's apron!*

My God, he might very well have missed it, and it probably would have been taken away for sure next week when the movers from the Salvation Army came..

He picked up the apron, and sure enough inside the left pocket was a pink envelope. It had a bobby pin slipped over the end. Henry looked at it, but didn't realize that the pin was intended to keep its contents from slipping out. It was the same letter he had seen and held in his mother's bedroom. When she snatched it from his hand she said that it was from her girlfriend. Henry was confused. Why would she want to give that to him? Surely this couldn't be what she wanted to give him. Maybe this is nothing after all…

He looked down at the letter and saw the red stamp across the envelope partially covering the addressee. The only name he could make out was "Pederson." Henry didn't take the time to look to the left corner and read where it was from as he was distracted by the bobby pin at the other end of the envelope,

He turned it over. "It's still sealed. She never even opened it. *I wonder why?"*

Still holding the envelope, Henry stepped backwards and sat down. Henry glanced at the letter again. He believed that the letter was his mother's, so he didn't think to look at the addressee's name.

He flipped the letter over again and as he debated if he should open the letter, the lilac scent, the warmth, and the heftiness of the envelope aroused his curiosity. Yet, he couldn't understand all the fuss over this letter and the apron. The attendants being frightened by it and Julean's presence… Why?

Henry looked down and absently tore open the end of the envelope opposite the edge where the bobby pin was. He pulled the letter out and laid the envelope back on the table beside him, unsuspecting that the envelope still contained a very important item.

The pale purple paper gave off a strong lilac scent.

"One of Mom's friends must like lilacs too."

He unfolded the letter and separated the two pages. His eyes at first noted the name at the bottom of the second page: *Love, Jenny*.

"Jenny? I never knew mom had a girlfriend by that name."

Fatigue and hunger were more on the doorstep to his brain than reading about some girl talk and distant friend of his mother's whom he'd never met.

As Henry stood, he skimmed its contents getting ready to discard it when an indescribable feeling ignited and crept forth from the very core of his being. His mind was in a daze, as if in a fog that spanned time. As haze lifted, it captured some distant familiarity – the handwriting, the sweet smell of lilac, its love filled contents.

"What on earth is this?" His mind reset, shifting from a letter to his mom from her girlfriend, into the reality of the moment; the surge of energy he felt moments ago accelerated from a crawl to an explosion, thrusting his head sharply back. He separated the pages, holding one in each hand. His eyes flashed to the signature again on the bottom of the second page – *Love Jenny* – and then to the top of the page in his left hand – *Dear Henry*.

"This can't be Jenny? My Jenny!? How could this be after all these years? Oh, how I waited for a letter from you. How could this be?"

Henry stood there frozen, unable to think or move.

Ever so slowly, he returned his gaze to the letter and read the writing at the top of the letter again, making sure that his mind was not just playing some trick on him: *Dear Henry*.

"It's true! This is incredible!"

Demanding more proof, he picked up the envelope to see who it was addressed to. As he did so, the bobby pin flipped off the envelope and something flew out cutting through the charged air. For a moment he thought it was the bobby pin, but it was a shiny object fluttering off, as if it had wings to the other side of the table.

"What is that?" Henry rushed over to the other side of the table and looked down. A shiny object reflected the light from the ceiling overhead. As he bent down, he hesitated and leaned closer.

"This just can't be! This cannot be possible!"

He picked up the pewter angel, his eyes transfixed on the sight before him...

Reality as Henry knew it faded away and was replaced by a spell that enveloped and carried him into a world far, far away – a world of guardian angels. An angel hanging on a Christmas tree in the window of Eaton's department store. There it was; his angel and Jenny's angel. It was exactly what he was looking for...*and here it was again...*

He brought the angel before him and read the inscription.

"Yes, it's the very same angel I sent to Jenny." He wondered if it was his and Jenny was returning it. He lowered the angel and studied the front of the envelope again and read the return address:

R.R. #21,
Ottawa, Ontario

He would have died to have known that address back then. His eyes lowered to the centre of the envelope.

"Yes, it is addressed to me," Henry said, with a tone of puzzlement. He furrowed his brow, *"Why on earth didn't Mom give it to me back then? It was mine. The letter I had been waiting for, for so..."*

For the first time in as long as he could remember, he was annoyed and upset with his mother.

There had to be some explanation.

CHAPTER FORTY-FOUR

As HENRY SAT down again, he laid the envelope on the table and picked up the letter and gave it a sharp flip. Years of being folded in the closed position caused it to spring back. His left hand grabbed the bottom edge of the letter and pulled down unfolding it all the way. He held the letter open in that position as he read in earnest.

December 18, 1956

Dear Henry

For days now I was thinking about writing another letter to you. I have always hesitated thinking perhaps you may have found another girlfriend. Today, however, my uncertainty went away, I was so excited.

Our school principal this year decided to have a Christmas tree decoration project to get us all in the spirit of Christmas. He had a huge evergreen tree set up in the foyer of the school. He then asked all the students to bring in an ornament and hang it on the tree. I took a metallic blue Christmas ball on which was a hand-painted image of Santa and his reindeers zooming through the sky. When I got to school and saw what my friend Tammy brought I just knew it was meant for me to send you this as a gift and write you one more letter.

I couldn't believe she had a pewter angel and with the perfect inscription on the bottom... When you read it you will know what I mean. Every night I pray to my guardian angel to protect you and to bring us together again. Oh Henry the gift is perfect and I just know it was meant to be.

All day, today, the snow was falling so heavily and covered everything in sight with a soft white cozy blanket. As night fell, the sky was still filled with millions of fluffy snowflakes... But moments ago when I looked out my bedroom window, the sky had cleared and the snowflakes turned into millions of twinkling stars. And most exciting of all, was the star to the east, it shone so brightly, tonight, and somehow I felt its beam was travelling to your heart telling you how much I miss you and my deepest wish that we could be together again.

The other day, I'll Be Home For Christmas was playing on the radio, it just sent goose bumps through me. Oh, how I wish you could be here at Christmastime. I so loved our summer walks together and can only imagine how wonderful it would be holding your hand in the winter time...and we could make angels in the snow so close together that our wings would intertwine... And to sit by the fire, listen to records and snuggle in your arms... Oh, how romantic it all would be.

Oh Henry, there is so much I want to say and tell you, but I am no longer sure of your love. If you have someone else please ignore this letter, I do not want you to feel bound to me. I want you to be free to choose. Since you haven't written, I cling to the hope that you still care, but I need to know.

You must be busy at Mr. Engelmann's store with Christmas just around the corner and everyone preparing for Christmas dinner. I remember how much you love working for him and what great business ideas you have always come up with. I so often think about how enthused you get when you think of something new to try. I just know that someday you will be a huge success in business.

School is going fine. The students are nice and I have made some wonderful girlfriends. The other weekend we had a sleepover party and we just had great fun. I like Ottawa, it is a pretty city, and I love how the Canal runs through the centre of the city. Last week when I went shopping with mom we walked through the park there and saw so many people skating...what a beautiful sight. I wish you were here and we were skating together.

I am so excited about the angel I am sending off tomorrow. As I write this letter, I am holding it in my hand. I want it to carry my love for you. When you receive it, you will feel my love by its warmth. I have already kissed it several times, too. You can just faintly see traces of my lipstick on the upper wing. Place your lips on mine. I just know my guardian angel will somehow return your kiss to me.

I made a special wish to the bright star of the east tonight, to send out my love to you. I hope and pray that you get this letter and my gift. Every night I pray for my guardian angel to talk to yours, so together they find some way to bring us to together again.

Even thought we are far apart, you are forever in my heart. I will love you always. Have a merry Christmas!

All my love,

Jenny.

The letter slipped from Henry's hands and fell to the table over top the angel. Tears spilled out his eyes; he could barely read the last paragraph. He pushed aside the letter exposing the pewter angel and picked it up, searching for the traces of Jenny's lipstick on the wing of the angel. The soft pink lip marks were still there.

Slowly, lovingly, he brought the angel towards him as if he were about to embrace Jenny herself. His lips tenderly touched her lips and his eyes closed forcing out the warm tears to gently roll down his cheeks mingling with the kiss. A warmth that he had not felt for a long time swept through him.

At that moment, *all time stood still.*

As Jenny was being wheeled out of the recovery room back to her room, she suddenly felt a soothing warmth emanate from the pewter angel. She could feel it against her chest next to her heart. She turned over and clutched the angel with both of her hands. She brought it up to her lips and tenderly kissed it. A warmth swept through, Jenny, and all memory and thoughts of her sickness vanished.

At that moment, *all time stood still.*

Reluctantly, Henry released the angel from his lips and studied it again. At first when he saw the angel, he thought it was the one he had sent to Jenny, but according to her letter it was an ornament her friend brought as a decoration for the tree at school.

But, but…how could this possibly be? How could Jenny have sent him exactly the same angel with exactly the same inscription…and send it to him at… He reached for the letter and read the date on the top: December 18, 1956. Henry looked up at the kitchen window above the sink allowing the light to help him recall and illuminate his mind.

"I think I mailed my letter to Jenny with the very same angel just two days before that date and that very same Christmas!"

The probability of such a coincidence to occur was astronomical!

An unearthly, yet warm sensation travelled down his spine. There were so many amazing happenings surrounding the purchase of the angel; the nickel he'd dropped into the Salvation Army pot, the Santa Claus alerting him to the angel crowning the Christmas tree in the Eaton's window, then Santa disappearing, the manager getting it for him and now...this!

Henry's feelings of warm love were enhanced with a growing surge of wonder, of mystery. Could there possibly be something supernatural going on here? He felt it back then and all through the years as well.

Am I really seeing Julean's spirit? Is she leading me back to Jenny along with my guardian angel?

It reminded Henry of the time Jenny almost had that terrible accident when crossing Victoria Avenue in front of Mr. Engelmann's store. How a car had been hurtling towards her and should have struck and killed her. Henry recalled the scene so vividly in his mind along with the fear he felt at the time gripping him. It was so real, he pushed the chair back and stood up, ready to run and save his Jenny.

Henry caught himself; shook his head and sat back down.

"She was saved by her guardian angel," Mr. Engelmann had said. It was the only explanation.

And now all this happening, what does it all mean?

He raised his head towards the window, again, and his brow took on a questioning deep wrinkle. There was another aspect of this that didn't make any sense either.

His mom knew how much he loved Jenny and how he yearned to receive a letter from her. Why would she have withheld this from him?

This is probably what she wanted to tell him. A week before she died she said twice that she had something to give him and tell him.

And on Monday, two days before their luncheon date, she reminded him again that when he comes home for his borscht soup to book off at least two hours...both times she was so serious that he could hardly wait to find out what his mother wanted to tell him.

Henry looked up and muttered into the stillness, "*What was it Mom that you wanted to tell me?*"

Henry knew his mother would never purposely hurt him or withhold anything.

"What on earth is going on here?"

Henry knew his entire life might have been so different. He could have been married to Jenny, have had different children, perhaps even lived in a different city.

Henry found himself in the midst of thoughts of what might have been. There was a fullness to his life and yet an emptiness. He knew what he had and where he had been over the past 24 years and now he tried to think how it might have been different.

No, he didn't want to go there now.

It would be a foolish idea and blemish the wonderful life he had with Julean. He had four great children and would not trade them for all the world. And, although Henry knew in his heart that his life and marriage had been happy and good, there was still that special spot in the recesses of his heart; that tiny light that never really went out over all these years. Julean knew about it even before we wed and unbelievably had been willing to share their marriage with Jenny.

How ironic was it that his mother had placed Julean's card and Jenny's letter in the same chest. They were sharing their same fate, together. Both had been a part of Henry's life and both had been removed from it.

Henry was overwhelmed by the discovery and how very real his love still was for Jenny despite his deep love for Julean. Perhaps, his feeling lonely since Julean's passing only enhanced those tender feelings of love he once had and why they lit up so readily.

And yet, it is Julean herself who seems to be leading him. She said she would, not only in the letter she had written to him, but also the last time they spoke in the hospital. Even in death his dear, sweet Julean is offering her love to him. Even in death Henry's love was increasing for Julean and the realization of what an incredible gem she was.

For the longest time he thought that Julean was leading him to Ivania. But it seemed to be going nowhere lately. Ivania definitely wanted a closer relationship, but how could he in all honesty, be true to her and to himself?

This is all so incredible! And yet, where can it possibly lead? Jenny could be married and a millions miles away. What is the sense of all this?

Henry checked his watch. This has been some day. He felt exhausted more from emotional overload than cleaning out the house. Perhaps he would stop for the day and head home. He wanted to read Jenny's letter over again and again.

He stood and stared at the pewter angel in his hands. The traces of pink lipstick on the wings had transferred to his lips. He ran his tongue over his lips and tried to taste Jenny's, but couldn't detect anything… only a memory tinged with a sweet lilac scent.

"Oh, Jenny," Henry said, as he brought the angel to his lips once again and tenderly kissed it. He picked up the letter, folded it and slid it back into the envelope. Before slipping it into his breast jacket pocket, he studied the address on the envelope and the special delivery stamp, again, and still wondered how it had come to land in his mother's treasure chest.

At the kitchen door he turned and looked back into the kitchen. He stared at the floor where his mother had lain. He imagined the attendants lifting her and the astonished look they must have had as his mother's apron unravelled from her waist before sealing her in the bag.

He shook his head and muttered, Amazing! As he turned out the light he whispered, "*Thank you, Julean.*"

Henry opened the screen door and walked out onto the landing. He inhaled the fall prairie air to clear his head. The cool autumn breeze and warmth of the sun soothed his troubled spirit.

"Just too many unanswered questions,"

As Henry made his way to the SUV the neighbour next door shouted to him.

"Hi, Henry."

"Hi Rose, how are doing?"

"I'm fine. Just wanted to let you know how sorry I am over your mom's passing. She was such an angel. I miss her deeply."

"Thanks, Rose, I miss her very much too."

"The last time I spoke to her was the day of our anniversary. My husband sent me a dozen red roses and there was an extra white rose in the bouquet. I felt compelled to give it to your mother at the time."

"Really?"

"She was so happy to receive it. It made her cry. She said that it was an answer to a prayer she had made to a saint called 'The Little Flower.'"

"Yeah, St Therese."

"Well anyway, she said she had made a decision 24 years ago that she always regretted and just that day she had vowed to make everything right. She considered the white rose as a sign her prayer had been heard."

"Oh my gosh, Rose, that's amazing. It sort of answers at least part of the questions that were in my mind. Now I am certain that the letter I found was what she had in mind to give me. When did you say you gave Mom the rose?"

"It was August 26, the day of our wedding anniversary. Like I said, the flowers were all so lovely. I wish flowers would last longer. Mine drooped, wilted and died about a week after."

"You're not going to believe this, Rose, the white rose you gave Mom is in a vase in her bedroom. The water dried up weeks ago, yet the flower looks as fresh as the day you gave it to her!"

As soon as Henry buckled up, he turned the key and the Escalade roared to life. He shifted into drive and let the vehicle roll ahead for a moment before he slammed on the brakes, launching himself towards the steering wheel. He set the vehicle in park, again.

Something struck him about what Rose had just said. His Mom regretted a decision she made 24 years ago. It made him re-think the date he had seen beside the stamp on the envelope as he stood in the kitchen just prior to seeing Rose. "I'm certain the delivery date of the letter was different than the date of Jenny's letter."

Henry pulled out the envelope and flipped it over to the front. The mid-afternoon sun shone through the open sun roof illuminating the envelope in his hand. It wasn't very clear …

"I'm sure it's August. Yes, August 26…I think. It could be 28…" But the year was clear. "1962." The moment the numbers tumbled from his lips it hit him like a locomotive going full speed.

"That was just days before Julean and I got married!"

Henry was so flabbergasted he didn't trust his own memory. He quickly took off his gold wedding band that Julean had given him the day of their wedding and read the date inscribed on the inside.

"Yes, September 9, 1962. Oh, Mom. That's why you kept it from me. *It was too late.* I was on the doorstep to be wed to another!"

How difficult a decision that must have been for you to make Mom and to keep it a secret for all these years. That's what you shared with Rose and been praying for…that was the decision you regretted for 24 years…Oh, Mom…of course, I forgive you!

Everything made sense now, except for one last thing – who sent the letter? It wouldn't have been Jenny, as she would have re-dated it and explained why it was several years late. No, it must have been someone else. Someone who came across it and decided to send it by special delivery just to make certain that he got it. Perhaps, that was one part of the puzzle he would never figure out.

CHAPTER FORTY-FIVE

THE DRIVE FROM his mother's place to the acreage took thirty minutes. Since Julean's passing the children were slowly moving out. Jeremy was the first to go when he married Camilla. Allison was next heading to Alberta to attend Bible College, and in another two years Lauren would be going to Montreal to continue her dance studies. The house was too big for just him and Justin, but Henry loved his studio and the beautiful view from its window. The uninhabited hills and valley along with the meandering creek below was truly inspirational and never failed to get his creative juices flowing.

After he fed the two dogs and four barn cats it was almost nine o'clock. He had eaten some snacks earlier in the afternoon when he got home and nothing since. In any case, hunger had left him and he needed rest more than food. He thought about phoning Ivania, but it was too late now, so he vowed to do it first thing tomorrow. She might even drop into the café. I'll let Jeremy know to alert me in the gallery if she does. He wondered where their relationship was heading. After discovering Jenny's letter today, it was obvious where his heart still lay.

Henry went into the living room and turned on the record player. The songs he shared with his two loves always gave him solace. The first record dropped and began to play… "While I give to you and you give to me, true love, true…"

He made his way out to the sun-room; his favourite room. The gas fireplace was on and its warmth welcomed him. As he walked over to the window and looked out over the valley below he hummed along to the song. The light of the moon dimly illuminated his Poustinia beside the glistening, meandering stream. He'd worked so hard to get it finished and yet he never used it. It was a good thing Father Engelmann enjoyed and regularly made good use of it.

Henry knew the Lord was calling him to it and what He would ask of him. His stomach tightened at the very thought of it. He knew his days were coming to a close, yet he wasn't ready to give everything up or away. He admired Eddy for doing what he did. Henry still recalled when they spoke earlier that spring what his friend's response was to why he retired before his 40th birthday…

"I'm thankful for every day and enjoy life to the full ol' buddy. Take it from me, sell the business, come to Jamaica and learn to smell the roses. You work way too hard, Hank. Time goes fast. From morning to night, I enjoy my life. And I'm surprised on how little I really need. Most people work and work and never use up what they have amassed and before they know it they are old and gone and never really appreciated what they had strived for, for all those years and years. The good life is right under their noses and they can't see it…or choose not to see it."

"Yeah, you're right Eddy, it's all about choice. Life is a series of choices. How many right one's you make determines your peace, quality of life, happiness and in the end which one of God's heavenly mansions you occupy."

Tears were on the edge of his eyelids as he listened to the songs. Julean's song, *Love Me Tender* was now playing. He reached in his pocket and took out her rosary and brought it to his lips. The ache for Julean was almost too much to bear.

He turned off the record player and flicked off the lights on his way back to the foyer. He climbed the stairs to his bedroom next to the studio. Pajamas on and teeth brushed, he sunk into the warmth of his water-bed. The wavelike motion of the bed lifted and then lulled him as the water settled.

He was tired and emotionally spent after the effects of today's shock and discovery. His inner world had experienced an earthquake filled with such a kaleidoscope of emotions. Emotions that he had buried and forgotten suddenly vibrated loose with the discovery of Jenny's letter, sending shock waves throughout his mind.

His mom had to have known that it would happen some day. She had probably felt the tremors for many years. He would never know if the letter he found was what she had planned to share with him a few weeks ago, but Henry felt certain that it was. It was amazing how Rose came by at just the right moment to share his Mom's regret over her decision. And the white rose, all part of God's divine providence… *unbelievable.*

The hidden waves in the water-bed responded instantly as Henry rolled onto his side. The warm rippling motion gently soothed away the tension and excitement of the day. He pulled what was once Julean's pillow towards his chest and tossed his arm over it so it rested on the pillow. His hand hung over the edge holding Julean's rosary. He softly whispered a soft thank you to his dear wife for helping him discover the letter. In death as she did in life she always supported him in all he did, even in his relationship with his first love.

He wanted to pray, but thoughts of the letter and its contents occupied his mind. He had read and re-read the letter eight times since he arrived home and almost had it memorized word for word. It was so wonderful to know that Jenny had loved him and missed him as much as he did her. And the incredible coincidence of the pewter angels still overwhelmed him. He felt certain that it could only have been their guardian angels that made such an amazing thing happen.

As he began to relax deeper into his ocean of calm ripples and emotions and memories, his thoughts drifted back across time reliving those wonderful months he had shared with Jenny. With Jenny, his summer had miraculously changed from boredom to ecstasy. As thoughts of her beauty, spontaneity, charm and blue, sparkling eyes crossed the screen of his mind he drifted yet deeper into that incredible summer.

As he crossed sleep's doorstop the words, "Quickly hold my hand," flashed into his mind. It echoed so real in the room he almost sat up. That incredible sensation he had felt then, as they'd held hands for the first time swept through him now. Henry hadn't thought of those magical words for years, and suddenly they erupted so strongly and vividly as if they were yesterday. Suddenly he realized he had dropped the rosary and found his hand in mid air. He brought his arm down and rested it on the pillow at the same time picking up the crystal beads.

His sudden movements caused the water to stir and rocked him again, calming him, soothing him. The thought of angels involved in their lives further assuaged him and before he drifted off a prayer he hadn't said in many days entered his mind:

> *Guardian angel my guardian dear,*
> *To whom God's love commits me here;*
> *Ever this day be at my side,*
> *To light and guard, to rule and guide.*
> *Amen.*

"ARE YOU CRYING, Camilla?"

Jeremy raised himself up and rested on his elbow, his other hand touching her shoulder. He could feel her sobs. "What's wrong, honey?"

"I know this is upsetting for you, but…I…I don't know who I am anymore, where did I come from? Who really are my parents? Oh, Jeremy, I just feel so uncertain about my origins."

"I thought we went through that, Camilla. For awhile you thought you were connected to that Hamilton lady and, heaven forbid, that Dad was the father. But Grandma straightened all that out. Dad's girlfriend name was Jenny and not Marjorie as you had suspected."

"Well, that may be, but I still think there is something there. It's just the way Dad looks at me. And I still can't get over that man at Father Engelmann's anniversary party either. You said his name was, Peter… he stared at me in the same way your Dad does. And then a little later I saw Dad talking to him and all of a sudden they stopped and stared back at me. Oh, Jeremy I just feel this is all connected somehow. I'm so anxious and panicky. The girls at work notice it too. And, and I've seen it in other girls who I have counseled."

"Well, honey, just because a man stares at you doesn't mean he's connected to you. You're a beautiful woman, a man would be crazy not to notice or even stare at you for that matter. Camilla, you're going off track, Valerie and Stanley Breckhart were your parents. It's just one of those quirks of nature that you look so different. Honey, you just have to accept that!"

"There's more to it, Jeremy, I looked at the family photos over and over and the albums I brought home after Dad's death. In every one there isn't a speck of similarity between us. It's like night and day. You would think there would be at least one tiny thing that we have in common besides our name. Look at your brother, Justin and your sisters. I can tell instantly that their father is your Dad. And when I look at photos of your mom, you have her nose, her eyes and smile and colour of hair. In all cases there are similarities of origin…in my case I can't see one!"

Jeremy shifted and laid back on his pillow to give his arm that he had been resting on a rest. He brought his other hand under his head and just lay there thinking on it all. He didn't know what to say to his wife.

"Geez, honey, this doesn't make sense. You're going to have to deal with this somehow. Maybe do a family tree history on your parents, just maybe there is a grandma or grandpa or even great-grandparents who you resemble."

"I did already. Mom and Dad's photo albums are full of pictures of their family and ancestors. They all look like each other except for me.

I look like a white lamb in a herd of black sheep!"

And before Jeremy could speak, Camilla went on, "And there is another thing, for as long as I remember Mom always told me that a stork brought me to them. I remember the first time she said that was when Mom read a book to me…I can't remember what the name of the book was, but I can still see the image in my mind of a stork flying through the air carrying a baby in a blanket dangling from its beak. Whenever I asked her where I came from that is what she would say, 'a stork brought you.'"

"Camilla, a lot of parents feel uncomfortable talking about the birds and bees. It was never an issue in our family, Mom made sure of that. But for a lot of parents it's difficult. I don't think you should jump to any conclusions—"

"Jeremy, she said a stork brought me up until I was fourteen and then I stopped asking as it embarrassed me to think that my Mom was still treating me like a small child. To me it means that Mom was indirectly trying to tell me that I didn't come from her but rather from someone else. And even when I was grown she couldn't take credit for my birth and kept saying I came from a stork…"

"Or from another mother…" Jeremy said, finishing what Camilla would have said.

"That's right! I just can't shake the feeling that somewhere out there I have a mother and a father who I have yet to find."

"But what if you're wrong honey…what if you're creating something out of nothing and this thing hangs over your head for always? I hate to see you so unhappy. It's not your usual self."

Camilla didn't answer. She lay there and began to cry again.

"Well, with your Mom reading about the stork all the time, that would explain why you have that reoccurring dream of a stork delivering a baby in a blanket."

"That's another thing, Jeremy the dream has changed. It's no longer a stork carrying the baby it's now an angel and who is the lady sitting in the gazebo surrounded by wildflowers? And now I am beginning to dream of that man, Peter, too. He seems to be waiting for the angel holding the baby as well…"

"Oh, geez…Camilla, this is getting out of hand."

"But, there's another thing that I haven't told you yet…"

"What's that?"

"It's Dad's strong box. It's packed downstairs inside some other boxes that the movers brought here after Dad died and we cleared out the house—"

"Oh, you mean, the green metal box? I remember packing that one myself."

"Yes, that's the one. Dad kept all of his important documents in there. You know, his insurance policy, title to the house and things like that. I remember taking out his will and before locking it again, I noticed a birth certificate and other letters in there that I didn't bother looking at at the time."

"So?"

"I think some of those papers have to do with me and I'm afraid to look at them. I went downstairs three times last week and I just can't make myself get the box and see what's in there…"

Jeremy squeezed Camilla's hand, "Oh sweetheart, I'm sure it's nothing, come, let's go down there right now and have a look, I'll be right with you, nothing to be afraid off."

"No, this is something I have to do myself…I'm too afraid, Jeremy. I think the answers that I'm looking for are there…but, I don't know if I'm ready yet to know the truth of who I really am…"

Jeremy rolled over and put his hand on Camilla's shoulder once more.

"You know, Honey, for as long as I can remember both my Mom and Dad always told me to pray to my guardian angel when I was worried about something. They are messengers from God and they can whisper things into our ears of what we should do. They also are there to guide and protect us. Maybe pray to yours, Honey. I still do to mine almost everyday. It was so drilled into me as I grew up. Let's say the prayer and go to sleep, Camilla."

Camilla reached her hand back to Jeremy and held it as both whispered the Guardian Angel prayer in unison:

> Guardian angel my guardian dear,
> To whom God's love commits me here;
> Ever this day be at my side,
> To light and guard, to rule and guide.
> Amen.

Chapter Forty-Six

Today, would be Father Engelmann's last official sermon as parish priest for St. Mary's Church. The recent celebration of his 25th anniversary as a priest gave testimony and witness to many of the things Father had accomplished during his tenure as a priest. The weddings, funerals, baptisms, confirmations, the home visits were one thing, but Father's confessions and homilies were heaven sent. How attendance grew and the many people that were healed physically and spiritually and came home to the church was nothing short of miraculous.

Henry, as well as hundreds of parishioners, had tears in their eyes as they watched Father as he followed the altar boys to the altar. It was obvious to all present that Father's love for the priesthood had never lessened over the years. Rather, his love for being a shepherd exhibited even more passion for his chosen work as each and every Sunday rolled around. The spring in his step always seemed livelier than the last time; his smile only grew broader, warmer and more benevolent. His love for the mass and the Lord only grew more fervent. His commitment to become like Jesus and follow in His Master's footsteps, more deeply sown.

All Henry could conclude was that Father was a Saint back from when he first opened his store until now. Henry loved his teacher then and only more today if that were possible. He was his closest and dearest friend and everyday Henry thanked God for blessing him with such a beacon of light to follow that has helped lead him on the path to righteousness.

Father surveyed his flock with eyes that reddened as his head scanned the people. Several times he tried to begin, but his voice caught each time. Finally, he began the mass by making the sign of the cross. Henry's heart went out to his mentor and friend. He knew how difficult it was for Father to leave his beloved parish. Henry was not alone, parishioners all around were drying their eyes.

After the Gospel readings, Father closed the Bible and slowly began to speak.

"From the first day that I came here until today it has always been my main mission and purpose to serve you through the Lord. To make certain that each and every one of you comes safely home to the Father so that along with Anna and me, we will all be together in His kingdom.

During this past week I pondered over what sermon I could leave you with that will help you on your life journey. And as always the Lord in His perfect timing through the scriptures in the gospel readings today has told me what to say.

"St. Matthew's sixth chapter versus 21-24 points to the pit-falls that grips our world today and the message I want to leave with you:

"Where your treasure is, there will your heart be also."
Matthew 6:21

And......

"If your eye is pure, there will be sunshine in your soul. But if your eye is clouded with evil thoughts and desires, you are in deep spiritual darkness. And oh, how deep that darkness can be!
Matthew 6:22

And......

"You cannot serve two masters: God and money. For you will hate the one and love the other, or else the other way around.
Matthew 6:24

"Over the last 25 years as a priest I have noticed many changes in the world that attacks values which we hold so dear. Back then stores were closed on Sundays, and Monday or Wednesday afternoons. It was a day of rest for family. People worked from morning usually from eight or nine until five or six. Wives stayed home to raise the children and make the home. Or in some cases the roles were reversed, but there was order.

"*Today the values of the world are attacking these personal values.*"

"Television, while providing some good entertainment is over-shadowed with violence, drugs and sex. Advertisements are working to make us discontent with our lot and are urging us to buy more and to keep up with others. Family dinners are less often as both parents are working and at times all hours. Many times children are left to fend for themselves. Sunday church attendance is declining; there is no longer respect for the Sabbath. There is less prayer in the home, and infant abortions are on the increase…where is all of this leading to?

"It is so important my dear brothers and sisters that we stop and become aware of what is going on or else we will get snared ever more deeply into the ways of the secular world while the spiritual side of our lives is increasingly in greater jeopardy. To say we have no time to pray or relate with God is very dangerous my friends. We must stop and examine the direction in which we are going before it is too late. The first scripture reading clearly reminds us what is most important in our lives;

"Where your treasure is, there will your heart be also."

Father stopped and reached for something underneath the lectern. Many parishioners leaned forward and squinted to see what he was up to. Father was holding an old style alarm clock and began by winding the clock. When it was fully wound he pulled up the button on top of the clock and then he slowly began to make a powerful analogy.

"Sometimes a message is best learned and remembered with a visual aid. I have set this clock so that it will ring at some point in my homely. No, it is not to remind me to stop as you have heard enough. Nor is it to alert you to keep awake during my sermon." Some chuckled and others smiled.

"Meine lieben freunde, when this alarm goes off it is to announce to all of us that many people have died. This may be something that we don't like to think about, but death is a part of life. Between now and the time it rings hundreds if not thousands of people will have passed on and…it even could be one of us."

Father set the alarm clock on the ledge and continued.

"When each of us is born our clock of life on earth is wound just once. There is no snooze button or second wake up call. *When it rings, we will be no more.* Our journey through life has run its course and our time on earth is over.

"For many of us we don't give this subject much thought. For one thing it is unpleasant to think of death even though it is a door through which all of us must go through. It makes us anxious and uneasy and yet if we acknowledge it, it can motivate us to live lives that God blesses and rewards. When that moment in time comes knocking on our door will our lamps be lit and will we be ready to meet our Maker? Or will we be caught in the darkness or shadows of life? Time may go on seemingly forever, but our time on earth is very short and if we look at it in terms of eternity, it is far less than the blink of an eye.

"Jesus said there are many mansions in the kingdom of heaven. Where do you want to spend it? Near Him or on the outskirts or…in the other kingdom? It all depends on what we treasure in the heart."

Suddenly the alarm went off! Many were startled by the sound more so than its significance. Father let the alarm ring and ring and then suddenly he raised his hand and came down hard on the button and instantly an eerie, dead silence spread throughout the church.

Father surveyed the congregation nodding his head and then with a growing grin on his face he said, "Although many people died before the alarm went off, fortunately, I see everyone is still here."

There were a few nervous chuckles and Father continued, "But I tell you that one day sooner or later our alarm will ring. Let this be a wake up call."

"Are we ready my children?"

Father paused for a moment and re-set and re-wound the clock and set it down.

"Just before the alarm sounded I was about to share a St. Peter story with you. I'm sure all of you have heard many jokes in that regard of someone who has died and was met by St. Peter at the pearly gates of heaven. The only thing about my story is that it may not be a laughing matter.

"There was once a very successful man that died and tried to bring all his riches on a huge U-haul trailer that he pulled behind his Cadillac. As he approached the gates of heaven the wheels of his car and trailer began to sink deeper and deeper in the ground and finally came to a halt. As he looked around he saw many others either on foot or in their vehicles that were stuck too. He was glad he had made it this far.

"There must be a lot of rain in heaven, he thought. He got out and trudged through the mud and eventually he, too, got stuck as the mud made its way to the top of his boots. He was relieved to see St. Peter in the distance and yelled out to him for help.

"I could sure use a hand, I think four angels could easily lift me out of this mess if you would be so kind as to summon them for me."

"St. Peter came to the man's side and advised him to back up and soon he would be on dry ground again.

"'But isn't this the way to heaven? I'd like to come in.'

"'Your name is Sydney Accumulate More, is it not?'

"'Yes, that's right.'

"St. Peter checked the big book again and said, 'I'm sorry Mr. More, but your name is not on the guest list.'

"'There must be some mistake. My name has to be on the list. I've been a good man and have worked very hard all of my life. Surely the Lord must be pleased with that.' And turning to his trailer he said, 'And look at all the gold and silver and money I have amassed, I will gladly pay my way in.'

"St. Peter shook his head and looked compassionately at the man.

"'Mr. More, one—'

"'Please, St. Peter, call me Syd,' said the man, hoping he could make friends with the holy man and perhaps better influence him.

"'Yes, as you wish, Syd. Hard work and all the money in the world however, cannot buy your way into heaven, there is only one way—'

"'And what is that?' asked Syd, the furrow in his brow deepening.

"'We must come to Jesus with a repentant heart and tell Him that we are sorry for our sins and invite Him into our hearts to be our Lord and Saviour. Did you ever do that?'

"Syd thought back over his life for a few moments and quickly said, 'I'm sure I must have said it more than once…and I know I asked to be forgiven for my sins several times.'

"'Yes, many come to the Lord during their lives, Syd, but they must be sincere and truly invite Jesus into their hearts. We know that you have heard Jesus is the way, the truth and the life and that no one comes to the Father except through His son. Jesus became man, died for our sins to pay our debt to the Father so that we might have life with Him in heaven. All the wealth you possess cannot pay for your or anyone's sins. It's a gift from Jesus to you as long as you accept Him with a sincere heart as I said.'

"'I am sure I did, St. Peter!'

"St. Peter raised his hand in front of Syd and in a flash of light Syd's life passed before him exposing what he treasured in his heart.

"'Here is the thing, Syd. A half an hour after you invited Jesus into your heart you went back to your old ways. You worked very hard however you never spent as much as a half of an hour praying to God nor reading the teachings of His son in the bible.'

"'But surely my hard work counts for something. And look what I have amassed…' Syd turned and once again swept his hand towards the fortune piled high on the trailer.

"'I am afraid you don't understand, Syd. Your wealth and possessions are worthless. All the things you strived for like so many of God's children have absolutely no value here.'

"*Only love counts.*'

"'My dear Syd, you came into the world naked and that is the way you come to the gates of heaven; naked. The only thing that you have of value when you come here is what is in your heart! Words, deeds, actions backed by a sincere heart to serve God and your neighbour has value; everything else counts for nothing.'

"As they spoke there was a constant stream of people going through the pearly gates. Some were trying to make it on foot behind Syd but most were flying through the air accompanied by their guardian angel. It had distracted Syd earlier but he was so focused on getting into heaven that he didn't mention it until now. He was bumped into by a low flying guardian angel that was lifting a man in his charge just high enough to skim over the ground.

"Syd had a quizzical look on his face as he turned back to the holy saint. 'Why is it that all these people are flying into heaven while I and many behind me are trudging through this wet dirt and ...' Syd looked behind him and then to St. Peter and continued, 'And where is my guardian angel? Didn't I have one while on earth?'

"'You ask many questions Mr. Accumulate More, or rather Syd, let me answer them one at a time. Look up and study closely the people entering heaven...what do you notice?'

"It was immediately obvious to Syd. 'They all have brightness about them...yes, and it seems that the higher they fly the brighter they are.'

"Syd looked down and continued... 'And the ones that come close to ground level...their brightness is almost gone...'

"Syd's expression turned serious as it began to dawn on him what was going on...

"'That is a very astute observation, Syd. Let me explain; the more a person grew close to Jesus on earth and filled themselves with His word, they moved ever more into God's light. Many ignored to do this and remained in the darkness. The apostle Matthew talks about this in the scripture 6:21 when he says;

"The eyes are the lamp of the soul. If they are clear then the spirit will be filled with light (God's word) but if the eyes are clouded (by the values of the world) the whole body is filled with darkness...'

"'You see, Syd, the eye's reflect what a man treasures in his heart. Those who understood this and placed Jesus at the centre of their lives are now reaping what they have sown during their life-time.' St. Peter looked up and continued, 'They were content with far less than you amassed for sure, but they were happier on earth than you and look at how many are coming in even as we speak. They have an automatic admission. Look at the aura of light around them and see how happy their guardian angel is as they escort them through the gates! They sought first the kingdom of God...'

"St. Peter didn't finish, he knew the man before him was beginning to understand, but the wisdom of God's word was coming too late.

"'Look! There is Isabel, look at her go and up so high! She is filled with so much light she almost blends into the light where God resides. And look there, her guardian angel can hardly keep up with her! Wow! She is so free! We knew she was always just one step on this side of heaven.'

"Syd had to admit that just the sight of her soaring through the heavens lifted his spirits. He had to ask. 'What did she do on earth?'

"'She had a car accident and was paralyzed from the neck down. She was in the prime of her life when it happened. Only 16 and yet, she accepted her condition and made the best of it.'

"'There was one thing however that imprisoned her. She couldn't forgive the person that caused her accident. Isabel was such a beautiful person deep down but the spirit of unforgiveness overshadowed it all. It's much like a room filled with beautiful flowers. If the light bulb burns out you can no longer see the beauty that was there. Slowly the spirit dies just like the flowers without the light.'

"'Then one day she accepted Jesus into her heart and asked to see the person who had been the cause of so much pain and long suffering and forgave him.'

"'Like I said Syd, that was some day. The entire heavens sang in praise of her coming home. After that, she never complained, was cheerful, kind, patient, in fact people loved to come see her and were so inspired by her attitude and acceptance of what life handed her. As I mentioned, too, she suffered much pain in life as well, but once again she accepted it and offered it up to God as a prayer to heal the world.'

"'In fact, Syd, the man that bumped into you a few minutes ago is one of the recipients of Isabel's offering and prayers. His guardian is taking him to a place where we he will be filled with more light so eventually he can fly on his own and make it into heaven.'

"'Is he going into purgatory?' Syd wanted to know.

"'Yes, that is a good way to describe it. It is a cleansing process of sorts. But what I wanted to say was Isabel's offering of her suffering to the Father was applied to him as well as to others who fell slightly short of entry into heaven. Perhaps his cleansing time will be reduced.'

"'Suffering is a mystery that is hard to understand and accept on earth and yet it does not go in vain if it's offered up.'

"'When Jesus became man He too, suffered and died for mankind. He too, offered it up to the Father and look at the good that came out of it.'

"St. Peter looked up at the continuous flow of earthlings into heaven and continued, 'It would have been impossible for them to enter the pearly gates if it had not been for Jesus paying their debt with His life to the Father.'

"Syd looked up and thought long and hard about what St. Peter had just said, tears beginning to rise.

"'And in regards to your guardian angel, Syd,.. unfortunately at the moment of your death, he was reassigned to another earthling…he tried so many times to prompt you on a more profitable path but you were always too busy to heed his warnings.'

"Perspiration was beginning to form on Syd's brow, he was slowly getting the picture of where he was at. If only he had taken the time to examine what he so treasured in his heart…

"He was beginning to now. He could see that there was no aura around him like those flying above. There was hardly any difference between his colour and the dirt he was sunk into.

"Desperately, he resorted to earthly methods.

"He turned and pointed to his trailer once more. 'All the gold and silver and money I have on the trailer I will give to God to pave more streets in gold. Send me to purgatory and take as long as necessary to pay for my sins. Please, St. Peter, ask God to have mercy on me.'

"'Oh, Mr. More, the streets of heaven may shine and sparkle like gold but they are paved with love. As I said, it is only acts of love that count…even a tiny, brief smile does not go unnoticed by the Father. Acts of kindness cause rejoicing in the kingdom and those who choose to forgive brings a smile on the Lord's face. Patience, generosity, prayer, time spent with Jesus…these are the things that lift one into the light!'

"'But I was kind…

"'Yes, but look over your past life and tell me what you see. We do not judge people who come to our doorstep. You are judged by your own words, deeds and actions and the way you lived your life.'

"Yes, he was kind but it lacked sincerity and most of the time it was to get something from the other or for show?

"'Look at your riches. How did you use your wealth? Did you give to the poor? Did you give to your starving and sickly brothers and sisters abroad? Did you feed the hungry, cloth the naked, help the sick?'

"Syd looked down; his true heart revealed that he had done none of that out of love and service to others for Jesus' sake. He was always self-centred and not God-centred.

"But he was growing more and more desperate…

"'But St. Peter, I often put a $50.00 bill in the collection plate when I made it to church on Sunday.'

"'But did it come from your heart Mr. More?'

"'Many people present knew of my wealth, I would look like a cheapskate if I didn't at least put something in the collection plate.' The words that came out didn't sound right, he wished now he hadn't said them and so he offered, 'But at least I did make an offering, doesn't that count?'

"'Well, Syd, generosity is best kept a secret if possible. When one makes a showy display of it you have already received your reward, have you not?'

"'But…but God says to use your talents and gifts… I worked day and night to develop them. What about that. I wasn't lazy like a lot of others.'

"'Yes, you have been a very diligent worker Mr. Accumulate More, but for whose benefit?'

"*It always comes down to whether or not it was to serve God and your fellow man or was it just for yourself?*'

"Once again Syd hung down his head; shame, regret and sorrow growing rapidly in his heart. His main goal was always on getting ahead, accumulating more. Even when he was in church on those rare occasions, even then his mind was on his bank account and how much less it would be with the money he put into the collection basket. His life before him revealed every secret, every thought and desire, every lie, every judgment, everything…*there was nothing he could hide like he did on earth.*

"His sorrow and guilt were mixing with a surging fear…a dread of what awaits him.

"The holy man before him knew his thoughts. He looked compassionately upon Syd…

"'Yes, Syd, you were a very rich man on earth, far more than many, but …spiritually you were bankrupt! Look at all the times, God in His divine providence tried over and over to make you aware of the danger besides your guardian angel. All the while your ears were deaf to the pastor's sermons and admonishments. Did he not tell you that your purpose in life was to serve God and your fellowman? Did he not tell you that the gifts he gave to you were not just for yourself? Did he not tell you countless times that you must repent of your sins and come to Jesus and accept Him into your heart as your Lord and saviour? You were told that he is the bridge that you must go over to come to the Father. He is the way, the Truth and Life. No one comes to the Father except through His son. If you did not do this and sincerely commit your life to obey his commands and establish a relationship with him what else can the good Lord say when you come to His home but...*I do not know you...'*

"Syd could see what treasures lay in his heart...the record was clear, every nook and cranny of his heart were exposed and there was no denying that spiritually his life was empty.

"'Is there any way St. Peter, I can make amends? Send me into purgatory, do whatever, but please let me in...'

"'I am sorry Mr. More your life has been lived so much in the darkness you wouldn't be able to survive in the light. Even the ones that fly so low are placed in a dim area and as they repent they are gradually filled with light. Slowly as they are purified much as a precious metal is they can rise and come out.'

"'As I have said Syd, we do not judge you but rather it is the life that you have chosen to live that now determines your fate. St. Matthew in his gospel warned the people on earth that they cannot serve two masters. They will either love the one or hate the other...'

"Syd fell on his knees. The scripture that he had heard several times during his life time glared at him now... What does it profit a man if he gains all the riches of the world but loses his own soul? The meaning hit his heart to the core but the wisdom came too late... if only he had spent time in prayer it would have come to him, but now...his time had run out.

"Syd lowered his head and begged and pleaded...

"But the saint was firm, 'As you go back you will slowly come out of the mud and the way is easier to where you are going. You are not alone Syd. As you can see to your right and left, there are many others who are stuck and will have to go the other way, too. The residents of that kingdom will welcome you with open arms...'

"With that St. Peter turned and walked away."

Just as Father picked up the alarm clock it went off startling him as well as the parishioners. "Ah, death can come just that quick." He pushed the button down and spoke softly.

"I say once again my brothers and sisters the clock of our lives is wound the moment we are conceived and when the time runs out there are no more precious moments of time to forgive, to show kindness, display a smile, be patient, to give generously of your wealth and time. Like Syd, we now walk towards our Lord and saviour to be judged by what we carry in our heart. It's that simple, my friends. We will be judged by that. We saw what treasures were in Syd's heart and hopefully we can learn from him. What treasures are in your heart that Jesus can reward? Don't be so busy amassing riches and immersed in the values of the world that you are caught dead to a life that God cannot reward.

"*There is still time for you if you have not yet come to Him. He is waiting for you...come home to Him.*

"Many people doubt the existence of God because they have never taken the time to come to Him. To know Him. To experience His love and thus don't take this seriously. The very fact that I am standing before you and you have the ability to see me, to hear me, to think and reason what I am saying and all the while trillions of cells are keeping your body and mind working in perfect harmony. This is a most incredible miracle. For anyone to think that this just happened on its own is as unwise and foolish to think that the jet plane that they see flying in the sky just suddenly appeared on its own as well. You would be quick to say don't be silly, Father, it was made by brilliant engineers and technicians and tradesman. But who made these people, I ask? Who supplied the earth with all the ores and elements so that all these fine machines and everything else can be made? Only the foolish would say that it just happened on its own and that there is no great all knowing intelligence behind it all.

"There is a God, meine lieben Geschwister in Christus, who is the creator of heaven and earth. He has designed and made things to follow a plan and order and purpose of which we are a part. Let us never forget that we are children of God here on earth to love and serve Him and others; to give our will to Him and to use our talents and gifts to collaborate with Him so that all people in the world can be saved.

"As you can see from the story, it's all about the light, my friends. It's all about living in the Light of Jesus who is the way, the truth and the life. We must remain in the vine to remain in the Light. Recognize our pride and our lofty thinking for what it is which keeps us from coming to Him. We cannot live a fruitful life on our own no matter how hard we try and no matter how much we own or possess, we will never be rich in spirit without Him. Syd may have been a very wealthy man but he was never content with what he had. Many have chosen to have less and were happier. The devil loves it when we fear poverty, and love possessions and strive to accumulate more all the while ignore the spiritual side of our lives. Riches and possessions become our God and not the real true God.

"Meine leiben kinder, when you awoke this morning I pray you were glad and rejoiced in it. This is the day the Lord hath made for you. You have been given the gift of another day to get your house in order. Think carefully your thoughts, words and deeds. If you do what I have urged you to do over and over throughout the years, to pray and meditate on the word of Jesus and His teachings and to offer up your day and will to Him and allow Him to work through you, you will be in good hands when that moment comes and the alarm sounds.

"*Your heart will be so full of the treasures that God can reward and the light shining within you will be so bright that it will lift you high into the heavens just like your guardian angel. And together you will sing praises to our Father forever and ever.*

With tears filling his eyes Father opened his arms to his flock, "I love you with all my heart and so does Jesus. There is nothing that would make me happier than to know that each and every one of you has come home to Him."

As Father went to his chair, Margaret came up to the podium and with the voice of an angel began to sing the song as Father had requested…

> *Softly and tenderly Jesus is calling—*
> *Calling for you and for me;*
> *Patiently Jesus is waiting and watching—*
> *Watching for you and for me!*
>
> *Come home! Come home!*
> *Ye who are weary, come home!*
> *Earnestly, tenderly, Jesus is calling,*
> *Calling, O sinner, come home!*
>
> *Why should we tarry when Jesus is pleading—*
> *Pleading for you and for me?*
> *Why should we linger and heed not His mercies—*
> *Mercies for you and for me?*

Time is now fleeting, the moments are passing—
Passing from you and from me;
Shadows are gathering, death-beds are coming—
Coming for you and for me!

Oh, for the wonderful love He has promised—
Promised for you and for me!
Though we have sinned, He has mercy and pardon—
Pardon for you and for me!

Come home! Come home!
Ye who are weary, come home!
Earnestly, tenderly, Jesus is calling,
Calling, O sinner, come home!

CHAPTER FORTY-SEVEN

JENNY DIDN'T GO home as soon as she had hoped. Further X-rays three days after her surgery showed another tumour developing on the right side near her liver. The doctors decided to start treatment immediately. So, instead of going home, Dr. Kreake insisted she stay in the hospital for the duration of her chemotherapy and radiation treatments.

Jenny had just completed her ninth treatment when Dr. Kreake walked into her private room. She was beginning to lose her hair and was totally exhausted most days.

"Hello, Jenny."

"Hi, Dr. Kreake."

Jenny smiled. She loved Dr. Kreake. He was the only thing that kept her going.

"I like your bandana. Blue is your colour."

And Henry's too.

"Thank you." Jenny touched the kerchief covering her balding head. "Mabel brought it for me the other day."

"You're a class act, Jenny, the most beautiful woman I know, besides my wife, of course."

Jenny blushed. "Thank you, Dr. Kreake."

Dr. Kreake smiled and then resumed his medical role. "We are going to terminate your treatments for now Jenny. The X-rays show that the tumour has stopped growing and in fact, is shrinking. We hope we got it in time. In a few days you will begin to feel a lot better and won't be so tired anymore."

"Hallelujah, praise the Lord," said Jenny. "Will my hair start to grow back?"

"It should within a few months."

Jenny stared into Dr. Kreake's caring eyes for a long moment.

"I would like to ask you something, Dr. Kreake. Please be honest with me."

"Of course, Jenny, what is it?"

"What are my chances? Really. Am I going to make it, or is this just a little respite along the way?"

Dr. Kreake looked at Jenny intently. He had told Jenny the truth about the tumour. They had succeeded in arresting it, but it may all have been too late. It was now in the lymphatic system and he wasn't quite sure if it was spreading to other areas in her body.

"Jenny, I am going to be honest with you. I just don't know what the prognosis is, as yet."

"Will I be able to go home, soon?"

"Jenny, I'm afraid you can't live alone. You will be looked after much better in a care home."

"But I love my home and all the flowers. I just have to go home."

"You need a lot of care, Jenny and if the cancer spreads or comes back you will need help. There are a lot of very good nursing homes I can recommend—"

"Oh, doctor, I was so looking forward to going home. What should I do with my home?"

"Have you got family?"

"Yes, I have a son, a daughter-in-law, and a grandson but—"

"But, what? They know you are in the hospital, don't they?"

Jenny didn't answer, right away. "No, doctor, I didn't want to tell them. I was hoping the surgery would correct everything and that I would have been home by now. I didn't want to worry them."

"Jenny, they are your family. They have a right to know."

Jenny's eyes went downcast as she lowered her head. "My son and I are not on good terms at the present and—"

"Jenny." Dr. Kreake looked sternly into her eyes. "This is no time for family squabbles. It's time for all this nonsense to stop. You need their love and support. Do you want me to phone him and explain the situation?"

"Oh no, I will. If, as you say, I will feel better in the next few days I will call him on the weekend. He should be home then. He's kind of a workaholic like his father."

"Well, Jenny, if I can help in any way just let me know. And please give the care home serious thought. You can always have someone look after your home for a month or so to see how things go and when you get better, then your home will be there waiting for you."

"Well, couldn't I get a nurse to live in with me?"

"Yes, you could do that, but you will get far superior help in the nursing home. And your chances of recovering and getting better are better there. Trust me, Jenny, many have tried to do it on their own. It's better in the care home. You will meet other people, you'll be properly looked after and your friends and I can visit you regularly and—"

"Okay, Dr. Kreake, I get the message. I'll give it some serious thought."

"I see you love flowers," he said, nodding his head towards the string of potted plants on her window sill.

"Yes, I love nature, flowers, plants, they are my life and I get so much spiritual sustenance from them. Mabel brought those over when she brought the kerchief."

"I can tell. Your face brightens just speaking about them."

Jenny smiled, but the effort took the rest of her energy and she sagged back on the pillow.

"Well, I must really be off and continue my rounds. I will see you, tomorrow. And please, phone that son of yours or else I will."

Jenny waved him off with an appreciative smile.

She had thought about phoning J.J. for several days now. Even though she often had visitors and spoke with Matilda and Chloe often, her heart missed the family connections. Would she and J.J. ever be able to reconcile? *What if she died before they could patch things up?*

"Oh, Jenny, don't think that way. The doctor just told you that the tumour is shrinking, and soon you will be up and around and back home. I won't need a nursing home. That's for older people, like my mom."

Jenny clutched her guardian angel dangling at the end of the chain on her neck. "Oh please, don't let this be the end. I want so much to live a little longer, long enough to see my daughter and perhaps meet someone to love, to share my life with. Oh guardian angel, my guardian dear, all my life that is what I wanted and somehow, when it is just within my grasp, the doors always seem to close."

Jenny was nearly asleep when the phone rang. She struggled to reach the phone on the table beside her bed.

"Hello," said Jenny groggily.

"Hi, Jen, this be Matti. Are you okay to talk for a spell or a minute or two?"

"Hi, Matti, yes, of course I'm fine. I always love it when you call."

"So tell me the truth, Jen, how you doin'? Are the chemo treatments helping some?"

"Yes, as a matter of fact, the doctor was by this morning and said the tumour has stopped growing and might even be shrinking."

"Well, let's be hoping and praying it shrinks to nothing and go back where it came from. Some far dark corner of the universe and not come knocking at our door ever again!"

Jenny smiled. "How are you doing and have you heard from J.J. or Nora lately?"

"No can't say that I have since last winter. Now that he be married and with his work, he don't come by this way too often anymore."

"You mentioned last time we spoke that you were going to tell James that I was in the hospital, I wonder if he told J.J.?"

"That I can't tell you, Jen. All those two ever talk about is business, business and more business. I think the world could be falling apart and all they would be concerned about is their business! Anyway, Mr. Hamilton didn't say much when I told him."

"Well, the doctor advised me to call J.J. and let him know of my condition, you know, just in case."

"Now don't you be talking that way, Jenny. You don't ever want that disease to think for one minute that it has the upper hand, you hear me!?"

Jenny let out a slight chuckle, "I can't ever see any sickness coming your way, Matti. Any ailment would be shaking in their boots at the front door to your body."

"Amen, I say to that, Jenny, and that's just the way I wants you to be. You just claim the promises of the good Lord and declare 'by Your stripes I am healed.' And mean it from the bottom of your heart, honey child."

Jenny chuckled again, "Oh, Matti, whenever you phone I feel uplifted. I truly wish I had the strength of your faith."

"You have, we all have! We needs to develop a close relationship with Him. So close that we believe and trust Him in everything. I believe that you are going to be healed of this thing or He be hearing from me real quick!"

"So how are Thomas and Ramon?"

"They be fine, it was so nice being back at the estate while Mr. Hamilton was convalescing from his bleeding ulcer. But for some reason or another he hightailed it back to the condo and brought me with him."

"How is James doing? Is he better? Is he healed?"

"As far as I can tell, he seems to be his ole self, working hard as ever. Most days, I be in bed when he comes home. He's going to work himself to death someday, that's for sure, Jen."

"Yes, he was never one for stopping to enjoy what he has, and the estate is so beautiful…"

"That's right, he be stopping for no man, but one day the Lord be stopping that man and he soon see who be the real Boss! Anyway, Jen, you must be getting tired and I have to fix dinner for the master. So you go right ahead and phone that boy of yours. If he's worth his salt he'll come and see you real quick. And if you wants me to come, I can take some time off. Just let me know."

"Thanks, Matti. I love you."

"And I love's you too, honey child."

As Dr. Kreake had predicted, a week later Jenny felt much better. So much so that she put off calling J.J.. She would rather call him with good news and not bad, and rather he reconcile with her because he wanted to, not because he felt forced to because of her illness. Deep in her heart, though, she knew that would never happen. The chasm was far too deep and wide for J.J. to attempt crossing over.

Thanks to his upbringing at the hands of his father, J.J. had acquired most if not all of his father's traits and that included his revulsion towards her. Jenny assumed he felt that way only out of loyalty to his father. And, she knew J.J. would always blame her for the failure of the marriage.

Jenny also thought of calling Mrs. Blake, she would be back from holidays now and hopefully could advise her on how to re-unite her and Camilla in a way that wouldn't interfere with Henry's family. Perhaps she should wait until next week and make sure the disease was arrested.

The following Monday, Jenny was feeling so good, she planned to ask Dr. Kreake if she could go home and perhaps be treated as an out patient. But when Dr. Kreake walked into her room the look on his face dashed all her hopes of going home.

"Oh, Dr. Kreake, please, not again."

He came over to her bed and reached for her hand that lay across the book she'd been reading. Jenny's heart rate skyrocketed and she lay back into the pillow so if she fainted, she wouldn't have far to fall.

"Jenny, the X-rays taken last evening show another tumour is developing in your chest just below your lungs. We don't want to start the chemotherapy again so soon, but we are going to try and treat it with minimal radiation and some new drugs that are just coming out."

"Are you sure?" Jenny asked, tears of hopelessness welled in her eyes.

"Yes, Jenny, I just viewed the plate before I came here."

"But…but how could it be spreading like this?"

"It's in your lymphatic system. We are thinking perhaps of operating and removing one of the lymph nodes under your left arm."

Jenny's hand fell from Dr. Kreake's. "Why is this happening to me?"

"Have you called your son, yet?"

"No, I thought I was getting better. I would sooner try and work out our differences when I am well, rather than hold my sickness over him."

"Jenny, now is not the time to be stoic. If you don't call him in the next few days, I will." Dr. Kreake looked at her sternly and then tightened his lips firmly for added measure.

"Aye, aye, sir," She raised her arm as high as she could – only a few inches – in a mock salute.

Dr. Kreake smiled and winked at her. "Don't give up hope, Captain. I've seen a few miracles in my time."

Jenny held out her guardian angel by the tip of her fingers. "She's watching over me." Jenny tried to smile, but it died within her.

Dr. Kreake bent down and had a closer look. "A pewter angel," then he read the inscription, "Watch over my beloved."

"It's from someone who loved me very much."

"And, I'm sure he still does."

CHAPTER FORTY-EIGHT

EVER SINCE DISCOVERING the letter from Jenny, it was all his mind could think of in the days that followed.

"I just have to try and find Jenny!" was Henry's first thought when he awoke.

If Julean hadn't vindicated him for having thoughts of his first love and encouraged him to seek Jenny out, Henry would never have allowed himself to contemplate such a thought. Discovering Jenny's letter had revived too many suppressed feelings: tears, heartaches, yearnings, memories, one after the other rushed back and filled nearly every waking moment of his day, and dreams at night. He just had to find some closure to all this.

It was just not fair to Ivania either. He turned down a dinner date twice last week and Henry knew that she sensed something was wrong and wanted to talk about it. It was the same when Julean came along. He was torn then between Jenny and her, and in the end, she stole his heart.

But could Ivania do the same?

Perhaps if he knew for certain that she was married he could make a decision and let it go.

Henry couldn't sleep last night. He thought of calling the company Jenny's dad worked for. He would start there. Henry was so excited he skipped breakfast and went off to work.

When he arrived at the gallery, he went directly to his office and closed the door. Even after all those years, Henry still remembered the name of Mr. Sarsky's company and the address to which he had sent all the love letters he had written. He picked up the phone and dialed information. Within minutes he had the phone number. Hopefully, since the company still existed, the Sarsky's did too.

"Mackurcher and Company, this is Diane. How may I direct your call?"

"Good morning, this is Henry Pederson from Regina, Saskatchewan calling. I am trying to locate a Mr. Ted Sarsky. I understand he is, or was with your company."

"I'm sorry, sir, there is no one by that name here. You must have the wrong company."

"No, I'm certain this is the right company and at one time, anyway, he was the president."

"I'm sorry, sir," Diane said, "I am not familiar with the name. I've only been with the company for less than two years, I will transfer you to the personnel department, and perhaps they can help you there."

"Thank you."

"Personnel," answered a terse male voice.

Once again, Henry introduced himself and asked about Mr. Sarsky only to get the same reply.

"I'm sorry, Mr. Pederson, there is no one here by that name. I have been with the company for over fifteen years and I have never heard that name."

"But this goes back perhaps 25 years or so ago."

"Well, let me check the computer files, and see if that name comes up."

A keyboard clacked in the background.

"Oh, you're right, Mr. Pederson, there was a Mr. Sarsky here in the fifties and he was the president. I don't know the history of the company that well, do I?" the personnel officer said, with a nervous chuckle.

"It also indicates here, Mr. Pederson that he had passed away in 1961."

"I see. Do you have a forwarding address or phone number?"

"Yes, but we are not allowed to give out information like that unless it's in writing and can show just cause. In any case, I'm certain it would have changed by now if that's any consolation to you."

"Well, it's really not Mr. Sarsky I was looking for, but his daughter. Oh well, thank you for your trouble."

"You're welcome, sir. I hope you find her."

Just as Henry was about to hang up, "Sir, Mr. Pederson, are you still there?"

"Yes, I am, I was just thinking about who else I could possibly phone."

"Yes, I might just have a lead for you."

Henry's heart skipped a beat and he sat up in his office chair, the receiver pressed tightly to his ears. "Please go on."

"Well, two days ago, a Ms. Elaine McIntyre called about her pension plan. She worked for the company for thirty-eight years. She was employed as the secretary to the president. And, let me see, now…by God, she was Mr. Sarsky's secretary. What a coincidence!"

Henry didn't consider it a coincidence. This entire matter had an undercurrent of the supernatural – he was certain of it.

"May I please have her phone number?"

"Oh my, I'm sorry, I got you all excited and now I realize we are not allowed to give out employees' phone numbers, either. Perhaps, give me your phone number and I will call Ms. McIntyre and tell her you called and that you are trying to locate Mr. Sarsky's daughter, if she is still around of course. I will leave it up to her to decide if she wants to call you or not."

"That's fine." Henry gave his office number. "Please ask her to call. Tell her it is very important to me."

"I will do that, Mr. Pederson."

Once again, Henry's destiny was in the hand of another. He could only hope his heart's desire would be realized. He picked it up again and dialed the Ottawa telephone information. He asked for a listing for Ms. Elaine McIntyre, but was told they had no listing.

Once again, Henry hung up the phone and sat back in his chair. "All I can do now, is wait. Hopefully, she will call."

Henry's disappointment dampened his excitement and finally turned into nervousness. He got up and paced the floor, hoping to settle himself down. There were cheques to sign and letters to write, but he was too agitated to concentrate on office work. The thought occurred to him to call Father Engelmann; talking to him had always calmed him down. Henry was surprised that he hadn't already called him to let him know of his discovery of Jenny's letter.

Henry told his secretary that he was expecting an important call and to interrupt and let him know should he be on the phone. Henry called Father's number.

"St. Mary's rectory, Father David speaking."

"Oh, good, I'm glad you answered," Henry blurted out, his voice filled with excitement.

"What is it, Henry?"

"Father, you will never believe what I discovered at Mom's place?"

"What did you find, Henry?"

"Well, Father, I went over to Mom's in the morning—"

"Yes, yes, so, what did you find?"

"Well, as I was saying, I went over to Mom's to start cleaning out her things—"

"You've said that three times, go on."

"And, when I got into her bedroom, at the very end of sorting things out, I found her treasure chest."

"What is a treasure chest, Henry?"

"Well, that's what mom used to call it. It is a pine chest in which she stored things she considered treasures of the heart."

"I see, so, what did you find?" Father asked again, his voice a little edgy.

"Well, I was just coming to that, if you wouldn't interrupt me—"

"Yes, yes, okay, I will just listen."

"Well, Father, as I took everything out of the box, at the very end I realized there was something missing. It was a pink envelope that I had remembered seeing that gave off a lilac flower scent. And then the thought occurred to me it might be in Mom's apron because the day I found her and was praying over her I smelled lilacs. But, then I realized the ambulance attendants took Mom with her apron still on, back to the funeral home and threw it away, or so I thought!"

"Henry, you are going on and on. Did you find the letter and is that what you want to tell me!?"

"Man, are you impatient, Father and…I must admit I am taking advantage of it."

"Yes, I suspected as much."

"Well, Father, a miracle happened and Mom's apron was left behind through Julean's doing, but I won't get into that…I found the letter! Father are you sitting down? It almost gave me a heart attack."

"Ach, meine leiber Gott! Tell me, Henry!"

"It was a letter to me from…Jenny."

There was a long silence on the phone. Father immediately knew it was the letter that Mary had confessed to him about just before she died. He could have shared Mary's side to Henry but was sworn to secrecy. In any case Henry had probably figured out what happened. He would just listen and see where this goes.

Father simply replied, "Oh, that Jenny."

"Yes, that Jenny, Father?"

"Yes. So what do you know of this letter, Henry?

For the next fifteen minutes, Henry explained how he had found it, why he thought his mother hadn't given it him and that it proved that Jenny had still loved him. He also said what Father wanted to hear over all the rest, that he understood his mother's reasons for not giving the letter to him, and that he had no animosity towards her whatsoever.

"I just phoned Ottawa, Father, I'm trying to track Jenny down."

There was another long silence on the other end of the phone.

"Are you sure that's a good idea, Henry? What if she has a family and—"

"Yes, Father, I have thought about that. If I learn she has a family, I will stop trying to reach her. I just thought that maybe there might be the chance that she is still unattached. And remember what I told you when Julean was in the hospital and she came out of her coma? She too, at the time, encouraged me to seek Jenny out. *Maybe there is something to this.* In any case, it might be nice just to call as a friend to say, 'hello.'"

"It is possible she is single, Henry, but very unlikely."

"Don't worry, Father, I will be very careful not to start something."

"Yes, I understand, Henry, but I am also concerned about you. I know how long you had waited for a letter from Jenny at that time, and how much you cared for her, but that was a long time ago and things have changed; people change, feelings change. For all we know, Jenny may not even remember you by now. Be careful, Henry. Don't get your hopes up too high or begin something you may regret."

"I understand your concern, Father. Well, I am expecting a call from a lady who used to be Mr. Sarsky's secretary back in the fifties. Hopefully she will know where things are at and maybe help me to bring some closure to all of this."

"Yes, perhaps."

"Well, I better get back to work, Father, thanks for listening."

"Yes, thank you, Henry, for sharing all this with me. I will keep you in my prayers."

"Thank you, Father."

ELAINE HUNG UP the phone. Henry Pederson had contacted her former employer looking for information on Mr. Sarsky. She had never forgotten that name – the boy whose letters she destroyed in the furnace. It had always bothered her. Elaine wondered if Mr. Pederson's call had anything to do with the two letters she had mailed? But that was at least 30 years ago. Elaine was about to forget the entire matter and resume her plan to take her dog for a walk, but something encouraged her to call him. Perhaps it might in some way absolve her of the wrongdoing.

Elaine picked up the phone and dialed the number the personnel officer had given to her.

"Henry's Gift and Clothing Boutique."

"Is a Mr. Henry Pederson in?"

"Just a moment, please, I will transfer you to his office."

"Hello, this is Henry."

"Good afternoon, Mr. Pederson. This is Elaine McIntyre calling from Ottawa. I was given your number to call. How may I help you?"

Henry was at a loss for words. How should he start this conversation?

"Thank you for phoning, Ms. McIntyre. I recently came across a letter in my mother's keepsake chest after she passed away. The letter was from Jenny Sarsky. I understand you once worked for her father, Mr. Sarsky?"

"Yes, that is correct." Elaine replied. "You only just received the letter, now!?"

"Yes. From what I've been able to figure out, the letter arrived shortly before my wedding and I believe that was why my mother held on to it. I was wondering, Ms. McIntyre, would you by chance know the whereabouts of Jennifer?"

"No, I'm sorry, Mr. Pederson, I do not know where you might reach her. I did run into her and her mother a few years ago while shopping downtown. Jenny looked as beautiful as ever. She is married, you know, and at that time, anyway, she had one child. Her mother wasn't in the best state of health and I recall she was living in a care home."

Henry was no longer listening. As soon as Elaine mentioned that Jenny was married and had a child, his heart sank. He had hoped against all hope that Jenny might still be free. Henry knew it was over. It would be unethical for him to interfere with her and her family's life now.

"Mr. Pederson, are you still there?"

"Yes, I am still here."

"Mr. Pederson, there is something else I would like to tell you if you have another minute or so."

"Yes, I have time, Ms. McIntyre."

"Mr. Pederson, I want you to know that it was I who sent that special delivery letter off to you. In fact, there were two letters, one addressed to you, and the other I believe was one which you sent off to Jennifer. I discovered them in Mr. Sarsky's wall safe just before he died and decided to send them off to their rightful recipients."

"So, it was you who sent the letters?"

"Yes, it was me. I know what your next question is and I don't have the answer. I don't know why Mr. Sarsky didn't send them off, but I do know it bothered him immensely."

"Did Jenny receive my letter?"

"I don't know. I sent it off to her home by special delivery, just as I sent the one Jenny wrote to you."

Jenny would have written me or gotten in touch with me if she had received the letter; I know I would have.

Her letter had probably been intercepted, too. But then again, as he thought further on it, had his mother given him the letter, would he have really pursued it being so close to his wedding and how in love he was with Julean. Henry began to more fully appreciate the complexity of this entire matter and the decision his mother had made on his behalf.

"Ms. McIntyre, do you ever recall seeing a box full of letters addressed to Jenny? It was addressed to Mr. Sarsky because I didn't have their home address. Did he ever give them to Jenny?"

Elaine realized that the Lord had opened the door for her to confess what still weighed so heavily on her heart all those years.

"Mr. Pederson, I have an awful confession to make to you, Mr. Sarsky instructed me to destroy that box full of letters. I had them destroyed in the incinerator in the basement of our office building…"

Henry was shocked speechless by that revelation. It was as if a part of him suddenly died.

After a long moment, Elaine continued, "If it's any consolation, Mr. Sarsky was terribly troubled by it all. For some reason he wanted communication between you and his daughter to be stopped and I don't know why. I simply did what I was instructed to do and it has bothered me to this day for carrying out that order."

"I understand," said Henry, almost in a whisper. All his love letters, all his words of hope and love had never reached Jenny and had gone up in flames…

"Thank you for sharing that with me, Ms. McIntyre, that was very kind and considerate of you."

"I'm ashamed to say this, Mr. Pederson, but there is a selfish motive behind telling you this. I just had to get it out. It's something which has been heavy on my heart for a long time. I just hope the truth hasn't hurt you too much."

Henry didn't answer directly, he sensed she wanted forgiveness and he responded in kind, much the way Father would have. "It's always good to know the truth, Ms. McIntyre. You did the right thing by telling me."

"Thank you, Mr. Pederson." The relief in her voice was very evident. "I wish you all the best."

"Yes, thank you, again, for calling and sharing. Good-bye."

Henry now knew the truth. It should have given him some measure of closure and freedom, but it didn't. He was still trapped with such a deep love in his heart for Jenny that he couldn't release. All he had was memories. He knew in his heart that if Jenny had received his letters things would have been very different.

The discovery of the letter had revealed just how deeply he still was in love with Jenny. He so wanted to hold her, to give and receive her love, as well. Instead, he seemed to be doomed to this emptiness inside, this horrible lack of complete closure and fulfillment.

Could he suppress all these feelings again and hope time will heal as before? Deep down though Henry knew that even time had lied to him and led him to believe it was over. It was clear however, the torch for Jenny had always been there in his heart, smouldering in the depths of his being like some dormant volcano ready to erupt.

What pained his heart even more was that his dear sweet Julean had to live with this for all the years of their marriage. That Julean had been the one to tell him that he hadn't healed as well as he'd thought. That she knew he still loved another. He recalled the words she spoke at the hospital that memorable day… *"You shared your love when your defences were down…your dreams revealed her to me. The eve of our wedding after we made love, I will never forget your dream that followed. I tried to wake you, but you were making love to Jenny in your dreams."*

Henry remembered that night all too well and the guilt he felt for days after for having such a dream and those that followed.

Henry shook his head and muttered, "Was it all for naught? Was Julean's painful endurance in vain? Was my longing and yearning for all these years to come down to this…that it was nothing more than a memory and will always continue to be?"

The hum of the fluorescent fixture above him penetrated the still silence. There was no silence however in Henry's mind; it was churning, examining every detail of his conversation with Ms. McIntyre searching for any clue he might still pursue. She did mention that Jenny's mother was living in a care home. He could call every one in Ottawa and assuming that Mrs. Sarsky was still alive he may track down Jenny that way.

But, no, to what end?

She was married.

It was not the right thing to do and he had also promised Father Engelmann he wouldn't take it any further.

Chapter Forty-Nine

J enny hemmed and hawed for two days before deciding to phone her son. Just thinking about it made her nervous all day. The clock on the bedside table read 8:00 p.m. Since they were an hour ahead in Ottawa, she assumed J.J. would be home from work by now. If he was like James, a fourteen hour day would be normal. She picked up the phone and her trembling finger dialed the number. She listened with immense trepidation as the phone rang.

"Hello?" answered a female voice. Nora, J.J.'s wife. Would she still recognize her?

"Hello? Is someone there?"

"Hi, is this Nora?"

"Yes, who is speaking?"

"It's me, Jenny."

"Who?"

"It's Jenny, J.J.'s mother."

"Oh, Marjorie Hamilton."

"Yes, it's Marjorie. I still go by my second name. Everyone calls me Jenny."

"I can call you, Jenny, if you prefer."

"That would be very nice, Nora. How is my grandson doing?"

"He is fine. He's sits up and is making attempts to walk. Oh they grow so fast."

"I would love to see him. Your mom and dad must be so proud of him."

"Yes, they are over all the time. Dad's planning an early retirement just so he can spend more time with him."

"Oh, that is so nice to hear, Nora. Do you think you and J.J. and my little grandson can come to Regina for a visit, soon?"

"Well, I don't know Marj—I mean Jenny. J.J. is so busy, I hardly ever see him. He is going to start taking over part of the company and he and his father are spending a lot of time together, making sure they are both on track. Well, you know how it is in business."

Jenny didn't answer. She knew only too well. It looked like a similar pattern was occurring in Nora's life as had occurred in hers. Memories of the spousal agreement she signed stabbed into her mind. Jenny wondered if she should alert Nora, but it was probably too late.

"Are you still there, Jenny?"

"Oh yes, Nora, I'm sorry. Is J.J. at home?"

"No, he isn't, but I do expect him any time now. It's almost nine-thirty, and he is usually home between nine and ten. How are you finding Regina?"

"I love it, here. It's a much smaller city than Ottawa, but the legislature buildings remind me of Ottawa, so it does feel a little like home."

"Oh, that's good."

"Yes, and I have made a lot of friends and I love my house and neighbourhood."

"Oh, that's nice." Nora repeated.

"I would sure like to see my grandson," Jenny said again, trying to extend the conversation. "So do you call him James the Third or do you have a nickname?" Jenny was curious.

"We call him Jimmy. J.J.'s dad said that would be best until he gets older and then wants to refer to him as James the third. It sounds odd, but I guess we can get used to it."

Jenny recalled only too well, James preferences and control over others names. Jenny still shivered each time James referred to her as Marjorie.

"Anyway, Jenny, I think I had written Jimmy on the birth announcement. And actually when it's in print, James 3rd looks quite impressive."

"Oh, I don't recall receiving one, Nora."

"I'm sure I asked J.J. to mail them. I wrote them out in the hospital while I was there. I had a few complications and had to stay in for almost two weeks."

Jenny was silent for a brief moment. She wondered if J.J. purposefully didn't send her an announcement.

"It must have gotten lost. In any case, I would love to see him."

"Perhaps you could come to Ottawa for a visit."

"I would love to, Nora, but I don't think that's going to be possible."

"Well, perhaps next month."

"I'm not sure if I can come then, either."

"You must be very busy."

"Well, not really it's just that I...am in the hospital right now."

"Oh, no, I'm so sorry to hear. What is the problem?"

"Well, I don't mean to alarm you or J.J., but I have cancer."

"Oh, that's too bad, Jenny, I hope everything turns out okay."

"So do I." Jenny's pillow called to her and she had to hold the receiver with two hands so she wouldn't drop it.

"Could you tell J.J.? And ask him to call me when he gets home? Or in the morning is fine, too." Jenny gave Nora the phone number to her room.

"Well, I better get to bed, I need my beauty sleep," Jenny said, with a tired chuckle.

"Well, I do hope you are feeling better, soon."

"Oh, I'm sure I will."

"Oh, Jenny, I think J.J. just came in. I heard the garage door close. Just a moment please."

Jenny's heart sank. She was hoping he would call later, fatigue and nervousness swarmed over her; she needed rest badly. Loud voices and unpleasant tones carried to the phone. Nora and J.J. were arguing and Jenny was able to make out parts of it. "It's your mother J.J., …you have to talk to her…"

"She's not my mother anymore…"

The words stabbed at Jenny's heart like a knife.

"Oh, J.J., please don't do this to me. I really didn't do anything wrong," Jenny whispered into the phone.

Finally, Jenny heard the phone move and clang on the counter.

"Hello, Marj."

He sounded just like James.

"Yes, it's me, Mom."

"So, why the call?"

"Well, I wanted to see how my grandson is and I wanted to talk to you. It's been over a year and—"

"Well, you know how busy we are, the company is growing so fast, Dad and I hardly get time to sleep."

"Yes, I know all about that. I was wondering, J.J., if you could come for a visit and bring Nora and my grandson of course?"

"Marj, I am way too busy at this time, maybe next summer."

By then it may be too late.

"Well, J.J., I am in the hospital right now. I had surgery last month to remove a tumour and it was cancerous."

Jenny wondered if in his silence, J.J. was thinking that she deserved to be punished for what she did.

"Did they get it all?" J.J. finally asked.

"No, they didn't, J.J., and the doctor informed me the other day that it has spread."

Again, J.J. said nothing.

"I would really appreciate it if you and Nora," she couldn't say the name James "and your son could come for a visit, even if it's for a day or so."

"I'm really too busy, perhaps like I said, maybe next summer."

"Well, if you can find the time to come, please come."

"We'll see," J.J. said, still showing no indication of warmth or understanding in his voice. "Well, Marj, I am very tired. It's been a long day."

"Yes, of course. I am sorry, J.J.. It's been nice talking to you," Jenny lied again. "Nora has my telephone number. Please call me at any time."

"Yeah, sure."

"Well…bye, J.J.."

Jenny was going to add that she loved him, but felt his depth of coldness still so strongly that any words of love or reconciliation at this time might just deepen the rift between them. Jenny heard the click in the receiver. Perspiration rolled down her back and arm pits. The receiver clung to her clammy hand, she had to use her other hand to free it. Talking to her son was like talking to her ex-husband, only worse. He was her son and she needed him and his love and support.

She felt so alone.

Jenny collapsed back on the bed, her strength depleted.

"Oh, Lord, why is all this happening to me? Are you punishing me? I've tried to be a good person, but even my own son has disowned me. I have lost all the people I have ever loved." Jenny couldn't finish. She just wept all the more. Tears seemed to be the only way her aching heart could find some measure of comfort and relief.

Both her hands came up to her chest as she turned on her side and drew up her knees. If only she could crawl back into her mother's womb and start all over. She felt the angel and clutched it tightly with her right hand.

"Oh, you are all I have left, please help me."

Fatigue and exhaustion overwhelmed her and within moments she had drifted off into a deep, deep sleep.

The next day Jenny awoke at nine. A nurse was standing at her bedside when she awoke.

"Well, you sure had a long rest. You slept for almost 11 hours. Dr. Kreake was here about two hours ago, but couldn't wait for you to wake up. He will be back later this afternoon on his way home."

"Oh, I'm sorry I missed him, he should have woken me."

"We have held your breakfast. I will call to the kitchen and have them send something up for you in about a half hour."

"Thank you. I'm not really that hungry, though."

Thoughts about her conversation with her son returned and feelings of hurt and sorrow accompanied them. How could they possibly make up when he was so antagonistic towards her? Tremors of apprehension that he would never understand her side and never forgive her, reverberated through her. His feelings of hostility and utter disrespect for her demonstrated the night before sent fresh tears flowing again. The brief respite of strength she had enjoyed and hope that she was getting better faded; thrust out by a heavy fatigue.

Twenty minutes later when nurse Edna came in with Jenny's breakfast, she was in a state of peaceful repose. Once again, sleep had temporarily suspended her troubled consciousness.

In the week which followed, Jenny started her new medication. The assault on her body was swift and immediate. She became sick and threatened to throw up each time she took the tiny blue pills. Thoughts of ever going home again faded; Dr. Kreake was right…a care home was now her destiny. She was glad that she had applied to several the previous week. Dr. Kreake had brought her a list and circled the ones that he recommended.

The Nunnery Care Home had called. They said that they could keep her if her condition didn't deteriorate further. They did however recommend the Santa Maria Home which happened to be second on Jenny's list. They had an opening coming up at the end of the month and she would need to respond within two weeks to hold the room for her. The third home on her list was full at present, but they put her on a waiting list.

"The Santa Maria Home is a very good care facility, Jenny," said Dr. Kreake. "You need to find some place, soon. The hospital has already extended your admission privileges much more than they are able."

"Nobody wants me anymore," Jenny tried to quip, but knew the sentiment was partially true.

"Oh, Jenny, it's not that, it's just that there is such a shortage of beds."

"I understand, Dr. Kreake, the hospital has been very generous with me. I have been here for almost two months. I told Edna, the day nurse to call the Nunnery. It was once a convent and has a chapel which appeals to me. They can take me right away. I can try it there for a month and if it doesn't work I'll go to the Santa Maria Home. But, what about my home? I can't expect my neighbour to look after it indefinitely."

"Well, Jenny, you just might have to sell it."

"You mean, make the care home my permanent residence?"

"For now, Jenny move into the care home, try it for a while, and see how it goes? You will know soon enough if you can go back home or not."

"Yes, maybe that's the best thing to do." Even that speck of a glimmer of hope brightened Jenny's eyes.

"So, your son knows about your condition?"

"Yes, I called him—"

"And, is he coming to visit you?"

"I am afraid not. He said he's too busy."

"Too busy! You tell him to get his behind up here."

Jenny's mouth twitched upward.

"Why don't you give me his number and let me call him?"

"Oh no, it will all work out, I'm sure."

"Kids," Dr. Kreake muttered, "You raise them, feed them, clothe them, care and worry over them and when you want them to reciprocate, they suddenly vanish."

"Oh, it's not that bad. Young people nowadays are very busy."

"Too busy! Bah! Everyone is striving to get ahead, accumulating more and not taking the time to enjoy and appreciate what they have, especially each other and family." Dr. Kreake was about to say more, but hesitated. Whatever he wanted to say stayed inside.

"I really appreciate your concern, doctor. In my experience, things have a way of working out."

TWO WEEKS BEFORE Halloween, Jenny was transferred to the Nunnery Care Home. The new medication helped stabilize her condition, but most days she still was too weak to get out of bed. The staff at the Nunnery were concerned that Jenny needed more care than their facility could provide

On one of his visits, Dr. Kreake managed to get J.J.'s phone number. Jenny asked him to explain her condition and ask if J.J. would come home and arrange for the sale of her house and that he was welcome to take what he wanted.

Dr. Kreake left his number several times, but his call was never returned. Dr. Kreake finally got through to J.J.

"This is James Junior, what can I do for you? I am very busy."

"I understand your mother has called and informed you of her condition?"

"Yeah, she said she has cancer."

"Her condition is very serious, in fact terminal. She could use the support of her family. Can I count on you and your family coming to visit and support her at this time?"

"Like I said earlier, I am a very busy man and—"

"I'm a busy man as well, Mr Hamilton but I have always considered family takes precedence over everything else. I would suggest that you don't delay and come quickly. I don't know how long your mother has and—" And this time it was J.J. that cut off Dr. Kreake.

"I'm very busy and I have many things in the works, I just can't drop everything—"

"Look, if you were my son and he showed this kind of consideration for his mother we wouldn't be having this conversation. We would be having one which would leave him so sore he wouldn't be sitting down for the next six months. I suggest you grow up mister and have a close look at your priorities and get your ass down here pronto!"

Dr. Kreake slammed the phone down, shook his head and walked down the hall.

The attendants around the nurses' station made every effort to contain themselves from jumping up and yelling out a loud hooray for the doctor!

Two DAYS LATER Nora called Jenny.

"Oh, it's so good to hear from you, Nora. I hope you have good news for me."

"Yes, Jenny, I was sure that J.J. wouldn't be able to get away. I don't know what your Dr. told my husband but when J.J. discussed with his dad what nerve the doctor had to talk to him in the way he did, Mr. Hamilton senior backed up the doctor one hundred per cent."

"So…will J.J. be coming?"

"Oh, yes, we all are! J.J.'s dad instructed him to leave as soon as possible. We plan to be there towards the end of October or the beginning of November."

"Oh Nora, that is the best news I have heard in a long time."

The news perked up her spirits. Perhaps there is still hope for us and it was so good of James to encourage J.J. to come!

Jenny wondered if she should tell J.J. about his half-sister? The question had plagued Jenny's mind for a long time. It would be so wonderful if they could meet. Yet, would even she and Camilla meet? Her strength was waning by the day. Would she have the strength or energy to try and locate Camilla. And, what good would it do now? It would only disrupt the girl's life. She obviously had such fond memories of her parents and to tell her that they really weren't her parents, and to learn she had a mother on the verge of death, ready to abandon her again, wouldn't be fair.

"No, Jenny," she chastised herself, "Leave things as they are." At best she could call Mrs. Blake at the agency and let her know the circumstances and that if Camilla were to ever inquire she should at least know she has a half-brother. Some family connection would be better than nothing.

But, how would her son take it? Would he even respond kindly towards Camilla? Or, would he respond to Camilla with revulsion like James did to her? J.J. was so upset and cold towards her, probably anything associated with her would be in his ring of wrath, as well. All her life she wanted a loving family so much, but all she'd experienced was anger, rejection, and hatred.

The family situation so agitated her that the attending nurse had to give her a strong sedative.

As she drifted off, her mind considered another possibility that assuaged her. Wouldn't it be something if she could see her two loves before she passed away? She had always prayed that Henry would be the father to her girl. If only they had made love that day in the park. Perhaps another kiss, another hug, and it would have happened. And as the medication flowed through her veins, she reached out to Camilla and Henry standing gleefully on either side, "Quickly hold my hands," …and, together, they hopped and ran barefoot through a meadow of wildflowers and there, on the other side was J.J., waiting with open arms.

It was all so perfect…if only in her dreams.

CHAPTER FIFTY

O N A TUESDAY evening the Diplomat Restaurant was quiet. Henry had requested a booth to sit at for more privacy and intimacy. Both of Henry's arms were extended across the table, his hands entwined in Ivania's. They were gazing into each other's eyes for the longest time as Henry searched for a way to share his heart. Ivania wanted to know exactly where their relationship was at. Although they had spoken on the telephone, they hadn't seen one another for almost a month. Ivania had known that Henry still wasn't over the loss of Julean but always suspected there was something else. Ivania needed to know...

Henry had always regretted not being more open with Julean. He thought the open truth would hurt his wife too much. He suspected she knew of Jenny but didn't realize the extent to which she did and the hurt it must have caused her by him being silent about it. Perhaps if he had shared his heart earlier on in their marriage perhaps it would have been easier to accept and deal with. In any case, it was happening here again with Ivania and he didn't want to make that same mistake again. It was only right to be totally open and honest to the lady who sat across from him.

Ivania had a strong constitution, but Henry could see fissures in her demeanour. She liked him a lot, probably loved him and wanted to give him so much more. But she needed to feel that same love in return.

Henry finally broke the silence and spoke from the heart. For well over an hour he shared everything. The day he and Jenny met and the incredible attraction that occurred between them in the grocery store. Their summer together, their separation, and how he never heard from her again. He thought he would never love another, until Julean came along. Feeling surely his heart would be healed, unbelievably the love in his heart for his first love just would not let go.

Henry shared how Julean knew of his feelings and coped with it right up to the moment of her death. Even in her final hours she encouraged him to find his first love or to find another. He gazed into Ivania's eyes in total sincerity and spoke softly, "I thought when you came along that I could begin again. You are such a wonderful lady and I am so fortunate that you came into my life. I am so fond of you but I just cannot let go of the past. When Mom died and I found the letter Jenny had written to me so many years ago, it was as if it were yesterday. My feelings erupted like a dormant volcano. My love for her has always been just below the surface. I just don't understand it, Ivania, how the love that began one summer when I was fifteen is as strong today as it was then?'

The flickering candle on the table caught the tears in Ivania's eyes. Behind the sparkle, Henry could feel the hurt and disappointment. She sat motionless and speechless.

What could she say?

She had tried everything to win Henry's heart, but her efforts were in vain. The words that finally spilled forth said it all.

"My dear, Hen-dry, the women in your life have too strong a hold on you for me to come in."

She squeezed both of Henry's hands and then withdrew them and hid them from view under the table.

They continued to stare at one another. Their meal had come over an hour ago and neither had touched theirs. The chilled white wine had warmed and remained untouched as well. Even the waiter had sensed something was amiss and purposely stayed away from their table. Henry wished the waiter was not so sensitive and would come to break the growing tension.

He liked Ivania a lot, and it pained him to see her hurt.

Finally, Henry withdrew his hands and turned to the waiter who was waiting for his cue. He quickly responded and came over.

"Can I interest you in a coffee or dessert?"

"No, that will be fine. Could I have the bill, please?"

"Certainly, sir."

The drive home was a repeat of most of their evening. They sat in silence as Henry sped along. Henry always dreaded this part of their dates as he sensed Ivania wanted a closer and more intimate relationship. He did too, but under different circumstances. It was so strongly entrenched in his character that sex was meant in a marriage setting where there was a commitment to love, honour and cherish one another. As much as he wanted to make love to Ivania he knew it would be for the wrong reasons and send the wrong message. It would be for personal gratification…

Ivania got that message long ago and tonight, especially tonight, was no different. When Henry took her to the door she simply turned and pecked him on the cheek. She gazed into Henry's eyes for a long moment and said, "Perhaps we can be friends…"

Henry just stood there, tightened his lips and almost imperceptibly nodded.

"Dad, are you okay?"

"I'm fine, son. But I've noticed you haven't been yourself for quite awhile. Is there something wrong?"

"Yeah, there is. I didn't want to trouble you with it. I don't want to worry you and with grandma gone you've got enough on your shoulders…I know how much you miss her."

"I do miss Mom, Jeremy, but if you're having a problem that takes precedence. Let's sit down and have a coffee."

Henry hollered for the framer to come up and look after the gallery. The two men made their way to a table and sat down.

"Can I get you both a coffee?" asked Tamara who was filling up the salt shakers nearby.

"That would be great," Henry said as he turned over the cup on the saucer. Jeremy did the same and Tamara immediately filled the cups with steaming coffee.

After Henry emptied a creamer into his coffee, he took a cautious sip and asked, "So what's troubling you, Son?"

"It has to do with Camilla and me. Actually it has to do more with Camilla."

"What's troubling her then?"

"Well, it's kinda, complicated and it even involves you…or it did."

Henry furrowed his brow and a puzzled look grew on his face.

"Dad, do you recall how often you said Camilla reminds you of the girl you went out with when you were a teenager?"

Henry nodded.

"And do you remember how many times you thought Camilla's parents didn't resemble her at all?"

"Yes, I do recall saying that, but I wasn't the only one. Almost everyone was surprised to see Camilla stand by her parents and claim that she was their daughter."

"Well that's just it. Camilla has also felt for as long as she can remember that she was adopted."

Henry had those same feelings and still does. Could it be possible that his intuition was right after all? Henry just stared at his son and nodded for him to go on.

"She is even having these dreams of a stork delivering a baby to some woman sitting in a gazebo surrounded by wildflowers. Camilla thinks she is the baby being carried by the stork to her real biological mother…"

"Really?" Henry didn't know what to say and Jeremy continued.

"I think it all has to do with her mother reading a book to her about a stork delivering babies. And lately it's an angel delivering the baby instead of the stork…but I don't want to get into that—"

"But how do I fit into this?" Henry wanted to know.

"You're not going to believe this, Dad. Camilla and me have argued over this but I think she is okay with it now. Grandma kind of straightened it out. Anyway, Camilla thought that maybe your teenage girlfriend that Camilla reminds you of is her mother…"

Those were Henry's thoughts for the longest time. Henry shook his head from side to side…

Jeremy grew agitated by his father's silence. "Geez, Dad, is it true? You didn't make that girl pregnant, did you?"

Henry's face turned red. "No Jeremy, of course not…"

Henry didn't know what else to say. He had always thought that Peter had raped Jenny and fathered a child but he couldn't say that to his son! It was all an assumption that wasn't based on any facts. And surely he couldn't even suggest such a thing to his son. The consequences could be devastating to Camilla.

"Of course not," Henry repeated more emphatically. "I think this is all some coincidence that Camilla happens to look like the young girl I dated at that time."

"That's what I think, too! But she won't listen to me. And now she thinks that her dad has some papers in his strong box that will reveal that she was adopted. We brought the metal box home after Stan died and have it stored in the basement but Camilla is afraid to look for some reason and won't let me either. It's all so weird."

"Look Son, since she was born and raised in Ottawa, tell her to contact Social Services there and talk to someone in the adoption department to see if her suspicions have any validity. Camilla has been involved with that kind of thing for several years working with pregnant girls. She shouldn't have any trouble sourcing it all out. It seems to me she is creating all these different scenarios in her mind that may have no truth whatsoever."

"Yeah, that's exactly right!" Jeremy exclaimed and then said, "There's another thing, Dad. Do you remember at Father Engelmann's anniversary party there was a guy there named Peter? I don't know his last name, but he was Eddy's best man at their wedding that morning..."

Once again Henry turned red...

This is incredible.

Jeremy stared at Henry for a moment and was going to ask what was wrong, but decided to say instead, "Camilla dreams of that man too, Dad. She doesn't know why, and that day at the party she saw you and Peter talking to one another and then saw the both of you staring at her...she wonders why?"

Once again, Henry felt cornered. He could never tell his son that Peter dreams of Camilla too and that Peter feels he raped Jenny, who Camilla thinks is her birth mother! *My God, this is getting out of hand. What is going on here?*

Jeremy stared at his father waiting for an answer. Once more he grew concerned over his silence.

"I was just trying to think back, Jeremy. I think we were talking of our children and I told Peter that Camilla was not my daughter but my daughter-in-law..." Henry shrugged his shoulders as if to say, that's all he could think of.

"Well, maybe I'll suggest to Camilla to check with the agency in Ottawa and hope that I can convince her to look in her father's metal box. This is affecting our relationship and it's got to be resolved."

"Would you like me to talk to her, Son?'

Jeremy gazed at his father for a moment, "No, let's see where this leads to. Maybe the agency can clear things up once and for all."

Chapter Fifty-One

"THIS IS BECOMING a habit, Father. This is the second time I've helped you move in almost twenty five years."

"I know. It must be a considerable burden on you, Henry," Father Engelmann quipped back. Henry and Father stared at each other and chuckled.

"Just wait here for a moment; there is a book in the study which I want to take with me. I'll just be a moment."

"Oh, that's fine, Father, take your time."

As Henry stood in the foyer he stared at the suitcase before him. It was the same one he had carried to the car for Mr. Engelmann after he had sold his grocery store and decided to become a priest. All of his worldly possessions: his Bible, the holy cross which hung in their bedroom, and his wedding suit, were in that suitcase.

Henry smiled at the thought. From a worldly point of view, one would say he really wasn't very successful. That he didn't have a lot to show for all these years. Most people amass a small or large fortune during that time and yet, Mr. Engelmann, or rather, Father Engelmann, still carried the same old suitcase with the same contents it had held twenty five years before.

But, what Father had gained over the years had made him perhaps the richest man in the world. He had freed himself from the pursuit of materialism and devoted his life to seeking and gaining the treasures the Lord gives to those who follow him. His sermon last Sunday was on that very topic. Wow, what a homily. It was his last message to his flock and still reverberated in his mind. One of the scriptural passages he quoted stung his heart: "What does it profit a man if he gains the whole world and suffers the loss of his soul in the process."

Henry had such a good teacher in Father, such a good example to emulate and still he struggled and toiled excessively in making monetary gain his chief goal. His worth, his value as a person, his success all seemed to be so inextricably tied up with what he owned and achieved.

Will he ever be able to really let go, become detached, content and make the Lord the first and sole centre of his life?

Well, Father Engelmann certainly didn't have two masters. He was living proof of one who had placed Jesus at the centre of his life.

Henry still couldn't believe that Father was actually retiring. After a lifetime with Anna and the grocery store and another lifetime dedicated to the Lord's service, it was time for Father to finally step down.

But was he really retiring?

He might have freed himself from most of his parish responsibilities, but almost daily he seemed to be expanding his outreach to another flock.

Wherever he felt there was a need, Father worked tirelessly to fill it. He visited all the hospitals and care homes. One would have thought he'd be exhausted, and would need to slow down and take more time to rest. Amazingly however, the more he gave of himself, the younger he grew, the more energy he received to do God's work. Henry still didn't know exactly how old Father was in years. He was getting up there, yet he looked in his seventies, and behaved like he was in his forties.

Henry was still amazed over the events that had led to Father's decision to retire. He could still picture Father Knuka standing there before the congregation waiting for the Lord to touch him in a special way and He did; Father Knuka was given the gift of tongues and filled with the power of the Holy Spirit.

It was shortly after that incredible happening, which many of the people considered a miracle, that Father Engelmann began to talk about leaving. It was the sign he had been waiting for; the church was in good hands and could be entrusted to the young priest.

Henry wondered what was keeping, Father. He turned and looked through the window out onto the front yard of the rectory. The long sidewalk leading up to the rectory made Henry think of the path Father would now follow. He recalled thinking those same thoughts when he dropped Father off so long ago. Henry knew Father would never retire from doing the Lord's work. The path before him would simply lead to another journey the Lord had prepared for him. Henry suspected the Lord had already shown Father what his next project was.

After a few more moments, he heard Father approaching from the end of the hall, whistling his favourite melody, 'His Peace is Flowing Like a River.'

"Oh, I'm so sorry, Henry," Father said as he stepped into the light of the foyer. "I went to see the cook to remind her that I wouldn't be here for supper, tonight, and…well, you know how hard it is to say good-bye."

"That's fine, Father. Are you ready to go?"

"I'm always ready to do the Lord's work, Henry."

Henry picked up Father's suitcase and made his way to the door. It seemed lighter than before, and by the sounds of it, all that was inside were his Bible and the cross.

"Boy, this gets lighter all the time, Father."

"It may not seem like much, but it contains all the wisdom in the world." Father winked at Henry and smiled. "When the movers moved my bed to the care home the other day, I sent my priestly clothes and my wedding suit along with them."

Henry smiled. He had guessed accurately the contents of the suitcase. It was lighter because his suit was missing. It reminded Henry of the first time he saw Father Engelmann wearing his wedding suit. It was at Mrs. Engelmann's funeral. Everyone expected to see Mr. Engelmann in a mournful state. Much to everyone's surprise, however, Mr. Engelmann wore both the attire and an expression that was more appropriate for a wedding than a funeral. His light tan suit with the bright yellow geranium in his lapel and his smile, contrasted with the congregants who were dressed in traditional black and saddened faces.

A feeling of uneasiness swept through Henry as he continued to think of Mr. Engelmann's suit as they walked to the SUV.

It wasn't the death of Anna that gnawed inside Henry's stomach, rather it was the unforgettable memory of the prince charming dream he had the day he met Jenny when he fell asleep before taking her to Balfour Collegiate. He had often wondered if the man wearing the yellow suit and yellow flower in his lapel lying on the bed of daisies where Jenny had lain was Mr. Engelmann, especially now that Mr. Engelmann was older and looked so much more like the man in his dream. The thought of the faceless man wearing a black cloak who held him back from getting to Jenny and the man in the tan suit, sent quivering coldness down his spine just as it had done back then. Henry was relieved as the clink of Father Engelmann's seat belt buckle snapped him out of his reverie.

"What is wrong Henry, you look flushed and feverish?"

Henry wiped the perspiration off his forehead with the back of his hand and shook his head. "Oh, it's nothing Father." Henry forced a smile.

Father studied Henry for a moment longer then turned and gazed once more at the rectory, "this has been a very good second home and now I am going to my third and…perhaps last."

Henry knew that last day would come, and preferred not to think on it. He fired up the engine.

Neither of them spoke as they drove to Father's new home, both absorbed in their own thoughts. When Father had first talked about leaving the parish, he had considered the option to go back to Gravelbourg and retire at the seminary or at one of the fine retreat centres on the west coast, but Father declined to go to either. He saw more beauty in reaching out to people in need than mountain scenery or living a secluded life in a seminary.

He had also considered going into a senior high-rise, which housed about hundred people or so. In the end however, the Archbishop knew Father would consider them all his flock and be just as busy as he had been in the parish, if not more. He convinced Father it would be too much for him. Reluctantly, Father agreed to a smaller facility.

An ambulance was parked in front of the Nunnery Care Home as Henry pulled up behind. Someone was either checking in or out, Henry thought.

"Well, here we are, Father, your new home."

Father was gazing at the ambulance, his lips moving in prayer… "Ah, yes, here it is my new home…"

Like the rectory, The Nunnery Care Home had a brick veneer and sprawled across two city lots. There were no windows facing the street and the oak door was devoid of windows, as well. It was almost like a fortress, shutting out the world outside. A long walkway led up to the door. In a sense, the similarity cushioned Father's transition into his retirement home.

As they walked up the walkway to the front door, it suddenly opened. An ambulance attendant was backing out guiding a gurney. An attendant was at the other end. Henry grabbed the door and held it open. As the gurney passed through the door it bumped into the door frame wobbling it. Henry instinctively reached out to steady it and in doing so touched the patient's arm. Instantly, an indescribable energy surged through him. He turned and looked at the patient, but all he saw was the back of the patients head wearing a blue bandana.

"My good Lord, what was that?" Henry muttered, the energy still zinging through him.

"Are you okay, Henry? You look so pale and white again…"

"Oh, … I'm fine Father."

Henry continued to stare at the attendants loading the patient into the back. He felt a strong compulsion to go to the patient. He let go of the door and when it slammed shut the sound snapped him back to the reality of the moment. He watched as the ambulance sped down the street, then slowly turned and rang the doorbell.

As they waited for an attendant to answer the door, Henry reviewed in his mind the reasons Father had selected this care home. First, it was near a Catholic church where he could attend mass if he wanted to. But more importantly, the care home at one time had been a convent. It was occupied by the Sisters of the Precious Blood. As time went on, fewer and fewer nuns were recruited and the ones there, were getting on in age, and were sent back to the Mother House in Ontario.

Father must have been reading Henry's thoughts...

"I would like you to see the chapel before you leave, Henry. It is one of the main reasons I selected this care home. I hope they will allow me to say daily mass."

The door opened and a young girl peeked out.

"Oh, you must be Father Engelmann, our new resident."

"Yes, that's me. I'm here to make my new home."

"Well, please come in, Father, my name is Angela."

"Your mom and dad must have thought they gave birth to an angel to name you that."

"Maybe so, Father, but my yelling and screaming soon made them realize otherwise."

They all laughed.

"This is Henry, Angela, I consider him my son. He is helping me make this move, today."

"Oh, that's nice. It's good to have some support when starting something new. But I assure you, Father, you will quickly feel at home, here."

"Yes, yes, I'm sure I will."

"Please follow me, I will show you to your room."

"I think I still remember where it is. I looked at it about three weeks ago."

They walked down the long hall which was flooded with light from a huge inner courtyard. All of the bedrooms lay around the perimeter of the care home with a large window facing the hallway to receive the light as well as the beautiful view of the flower-filled courtyard. The rooms also had a small narrow window facing the outside, but it was more for ventilation and didn't interfere with their privacy. The doors to most rooms were open and occupants just stared with a blank look as they walked by, probably wondering what a priest was doing there.

They turned at the end of the hallway and passed the kitchen, bright and sunny, as it too faced the courtyard. They stopped and briefly looked at the huge table.

"The table of the Lord," Father muttered under his breath, "I shall soon meet my flock."

When Father Engelmann turned towards her, Angela took that as her cue to continue on.

"Well, here it is," said Angela, as she stopped, turned, and with the same motion swung her right arm towards the open door to Father's room. Father passed by her first then Henry followed. Henry didn't tell Father that he had already been to this room. He had stopped by two days earlier to hang a painting.

It was a fairly large room, with a single bed against the far wall. A night table with a lamp, which was turned on, stood next to the bed. It gave off a nice warm yellow glow and provided a welcoming atmosphere. Father's chair sat next to the table and lamp. The window just behind the chair was larger than the ones in the other rooms and faced south. That was another reason why Father liked this care home.

Father hadn't noticed his special surprise yet, as they studied another painting Henry had given him shortly after he moved into the rectory. It was a prairie landscape with a full crop swaying in the summer sun. It was ripe and golden and ready to be harvested. In the mid-ground was the town of Lipton with its three grain elevators, several homes and buildings, and the town church just off a bit at the edge of the town. The care home must have hung it after Henry had brought in the other painting.

The landscape painting hung above a chest of drawers, covered with a long table cloth which Henry surmised Anna had crocheted. On top, sat a single, framed picture of Father Engelmann and Anna on their wedding day. There was no television set, no radio. Henry knew as soon as he left, Father would immediately have his Bible out of the suitcase and onto the night table beside his chair.

"Well, Father, you should be very comfortable, here."

"I feel like I am in the Hotel Saskatchewan, spoiled already." Father turned towards Angela to thank her for showing him to his room, but she was no longer there. It was then that he noticed the other painting on the wall across from his chair.

He was silent for a long moment as the memory of that poignant scene consumed him. "Jesus, Mary and Joseph help me. Ach mein lieber Gott" He took a couple of steps forward, and then a few more until he was but three feet in front of a scene that captured the love he and Anna had shared even in death. It was a moment frozen on canvas and now melting in Father's heart.

It was just as Henry had burned it into his memory and then sketched it in his room the morning after Anna had died. Henry knew it would not be a reminder to Father of Anna's death, but rather of the life they shared, and the eternal life Anna was enjoying with her Lord. In the centre of it all was the holy cross – the Giver of life, the One in the centre of their life and their marriage.

Only now as Father wiped away the tears blurring his vision did he see his guardian angel faintly superimposed against the background behind him. And on the other side of the room in the painting was Anna's protector, as well, welcoming her.

"Henry, you have captured it all. You are a Rembrandt!"

Father turned towards the master painter and they stepped into each other's arms and wept.

"Words fail to express my gratitude, Henry."

"If only my heart could speak."

Angela tapped lightly on the door not sure if she should interrupt Father and Henry. They parted and looked through tear-filled eyes at their lovely young host.

"I was just admiring the painting Henry has done for me—"

"Yes, we all saw it the other day when Mr. Pederson brought it in. It is truly so beautiful. You must have loved your wife so dearly, Father. It still brings tears to my eyes seeing you hold her hand."

"Yes, she is and always will be my first and only love."

"And the angels!" Angela blurted out, "Makes it perfect. I pray to mine every night." Her eyes, when she said that, brightened so much Henry thought they would pop out of their sockets.

"Do you want me to show you the rest of the place before dinner, Father?"

"That's not necessary, Angela, I was already given the tour."

"Well, Father, if you want to unpack…" Henry caught himself. What was there to unpack – his Bible and the cross? That would take all of two minutes.

Father smiled.

"Oh, I can do that later, Henry. Come, let me show you the rest of the place. I will give you the tour the owner gave me the other day." Father said, as he briskly walked past Henry and out the door of his new home.

They retraced their steps of fifteen minutes or so ago, but this time instead of turning left at the end of the hallway, he went straight ahead into what could be considered a family room.

"This is where we all hang out," Father quipped as they entered. "This is where you can relax, watch television, play cards and all that."

The television at the far end of the room was turned on, surrounded by several chairs and two couches. Every spot in the room was occupied by a sleeping resident, but one. The resident watching TV turned towards them and smiled as they walked in.

"Hello, I am Father Engelmann, or David." He extended his arm to her. She hesitated then extended her hand to Father's.

A look of consternation gradually turned into a smile. "I'm Frances."

"I'm very pleased to meet you, Frances. I just moved in and I am showing my good friend Henry, around."

Henry stepped forward and shook Frances' hand, as well.

She nodded and smiled without saying a word then turned her gaze back to the television. Father and Henry looked at one another.

"Come, let me show you the Chapel."

Father walked past Henry and led him down the hallway to a closed door at the end. He opened the door, stepped inside, and disappeared. Henry jogged to catch the door before it closed. Father was already in a state of prayer before a lifelike crucifix hanging just behind the altar. It made Henry happy to see something Father loved and was familiar with. He loved the Church. This would make him feel truly at home.

Stations of the Cross lined the walls on either side and moveable chairs were neatly placed in rows facing the altar. Henry tried to visualize the nuns praying there every day and a priest coming from the parish down the street to say mass for them. There probably hadn't been a mass in the chapel for a long time. But there soon would be one with Father living there.

It was going to be quite an adjustment for him. He could have stayed at the parish longer, but he felt called to this, to enter a care home. What on earth would he do here? The people were all so old. But, then again, so was Father. He just didn't seem old. He was so active and alert. He didn't really belong here. But Father and his Lord knew best.

"This is a very beautiful chapel," whispered Henry, finally breaking the long silence.

"Yes, very nice, Henry. I feel comfortable, here. This is precisely where the Lord wants me. Soon you will see and understand. To me it's like watching a show. The Lord is the producer and director. It's always so exciting to see the movies unfold and play before my eyes. I simply listen to what he instructs me to do and then play out the scene. I give him an Oscar award for every performance, every movie he creates and I am always in awe of how creative He is in dealing with life's challenges. You will soon see!"

"I have seen it many times, myself. I am as anxious as you are to see what the Lord has planned for this care home now that you are here. I think I will leave now, Father. I have things I need to do at the farm and Coco and Ginger need some attention."

"Has Coco settled down a bit? She gets so excited when I come out there."

"No, it takes years for chocolate labs to stop jumping up and down. The Golden Retriever on the other hand is the complete opposite, very calm. Yet, I must say that Ginger too gets very excited when I take them for a run. I love to see them run full stride beside the quad… Actually, Father, would you like to come out and spend the evening, I can drive you back in the morning?"

"No, thank you, Henry, I think I would like to spend the day here and have dinner with my new family."

"Yes, of course."

"I would like to spend a few days in your Poustinia before winter sets in, if I could. Three days there beside the still water, nature, and only God's word for sustenance, and I feel renewed and ready again to do the Lord's work."

"Of course, Father, I'm so happy someone is using the prayer house. One of these days I will have to start using it myself. I know the Lord has an important lesson to teach me."

"Take the time then, to learn it, my son. *The day will come all too soon when school is out and we are accountable to the Teacher.*"

Henry looked at Father knowing full well what he meant then walked towards him and hugged him.

"Thank you, Henry, for bringing me here and for that wonderful painting. I know how busy you are." Father shook his head in appreciation.

"You're welcome, Father, each brush stroke was a prayer of thanks to you and Anna."

Father walked Henry to the front door.

"See, if I had taken up driving a car, I would have brought myself here and we wouldn't have had this time, together. It's a good thing I'm always dependent on someone," said Father.

"Yes, Father, and I so look forward to driving you wherever you wish or want to go. The pleasure is always mine. May God bless your new home, Father."

"Thank you, Henry." Father patted Henry's shoulder.

"I'll see you this week sometime, Father."

Father held the heavy oak door open and watched Henry walk out to his SUV.

"Thank you, Lord," Father murmured, "For blessing Anna and my life with such a wonderful son."

CHAPTER FIFTY-TWO

IN LESS THAN twenty minutes Henry entered his acreage. The dogs had heard him and charged towards the SUV. As he drove down the lane by the barn, his two quarter horses were grazing in the pasture beside. He honked the horn and Valley Seeker looked up for a moment, but quickly resumed her munching.

Henry slowed his vehicle as the dogs playfully nipped at each other near the front tires. Just before a large group of trees and shrubs, the lane took a sharp turn to the left and opened up to the view of the cedar log home and the sprawling valley all around. It was for that reason Henry named his acreage, Sudden Valley Ranch. For the flat prairie to suddenly give way to such an incredibly beautiful view of the valley was totally unexpected and always a shock to visitors seeing it for the first time.

It was a gorgeous, late fall day and Henry decided to follow through on his plan to give the dogs a run and head down into the valley. He quickly changed into jeans and a sweatshirt then hurried outside. The dogs heard him coming and sensed an impending run. They barked and jumped up like two overexcited children as they followed him to the garage.

As soon as the vehicle fired up, the dogs' excitement escalated into pandemonium. Henry burst out of the garage and watched as the dogs' uncontrolled pent up energy transformed into long graceful strides, going full out just to keep up with the speeding quad. Very quickly their tongues were hanging out and white saliva began to form. It was beauty in motion and Henry never tired of watching them run. When he slowed down a bit, the retriever caught up to Coco and tried to bump her and slow her down to get into the lead, but Coco just darted forwards always staying just enough ahead not to be thwarted by her mate.

When Henry and his family first moved to the acreage, he had a contractor cut a road around one of the hills near the home which led down to the valley bottom. As the road descended, the shoulder dropped sharply into a deep gorge. On this trip, Henry drove precariously close to the edge, heightening the sensation of danger. The air cooled as he followed the winding road to the valley floor. The dogs anxious to cool off, reached the bottom long before he did and were already swimming in the creek like two beavers.

Henry pulled up beside the water and turned off the engine. Even though his home sat on the side of the hill and had an incredible panoramic view of the valley, the view, atmosphere, and perspective of the valley from this vantage point nestled amongst the lush green grass and hills was one of peace and serenity. It always reminded him of the 23rd Psalm and many times Father made the same comment:

> Yahweh is my shepherd,
> I lack nothing.
> In meadows of green grass he lets me lie.
> To the waters of repose he leads me;
> There he revives my soul.

Perhaps it was this ethereal setting which led him to build the Poustinia. The creek that meandered through and divided the valley, led both into and out of a naturally occurring pond. It was on the edge of this large body of calm water where Henry's prayer house was situated. He gazed at the cabin's mirror reflection in the still water. Occasionally, a dying ripple from the dogs swimming nearby brought a sense of life to its reposeful state.

Henry alighted from the quad and walked around the pond to the Poustinia. Unfortunately, neither Henry nor his family had used the house once completed. Only Father Engelmann had used it. Henry, much to his chagrin, was always caught between two magnetic poles: the attraction of his Lord and the strong pull and lure to the ways of the world. He couldn't believe that at his age and stage in life he still hadn't come to terms with the most important decision of his life.

He stepped onto the deck and drank in the magnificent view before him. Most of the trees and shrubs covering the hills had lost their late summer olive green shade and turned into the bright yellow, ochre, vermillion and red colours of fall. It was how the deep purple and crimson chroma of the leafless brush and thickets harmonized in between in a spectacular array of colour that took his breath away.

Henry staggered, drunk by the beauty of nature's profusion of brilliant pigments across the valley, and as his eyes lowered to the reflection in the placid pond, only to see those dazzling hues repeated once more. Complete intoxication overtook him. If only the prairie wind could be quieted for a spell and allow these autumn leaves to peek through the white snow of winter, what a rich warm season it would be.

The dogs were out of the water on the other side of the creek chasing some scent until Coco saw her master sit on a wooden chair and launched herself towards him; Ginger followed. Within moments, the dogs were on the deck showering Henry as they shook the water from their fur.

"Enough," Henry cried. "Lay down!" It took several more commands before the dogs finally settled on the deck and basked in the sun.

Henry rested his head against the reclining back of the chair and watched swallows swoop down on the water and scoop up insects from the surface. It was fascinating how the graceful birds slipped through the wind barely touching the water, and when they did the sun danced off the tiny splash like a diamond. It was all so beautiful, but his eyes grew heavy and fluttered. Before they closed he captured the serenity of the scene on the inner screen of his mind.

The word tranquility became a temporary mantra that captured the moment; unhurriedly, almost sluggishly he rolled this most beautiful and melodic word over and over, spreading a soothing balm throughout his being, filling him with an indescribable peace. His thoughts thinned, slowed, quieted; becoming ever more in harmony with the stillness.

"Yes," murmured Henry, "to the waters of repose He leads me."

Having attained that quiescent state, he drew from the unlimited source of energy found in the essence of silence and heard the deeper sounds of harmony and beauty that are of God. He was in perfect peace by keeping his mind on his Lord. At once he saw the truth: God alone is sufficient.

Immersed in quietude, Henry fell into a trance-like state. He was at one with what is. The scripture he so often spouted took on new meaning: Be still and know that I am God.

"OH, THERE YOU are, Father, we were looking all over for you. I saw Henry leave over an hour and a half ago and I thought you went back to your room."

"Yes, yes," said Father Engelmann, "I thought I would talk to the Lord for awhile, I never realized it was so close to dinner time."

"Everyone is already seated and some have started to eat. Please come, I would like to introduce you to everyone."

"I will be there momentarily."

"Good, we are having pot roast, tonight, and Agnes makes a terrific gravy."

"I can smell the roast, now that you mention it."

Angela looked at Father and smiled then turned and walked away. Father turned back to the cross behind the altar. He had been so deep in prayer he hadn't realized how quickly the time had gone.

He made the sign of the cross, genuflected. "Help me to relate to these people, Lord. Bless this house and watch over Henry as he drives home. Or, should I say, thank you for watching over Henry as he drove home."

Father left the chapel and hurried towards the dining room just off the kitchen. When he got there, everyone was seated and the cook was just setting out the plates.

"Oh look," said Angela, "here is Father Engelmann. You can sit over there." Angela pointed to the empty chair between Mr. Lure and Mrs. Lawson.

"Yes, thank you," said Father. After Father was seated, Angela introduced him to all the residents.

"Well, everyone, this is Father Engelmann. Father said you can call him Father Engelmann or David, whatever you wish. He was the priest at St. Mary's Church and has decided to retire and live here. Father, this is Helen."

Angela stood behind Helen and put her hands on Helen's shoulders then moved to next person. "This is Elizabeth. She moved in here about a month ago. She is settling in very nicely." The next person was Johnny Louis. He was in a wheelchair and wasn't sitting on a wooden chair like everyone else.

"Hi, Father," said Mr. Louis, "welcome to our home."

"Thank you, Mr. Louis."

Angela moved entirely around the table. As the people were being introduced, some greeted Father while others were already eating, and didn't even bother to look up. Finally, Angela stood behind Father and patted his shoulders, "Welcome again, Father. Enjoy your first home-cooked meal at Nunnery Place."

"Thank you, Angela."

Without further ado, Father bowed his head and then said, "In the name of the Father and the Son and the Holy Spirit. Dear Father, we thank you…"

A fork clattered onto a plate, as Millie, so shocked by hearing someone say grace, just looked up and stared at Father. Mr. Louis hadn't started eating, yet, and most everyone else stopped eating as well, their food and forks somewhat suspended in different positions, all except Margaret, who just kept on eating, not out of disrespect, but because she was a little hard of hearing.

"…Lord for this food. Bless our conversation, and all the wonderful people at this table. And bless Angela and the cook who prepared this meal. We ask this blessing in Jesus' name. Amen."

"Amen," said Mr. Louis, as he looked up at Father and smiled.

Father picked up his fork and knife and cut into the roast beef. Everyone was busy eating, so no one spoke. All focus was on eating as if this was the only pleasure they had left. There were eleven residents seated at the table including Father. There was one empty chair near the end of the table. Father was later to learn that that was Norma's. She was out for dinner at her son's home and would be back before bed.

Father felt a little uncomfortable just sitting there and eating without the accompaniment of conversation and sharing. After several mouthfuls, and still no one speaking, Father finally said, "Well, Mrs. Lawson, have you children in Regina?"

Once again, everyone stopped eating except for Margaret. It was unusual for someone to speak at the table.

"Why, yes, Father, I have two children, a son and daughter. My son lives in Calgary, but my daughter lives here in Regina."

"So, does she have children?"

"Yes, two boys, I think they are 8 and 9."

"Well, they must be quite something."

There was a long silence and finally Mrs. Lawson spoke. "Well, they don't come and visit that often. They are very busy, you know how it is with young families, nowadays. They have so many activities planned, lessons to take…and…" Mrs. Lawson's voice trailed off, carrying a tone of disappointment.

Father sensed she was lonely, but didn't want to pursue it, yet.

"And, you, Mr. Louis, how long have you been here?"

"Oh, it's been at least eight years. Ever since my car accident, I needed someone to help. I tried living at home with mom, but she is getting on and can barely look after herself, so here I am giving Angela a rough time, every day."

Angela caught the tail end of that comment, as she picked up an empty plate and set down a bowl of jelly in front of Helen at the same time.

"Oh, you're pretty easy to look after, Johnny Louis."

By the time dinner and dessert was over, Father tried to talk to everyone at the table. Some responded, but most of them were very abrupt, answering yes or no without really engaging in a conversation. By the time Father got to his dessert, only two people were left at the table; Mr. Louis and Margaret, who was sort of dozing off.

"Would you like to sit in the TV room, Margaret?" Angela asked, almost yelling.

Margaret startled awake. Angela put her hand on her shoulder and gently shook Margaret's shoulder. Margaret looked up at Angela. Angela repeated her question and Margaret nodded. Angela helped Margaret up and together they walked out of the kitchen and down the hall.

"Well, Mr. Louis, it's a lovely evening to sit out in the courtyard and have a cup of tea, shall we go out and watch the sun go down?"

"Oh, no thanks, Father. There is a TV show coming on in 10 minutes that I want to watch. But you go ahead. Perhaps I will see you later."

"Of course, Mr. Louis. May I call you Johnny?"

"For sure, Father. Mr. Louis is way too formal for me."

Father smiled. Angela appeared again bringing his tea.

"Oh, I think I will have my tea in the courtyard."

"I'll carry it out there for you and set it on the patio table."

"Thank you, Angela. That is very kind of you."

Father followed Angela outside.

It was a gorgeous late fall evening and the air was unusually still for the prairies since the courtyard was surrounded by the care home, keeping the stronger breezes out. The sun was far off to the west and low in the clear cloudless sky. Only half of the courtyard at that time could still catch the sun's light. The shadows of the tall pine trees crept across and up the east wall of the care home further shielding out the pleasant rays of the sun. Father felt the chill and knew he wouldn't be out here for long.

He turned one of the four chairs by the table and sat down. He sipped his tea and gazed at a huge patch of flowers enclosed by a concrete border. Most of the petunias and geraniums were wilted and dead. It looked as though someone had brought out house plants to extend the growing and flowering season. A small area of ground near the north wall looked as if someone put in a garden and hadn't cleaned up the dead stems and leaves. A barbeque stood near the door next to the kitchen.

"Well, Lord," he said almost audibly, "Thank you for bringing me here." Sounding like he was a parent of a slew of offspring he rambled "It's good that there is a place to go when we get old, when we become too much of a burden for our children and yet, we've looked after them…"

Father was thinking of Mrs. Lawson and her family that doesn't come that often to visit. Two or three of the other residents made similar comments. "Yes, we bring children into the world and sacrifice so much to raise them, to clothe them, feed them, educate them and then off they go; get married, raise children of their own and soon we are forgotten. In our later years most of us need help, but where are the children?"

Father remembered only too well how in the old country, children, parents and grandparents lived together as a family, caring and looking after each other. The elderly were revered, honoured, and respected for their wisdom. Nowadays, it was almost as if the old folks were castaways, forgotten people, put out to pasture and someone else was assigned the burden of tending to their care until death consumed them.

"Oh, David," Father mumbled, "Don't be so hard on this younger generation, like Mrs. Lawson said, they are too busy trying to make a living and getting ahead. But does it have to take top priority over their aging parents? We need each other. I can see the loneliness in their eyes. Their life is like a slow burning candle just waiting to be snuffed out. I've seen it in so many care homes during my visits. All too many children have almost abandoned their parents."

Father knew why the Lord had led him here instead of some secluded seminary or fancy retreat in the mountains. He took another sip of his tea; there was no need to cautiously drink it, it was as cool as the growing chill in the air.

He set his cup down and looked at the chair next to him as if occupied by his Lord and asked straight out, "What can we do, Lord, to make these places fun, full of life, full of hope, full of love, full of you, Jesus. What is it that I can do?"

Father felt warm as he got more fired up. The message was coming in loud and clear. "St. Francis of Assisi said it centuries ago in his wonderful prayer:

> Lord, make me an instrument of Your peace.
> Where there is hatred, let me sow love.

Where there is injury, pardon,
Where there is doubt, faith,
Where there despair, hope,
Where there is darkness, light, and where there is sadness,
joy.
O Divine Master, grant that I may not seek to be consoled,
As to console;

To be understood, as to understand;
To be loved, as to love;
For it is in giving that we receive –
It is in pardoning that we are pardoned;
And it is in dying that we are born to eternal life.

"Yes, Lord, I understand. I know in my heart what it is that you want me to do. *Make me an instrument of your peace. Let me bring light, hope, faith, consolation, joy, let me bring love!*"

IT WAS EITHER the growing coolness that restored him to the presence of the day or the eerie sounds of a pack of coyotes downstream piercing the stillness. The dogs leapt to their feet and barked their way into the chorus. After quieting Coco and Ginger, together they entered the Poustinia. Henry flicked on the light and made sure everything was ready for Father.

In the living room the two chairs in front of the patio doors facing the pond looked as if they hadn't been moved or sat in since he bought and put them there well over a year ago. He parted the French doors and peeked into the bedroom; the bed was neatly made and a Bible was open on the table beside a large picture window that faced the brook meandering up the valley. Father often remarked how much he liked to read and look at that view. He felt certain that many times he could see the Lord walking on the stream coming to visit him.

On the way out, Henry checked the fridge. It was completely empty save for four bottles of water. That's all Father ever requested when he was here for his three-day retreat. Henry surveyed the living room once more. Crucifixes were above each doorway, with a five foot high one on the wall next to the entrance on the west side. A small altar stood below the cross with a clay chalice centred on the table. Henry remembered the day he hung the huge cross and saw the radiance of a saint reflected on Fathers face. As soon as we brought in the small altar, Father said mass as if he could not wait another minute to eat His body and drink

His blood. Henry shook his head in awe at the faith of that holy man.

The wall opposite the patio doors had shelves filled with books all related to the Lord, and a stereo with many relaxing CDs, but again, Father never listened to music or read anything but his Bible. The song of silence and his holy book contained everything he needed to hear, to know and more.

Henry smiled as he recalled the last thing Father said when they departed this afternoon, he wanted to go to the prayer house before winter set in so he could get regenerated for a fresh task. What were he and the Lord up to now?

Henry hit the light switch then stepped outside, his furry companions following.

"What an incredible sight," muttered Henry as his eyes took in the beautiful valley filled with the hush of evening time. Somehow it filled him with even more peace than the view which had enraptured him earlier. He realized that it was at twilight that nature reaches its own quiescence.

It wasn't just the soft light when the sun sunk below the horizon. It was the all-pervading atmosphere that arrested one's troubles and cares. Details which busy and preoccupy the mind during daylight were diminished, almost totally obscured by the growing shadows of the night. The reflection of the distant hills in the silvery water of the pond was reduced to a simple shape of rich darkness contrasting sharply with the light of the rising moon. All the clutter of life disappeared, suggesting timelessness, simple clarity, oneness.

Without the water, Henry's artistic sense thought, the beauty of nature, especially during this special time of day would lack life. In the same way the eyes are the windows to the soul and give man a sense of being alive, the glistening, sparkling and sheen of the pond, lake, stream or sea were the eyes of nature and gave it its spark of being, as well; otherwise the earth lay asleep, hiding its soul!

Henry felt exhilarated at the thought.

He hadn't felt so refreshed for as long as he could remember. It was a wonderful day and he vowed to have more of them. A buoyant energy of spirit filled him as he stepped off the deck and followed the dogs on the moonlit path to his quad.

"Aha, this is Father's secret to renewed strength and vitality," Henry chuckled. "No wonder he makes this retreat twice a year."

Just as he arrived at his vehicle, he noticed a V-shaped stream glimmering in the pond. If it had not been for that almost imperceptible ripple catching the light, he would never have noticed a beaver cutting through the water. He breathed in the crisp cool air of the glen, the atmosphere redolent of the pine trees he planted there over twenty years ago. All was quiet, save the natural sounds of the valley and the gentle panting of his protective escorts. As the darkness of the evening grew, more and more stars blossomed in the infinite meadows of the sky until the heavens were ablaze with millions of twinkling diamonds.

"How? How can anyone not believe in You?" whispered Henry. *"How can the very being you created dare to question Your existence?"*

The babbling water trickling through the nearby beaver dam seemed to concur Henry's observation.

Reluctantly, he pressed the starter, shattering the spell of it all. As he ascended the winding road, he took with him a peace that no amount of money could buy. He understood why Father needed this retreat. It was his fountain of youth that gave him the energy, vigour and perhaps most of all the peace of his Lord which he gave freely to all who came his way.

Henry knew the Lord was patiently waiting for him to make that retreat, too. He felt the gentle tug almost daily, and he knew Father was praying for his salvation. He could feel the energy of Father's petitions on his behalf. Twinges of guilt and thoughts of self-condemnation swept through him for his lack of commitment.

Above the sound of the roaring quad as it sped to the top, Henry cried out, "Oh Lord, give me the strength of conviction to place you completely at the centre of my life. Grant me the courage to follow Father's footsteps!"

The echo of his plea resounded like thunder throughout the valley.

Chapter Fifty-Three

T HE DAY AFTER Father had said grace at dinner, Angela talked to Doris, the director of the care home, and Hazel, the supervisor, about the issue.

"Did anyone object?"

"No. Some kept eating and some stopped and listened."

"Well, this was a Catholic facility at one time, but now it's non-denominational. It's safer not to try and get too religious or preachy, yet I know they are all Christians and God-fearing people. Frankly," continued Hazel, "I like the idea of them saying grace at the table. It's like family and it may help to bring them closer together."

"Or further apart," Doris countered. "Did you see or feel that anyone was offended by Father's prayers?"

"No, I didn't."

"Did anyone participate?"

"No. No one joined in either, but most stopped eating and listened except for…"

"For who?" asked Doris.

"Margaret."

"She probably couldn't hear him," said Hazel.

"That's what I thought," Angela concurred.

"Well, perhaps it won't hurt any," concluded Doris. Reflecting on it further she added, "Let's monitor it closely for a few days and see where this leads to. If it becomes a problem I'll talk to Father about it, right away."

DURING THE FIRST few days at the care home, Father considered himself a student. He learned the routine and made a point of meeting everyone either in their room or the TV room. Soon he knew their family backgrounds and their aches and pains. The residents were surprised to suddenly see someone take such an interest in them and quickly began to trust their new member. Father also began to take some of the residents for a walk down the hallways. His favourite pathway was towards the chapel. Several of the residents hadn't even known it was there.

After breakfast that morning, Father took two of the more elderly residents by the hand and invited them to go for a walk with him. After they had expressed some aches and pains at the table they consented to talk to Jesus about them.

"Hello, Jesus, how are you on this fine day?" Father said as they entered the chapel. "I have two guests for you to meet, today. This is Margaret and this is Greta."

After they were seated, Father began to pray on their behalf. "Dear Jesus, Greta has a sore back, would you be so kind as to rub it a little with your love. Soothe it with your warm and gentle touch. Thank you, Lord. Greta and I appreciate that very much."

Turning to Margaret he asked, "Is there anything you wish to pray or thank the Lord for?"

Margaret not used to this kind of conversation put her head down and softly said, "No, I'm fine."

After a minute's silence, Father said, "Well, Greta, we can go, now. Does your back feel better?"

"Yes, Father, much better." She looked to the cross above the altar, "Thank you, Jesus."

Greta turned to Father and smiled as she squeezed his hand. "He never lets you down does He, Father?"

"I've never known Him to, Greta."

"Well, let's get back to the family room and see what Angela has planned for us."

Most days the care home had an activity or two planned, such as playing cards, doing crafts, drawing and painting and also exercising. The care home made every effort to provide something for the residents to do. But the activities were routine and mechanical. The staff continued with these events more so out of a sense of duty and job requirement. Father felt the activities and relationships were superficial and lacked that personal touch that stirred the heart and soul.

"What we all need," concluded Father, as he sat in the chapel talking with the Lord, "Is to put You into the heart and soul of this care home. We need You to fill our hearts to overflowing, to banish the loneliness, to make us truly a family. We also need to reach the people outside these walls and remind them of their parents, their brothers and sisters, their aunts and uncles. We need to remind them of their responsibilities, their great need to love and care for those in the care home.

"Children need to understand that all too soon they, too, will be in one of these homes waiting for someone to come through the door to hear their name being called by a loved one, or a relative. A sign that they are still cared for, not forgotten. My Lord, we'd better get busy."

Father Engelmann scheduled an appointment with Doris for Thursday morning.

"Come in, Father, have a chair. Close the door, if you wish."

"Oh no, that's not necessary. I have nothing to say that needs to be private."

"Well, I see you are settling in quite nicely."

"Yes, it's not too much of an adjustment from the rectory. Just a lot more people to talk to during meal times."

"So, how are you finding everything? Is there anything you need or want to make you more comfortable?"

"Well, in a way there is, Doris." Doris straightened up in her chair and moved a little closer to her desk.

"It seems a shame, Doris, that we have such a beautiful chapel and it isn't used for anything and especially for what it was built for, to celebrate the Holy Mass."

"Well, Father, there are not enough priests out there to come here and say mass. Like everyone else nowadays they have no time."

"But I do, Doris, I have all the time in the world, at least what time the Lord has left for me. I was wondering if I might say mass in the chapel, every morning, and if I may invite those who would like to attend?"

Doris stared at Father.

"You know, Father, the last time a mass was said in the chapel was when a nephew of one of the residents, who was a priest, offered to say mass during his Christmas visit. It was such a joyous occasion and the chapel was packed."

"It could be again, every day!"

"Well, Father, as long as we don't make it compulsory, and don't force anyone I can't see why you can't say mass."

Father smiled, "That's very understanding, Doris, the good Lord will bless you for this."

Doris returned his smile.

"And, while you are so obliging," Father continued with a twinkle in his eyes, "There is one other request I would ask." Father noted her hands gripping the edges of her desk. Clearly she was unaccustomed to residents entering her office and asking to do something.

"What else is there, Father?" Doris cautiously asked.

"Well, since the chapel is only used in the mornings for mass, it's a shame that it remains empty and unused for the rest of the day. I was wondering if it might be used in the afternoon to have Bible study and sharing? We would schedule them around any activities the care home already has. This, too, would be strictly voluntary, of course."

Doris sat back in her chair, her shoulders lowered and her hands released their grip on the desk.

"The chairs in the chapel are individual and can easily be moved so we can sit in a circle. And that beautiful Heintzman piano in the corner would be just wonderful for a sing-song or two, don't you think?"

"Well, yes. It may need a tune up."

"I know just who can do it. Mr. Schmidt tunes the piano and the organ at St. Mary's Church whenever we need him."

Doris looked at Father thoughtfully, with a slight smile on her face. He could tell she was almost as excited as he was.

She leaned forward in her chair. "Well, Father, what you're suggesting would certainly introduce a lot of change. That would get the residents talking for sure."

"Well, isn't that what we want? Something to stimulate the blood a little and maybe get the feet dancing. That is, if it's okay with you if we dance in the chapel." Father winked, his eyes twinkling.

Doris chuckled a bit, "That's assuming some decide to attend of course."

"Well, Doris, let's keep that up to the Lord. If we do our part, let's put our faith and trust in Him to do the rest."

Doris shook her head in astonishment. Her smile deepened.

"Well, Father, once again I can't find any objection. The only restriction I would place on any of this is that the residents are free to choose. No coercing or coaxing; if they want to go and attend fine, if not, just leave them alone." Doris looked directly at Father with a semi-stern look on her face.

"I assure you, Doris, what you are asking is totally in the hands of the Lord. I am only an instrument of His peace here to do His bidding. Who He wishes to bring into my path is His business."

"Well, fine, then. You can put up an announcement on the bulletin board and I will also mention it to all the residents during lunch, tomorrow. I will stress that this is completely voluntary and if anyone has any objections to it to please come and see me. Is that okay with you?"

"Oh, yes, Doris, that is very satisfactory to me."

Doris smiled then cringed as she asked, "Is there anything else?"

"That is all, for now," he said with another wink of his sparkling eyes.

"Thank you for coming in, Father. Please feel free to see me at any time. I am very happy you decided to come to our care home, I truly hope it does become a home to you."

"I assure you, Doris, it already has. I can hardly wait to say mass in my Father's house."

Father got up and just as he was about to leave, Doris said, "Father, do you still make hospital visits?"

"Yes, I do,"

"The reason I ask, is that we had a resident here who was returned to the hospital but may have been transferred to another facility already. She needed more care than we could provide. However, I noticed on her application form that she is Catholic and if by chance you are visiting the General Hospital, I thought you could drop in and see her."

"Yes, yes, of course. Do you have her name?"

Doris sorted through some papers on her desk and found the one she wanted then jotted down the name on a Post-It note.

"Thank you for coming in, Father, it was a pleasure talking to you."

Father smiled, "It was a great pleasure talking to you as well, Doris."

He turned and as he walked out of the office, he glanced down at the paper which Doris gave to him and read the name of the patient ... Marjorie Hamilton.

"SLOW DOWN, FATHER, I've never heard you so excited." Henry was sure Father was jumping up and down on the other side of the phone.

"Henry, I can say mass here! The director also said I can start a Bible study group and I found some vestments in the small room next to the chapel, they must have belonged to the pries—"

"Father, just hold it for a minute, I can't understand your jabbering." Father was breathless and sounded about to keel over. "So, you can say mass in the chapel and start up a Bible class?"

"Yes, yes, see how quickly the Lord works. I couldn't find any chalice, bread or wine though and I was wondering, Henry—"

"If I would buy you some wine?"

"Yes, yes, how did you know?"

"And you like the Jewish wine, Manischewitz."

"Henry, you are reading my mind."

"And, we have some beautiful goblets in the gallery that one of the potters brought in that would make—"

"Yes, yes!" Father exclaimed. "A goblet molded and created by an artist to be used in the house of the Lord. Yes, perfect, Henry—"

"And the bread, do you want me to pick some up at St. Mary's?"

"Yes, Henry, if you would be so kind as to stop at the church, Father Knuka will give you some."

"No problem, Father. I won't be able to make it this afternoon, but will see you sometime tomorrow. Will you be there all day?"

"Yes, I am planning to visit the Santa Maria Home on Friday right after mass to make a visitation call, and the General Hospital in the afternoon, to visit a lady who has cancer."

"How is everything else going, do you like it there?"

"Oh, yes, Henry, the Lord and I have big plans."

"I'm sure you have. Well, we are quite busy here, today. The café sounds packed. It is so loud with chatter you're beginning to fade out. I think I'd better see if they need any help and say 'hello' to my customers."

"Yes, that's very important, Henry, to make your guests feel welcome and to—"

"Serve. That's what it's all about, isn't it?"

Father remained quiet for only a moment and then quipped, "I taught you very well."

"Yes, indeed, Father, you did, and I am still learning. See you, tomorrow."

"Yes, I am looking forward to your visit already."

CHAPTER FIFTY-FOUR

J ENNY COULD HARDLY wait for J.J. and his family to arrive. J.J. had left a message with the administration office that they would arrive October 28th. After calling Air Canada, Jenny knew the plane arrived at 9:40 a.m. and so she could expect to see them before noon.

First thing that morning, Jenny changed from a white gown into a pair of pink lounging pajamas and matching robe. Her hair was so sparse and raggedy she had it all shaved off a week ago and asked Mable to buy six different coloured bandanas. With the outfit she had chosen to wear she put a pink bandana on her head. Jenny was all set to meet J.J. and his family in the visiting room rather than in her bedroom. She wanted to look healthy and fit, rather than sickly and drawing sympathy.

In spite of her critical illness, Jenny on the whole did a very good job camouflaging it. But by 10:30 she was so exhausted from the hustle and bustle to appear healthy and normal that the room began to spin. Fortunately, she was right beside a chair and put her hand on the arm rest and turned herself around so she could collapse into the chair.

A nurse walking down the hall saw Jenny through the open doorway slouching in the chair. She rushed in and caught her just before she fell onto the floor. The nurse pushed Jenny in the chair over to her bed allowing Jenny to fall face first onto the edge of the bed. The nurse was able to reach the emergency cord and buzz for help.

They slipped off Jenny's robe and got her into bed. Jenny was semi-conscious and winced with pain each time she moved. She was breathing excessively hard and her heart was racing. Another nurse brought in a needle with a combination of pain killer and sedative. Within minutes Jenny was breathing regularly once more, but her eyes were getting heavy. Sounds and chatter in the room grew faint and then completely silent as she fell into a deep sleep.

Around 11:30, J.J., his wife and son entered the nursing home. They thought they would briefly visit Jenny before going to the hotel where they had made reservations, despite Jenny's insistence that they stay at her home.

"We are here to visit Marjorie Hamilton," J.J. announced to the receptionist.

"Are you relatives?"

"Yes."

"Oh, you are her son? I have a note here that she was expecting you and to send you right up to her room. Just one moment and I will call up to the nursing station"

"Hi, Jan, this is Noreen. Jenny's family is here. Oh, I see, around 2:00. Okay, I will tell them."

Noreen put the receiver down and looked up at J.J.. "Apparently she was all ready to see you, but had a fainting spell. They gave her a sedative and she is asleep. The nurse on duty says your mother would be able to see you around 2:00 this afternoon. Would you be able to come back then?"

A mild cuss passed J.J.'s lips.

"So? What should we do, Nora?"

"Well, this would be a good time to check in at the hotel. We can change, have lunch and be back around that time. It will be all right, J.J.. She needs her rest."

"Well, let's go then," said J.J.. He turned to the nurse, "Would you please call us a cab."

"Certainly, we usually call Co-op, will that be fine?"

"Yes, any one will be fine. Let's wait outside, Nora. I don't like the smell of nursing homes." He walked past Nora and his gibbering son and led the way back to the front door.

J.J. AND NORA returned at 2:30 p.m.

J.J. approached the desk and rested his elbows on the high counter.

"Is Marjorie Hamilton able to see us, now?"

"Yes, I called up and she just woke up and asked for you. Her room is 207 on the 2nd floor. There is a stairwell just down the hall," Noreen pointed, "Or, if you wish, just past the stairs and to the right is an elevator."

"Thank you," said Nora.

"Let's take the stairs. We'll probably have to wait an hour for the elevators in this place."

"Oh, J.J., I'm sure the elevators work fine, but the stairs will do. I like the exercise after sitting on the plane all morning,"

Without any further comment, J.J. marched down the hall, leaving his wife trailing behind.

A NURSE HAD turned up Jenny's bed slightly so she was in a better position to visit. The sedative they had given her didn't quite alleviate her jittery nerves. Heavy footsteps drifted into the room from down the hall. *Oh, I hope I look fine,* was the last thought Jenny was able to ask herself, as J.J. turned into her room followed by his wife and son.

Jenny and her son just stared at one another.

God she looks old, and tired and so thin, thought J.J., a feather would probably knock her over.

"Hello, Marj."

Jenny smiled and opened her arms to receive him, but he just stood there.

Nora, seeing her husband's reluctance to greet his mother with a hug, walked past him.

"Hi, Marj, I hope I can call you that. I just can't believe we have not met yet! I'm a little uncomfortable with calling you mom, just yet, anyway." She extended one hand to Jenny and held onto James the Third with the other. "This is your grandson, Jimmy."

"Oh my, what a handsome young lad you are. Here, want to come to grandma?" Jenny lifted her arms, but Jimmy drew back and winced.

"Oh that's okay. Let's give it a little time. Come sit down. Take a chair, Nora. I asked the nurse to bring in another one."

Nora pulled the chair a little closer to Jenny while J.J. stood at a distance and remained unresponsive.

"I had it all planned this morning to greet you in the visiting room, but somehow wasn't able to make it. You know how grandmas can get at times." Jenny tried to make light of it.

"How are you feeling, Marj?"

Jenny wished her daughter-in-law would call her Jenny as she had on the phone, but thought better not to correct her. She longed for J.J. to call her mom, as he had when he was little.

"Oh, I'm fine, just a little tired, that's all. But I am so glad you came. So you decided to check into a hotel?"

"Yes, Marj," said Nora, "It's a little more convenient and the room is very nice."

"Yes, the Hotel Saskatchewan is a very old and prestigious hotel. The Queen of England, always stays there when she visits Saskatchewan I've been told. So, how are you, J.J.?" asked Jenny, turning to him with a smile.

"Busy, very busy."

"Well, I am so glad you took a little time to come and visit."

"I understand you want me to look after your house. Are you sure you want to sell it?"

"Yes, I won't be able to go back there anymore. I thought about getting a full-time nurse and living at home a little while longer, but I think this is better, and my doctor thinks so, too. On the end table…" Jenny turned slightly and waved her arm with effort towards the table beside her, "is an envelope with the house key and the security code. Maybe later today or tomorrow you and Nora can go there. The antique furniture is very beautiful and you're welcome to—"

"No, we are not interested in the furniture, Marj, we have our home furnished the way we want it. So, what do you want for your house?"

"Well, I thought perhaps you could discuss that with a realtor and see what the market value would be."

"And what about the contents?"

"I thought you might want some of it. If not, we could sell it."

"I really don't have time to wait around and sell old furniture."

"J.J., it's not old, it's antique," Nora corrected.

"Well, don't get any ideas, Nora, I won't have any of that stuff in my home."

'My home' as opposed to 'our' home. Jenny sensed that Nora was not as naïve as she had been, but was heading towards the same fate. Jenny tried to sit up a bit more, but just didn't have the strength. She put her arms out to Jimmy again.

"Would you like to sit with grandma a little?" James still shrank away. "Well, maybe tomorrow," said Jenny.

"He just needs a little time," said Nora.

J.J. appeared as a statue, making no effort whatsoever to keep the conversation going or show any interest in his mother. His stony-hearted attitude infected the atmosphere with a coldness that grew more frigid with each passing minute. He looks so young and…immature to be a father…

Nora rose from her chair.

"Well, Marj, perhaps we should go, you seem a little tired and with the excitement of us being here, we should let you rest a bit." Nora reached for the envelope on the end table. "We will visit your home, this afternoon, call some realtors and begin making arrangements to sell your home."

"Feel free to take anything you wish."

Before J.J. could say something rude, Nora said, "We will look, Marj. Thank you so much for the offer."

Deep hurt and rejection swept through Jenny as her son turned and walked to the door without so much as shaking her hand or saying good-bye.

"Good-bye, J.J.."

Nora stepped forward and took Jenny's hand. "It was so nice to see you, Marj." It was obvious Nora was trying to compensate for J.J.'s rudeness and shift attention away from his coldness. As Nora was about to turn away, Jimmy reached out his hand towards Jenny.

"Aah," Jenny said, "That's my boy," and quickly she reached up towards her grandson. Nora moved a little closer so Jenny could touch her grandson.

"Oh, Jimmy, thank you, it won't take long for you and me to become friends." Jenny winked at him and gave a sincere, genuine smile.

J.J. oversaw the scene with a cold, blank detached look on his face as if annoyed by his son's action.

"Well, let's go, Nora. We have a lot of things to do."

"Thank you, again, for coming, and thank you, J.J., for looking after the sale of my house."

J.J. didn't answer, but walked out the door ahead of his family.

A gush of tears spilled down Jenny's cheeks even before Nora walked out of the bedroom door.

"Oh God, what am I going to do. J.J. is so angry towards me; I find it so hard to accept his coldness. I must find a way to reconcile with him before he goes back. If we don't, I'm afraid we may forever be in this unforgiving bondage to each other. Oh, God, please let us make up like mom and I did."

Jenny reached for her pewter guardian angel on the chain around her neck and continued to whisper softly, "Please, I wish for you to help, too…"

The angel felt warm and soothing. She brought it up to her lips and as she kissed the angel, Jenny began to imagine Henry kissing it the day he sent it off to her. The thought gave her some warmth and comfort, a respite from the lingering chill left behind by J.J.'s distressing visit.

Jenny rolled onto her side as fresh tears were absorbed into her pillow. She closed her eyes and made one more request of her guardian angel. It was an odd request not really related to her son's visit and yet, perhaps it was.

"I wish with all my heart that, someday, Henry will find me and kiss me as tenderly as he did this angel."

Jenny held onto to that thought for but a moment or two before sleep rescued her from the heartless encounter with her son.

Shortly after seven, Matti called.

"Hi Jen, how you feeling this evening? Can we chat for a few minutes?"

"Thank you so much for calling, Matti. I look forward to chatting with you. It's always so uplifting."

"I be uplifted, too, when that disease lifts itself right out of you. In fact I see your angels taking it away. If I were in your backyard I would run first thin' to the Angel of Thanksgiving and put in a beautiful bouquet for you in thanks."

"That's beautiful, Matti."

"Yes, ma'am, we trust in the Lord's promises, Jen. He came so that you might have life and have it abundantly. All things are possible through Him. Keep the faith strong in your dear angel heart!"

"Oh, Matti, you sound just like a preacher." Jenny chuckled.

"It be my second calling, for sure. At times at our church services, I get so filled with the spirit, the preacher have to come to me and tell me to keep it to myself for a spell so he can finish the service!"

"I can just picture you singing and dancing, raising your hands in praise, thanking the Lord for all your blessings!"

"You got that right, honey child. It don't take much to get me fired up. So you lift any little ache and pain up to the Lord, Jen and believe with all your heart that his sweet healing power is washing through you right this minute. Why I can see the Lord's angels taking it away now just like I said before. Oh my, that must be Gabrielle, he looks so powerful…he'll get the job done, for sure."

"I can just picture it, Matti."

"That's the idea, Jen, see it leaving. This be the time for serious trust and faith, Jenny. You can't be wishy washy. Remember, the Lord says if you have faith the size of a mustard seed, why you can move a mountain and throw it into the sea. And that's what we be needing right now, Jen! Faith!… Believe!"

"Oh, Matti, like I said, I find chatting with you so uplifting. I wish I could say the same thing when I talk to my son, and by the way how is James doing?"

"He be fully recovered from his operation and have to say he be recovering from himself some, too."

What do you mean, Matti?"

"Well, ever since moving back to the estate last summer he seem to be changing and thank the good Lord, for the better. For a while there we all thought we be moving out and then a while later he settled down. I think he be learning to enjoy the estate since being away from the business."

"It must have been such a shock for James to learn he had prostate cancer."

"At first he was treated for a bleeding ulcer and he did feel better after resting on the estate last June, but no sooner had he gone back to work than he learned he had the same disease as his father did. He sure does hope they got it in time."

"Yes, I do too. It must be so hard for him to slow down. I can't believe that he has."

"The doctors tell him straight out he has to take time off or the Maker come calling real quick… I know I shouldn't be gossiping, but maybe this cheer you up a bit. Apparently that girl Susan Mr. Hamilton be seeing double cross him. Heard him say to J.J. that she asking for three million dollars or else she tell about his Swiss bank accounts and I do believe he also mentioned my island, Jamaica of all places. Why he be stashing money here and there by the sounds of it. Don't know what it's really all about except it have something to do with not reporting money to the income tax department."

"Oh, Matti, poor James. That's all he needs at this time."

"No, Jen, good for James. Having his nose in his business all the time and trying to make more and more money day and night just gives him one big headache after the other and an ulcer to boot. Just what he needs is to stop and smell the roses. The Almighty be zapping him in all the right places, that for sure…and you know something, Jen, I think the good Lord has. Last night when Mr. Hamilton was talking to J.J. just before he hung up he says to his boy that the only woman he would ever trust was Marjorie. And what he said next will make your day, honey child. Why Mr. Hamilton say to his son, you treat your mother right when you be visiting her. It sounds like he be there in Regina."

"Yes, they came in yesterday. I was so glad to see him and his wife, Nora and little Jimmy. Just before they left, my grandson reached out too me. Oh it gave me such joy to touch him. I hope he will come to me today."

"So, did Jimmy senior come to you, that be the million dollar question?"

"I'm afraid not, Matti. He is so cold towards me. I don't think he will ever forgive me for breaking up the marriage."

"You didn't break up anything, Jen. That marriage was broken from the very start. That boy should open his eyes before it's too late and see the angel he has for a mom."

"I just don't know what to do, Matti? There's that saying, you can lead a horse to the water but you can't make him drink."

"My daddy had a remedy for that saying, Jen. When I did something stupid and wouldn't drink from the trough of life, he would say, Matti let's go out to the woodshed and have us a meeting, there is something we need to discuss. Only thing was a tree branch did all the talking. I can hear my daddy say to this day, 'Matti, this hurts me more that it does you. But I love's you so much I just have do it.' I tell you, Jen, my behind remembered them there discussions better than any talkin'. Seems to me, J.J. had many meetings and discussions when he grew up, but most of them be of the wrong kind, know what I'm saying?"

Jenny was chuckling again. She just loved it when Matti called. She was feeling so much better.

"I have asked J.J. and Nora to go to my house and take what they want and put it up for sale. Looks like I won't be going back home anymore—"

"Now see, there you go again, Jen. Putting the cart before the horse. You are going to get better. You'll be sorry when you walk out of there and have no place to go. Oh, Jen, do you have to sell that home? It be so beautiful and everything fixed up so nicely just the way you wants it."

"I think it's for the best right now. There are other houses and furniture to buy if things turn out."

"I have to say it again, you be sorry when you walks out of there and have no place to go."

"You just may be right, Matti—"

"I know I'm right, it's getting you to think that, too!"

"Well, I just hope J.J. looks after everything and for now I think that's the best thing to do. I just hope when they come back in the morning things will go better than they did today."

"Well, if they don't tell J.J. I would like to have a discussion with him when he gets back to Ottawa. The kind me and my daddy used to have."

Jenny laughed. "Thanks for calling, Matti. I hear the nurse coming with their trays filled with medicine."

"The kind of medicine you need honey child is large doses of the Lord's faith. There is a scripture I'd like to share with you from Mark's gospel:

"'What things soever ye desire, when ye pray, believe that ye receive them and ye shall have them.'

"See Jen, if you pray for healing but don't believe it in your heart your words are idle. Like I said before, I see the Lord spreading his healing love all over you. Can't you just picture his big powerful angels surrounding you and taking all your aches and pains from you on their wings and flying far away with it never to come back. Trust in Him, Jen, with all the beautiful goodness that is in your heart and don't let these present circumstances affect your thinking, know what I'm saying?"

And after a moment of silence Matti said, "I be calling tomorrow night, Jen, when we tune in to another sermon from Ottawa, the Hour of Power by pastor, Matilda Belafonte…I love you, Jen."

"I love you too, Matti, with all my heart."

CHAPTER FIFTY-FIVE

JENNY WAITED ALL morning for J.J. and his family to visit, but no one showed up except Dr. Kreake.

"I heard you had another fainting spell, yesterday."

"Oh, those darn nurses, telling on me all the time. Nothing is private anymore."

"No, I have spies and guards keeping a close eye on you." Dr. Kreake said, with a kindly smile on his face. "I also learned that your family came. How did that go?"

"Not very well. J.J. still blames me for the divorce between his father and me and…he just doesn't want to forgive me. He just won't listen to reason or my side."

"Well, Jenny, kids will do that at times. We can be so cruel to each other. Sometimes we treat our own family worse than our enemies. Eventually, time will heal all, Jenny."

"But I am running out of time, I can't wait too much longer." Jenny tried to say it in a joking manner, but she knew Dr. Kreake knew not only the sad truth in what she said, but the deep hurt in her voice.

"Do you want me to talk to him?"

"Oh no, J.J. would resent that, but thanks anyway. Perhaps I will see if he and I can talk alone, if he comes back this afternoon."

"Well, don't get too upset by all this, Jenny, you need your strength." Dr. Kreake patted his favourite patient's hands, and tenderly and fondly smiled. "I'll see you in a few days."

"Thank you so much for coming."

Jenny finished her lunch shortly after 1:00 p.m. and had just picked up a book when she heard familiar footsteps tromping down the hall. Instantly, the energy her body was using to digest her meal turned into hypertension.

"Oh, I hope J.J. will be more receptive, today." Fully expecting J.J. to enter first, Jenny was pleasantly surprised to see Nora's friendly face pop in.

"Hi, Marj. Is it okay for us to come in?"

"Of course, please come in. I've been waiting for you all morning."

Nora came and a few seconds later J.J. followed holding his son. It was obvious he felt awkward and uncomfortable in doing so.

"Hello, Marjorie," he said, his tone formal and cold.

"Good afternoon, J.J.," said Jenny, "Oh, it's so nice to see you all back. Please come closer, J.J.. Jimmy, do you have a hug for grandma, today?"

When J.J. made no move to bring neither himself nor James closer, Nora quickly lifted James from J.J. casting him a furtive glance that would have melted an iceberg, but not J.J..

"Oh, men," Nora remarked as she carried Jimmy over. She feigned a chuckle, trying to erase J.J.'s rudeness and the redness from her face. "Say 'hi' to grandma. Come on Jimmy. Wave."

Little Jimmy studied his grandma and much to J.J.'s chagrin held his hand out.

Jenny immediately reached up. "Aah, come here."

Nora stood Jimmy on her bedside and as painful as it was, Jenny twisted her body and sat up a little more to support her grandson. Nora held on. She could see Jenny was uncomfortable, but wanted to help as much as possible as her son and his grandma bonded.

"My, my you are such a handsome little boy, such nice dark brown eyes and light brown hair." Little James looked a little more like Nora than J.J., but she didn't comment on it.

"Let's sit you down beside me."

Nora helped adjust James to sit on the bed. Jenny raised her arm around him and pulled him in towards her in a sideways hug.

"Oh, I just love you. I could eat you up, yes I could," said Jenny, lovingly shaking the little bundle in her arm from side to side. "So, what were you up to this morning?"

The sides of J.J.'s lips curled as if to smile then quickly evened out to his stiff abrupt businesslike manner. "We went to your house, yesterday, and found your Agreement to Purchase and other legal documents relating to the purchase of that property when you came to Regina. You bought it through Remax. I phoned them this morning and met with a Ben Walker at the house around 11:00 a.m., this morning. Apparently it's the same salesperson who was involved with your initial purchase."

"He couldn't get over how much you improved the property and especially the landscaping," Nora said. "He said your yard work is so appealing it should easily fetch you an extra fifteen thousand to the value alone. J.J. and I still can't get over how reasonably priced homes are here compared to down east. Your house would be valued at least twice as much in Ottawa."

"In any case," J.J. spoke again, "We listed it at $225,000 and an additional $15-20,000 for all the contents."

"Oh, J.J., the furniture is worth much more."

"Maybe so, but I don't have time to sell the furniture piece by piece. I called an antique dealer, who would take it on consignment, but it may take months to sell everything. This way, it's quick, and it may be an enticement for the person or family interested in the house to purchase the property."

"Yes, that's true, but are you sure there is nothing you would like? The curio cabinet is a real find and the Victorian chair in my bedroom is very rare—"

"No, Marjorie, we are not interested in any of it. We have our home and furniture the way we like it."

"Oh, Marjorie, some of those pieces are very nice. It's just that J.J. likes modern furniture."

Just like his father. Jenny could see Nora would have taken some of the antiques, but didn't dare go against J.J.'s wishes.

"Well, were there any pictures or any pieces of art that you might want?"

Once again, J.J. blurted out, "No, we looked and there really wasn't anything."

"What about my personal things, notes and so on."

"Well, we will go back later, today, and sort through all your things," Nora said, trying to pacify Jenny's obvious agitation over J.J.'s lack of consideration.

As much as she wanted to go through the papers herself, she was too weak to carry out that chore and was now forced to leave it up to her son who didn't seem to give a damn about anything of hers. Jenny hoped Nora would treat her possessions with more care and discretion.

"There is one more thing you may want us to do and that is to hire a lawyer to draft up documents granting me power of attorney and executor of the estate in case you can't look after the sale and so on."

J.J. was kind enough not to say if you're too sickly or lose your mind.

Jenny thought a brief moment. "Yes, perhaps we should do that, J.J.. You're used to business and contracts and such. Yes, maybe you should look after it all."

"Well, as soon as we get back to the hotel, I will call around unless you have a lawyer?"

"No, not really, just the one that did up the purchase of the house."

"Yes, it's Peter Dalham, I remember seeing it with the other papers. I will phone him. I'm sure he is capable of drafting up the papers and we will bring them around in the morning for you to sign."

Jenny felt a little queasy about doing all this so quickly. She still felt that she was mentally capable of carrying this out, but physically she didn't have the strength. She would have to go along with this, just until she got better.

"Well, how is my boy doing?"

Jimmy was playing with the book at Jenny's bedside. One of the pages began to tear out, but Jenny didn't mind.

"Oh, you're so good and patient listening to us grown ups talk about such boring things. I wish I were able to have done some shopping and get you a nice toy or two."

"He has more than enough, Marj," said J.J..

"Perhaps, but I would like to spoil him a little. Grandmas have that privilege, you know."

"Well, if we are going to get a lawyer for you and get this power of attorney matter straightened out we'd better go."

"But, J.J., you just got here—"

"You also want us to sort things out at the house, too, we don't have much time. Our flight leaves at 5:20 p.m., tomorrow. By the time I return the rental car and get out to the airport, we may run out of time."

Jenny looked at J.J. and said absently, "Yes, we are running out of time. Is there any way you and I can talk in private for a few minutes, J.J.?"

"Perhaps tomorrow, Marjorie, there is too much to get done."

Jenny looked so disappointed, her eyes pleading for some sense of reconciliation and understanding between them. J.J. stared at his mother unmoved.

"I'm sure J.J. will have time, tomorrow, Marjorie. Oh, Jimmy, you mustn't tear your grandma's pocket book. I'm so sorry, Marjorie."

"Think nothing of it, a little tape and it will be good as new. I'm almost finished that book, anyway."

J.J. turned towards the door. "Well, let's go, Nora."

Nora kissed Jenny's cheek before picking up Jimmy. "Hope you are feeling better soon, Marj."

Jenny looked up at her and said, "Thank you."

"We will see you in the morning, Marjorie," J.J. said, as he disappeared out the door.

Nora smiled. "Say good-bye to grandma, Jimmy."

Jenny waved and threw him a kiss. "Bye, Jimmy."

Nora and her son disappeared out the door. She heard some impatient and angry remarks by J.J. and an ensuing altercation that faded as they walked down the hall.

Jenny felt empty inside. She had so hoped to talk to J.J., but it was not to be. Not for today, anyway. Slowly, she got out of bed and limped over to the window that overlooked the parking lot. From the rear door of the nursing home J.J. emerged. The door slammed behind him. Then Nora came out, holding James. Their relationship seemed as distant and estranged as hers and James had been.

"Oh, Nora, you may suffer the same fate as I did," Jenny murmured. It was too bad she didn't live closer. She might, in some subtle way, have been able to alert Nora, offer suggestions of what she might do, where she had failed to act in her own marriage. To make sure, their home and belongings are in both their names and not owned by some uncaring corporate third party.

Jenny wondered if it was wise to agree to give J.J. power of attorney. *Does it really matter? It doesn't seem like I'm going to be around much longer.* The thought sent shivers down her spine. Perhaps, though, she could provide for Nora and her grandson should some prenuptial agreement be in place that leaves them in a predicament. When the lawyer visited, tomorrow, she would ask to see him privately about changing her will.

Chapter Fifty-Six

ONCE AGAIN, JENNY waited anxiously for J.J. and his family. It was almost 10:30 a.m. and still no sign of them. If they would at least phone. She had prayed since she woke up that she and her son could reconcile and free themselves from the terrible bondage that separation and unforgiveness had kept them in.

Jenny knew her son was suffering as well, but was too proud to admit it. He simply doesn't realize how his anger, hatred and unforgiveness was cheating him out of a happy life. His future will forever be shaped by this present turmoil. *Oh Lord, please help him and...us.*

Jenny knew that unless they healed their relationship she could never tell J.J. of his half-sister. It would be so wonderful for him to know of Camilla and that she was a part of their family. It concerned Jenny that if Camilla ever searched for her birth mother and she were gone that J.J. would never accept his step-sister. And if Camilla approached J.J. without their reconciling, he probably would hold it against her. He would see Camilla as the result of her mother's promiscuity only adding more proof of her illicit relationship with the bookstore dealer. The entire situation was a mess and Jenny simply didn't know how to deal with it. Nervous exhaustion crept in, but she didn't want to ask for a sedative. If she fell asleep they might just come and go and not wake her.

At noon, an attendant brought Jenny her meal.

"Hi, Ms. Hamilton, I hope you're hungry. The asparagus smells so good I'm tempted to snitch some."

Jenny smiled and remained silent. She was trying to conserve all of what little energy she had left. The lunch before her grew cold and remained untouched. She felt so forlorn, lonely and rejected. For the first time since leaving James, her centredness was threatened and feelings of unworthiness attacked her self-image. J.J.'s behaviour and cold attitude saddened and wounded her. For twenty two years, she'd put up with that kind of a relationship in her marriage and now it was perpetuated by her son. He was the perfect clone of his father. James had taught J.J. very well.

The minutes ticked away and grew into an hour and then another. Finally, shortly after 2:00 Jenny heard them approaching her room. By now she was tired and exhausted from the waiting and the tension she was experiencing over their relationship. This time, J.J. walked in first with Mr. Dalham behind.

"Hello, Mrs. Hamilton, it's been awhile since I saw you."

"Hello, Mr. Dalham."

"So, how are you feeling?"

"Way too exhausted to go through with all the paper work about to take place. I'm so glad to have J.J. home to help me." She looked appreciatively towards J.J..

"Hi, Marjorie," said Nora, as she entered, holding James the Third.

"Hi, Nora." She looked a little tired. She hoped they weren't quarrelling on her part. Turning back to Mr. Dalham, Jenny asked, "So, do you have some papers for me to sign?" She wanted to dispense with that as quickly as possible.

"Yes, J.J. told me that you wished to give him power of attorney to look after your estate."

"Yes, that is correct."

"It is my duty to inform you, Mrs. Hamilton, that once you sign these papers J.J. will have the right to deal with your estate as he sees fit."

"Yes, I realize that."

"I might also add that at any time while you are able, you can terminate this agreement if you feel he is not acting in your best interests."

"Oh, I'm sure J.J. will do a fine job." Although Jenny indicated trust in J.J., she was relieved by Mr. Dalham's comment.

Mr. Dalham rolled the eating table over to Jenny's bedside. He opened his satchel and pulled out a small tape recorder, turned it on and set it on the table. "I'd like to record the conversation just as a backup in case there is any dispute down the line. Is that okay with you, Mrs. Hamilton?"

"Yes, that's fine."

Mr. Dalham looked towards J.J. and he nodded. He turned back to Jenny. "J.J. signed these papers in my office. Please look them over carefully, I think I have all the information correct. Your full name is Marjorie J. Hamilton and your birthday is 1941, March 20th."

"Yes, that is correct."

"I have your social insurance number on file from last time." He handed the three papers to Jenny.

"I will never be able to read all this."

"Essentially, Mrs. Hamilton, you are giving complete power over to your son to look after your affairs. Now, until such time as you are completely unable to do so, you can still override his wishes if you so desire and you can also remove his power at any time,," Mr. Dalham reiterated.

Jenny stared at the lawyer and was reminded of the last time she signed the spousal agreement without fully understanding the meaning of what she was signing. *She hoped she was doing the right thing.*

"So, where do I sign?" Jenny said. Time was running out and she still wanted to talk to J.J. alone and spend some time with her grandson.

Mr. Dalham flipped the papers to the last page. Jenny saw J.J.'s signature on the paper and Mr. Dalham's signature beside as a witness. Jenny picked up the pen on the table and signed the paper. Mr. Dalham took a duplicate set from his briefcase and asked Jenny to sign a second copy.

"Most institutions take a duplicate copy, but some still insist on seeing the original, should J.J. have any difficulties securing your funds to look after you when you require it."

After Jenny signed the papers, Mr. Dalham witnessed it. He placed one copy in a brown envelope and handed it to J.J.. The second copy he kept for his own records. He turned off the tape recorder and returned it to his briefcase. "It's been a pleasure seeing you again, Mrs. Hamilton."

"Perhaps in a week or so Mr. Dalham if you can make the time, I would like to see you again."

Mr. Dalham studied Jenny for a moment.

"It's in regards to my will. There is something I want to add."

"Certainly, Mrs. Hamilton, I will call ahead, next week, and make an appointment with you."

"Thank you, Mr. Dalham, it was very kind of you to come to the nursing home."

"No problem, Mrs. Hamilton." He turned and shook hands with J.J. and Nora and touched little Jimmy on the head and left.

"Well, I'm glad that's over with." Jenny felt tired, hot and flushed.

"Are you okay, Marjorie?" asked Nora, as she walked over to where Mr. Dalham had stood before.

"Oh, yes. All this business, papers and such, it's all too much for me."

"Yes, I know what you mean. J.J. looks after all that in our household, too."

That last comment only added further tension to Jenny's nervousness. She wanted to encourage Nora to take an interest in the family finances, but now was not the time. She turned to J.J..

"Thank you for coming to Regina and helping me with all this, J.J.."

J.J. nodded with a look of indifference.

It was almost 3:30 p.m. "Oh my, it's getting late, I so hoped you would be able to come this morning."

"By the time I signed the listing papers with Ben Walker and then meeting with the lawyer, it took up most of the morning."

"Here, Nora, please push the table away and bring Jimmy down to me. How is my boy, this afternoon?" Jenny said, as she received Jimmy beside her in bed. She gave him a hug and kissed his cheek. "Oh, I could spoil you in no time." She tickled him in the tummy and he laughed. Jenny did it, again, and little James laughed harder. "Oh, that's my boy." Jenny hugged him, again.

J.J. hopped from one leg to the other. Jenny knew he felt uncomfortable and wanted to leave.

Oh, J.J. How simple and easy life can be, how happy we can be. Please don't let this opportunity of healing slip away. Lord help him come to me, let us both feel liberation and freedom from the past. It will cripple J.J. and doom us to a life of mediocrity and regret.

Perhaps J.J. felt her mind messages of hope for peace between them, but the only awareness he gave of anything to was his watch.

"Oh, I can't believe it's time for you to go. This is all so quick; hardly had a chance to visit. Did you manage to see a little bit of the city?"

"There's not much to see," J.J. said. "We can't believe how dead everything is after 5:00 p.m. The streets are deserted."

"Yes, the downtown shuts down pretty quickly, but there is still a lot of activity, especially in the south and east ends of the city. People usually stay closer to home rather than come way back downtown after work."

"But it only takes a few minutes, not like in Ottawa where it can take an hour or more," challenged J.J..

"Well, that's the difference between a large and small city."

"I can't believe you moved here. There's nothing—"

"Oh, but I love it, here," interjected Jenny. "I like a smaller city. Since spring I have made some very good friends. It's so easy to get around and there's theatre and the library and very nice restaurants, just like in a bigger city, only on a smaller scale perhaps."

"Well, you would never get me moving to a place like this. And flying here, I noticed there is no landscape to speak of, just flat land, don't you miss the trees?"

"Actually, the city and the prairies grow on you, you can see for miles and miles, almost to the end of the world and the sunsets and sunrises are spectacular."

"Well, the sunsets in Ottawa look pretty good to me."

"Now, J.J., Marjorie likes it, here, and that's the important thing." Nora interjected, once again trying to come to the rescue. "Actually, Marjorie, I like small cities, too. I would feel very safe here raising a family."

"Ottawa is safe, too. I'm sure the crime rate is about the same," J.J. countered.

"Well, enough of that, when are you coming back for another visit?"

J.J. didn't answer.

"Maybe next summer we may be able to come back, again," said Nora and then her eyes brightened with hope. "Perhaps you will be well enough to come to Ottawa."

"Yes, I sure hope I get over this nonsense. I would so much like to travel and see all the places I've only read about in books. But authors have a way of making everything sound so exotic and romantic. I get easily drawn into that."

J.J. shuffled. Jenny realized that he took her last comment as confirmation that she was easily drawn into romantic ventures, especially with the bookstore dealer. Jenny quickly changed the subject.

"I suppose you are very busy at work, J.J.."

"Yes, very busy, Marjorie. I am taking over more and more responsibility since dad's operation."

"Oh? What kind of operation, J.J.?"

J.J. hesitated and then said, "He had cancer removed from his prostate. The doctors got it all and he's back at work, now."

"I'm so glad he's better."

J.J. stared at his mother questioning her sincerity.

Once again, Nora came to the rescue. "Yes, J.J. is hardly at home—"

"Well, someone has to make a living."

"Really, J.J., I suppose what I do isn't considered work," she tried to say in a teasing way.

J.J. shook his head.

Jenny couldn't get over how much J.J. was like his father. Mr. Know It All and perfect in every way, no time for anybody or anything. It's all work, and more work, and business and more business.

"Will we be able to have a little private chat before you go, J.J.?"

J.J. winced.

Nora looked at J.J.. "We do have a little time. I will take Jimmy for a walk down the hall and you can have a talk—"

J.J. checked his watch again, "It's almost four, we have to get to the airport, return the car, and it would drive me crazy if we missed our flight and had to stay another night. Maybe next time, Marj," said J.J. tersely and with a furtive glance her way, "We really must go now."

Nora looked upset with him and lowered her head trying not to show her disappointment. Jenny too, used every ounce of strength she had left to hide her distress and fend off complete devastation.

"Well, it's been so nice to meet you in person, Nora, and to finally see my little treasure, here." Jenny looked down at Jimmy and squeezed him.

"Yes, it's been so nice to see you, too, and you're right, we must see each other again, soon. That's what family is all about." Nora said, not daring to look at J.J..

J.J. shuffled, again, holding back a remark his wife would surely hear as soon as they left.

Nora hoisted Jimmy onto her hip. "Say good-bye to grandma. Well, good-bye, Marjorie. I wish you all the best. I will keep you in my prayers."

"Thank you, Nora." Nora bent down and kissed Jenny's cheek.

Jenny reached out and touched Jimmy's head at the same time. J.J. was about to turn and walk out when Jenny said, "Please, J.J., come over and give me a good-bye kiss?"

J.J. looked at her.

"Please, J.J.," Jenny pleaded.

Nora glared coldly at her husband almost in disbelief. J.J. shuffled a bit and then walked to her bedside. Jenny grabbed his hand. It felt stiff and cold. She reached up towards him with her other arm. J.J. bent down and rather than kiss his mother, he turned his cheek towards her. Her trembling lips touched his cheek briefly and he immediately straightened. They looked at each other for a brief moment. Jenny was still holding onto his other hand and could feel him resisting slightly and then he pulled his hand free.

"Thank you for coming, J.J., and thank you for looking after everything for me. I really need you. You're all I have."

J.J. didn't respond for a long moment. "Take care, Marj."

"Oh, please, J.J., call me 'Mom.'"

J.J. looked at his mother. "Yeah, sure." For him to swallow his pride and give in to his dying mother's final request was as impossible for him as it would be for Jenny to hate. His heart had hardened too much under the tutelage of a father who was incapable of instilling love for others.

Nora had tears in her eyes in embarrassment and disgrace over her husband's lack of compassion, and heartless behaviour. She wanted to call Marjorie, Mom, but didn't want to upstage her husband or force him into yielding to his mother's request. It had to come freely, from his heart to be of any value.

"Bye, Mar…Jenn. Yes, bye, Jenny," Nora dared say, offering some consolation, as she walked out of the room.

Nora's gesture pushed tears to the edge of Jenny's heart. Fear that she would never reconcile with her son before her death gripped her stomach into such a tight knot it restricted her breath. She brought both of her hands up to her chest and with her right hand she clutched her guardian angel.

"Bye, J.J." Her lips quivered, her eyes begged for some sign of love and warmth.

J.J. just stood there, frozen in time. At that instant he had the power to change destiny for himself, his mother and not only be a model for his family to admire, but change his own family life for the better. He didn't realize how close he was to what really mattered in life. It was right under his nose and he didn't see it. Love, family, forgiveness, understanding, kindness were the values that would give him happiness and true success.

In his world, however, such ideals and principles were almost alien to him. His values were based upon pursuit of money, wealth, possessions, acquisitions and retaliation. He had bought into the belief that happiness would soon be his. One more buyout and he would be at the top, but it never was. The void he was trying to fill could never be filled. He was trapped in a vicious cycle, always in pursuit of a false dream, an illusion.

J.J. looked into his mother's pleading eyes. He knew what she wanted to hear. She wanted to hear that she was loved, a word of affection, but all he said was, "Good-bye." Neither 'Marjorie' nor 'Mom' could further utter from his stiff cold lips. He turned and walked out the door, not realizing he'd failed to close the biggest deal he could ever have made in all his life. Just a few words of kindness and love could have purchased him a treasure beyond his wildest dreams.

Jenny held back for as long as she could until they were far enough down the hall before she burst into tears of sadness and sorrow, her feelings of utter despair.

"Oh, God, why is this all happening to me?" Her knuckles turned white as she squeezed the pewter angel in her hand, trying desperately to wring out any love she could. Even the metal angel gave her more comfort and warmth than her son, her own flesh and blood.

In the days which followed, Jenny was too sick and heavily sedated to think about her home. She didn't know that J.J. had never gone back to her house and sorted things out. All of her private things were left exactly as they were. Potential buyers and real estate people traipsed in and out, uncaringly handling Jenny's precious things. Whoever would purchase Jenny's house would literally take possession not only of the house, but another person's inner life as well.

Many people viewed the house and had very positive comments. In fact, most ranted and raved over the layout design and the tasteful furniture. The realtors were surprised it hadn't sold instantly. Perhaps if it had been summer time and people had seen the beautiful garden Jenny had created, the house might have sold sooner. But perhaps, it was just waiting for the right buyer, a very special buyer who would completely appreciate the house and the treasures therein.

CHAPTER FIFTY-SEVEN

WINTER ON THE prairies can be a punishing ordeal when the temperature drops and the winds pick up. Since the beginning of December, prairie folks had braced themselves for the bitter cold to arrive, but days before Christmas it had still not yet come, at least not in full force. The temperature hovered around 10 degrees below freezing, but it hadn't snowed, and without snow covering the landscape, it just didn't seem like Christmas.

Finally, one morning, Regina residents woke up to their winter wonderland. Huge flakes tumbled from the sky and by the time Justin opened the gallery at 9:30 a.m. at least 10 inches of snow had fallen and traffic was almost at a standstill.

When Henry arrived at the shop, snow was beginning to gather where Justin had already shovelled.

"Hi, Dad. Mr. and Mrs. Clarke just purchased a painting of yours for their daughter and her husband, and would like you to personalize it."

"Certainly, I'll just be a minute." Henry shook the snow from his coat and hung it up. He headed back to the counter and extended his hand to the Clarkes.

As Henry began to personalize the back of the painting, Ben Walker entered the gallery.

"Hi, Ben," Henry said, as he glanced up from writing the note. "I'll just be a few moments."

"Hello, Henry, take your time. I'll just browse for a while. I love looking at your paintings."

After Henry signed the back of the painting and a book for the Clarke's, he handed them both to Justin to gift wrap them. He thanked the Clarke's, and then approached Ben, who was examining one of Henry's new Giclees.

"Well, Ben, haven't seen you in a spell. How are things going?"

"This is nice, Henry. I haven't seen these before."

"They just came out. I reproduced my last two originals directly onto canvas. I am pleased with the colour and quality of the reproduction."

"Yeah, they look just like an original, in fact, I thought they were."

"Good-bye, Susan, Paul," Henry said, as the Clarkes passed on their way out.

"Bye, Henry, thanks again for personalizing the painting, it will mean a lot to them."

"The pleasure is all mine. Merry Christmas."

"Merry Christmas to you, too."

Ben and Henry walked over to the counter where Justin was standing.

"Hi, Ben," said Justin, as he put out his hand.

"Hi, Justin, how are you doing?" He gave Justin's hand a firm shake.

"Good. Selling any gingerbread houses?" quipped Justin.

Ben smiled, "I wish I could. Sales go down at this time of year, it will pick up again in the New Year."

Just then Jeremy walked into the gallery.

"We might need to get a new dishwasher, Dad. You may want to have a look at it. Oh, hi Ben," said Jeremy as he extended his hand.

"Haven't seen you in a long time, Jeremy, seems every time I'm in the restaurant you're on a day off."

"I don't think so Ben, or at least my wife wouldn't agree with you. Running a restaurant is a full time business. I must have been in the kitchen when you were in."

"So, what brings you here, Ben? Interested in one of my originals?" Henry chimed in.

"I wish I could afford one, I'd be the first in line. The reason I am here is a house came on the market awhile ago and I think you may want to have a look at. It's in an excellent area, a very nice bungalow and the price is quite good."

"How long has it been on the market, Ben?" Henry inquired.

"Only a month or so. I thought for sure it would sell in the first week. One person was very interested, but the financing fell through."

"Well, Ben, I am not really interested in purchasing any more properties, but perhaps Jeremy might want to acquire another revenue property."

They turned to Jeremy.

"Would you like to have a look at it?" asked Henry.

"Yeah, I'd like to see it."

"Well, then, why don't the three of us have a look at it. We'll meet you at the house around four this afternoon?"

"That sounds great, Henry. Here's a feature sheet. The address is at the top. See you both there, then, around four."

"Right, bye for now."

After Ben left, Jeremy and Henry studied the sheet.

"That's a nice looking bungalow. I like the steep roof and all the stone work, it sure gives it a quaint look. Too bad the snow is covering up all the landscaping. The low, stonewall fence at the sidewalk is great, it almost feels like you're entering an estate. It's impressive, very nice exterior and looks like the interior might have a nice layout, too. Well, we will know soon enough if it's a good buy or not." Henry placed the sheet on the edge of the counter and followed Jeremy to the kitchen to examine the dishwasher as they braced themselves for another busy day.

Shortly before four, the Pederson's pulled up in front of the bungalow on Hill Avenue. Ben was already in the house, his car parked on the street. The winding walkway to the front door had been cleared of snow but was filling up again. Only hints of the green evergreen trees peeked through the white blanket of snow. The connecting roofs were laden with snow as were all the shrubs and cedars wrapping around the front of the house.

Henry and Justin walked in single file up the cleared path. Ben opened the front door as they stepped onto the landing.

"Hi, Henry, Jeremy. I see you found the place okay. I was worried the snow might bury the city by this afternoon. It's quite a snowfall we are having."

"Yes, it sure is," said Henry as he stamped his feet on the landing.

Ben took his coat then Justin's and hung them in the front closet. They took off their shoes, even though Ben said it wasn't necessary. Henry cleaned the snow and moisture off his glasses with his handkerchief.

The agent stepped back as Henry brushed past him into the foyer then entered the living room. His first impressions came from the furniture rather than the house itself but even more so the fragrance in the air. He had smelled it as soon as he entered the house. Plants and flowers were everywhere and so discreetly placed that it complimented rather than detracted from the furniture. Everything looked so elegant and tastefully arranged. It instantly appealed to him. In fact, it made him feel totally at home.

An all encompassing but strange calm settled over him as he gazed around the room. The antique furniture was exquisite and the fine craftsmanship of the chairs and tables exuded an inherent aesthetic beauty. Solid wood, carved with sensitivity and design, not even close to most of the best furniture on the current market.

Henry couldn't get over the flowers blooming and how the air was mixed with so many different scents…it was intoxicating and yet, *amongst the heavenly air surrounding him a faint scent was triggering a memory. His nostrils quivered.* He felt like a hound dog highly trained to sniff out opium amidst thousands of odours.

What was this faint scent that stirred him?

Goose bumps formed on his skin. He felt the hair at the back of his neck rise and just as a memory of the fragrance began to surface, Ben broke the spellbinding reverie of the moment.

"Nice layout, isn't it?" Ben commented from behind him.

"Oh, yes, Ben," Henry mumbled as he actually started to look at the house interior itself.

At the end of the living room was a natural stone fireplace with a beautiful mahogany mantle. It was snuggled in between bookshelf units on either side. An original painting hanging above the mantle caught Henry's interest. He went over and looked for the name, but didn't recognize it. The artist obviously sensitive to light caught the sunlight on the lake in the landscape magnificently. It was definitely a painting he would have purchased as it reminded him of the serene view of his pond in the valley near the Poustinia.

The grate which held the firewood had curved legs and a curved front; very unique, as was the ornate screen sitting on a strip of ceramic tile in front of the fireplace; these items were handmade and antiques in their own right. The utensils hanging near the opening of the fireplace were all part of the set as their shape, design, and artistically hand-carved oak handles carried the same craftsman's touch.

"Absolutely beautiful," Henry murmured.

A very comfortable armchair sat in front of the fireplace. It looked so inviting; he could have sat down immediately and started to read the book resting on the round end table next to it. The book was open and lying face down, Henry wanted to go over and read the title, but held himself in check.

The dining room grew out of the end of the living room separated by an arched opening with pillars on either side. A crystal chandelier hung from the ceiling, almost perfectly centred over the antique dining room table. The coving around the ceiling reflected an earlier time, perhaps the thirties or forties and in superb condition. The tripod legs at either end of the dark mahogany dining room table and the way they flared out into brass-covered claw feet intrigued him. The high backs and seats of the chairs were covered with dark chocolate coloured leather. The accompanying sideboard and china cabinet were both supported by flared legs, as well. Henry couldn't believe that such fine antique pieces of furniture were in the same house. It must have taken the owner years to find such rare pieces and to combine them together so tastefully.

Jeremy and Ben had walked ahead into the kitchen. They were talking about something, but Henry was so mesmerized by the antiques he didn't know what they were discussing. It would take him hours just to fully examine and appreciate the furniture. He was just about to more thoroughly study the intricate mullion bars over the curved doors of the china cabinet when his son called him.

"Come on, Dad, we have to get back to the gallery, soon."

"Yes, I'm just so taken by the antique furniture, such absolutely beautiful pieces." Reluctantly, Henry tore his eyes away from the unusual shape of the brass pulls of the cabinet's drawers and walked into the bright kitchen.

"Jeremy and I were just talking about the fridge and the range. They are actually quite modern, yet have an old style about them. Works very well with all the old furniture and light fixtures."

"Everything is just fantastic."

"Wait till you see the bedroom," said Ben, "I brought my wife here, this morning, to show her the house. She instantly fell in love with the bedroom furniture. We are hoping whoever buys the house will sell us the set."

"What do you mean, the buyer selling you the bedroom set, you mean the seller?"

"No, I mean the buyer. Oh, didn't I tell you, the price of the home includes all the furniture?"

Henry could barely believe what he had just heard. He stepped back.

"What on earth do you mean, Ben? You can't be serious. Surely no one in their right mind would give up all this incredible furniture with the house sale."

"I'm dead serious, Henry. Absolutely everything in the house goes with the sale, exactly as you see it."

Henry was momentarily speechless. Why on earth had this house not sold yet? Surely other people must see the tremendous value.

"So, tell me, Ben, what is going on, here. Where are the owners and how can this possibly be?"

"Well, apparently the lady that owned this house took ill and had to move into a nursing home. When her son came from down east for a visit, she asked him to sell the home. I guess her illness is terminal."

"Well, doesn't her son want any of this furniture or some of his mother's things?"

"Apparently not. In my discussions with him, I got the impression that he doesn't like antique furniture at all. He's quite young, actually and I guess he and his wife are into modern furniture. And for his age, he seems to be an important business man and doesn't have the time to go through any of this. He just asked me to find a buyer for the house and to price everything into it. It's hard to put a price on all this stuff. At the end of the day, her son simply said to add $15 to $20,000 onto the price and let it all go. He didn't have time to spend selling each piece or dickering with people. 'Just sell it all,' were my final instructions on the matter."

Henry studied Ben for a long moment, making certain that he wasn't pulling his leg. Ben's expression confirmed that he was dead serious.

"This is unbelievable. What do you think, Jeremy? This would be a very good investment."

Jeremy looked at Ben and then at his dad not sure if he should say what was on his mind. "To be honest, Dad, I don't care for the antique furniture, either. It's a nice house, but I don't know. It's a little old style, Hill Avenue is a busy street. I don't know. It's a very good deal...it, it just doesn't seem to appeal to me."

Once again, Henry couldn't believe what he was hearing. *This is the buy of the century!* Why couldn't he see the value here?

Henry was mystified.

And yet, if his son couldn't see the value, perhaps this in part at least explains how the owner's son didn't, either, or the other potential buyers who had already viewed the house and its contents. It never failed to intrigue Henry how one person could see a treasure in something, while another person could see the opposite.

Henry shook his head. How many times had he witnessed this perception especially during his counseling years and the resulting misunderstandings and problems.

"Are you sure, you are not interested in this house?"

Jeremy shook his head with a slight smile on his face.

Henry walked over to the kitchen sink and rested his hands on the edge. Thoughts of his mother doing that very same thing in their gently drifted into his mind. She seemed to do her best thinking there with her hands in the water washing something or other. He felt her presence as he looked out the window and surveyed the huge back yard.

Although everything was covered with snow, Henry could imagine what lay underneath by the impressions of the snow above. It was obvious a winding path led to a gazebo way in the back yard. Flowers and hedges lined the walkway on either side. The tall, old evergreens lining the west and east side of the yard would provide shade, privacy and a cozy seclusion. If this were his back yard, he would have done a very similar thing. He could just picture himself strolling down a winding path and then sitting in the shade or light of the gazebo to rest or read or meditate. It was perfect.

As Henry stood there, he realized that his appeal for this house was not just the house *per se* and its contents, but the overall general feeling it gave to him. Never before, other than when he walked into his mother's kitchen perhaps, had he ever felt so completely at home.

An unexplainable peace, a oneness, a mysterious connection with this home swept over him. It's almost as if he had discovered his other self or his whole self.

Just as Henry was about turn back to Jeremy and encourage him to buy the house he saw a shadow streak across the back yard. He leaned forward and saw Julean's spirit. He gasped. He heard one of the men behind ask if he was okay but their words of concern quickly faded away. She moved to the right of the gazebo and disappeared…

What Henry saw next overwhelmed him even more and the blood drained from his face. Beside the gazebo, half-buried in the snow, its white colour blending into it emerged an angel with beautiful wings holding a basket that caught a high fluff of snow from the day's snowfall. Perhaps more than the house, the furniture, the incredible price, *it was the guardian angel beckoning him to his new home.*

"Unbelievable."

"Dad, we really have to get back to the café and gallery."

Henry tried to register in his mind what Jeremy had just said, but he was so engrossed and overtaken by this strange feeling growing within him it took several moments to return to the reality of the moment.

"Dad, did you hear me? I have to get back and close the café…"

Henry turned and looked at Jeremy and then at Ben. They were both looking at him intently. Each for different reasons. Ben was wondering if the property was enticing him and Jeremy was trying to figure out what he could possibly see in this old house filled with all of this old stuff.

"Do you want to see the bathroom and the bedroom, Henry?" asked Ben.

Henry could see Jeremy wanted to get back to the cafe and he didn't want to rush seeing the rest of the house. He wanted to savour it all, appreciate every item, every nook and cranny. Absolutely everything!

"Look, Ben, we need to get back to the store, and I don't want to rush this, but let me say I am definitely very interested. I promised myself not to buy any more houses and get back to my painting, no more distractions, and yet here I am, trapped again by such character, architecture and design. And all this beautiful furniture comes with it. *How can I possibly turn this down?"*

He spun around to take it all in again. "*It feels like home!* I'm almost certain I will take it, Ben. I would however like to come back one more time."

"Sure, Henry, whatever you think. I can give you the key to the house. Come back either tonight or tomorrow and go through it at your leisure and get back to me."

"Thanks, Ben, I'm going to take you up on that."

Ben reached into his pocket and pulled out a set of keys. He took one key off the ring and handed it to Henry.

"Here you go, Henry, it's all yours," he said with a smile.

"You know me too well, Ben, you're a good salesman."

"And so are you, Henry. We both know how sales work. It's the same as when you let a customer take a painting they are interested in home on approval. Once there, chances are they are going to keep it."

Henry nodded and smiled. "You're probably right, Ben. Well, let's go, son."

For the most part, Justin and Henry were silent as they drove back to the gallery. Jeremy was definitely not interested in the house, he was adamant about that.

"Are you sure you want that house, Dad? It will require some work, and we all know how you are, once you get an idea, God knows what changes you will make to that place."

"Oh, I don't know, Jeremy. I really like the house just the way it is, it's hard to explain, there is just something about that place that I find very appealing, in fact, I feel such a strong attraction to it."

"And, what about all that old furniture...I mean antique furniture. What on earth are you going to do with all that stuff? There's an entire house full of things. You already have too much at the farm that you have collected over the years."

Henry thought about what Jeremy said. It was true, he had more than enough furniture and art and yet…

"I don't know, Jeremy, I just don't know what I would do. Perhaps just leave everything the way it is. I don't think I would want to make even one change to it. Everything I saw so far appeals to me just the way it is. Maybe I would buy it and keep it as a city home, a place where I can come to on days like this for example, when it's too blizzardy to go home. Or, a retreat of sorts, when I want to get away from the gallery for a while."

"I don't know, Dad, you can just as easy go home, you know. You already have a retreat in that prayer house you built and don't seem to use. Why take on another house to look after?"

"Yes, I know, son. Yet, there's something about it. I just can't put my finger on it. It just feels too good to be true."

CHAPTER FIFTY-EIGHT

THE NEXT DAY Henry and his staff were very busy. The snowfall had put everyone in the Christmas spirit. Henry was physically there, but not mentally. He couldn't get that house out of his mind. He had wanted to go back there first thing in the morning, but right from the start customers flooded in and didn't stop coming until mid-afternoon.

"Is something bothering you?" asked Shelly, "You look like your mind is miles away from here."

"You're too perceptive, Shelly. I am preoccupied with a purchase I'm considering. I have been thinking about it all day."

"I could tell something was bothering you. You were not your usual self with the customers, today."

"It's that obvious is it?"

"I'm afraid so, Dad," Justin concurred with a smile.

Some things never change. His mom and Mr. Engelmann had always told him that he was an easy read. His thoughts and feeling always dangled out there for everyone to see.

"Well, I think I am going to call it quits for the day. I'm sure you and Justin can handle everything."

"We do it every day."

"Right," Henry said, taking the hint that he was dispensable.

Before another customer came in, Henry grabbed his overcoat and rushed out the door. He just had to see the house one more time. Was the attraction he felt yesterday still there, or had it all been just a figment of his imagination?

His shoes filled with snow as he climbed through the foot high drift of snow on the sidewalk leading up to the front door, the key already in his hand. He stomped his feet, unlocked the door and stepped into the foyer. A table lamp on top of a round table next to a reclining chair was on. It cast a soft, warm glow in the room, welcoming him home. He slipped off his shoes then his overcoat, which he hung into the open closet. He turned and looked into the living room.

Furniture stood out that he couldn't remember seeing, yesterday, like the sofa, the long console holding the record changer, and the low round antique table next to the front windows completely covered with plants. The owner sure must love plants. They were all over and yet displayed in such a tasteful way. Henry stood for a moment admiring the many different varieties on the table alone.

And then just like yesterday, a faint scent seemed to emerge from a multitude of fragrances that stimulated his senses. What on earth is that odour…?

Oh, it will come to him, he thought as he deliberately focused on the furniture.

There, in the corner, was a tea caddy. How on earth did I miss that beautiful piece yesterday, he thought? Mint condition. Not a scratch on the flawless dark walnut finish. The caddy, supported by two, 12-inch-diameter wheels at the back and smaller ones in the front gave him a clue as to the age of piece. Hand carved spokes like that must go back close to 100 years. It alone would fetch well over $5000. How on earth could the owner's son give up such an exquisite piece of furniture?

Henry almost missed the tray on the second shelf of the caddy. He pulled it out and set it on top. It was a serving tray made out of walnut, all hand carved with ornate wood handles on either end. A quarter inch thick glass covering the bottom of the tray was cut precisely to follow all the curves and lines of the tray. The flaws in the glass confirmed that this item too was of an earlier period. He just shook his head in disbelief at such a treasure.

Even though the house and its entire contents were up for sale, Henry couldn't help but feel that he was intruding. A person's entire life was intricately tied up in their home and belongings. It reflected their likes, tastes, what appeals to them; purchases contain memories of places where they have been, travelled to, heirlooms, family treasures. He should definitely feel out of place and yet, just like the previous day, he felt completely at home.

Everything seemed to reflect his tastes, his likes, almost as if it were he who had made all of those purchases and collected all of those fine antiques.

How could this possibly be? He absently walked over to the chair in front of the fireplace. The open book lying face down on the end table that he had noted the day before drew his attention, again. As soon as he picked it up he recognized it, 'Mere Christianity' by C.S. Lewis. He had just finished reading that book for the second time less than three weeks ago. He further noted as he turned the pages, the owner also underlined certain passages, a practice which he followed, as well. *How strange all this was. It felt so right. He put the book down and saw the pencil. It could very well have been his.*

Henry entered the dining room and began pulling open the drawers of the sideboard. Sterling silver cutlery in the end drawers immediately glistened as they caught the light of the chandelier. Linen and a huge assortment of candles filled the middle drawers while crystal vases of all shapes and sizes stood hidden behind the doors below the small top drawers.

It didn't make sense that he should be the recipient of heirlooms which should be willed to some child or relative and yet, perhaps in a way, it was good that someone like himself, who appreciated it so much should take possession of it.

He was beginning to feel obligated to buy the house and take charge and responsibility of all these rare and precious contents.

There was so much more to look at in the dining room, but he was anxious to see the bedroom set since Ben and his wife were quite excited about it. He couldn't resist running his fingers down the edge of the ornate moulding surrounding the large bevelled mirror over the sideboard before turning into the kitchen. The same feeling made him stop and take a quick peek into the china cabinet in the corner.

"Unbelievable," he uttered. Even a cursory glance revealed the quality and value behind the curved glass doors. It was overcrowded with crystal and fine bone china. It would take him hours to go through this cabinet alone to appreciate the collection contained therein.

And again the scent came into his awareness, as he entered the kitchen. It seemed to be getting stronger…

Drawn to the kitchen window he gazed outside. His eyes scanned the backyard and quickly rested on the angel. The light bouncing off its white marble surface was spectacular.

"Just beautiful," Henry whispered. A vision of a guardian angel.

He searched for Julean's spirit but felt certain it had merged with the angel before him.

Reluctantly he turned back into the kitchen as if drawn by the scent. It suddenly struck him why it had seemed so bright when he entered the kitchen yesterday. The completely white paint of the walls and the kitchen cabinets gave the kitchen such a clean and pristine look, accented by the colourful geraniums on the window sill and paintings on the wall. It appealed to him even though it contrasted so differently to the rich mellow cedar wood of his log home in the valley. It would be a drastic change, but a nice one. A nice alternative when in the city.

Just as he was about to leave the kitchen, Henry noticed a cook book open on the kitchen counter. The owner must have left in a hurry, almost as if she didn't have time to put things away. Just leaving like that so suddenly, in the midst of daily living. It must have been so difficult for her. The hair on the back of his neck curled as he glanced at the recipe. It was the same recipe he followed for the Chicken Marsala with mushrooms he made the other night at the farm.

He looked up and went to the window. His eyes immediately rested on the angel and like yesterday was overwhelmed by its beauty. Julean had wanted to make sure he saw it, he felt certain. She knew how much he loved angels. His eyes swept the back yard in search for her spirit but was drawn back to the marble angel.

"Unbelievable..."

Henry wanted to open the cupboard doors and see what was inside; open the drawers and discover their contents, too, but he was now drawn to see the bedroom. The excitement he felt as kid at Christmastime flowed through his veins. It seemed like he was being bombarded by one gift after the other. He could hardly wait to see what was in the next drawer or behind the closed door. What an intriguing Christmas present this would all be. He had not felt so exhilarated in a long, long time.

On his way down the hall the scent was growing stronger...yet it was still overshadowed by the herbs and blooming flowers that filled the house, without which he felt sure he would have recognized the scent immediately. Searching his memory, he walked slowly as he made his way towards the bedroom.

He stopped and peeked into the bathroom. He flipped on the light and as he had expected, it contained a pedestal sink with a high ornate back with a matching toilet and tank. The tub was free standing, supported with large beautiful brass-clawed feet. A circular ring canopy hung from the ceiling which supported a shower curtain with a light floral pattern. All the taps, the shower head and even the handle of the toilet tank were solid brass. All of the fixtures were in excellent condition considering their age. Very elegant, indeed.

The layout of the three bedrooms was well designed. The main one was straight ahead. Now that he remembered the exterior, this room must be the one with the bay window. The other two bedrooms were down at the opposite end. He wanted to see the bedroom set that Ben had spoken of and the closer he came to the bedroom the stronger the scent became.

He hesitated at the door then opened it into a spacious main bedroom. As he had suspected straight ahead was the bay window. The shades were drawn so most of the light crept in from the hallway. He fumbled for the switch, flipped it on, and was instantly spellbound by what he saw. It almost made him dizzy as his eyes swirled around and around then back and forth, trying to take it all in.

The vanity dresser, the high chest of drawers and the bed itself were a set. They were all mahogany and stained deep burgundy. The supporting legs of each of the pieces were similar except for the height. After that, each piece took on its own unique distinctive appearance and design. The large headboard had the shape of several flower petals, like a group of petunias overlapping one another so naturally. Henry tried to smell the scent. He marvelled at the exceptional craftsmanship.

The foot board was simple with straight lines, clearly not wanting to steal any attention away from the intricate head board, but it too carried a design in its shape. Its top edge curved into the bed and continued to curve in an almost elongated 'S' shape as it made its way to a crowned bottom, supported by curved legs with hand-carved crow's feet. Henry's heart double-beat at the sight. No wonder the agent and his wife were interested in it. But how on earth could the owner's family bypass such a treasure.

"There must be a story behind all this."

The bed itself had several pillows stacked behind one another. It appeared so inviting and comfortable. The comforter was fluffy and soft and its floral pattern complimented the design on the headboard, almost as if it grew out of the comforter itself. What excellent taste to put the two pieces together like this. Henry sat on the edge of the bed. He sank his hands firmly into the comforter shifting his body around.

The reflection in the vanity mirror startled him until he realized it was him. He pictured the old lady sitting at the dresser putting her make up on, the antique lamps resting on each side of the dresser top with their frilly lampshades giving light to her features. She must have loved this room and her home. It was all so exquisite, so tastefully done.

Henry saw himself get up and walk towards the mirror. He held the reflection firmly in his sight and as their eyes met he asked pointedly, "Do you really want this home? You don't need another acquisition. Just the other day at the Poustinia didn't you realize that all this property and materialism was keeping you from the Lord?" Henry looked away, afraid of the answer, only to allow his gaze to rest on two chairs on the far corner of the room separated by a small round table. The distraction relieved him from the calling of one Master, but drew him back to the other.

"My God," Henry blurted, the Victorian chair covered with brocaded satin was clearly from the 18th century. It was similar to the two in the living room only less ornate and more petite. The rocking chair on the other side of the table was also an outstanding period piece so unique in design.

"What am I going to do, Lord? This house is filled with such treasures. They are objects of art that have always given me much joy and spiritual sustenance." As his eyes returned to the mirror a convicting thought stared back at him, "Is not the Lord alone sufficient?"

His hand brushed by the hand-carved frame of the mirror and flicked off the bedroom light hoping to escape in the darkness. The glint in his eyes, however, caught by the light from the hallway glared back at him like two headlights.

It is easier for a camel to walk through the eye of a needle than it is for a rich man to enter the gates of heaven.

"But, Lord," Henry dared to ask, "Did not You derive great satisfaction from your creation? Did You not say it was good? Can man not take joy that results from the creative abilities you have granted us?"

A small voice answered as he walked down the hallway. "But when is enough, enough? You have more than you need, now, and isn't this pursuit for more just an illusion, an empty hole that can never be filled? Isn't this just another detour from the true path to peace and your true purpose?

"Yes, but isn't this part of your purpose for me. Why was I brought, here? It was not for my son, it was obvious that he didn't want the house. It was beckoning to me, Lord. I have not felt such peace in a long time. And the angel in the backyard, your very messenger, it was as if the angel had spoken directly to me, welcoming me home."

On and on the debate raged in his mind swaying him first this way and that. Absently he slipped into his shoes and overcoat and just as he had his hand on the door knob ready to leave, it hit him…!

Lilacs!

It had hit him immediately when he opened the bedroom door, but the sight of what he saw had overwhelmed him so much, it temporally overshadowed what he smelled from the moment he came into the house yesterday and today! The scent was lilacs…

Without taking off his shoes he made his way back to the bedroom, focused now on the fragrance. The scent was increasing and sure enough once in the bedroom the fragrance overtook him. The hairs at the back of his neck began to rise as they did yesterday, only now he knew why. The lovely scent went into his nostrils but didn't stop there. It went beyond his ordinary senses and thinking and stung his heart so sharply that instantly he knew the memory that the fragrance had revived of so long ago…

It was the memory of his first love…a memory of Jenny.

How Henry drove back to the gallery was a mystery to him. He couldn't remember getting into his car, turning on the motor, driving… nothing!

The only thing he recalled for sure was that he had finally made a decision.

He did however, chastise himself for being so preoccupied, he was lucky he didn't have a serious accident.

After he took off his coat, Henry retrieved a business card from his sports jacket pocket and dialed the cell number on it.

"Hello?"

"Hi, Ben, it's Henry, I guess you know why I am phoning you."

A tense silence zinged through the line while Henry pleaded softly with the Lord:

"Forgive me, Lord, it is you I deeply love, but I just have to make this one last purchase. My heart tells me it is a gift from You. I feel your messenger telling me that that is so."

"What did you say Henry? I could barely hear you."

"Sorry, Ben, I was just thinking out loud. It comes with old age."

"Yeah, I know what you mean. It's when you start answering yourself that you're in trouble."

"Well, I guess I'm in deep trouble."

They both laughed helping to relieve some of the building tension. Ben held his breath waiting for Henry's decision.

"I'm going to buy the house, Ben."

He let out a long silent sigh, "I knew you would, Henry. Is there any chance we can buy the bedroom set?"

"Not a chance Ben, I wouldn't break up the collection of furniture in that house for anything. I will treat each piece as if they were my own."

"And, they soon will be," answered the realtor.

AROUND ELEVEN THE next morning, Ben walked into the gallery carrying his attaché case. He plunked it on the counter and brushed away a few snowflakes with the back of his hand.

"Well, Henry, I called the care home this morning to see if Mrs. Hamilton could respond to accept your offer to purchase the home, but the nurses on duty said she was too ill and asleep, so I called her son down east. He instructed me to fax the Offer to Purchase form to him and he would sign the Acceptance Agreement and return it, right away. Apparently he has power of attorney over his mother's estate. He will also mail the original copies."

Ben pulled out the forms. Everything was already filled in just waiting for Henry's signature. Henry carefully looked over the form. *Marjorie J. Hamilton.* 'J' for Jane? He scanned the page; the amount of the offer was what the purchaser asked for, so no counter offer would ensue. Although Henry had usually put in lower offers in the past when purchasing properties, it had never even entered his mind to do so in this case, as he already felt he was getting it for a huge bargain.

There were no conditions placed surrounding the sale. Ben knew Henry wouldn't have any problem in financing the purchase and the inspection report indicated the house was in fine condition. The basement and foundation were solid, the plumbing and electrical wiring were updated, and the walls and ceiling well insulated to present day standards. And most important of all the offer stated clearly that all of the contents as-is, were included in the price.

"Well, everything looks fine to me, Ben. The same as we discussed. I still find it hard to believe that absolutely everything comes with the house. You're certain neither Mrs. Hamilton nor her son wanted anything?"

"Apparently not, Henry. I guess Mrs. Hamilton is very ill. As I said, I believe it's terminal. And the son doesn't want anything except the family photos."

"I feel guilty buying this home with all of these things in it."

"Well don't, Henry. Mrs. Hamilton's son gave me specific instructions as to what was included in this sale. I told him who you were when I called this morning and how much you appreciated all the fine furnishings. He seemed pleased with that and hinted that you exercise discretion in destroying any personal letters or papers of his mother's. In any case, except for a few photos and a photo album which I am going to send to him, you take possession of everything else."

How could a son rely on a complete stranger to go through his mother's personal belongings and decide what to destroy or not?

Henry shook his head and muttered, "Unbelievable," under his breath, as he put his signature to the Offer to Purchase form.

"Yes, Henry, you just bought yourself an unbelievable Christmas present. I'm sure you will be discovering and opening things up for many weeks to come. God only knows what you will discover in this house."

Without thinking, Henry responded, "I don't think anything can ever top the discovery I made after my mother passed away."

"Well, Henry, you just never know. You might find some similar hidden treasures, beyond your wildest dreams, there as well."

With that, he closed his attaché case and shook Henry's hand.

"Congratulations on your fine purchase, Henry."

"Thank you, Ben."

Chapter Fifty-Nine

J AMES STOOD AT the front door to his estate at Greystone Manor and gazed outside. It had snowed most of the morning and he was fascinated with the ease at which Thomas shovelled the snow off the entrance landing and stairs. He had never held a shovel in his hands nor had he ever even looked at a shovel closely in his entire life. He would have thought it was hard labour using a spade and yet the relaxed manner and skilled movements of his employee touched him at a level that was unfamiliar to James.

It was like watching a fine oiled machine move with a steady rhythm similar to that of a pendulum. His arms and shovel moved back and then forward scooping up the snow and tossing it off to the side all in one smooth motion. Back and forth went his arms and shovel as he worked his way down the steps almost effortlessly. The sight mesmerized and relaxed James. He would never in his wildest dreams ever have thought that an act of menial labour would captivate his attention.

Thomas's breath made visible by the cold air showed no signs of exhaustion…his breathing clearly was smooth and steady. James knew if he were at the end of that spade he would be huffing and puffing from over exertion. Just hustling from his office to the board room or to one the executive offices sent his frazzled nerves in a tizzy and his heart racing. He could easily see the difference between the calm, relaxed demeanour of the man in front of him and the stressed out life style that he had been living. It was no wonder that all of the doctors in his care agreed that his over exertion and stress at his business was the main reason a tumour had grown on his prostate gland.

To get James to agree to withdraw from his business to rest and recuperate after his surgery for the next six months was no easy task. He knew however, if he didn't the consequences would be fatal. He was on a one way road that would lead him to a resting place next to his father.

James had never thought of his immortality before. He was always able to get everything he wanted in the bat of an eye. Money, wealth, prestige, influence, distinction, fame could buy anything. These were the elements of life he knew and controlled. But death was another matter. Death was the great equalizer; it brought everyone down to the same level regardless of status or power.

Something totally unexpected came out of nowhere and hit him on his blindside. An illness had brought him to his knees along with the painful realization that he could go through the same door that his father and mother and brother had gone through or perhaps he could prolong his existence by co-operating with life from a totally new perspective.

The first two months drove him and his staff crazy. Matilda threatened to leave and Thomas was on the verge of doing so as well. If Thomas hadn't loved the estate and the gardens as much as he did, he surely would have been gone.

But slowly James began to unwind.

He read a book; it was the first novel he had read since he was eleven years of age. It wasn't great, but the story held his interest. He would have much preferred a text on economics, business administration or how to keep the competitive edge over his rivals but he knew such books just got him all riled up. Most of the authors of those books didn't know what they were talking about. All theory and little if any real pragmatic advice. He had forgotten more about surviving and winning in big business than all of his professors knew put together. But his doctor suggested that he just let those thoughts go and learn to enjoy the moment.

James began to stroll down the paths of the estate gardens as the summer came to a close. At first the sight of the wildflowers bothered his sense of order immensely and so did the fragrance they gave off. He was still amazed how quickly they grew back after he had ordered Thomas to till them up when Marjorie left the estate. He didn't understand how such a thing could happen, but it did. It had spooked him... something that rarely happens to him. Usually it was he who spooked others by his business sense and ability to forecast problems and when to buy and when to hold and when to sell.

But this was different...something alien to him just like the way Thomas handled the shovel.

The butterflies initially bothered him, too. At first he wore a net over his head and gloves to keep them from landing on him. But that fear gradually faded away and when the Monarchs left for the winter to make their trek back to Mexico, he missed them. He never told anyone, but secretly he was looking forward to their return in late spring. He was glad that the milkweed plants grew back along with the wildflowers.

But it was the bouquet that Marjorie had left him in the Angel of Thanksgiving's basket that totally went beyond his comprehension. How the flowers lay in the basket for weeks without watering and remain as fresh as the day Marjorie had placed them there was mind-boggling and totally unexplainable.

Thomas said it was due to an act of love and thanksgiving.

James would never forget that moment. As alien as it was to him he had to agree with the gardener. How she could do such a thing after the way he treated her over the years touched him at the very essence of his being. That warm feeling surging through him wanted to grow and bloom but he was afraid of it and in the presence of his employee the scene in his mind's eye overwhelmed him.

Thoughts of Marjorie lying to him that she was a virgin and keeping her rape a secret from him was all it took to overcome the miracle before him and reject it all with revulsion. The sight of the flowers shrivelling and dying before his eyes was both satisfying and torturous. It pleased him that he had the power to destroy things that bothered him and yet it was painful to let go of the momentary feeling that had accompanied such an extraordinary act of kindness and...love.

Perhaps if Thomas had not been present he would have savoured that moment of ecstasy for a while longer, but he couldn't handle the moment. Just like he could never handle or control Marjorie. There was something about her that he wanted out of his life and at the same time drew him back again and again.

What was it?

He noticed it straightaway after she left that a special presence left as well. The estate had never been the same again. He noticed it in the workers instantly. A light had gone out in their eyes and along with it an inner joy of being around a beautiful person had disappeared. Marjorie possessed something that drew others to her without any other effort than just being herself. It was the complete antithesis of the world in which he lived. Yes, he could get people to come to him at his every call too but his control was achieved through the use of power, money and fear.

Each day James walked the grounds trying to capture what once was there. He searched all the flowers in the garden, he looked up to the flitting butterflies, perhaps a part of it was in the Angel of Thanksgiving …but it was gone. He was certain that special something was in all of these things but was activated in her presence, in much the same way something touched him deep inside when he was in her presence as well…*it was in her unwavering acceptance of him.*

How he tried to rile her, to engage her in battle, to find something to attack but there was only a calm peace and acceptance. Marjorie had something that he was searching for now. He wondered if he had not married Marjorie if he would have been brought to this point in his life to be searching for something that stirred him yet he was unsure of what it was.

His entire life lately seemed to be going upside down because of the aftermath of her life on the estate. A strange new world was knocking at his door and yet was it really all that new? It was there from the moment he had met Marjorie but didn't understand it and never took the time to appreciate it or let it be part of his life. The bouquet that she had left for him awakened him to that unexplainable feeling at his core. It was for just a fleeting moment and …*he wanted it back.*

James opened the door and called out to his employee, "Thomas, when you finish the last step come in and I'll have Matilda make us a coffee."

Thomas looked up at his employer with a puzzled look, "Why that is very kind of you Mr. Hamilton. A warm cup of coffee would take the chill off my bones…I will come in the back way shortly."

"No, come in the front Thomas, it's shorter…ple…please."

Thomas looked at James, holding the puzzled look on his face a bit longer and then Thomas smiled and nodded his head.

James made his way into the kitchen and asked Matilda to make coffee for him and Thomas.

Matilda assumed the Thomas that Mr. Hamilton was referring to was some kind of client of his.

"Shall I bring some pastries into the den for you and your guest, Mr. Hamilton?"

"No, we'll have it in the kitchen. I'm beginning to enjoy the light and warmth of the sun through the windows. And some of those chewy oatmeal cookies would be nice, Matilda."

Matilda had noticed something different about her master for several weeks now—"He ain't his usual self that for sure, she thought, as she made her way to the cupboard.

A few minutes later she heard the front door and rushed to greet Mr. Hamilton's guest.

"Oh, that's okay, Matilda, he knows the way in."

Matilda still went to the door and was shocked to see Thomas enter.

Matti whispered, "Thomas , what you be doing coming in the front door!?" She turned and pointed her finger to the kitchen, "Mr. Hamilton sitting in the kitchen, you best come around the back way before he sees you."

"Oh that's fine Matti, Mr. Hamilton is expecting me."

"He is…? You be the Thomas he be waiting for!?"

Thomas grinned, tilted his head and nodded.

"Well, my sweet Jesus, now I done seen it all…"

Thomas brushed past Matti and made his way to the kitchen leaving Matti standing there in a quandary.

"Take your jacket off and sit down, Thomas."

"Thank you, Mr. Hamilton," Thomas said as he rubbed his hands and then began to take his coat off.

"I drink my coffee black, Thomas, what do you take in it?"

"Sugar would be just fine, Mr. Hamilton. My wife tells me time and again that I'm not sweet enough." Thomas chuckled, but James didn't seem to see the humour in what he said.

"Matilda, would you get some sugar for Thomas? … Matilda…did you hear me?"

Matti was dumbfounded by what she was witnessing… "Yes, I be getting it real quick…" She hurried to the cupboard.

"So tell me Thomas, the angel statue that you and Ramon crated and sent off to Marjorie, do you recall where you got it from?"

Both Matti and Thomas looked surprised as they gazed at their employer wondering if they had heard right.

"I don't exactly know where it originally came from, Mr. Hamilton. I first saw it at the Memorial Gardens cemetery. It was shipped there by the sculptor. Apparently the man who commissioned the statue died and never came to pick it up and so he just sent it off to the cemetery. It was a fine expensive work and unbelievably the cemetery only wanted the freight paid and that happened to be the exact amount of money I had in my wallet. I still don't know why they didn't keep it themselves as it would have made a fine addition to the cemetery. But all the staff here as well as Carlos went in on it as a gift to Mrs. Hamilton knowing how much she loves angels."

"Yes, she does love angels," confirmed James.

"What we later learned however, makes this story even more unbelievable. The man who commissioned the statue in the first place was

Miss Jen…, I mean Mrs. Hamilton's father. We also learned that the sculptor saw the spirit of Mrs. Hamilton's father in the quarry and it spooked him."

"And that's why he sent it to the cemetery, to get rid of it…"

Thomas took a sip of his coffee and answered the question. "I believe that's correct Mr. Hamilton, and I just came along a day after it arrived at the cemetery."

"That is some story, Thomas."

"Yes, we all feel it was God's divine providence to find a way to have it brought to the rightful person it was meant for."

James furrowed his brow and was going to ask Thomas what he meant by that when J.J. came through the front door. As soon as he entered the kitchen he stopped dead in his tracks.

"What the hell is going on, James?"

"What does it look like, I'm having a coffee."

"With the gardener?"

J.J. looked at Matti and then Thomas and then his father, "I couldn't get a courier to deliver this contract to you today because of the snowy road conditions and so I brought it myself . The contract needs to be signed and returned by tomorrow. Let's go into the den."

"This is fine here. Did George okay it?"

"Yes, he and several other lawyers reviewed it and said everything looked good. You don't want to discuss this in front of the staff, let's go to the den."

"Does it have to be witnessed?" James wanted to check for sure.

"George said it would be okay as they have enough of your signatures on file, however he did say that one of the staff could witness it."

"Well, give me a pen and let's do it right now."

James flipped to the eighth page and signed the document. He passed it over to Thomas, "Would you witness this, Thomas. It has to do with "cryonic suspension." A person gets frozen at an extremely low temperature and then gets unfrozen at a later date when a cure exists for an incurable disease. It's hard to believe that cancer research scientists still haven't figured that out yet. Well this may be one way of beating that damn cancer should it come back. Are you familiar with this procedure, Thomas?" James turned to Thomas and passed him the pen.

"Geez, James, I wouldn't be talking about this with the staff." J.J. interjected with a scowl on his face.

James looked at J.J. "It's okay, J.J." He then turned back to Thomas and asked again, "Have you heard about this, Thomas?"

"I've read that it can be done Mr. Hamilton, but I have to say, I don't understand how they can do that once you've expired."

"Well that's what has concerned me and the legal department. The timing is critical. Once the heart stops beating, you are pronounced legally dead but the brain is still functioning for several minutes longer. It is at that point the firm I have this contract with takes over. Their team guarantees that they can stabilize the body by supplying the brain with enough oxygen and blood to keep it going until it's delivered to the suspension facility where the freezing begins…"

"Good, Lord…!" muttered Matilda.

"Look, James, I have to go. This has used up three hours of my time. I won't get home until eleven tonight…Nora's not going to be happy."

James took the contract, got up and handed it to J.J. and the two walked to the front door. Thomas and Matti heard bits and pieces of the two men's conversation.

"…You're losing it James, having a coffee with the gardener…"

"J.J., have you ever talked to Thomas? It's the most relaxing conversation I have ever had in all my life. There's an easiness about the man that is hard to explain. He almost lulls me to sleep…

"Anyway, how is Marjorie doing?"

"I don't know. I haven't called since we came back from Regina. She wasn't doing so well when we were there."

"Look, J.J., call her tonight. See how she is doing…she is your mother."

"You call her. I don't want to get in between you and her. You have always discouraging me from spending too much time with her and now…you call her."

"J.J., I was wrong—it might be a good idea to take some time off and go back and see her again."

"Look, James, I have to go. I have too much to do at the office…"

"Come into the den for a minute, J.J."

J.J. followed his father into the den and closed the door. Matti and Thomas overheard the two men have a heated exchange and then J.J. opened the door and stormed out slamming the front door behind him.

Thomas was just getting up, ready to go as well, when James returned to the kitchen.

"Thank you for the coffee, Mr. Hamilton. I best be finishing the walk."

"Have another coffee, Thomas, there is something I want to ask you."

Thomas sat down slowly and kept his gaze on James, a puzzled look growing on his face. Matti brought the pot of coffee over but Thomas covered the cup with his hand and shook his head.

"I hope that cryonics works according to plan, Thomas. It costs a lot of money to do something like that. It's amazing what one can do with money…"

"Yes, I am sure it carries power, Mr. Hamilton." Thomas couldn't believe he had just said that; this was such an unusual discussion but then it got more to his liking.

"Tell me, Thomas, the angel statue that you and Ramon crated and shipped off Marjorie…"

"Yes…"

"You say the sculptor had it shipped to the cemetery. Would you be able to find out the artists name and how to get a hold of him."

"I could call Frank and see if he can find out that information. He works for the Memorial Gardens Cemetery."

"I was thinking last fall as I sat in the Gazebo that it just doesn't look the same without the statue. I only saw it a couple of times but I have to say it made an impression on me. It added a kind of life to the garden."

"Oh, how Miss Jenny loved that garden and angel, Mr. Hamilton… oh, I be sorry for interrupting…" Matti turned back to the counter and continued peeling the potatoes.

"No, that's okay, Matilda." Turning back to Thomas he continued, "Look into it for me, Thomas and let's see if we can restore the garden the way Marjorie had it…"

Thomas looked long and hard at his employer and he worked hard to suppress a growing lump in his throat. "Yes, I will check into it first thing in the morning. Having an angel back in the garden would make Miss Jenn…, I mean Mrs. Hamilton very happy. I'm sorry, Mr. Hamilton I meant no disrespect…Mrs. Hamilton preferred to be addressed as Miss Jenny."

I understand Thomas, on several occasions over the years I heard you address Mrs. Hamilton that way. It was never to my liking but I chose to ignore it. However, I must say that these past few months my thinking on a lot of things has changed. In fact Thomas, I would prefer if you addressed me as James from now on…"

A glass bowl full of peeled potatoes fell to the tiled floor shattering into a thousand pieces.

Thomas and James were startled and turned to Matilda. She held both hands to her wide open mouth…

"Oh, I be so sorry!"

James raised his right hand and waved it off as if it was nothing.

He and Thomas bent down and began picking up the pieces of broken glass.

Matti stared in disbelief, unable to move…

Could this be the same Mr. Hamilton I knows?

CHAPTER SIXTY

EVERY TIME FATHER Engelmann visited hospitals and care homes, the loneliness of the people ate at his heart. Their eyes were empty, vacant, totally consumed by nothing, and revealing a physical body devoid of a meaningful existence. When he walked into their room, their eyes lit up and the boredom on their faces fell away, erased by a sincere appreciative smile like a starving person being offered a morsel of food. But, in this case, the food these people needed and wanted was *love*.

His only answer to it all was to try to come more often and visit as many residents/patients as he possibly could. Father dedicated at least three days of every week to hospitals and care homes. But despite his efforts, it always bothered him that he couldn't see more people. The needs were so great and many. He loved bringing cheer into the life of an aging person, showing them that someone cared, that Jesus loved them, that they were precious children of God and not some castaway because they were no longer useful to society.

For too many, life had become a hollow existence, just another stepping stone towards the end of their time on earth. Many had no one. Day in and day out, they sat waiting for death to claim them.

For many days, Father had had trouble sleeping, burdened with the desire to bring joy to those people, but knowing that he couldn't do it alone. He needed help. There were never enough volunteers…the needs were great and the shepherds were few. Whenever Father happened to meet relatives or children, he confirmed how wonderful it was that they had come and how much their parents or uncle or aunt appreciated it. He affirmed that they would be so blessed in heaven for coming, and encouraged them to come again and to tell others to come.

It seemed to help. The family would come the next Sunday and the following month, but after a month or two, the visits stopped, again, until the next major celebration: Christmas, Mother's Day, Father's Day, Thanksgiving and birthdays. It almost seemed that children or families needed to be reminded of their loved one in the care home. It wasn't that they didn't care necessarily, but that living, making a living, raising their children got in the way and with both parents working, they tended to want their weekends to themselves. If they weren't too tired to visit, they had other plans which would be more rewarding, bring them more happiness and more entertainment.

Seeing an elderly person was boring and uninteresting. Within two minutes, one had heard it all: "What did you have for lunch, today? Are they treating you well? How do you spend your days?" The answer was always the same: "Yes, the meals are good. Oh, some meat and potatoes," or…"I can't remember. Played cards, did a painting of a house. Oh, I threw it away." Very quickly the conversation would come to an uncomfortable end and everyone would sit in silence. "Well, I'd better go. I have to pick up the kids," or "I have an appointment." Any excuse to justify leaving as quickly or as soon as possible.

On Sunday, Henry attended Father Engelmann' Mass at the nursing home. The chapel was packed when he arrived and he was lucky to find a place to stand at the very back. Mrs. Lawson led the congregation in prayer for the needs of the world, for the needy, the sick, the hungry, the aged, all the families and the many challenges they faced. Then they said another decade of the rosary. Various people in the church lead by saying the first half of the prayer and then the congregation together would say the last half.

The response, involvement and participation of those present was almost deafening. The prayers were said with such fervour and meaning that the fifty or so in the chapel rivaled the 750-person congregation at St. Mary's.

Henry couldn't believe how involved everyone was, not half-heartedly, but with their entire being. Father Engelmann had given them something to live for, he gave them meaning. They were there to pray to their Lord and to pray for the needs of the world. In an incredibly short time, Father had helped them to rediscover the love in their hearts that had been buried by their mundane existence. In a sense they were reborn, living fully with purpose in the present moment, instead of despairing over the past or looking forward to a future that would only guarantee them death.

When mass started, jubilation began in earnest. Johnny wheeled his wheelchair over to the piano and banged out a lively tune, and like Jerry Lee Lewis, his fingers danced across the keys. Henry watched in awe as the awkward, out-of-time movements of their stiff, arthritic bodies and shuffling feet, suddenly wanted to dance. Adrenalin, long dormant, chugged through their constricted veins and arteries. It brought tears to Henry's eyes. A body may get old, but inside everyone wanted to live, and to enjoy and participate in life. To love and be loved. Everything else is really meaningless.

With everyone gathered, there was only a very narrow passageway for Father to walk from the back and make his way to the altar. They sang Lord of the Dance as he entered and by the time Father got to the front everyone was not only singing to the song but also clapping. It was heart moving to witness so many of the residents clapping and acknowledging their joy and participating in the mass. Unbidden tears surfaced as he gazed upon this incredible sight.

When the song ended, Father looked out at the sea of happy people and smiled.

"Good morning, my brothers and sisters in Christ."

"Good morning, Father," the congregation resounded.

"I see some new faces, here this morning. Welcome to our humble chapel. Thank you for coming. Today is the feast of St. Francis and do I have something to tell you about him, and also something that the Lord hasn't revealed to me, yet, but he will when it is time to speak…"

The singing and dancing and homily that followed was so touching and stirring, Henry left wanting to be a saint from that moment on.

After mass, the people streamed out, joy written all over their faces. They greeted one another and hugged. Some held hands as they walked down the hall, some stayed behind to talk to Father. Many approached Henry to introduce themselves and invite him to come again. It was almost as if they were there to visit with Henry, and to cheer him up, rather than the other way around. They had been provided an opportunity to serve again, and with that opportunity came the desire to live again.

Finally, Father and Henry were able to speak to one another.

"How about going to the café for breakfast?"

"That sounds wonderful, Henry. A bit of fresh air and breakfast in your fine café would be a very special treat."

As they passed the open bedroom doors, every resident bellowed a greeting to Father. It was as if the Pope himself were walking down the hallway. What a difference from that first day when he had brought Father to the care home.

"It didn't take long for them to fall in love with you, Father."

"Yes, and I love them also."

THE CAFÉ WAS busy with after-church customers. Like the chapel, the café was a gathering place for parishioners of the downtown area. They were like family, and as Father and Henry walked in, the customers greeted Henry in a similar fashion as Father's people in the care home greeted him.

As they sat down for breakfast, Father shared with Henry his concern about all the care and nursing homes in the city and about how he could possibly reach more of the families and get them to visit the aged in these homes. He shared his idea with Henry about starting a tour for not only the Catholic churches, but the other denominations as well. He wanted to talk to all the churches about the need to visit those in the care homes. He called his talk, "The Forgotten People."

"My only fear is that it will be short lived. It might encourage some to come out, but as I have found out, even when I encourage those who visit to come back, they do so for a visit or two and then stop coming again until the next special occasion. In between there is nothing, just empty time. They're forgotten."

"That's it, Father!" Henry blurted out. "It's all about marketing!"

Father looked at Henry and recognized the young bright business partner he hired to work in his grocery store. Memories flashed through his mind remembering Henry's excitement over a new idea to improve the business. The same excitement surged through him now. His eyes widened and brightened in anticipation.

"What is it, Henry? How do you mean? Surely not market the old folks? We're not for sale like some commodity."

"No, no, that's not what I mean, Father. What I am getting at is essentially the same as what you are proposing. You want to tour the churches and promote visitation amongst the people and how important it is not to forget them."

"Yes, yes," Father said, sitting on the edge of his chair.

Henry took a mouthful of scrambled eggs delaying his answer. He loved to see Father get excited.

"Go on, Henry. I'm an old man and I don't have time to waste. Tell me, what is in that clever business mind of yours?"

Henry smiled, "Well, Father, you said that people come to visit when you talk to them and encourage them to do so, right?"

"Yes, yes."

"And, you said it picks up again when the care home sends out an invitation to come for a free meal and celebrate Thanksgiving or whatever."

"Yes, yes."

"Well, Father, the answer is simple."

"Henry, please get it out."

Henry held back a chuckle. He so much enjoyed playing with Father and seeing the look in his twinkling, inquisitive eyes. Henry easily visualized how Father must have looked as an excited child waiting to hear a surprise.

"What we need to do is to send out a monthly newsletter, a constant reminder of the people in the care home. We need to get volunteers to write it, conduct interviews with the people there and get ideas from the people in the care homes as to what they would like to say. We need jokes and funny stories from the heart about the successes of the people. Have special sections in there in which residents remind their children of things they need, or their birthday, or their children's birthday. It would be exciting for the elderly to see their name in print.

"Folks need to hear about your chapel. We need to go to businesses who cater to seniors' needs to place ads in the newsletter to help pay for the cost of printing. This way, both the seniors and the young people know the needs of the aged, what gifts to buy on birthdays. We need to offer advice to young people on what to say when they visit, how to make a two-minute visit last for a meaningful half hour, we nee…"

"Hold on, Henry. Wait a minute. You are so blessed with ideas. This is wonderful. I am so excited to start, I can't sit on my chair, anymore. How do we begin all this, Henry?"

Father searched Henry's eyes for a clue.

"Well, Father, first we need to get volunteers and form a committee to do some leg work. We need an editor, printer, writers, journalists, researchers, interviewers and interviewees. It will take time, but it can be done. Perhaps when you start your tours, you could mention this idea and ask for volunteers. Someone in the congregation may have a printing business, and other business people may want to place ads in there relating to special beds and chairs, vitamins, new medications for different ailments, café certificates—"

"Yes, yes, that's it, exactly," Father blurted. "Now we're on track." Father beamed at Henry, "This is like the good ol' days. I just know my Anna is so happy to see this, too."

Father looked deeply into Henry's eyes, "I said it to you back then on at least two occasions, you are a good man with a good heart. The Lord has so richly blessed you and you haven't let Him down. You have been faithful and used all the talents he has given you and not squandered a one." Father reached across the table and patted Henry's hand.

"Thank you, Father."

AFTER BREAKFAST HENRY dropped Father back at the Nunnery Care Home. They both were silent for the longest time, each absorbed in their thoughts. Henry assumed that Father was mulling over what they had talked about in the café.

"So, tell me, Henry. Were you able to track down where Jenny lives?"

Henry was taken aback by his question and interest. He had meant to tell Father what he found out from Mr. Sarsky's secretary, but had forgotten. He hadn't shown Father Jenny's letter that he had discovered in his mother's treasure chest either.

"Well, it's funny you should ask, I was going to tell you about it over breakfast this morning, but then we began talking about your concern over care homes. It slipped my mind."

"I did get a hold of Mr. Sarsky's secretary. She did not know where Jenny lived now, but did inform me that she had married and at that time had one child, a son."

Henry waited for Father's reaction even though he knew what would be in his mind. When Father didn't respond Henry continued, "As soon as I heard that she was married, I immediately knew it was over and dropped the whole matter right then and there."

Before Henry could say any more, Father turned and patted him on the shoulder. "Yes, Henry, that is the best thing to do. It was so long ago, so many things change in our lives. It may not be the same anymore, at all. She may have even forgotten all about you."

"Well, what encouraged me to try was the letter I found in mom's treasure chest that I told you about. It was filled with love and revived so many memories. At least I found out that at the time, anyway, she still cared for me and hadn't abandoned me as I had thought."

Henry pulled out the letter from his jacket pocket. "I still carry it around with me. Read it and you will see. She still loves me."

Father reluctantly took the letter. "But, Henry, that was so long ago. People change."

"Maybe so, Father, but just read it."

Father unfolded the letter and read it. Henry remained silent, but glanced at Father trying to read his expression. At least twice, other drivers honked at Henry as he drifted into their lane just as he tried to drift into Father's thoughts.

"It is a very beautiful letter, Henry, filled with love and yearning just as yours were to Jenny. But for some reason, it was not meant to be. One reason is that you found Julean, a lovely girl whom you loved very much, and look at all the fine children you and Julean had and raised…"

"When Julean came into my life I loved her deeply and considered my relationship with Jenny over. And you're right, I had a very rich and wonderful marriage with Julean and together we raised four beautiful children. But after finding that letter and with Julean gone now and feeling lonely, well, I guess one never gets over their first love. It just seems that all those feelings I had, came back so strongly. I just had to try and find Jenny, or at least find out if there was the possibility that she was free and unattached."

"I know how you feel, Henry. When Anna passed away, I was so lonely for the longest time…and even, today, I still think on her and wish she were here to talk to. But this is another matter, now, we both know Jenny is married and as you have decided, it's best to leave it alone."

They fell into a long silence. Henry knew that Father was reflecting on the matter and that the discussion was not yet over. He sensed Father's uneasiness and waited patiently for him to express his concerns.

"Perhaps, Henry," Father added finally, "It may be a good idea not to carry the letter with you anymore. To keep entertaining something that has no future is not good. This could easily fill you with regret, ifs and buts, and might lead to future action which may cause problems. Put it back into Mary's treasure chest. She made the right decision at the time to do so and it may be wise for you to follow her example. Put it where it belongs, it is a treasure of the heart and it belongs in your treasure chest, now."

"Yes, I know you are right, but somehow I just can't let go of it. And look, Father…" Henry said excitedly, as he reached inside his shirt and pulled out a pewter angel hanging at the end of a chain around his neck. "Look at the angel Jenny sent me in this letter. It is identical to the one I sent to her only a few days before, that same Christmas in 1956!"

Father glanced cursorily at the angel. Henry could see Father's concern and tucked the angel back inside his shirt. He also took the letter from Father's extended hand and slipped it back into his pocket. "There is one other thing, Father…"

Father turned and gazed at Henry once more. The concerned look he had over the matter had still not left him. "And, what might that be, my son?"

"Remember when we packaged and shipped all the letters I had written to Jenny in care of Mr. Sarsky's office?"

"Yes, I recall it very well, Henry."

"When I spoke with Elaine, she told me she took the entire box down to the basement in the office building and burned them all in the incinerator. Mr. Sarsky had instructed her to do so. I couldn't believe my ears when she told me that, Father. How could he have done such an awful thing?"

Father shifted in his seat. Father's voice was soft now, tender and came from within his caring heart.

"Henry, I have told you this many times before and it is important for you to fully understand it now. All of us see things from our world, the reality we have created for ourselves. What seems so very wrong to us can be so very right in the eyes of someone else. We all make decisions based upon our own values, beliefs, conditioning, and experiences.

"Mr. and Mrs. Sarsky's past life up to that point in time was such that they decided it was for the best to stop communication between you and their daughter. It may not have been the decision that I would have made, but I had a different past than the Sarskys and so my reaction would have been different.

"Don't be controlled by another person's reality or blame them for it. It will rob you of joy and give even more power to what they have done over you. Don't you see, Henry, each moment can be a new beginning! We can choose to accept, forgive and let go and live fully and freely in our precious present moments. Don't crowd your life with yesterday's baggage or what might have been. Don't be controlled by others decisions. Live fully in the now and you will always have a wonderful past and an unbelievably good future."

Father was on a roll and wanted to make certain Henry didn't regress back to an unforgiving heart over all this. It was as if the Holy Spirit was constantly whispering thoughts of wisdom to him. His words hit home just like they did in his school of life behind the grocery store. Henry smiled. The sun streamed in through the open sunroof of the SUV, just like it did on them back then when they had sat on the weathered grey crates. How easily it was to succumb to old thoughts and ways of reacting, spending countless precious minutes, hours, and days trapped in feelings of resentment, self pity and anger and all for naught over another person's reality and beliefs over which he had no control.

And just as they pulled up to the care home, Father reminded Henry of the most important lesson of all, "This is why, Henry, it is so important to pray and meditate every morning. In the stillness and silence you will touch within you the kingdom of the Lord. He will reveal the thoughts and actions you need to address not only in the silence but in His word. The Bible has stood the test of time and we can trust every word. *Its message is clear: to forgive and be free of the past so you can love. That is the key to inner peace, to a happy life.*"

"You know, Father, last Sunday I took the dogs down to the creek and visited the Poustinia. It was such a beautiful day and as I sat on the deck I became overwhelmed by the calmness and beauty of nature. I can't remember when I was so deeply filled with peace."

"You tapped into the Creator of all things. The source of love, joy and beauty. Each morning, I try to fill myself with that peace, but I must admit it is when I spend three days in the Poustinia that my spirit is completely renewed. It is as you say, in the calm, stillness, and beauty of nature we come face to face with our Lord. We commune in the silence and the wonder of His creations.

"Perhaps, Henry, the Lord gave you a taste of what you will find if you take a retreat with Him." Father winked at Henry then got out of the car.

Henry watched as his teacher walked up the path to the care home and entered. Father was so filled with the peace of the Lord that an aura of light surrounded him. He had wanted to tell Father about the house he purchased, but decided to leave it for their meeting next Sunday. Talking about Jenny's letter had been enough for today.

FATHER THOUGHT ABOUT his conversation with Henry as he stood in front of the dresser in his bedroom. That entire experience of the letters and what occurred had not been the best for him. Perhaps he would offer tomorrow morning's mass up for Henry and ask the Lord to give him strength and wisdom to forgive and move on.

Absently, he removed the bulge of papers and notes he had collected over the past several weeks from his trouser pockets. Most of them were reminders of what he needed to do, who to see, who to talk to. As he sorted through the papers, he came across the name of the person who the care home director asked him to see during his visit to the hospital.

Ah, yes, tomorrow I will see her.

Lord, I pray that Your healing power and love wash over Marjorie Hamilton.

CHAPTER SIXTY-ONE

"HELLO, NURSE, COULD you please tell me what room Marjorie Hamilton is in?"

"Certainly, Father...I don't see her name as being registered here."

"I believe she is being treated for cancer. Maybe she has passed—"

"I will call up to oncology." After a few moments, the nurse addressed Father again. "She was here, but was transferred to the Santa Maria Care Home. I hope you didn't come all this way to see her."

"Well, I did come to see her, but there is also another patient I wanted to visit."

IT WAS ALMOST 5:00 p.m. when Father left the hospital. The cab was already waiting for him. They would be serving dinner soon, and he had hoped to work on his "The Forgotten" speech and talk to Father Knuka about his and Henry's idea for drawing attention to the plight of the elderly. He would have to visit the lady with cancer tomorrow.

THE NEXT DAY, Father reviewed his visitation schedule at the Santa Maria Home.

First on his list was Mr. Miller who had just returned from the Grey Nun's Hospital following removal of a tumour from his prostate gland.

An hour later, Father finished visiting with George and Edna on the fourth floor. Marjorie Hamilton was next on his list and, luckily, was next door to Edna. After uttering a brief prayer and taking a deep breath, he entered the room.

She was sleeping. He stepped closer debating if he should wake her. She looked thin and frail, her skin pallid yet she was still quite an attractive lady. Her bandana had slipped off and Father noticed that she was bald. She looked so peaceful and not in pain as so many of the cancer patients he visited were. As he was about to turn and leave, Jenny opened her eyes. She blinked several times.

"Who are you?" Jenny asked, her voice croaky and dry. She raised her head, "Oh, you're a priest! Are you here to give me the last rites!"

"No, no…I was about to leave. I didn't want to wake you. I usually come to the Santa Maria Home twice a week and visit as many patients as I can just to say hello and see if there is anything I can do for you."

Jenny smiled, "That is so nice of you, Father."

"So, how are you feeling, Mrs. Hamilton?"

"Oh, please call me, Jenny. Mrs. Hamilton sounds too formal and life is much too short for such distant greetings."

"Well, you can call me David if you wish."

"No, I like Father, it makes me feel more like I am in God's hands."

Father smiled, "Did you say, Jenny? I note on the list it's Marjorie." Father thought he better make certain.

"Yes, Marjorie is my first name and Jenny my second. It's just that I prefer my second name."

"I see. Well, then, we shall call you Jenny. It reminds me of a very special young girl I once knew a long time ago."

Jenny winked at Father. "Well, she mustn't have been special enough to keep you out of the priesthood."

"Oh, I didn't mean it in that sense," He was about to explain that the Jenny he was reminded of was Henry's sweetheart. "Oh, we'd better not get into that. Tell me, how are you doing?"

"Well, Father David, I really wish I could say 'great,' but the truth of the matter is that I am not doing so well. I've tried to fight this silly disease, but it just keeps coming back, and I get weaker all the time. But, thank God, I am still here and I try to make the best of each day."

Father didn't say anything, he just smiled.

"What parish are you from?"

"Oh, I don't belong to a parish, anymore. They kicked me out a few months ago and actually I live in a care home now. The Nunnery Care Home."

"Isn't that something, I was in there but only for a week. I was too sick and too much of a challenge for them."

"Well, Jenny, they are more equipped here to provide better care."

"Yes, I know, and the nurses are so nice. Actually I feel blessed to be here."

"Do you have any family?"

"Not in Regina. I do have a son in Ottawa. He was here for a visit a little while back with his wife and my grandson." When Jenny spoke of her grandson, she smiled and her blue eyes lit up and came to life.

There was such a familiarity about her. She reminded Father of someone, but he couldn't place her.

"It's unfortunate that they don't live closer. Do you have relatives, here?"

"No, just a lot of very good friends, they are always coming to visit me."

"That's good."

A nurse walked into the room carrying a tray full of small white paper cups.

"Hi, Jenny, it's time for your medication."

"Well, I best better be going, Jennifer. I am back this way, again, next week, is it okay if I drop in then for a few minutes?"

"Oh, that would be wonderful, Father. Perhaps sometime in the near future you will hear my confession, if you still do that."

"Yes, yes I do, Jenny, I would be happy to hear your confession, tell me when you are ready." Father smiled.

"You will never be the same after you hear what I have to tell you," Jenny quipped.

"No, Jenny, I'm certain there is nothing in that mind of yours that I have not heard before in my lifetime."

"Don't be too certain, now," Jenny said, again, with a wink.

Father smiled. She was gravely ill and yet she exuded such life. Father turned and left the room, carrying with him such a strange feeling that somehow he had met Jenny before, but when, and where?

Yes, she reminded him of the scripture he likes so much, Proverbs 13:15, *a happy heart makes a cheerful face!*

Chapter Sixty-Two

CAMILLA STARED AT the large cardboard box for over fifteen minutes. For almost a week she had stood at the door to the basement unable to go down. She knew her father's strong box was packed away in one of the cardboard boxes that the movers had delivered last year from Victoria when she and Jeremy cleared out her father's home after his death.

Finally, Camilla mustered up enough courage to at least go downstairs and look at the box. She took the day off from work so she would be alone while Jeremy was gone and Josh at day care. Slowly she made her way to the basement her heart beginning to race faster and faster.

Camilla felt certain the metal box contained the information she desperately wanted to know, yet she was so afraid of what she might find. Ever since she had married Jeremy, she'd always felt uncomfortable in his father's presence because of the way her father-in-law stared at her. She reminded him of someone he once knew and later learned that it was his girlfriend named Jennifer.

She had gone over this so many times in her mind and with Jeremy. And with her growing feeling that she was adopted, the matter became more complicated and serious. The facts seemed to support her concern. She recalled Grandma Pederson saying Jenny left for Ottawa in 1956, two weeks after school started and never heard from again. If Jenny was pregnant she would have given birth in the spring of 1957 the exact year and time of year she was born.

It was clear to Camilla as well that Henry still cares for Jenny. He just has that look in his eyes. It must have been quite the summer romance. It seemed very probable to Camilla that Jennifer carried Henry's child which could possibly be her!

If that were the case…Jeremy would be her half brother…! The very thought sent chills up and down Camilla's spine. It could be devastating to have such close family ties. The blood relationship could have severe consequences on their children. She wondered how this might even affect Joshua!

The only consolation in this scenario was Peter. The moment she saw him she felt an eerie feeling that she knew him or was related to him in some way. She saw her features in him; his eyes, and although his hair colour was not blonde, his skin colour was still very similar, as was the shape of this mouth and how his lips turned up when he smiled. She couldn't stop staring at him and burning his image into her mind.

Could he somehow be related to her? Could he be her father? Camilla now dared to ask herself. At least if he were, it would be better than having her husband's father be the one!

Her biggest fear was that the metal box would identify Henry as the father. *She would sooner not know, than to know that really was the case.* "Camilla, you are being so silly! This is all conjecture! You may be torturing yourself over nothing! You just have to get to the bottom of all this. It could all just prove to be a figment of your imagination!"

Camilla inched her way to the cardboard boxes that had the contents marked on the outside. There were five boxes in the basement and this one contained the metal box.

Camilla whispered a prayer to her guardian angel to protect her, to guide her and to help her.

Camilla cut the string and the flaps opened slightly. She opened them all the way and at the very top in the far corner of the box was her father's metal strong box. She lifted it out and carried it upstairs.

Once again, Camilla agonized over whether she should open it or not. She sat down at the kitchen table and just stared and prayed that whatever she would find would not include her father-in-law.

She checked the kitchen clock. It was almost three thirty and Jeremy would be home in a couple of hours along with Joshua. If she was going to look, she would have to do it now.

Camilla stood next to the table and opened the box. One by one she took everything out and laid it on the table. The first item she grasped looked like some kind of certificate. It was hers…

Camilla Sarsky
Born May 24, 1957

This was almost the same as the one she had except for the last name. On hers it was Breckhart.

Camilla let out a sigh. She fully expected that she was adopted and rather than being upset by this revelation, she felt relieved to finally know the truth.

And how could she be angry or upset?

She had been so loved and brought up with such caring parents. And perhaps, what was helping her to be so understanding was that she had met so many girls in her counseling work who were also adopted and found out either this way or by someone telling them.

Camilla was also aware of the general practice at the time to keep everything in such secrecy. Parents were almost advised to keep things private unless the child asked and even then, was it wise to tell the child? Fortunately, thinking on that matter had changed so much.

One thing was clear; she was adopted. The name Camilla Sarsky and date confirm that this was her birth certificate.

So far so good, Camilla thought as she dared to venture on until a disturbing thought came to mind. She wondered if Henry's girlfriend's last name was *Sarsky*? She and Jeremy had forgotten to ask Grandma Pederson that, that day. At the time, all they wanted to know was if Henry's girlfriend name was Marjorie and Mary informed them it was Jennifer and at times Henry called her Jenny. They should have asked what Jenny's last name was.

How would she find out?

She could ask Henry but then, depending on what she discovered still in the box, it might not be necessary. Perhaps she would still be able to learn what her mother's first name was…

The next item was a letter which would send Camilla into a swirling spiral of confusion.

Camilla began to read a letter addressed to her adoptive parents from the Social Welfare department explaining that the adoption was based upon two conditions. If the child was a girl she would have to be named Camilla, if a boy it would be Henry…HENRY! The name exploded in her mind…she just had to know the mother's first name!

Camilla quickly scanned the letter she was holding. It didn't reveal the mothers name, but the next one did…!

It was a form that the mother had signed relinquishing her child for adoption…

Marjorie Jennifer Sarsky.

Tears filled Camilla's eyes as her mind blitzed through the possibilities; Marjorie was the name her father had written on the slip of paper just before he died and Jennifer was the name that Grandma Pederson said was Henry's girlfriend.

Did Marjorie Jennifer marry someone named Hamilton? That would explain the name change and was Henry's girlfriend's last name,

Sarsky? If so, why didn't he call her Marjorie or…did he prefer to call her by her second name?

And to make it a condition that if it was a boy to name the child *'Henry'* would seem to indicate that Marjorie wanted to honour the father…Oh, my…

Panic began to zip up and down Camilla's spine.

Everything seemed to indicate that her worst fears had come true. But Camilla knew this was too important a matter to leave any doubts. She just had to know first and foremost the last name of Henry's girlfriend. She could ask her father-in-law directly but was afraid to in case Henry was the father…and then what!?

Camilla didn't dare want to think of the consequences at this point.

It would all be so devastating! How could she possibly tell Jeremy that he might be her half brother!

Oh my God this is so incredibly…terrible!

Anxiety mixed with fear, and dread swept through Camilla. She looked at the clock. It was after five and her son and husband would soon be home.

She had to get a hold of herself.

She started to put the items back in the box and another thought came to her that promised some solace.

Yes, there was one other possibility…*Peter!*

Where did Peter fit into all this? Why did she feel he might be her father? *It felt so right.* He looked like her in so many subtle ways. And why does she dream of him in the same scene as the one with the angel holding the baby flying to the lady in the gazebo surrounded by wildflowers?

Oh please let him be the father! The mere thought of Henry being her birth father sent her into a spiraling vortex. The bright, sun-filled kitchen began to dim…

She checked the clock. Jeremy would be home in minutes.

Camilla quickly replaced the remaining items in the strong box, closed it and took it into Joshua's room. She hid it on the top shelf in the closet and put a teddy bear in front of it.

Just as she returned to the kitchen Jeremy and Joshua came in the front door. Camilla could barely greet either of them; she was in such a state of confusion with so much anxiety and panic filling her spirit. She went to kiss Jeremy trying desperately to keep her emotions in check and looked into his eyes. The thought that he was her brother sent her into a fit of tears. She looked down at Joshua and the close possible blood lines…she gazed back at her alarmed husband and whispered, "Oh, Jeremiah!" before turning to run off to their room.

Jeremy looked on in shock.

Joshua looked up at his dad and asked, "What's wrong with Mommy, Daddy?"

Chapter Sixty-Three

IT WAS SUNDAY morning and Father Engelmann was about to give the speech he had prepared for all week. It was like old times to see Father Engelmann and Father Knuka officiate the mass together and it was obvious that both celebrants as well as the parishioners enjoyed seeing them together again.

After Father Knuka read the gospel he informed the congregation how happy he was to have Father Engelmann back as a guest speaker to talk about the needs of care homes. And without any further ado, he went to his seat as Father Engelmann made his way to the pulpit.

Henry always loved to watch Father get ready to deliver his sermon. His unhurried manner seemed to create a positive tension; people usually sat up and became alert. It was as if Father was addressing each one individually; sensing and almost feeling the breath of those present, establishing a special rapport or bond between them. This affinity permeated the air. The presentation was very close and dear to Father's heart, Henry just knew it would be a godly talk.

"My dear brothers and sisters in Christ, the topic this morning, is something I call 'The Forgotten People.' In some cases, they could almost be referred to as 'The Castaways.' Who are these people and how and why does this concern you and me?

"Over the years, I have seen many of my parishioners grow old along with me and many of them reach a point where they are ready to move into a care home, either because of sickness, or because they simply don't want to live alone any longer. Sometimes, it's because they don't want to live alone, but sometimes it's because they can no longer look after their homes or themselves any more. In either case, this becomes a concern not only for themselves, but for their children, relatives, families and in many cases society in general as well.

"It is good to be reminded that we are indeed brothers and sisters in Christ. That we are our brother's keeper, and that we do have a responsibility to visit the shut-ins and the sickly and the aged. It's very easy to give money, to pay for the keep of our parents and to let some care home look after them, but to give of our time, to visit or to volunteer, or help out, and the need we all have to serve in this way, is the topic for today's discussion.

"Perhaps some of the biggest concerns or problems the aged feel when they go into these homes, is that they are no longer needed or have any purpose. They feel old and begin to believe that they have been let out to pasture, where they will graze for awhile and then die. A major symptom that I see in their eyes is loneliness...mainly because the visits from their families are less and less. No one has time, and soon, they become forgotten, perhaps not completely, but for all too many there is no one, and they are truly, completely forgotten.

"There is great sorrow and sadness to walk down the hallways and see many aged staring off into space or sleeping hour after hour. Yes, there are activities and things provided to do, but there is nothing that can replace the human touch, concern and love by coming to visit, developing a relationship and giving of yourself to our seniors.

"The purpose of this talk is not to instill guilt, but to make us all aware and to understand the need that is there and to commit to fill it. Hopefully not out of guilt or a sense of duty, but because of our love, and appreciation of the aged and for what they have done. For all the years while we were growing up, they tended to our cares and needs. And now hopefully we can reciprocate because we realize that it's now our turn to understand them, their needs, their feelings, and to care for them in any way we can in the twilight of their years.

"They know their time is running out, whereas we have lots of time, we're young and these thoughts don't enter our mind, but someday all too soon, we will be where they are, feeling what they feel, thinking about the end, that it is near...they are lonely, all alone, some afraid...forgotten, cast away.

"It is very important to be role models for others and for our children. To show them our responsibility and theirs too. To show our commitment to love and appreciate our parents or relatives or the aged. Our children should see by our actions, not just words that we care and have a responsibility. Someday soon, when our turn comes around, our children will remember what we have done and hopefully come to visit us as well. Remember, we always reap what we sow. Plant the seed now, today. What goes around, comes around...don't be one of the 'forgotten ones.'

"When we were young, who was always there for us? Protecting us, consoling us, buying our clothes, caring for us until we were old enough? And even then, did it stop? No, we still had wants, needs and fears. And once again in our teenage years and even beyond when we may have had troubles with marriage, or boyfriends, or school or our job, who was there ready to support and bail us out? Now it's our turn and unfortunately where are so many of us now? Too busy, no time? Many times, they had no time as well, but they made time, they didn't abandon us. No, they made us their priority. Are we making them our priority now?"

Father hesitated, he looked across the sea of faces before him with a penetrating gaze, allowing the parishioners to look deep within themselves and to answer the question he just posed. And then he went on...

"The aged have lived a full life. They have been around the track over and over again and they have learned a thing or two from life, from their failures and their successes. We don't have to invent the wheel over and over again. We can learn from their wisdom and their mistakes. They are not too senile. A mother is always there to give chicken soup from the heart, and a father, his wisdom and know-how, too. The aged are a huge resource of knowledge and understanding. Never forget that or take it for granted or discount it. They have time to listen, to give, to be there for us and it will always come from the heart.

"All too often I witness nurses, caregivers, or children talk condescendingly towards their elderly parents as if they knew better or knew what was good for them. For many seniors they have lived through more, seen more, forgotten more than the young will ever know. Always respect your elders and their wisdom. Just like you wanted to be treated as an equal as you grew up, so, too do seniors in their declining years want to be treated that way and to feel that they are needed.

"Can you imagine how good it makes one feel to be needed or that they can help? Isn't that better than to feel you are no longer useful to anyone, no longer needed, that you can't help anymore, that you're too old, getting senile, 'out of the loop' as they say?

"My dear brothers and sisters visit the aged, share with them, talk about your real concerns, not just surface talk, but real talk, as if you were talking to a friend. You may be pleasantly surprised by the sincere response and care you will receive, the wisdom you may learn. And most of all, the deep friendship you will establish. Some of the best friends I have made are in the care home. They have helped me immeasurably, and you just may find that you will look forward to your visits with them more than they do.

"So my friends, whether or not you have parents or relatives in a care home, or living alone in their own home, this applies to all of you and your children. Parents love to see their grandchildren and are so proud of them. They love to see a friendly face come into their room or their home week after week. They love to know that they are still remembered and cared for. And when we think about it, isn't that what all of us want…to be loved? So, don't forget the aged. The benefits will be immeasurable. You will be richly blessed. In them you will find a trusted friend, a counselor, a grandfather or grandmother you never had but wished you had. You will also find wisdom, understanding and love."

And then Father went on to explain about the idea for the monthly newsletter, and the need for volunteers and businesses to come forward who could help. He pointed out the need for such a newsletter, to continually keep in the fore the aged, the sick and the needy, that they not be forgotten. Such a newsletter would give families and volunteers ideas about how to make their visits fruitful and meaningful. What to talk about, games to play, books to read to them, how to offer to get supplies for them, and how to involve them in outings and family life.

Father finished by blessing all the people and asking once again for volunteers. That they search their hearts for the Lord's calling to help out in this worthy cause and if not, that they would set aside some time to visit.

 Henry remained on the sidelines in the aftermath of Father Engelmann' speech to the parishioners at St. Mary's, for forty-five minutes, Father was showered with praise and glory for his work with the elderly, and bombarded with questions from those who wanted to volunteer. Eventually the crowd dispersed and Henry took Father to the café for breakfast.

Once they'd placed their breakfast orders, Henry asked Father how it felt being such a hero and so admired.

"Oh, Henry, it's not for me, but for God's glory."

"That must be so hard to do, Father. I'm sure you receive compliments and praise every day. How do you keep it from swelling your ego?"

"You mean, keep it from going to my head?" Father smiled. "It is a difficult thing to deal with and one of the paradoxes of human life. Our purpose is to love and serve our Lord and others, and yet by nature we are self-centred. We so much want praise and glory, to be recognized, to meet our needs and act always in our best interests. If our Lord had not given us a free will, it would have been so much easier. He could have made us to love and serve, but then we would be like robots. No, God made us free to choose and to serve him and others, and we must choose to do so. We must daily die to ourselves and our needy flesh."

"Do you mean it is never over? Surely you have won the battle. You're the most humble man I know."

"Ssh, Henry. No man is free from sin except our Lord. It is over when we take our dying breath. Our ego can never be defeated try as we might to bridle or bury it. Some days we are a flower revealing God's glory, but in the shadows of the petals a weed is always lurking to steal some of the sunshine for itself.

"Each night I try to rid myself of praise or accolades, but in the stillness of the night when the mind is quiet and asleep, it is the heart which is closer to God than our mind that speaks and reveals our sin. Just when we think we are there and have won the battle, a truth pierces the darkness and we realize that the sin of pride has its roots even in excessive attempts to be humble."

"Then you are damned if you do and damned if you don't," Henry blurted out seeing the folly of it all.

"It is good for you to see that I am not perfect. There is a little of the Pharisees in all of us. We may think we are holy and pure and free of sin, yet all the while we walk in the dirt of this earth. Pride, is the curse of our first parents. As I have said over and over, Henry, we must daily acknowledge our sinful and weak nature and become completely dependent upon Him. Only when we are aware of how far we fall short can we truly seek his strength and become an instrument of his peace. It is the only way."

Henry fell into a deep silence, not knowing what to say. Even Father's admission of being a sinner was so admirable and lovable. Father could so easily hide behind his good works and sit in judgment of the pitiless creatures around him who fell time and again, and yet in his weakness he gave hope. It suddenly occurred to Henry just how total honesty of oneself could bring greater comfort to others, than just revealing the saintly side.

Father continued as if reading Henry's mind. "It's important not to complicate this, Henry, and give up. We are human and we are far from perfect, but we are all children of God and He loves us despite our failings." Then, bringing his hands together and cupping them as if holding a heart he added, "Harden not your heart. Keep it soft, pliable so the Lord can keep working on us. The sooner we realize that we need

His strength and place Him in the driver's seat we go into a direction that will fill us with peace. His vision is crystal clear; when we drive, the windshields are always murky and we weave off the path, get stuck and many times—"

"Yeah, I know…fall into the ditch."

An expression of joy promenaded over his face. "Oh, Henry, you know me too well." Father chuckled and then added, "Everything I have, including my very existence, is from the Lord. My purpose while on this earth is to use these gifts to serve, love and honour Him. Whenever I receive praise, I always repeat to myself, 'not for me, Oh Lord, not for me, but glory to your name.' And even the pride that is in that statement I offer to Him. St. Francis' prayer of peace recognizes the path the Lord wants to lead us on."

"Yes, it's such a beautiful prayer and, you're right, it is a perfect guide. Where there is hatred, despair, darkness, doubt we should bring peace, faith, light and hope—"

"Yes, yes, with the strength of the Lord within us we can do that. We can seek to console and understand rather than be consoled or understood. For it is in giving that we receive—"

"It is in pardoning that we are pardoned—" Henry chimed in and then almost in unison they said, "And in dying that we are born to eternal life." They stared at one another and laughed.

After reveling in that delightful moment for a time, Father said, "I say that prayer at least four times a day and sometimes more. I can never be reminded enough of my purpose. At the risk of sounding like a broken record, the key to all this—"

"…is starting one's day in the right frame of mind," Henry concluded. "Meditate, be still and hear Him speak, read the Bible, fill my mind with His words, His energy, His strength and then I will be focused and ready for the day and prepared to carry out St. Francis's guideline to peace."

Father shook his head and beamed as if struck by the sun, "There is nothing left to teach you! You have learned the art of living in two worlds at the same time; the world without and the world within—"

"Yeah, only all too often I allow the world without to overshadow the world within."

"Yes, it's a delicate balance to live in two worlds at the same time. But if you faithfully start out the day, as you say, by filling up on God's peace and staying connected to it, this peace shines and flows into the world. In this way we can bring hope and love into a world that needs healing, and fulfill God's commandment to love and serve Him and others. We become His co-workers to make the world as he intended."

Henry noticed tears well up in his mentor's eyes. His followed closely behind.

"How did we get into such a lofty philosophical discussion?" Henry said with a chuckle.

"It's good to discuss what is really important in life, and what we said isn't so lofty, carrying out the holy saint's prayer is very close to the ground. Is not showing kindness rather than anger or indifference more profitable for the heart and soul? Spreading joy more uplifting than gloom and sadness? "

"Isn't it funny, Father, what we are discussing is so true and I am fully aware of it and what I should be doing and yet, I still seek recognition, approval of others, the desire to make more money, accumulate more."

After a moment of silence and holy reflection Father said, "It sometimes seems like we are going around in a circle. But, as I said, this is a lifelong process, and the fact that you recognize your weaknesses and acknowledge them means you can then turn them over to the Lord.

"Henry, you are a child of God first and foremost. Each time we fall we stumble forward, sometimes a lot and sometimes a little. But each time we inch closer to who we are. Someday Henry you will be in complete harmony with who you are. Eventually, you will walk in ways that reflect completely your inheritance. Pray that day comes sooner rather than later. Through prayer, and releasing your will to Him, the Lord will guide and strengthen you, and gradually your days will be filled with more and more peace."

Father paused and then as if he received more words from heaven, he went on. "Our worth, our importance, our happiness we sadly believe, is equal to what we own. Our possessions, our rank in society, our belief that this will give us freedom and happiness is all an illusion one, unfortunately, that is so ingrained in us, that most of us go through our entire lives never realizing it. We live an illusionary life until we fully realize just what we have been talking about, that true happiness, joy, inner peace does not come from without, but from the wellspring of our Lord that is within all of us. We foster and nurture this interconnectedness through our thoughts, words, and deeds. Just like St. Francis instructs, this is what is really real. Put Him first, stay connected to His peace and all else will fall into place and assume its proper perspective and importance in life."

Father gazed at Henry intently as if trying to read his thoughts. Henry did not seem as attentive as before. A smile formed on Henry's face, tainted with a tinge of embarrassment, almost apologetic. Father leaned closer and studied him even closer now.

"Well, Father, after listening to your reproof about the accumulation of wealth and possessions, I feel guilty about telling you that I purchased another house."

Father raised his eyebrows, concern gathered in the corners of his eyes as he threw a cutting glance at his faltering protégé and after a deliberative moment he said with a voice that betrayed his agitation.

"My, my, Henry, you have more than enough and looking after your business is so demanding of you. *For what purpose?*"

It seemed like the entire previous discussion hit a brick wall. Father looked perturbed and not at all happy. Perhaps the only good thing behind this revelation was that it was a perfect example of what he had just chided Henry about.

"Really, Father, my motive for this house is entirely different than my other purchases."

"But, how can they be different?" Father lamented, his voice rising slightly, carrying a scolding tone.

"No, Father, I am serious. I never planned to buy any more properties. It was really intended for Jeremy. But he wasn't interested and in the end, I decided to buy it; I couldn't resist. It was the strangest purchase I ever made.

"The lady that owned it suddenly became ill and went into the hospital and apparently never got out. She was forced to sell her home just as it was the day she walked out and went into the hospital. What is so strange about this, Father," Henry said excitedly, "the purchase of the house included everything in it, lock stock and barrel. And what is even more bizarre, is that all the antique furniture, her taste in colour, the layout of the home is so appealing to me, it was almost as if I walked into my own home. As soon as I entered that house, Father, I felt at perfect peace, just as I used to when I walked into Mom's home when she was alive!"

Father gazed at Henry with one of his unreadable expressions, trying to stay neutral, non-judgmental and as non-interfering as possible.

"And, you should see the antiques, Father. Every piece is incredibly rare, an unbelievable purchase."

Father nodded.

"I know what you are thinking, Father, and in a way I can't disagree, but to me, I didn't just buy more things, but something which seems to touch the very core of my being. Everything about the house exudes such peace and aesthetic pleasure for me, it's almost spiritual, Father. In a sense it seems to give me a respite from my business, a little getaway from it all. I know I would never want to renovate this house. I plan to leave it just as it is."

Father raised his shoulders, took in an almost imperceptible deep breath and slowly let it out as his shoulders gently settled back.

It was his way of accepting the moment.

He had said his piece and now it was up to Henry to be free within his decision. As resistance to all of Henry's rationalizations faded, Father's concern turned into a peaceful benevolent smile.

"It's hard to explain, Father, and even harder to understand that somehow the old lady who owned this house and I have some kind of connection beyond the coincidence of the furniture, similar taste and on and on. It's almost like she is some kind of kindred spirit, a once-in-a-lifetime happening where a person, a complete stranger almost seems to be one's other self! It's like…an angelic occurrence!"

Father leaned forward and in a voice that was calm and accepting said, "Henry I've always prayed for your success, not as the kind the world gives, but in achieving happiness and peace of mind. Perhaps, there is more to this purchase. Let us wait and see if it's part of God's plan for you."

Father's comment seemed to support the strange wonderful feeling he had. Maybe this purchase had some divine intervention.

"Well, enough of this, Father, I thought your talk at church this morning was very effective. I'm certain you will get a lot of volunteers. If you need my help in getting it all organized and started I will be very willing to give you a hand."

"Yes, thank you, Henry. I know I will need your help, just judging from the people that approached me after mass and offered their services, too. Perhaps the first thing we need to do is start up a committee and appoint a chairperson who will then appoint someone to screen all the volunteers and assign them to different positions that they are skilled for."

"Yeah, that will be a big job, but not an insurmountable one," Henry said. "Getting key persons in place from the start will be very important to getting the project started off on the right foot."

"Well, I know the Lord will lead us every step of the way. I am speaking at the Blessed Sacrament Church next Sunday, and Holy Cross the following Sunday and after that—"

"You sure don't waste any time."

"I have no time to waste, and the needs of people are so great. Every time I visit one of the care homes, I come in contact with another who needs support and love. Just last week, I visited a lady Doris suggested to me. The lady has terminal cancer, the poor dear, but she exudes such life even though she is so sick and interestingly, Henry, her name is Jenny."

Henry raised his eyes just at the mention of the name.

"Well anyway, Henry, the needs are so great, so many people to serve and attend to."

"Yes, Father, there are so many needs, so much suffering out there; I often wonder why the Lord allows it all."

"Now, Henry, it seems to me that we have discussed that somewhat and it's getting too late to get into that again. I'd better be getting back to the care home; I need to have a nap before I visit a few people this afternoon."

Henry shook his head, in disbelief. Where did Father get the energy and drive from?

From the Lord, who else?

IN THE WEEKS which followed, Father toured all of the Catholic churches as well as other denominations. He was invited to the United Church, the Synagogue, and several Baptist churches. Within a month he had more volunteers than he knew what to do with. Henry helped establish a committee and in no time at all a small, but effective, publishing company was up and running. Unbelievably, on the fifth week, the first newsletter was printed and sent out to all the families and relatives on file at most of the care homes in the entire city. The results were immediate. Owners and directors of the various care homes had never seen such overwhelming attendance to their care homes in the week which followed.

"Now we just have to keep this sort of response up. This will be our challenge in the weeks and months ahead," said Father encouragingly to all the volunteers.

The newsletter was light in spirit; full of fun, filled with coupons, jokes and funny and interesting anecdotes. The titles were so off the edge that one felt compelled to read it. For example, 'Henry of Henry's Café is giving away free food to seniors…Is he losing his mind?' Or,

'Why is John Burton at Mackenzie Jewelers serving customers in his gold shorts?' Or, 'Mrs. Schmidt has a real surprise for her son, Ron. He'll never forget her birthday again!'

And as Father had suggested in his talks, the newsletter contained special sections like, Tips from My Home to Yours, Chicken Soup From Grandma and Grandpa, Advice and Wisdom from the Heart. In a way it was like an Ann Landers section in which problems could be stated and then advice was given, tapping in on experienced advice and know-how. Ideas as to what to discuss and what to do when visiting. How to relate to people who cannot read, or are bedridden, what games to play with them and on and on.

It was amazing to see the transformation in many of the seniors and in morale as a whole which improved so quickly and significantly. The care home directors and members of the newsletter began to realize what Father had seen all the time. The residents needed something to look forward to and to have purpose, the sense that they were still useful and contributing members of society.

All residents were asked to participate in the newsletters by submitting stories and anecdotes. A buddy system was set up where a healthier, more able resident would become friend and assistant to one less able and help them along. The newsletter encouraged families not to forget to include their parents or aunts and uncles in care homes on outings to movies, theatre, or family dinners, or just even an evening out to visit. Residents were then encouraged to share their outing or experience. Awareness was definitely a key to making it all work, but a constant reminder like the newsletter to keep it all in the fore was absolutely essential to keep everything well-oiled and primed.

CHAPTER SIXTY-FOUR

JEREMY SEARCHED HIGH and low for Stan's strong box. He knew that Camilla must have found something in there that upset her immensely. The last few weeks had been terrible. It seemed like their marriage was falling apart. Pleas to discuss it, buying her flowers, offering to go out, nothing seemed to appease what was troubling her so deeply. If only he could find the metal box. Hopefully whatever she found was still there.

He had just gone through the basement again, and had searched every nook and cranny. The box seemed to have vanished. If only she would talk to him about it. But every time he tried, she'd break down and cry.

The only consolation was that lately Camilla had seemed to be settling down to being her old self. But Jeremy knew it was only an act to make him feel better. He knew his dear wife too well. It was more superficial that real. He could feel it all just simmering beneath the surface, ready to blow at any time.

Jeremy suspected it was something to do with his father, but the thought that he was somehow involved, seemed not only remote but preposterous. He went over and over the conversation he'd had with his dad and there was nothing that tied him to his wife, through his teenage girlfriend, whatsoever. Dad did suggest that Camilla see someone in Social Services. But it was Jeremy who decided to speak to someone there. Perhaps they not only could help to clear this all up, but they could also offer him some advice and help as to how best deal with Camilla himself.

Ironically, Camilla had already thought of the same thing, and had been in to Social Services just two days before. Irene Gilmer, a counselor with Social Services however, thought it best not to reveal to Jeremy, the confidentiality of his wife's visit. Ms Gilmore suggested to Jeremy the same advice and information as she had to his wife.

"It's important for your wife to know all the facts surrounding her birth and her parents, and to know for certain that she was adopted.

For her to be able to work through all of this she needs all of the information, and then and only then can the process begin to work through. This may involve searching for her birth parents…if in fact she was adopted, Ms. Gilmore hastily added. Although she already knew from Camilla that she was indeed adopted, she thought that the revelation should come from Camilla rather than from her.

"What I can do Mr. Pederson is give you the phone number to Mrs. Blake in Ottawa. She works in the department of Social Services and deals with adoptions issues. I would suggest that you give the number to your wife to call. The sooner this issue is dealt with the better.

"Yeah, it's starting to creep into our marriage, big time. Camilla is so troubled by this and frankly, so am I."

"That's very understandable. Like I said, the sooner your wife knows all the facts the better and then the healing and accepting part of this matter can begin for all concerned.

CAMILLA READ AND re-read all the information that was in her father's strong box. Unfortunately there was nothing in there that revealed who the father was for certain. There was no mention of the name "Peter," only the mention of the name "Henry" in the conditions section. If it was a boy it must be named, Henry.

At this point there was still hope that Marjorie or Jennifer, her mother, simply wanted to have the child named in memory of Henry and the love they had shared that summer, and it was nothing more than that. It was possible she had an affair with some other boy in Regina before she left, but according to Grandma Pederson, Jenny and Henry had been inseparable, which made the likelihood of another boy very remote. Plus, the way Henry still looked at her, told Camilla that theirs had been a very serious relationship indeed.

So, the only other possibility, reasoned Camilla, was that her mother had met another boy in Ottawa very soon after arriving there, and had sex with him. It would have had to happen sometime in September as she was born on the 24 of May.

But it seemed, from what little she knew, that it was highly unlikely that Jenny would do that. The scenario with Henry would make more sense. A summer romance and an ensuing love affair.

She got the phone number and the lady's name to call in Ottawa from her friend Irene Gilmer, and bless his dear heart, so did Jeremy. He went to see Irene a few days after she did. He was so concerned. He just wanted to help.

"I feel so badly to put him through all this," Camilla lamented.

Camilla, like Irene, knew that it was best to get all the information out as soon as possible and deal with whatever they find out in an open and honest manner. Camilla was going to call Mrs. Blake but what could she possibly tell her beyond the information she already had? Maybe they would have the name of the father, but more than likely the father's name would be confidential and not disclosed to the adoptive parents.

However, there was still one person to whom she could go to in confidence first before following up with the agency in Ottawa...Father Engelmann. He had been with the Pederson family right from the start. I don't think there is anything that Father doesn't know about Henry, thought Camilla. Surely, Father would know the name of Henry's teenage sweetheart.

"Hello, Father, this is Camilla, I was wondering if you had some time to see me this afternoon. I can get away from work at three thirty. It will only take ten or fifteen minutes of your time?

"Yes, of course, Camilla. I am visiting a few people at the Santa Maria this afternoon but I can be back at the care home by that time."

"Thank you so much, Father. I will see you then."

"Hi Father, I hope I'm not interrupting your busy schedule."

"Not at all. Please, come in, let us go into the sun room, no one is in there right now. I love the warmth the room has at this time of day."

"I love the sun, too, Father."

Camilla followed Father and then sat down at two comfortable arm chairs beside one another.

"So, Camilla, you are a busy mother and still have time to help out counseling troubled girls."

"Yes, the pregnancy rate is increasing and so too are the problems it brings. Many keep the child they are carrying but many struggle with the decision to give up their baby for adoption and others choose abortion."

Father shook his head and said sorrowfully, "Ah, yes, for a young girl or a lady of any age to be faced with the decision to end the life of the infant they are carrying is a very deplorable situation to be in."

There was a long silence before Camilla spoke, "Yes, Father it is so sad..."

Camilla shook her head and wanted to continue that discussion but thought she better get to the reason for her wanting to see Father.

"Father, I am here on a confidential nature…" Camilla studied Father, and he nodded,

"Of course, Camilla, please go on."

"This may seem like an odd question to ask, but do you recall the name of the young girl that Jeremy's dad, or rather Henry, my father-in-law went out with way back when he was fifteen years old?"

The furrows in Father's brow deepened. He studied the young lady next to him and wondered where this was leading.

"Yes, her name was Jenny…"

Camilla sat on the edge of her seat waiting…

"And her last name was…?"

Father continued to study Camilla. He knew Jenny's last name, how could he forget? How hard he and Henry tried to get Mr. Sarsky to give Henry's letters to his daughter. Why would Camilla want to know the name of Henry's girlfriend all those years ago?

"Yes, her name was Jenny Sarsky."

No sooner had the words left Father's lips than an arrow pierced her heart.

Henry was her father!

"Camilla, what is wrong?" Father leaned forward and took hold of her hand. "You look so troubled…what meaning does the name hold for you?"

Oh, what could Father do other than be totally upset if I told him that Henry was my father and that Jeremy was my half brother, thought Camilla? There wasn't anything Father, or anyone could do for that matter. What was done was done…but, but what about Peter? Why does his name keep coming up."

Tears were in Camilla's eyes as she asked the next question, "Does Henry have a friend named, Peter?"

Father imperceptibly shook his head, where on earth is this going? The only Peter he knows is Eddy's friend who was also one of the boys that took Jenny to the park that night. It was never established what really happened. Surely he could not relate such unsubstantiated information to Camilla.

"Yes, Camilla, the only Peter I know is the one who came to my anniversary. He was Eddy's best man and as I understand it Henry did meet him as well and so I suppose in that sense, Peter is Henry's friend. Why do you ask, Camilla"

Camilla was finding it harder and harder to sit still. The thought that Henry was her father had her so anxiety filled, she had to leave. Perhaps she should speak to Irene Gilmer again, or even better call the agency in Ottawa. Maybe, just maybe, either could help her to make some sense of all this.

There was only one further question she wanted to ask of Father, "You said Henry's girlfriend's name was Jenny Sarsky. Could it have been Marjorie Jennifer Sarsky?"

Father tightened his lips wishing he knew what was troubling Camilla so deeply, "No Camilla, I never heard of the name Marjorie connected to Jenny Sarsky in any way. As far as I know the young girl's name was always Jenny or Jennifer Sarsky." The only Marjorie he had heard of lately was the lady he was visiting in the Santa Maria Home, *Marjorie Hamilton.*

Camilla rose and extended her hand, "Thank you so much Father for your time, I really must get home and prepare dinner for my boys."

Father knew something very powerful was in Camilla's heart. He wished she would share it with him. "You're welcome, Camilla. Please come at any time, everything we discuss is between us and I am here to help."

"Thank you so much again…and it's okay, I can find my own way out."

With that, Camilla rushed off leaving Father standing there scratching his head.

CHAPTER SIXTY-FIVE

FATHER ENGELMANN ENTERED the hospital bedroom and held the doorknob as he surveyed the room. The curtains were drawn, casting a very dim, soft light over the interior. Very similar to a confessional booth, thought Father. It was almost as if the attending nurse was preparing the room to hear Jenny's confession.

"Hello, Father," said the nurse as she passed by, carrying a tray with a syringe and medication vials on top.

Jenny turned her head towards Father and managed a tender smile as he sat in a chair next to her bed.

"Thank you for coming," said Jenny, almost in a whisper.

Father smiled and nodded slightly. Over the past few weeks, they both had grown very fond of each other. Father held such compassion for Jenny and felt the pain she was going through. Often in his prayers for her, he would ask the Lord to give him her pain, give him her disease, take his life and give Jenny back the life she so much desired. He struggled to control his emotions at the sight of her with the IV, catheter tubes, and monitoring wires protruding from her frail body. The room was quiet and still, filled with a restful peace.

"I'm sorry, Father. I wanted to be so alert and ready for you, today. But my medicine was wearing off just before you came in and the nurse had to give me another shot. I don't know how long I'll make it."

Father took Jenny's hand in his. "Then, let's use the time we have, Jenny. We have some privacy here now. Is there anything in your heart which you would like to let me know and receive forgiveness for from our good Lord? Whenever you are ready…"

From years of conditioning in her elementary school upbringing, Jenny squeezed Father's hand and began to recite the prayer one says when going to confession.

"Bless me, Father, for I have sinned. It has been several years since my last confession…and these, Father, are the sins I ask forgiveness for. I ask, Father, for forgiveness for the lingering feelings of anger and resentment towards my previous husband and our failed marriage. I know he had to be the way he was, from the way he was brought up. I understand and learned enough about life that James has to be James. I know too, Father that much of it was a facade covering the real James that the Lord created. Someday he may see the James that I always tried to see. I forgive him for all the hurts I felt in our relationship and I ask pardon and forgiveness for all the wrongdoing and the way I contributed to that relationship."

Jenny's breathing was laboured, but she went on, "I ask the Lord to lift all my feelings of pain that I feel between my son and me. I want the Lord to know I forgive my son for not forgiving me and perhaps J.J., too, has to be the way he is now, and I ask you, Father, to pray that before I die, my son and I reconcile. He came to visit me a few months ago and it was so painful to see him go, in such a cold, unforgiving, unloving way. I so need to feel, Father, that he no longer harbours any unforgiveness towards me. I don't want him to carry that sin.

"And…and perhaps, Father, my greatest sin is that I so desire the love of a man who is married."

Father was momentarily taken aback by Jenny's confession. How could someone in this condition even have such a thought? How could she possibly be a threat to anyone? He felt a loving heart, one which was filled with care, concern, kindness; one which never could harbour unforgiveness, ill will or hurt anyone. No, in all the years of relating to people would he have ever considered Jenny as one who would interfere in another's marriage.

Father raised his bushy eyebrows and gazed over at Jenny. In the dim light, he saw that perhaps his assessment had been questionable. Streaks of shame and guilt ridden tears glistened in Jenny's eyes as they rolled down her sunken cheeks.

She squeezed his hand and he knew that she was looking for understanding from him. Father placed his free hand on hers gently patting it.

"Father, I have only known two loves in my life. The one was my former husband, but I realized too late that he was already married… to his business. Even before we wed, there were such strong signs of his almost complete commitment to his company. I thought he would change but unfortunately he didn't.

"And the second man was the love of my youth…my first love. We were so in love, but we were young and at that time my parents moved and somehow we lost touch. Over all those years, Father, in my loneliness with my husband and our failing marriage, how I yearned to be with my first love. It was all I knew, it was the only relationship I could fall back on. My fantasy of being with him seemed to fill the emptiness, the void in my heart... But, Father, he betrothed another and...and has children."

A waterfall of tears cascaded down her cheeks and trickled onto the pillow.

"Oh, Father, I love life so much and yet it doesn't seem to love me. I want so much to love someone, to hold and be held, to kiss and be kissed, to look deeply into someone's eyes and see that care and love reflected... mirrored back..., but there is no one. My life is slipping away minute by minute. The only one who ever gave me that kind of love, Father, was my first love.

"He is the only one I think about, dream about and so desire. I know it is wrong; only an illusion, but how else can I support my broken heart? There is no one else who can fill the emptiness."

Father was smitten by her anguish, her heartache, her utter desolation. Father understood loneliness. Even though Anna had died so many years ago, the love and companionship they shared so often beckoned him. At night when the busyness of the day was over and he lay in bed enveloped by the darkness, he still reached out for his love's hand.

If only he could hold her, sit on her bed and cradle her in his arms, to comfort her. His heart went out to Jenny so deeply, wanting to give all he had, yet he thought better of it. She was in so much pain, and all the tubes and cords going to her body monitoring her sickness. No, it was too dangerous. Father just pressed Jenny's hand between his with increasing tenderness. He slowly nodded his head. Tears of empathy overflowed and began to drip down onto his hands intertwined with Jenny's, cascading down their fingers, giving some measure of warmth and comfort.

By now Jenny was spent, nearing exhaustion. The narcotic had spread throughout her body, lifting her pain, clouding her mind with a false euphoria. The kind of ecstasy Jenny so deeply wanted was not from the rapture of a drug, but the touch of a real hand...Henry's hand. It was he who could send her off into oblivion. It was only he, who could fill the emptiness lying just below the surface of a medication which was only camouflaging her real heart's desire.

Father looked lovingly towards this frail, helpless body, sunk so deeply in her bed, the covers barely revealing the presence of a body underneath. He saw Jenny reach up towards her chest and grasp a metal object that was hanging from a chain around her neck. It was silver but he couldn't recognize what it was. He tried to see it, but Jenny's fingers were wrapped around it and the room too dim. For a moment he thought he had seen it before, but it was hidden from view too quickly by Jenny's grasp.

Jenny was drifting, being transported into another world, she was no longer aware of Father's presence or that she was going to confession. Yet there was a yearning, so desirous in her heart that not even the morphine could suppress. As she clutched her guardian angel, Jenny made the same wish, she wished so many lonely days and nights before. She knew she shouldn't hold such a wish in her heart, but it was the only thing which sustained her.

"Oh, dear guardian angel, I so wish before I die to be kissed by my first love...my dearest beloved...my dear sweet...Henry..."

Father strained to hear what Jenny said, thinking it was still part of her confession, but her words were too soft. All he could make out before she drifted off, was her wish to be kissed by... it sounded like ... her first love—

"Oh, Camilla, please come to me, too. Forgive me for giving you away. I did not abandon you..."

Father leaned forward again, he was certain he heard the name Camilla. "Is Camilla your child, Jenny? Did you give her up for adoption? Is that what you are saying?"

Jenny remained silent and Father knew the drugs had taken over.

Camilla was such an unusual name. Father liked it the moment he was introduced to Henry's daughter-in-law. But Camilla had never spoken about being adopted...

What a coincidence Father thought that Jenny should mention her daughter, Camilla and just the other week when he met with Henry's daughter-in-law she wanted to know the name of Henry's girlfriend, Jenny Sarsky.

The link was so close to Father, just a breath away, but the thought of the two being connected was too remote, too improbable to even give it any kind of consideration.

"Oh, Lord, I couldn't hear all she said and wished for...and I do not understand it. But I know nothing passes your discernment and you hear everything that is in the heart. And I am certain, this poor, dear sweet lady's last thoughts came from her heart.

Whatever she wished for, I pray you grant her what may very well be her last wish."

Chapter Sixty-Six

At Henry's new home, he was making discovery after discovery. He was falling in love with an illusion, a kindred spirit of sorts whose house he had the good fortune to purchase. Henry visited the home daily, just to feel the peace and spiritual sustenance he derived from it.

Everything he looked at, every book he picked up, every item he discovered in a room, a box, or a trunk immediately appealed to him. He could no longer tell if it was the object itself, or the sense of feeling the touch of the previous person who had owned and held it. Henry was going beyond the physical, natural world and entering the supernatural, trying to connect with the person behind it all.

Who was the wonderful lady who owned all these things? Who mirrored back to him such a strong unexplainable attraction?

The books especially overwhelmingly appealed to Henry; most had to do with spiritual or personal development. Remarkably, many of the books Mrs. Hamilton had in her book cases were ones Henry had in his, as well. Books by Eric Fromm, Maslow, *The Old Man and The Sea*, *Catcher in the Rye*, Rollo May, C.S Lewis, and on and on.

Every day, Henry took another book from the bookshelf in the living room or the second bedroom which Marjorie had converted into an office. It was incredibly amazing to find another person with tastes and likes so similar to his, particularly at the cognitive level. Henry was filled with the wonderment of it all.

With each visit, Henry struggled to accept that it was now his house, his home. It really was someone else's home, and by some good fortune he had come into this windfall through the misfortune of its owner. He had literally walked into a home that only existed in his dreams. Everything he ever wanted in a home was phenomenally here – no – somehow strangely here.

Henry was becoming so in tune with the spirit of the previous owner that he found himself unconsciously talking to her. He secretly hoped she would be there; he wanted so much to meet her, to see her, talk to her, share with her, read to her…to hold her.

Henry searched in vain for a photograph of her, something more concrete to relate to, more so than objects and furniture, but he couldn't find any photos. All Henry could do was conjure up some image of Marjorie; a lady of grace and beauty, elegant, dignified and tasteful in every respect. A lady who loved life and tried to understand it. A lady who sought self-improvement and spiritual growth, who was hungry for knowledge. Every book he picked up was a clue to her inner mind… her being.

What Henry didn't fully realize however, was that his imaginings were invoking an image of what his first love might be like. Ever since discovering Jenny's letter in his mother's treasure chest, Henry had been subconsciously trying to bring her into his life some way. He knew she was married and that he could no longer have her in real life, but after purchasing Mrs. Hamilton's house and discovering this inconceivable sense of appeal and inner peace in this new environment, his mind somehow found an outlet for his desire of Jenny, in Marjorie Hamilton!

One day, Henry called the Santa Maria home, inquiring about Mrs. Hamilton. For weeks he was hesitant to call, he was afraid that the fantasy of the person he had conjured up in his mind might not fit the illusion. That Marjorie Hamilton was old and unattractive…and not on the high pedestal he had built up in his mind to be that of his first love. He felt so at peace with his imaginings and the comfort he derived from these fantasies as an outlet for his subconscious desire for Jenny. It would crush him to discover something different. His world would collapse; he did not want to experience any let down.

He was almost relieved when the nurse at the care home informed him that Mrs. Hamilton was too ill to have visitors and that only members of the family and those requested by Mrs. Hamilton herself were permitted to visit. Yet, Henry felt like a member of her family. He felt he knew Marjorie perhaps better even than her own family, who didn't seem to want anything of hers.

And yet Henry desired everything of hers, even Marjorie herself.

CHAPTER SIXTY-SEVEN

AFTER FATHER'S VISIT yesterday and her confession, Jenny was spent. She not only slept right through dinner time but through the entire night as well. Today was the first time in days that Jenny felt alert and rested.

A respite Jenny was thankful for, as she was about to be visited by one of her favourite people.

"Chloe! Oh, it's so wonderful to see you!" Jenny exclaimed as her adopted niece walked into the room.

"It's so good to see you too, Auntie!"

Chloe rushed over and gingerly hugged her dear aunt.

"Dad was trying to come as well but is just finishing with the conference and promised to be here early next week."

"That will be wonderful, I haven't seen Robbie since Tammy passed away…Oh, I'm sorry, Chloe."

"That's okay, Auntie, I miss Mom terribly but I have accepted it…so how are you keeping, Auntie?"

"Well, I'm hanging in there. The prognosis doesn't look that promising but I keep hoping and praying for the best."

"Dad and I have too. You are constantly in our thoughts and prayers."

"That's so wonderful Chloe. There's a lot of power in prayer."

"There sure is. Daddy is the biggest believer in that for certain!"

"So how long are you staying and where are you staying? You could have stayed in my house, but I sold it late last fall."

"That's fine, I'm staying at the Regina Inn downtown. It's a nice hotel and the room is comfortable. Anyway, I thought I would stay for a week or two. We are on our semester break and since I'm so smart I can skip most classes!! Ha, ha. Actually I brought some of my studies with me. I'm sure I can manage and thought it would be good to visit in person as most of our talks are over the phone."

"Oh, Chloe, come here and give me another hug, it's so good to have you here. I miss family, Mom, J.J. and his family, and…" tears surfaced in Jenny's eyes.

Chloe moved a chair over to Jenny and took her hand as she sat down.

"Are things better yet between you and J.J.?"

"No, I'm afraid not. He is so distant and cold towards me, Chloe. I don't know how to break through that rigid barrier of his. He blames me for the demise of our marriage and won't listen to my side of the story. He totally misinterpreted what he saw."

"That's the kiss the book store owner gave you on the cheek when you said goodbye to him?"

"Yes, as soon as I found out he was married I told him that we couldn't see each other anymore and that I always considered our relationship only as a friendship. He however, considered it to be more, and just as I was about to leave he reached forward and kissed me on the cheek. Unfortunately, at that moment J.J. came into the store looking for me and saw it. He called me such an awful name at the time."

"Oh Auntie, do you want me to talk to him, perhaps he will listen to me?"

"Yes, if you want, that might help. I would so much like to see him and make up before anything happens to me…"

"I will call him from the hotel tonight. Have you got in touch with your daughter, Camilla, yet?" Chloe wanted to know.

"Oh, Chloe, that is on hold too. I was all set to phone Mrs. Blake last September when she returned from holidays to help me make contact with Camilla rather than just pick up the phone and call her. I also wanted her advice on how to relate to Camilla so as not to interfere with Henry's family…you still recall that Camilla is married to Henry's son and that Henry and I were teenage sweethearts?"

"Oh yes, Henry was your first boyfriend that you met here in Regina before moving to Ottawa. I recall you and Mom sharing that with me."

"Do you see what I'm up against? I would hate for Henry to still have feeling towards me like I do for him. I don't know how best to relate to my daughter under the circumstances. And now with this disease coming along I just don't know what to do. I abandoned her once and if I contact her and should the worst happen and I die, she might feel like I have abandoned her all over again. I would hate to break the news to her that her parents who she loved all her life were not hers and then I die and leave her hanging in limbo. I thought it best to just leave her have pleasant thoughts of her parents and not complicate her life."

"I understand what you're saying Auntie, but I have counseled so many girls who were adopted and they have this uncanny feeling that they were even before they were told. Whether you tell Camilla or not she may already be going through an emotional struggle. I think it would be best to call Mrs. Blake and tell her your condition and get her advice on the matter. If I were Camilla, Auntie, I would want to know who my biological mother was. If the disease should overtake you Auntie, and we will pray night and day that it doesn't, but even a day with your daughter would be so healing for the both of you."

"Yes, I suppose you're right, Chloe. I never thought that Camilla might be having doubts of her origin. It is something that could plague her for the rest of her life. Yes, Chloe, before you leave, please help me call Mrs. Blake and get the ball rolling. Some days like today, I feel fine, but some are horrible. So the sooner we do this the better."

"I know Henry wasn't the father, Auntie and I know you have forgiven the man who fathered Camilla, but have you ever found out who he was? Once again, girls who I have counseled want to know that just as much as they want to know who the mother was."

"See it was divine providence that you came Chloe. You are giving me such clarity on all this. I can totally understand that an adopted child would want to know both of their parents. And yes, I'm pretty sure I do know, Chloe. His name is Peter. He has become a pastor and lives in Calgary. I think I told you in one of our conversations that Matti came to Regina to attend her sister, Coreena's wedding."

"Yes, and some priest was celebrating his anniversary at the same time."

"Yes, that's right. Well, anyway, Coreena married a man named Eddy Zeigler. Unbelievably, and I haven't told this to Matilda, it was he and his friends who attacked Henry and I when we were coming home from the show that summer. Eddy was dropped off at his home, but his other three friends came back and attacked us again. This time they took me to the park. One of the boys raped me and fathered Camilla."

Chloe's eyes grew wide as the story unfolded, "Go on, Auntie." Chloe moved closer to the edge of her seat. "How do you know which of the three boys it was?"

"Well, when Matti was at the anniversary party for the priest whom all of them seemed to know, Matti met all three of the boys as they were invited to Eddy's wedding as well. In fact, Peter was Eddy's best man at the wedding. According to Matti, the three men were all gentlemen but the one she liked best was, Peter. It just so happened that when she and Peter and his wife were talking they were overtaken by the presence of a young blonde haired lady standing beside her husband no more than ten feet away. Henry and his wife were also standing next to them as well. Anyway, Matti said she instantly knew that the blonde lady was Camilla because she looked so much like me. In fact for a moment there Matti said, she thought it was me at the party!'

"Oh, my God, Auntie."

"But what surprised Matti just as much was how intrigued Peter also was with Camilla. He couldn't get her eyes off her and told Matti that he has dreams of a girl who looks just like her. Matti thought Peter was troubled by something which she couldn't explain. She wanted to talk to him about it, but it was getting late and she wanted to come and see me for a visit as she was flying back to Ottawa the next day."

"That's an amazing story, Auntie. But can you see how Peter is dreaming of Camilla? Can you understand how that other sense operates in one's life that is unexplainable? It's quite possible for Camilla to be going through the same feelings and struggle. It's an uncanny thing, Auntie, but I have seen it so many times."

"Oh Chloe, I think you are so right, why didn't I think of that before? Yes, yes, look in the top drawer and get my little phone book out. I have Mrs. Blake's number in there."

Chloe opened the drawer and saw a tattered looking letter.

It was from Henry...

LATER THAT EVENING as Jenny drifted in and out of sleep Chloe went to the window and gazed out. Since the lights were off, Chloe could easily see out into the night sky. She was thinking of the conversation they had had with Mrs. Blake. She too thought it was best that she call Camilla and explain the situation, and tell her that if she wanted to visit her mother she should do it soon as she was seriously ill. Mrs. Blake was going to call them back and let them know how it went.

Just as Chloe was thinking on these things she was startled by her auntie's voice.

"Do you see the first star of the east, Chloe?"

"Oh, you're awake. Yes, I do see it, Auntie and it's shining bright as ever. And, I know what you are thinking."

"Oh, so you're clairvoyant as well as being such an angel."

"When Mom was alive, she always invited me to say a prayer for you when we were sitting outside as the first star of the east appeared. She told me that the star of the east was your and Henry's star and that you could feel each other's love through the star's shimmering rays coming to you. Mom shared the secret wish you held in your heart that it is your deepest desire to gaze into Henry's eyes once more and kiss his tender lips. That is so romantic, Auntie."

Chloe turned to her auntie to see her tear filled eyes glisten in the dim moon lit room.

"Oh, Auntie, I am going to say the prayer Mom and I said beside the guardian angel prayer whenever we thought of your wish:

> *Star light, star bright*
> *First star I see tonight*
> *I wish I may, I wish I might*
> *Have the wish I wish tonight.*

"I so wish that the wish my dear Auntie Jen has held in her heart for so many years comes true. Bring her daughter Camilla and her first love back to her so they can gaze once more into each other's eyes and feel their warm embrace and touch of their tender lips."

"Oh, Chloe, that is so beautiful. I made that wish upon a shooting star once. Tammy maintained that it would come true some day. Hers did."

"Yes, she shared that with me too, Auntie. She wished that she and dad would get married and they did. She said she saw a bunch of shooting stars which had reminded her of the wish and shortly after Robbie phoned her. The rest is history...

Just then, Chloe turned her attention back out of the window as the sky seemed to light up with streaks of light. Miraculously, Chloe immediately knew what she was witnessing.

"Oh look Auntie, the sky is ablaze with shooting stars. I have never seen so many at once! It's such a kaleidoscope of colours."

Chloe ran to Jenny's bed and cranked up the head board raising Jenny so she could see. Jenny saw just the tail end of the spectacular show.

"Oh Chloe, do you think it's possible? Your mom told me to watch for the kaleidoscope of shooting stars to remind me of the wish I made..."

It was almost like a fourth of July celebration! Stars whizzing this way and that, lighting up the sky!

Was it possible that over all of those years wishing upon star after star after star it was like all her wishes had been saved up and released all at the same time in this one instance...?

Once more, despite her illness...Jenny, was filled with burgeoning hope.

Chapter Sixty-Eight

S INGING AND DANCING from the chapel to the left of the front entry way led Henry to Father Engelmann. Chairs had been rearranged into a huge circle. Most of the people were standing in front of their respective chairs, while those who had difficulty standing were seated. Johnny was at the piano banging out a tune, shimmying and shaking in his wheelchair. Father Engelmann was at the end of the circle nearest the altar, his hands raised in unison with many others who were also praising and honouring their Lord.

Wow, what a sight. This is what heaven must be like.

They were just winding up their Bible study for the day so Henry walked in and stood behind one of the ladies. He began singing and clapping with those gathered and felt his quiescent mood instantly lift. Perhaps that was what he needed more so than talking to Father Engelmann.

Henry had called him earlier that morning, asking if he had time to see him about a certain matter. It seemed odd that he should have to make an appointment with a senior well on in years...

It made Henry think again, how old is Father? One would think that he had all the time in the world on his hands. But not Father; grass could not grow under his feet. His days were full and seemed to be getting even busier, if that were possible.

However, Henry had noticed a weariness in Father lately. With his final goal being accomplished, or at least attended to, he seemed ready to retire or at the very least let up a bit. In any case, he had never known anyone, who gave life everything they had like Father.

After a reflective prayer to end the prayer session that just wanted to keep going, Father and Henry headed out to the sun room. Even though it was bitterly cold outside, the bright yellow room with an almost complete wall of glass, faced the sun-drenched courtyard and emitted a welcoming warmth.

Angela brought them each a cup of tea, while Father updated Henry on his tours of the churches and the monthly magazine. Then Henry began to talk about his real purpose for wanting to see him.

"You know, Father, when Julean was alive and became ill, I never thought about wanting anyone else. Even after her death, I continued to think that there would never be another to replace her or fill her position in my life…or that I would even want to pursue another relationship. There simply was no desire or room for anyone else. However, finding Jenny's letter after mom died and now purchasing a house that elicits such desirous feelings for someone who seems to be so close to my way of thinking, feeling, perceiving… Well, perhaps Father, there could be another who I could share the rest of my days with."

Henry studied Father for a reaction, but there was none, just a benevolent smile, going with the flow of the moment.

"Time can do many things," Henry went on sounding rather philosophical, "it can heal and it can make you change in ways that you never thought possible. I recall vividly how Julean expressed to me in her final days that after she was gone that I might find another and that I was free to love someone else, perhaps not like us, but in a unique and different way and that I need not feel guilty about it. She even suggested Jenny if she were available.

"At the time, I discounted her words as unnecessary, that I would never want anyone else. Even when Ivania came along, as wonderful as she was, she could not attract me enough to get over either Jenny or Julean. Ivania noticed it straight off and that is why we eventually decided to just remain as friends for the time being.

"But now, Father, I am not so sure. When I discovered Jenny's letter it seemed as if my life had come alive again. Even though I know she is married just thinking of her makes my heart soar. And now the house I bought from this lady attracts my heart as much as Jenny. It's unbelievable Father, but either Jenny or this lady could easily find a place in my lonely heart.

"In a way, I don't feel any guilt over thinking such thoughts about Jenny, as she was my very first love. She came into my heart long before Julean and even Julean herself tried to relieve me of any guilt for entertaining such an idea. I thought for the most part I was over Jenny, but like I said, after finding the letter, I couldn't believe how all those feelings of my youth flooded back. That's why I had to try and find her, to see if there was the remote, hopeful chance that she could possibly be unattached. "But as I told you, Mr. Sarsky's secretary informed me that she was married and had a child and that put an end to my search. At least that is what I thought."

Father raised his eyebrows and his eyes studied Henry intently.

"When I purchased the house on Hill Avenue, it was like I found my other self. It's so incredibly amazing, I can't put it into words. It's like I have found the girl of my dreams. Even though I have never met her, I seem to know her through her home and everything that is in it. It's me, Father, it all reflects me!

"How could our likes, tastes in everything and even her books be so similar to mine or what I would have bought? How can it be possible?"

Father stared at Henry, his eyebrows knitting closer together.

"And lately, Father, I find myself feeling desirous of her. Even though the realtor told me she is old and sickly, I perceive her in my mind as healthy, younger, more my age and that we have this wonderful relationship. I try not to think about it, but it just keeps coming into my mind. In fact, the other day I called out her name as I entered the house."

Henry felt silly and somewhat embarrassed that he had shared that. He could sense Father's disquiet, and was cautious now about revealing all that was really in his heart. An uncomfortable silence fell over the room.

Father reflected thoughtfully for a long moment and then he finally said, "It may not be my place to suggest this, Henry, but perhaps you should consider going out with other ladies. Maybe Ivania just wasn't the right lady friend. You have mentioned to me before that other women who frequented your store have hinted at going out with you. A date perhaps," Father added, with a wink in his twinkling eyes.

"But I never really had any interest or desire, Father. I seemed very content with my life, having you, Mom, my children, and the business. This was more than enough. Sure, I dated Ivania, but it too soon fizzled out. But ever since mom died and I discovered Jenny's letter, something has changed within me. You have no idea how I loved Jenny and I'm sorry to say this, but I still do."

Henry clutched at his shirt as he spoke those words. Father could see it was not the shirt Henry was holding onto, but the pewter angel he received from Jenny.

The truth was beginning to dawn.

Henry expressed his love for Jenny so deeply, Father felt his yearning at the core of his being. Just as Father was about to empathize, Henry went on with what actually was becoming a confession.

"I know I shouldn't desire another man's wife, but I feel Father… that I am…"

Henry's voice trailed off slightly, he knew he was going around in circles repeating himself but he wanted to prepare Father…he was hesitant to go on, but knew in his heart he had to say it, express it, it was too dangerous to keep inside.

"I think what is happening, Father, is that being surrounded by all the things I love, I am making Jenny to be the lady who previously owned the house. I am trying to camouflage my desire for Jenny who is married, by desiring this lady who I think is widowed. And what is even more incredible, is how *I have this growing desire to want to kiss her.* I know, Father…," Henry lowered his head in shame and embarrassment, "I know I need forgiveness for entertaining these thoughts, but my heart pains so. I feel helpless, and…"

Henry fell silent. *The knuckles of his hand clutching the angel through his shirt turned white as if trying to squeeze Jenny from the pewter ore itself.*

HENRY TURNED INWARD, as Father looked at this hurting man whom he had adopted as his son some thirty or so years ago. When Henry hurt, so did he.

Father was relieved that Henry shared what he was beginning to suspect. Henry was treading on dangerous ground. The fact that Henry was aware of it lessened his concern.

Father could see and understand, though, how such a deep unresolved love between two young people without closure even after all those years might be transferred in this unusual way.

Henry's sorrow and guilt for desiring another man's wife and seeking forgiveness caused Father to think that perhaps Henry was in essence going to confession. After he silently said an absolution and prayer for Henry, he began to think about how remarkably similar Henry's confession was to Jenny's confession he'd heard just the other day in the Santa Maria Home. *Both she and now Henry desired the love of a married person. Both yearned to fill the emptiness, the loneliness in their hearts. Both desired to be kissed by their first love…the love of their youth.*

Once again Father broke the silence by offering another suggestion that was even more strongly rejected in Henry's mind.

"Perhaps, Henry, you should sell this house. I am concerned where this all might lead to—"

"Oh, Father, I couldn't. I understand the danger of losing touch, but there is something so strangely wonderful going on here, I just can't explain it. It's like I am surrounded by and being led by angels…it's… it's…an angelic occurrence!

"No, no, Father, definitely not. I just couldn't give up this home. I have found something so rare and special, almost a second chance at life."

"A second chance at what kind of a life? It's all make believe," Father blurted out.

They locked gazes, each adamant in their position and their perception of the situation.

"What if, Father…I mean just suppose I were to marry, again. After we all die, whose husband would I be? Would I go back to my first wife, Julean, or would I be Jenny's…I mean the other lady's husband in the hereafter?"

Father studied Henry. He knew what was in his heart. Surely he wouldn't go after Jenny, knowing that she was married. It wasn't Father's place to sit in judgment. Henry had asked him a question.

"After we die, Henry, there is no need to concern ourselves with marriage. The Bible clearly tells us that things will be quite different when we go to heaven. We will see each other, our parents, relatives, wives, husbands, but in another way."

Father turned and reached for the Bible on the end table next to him. Within seconds, he found the passage. Clearing his throat and settling his spectacles more firmly on his nose, he read Matthew 22; 24-30.

"Teacher," they said, "Moses taught: 'If a man who has no children dies, his brother must marry the widow so they can have children for the dead man.' Now, there were seven brothers who used to live here. The oldest got married, and died without children, so he left his widow to his brother. The same thing happened to the second brother, to the third, and finally to all seven. Last of all, the woman died. Now, on the day when the dead are raised to life, whose wife will she be? All of them had married her!"

"Jesus answered them: 'How wrong you are! It is because you don't know the scriptures of God's power. For when the dead are raised to life they will be like the angels in heaven, and men and women will not marry….'"

"So, that is your answer, Henry. Marriage will not exist as such in heaven."

Henry looked at Father, having heard the answer, and knowing what Father really was thinking about.

"You needn't worry, Father, I have no intention of pursuing a married women, be it Jenny or any other."

Father smiled.

LATER THAT EVENING after Justin and Lauren went to bed Henry always enjoyed the chance to have some time to himself and listen to his two favourite songs. Love Me Tender had just played as he walked out into the sun room. He decided not to turn on the lights but felt prompted to just gaze out into the cloudless sky.

He heard the next record drop and begin to sing his favourite song…

> *"Well I give to you and you give to me…true Love, true love, and on and …*

Unbidden tears came to Henry's eyes as he stood in front of the large glass window in the darkness. Thoughts of his first love surfaced so powerfully his heart began to ache. The wonder and awe of purchasing the house and the spiritual connection he made to the previous owner was such a mystery to Henry, yet so palpable it was real. Had he gone too far in thinking that Marjorie was Jenny?

Was the love in his heart so deep and strong that he would do anything to make it all real…?

Henry looked outside to see if he could see their star but the sky had blossomed into millions of twinkling stars each seemingly begging Henry to make a wish…

> *"and on and on it will always be, true love, true…,"* Bing crooned. .

Henry felt Julean's presence and he recalled a verse she had taught him and the children.…

> *Star light, star bright*
> *First star I see tonight*
> *I wish I may, I wish I might*
> *Have the wish I wish tonight.*

Oh star of east I know that you are out there, I wish with all my heart that it would be possible for my Jenny to come back to me…

No sooner had the words tumbled from Henry's lips then suddenly… a kaleidoscope of stars from everywhere burst into the sky! He had never seen such a dazzlingly display of colour. One shooting star after the other streaked across the sky. Just when one fizzled out another took its place. Each time the dust from the star filled Henry's heart with wonder and joy! The tears sitting on the edge of his eyelids spilled over and flowed glistening in the moonlight…

"...for you and I have a guardian angel on high with nothing to do, but to give to you and to give to me love forever true..."

Oh dear guardian angel, please give me my *true love*...

And there before him stood Julean. She softly smiled and passed through the window as if air and flew swiftly into the star studded sky...

Henry was filled with burgeoning hope...

CHAPTER SIXTY-NINE

"HI MATTI, THANKS for calling."

"Just wanted to know how you be feeling, Jenny. I've been thinking and praying for you all day. I even told the Boss upstairs he better get to healing my best friend or He's going to hear from me, big time!"

Oh, Matti, you are my best medicine, that be for sure," Jenny said trying to lovingly imitate her good friend.

"I'm doing as fine as can be expected. I have decided to go off all support and treatments in a few days. I don't think they are helping and it just makes me feel so drugged and fatigued. If I'm going to see my Maker I'd like to go out with my eyes open."

"I know what you mean. It's down right frustrating that after all these years of research and study you'd think smart fellows like them scientists and doctors would have figured this sickness all out by now. I hopes they not be sleeping on the job."

"I don't think so, Matti, it's just that there are so many different forms of cancer and depending where it strikes…I guess it's all more complicated than we think. Anyway, I am very grateful for my doctor. I have to admit, I love him to bits and if he wasn't married I'd be flirting with him until my dying breath!"

"Now don't you let Henry hear you say that, your heart tells me over and over that he be the one and only man in your life. I'm feeling he still keeps a secret corner of his heart for you, too, Jen. But that only be the natural thing, I can't see how any man that knows you couldn't be smitten for life!"

"So have you seen J.J. lately?" Jenny asked, subtly changing the topic.

"Yes, J.J. was at the estate a couple of weeks ago. He brought some papers for Mr. Hamilton to sign. He be thinking of freezing himself the moment his heart stops beating and before his brain stops thinking. He figures they can suspend him somehow until them scientists come up with a cure. Then when the doctors know how to fix him up they will thaw him out and bring him back to the land of the living. Good Lord, at the rate them scientists are working on this cancer thing, Mr. Hamilton be sleeping a long time."

"Oh, my…I can't imagine a person being frozen and placed in some drawer and then coming back. It gives me the chills, Matti, just thinking about it."

"Me, too. I just wonder what the good Lord has to say about all this. You know, Mr. Hamilton trying to delay his final judgement like that. Why with all the money that man has he can stay frozen until all hell freezes over."

"Oh, Matti…" Jenny chuckled… "that James, what will he think of next?"

"But I must say, Jenny, like I said to you before, he be changing some. Since coming back to the estate last summer I noticed a huge difference in his disposition. Kinder and more accepting somehow. Why, the day J.J. brought them papers Mr. Hamilton invited Thomas in for a cup of coffee. The two sat in the kitchen and had a discussion like they was two old friends."

"That's wonderful, Matti. Perhaps getting away from the business and enjoying what he has is beginning to rub off."

"That be for sure, Jen. He told Thomas he wanted to restore the garden just like you had it. He even wants to get another angel statue just like you had, too."

"Oh, Matti, that makes my heart sing. That's wonderful news."

"What took the cake, Jen, was when Mr. Hamilton asked Thomas to call him James from now on. I thought I be having a heart attack right then and there. I be so shocked I dropped a glass bowl filled with peeled potatoes.

"Scared the dickens out of the two men. I'm still not over it. I just don't know where this be leading…but he shore seems to be heading down the right path."

Jenny was so overwhelmed with what Matti said, tears surfaced in her eyes. "I don't know what to say, Matti…it all sounds so wonderful."

"Things improving around the household. We all be relaxing more, know what I'm saying?"

There was a silence over the phone line. Jenny was momentarily too choked up to speak.

"What I started to tell you was about J.J. and then I be sidetracked with this freezing business. Before J.J. left that day, I hear Mr. Hamilton tell his boy that he better call you. They then had some words about that and it ended by Mr. Hamilton saying he was wrong the way he be treating you and then J.J. left. So that's all I can be telling you. Sounds to me like the boy still hasn't called you…?"

"No, unfortunately he hasn't, I pray everyday that he does. But that is so wonderful for James to support me on this…I am just so happy to hear that. Oh. Matti, do you think J.J. might still come…?"

"Can't say. After Mr. Hamilton say that, there was a lot of exchange between them behind closed doors. Some of the words that Mr. Hamilton say, I can't repeat. But the meaning of it all was, that J. J. better learn to appreciate his mama. To be honest, Jen, it's the first time that the estate sounded like a home."

"I find that almost unbelievable, Matti, it's like music to my ears."

"Now, I can't promise that boy of yours will come to see you. He filled with a lot of pride, just like his daddy. Sometimes they'd have to hit some kind of bottom in order to bring sense to their steel hard heads, you know what I'm saying?"

Jenny chuckled for the first time in days, "Yes, Matti I know what you're saying all too well."

"Anyway, here's even more good news and the purpose of my call. I told Mr. Hamilton that you weren't doing too good and that I would like to visit you for a few days. Now, I fully expected a blast, but instead Mr. Hamilton said, he was going to suggest that very thing. That I could do a lot more for you than all them doctors put together. He told me to get a ticket straight away and stay as long as I needed to…"

Jenny let out a yelp that almost collapsed Matti's ear drum.

"That's wonderful Matti, Oh I can't wait for you to be here. And guess who else is here…Chloe! She came a few days ago. Oh my heart is starting to sing again, Matti. My two favourite people at my side… Oh thank you, Matti, I love you so much!"

"I love you too, Jen, and I can't wait to see you and Chloe, it be like one big family re-union. I should be there by the weekend."

"And Matti, would you please tell James, thanks, that it is so kind of him…and give him a big hug for me."

"Now, I carry out your first request Jen, but there is no way I am going to wrap my arms around that man…no sir. Even I have limits!"

The two girls laughed and then hung up.

CHAPTER SEVENTY

T HE GALLERY BUZZED with activity all morning then turned even crazier after lunch. The café was packed; meaning people had to wait to be seated. Many of those waiting browsed the gallery until a table came available.

By one o'clock, Henry was exhausted. Talking to customers, autographing his books and prints, and helping out in the café, had drained him. He longed to get back to Marjorie's house where he always found a quiet respite from the business.

Finally, Henry was able to make a quick exit out the rear of the café. It was a beautiful sunny afternoon, almost too nice for the second week in April. March had come in like a lion and out like a lamb. Only two weeks ago everything had been covered with snow and freezing cold. But a Chinook from Alberta had melted the snow in no time. It seemed more like July than early April.

In any case it was a perfect day to play hooky, something he should do more often. He knew he was working too hard, but without Julean and the kids at home, he found the interaction and satisfaction of working at the shop more enticing than retiring from it all.

But the anticipation of further exploring Marjorie's house easily pulled him away. He was anxious to go through the cedar chest which he'd opened yesterday in the basement. It was filled with numerous outfits for a growing child. Henry guessed the outfits were meant for an infant to at least a seven or eight year old. The older outfits clearly were all meant for a little girl. The infant ones could have been for either sex but probably for the same child.

Henry liked one outfit especially; a bright yellow sun dress with white daisies all over. Maybe it was the little tag that Marjorie had written on it that appealed to Henry the most: *To my beautiful wild-flower!* There were quite a few toys as well and some boxes that he hoped he would get at today.

After all these months, he was still discovering things. And no matter what he found, it all appealed to him. It was almost like opening boxes of things which he had purchased a long time ago, and was just now getting around to opening what he had stored away.

Henry could hardly wait to get to Jenny's house…that is Marjorie's. Over the last week or so he had such a strong compelling desire to go there, a pull that seemed stronger by the minute, almost like a gripping urgency in his gut, drawing him back day after day.

Along with his daily visits was the increasing fascination to go through all the drawers, boxes and closets in the house. He surmised that this feeling had to do with his desire to know everything about Marjorie. Lately however, it seemed more like a compulsion to look for something or…was it something that wanted to be found?

The warm breeze coming in from the sunroof felt good after a long cold winter. His thinning hair fluttered in the wind as he drank in the dry prairie air. He was enjoying the spring day so much he hadn't realized that he had travelled all the way down Albert Street to Hill Avenue. He turned right on a green light at that intersection and sped to Marjorie's house.

All the way as he walked up the winding sidewalk to the front door, he wished Jen-Marjorie were there waiting for him. He was tired and lonely and ached to be loved and held.

As he stood at the front door, the emptiness inside subsided and began to be replaced by a feeling of anticipation, that something unforeseen was waiting for him inside. It was growing so rapidly that it overwhelmed him. He unlocked the door and stepped inside.

Henry surveyed the foyer and parts of other rooms that he could see through the open doorways. As usual however, nothing had changed. Everything seemed the same, there was just a stillness filled with peace and silence. The lilac fragrance in the air seemed stronger than usual. Or was it due to his heightened senses?

It was exactly as Marjorie had left it; he hadn't changed a thing over the months he had been coming, except for the odd book or half-empty glass or coffee cup here and there.

He closed the front door and was going to go to the basement and look through some more boxes down there. As he walked past the entrance to the living room a shadow streaked across the room. His eyes followed it to an easy chair where he felt Marjorie had always sat…Julean…is that you? Henry looked again…he could have sworn Julean was sitting in the chair. He went over and carefully touched the seat of the chair and then sat down. He shook his head and looked at the antique round end table just beside the chair. It was a beautiful table with a drawer in front. Henry always admired the table whenever he sat in the sofa across the room. It was supported by four curved legs fanned out to the floor with their tips covered with brass claws.

There was something familiar about the table; he felt that he had seen it somewhere before. He ran his hand over its shiny surface and thought about the fine workmanship that no longer marked modern furniture. Henry opened the drawer and was surprised to find the Sunday Sun magazine inside with his interview. He smiled at the thought that Marjorie had read it. Perhaps she knew him better than he did her. At least she could see a picture of him on the front cover. Henry turned to the article of his interview on the third page and scanned it.

If she had read the article, had she also visited his gallery? Perhaps he had talked to her without knowing it. The feelings of being connected to Marjorie strengthened with this revelation. Henry shook his head as he marvelled over the serendipity of it all.

As he was about to put the magazine back into the open drawer, he noticed the brass plate adhered to the inside side of the drawer. It looked similar to the one that was on the inside of the roll top desk he had purchased from the antique dealer at Old City Hall.

Henry leaned forward and read it to make sure:

Manufactured
By
The Kroehl Brothers
1938
Minneapolis, Minnesota

Henry immediately recalled what the store owner said "Not only were the Kroehl Brothers fine craftsmen but they were also known for their secret compartments in nearly every piece of furniture they built including chairs, beds and even dining room sets."

The feeling of anticipation he felt when he came into the house earlier now escalated to the point he could no longer contain himself, *"Could this table also have a secret compartment!?"*

Henry slid his trembling hand slowly inside feeling for a round brass ring…and there it was. He could see it in his mind's eye.

"Oh, my God, what would he find?"

He inserted his finger in the ring and felt not only the cold touch of metal but the warmth of Marjorie's touch zinging through him. He felt almost helpless to pull the ring.

He heard the "clunk" of the trap door open exposing the secret compartment.

He fully expected to pull out a wooden box like the one in his roll top desk but there was no knob or handle to pull on. It felt like a book. He worked his fingers under it and pulled it out.

It was a diary.

He stared at the diary in disbelief. The top and back were hard thick covers topped with brown leather. The words, 'My Diary,' were stamped in gold on the front. Most of it had come off. The corners were dented and worn exposing the cardboard paper core underneath the layer of leather covering. For the months he had been coming to the home, he had never once contemplated searching for a diary

Henry was amazed at the workings of divine providence. How he was filled with such an urgency to get here today. Almost as if time was running out and he was supposed to find this diary. Had he not purchased the roll top desk a year ago preparing him for this moment, he would never have known of the existence of the secret compartment let alone this diary! Julean…in both instances she had alerted him. Henry was in awe of it all.

What a discovery…he felt certain that he was led to find this…why?

He thought he knew most everything about Marjorie from her books and personal notes and recipes …but this, *"Oh, my God, this would reveal her heart."*

He stared at the diary on his lap. It seemed to be divided into two parts; each secured by a leather tab.

The latch on the front cover opened when he pressed the button. Hesitation rippled through him. He had just opened a private journal. Did he have the right to open it? Normally he would have respected the privacy and sought to return it to the owner or a next of kin or even destroy it, yet he felt compelled to open it. Both his guardian angel and Julean led him to discover it, *he was certain of it.*

And besides it seemed her son was not interested in anything of hers and during the months that he had come to the house he probably got to know Marjorie even more intimately than her offspring. It probably had to do more with her teenage life anyway he rationalized.

The urge to continue nudged away his hesitation. From the moment he had entered Marjorie's home that afternoon he had been under the umbrella of his guardian angel and on the verge of something that would affect his life and perhaps…change it forever.

He was certain of that, too!

Chapter Seventy-One

FATHER ENGELMANN DECIDED to head back to the Santa Maria Home just to see Jenny. Their visits tended not to last too long as Jenny would often slip into a medication-induced reverie similar to the one he had witnessed following her confession. In any case, Father saw the disease's grip on her accelerating and just wanted to be there for her as much as he could.

"Oh, I am so glad you stopped in, Father," Jenny said, as he entered. "I need you to help me with a certain matter." Jenny continued then paused, trying to catch her breath. Every word she spoke required effort and like the other day, her voice was low and hoarse. Jenny's eyes moved off Father's towards the bedside eating table. Father's gaze followed and rested on some papers.

"I want you to witness that I still have all my marbles, that…I am of sound judgment…and, that I no longer wish to be supported by any machine when the end is certain."

Father smiled and nodded. "Yes, Jenny, I know everything is okay in your heart and…upstairs."

Jenny tried to appear buoyant, but her inner strength was failing. She blinked several times to keep her eyes from drooping closed from the medication. She took a long deep breath sucking in energy from the air and raised her right hand motioning Father to bring the pen and papers to her. Father slid the table in front of Jenny, picked up the papers and searched for the one which required her signature.

She fumbled for the pen then slowly and deliberately signed the dotted lines. Father placed his hand upon hers guiding it through the motions. The only letter that was really discernible was a J, the rest of her signature went off at an angle in the form of hieroglyphics. It was only important that Father knew she had signed it. He took the pen from Jenny's hand along with the papers and studied her for final confirmation. As soon as Jenny nodded, he witnessed her request to die naturally.

Father rolled the table off to the side and pulled up a chair in its place. He sat down at Jenny's bedside and placed his hand on hers. Jenny opened her eyes and gazed tenderly at Father. "There's another favour I require, Father."

"Yes, of course, how can I help?"

Once again, Jenny raised her hand and pointed to the end table beside the bed. "In the drawer is an envelope addressed to my lawyer who is the executor of my will. Over the past few weeks one of the nurses helped me write my life story…"

Father reached over and secured the large 8 x 11 brown envelope. It was thick and surprisingly heavy.

"Perhaps it will be a New York number one bestseller." Father quipped.

Jenny's eyes remained closed, but her lips formed a slight smile,

"Yes, I hope I can make a tour and do signings." Jenny's expression turned serious, "I've never told you, Father, but when I was a young girl of fifteen I had an unfortunate circumstance which resulted in my getting pregnant. I was too young to keep the baby and gave her up for adoption—"

"Yes…Camilla. Is it not?"

Jenny's eye's opened. "How did you know, Father?"

"You mentioned her name during your confession."

"Oh my, I hope I didn't reveal every dark corner of my life?"

"No, no, Jenny…I'm sure the good Lord sees only light in your life."

"I had hoped that someday I would see my child, but I guess we will have to meet in heaven. In any case, I wanted Camilla to know about her mother and explain the circumstances around her birth and adoption. Since learning of my illness, I thought it best not to disrupt her life with the news that her parents were not really her birth parents, but after speaking with my niece who counsels pregnant girls I thought it best to try and let my daughter know who I am and that I would love to see her if she was willing. I called the social welfare department to contact Camilla and let her know. I informed the agency as well that if I am gone, they were instructed to direct my daughter to my lawyer who will give her the envelope I gave to you."

"I'm certain God will turn this all out for the good—"

"Well, He'd better work fast, Father!"

"I will pray for a wonderful re-union between you and your daughter. That was a wise decision to let Camilla know."

"Thank you, Father. I only wish that my son and I could reconcile as well. It would be so wonderful for us and for him to meet his half sister.

Would you pray for that as well, Father."

"Yes, I will also say a mass for your wish, too."

Jenny winced and shifted slightly trying to find some comfort in another position. A glass of water with a plastic straw in it sat on the table; Father reached for it and directed the straw to her mouth. She sipped slowly and winced again as she swallowed.

"Have you met my niece, Chloe, yet?"

"No, I am the only one in the room. Has she come to visit?"

"Yes, she must have gone for lunch. I hope you meet her, she is a wonderful girl. Matilda, is also coming to visit in a few days. It is so good to be surrounded by people you love."

"Yes, it is, Jenny."

A streak of pain crossed Jenny's face. She was tiring and was using every bit of strength she possessed to stay awake.

Father tried to be consoling and perhaps offer some solution that might speed things up.

"That was a very thoughtful thing you did, Jenny, to write a letter to your daughter, but perhaps I can find her and bring her to you…"

"I thought of that, Father, but my life gets complicated. In my confession I do recall telling you that I had a love of my youth whom I still desire…"

"Yes, I remember, Jenny."

"Well, that man, Father, turns out to be Camilla's father-in-law. I don't want to disrupt his life or marriage. My son still blames me for being the cause of breaking up our marriage. So, I decided to keep it secret until I was gone."

"Oh, Jenny, I'm sure everyone will understand under the circumstances and be so happy. Are they near? What city does your daughter live in?"

Jenny's voice was dry and hoarse: even her lips were becoming chapped. Father reached for the water again, and she flinched with each sip.

"That's the unbelievable part, Father. They all live here in Regina."

"So near and the Lord has not prompted you to call them?"

"Several times before I became sick I wanted to, but now I think the letter you have will be the best for all concerned and perhaps the welfare agency can explain it to all concerned—I"

"Are you certain this is the way you want it to be? Tell me who they are and I can explain and quickly bring them to you…"

"It has always been my heart's desire to see my two loves, but it's all too late and this is for the best."

Jenny was tiring and Father could see the pain was increasing and she would require her medication soon. He wanted to press Jenny and get her to reconsider, but if that is what she wanted he would have to respect her wishes.

How life can spin a web that has so much love and yet filled with so much sorrow. As incredible a story as it was, *Father somehow felt that he had heard it all before.*

Exhaustion was overtaking Jenny. Her energy was all but spent in talking to him and coping with the growing pain. Father remained silent as she drifted in and out of consciousness. Suddenly she stirred and fumbled for the pewter angel at the end of the chain hanging from her neck. It sparkled in the dim light and obviously soothed her. Her features relaxed and as sleep was about to take her, her true desires became known.

Father leaned forward straining to hear the prayer she began whispering to her guardian angel. All he could make out was that she wished to be kissed by someone, but who did she say? It surely must be her first love.

"Who is it you desire, Jenny?"

He studied her intently hoping for some clue, but she did not respond.

He gazed down at the sealed envelope still in his hand. It held the answers he wanted to know; it would have Camilla's last name and address and thus identify the last name of the father-in-law – Jenny's sweetheart. Father so much wanted to grant Jenny's final wish. But time was running out. Father gazed with tender compassion upon Jenny as she clutched her angel; her knuckles white from the fervour of her heart's yearning.

It triggered a similar memory...but when and where?

Tears flowed from Father's eyes as he looked up and soulfully pleaded, "Lord, will you forgive me for breaking the seal of this envelope?"

When Father left Jenny his mind was buzzing. The predicament that people find themselves in. That poor woman lying on her death bed yearning for her daughter that she gave up for adoption to come to her.

Death is at the doorstep.

Oh Jesus, heavenly Father, please allow this dear soul to die in peace and for the daughter to also live in peace having at least met her mother for as long as time permits.

As Father made his way down the hallway he saw a smiling young lady coming towards him.

"You must be Father David? Auntie Jen said you have a wonderful smile and she is right."

"And you must be Chloe?"

"That's me, I'm the mischievous girl that Auntie had to put up with when I visited her in Ottawa for many a day when I was a toddler."

"That's not what I hear. Over the past few months Jenny has spoken so kindly of you and I believe your Mom's name is Tammy…?"

"Yes, that's right but Mom or rather Tammy has passed away and Auntie Jen has become my Mom."

"That's good and it's so good of you to be here. Jenny needs lots of love and support."

"Yes, she needs a lot of prayers, Father. I wish my faith were stronger, so I hope you have her in your prayers."

"I do, Chloe and I know the Lord hears yours as well. He listens to your heart and I know you want your Aunt to be healed just as I do."

Chloe's eyes filled with tears. "Oh, Father, I don't know what I would do if I were to lose Auntie. We are so close and like I said she is just like my mother."

Father took Chloe's hand and squeezed it. "Trust in the Lord with all your heart, Chloe, things will work out."

"Thank you Father. I better get back in there. Oh by the way, did Auntie tell you her friend Matti is coming from Ottawa tomorrow?"

"Yes, she did mention it. And I do remember Matilda. She is Coreena's sister, Eddy's bride. Yes, yes, I remember them well at my 25th anniversary party."

"I've met Matilda but not her sister. Now if you want to see someone filled with faith Father wait till you see Matilda in action. She is something else. Even more fervent than my Dad."

Father smiled. "Well I must be going too. So nice to see you Chloe."

Father gazed at the envelope in his hands as he made his way to the front entrance door. He could easily find the answers he needed to know who these people were and search them out. But it was wrong to look into someone's private affairs without their permission.

He checked his watch; three forty five. There was still time to see one more patient at the General Hospital before dinner. He promised Gertrude he would stop in today.

"Hi Bruce, thank you for waiting."

"No problem, Father, glad to be of service. Back to the Nunnery?"

"Could I trouble you to stop at the General Hospital, I just want to run in for a few minutes to see a patient that is scheduled for surgery tomorrow morning, I would like to pray for her and wish her well."

"No trouble at all. So, this has been a busy day for you?"

"Yes, I must admit I am feeling tired. Perhaps I will retire right after dinner. I guess my years are catching up with me."

The taxi pulled up to the front door. "I'll wait for you in the taxi waiting area."

"Thank you Bruce, I shall be no longer than fifteen minutes."

"Take your time, it's not busy at this time of the day, and I have a book I'm reading."

As Father made his way to the front door, weariness was weighing on him. Who should come out but, Camilla!

"Hi Father, going in to see someone?"

"Yes, yes, Camilla, how nice to see you. Hope you were not here for yourself?"

"Oh, no. One of the girls at the school started to haemorrhage and we drove her here rather than call an ambulance. We are only a few blocks away."

"You have been on my mind since out last visit. You wanted to know the name of Henry's girlfriend, Jenny Sarsky."

"Yes, it's a long story, Father, but since our talk I found out that I was adopted. I had always suspected it but I found some papers in my dad's metal storage box after he died that confirms I was. I'm just trying to track down my biological mother. I called the social welfare department in Ottawa last week and am just waiting for them to call back. Anyway I think I know her name."

"Yes, last time we spoke you also mentioned the name, Marjorie, does that name have anything to do with all this?"

There was a long silence and then Camilla said, "I'm not one hundred percent certain, Father, but I think she lives in Ottawa and her name is, Marjorie Hamilton..."

Father stared at Camilla and his mind went blank as if in a state of shock. He was so weary and had so many names bouncing around in his head he just couldn't think clearly. What Camilla said registered, but his mind couldn't connect the dots to the Marjorie Hamilton he was seeing. His mind kept thinking 'Jenny Hamilton in Regina at the Santa Maria Home.'

The connection that they were speaking of the same lady was the fur-thest thing from Father's mind and yet...

"I have to run, Father, I will keep you posted. I hope the agency calls today or tomorrow."

CHAPTER SEVENTY-TWO

THOUGHTS THAT ANGELS were in the room directing him would normally spook Henry, yet the feelings aroused were warm and gentle, encouraging him to go on.

He flipped the cover of the diary open to the first page which gave a clue as to Marjorie Hamilton's age:

To Marjorie

On your first teenage birthday of thirteen years, March 20, 1954!!

Happy birthday, honey!

Love, Mom and Dad

A quick calculation told him that Marjorie would be 45 years of age now, the same age as he! The realtor had told him she was a lot older, probably a result of her illness.

Henry picked up the diary and flipped quickly through the pages allowing only cursory glances. He purposely did so, trying to slowly overcome any feelings of guilt for reading someone's private thoughts. The pages were old and yellow. A few were quite shriveled and wrinkled from being wet. Perhaps a drop of tea or maybe from a few shed tears. He opened and closed it at random and read the different notations. It quickly became evident the diary was not kept on a daily basis. Sometimes a month or two elapsed between entries.

The notes were general, not really revealing anything to gossip about. Things like what she did that day, what she was looking forward to and so on. Some entries, however, were personal and expressed sorrow that they were moving once more, but again, very general.

The second part of the diary could prove to be a different matter.

The inscription embedded into that cover just above the latch read:

MY PRIVATE THOUGHTS

To Which I Only Hold the Key

There was no button to push; the only way to release the tab was to unlock it with a key. Henry recalled seeing a paper pocket glued to the inside of the front cover. He flipped back and his memory proved correct. He retrieved the tiny key from its pouch and flipped back to the second part of the diary. It had his full attention now along with a growing curiosity. The first part did not seem so intrusive or invasive and helped to relieve his guilt feelings for prying into the personal life of another.

But now he held the key to Marjorie's inner most thoughts, her private thoughts. He wondered if the diary would confirm and fit the vivid image he had conjured up over the past months or reveal something that would possibly mar the fantasy he had created. Everyone had skeletons in their closest, was he about to learn about Marjorie's? In any case he had to find out. He had fallen in love with this lady and felt possessed by a selfish desire to know everything about her. Even his guardian angel seemed to be prodding him onward.

Henry's heart raced with excitement as he inserted the key and with the lightest turn the leather tab snapped back, freeing the pages in the back section. A burst of air fanned his face. Perhaps it was his desire to know more of Marjorie's recent past that caused him to go further to the back of the diary. Expecting to read of some recent romance or hidden desire, Henry was completely taken back by the first line Marjorie wrote there on June 12, 1986:

Today my son testified against me, it all has to do with that day he called me a whore.

This was so unexpected. Even the use of the word 'whore,' went against the graceful vocabulary he expected Marjorie to possess. He hoped the remaining page would offer some explanation that could possibly justify such a deplorable accusation. He felt the hair curl at the back of his neck, his shoulders tensed at the very thought of a son being so cruel and disrespectful to his mother.

Henry took a deep breath and read the entire entry:

I could see the deep hurt in his eyes as he told the lawyer that I was the cause for the demise of the marriage between his father and me. J.J. still blames me for the divorce. He simply refuses to understand my side of the story. His father and I were married by certificate only. James' real wife was the company. I knew it before and immediately after we were married. Not even our first honeymoon day was free of James' making business decisions.

I was so hoping when I became pregnant with J.J. that things might change, but they only got worse. While J.J. and his father grew closer together, James and I grew further apart. Today's court hearing clearly showed J.J.'s support for his father. It was so sad to see our son come between us in this way.

This was a whole other side of Marjorie he had never suspected. In his mind, Marjorie had had everything and yet, she was lonely and estranged. It's funny how people you would least expect to be unloved sometimes are. He read the next page:

I guess out of loneliness, I began to develop a close relation-ship with the proprietor of a corner book store. I have several girlfriends, but it just isn't the same as male companionship. I longed for affection, to be held, and loved., Patrick is warm, affectionate, and loving. Unfortunately I had little in common with James, but with Patrick, he loved books as much as I do. I think it was this common ground which drew us together.

Unfortunately, Patrick was married and as soon as I discovered it I told him I could no longer see him. It is very unfortunate that J.J. walked into the bookstore when he did, in time to see Patrick give me a peck on the cheek as a farewell gesture.

Perhaps it was for the best that J.J. told his Father a distorted fact that his mom was cheating on him. I believe J.J. thought it might encourage his father to pay more attention to me, but instead James immediately called for a divorce.

Henry laid the diary on his lap. He felt such an emptiness in Marjorie's life. How wrong was his perception of her? He shook his head in disbelief. And the way she wrote in her diary was unusual, a catharsis of sorts and almost as if she were talking to a friend.

What led up to this? Henry wondered as he flipped back a few pages and read another entry. This one had to do with how she met the book-store proprietor:

Today, as I was looking in the used book section at Dole's Book Shop, I was startled from behind by Patrick. He asked if he could help me. I told him the name of a book I was looking for that was mentioned on a talk show that I had recently viewed. He said that he hadn't heard of it, but would phone some of the other stores to see if they might have a copy. We had a very nice discussion on inspirational and self-help books. He suggested several others he had read and found helpful.

I was surprised how quickly we hit it off and talked about books that would help us in our life journey and the challenges we all face. We both seemed very relaxed and natural in doing this.

Patrick is younger than I. I find him handsome and especially like his soft low voice and the way he looks at me when we speak. He seems so interested in what I have to say and makes me feel as if I am the only one in the store. Even when it is crowded. I haven't felt this much attention by a man in years. I like him...a lot.

It was evident from the entry that Marjorie was lonely and that her husband James wasn't fulfilling her needs. The next two entries confirmed that conclusion. She spoke more intimately about the relationship she had with Patrick. She looked forward to going back to the bookshop and tried to find some reason and excuse to do so. One sentence she wrote, spoke volumes of their growing relationship and of her existing one with her present husband, James:

"Patrick makes me feel special. No, it's more than that, he makes me feel like a woman again."

The two entries after that brought Henry back to the first entry he'd read.

Henry closed the diary and laid his head back against the high back of the armchair and thought about marriages, children, and the problems families invariably have in close relationships. He thought about some of the problems and misunderstandings he had with his children as they grew up and about all the problems he heard and dealt with as a guidance counselor of teenagers. Time and time again, he had seen huge walls build up between parents and children mainly due to misunderstandings; seeing things from their world, their perception, wanting their needs met and not seeing things from others point of view. Often we treat our worst enemies better and with more consideration than we do family members.

If her husband had been more supportive of their relationship none of this would have happened. But, then what right did he have to judge not knowing all of the circumstances. From what he had seen and the counseling he had been involved in over the years, in all too many marriages no sooner was the honeymoon over than couples forgot the vows they made. They took each other for granted, daily neglects insidiously built up, little hurts, resentments, pouting, anger, lengthy silences, until eventually there is a distant, cold and unfulfilled relationship. From what he had just read, Marjorie's marriage was a perfect example of needs not being met.

Henry recalled the analogy Father Engelmann used for a good marriage in one his homilies about five years ago. He likened it to making a double loaf of homemade bread. It was such a vivid comparison that parishioners still talked about it. Henry had to agree as he thought about it that there was nothing like the smell of homemade bread baking, just as it is to be greeted with a warm loving embrace.

Henry flipped the pages back to another section of the diary and read something that intrigued him. It had to do with something related to her name, that she really liked to be called Jenny rather than Marjorie, but her husband liked her first name, Marjorie, and told her to use it when signing legal documents. "

Henry jumped as the phone jangled. An extension phone was just on the table next to him. He reached over and retrieved it.

"Hello."

"Hello, is this Mr. Pederson?"

"Y…yes, who is speaking?" Henry was surprised that someone other than his family or staff knew this number.

"The lady at your gallery gave me your number, I hope it's okay for me to call you. This is Angie Fraser, I am Peter's wife…"

"Oh, yes, Eddy's friend."

"Yes, that's right. The reason I am calling is that Peter was admitted into the hospital today to start chemotherapy treatments. I believe his illness in his case is due to the guilt he feels over what happened that night that he and his friends came across you and your girlfriend Jenny." Angie began to cry.

Henry was surprised by Angie's openness, and thankful at the same time that Peter had shared that incident with his wife. He had just been thinking about marriage relationships. In spite of the circumstances he felt that Peter and Angie had a very good, open, honest relationship.

"Thank you for phoning, Angie and sharing, I understand your concern...what is it that I can do?"

"I think Peter desperately wants to talk to Jenny and ask her for forgiveness for what he did that night. Since you and Peter spoke at Father Engelmann's anniversary party have you learned of Jenny's whereabouts?"

"No I haven't, Angie. I wish I did too." Henry wondered if he should share what he knew about Camilla and her concern that she might be adopted after all. Henry didn't know if there was any truth or validity to that.

As if reading Henry's thoughts, Angie asked, "Do you recall speaking with Peter about a young lady he saw at the party? I believe her name was, Camilla and she is your daughter-in-law."

"Why yes, Angie, in fact I was just thinking of her as well."

"Peter dreams of her all the time and his dreams are changing..."

"Oh...?"

"He now dreams of her the way he saw her at the party. She is walking towards a small round structure...I can't think of what they call those things that usually sit in a garden area?"

"Yes, a gazebo is what I think you are referring to."

"That's right, Hank. Camilla is walking towards a gazebo and Peter thinks he sees her twin sitting in the gazebo. Does Camilla have a twin sister, Hank?"

"No, I think Peter is seeing Jenny. Camilla looks very much like Jenny. That is why I have always thought that Camilla was Jenny's daughter. But when I met Camilla's parents I had to give up on that idea as she claimed that Valerie and Stanley Breckhart were her parents but...something has happened lately which may throw new light on all this."

"And what is that?"

"Well, I may be speaking too soon and I don't want to build up hopes, but I recently learned from my son that Camilla feels she is adopted and was going to check into that. That was a few weeks ago so I am assuming nothing ever came of it. But you know the old saying, where there's smoke there's fire."

"Oh, Hank, perhaps speak with your daughter-in-law. Peter is so ill and I fear for him. He desires forgiveness...wouldn't it be something if that young lady was Jenny's daughter after all?"

"Yes, Angie, it sure would be something!"

No sooner had Henry hung up the phone than it rang again.

"Hi, Henry, it's Shelly. Sorry to bother you, but could you please come to the gallery. Some people from Vancouver just purchased one of your original paintings. They are very excited to meet you and would also like you to personalize the painting for them. It's an anniversary present to each other."

"Certainly," Henry replied, "I'll be there in ten minutes."

As Henry hung up the phone, he noticed a change in light in the kitchen at the end of the hallway; he was drawn to it. The late afternoon sun was flooding the backyard and some of the rays streamed through the kitchen window above the sink. He walked over and peered outside to see beams of warm sun coming between two large pine trees and resting on the seat of the bench in the gazebo. What a perfect time to be there and reading.

I bet this is what Marjorie had in mind when she had it constructed. If he didn't have to get back to the gallery he would have really enjoyed going outside and reading the diary there for a while.

Just as Henry was about to turn and leave his eyes were attracted to a bright glimpse of colour against the glistening white snow. The snow which was piled high in the basket belonging to the marble angel had melted and now was filled with what looked like a fresh bouquet of flowers. He wondered if they were real.

He headed out the patio doors and stepped out onto the deck. There was still a lot of snow in the yard, but it had gone down considerably. Parts of the winding stone path leading to the gazebo were now exposed as well as some of the brush and decaying flowers on either side.

Henry made his way down the steps and followed the lane to the angel beside the gazebo. He couldn't keep his eyes off the colourful flowers; they just had to be artificial.

The snow quickly worked its way into his shoes as he stepped off the path and plowed his way through the foot-deep snow, stopping just short of the gleaming white angel. Henry touched the velvety soft bell-shaped flowers in the basket along with some yellow daisies. He didn't know their name, but they were all real; a beautiful mix of flowers in pastel shades of pink, mauve, and blue. And he loved the brilliant red poppies against the blue delphiniums. He was awestruck by this absolutely dazzling fresh bouquet! He wondered who could have put them there? There were no footprints in the snow anywhere in the backyard except his own!

His mind swirled, again. How could this possibly be? Could Marjorie have put them there before winter and they somehow froze?

No! That was months ago. She went into the hospital last fall. The flowers would have wilted and died within days and there was very little snow until mid-December.

Henry raised his gaze from the flowers to the angel's face that carried an almost imperceptible Mona Lisa smile. The feeling of angels flying around inside the house and outside overwhelmed Henry in a strange wonderful way.

He reached up and through his shirt grasped the pewter angel hanging from his neck and softly whispered, *"Could this be a miracle?"*

Chapter Seventy-Three

CAMILLA TOSSED THE book she was trying to read on the coffee table. She just couldn't concentrate on anything. Last week she had called the Post-Adoptive Registry and asked for Mrs. Blake, the lady Irene Gilmer had suggested to call in regards to her adoption, but her call still hadn't been returned. Camilla was certain that Mrs. Blake or someone in that department would provide her with the information he needed to know. Since Ottawa was where she was born and also where Mrs. Hamilton was from it seemed the logical place to start. Since the agency still hadn't called, Camilla phoned again that morning. She was informed that Mrs. Rita Blake, would return her call later in the afternoon.

The tension and anxiety of waiting for the agency to call was driving her up the wall. This entire matter has been so hard on Jeremy as well.

Oh, please call...

Camilla checked the time, three forty-five. That would make it four forty-five Ottawa time. She felt certain they closed at five. Camilla was pacing the floor when the phone rang. Her heart skipped a beat. She took a deep breath then rushed to the phone.

"Hello?"

"Good afternoon, this is Rita Blake calling for Camilla Pederson. Would she be in?"

"This is Camilla. Thank you so much for phoning." And before Mrs. Blake could speak, Camilla, so anxious to get the facts out in the open and to know the truth, rambled on. "My parents' names are Valerie and Stanley Breckhart. Both of them passed have away recently, and upon my father's passing I discovered something that proves I was adopted, something I had begun to suspect. I'm sure if you check your records, Mrs. Blake, you will find a file under the name of either, Stanley and Valerie Breckhart or Marjorie Jennifer Sarsky."

"Yes, Camilla, I am very familiar with your file and expected you to call some day. Even if you hadn't, we were going to call you."

"You were?"

"Yes. Normally under such circumstances I don't give out information over the phone but there is an urgency surrounding this matter which I will come to. I am happy to hear that you already know of your adoption which makes this conversation less sensitive…"

"I am a counselor as well Mrs. Blake and I fully understand the need for caution in such situations. However, I want to assure you I am fully prepared to discuss all aspects of this matter with you. So please be frank and fully open with me. I have waited far too long to know who I am."

"Thank you for sharing that with me, Camilla. So, since you mentioned her name, I gather you know the name of your biological mother is Marjorie Jennifer Sarsky. Do you know any more than that?

"When Dad passed away last year I found his storage box in which he kept his important papers. I finally had the courage to look in it this past summer. I've been wondering for a while now, if the reason I look so different from the rest of the members of my family, isn't because I'm not actually one of them. I have a different build, different hair colour, and a different complexion from my parents and other relatives. So, to tell you the truth I was almost relieved to finally find evidence in my Dad's metal box that I was in fact adopted. There was some correspondence surrounding my adoption, as well as my birth certificate. But really, beyond my mother's name I don't know much else."

"Well, I can tell you that her last name now is not Sarsky, she was married and so her last name changed to Hamilton. I can also tell you that our records show that your mother inquired about you several times before you were eighteen and once again after she got married to Mr. Hamilton who, by the way, is not your father. However, it was only last year that Marjorie Jennifer Hamilton officially initiated the search for you.

"She requested that we contact your parents, first, to ascertain if you had been informed of your adoption before trying to make contact with you directly. I received a call back from your father letting us know your mother had passed away and that it was always their intention to let you know of your adoption, but they decided to wait until any inquiries were forthcoming. Why disrupt the family, they reasoned, if it wasn't going to go anywhere? But then they realized that decision should really be up to you.

"Your mother passed away before she could let you know and your father told us he simply put it on hold until we wrote to him of your birth mother's intention to seek you out. In any case Camilla, your dad welcomed Ms. Hamilton's call and requested to speak to her. I know they did speak, but in the interim, before he was able to speak to you about your adoption, unfortunately he passed away and the two were unable to follow through as they had planned."

"And, that's when I got the call from Mrs. Hamilton asking for Dad."

"Yes, from what I later learned from Jenny that is the case."

"You know, although I only spoke a few minutes with Mrs. Hamilton I still felt such a strong connection to her…"

"Yes, I've run into similar encounters like that in other cases over the years."

"I noticed you called her Jenny, Mrs. Blake. Why not Marjorie?"

"She indicated right from the outset, that although Marjorie was her legal name, she much preferred to be called by the shortened form of her second name."

"That explains another thing that I was not only confused about but also dreaded to know…"

"I don't understand, Camilla?"

"Before I explain that to you, can you tell me first who my father is…? Was it, Henry!?"

Mrs. Blake checked her files and then said, "Our records show that Henry was a boy that Jennifer was very fond of—"

Camilla swallowed hard not wanting to know, yet she knew she had to know the truth. "Mrs. Blake, is Henry…my father?"

"Our records show that the father is listed as "unknown." Apparently there were some circumstances surrounding the pregnancy which I am not at liberty to discuss with you. That is something you will have to talk over with your biological mother if you wish to pursue this."

"I need to know for certain, Mrs. Blake, that Henry was not the father."

"Like I said, our records indicate no, however, Jenny could have been protecting Henry. But in all our discussions with Jennifer over the years when she phoned to see if she could seek you out she always maintained that Henry was not the father. Why is this so important to you, Camilla?"

"My husband's father's name is Henry, and in the summer of 1956 he had a girlfriend named Jennifer Sarsky, but Jenny moved to Ottawa that fall never to be heard from again. Ever since I married into the family and even from the first moment my husband introduced me to his dad, it was as though he was seeing a ghost from his past. Jeremy's dad, Henry, said that I look just like the girl he once knew when he was fifteen. Since I already had strong feelings that I was adopted and the way Jeremy's dad looked at me when we visited, I began to suspect that perhaps Jennifer Sarsky was my mother. The timing would have worked out perfectly, because I was born in the spring of 1957. What confused me however was the name Marjorie as Henry only knew of his girl-friend as Jenny. But now that you have explained that she preferred to be called Jenny, it's possible that…"

Camilla couldn't finish.

Mrs. Blake saw where this was going. "So Camilla, your worst night-mare, is that Henry, your father-in-law, is also the man who fathered you?"

"Oh Mrs. Blake, the thought of my husband being my half brother terrifies me, I just don't know what to do…"

"Camilla, I understand your concern but we have to go by what the file says. Henry was not indicated as the father."

It gave Camilla a glimmer of hope, "Is the name Peter in your files?"

Camilla heard papers shuffling and finally Mrs. Blake said, "No, that name nor any other man's name beside Henry's is in the file. Why do you ask?" Rita wanted to know.

"Last summer there was a celebration for our parish priest's 25th anniversary in the priesthood. My father-in-law Henry, his best friend Eddy, and another friend of Eddy's named Peter were all there. When I arrived, I noticed that Peter kept staring at me. At one point our gazes locked and I swear I felt the same kind of instant connection I felt over the phone when Ms. Hamilton called. Looking at him closely, I saw features of myself in him, and for the first time in my life, I felt like I resembled someone. Later I saw Peter and Henry talking, and when they both turned to look at me in unison, I would have sworn that they were talking about me."

"So, you think that maybe, this Peter is your father?"

"I don't know, Mrs. Blake. How can a man just come out of the blue like that and yet I feel that there's this strong connection between us?"

A long silence passed through the lines and Camilla continued, "So, Mrs. Blake, why haven't I heard from my real mother, yet?"

"Things are a little complicated Camilla. I received a call from your mother just last week. She wanted so much to make contact with you, but…I'm sorry to tell you this, but she contracted cancer last fall and was hospitalized. The cancer now has spread and unfortunately her situation is now terminal. She thought it best not to contact you under the circumstances. Why let you know only to leave again? And why disrupt the pleasant memories you had with the parents who raised you? She didn't want to disrupt your life in this way… Are you okay for me to go on?"

Even though Camilla never knew her mother, hearing that she had cancer and was about to die, filled her with sorrow and tears.

"Yes, Mrs. Blake, I'm fine, please, go on."

"As I was saying, Camilla, your mother called me just last week and it was to tell me she had had a change of heart. She said that if we could find you or if you should ever call while she was still alive, that it would be better for her to meet you in person, and answer any questions you might have, rather than have you spend the rest of your life wondering about her. In the event that she died and you inquired, then we were instructed to direct you to her lawyer. Apparently she's written about the circumstances surrounding your birth and adoption and also a little about her life."

Stunned by all she had learned, Camilla couldn't help think of what had brought her to this time and place.

"You know, I only had vague suspicions and a feeling of not belonging in my own family before this. I would never have pursued any of it or searched for the truth, if it wasn't for the dream."

"And what is that dream, Camilla?"

"Well, it may take a few minutes and I've already taken up so much of your time,…"

"That's perfectly fine, Camilla, this is much too important to leave for tomorrow. Please, go ahead and share your dream, I'm interested in hearing about it."

"Well, up until my early teens, whenever I asked my mother where I came from she would always tell me I came from the stork. When I was little she would show me a nursery book which showed pictures of a baby that she said was me, being delivered by a white stork. I loved that story, and the pictures showing me being carried by a sling at the end of the stork's beak, flying through the air and landing on the doorstep of my parents' home. It was so real to me that I firmly believed it and dreamed about it for years. But as I grew older, and started questioning my mother about where the stork had gotten me from in the first place, she was reluctant to talk about sexual matters and simply dismissed it with a casual remark that I would know soon enough. Looking back, I think it was not so much that she was uncomfortable talking about sex as it was a reluctance to take credit for giving birth to me. Are you still interested in this, Mrs. Blake? Should I go on?"

"Yes, this is quite fascinating, please continue."

"As I grew older I stopped having that dream, at least until this past year after dad died, but this time, when it returned, it came back in a different form.

"In this new dream I am still wrapped in a blanket and still flying through the air, not by a stork but rather by an angel. Her hands are cradling me in outstretched arms as we sail on the back of the wind. Her long golden hair and gown fluttering in the breeze, and in the distance I can see a most radiant woman with arms outstretched, standing at the opening of a gazebo beckoning me to come home.

"And there are wildflowers, hundreds of them as far as the eye can see dazzling with such brilliant colour that I can barely keep my eyes on the woman. Tears of joy are glistening in the bright light as they flow down her cheeks...and now, here is the astounding thing, Mrs. Blake, but as we get closer and the woman's features become more distinct I am shocked to see that the she looks just like me, and just as that realization hits, I wake up.

"How could I be delivered to myself? To me the only explanation is that perhaps the woman of my dream is actually my real mother."

Mrs. Blake listened silently in awe as the story unfolded.

"Thank you so much for sharing that with me. I think it's my turn to become emotional. Your dream is so clear to me and it will be to you as well, as I relate a little more of what your mother told me in our past two conversations. Your mother loves gazebos, wildflowers, and angels! She also related to me that she always considered you her beautiful wildflower. Do you see how this all fits in?"

"Oh, my gosh, I love all those things as well!"

"Just before your mother went into the hospital she had a round gazebo built in her backyard and surrounded it with wildflowers. She loved to sit and read there and be surrounded by nature. That's the way she had it when she lived at home when she was young in Ottawa, also when she was married and lived on an estate just outside of Ottawa. Just next to her gazebo is a large white marble statue of an angel holding a basket. She calls it the Angel of Thanksgiving. Apparently not for receiving gifts from the angel, but for offering up wildflowers in thanksgiving for all the wonderful blessings she receives in her life."

"What a lovely thing to do. The angel, the wildflowers...and we had a gazebo built last year too. Could it really all just be coincidence?"

"Wait there's more," Mrs. Blake continued. "The day she entered the hospital she told me she had placed a bouquet of flowers in the angel's basket for you and her first love. She asked for a miracle – that she would be reunited with you both before she passed away—"

"Oh no! I just have to see her.

"Mrs. Blake you mentioned that my Mom placed flowers in the angel's basket hoping to be reunited with me and her first love.

"Do you think that her first love is my father?"

And before Mrs. Blake could answer, Camilla continued, "Oh, I just hope and pray it's not my husband's father. The only glimmer of hope is that it might be Peter. The reason I say that is because in the dream that I just described to you, Peter is now also in the dream at the far end of the wildflower garden and his arms are outstretched as well, ready to receive the baby from the angel!"

There was dead silence. After considerable consideration of the facts Rita responded with reserved discretion.

"Camilla, since your birth mother is still alive and able to answer that question, I will leave that up to her to relate to you. In the event that Jenny passes on and you still don't know who your father is, call me and we will have another chat.

"So let's cross that bridge when we have too. If it's any consolation to you Camilla, I have a feeling that Jenny was telling the truth that Henry is not the father. And as I said earlier, there is something on file here that I still have not shared with you and that is the circumstances surrounding your conception. Hopefully Jenny will share that with you and then you will understand why I still believe that it is someone other than your father-in-law who is your biological father."

Camilla could no longer hold back her tears. It was all too much.

"When your call came through, this morning," continued Mrs. Blake. "I called the care home where Jennifer last phoned from. I wished to speak with her and make certain she was still willing to see you if you called. I was informed however that she was too ill at that time to speak to anyone. I therefore took it upon myself, based on her last instructions to me to let you know where she is since she is still alive.

"Should you decide not to pursue this she did want me to personally tell you that she always regretted giving you up for adoption and that you were in her mind and heart each and every day of her life and that she loves you more than you will ever know."

Camilla couldn't speak for the longest moment.

"In what care home is she in, in Ottawa?" Camilla inquired between sobs.

"What?"

"What care home is she in, in Ottawa? I need to see her as soon as possible."

"Oh Camilla, I can't believe I haven't told you yet, you're not going to believe this, but she's not in Ottawa, she's there, in Regina. Stanley told her you live there, and after her own mother passed away, Jenny moved to Regina in the hope of meeting up with you."

Camilla was momentarily speechless.

Her real mother was here in Regina?

"But…that's unbelievable."

"Yes, it is amazing how these things happen. When a person has a dream in their heart for something, somehow God and the entire universe all seem to work together to make it come true. I've seen it happen over and over and am still in awe how events are created to make one's dreams come to pass."

"But Mrs. Blake, she called my Dad almost a year and a half ago, she could have easily followed up on all of this back then, before she was ill. Why didn't she? Why has she waited so long?"

"In a way it's a similar concern that you have over who your father is. Because she and Henry were once sweethearts, Jenny was worried that she might cause trouble between him and his wife. It was something she was very adamant about not doing."

"But Henry is no longer married," exclaimed Camilla. "His wife died several years ago."

There was a long silence before Mrs. Blake spoke again. "Camilla, you need to go to your mother's side and tell her. Tell her that Henry is widowed, that he's no longer married. I have a feeling you will make her extremely happy. But time is of the essence, please don't delay."

Of course, but you haven't yet told me what care home she is in?"

"Yes, let me see now…"

Mrs. Blake shuffled papers around."Here it is… It's the Santa Maria Care Home."

"I know where that is…"

"Try to go first thing in the morning. She is quite ill by the sounds of it and she may be most alert in the morning after a long night's rest."

"Yes, of course. Oh, I can hardly wait!"

"I do hope and pray everything turns out well. It's been such a joy meeting and talking to you on the phone. Please don't hesitate to call me at any time. I know what you are going through as I…was given up for adoption at one time, too." Camilla could sense Mrs. Blake's emotion rise. There was silence for the longest moment as they all seemed to share one thing in common.

"Thank you so much for all your time, Mrs. Blake, it was so kind of you. I would never have understood the dream I was having without your input and the other information you gave was so helpful, as well."

"You are most welcome, Camilla, and as I said, please call me at any time."

Camilla hung the phone up and stood up. She heard a noise and turned slowly to see Jeremy standing in the hallway, a look of both worry and amazement on his face.

"How much did you hear?"

"I heard it all…"

"Oh Jeremy I'm so sorry, I wanted to tell you that I had found proof that I was adopted, and that I knew who my real mother was, but …"

"But you still don't know who your father is. I don't know either Camilla, I only know that it could never have been my father. That's just not the kind of man he is. As strange as it might be, it just could possibly be Peter. But I think the only way we'll know for sure is for you to go to the care home tomorrow, meet Jenny, and find out from her."

Jeremy took her in his arms and held her tight.

"I love you so much, Camilla. Do you want me to come with you in the morning?"

"No…*I think I need to meet my birth mother alone.*"

Chapter Seventy-Four

Henry placed the diary on the end table next to his favourite chair in the sun room. He was glad he had brought it home and fully intended to read it, but it was getting late and he was exhausted. The room was still quite warm from the heat it captured during the day. Henry opened the patio doors slightly, returned to his chair and plopped into it.

"Boy does that feel good."

"Goodnight, Dad," hollered Justin as he followed Lauren upstairs to go to bed.

"Goodnight, kids."

Henry would normally be following the children but he was still too wound up from the day's events. The tension and aches oozed out of his legs as he nestled into the chair. Thoughts of discovering the diary in a secret compartment of a round table in Marjorie's house still overwhelmed him. Clearly it was divine providence that he purchased the roll top desk and first being alerted to it by Julean. And again today how he felt her presence along with angels.

He reached over to the end table and picked up the letter she had written to him before she passed away and read it through. He went back to the part where she said that she would help him find another love in his life:

> "When I go to heaven I will ask the good Lord's permission to guide you to another love and perhaps the girl of your youth is waiting for you. I pray that this is the case and I will do all I can to bring her back to you."

Amazing!

Henry thought how his dear wife both when she was alive and even after her passing to the other side she is still so supportive and…

Was this all a figment of his imagination? Would God really give Julean permission to guide him back to Jenny? He had thought for the

546

longest time it was Ivania but Julean seemed to be discouraging that. It all seemed so incredible yet Henry could feel her presence and he was certain that he saw her spirit.

Henry recalled the times when she was there; helping him to forgive John McBryne, leading him back to the star of the east and the day she guided him to turn and look at the lady who had pulled up beside him…Henry still wondered if it had been someone that looked like Camilla. He feels his wife's presence so much lately and even now she was in the room with him…he just sensed her presence.

There had always been this supernatural side to his life for as long as he could remember. It seemed to start when he met Jenny. Yes, the moment he gazed into her eyes something spiritual happened. *Henry was certain of it.* He could still feel that energy flow through his being. How his eyes stung as if something were caught in them for days after. From that moment on he was in love and even after 30 years of being separated from his Jenny, he still felt that love as if it all happened yesterday.

And Mr. Engelmann came next into Henry's life. The incredible relationship he had formed with the wise elderly man and the life lessons he had learned. It was he who reminded Henry of guardian angels and …and that day Jenny almost got hit by a car…Henry shook his head at the very thought of it. It was a miracle, no two ways about it. It was then that Mr. Engelmann seemed to appear at his side and tell him 'it was her guardian angel that saved her…that he needn't worry. Incredibly Henry later learned that Jenny had thought so too! Henry shook his head again as he remembered that and the many incidents which followed; his guardian angel, the pewter angel, the star of the east and feeling Jenny's love and Julean's presence and…and what about the fresh bouquet of flowers in the angel's basket in Marjorie's backyard that Julean alerted him to…these thoughts overwhelmed him.

Henry didn't understand it all but somehow he felt blessed by it all.

He rested his head against the back of the chair in a state of awe.

The grandfather clock in the living room chimed one, two, three… before the harmonious sounds struck ten, Henry was lulled into a deep, deep sleep.

Sometime in the wee hours of the morning, Henry found himself back in Marjorie's home. She was sitting at the dining room table with her back to him. Her wheat-coloured hair hung just short of her shoulders. Henry tried to see her face reflected in the mirror across from her on the wall, but he was at the wrong angle. As he walked further into the room she stood and rushed into the kitchen. He followed, turning on the lights as he went along hoping to catch a glimpse of her. In the kitchen he tried to overtake her, but she sped into the bedroom and closed the door.

Henry hurried to the door, knocked and stood there. After several minutes and hearing no response, he opened the door and entered the dark room. The lilac perfume hit his senses instantly and his thoughts were distracted…Jenny? …no…Marjorie?

The odour was making him dizzy with feelings of love. His eyes searched the room. There, in the corner she stood, her silhouette revealed by the moonlight entering from the bay window.

Turning on the lights was of no help to Henry as she faced the wall. He called out to her, "Marjorie, Marjorie…" but she did not respond.

Hesitantly, Henry walked over to her and took hold of her arm and gently turned her towards him. When her face came into view he was so startled that he snapped his head sharply up and back against the backrest of his chair. The last thought he had in his dream caught in his consciousness, as he became wide awake.

Could Marjorie Hamilton really be Camilla Pederson? My daughter-in-law?

That was absurd.

But what about Peter's dreams? They seemed absurd as well. He recalled the conversation he had with Angie yesterday. Peter was so certain he fathered a child that night he and his friends took Jenny to the park. For years he dreamt of a little girl with blond hair and blue eyes and how certain he felt Camilla was that same girl…Angie said Peter now dreams of Camilla. It all seems so weird…

And…and what about Camilla? Is she adopted? Do all these things have any reality or is it all an illusion driven by feelings of guilt, sorrow for past mistakes…searching for truth.

Henry's head began to ache again, his thoughts overwhelmed him. He wanted to be soothed by pleasant thoughts. Thoughts he had just moments ago.

He closed his eyes and desperately hoped to recapture his dream. It didn't matter if it was real or not. The feelings of love he felt for Jenny when he whiffed the lilac perfume intoxicated him into a momentary rapture of a love he longed to bring back into his life.

"Yes…" Henry whispered as he lulled himself back to sleep. It was early summer and the lilacs trees were blooming. Jenny couldn't be happier. She raced over to the shrub and picked a lilac. She inhaled its scent deeply.

"Here Henry, isn't its fragrance so wonderful!"

Henry had to agree…it sent him soaring or… was it really Jenny that sent him reeling? There she was picking another lilac flower from the tree and began chasing the butterflies down the wooden sidewalk on Broder Street.

Henry was so in love he began to fly like an angel…it was the only way he could catch the love of his life.

Chapter Seventy-Five

Three-thirty in the morning, the phone rang. Even though the volume had been turned down so as not to disturb the other residents, Father Engelmann heard the ring. In fact, he was already awake thinking about the sealed envelope on the night table which held the information he needed to fulfill Jenny's heartfelt wishes and prayers.

He rolled over towards his night table and thrust his hand through the darkness of the room towards the phone.

"Yes, this is Father Engelmann," Father whispered quietly into the phone.

"Good morning, Father, this is Chloe, I'm Jenny's niece at the Santa Maria Home. Do you remember me?"

"Yes, yes, what is it, Chloe?"

"I am so sorry to wake you at this time, but Auntie Jenny has been asking for you since midnight. She would like you to come and give her the last rites. I wouldn't have called you, but she is so agitated and gravely ill."

"Yes, it was good of you to call me, Chloe. I will be over very shortly."

The dial tone pierced the stillness of the night. It was an eerie sound, almost like the steady tone of a cardiac monitor when the heart of a patient stops beating. He had heard that sound many times over the years when tending to his sheep and they had passed on to meet their Shepherd. Father got up and sat on the edge of his bed, still holding on to the phone. A soft peaceful glow filled the room as he instinctively reached for the lamp switch with his free hand and turned on the light.

It was about this time – though usually a half-hour or so later – that Father would get up to begin his morning prayers and meditation. The reading of his breviary would have to wait until later in the morning. While still holding the receiver, Father gazed at the envelope Jennifer had given him for a long moment and then called for a taxi. That done, Father hung up the phone and dressed. In the closet was a small black satchel he hadn't needed for almost four months. After checking its contents, he closed the leather bag, then switched off his lamp and left the room.

He passed the front door as he detoured to the chapel.

"Good morning, Lord." At the foot of the altar, Father genuflected and made the sign of the cross. Then he stood and walked over to the altar, put his bag down and opened it. A small brass vessel immediately shone inside the bag as it was caught by the overhead light. He took out the little shiny container, unscrewed it, and went over to the tabernacle. The key was still in the keyhole, Father unlocked the curved door and took out the ciborium which had several consecrated Hosts from the previous day's mass. He lifted the arched cover of the cup and reverently bowed his head at the mere sight of the round white flattened bread.

"This is the body of Christ," he said, under his breath and made the sign of the cross. He placed one of the hosts into the brass container, returned the chalice to its holy chambers and the small vessel to his satchel.

Just as Father reached the front door, he saw the lights of a car approaching. "Ah, that was good timing."

The taxi driver leaned over and opened the passenger door just as Father was about to open it.

"Good morning, Father, I see you got the graveyard shift, too."

"Good morning, Bill. Yes, someone is very ill and needs last rites."

Father reflected on Bill's remark…. "graveyard shift." Everything so far that morning had been so ominous – the chilling sound of the telephone dial tone and now Bill's comment, all suggesting death. Father hoped it was not a foreshadowing of what was to come as he settled restlessly into the seat. His head jerked back as the cab sped off.

"Well, Father, the only good thing is every time someone dies, someone is being born. There is joy and sadness going on all the time."

"Yes, that is true, Bill, but there is joy in death, too. It's a time when all suffering is gone, all the cares are over and we enter into our final eternal home with our Lord. It is truly a time to celebrate."

After a lengthy reflective moment, Bill responded, "Yeah, I suppose so, never thought about it in that way… Hmm, joy and celebration in dying."

They remained silent for the rest of the trip. Father was praying for Marjorie or…Jenny…Hamilton. What was it that was tugging on his memory? The name…and what was it that Camilla said yesterday about her being adopted…?

"Good morning, John," Father greeted the night attendant at the front reception desk.

"And, good morning to you, too, Father. Up and at it early today, I see."

"Yes, yes, there is always a need, John."

Nurse Dolan, looked up towards the elevators, when she heard the bell sound. The doors of the elevator opened and Father Engelmann emerged. If it were not for the white collar, one could have mistaken him for an old-time country doctor carrying his medicine bag, making an early morning house call. In a sense, Father was a doctor, only his satchel carried medicine not so much for the body, but more so for the soul.

"Good morning, Father, thank you for coming," said Betty, with a smile.

"Good morning, Betty. Is Jenny still in room 455?" Father asked, as he whizzed by.

"Yes, she is awake and waiting for you. She seemed so happy to learn you were coming. Her two friends are with her as well."

When Father entered Jenny Hamilton's room, he expected to see a monitor or at least an intravenous tube going to Jenny's body, but there was nothing. Then he remembered helping Jenny sign some papers, last week, terminating all life support equipment when the end was near; she wanted to die naturally.

Chloe and Matilda were seated on the other side of the bed leaving the side nearest the door for Father.

"Hi Father," said Chloe.

"That was good of you to come," said Matti. "You be a tireless worker for the Lord, that for sure. Be it best to go to the waiting room or can we stay…?" Matti wanted to know.

"You both can stay if you wish. Jenny knows you are here and feels your love and support."

Father simply nodded as he looked down on Jennifer. The lamp on the end table cast a soft glow on Jenny's sleeping face. Father walked over to Jenny's bedside, put his satchel on the chair then gazed down at her. Jenny was a very beautiful lady, wanting so much to love and be loved. It was at times like this, when he saw how sickness and suffering took hold of a life and sapped it for all its worth, that he dared to question God's wisdom in it all. How Jenny fought the disease, day after day, until finally there was just no strength left.

Father felt himself sinking and quickly reminded himself of a passage, "My ways are not your ways," and that, immediately put a stop to such thinking. To further reinforce his defensive thoughts, he recalled other passages to combat his moment of weakness. Father had learned over and over in his lifetime that one must be ever ready to do battle and have a plan in place. Softly, Father began to recite scriptures of comfort:

> *"We have an everlasting home in heaven.*
> *We shall be with the Lord forever.*
> *We shall see God as He really is.*
> *The Lord is my light and my salvation......*

And each time Father quoted a passage, he identified their references ...2 Corinthians 5:1, 1 Thessalonians 4:17, 1 John 3:2, Psalm 27:1...

> *To you Lord, I lift up my soul. Psalm 25:1*
> *Though I walk in the shadow of death,*
> *I will fear no evil,*
> *For you are with me...Psalm 23:4.*
> *Come...*

Jenny moaned and opened her eyes.

"What a beautiful sight to wake up to, Father." Her voice was low and hoarse. She gazed lovingly at Father and he did likewise towards her. A deep love and friendship had developed over the few weeks he had visited her. Father would have given anything to see Jenny get well. She was included in every mass he'd said from the very first day he saw her. No, in fact, from the day he was given her name as a patient to visit from the director of the care home he had been praying for her. Everyday he pleaded with the Lord to heal her...until Father relented: not my will, but Your will be done.

Her gaze held so much suffering. Father reached out and laid his hand over hers. She was too weak to respond, she only smiled and nodded her head ever so slightly.

"Thank you, Father, for coming. I feel the Lord is coming to get me, today."

Father just looked down at Jenny and smiled. After a brief moment, he said, "I would like to anoint you with holy oil, Jenny. I also brought communion for you."

"Oh, thank you, Father, I was hoping you would."

Father turned towards the chair, opened up his satchel and took out a small jar containing oil, opened it and placed it on the night table.

He did the same with the brass vessel that had the Host. Next came the white vestment scarf which he kissed and put around his neck. Finally he retrieved his Pastoral Care Book and opened it to a place marked by different coloured ribbons.

Wearing a warm compassionate smile, he looked down at Jenny, hoping that what he was about to do would offer her hope and instill some measure of faith. Over the past years, he had witnessed many miraculous healings. His reminder of some of those healings, prompted Father to say the prayer of faith. He bowed his head and, in a tone which was barely audible, he said, "Oh, heavenly Father, in James 5:14-16, you told us that when one is sick, that we should pray for them and pour oil on them, anointing them in your name. If it is in your will, oh Lord, I ask that you restore Jenny to health."

"Yes, Lord, we be claiming your promise…" Matti said with conviction.

He knew Jenny was on the verge of death, yet, he believed all things were possible through Christ.

Father's gaze returned to the open book before him and he began the last rites:

"We have come together, oh Father, to celebrate the sacraments of anointing and Eucharist. Christ is always present when we gather in his name. Today, we welcome Him, especially as Physician and Healer. We pray that Jenny may be restored to health by the gift of Your mercy and made whole in her fullness."

Once again, Matti, said, "Yes, you be the great Physician and Healer. Come now sweet Jesus, do your healing…"

Father stopped for a moment and looked down at Jenny. Her eyes were closed. Father did not know if she was asleep or awake. He continued to pray.

"Father, you raised your Son's cross as the sign of victory and life. May all who share in His suffering find in these sacraments a source of fresh courage and healing. We ask this through our Lord Jesus Christ, your Son, who lives and reigns with you and the Holy Spirit, one God, for ever and ever."

"Amen," came Jenny's weakened voice from the bed.

"Amen, amen!" echoed Matti.

Once again, Father looked at Jenny and warmly smiled. She half-opened her eyes and reflected his love. Father decided to shorten the liturgy of anointing, skipped the next few prayers, and got right to the anointing itself. He could see it took all of Jenny's effort just to stay awake.

He held the book in his left hand then placed his right on Jenny's forehead:

"Praise to you, God, the Almighty Father. You sent your Son to live amongst us and bring us salvation. Praise to you, God, the only-begotten Son. You humbled yourself to share in our humanity and you heal our infirmities. Praise to you, God, the Holy Spirit, the Consoler. Your unfailing power gives us strength in our bodily weakness. God of mercy, ease the sufferings and comfort the weakness of your servant, Jenny, whom the church anoints with this holy oil. We ask this through Christ our Lord."

And, once again, Jenny surprised Father with, "Amen."

"Oh, yes sweet Lord, Hallelujah."

Turning to the end table, Father took out the cotton which was in contact with oil in the jar. It had already been blessed by the bishop of the archdiocese on Holy Thursday prior to Easter Sunday especially for that purpose, but Father so desired Jenny healed that he blessed the oil again for added measure. Father began to fervently pray from memory for blessings and healings. With each request Father asked for, Matilda added "Yes, Jesus, you be doing it now…"

"Oh God," Father began, "of all consolation, you chose and sent your Son to heal the world. Graciously listen to our prayer of faith; send the power of your Holy Spirit, the Consoler, into this precious oil, this soothing ointment, this rich gift, this fruit of the earth. Bless this oil (over which Father made the sign of the cross) and sanctify it for our use. Make this oil a remedy for all who are anointed with it; heal them in body, in soul, and in spirit, and deliver them from every affliction. We ask this through our Lord Jesus Christ, your Son, who lives and reigns with you and the Holy spirit, one God, for ever and ever…"

And a very weak, but appreciative voice from the bed responded, "Amen."

"Amen, thank you sweet Jesus," Matti whispered.

Father squeezed the cotton, releasing oil onto his thumb and forefinger, then anointed Jenny's forehead with oil, making the sign of the cross and said, "Through this holy anointing may the Lord in his love and mercy help you with the grace of the Holy Spirit."

"Amen," said Jenny attentively.

Father anointed Jenny's hands with oil as well.

"May the Lord who frees you from sin save you and raise you up."

"Amen," said Jenny, her voice no longer audible.

Matti answered for her dear beloved friend, "Amen…"

Father stood erect and returned his gaze to the pastoral book to say the prayer after the anointing.

"Let us pray:

"Lord Jesus Christ, you chose to share our human nature, to redeem all people, and to heal the sick.

Look with compassion upon your servant, Jenny, whom we have anointed in your name with this holy oil for the healing of her body and spirit.

"Yes, sweet Jesus…"

"Support her with your power, comfort her with your protection, and give her the strength to fight against evil.

"You be strong now, Jenny, Jesus here to help you…"

"Since you have given her a share in your own passion, help her to find hope in suffering, for you are Lord for ever and ever…"

"Yes, our comfort may be hurting, but our joy for you Jenny be filled with praise!"

Father waited for Jenny's response, but there was none. He looked over his book and down on Jenny. Her eyes were closed. Again, it was impossible to tell if she were awake or asleep.

Holy Communion was next, but he didn't know if he should disturb her or not. Her chest slowly rose and fell; there was still time for the Eucharist. Perhaps she should rest. Father decided to say the Lord's Prayer. Both Chloe and Matti joined in:

"Our Father, who art in heaven, hallowed be thy name, thy kingdom come, thy will be done, on earth as it is in heaven. Give us this day our daily bread and forgive us our trespasses, as we forgive those who trespass against us. And lead us not into temptation, but deliver us from all evil—"

"Amen," said Jenny, startling Father and the other ladies.

"I am so happy to see you awake, Jenny, would you like to receive communion?" Father asked, before she could drift away again.

"Yes," said Jenny softly, nodding her head ever so slightly.

Father quickly returned his attention to the end table and picked up the brass container with the Host. He turned back to Jenny, took out the Host and raised it up.

Jenny stared at the Host as Father said:

"This is the Lamb of God who takes away the sins of the world.

Come to me, all you who labour and are burdened, and I will refresh you."

As Father lowered the host and brought it towards Jenny, she responded, "Lord, I am not worthy to receive you…but only say the word and I…shall be healed."

It touched Father's heart to see the immense effort Jenny exerted in saying those words. Tears filled his eyes as he placed the Host on her parched tongue. Both Chloe and Matti were sobbing.

"The body of Christ," was all Father could say, he was too choked up to say any more.

Jenny received her Lord and closed her eyes. She was spent. Every ounce of energy, gone.

Father straightened himself and turned towards the night table. He put the lids back onto both vessels and returned them to the satchel then removed the vestment; he kissed the cross on it and returned it to the bag as well. Once more he picked up the book and said a prayer which follows communion:

"All powerful God, through the paschal mystery of Christ your son you have completed the work of our redemption.

May we, who in these sacramental signs proclaim his death and resurrection, grow in the experience of your saving power.

We ask this through Christ our Lord…"

Father waited for Jenny's response, but there was only the sound of very shallow breathing. Father continued:

"All powerful God, we thank you for the nourishment you give us through your holy gift.

Pour out your Spirit upon us and in the strength of this food from heaven keep us single-minded in your service.

We ask this in the name of Jesus the Lord…"

"Amen…" this time Matti completed the response for Jenny.

"All powerful and ever-living God, may the body and blood of Christ your Son be for our sister, Jenny, a lasting remedy for body and soul.

We ask this through Christ our Lord…Amen."

"Amen, and I be saying it again, Amen…sweep your healing into this child oh Lord…" said Matti, before she broke down again.

Father slowly closed the book and brought it towards his chest. He looked lovingly at Jenny. He felt as drained as Jenny appeared. The sorrows of earthly life had deeply pierced his heart. Tears rolled down his cheeks and fell upon the book, wrinkling more pages. He likened it to the time when Jesus came to the tomb of Lazarus, his beloved friend, and was so moved that He restored Lazarus's life. Father, too, loved Jenny, he now pleaded with all his being that the good Lord might do the same…to heal her, make her whole.

What Father saw before him, however, was a far cry from a miracle. Jenny was dying and he felt helpless, but to trust in the Lord. His heart ached so it threatened to break. Energy had left him only adding to the weariness he'd been feeling lately.

Father slowly raised his right hand and blessed Jenny.

"May the Lord be with you and protect you. May He guide you and give you strength.

"May He watch over you, keep you in His care, and bless you with His peace.

"And may almighty God bless you, in the name of the Father, and the Son, and the Holy Spirit…"

Father waited a moment, hopeful for a response then said, "Amen."

It was finished. Father placed his book into his satchel and closed it. He set the bag on the floor and pulled the chair up beside Jenny's bed and sat down. Fatigue and exhaustion overwhelmed him. He knew he should go home and rest, but he couldn't leave her side. He placed his hand over Jenny's and began reciting scriptural passages as he had when he entered the room:

"I believe that I shall see the goodness of the Lord in the land of the living. Psalm 27:13

Come, blessed of my Father, says the Lord Jesus, and take possession of the kingdom prepared for you… Matthew 25:34

The Lord Jesus says, today you will be with me in paradise. Luke 23:43

In my Father's home there are many dwelling places, says the Lord Jesus. John 14:2

The Lord Jesus says, I go to prepare a place for you and I will come again…to…take you myself…John…"

Father could barely go on, his heart felt too heavy. He recalled when Anna died how he lain on the bed after the attendants removed Anna's body.

Now, for the second time in his life, Father cried out as he did then, "Oh Father in heaven, come and take me, too…" He hung his head and sobbed.

Father felt someone's hand on his shoulder, slowly nudging him…

"Father, Father, I think you need some rest."

Father looked up at Dr. Kreake looking down at him.

"Oh, good morning, doctor, I must have dozed off."

Father stood and shook Dr. Kreake's hand. "How is our Jenny doing?" inquired Father, knowing the answer and yet wanting to make conversation.

Dr. Kreake just shook his head.

"I just came to check on her before I made my morning rounds. She is refusing all medication and life support."

Father slowly shook his head, "She is ready to see her Lord."

There was a lengthy silence. Father looked at his wrist watch, "Oh my, it's only 6:00 a.m.. You do get started early."

"Well, I must admit, I am earlier than usual, today. Jenny hasn't been well. I wanted to see her before I got started."

"Yes, I understand, I want to be with her and support her as well. She is such a lovely lady."

Dr. Kreake smiled then moved to Jenny's bedside.

Chloe and Matti were standing on the other side of Jenny's bed, tears flowing from their eye's. Matti's rapidly moving lips, although silent, reflected fervidness.

Father didn't even know the ladies were still present in the room until he felt the power of Matilda's faith…

"Ah, good morning girls. I see you are both still here."

"It's good to be here, Father, beside my sister's side. Oh my sweet Jesus is going to heal Jenny. I just knows it…"

Chloe remained silent as her hand softly assuaged Jenny's shoulder.

Father nodded and said, "Well, I best be going." Father picked up his satchel, turned to Jenny and stared for a long time. Her left hand must have found its way up to her chest while he was asleep. She was clutching onto her pewter guardian angel. She was still wishing for someone to come and give her a kiss. It reminded Father of the envelope Jenny had given him.

He'd struggled for hours the evening before deciding whether to open it or not and find out who her first love was. Perhaps he would peek into the envelope…it could be part of the Lord's plan.

Fresh tears welled up in his eyes. If it is your will oh Lord, restore Jenny. Bring back her health and life. Let her serve you a little while longer…if it is your will… "God be with you," he whispered then turned and walked out.

Father walked wearily down the hospital corridor, completely drained and exhausted. How deeply he prayed for a healing, a miracle. He had given it his all, but it was not meant to be. Nurses, doctors and aides bustled back and forth tending to their duties. Father was oblivious to it all. He felt in his heart that the end was near, but not only for Jenny.

A brightness glowed about him as he trudged along.

CHAPTER SEVENTY-SIX

EVEN THOUGH THE shadows of the night still covered the valley, the birds had anticipated the light long ago and were already chirping their greeting to the impending morning.

Henry was still asleep in his chair in the sun-room as the sun peeked over the horizon and a ray of light streaked into the room. The sudden brightness stirred him and he gently awoke to the sounds of nature. He shivered. The fireplace was on, but it couldn't keep up with the cold air pouring in through the open screen door. He quickly got up to close the patio doors.

A thick mist spread over the entire valley floor. Whenever this occurred, it always reminded Henry somehow of a cloud that got too heavy and fell from the sky. Even though he felt chilled, he couldn't help but step outside and seep in the peace and calm of the early morning. There is such a spiritual presence at this time of day. Truly meant for praying and meditating, preparing for the day ahead. His thoughts were suddenly broken by a skirmish at the bird feeder.

A group of sparrows where trying to fend off a woodpecker who was using his size to get more than his fair share of the sunflower seeds. Even the birds have their quarrels. It reminded him of Marjorie and her son, but...he didn't want to go there, now.

Rather, he breathed the fresh air deeply into his lungs and surveyed the valley once more. As the rising sun burned off the fog, shadows of trees and hills emerged like ghosts before his eyes, almost as though being created for the first time. He wondered if that is what it was like when God created the earth out of the purity and depth of His thoughts. No wonder He saw that it was all good. Henry felt so blessed that he lived in this little slice of heaven.

The sound of the creek rushing over the beaver dam drifted up to him from the valley below. He couldn't see it through the mist, but its sound indirectly instilled a feeling of calm. The calm did not come from the turbulence of the water falling over the dam, but rather, the still water in the pond just before the dam. It reminded him of the 23rd Psalm and he softly muttered under his breath, "He leadeth me beside the still waters…and gives me rest." Seeing his breath in the cool morning air as he spoke reminded him of how chilled he really was.

Henry picked up a blanket and warmed it in front of the fireplace for several minutes then spread it over his chair where he nestled into it, his bones drawing as much of the warmth as they could. His joints and muscles were sore and stiff from sleeping in the chair all night. He should have gone to bed, but the dream he had so unnerved him that he wanted to get right back to sleep and continue the dream. The shock of seeing Camilla as Marjorie might not be so far fetched as he had thought. She looked so much like Jenny and for months, now, he had been fantasizing about Marjorie, desiring Jenny, that it was just natural for him to see Camilla there.

The old Westminster wall clock in the sun room read 7:28 a.m., still enough time to read some more of the diary before having to head in to the Gallery. As he reached for Marjorie's diary on the end table next to him, he wasn't certain any more if he wanted to know the truth about Marjorie as he was comfortable in the fantasy he had created and felt safe within its boundaries. Whatever scene or scenario he wanted to conjure up for the day was easily in his control.

But now, he was facing the real Marjorie. The story of what had happened between her and her son had already upset him. Truth and consequences were at the doorstep and once he opened the diary his fantasies would be all but completely shattered. It could set him adrift again like a leaf in a prairie wind, completely at the mercy and hands of destiny.

Fear and trepidation had set in and he no longer felt the eager desire to read the diary and yet this foolishness had to end. Father was right, as usual. The notion that Marjorie and Jenny were one in the same, was a figment of his imagination, an illusion and began to concern him.

"Better snap out of all this before you lose touch." The real Marjorie was just some very sick lady in a care home and not the Marjorie he had created – an ideal Marjorie with similar tastes, likes, dislikes, character and even looks to that of the love of his youth. Whether it would destroy the wonderful world he had created or not, it had to end.

Henry slowly opened the diary to the section labeled private thoughts. Instead of flipping randomly through this section as he had the day before, he started from the beginning. That way, he'd know the truth. The first few entries had to do with her 15th birthday and people she invited to her party. In the next she described her feelings about having to move again. She loved Vancouver, had made friends and now her father was being transferred to Regina, some city in Saskatchewan that she knew nothing of. She dreaded to move there and start all over again.

The next entry however, immediately caught his attention:

July 6, 1956.

I think I am really going to like it here in Regina after all. I just met this cute boy at a grocery store. I helped him pick up cans of salmon that he knocked over. Oh, I can't explain how wonderful it was to look into his eyes! I still can't get over it...

He walked me home and I held his hand as we crossed a busy avenue. It felt so romantic. After lunch, he is going to take me to Balfour Collegiate to register, I can hardly wait. Perhaps we will hold hands, again.

Oh yes, his name is Henry.

Henry jumped up, making certain he was awake and not just having another dream. Marjorie was Jenny!? Still in a state of disbelieve, he re-read the last sentence several times. It was right before his eyes in black and white. He had suspected it, felt it in his bones, dreamt about it, fantasized about it, even thought he was losing touch with reality and here he had been right all the time.

Marjorie Hamilton was Jenny Sarsky!?

Henry paced the floor, trying to work out the tremendous surge of energy sweeping through him, as he leafed through the next few entries. Each one confirmed the awesome truth that Marjorie was Jenny! Their walk home in the storm, getting soaking wet, running barefoot on the grass. Their summer walks, the movie outing, their first kiss...

It was all there!

He visualized and savoured each flashing memory as he read. He was so elated he thought for certain he would float and then he read an entry about their parting in September. Oh the aching pain and sorrow that she described over their parting...it stabbed his heart, too.

He dropped into his chair; weakness crashed down upon him as he felt the loss and sadness sweep throughout his being. Her words of how heartbroken she was to move away almost split his heart in two. The pages blurred as tears gushed out from a new level of depth that had been buried since then.

A piece of his heart had been buried there, too.

The rueful, agonizing days, months and years that followed that wonderful summer, never to hear from his beloved again so overwhelmed him at that moment his body began to shut down. He sat still, motionless for the longest time until his mind was completely devoid of all thought. His breathing was slowing and so quiet the only sign that he was still in the land of the living was the slight rising and falling of his chest. It seemed as if all the human energy he possessed had dissipated and if he were to go on being his strength would have to come from another source.

As he sank deeper and deeper into the stillness of his mind a thought formed seeking expression, while simultaneously an image of someone evolved at the same time. Both were blurry, vague, and distant like a telescope gradually coming into focus. The sound advanced faster and the word "quick" …no… "quickly" formed in Henry's conscious mind. It repeated itself over and over again, getting stronger and stronger, the repetitions in tune with the faint sound of the back and forth swing of the pendulum in the grandfather clock just around the corner in the dining room. Quickly…quickly…quickly, over and over it chimed. He felt helpless to change the pattern. It seemed as if he had lost control of his thoughts.

He remained surprisingly calm and followed the flow of whatever it was that was happening then, suddenly, the remaining sentence came into his mind along with an image of …Julean. There she stood in front of him with smiling happy eyes beckoning him.

"Come, Hank, I will take you to your first love." Julean reached out her hand and then… he heard his first love…"Quickly, hold my hand!"

And as he had so many times during that memorable summer, Henry thrust his hand out to his beloved…but it passed clear through Julean's hand and came crashing down on his lap. It brought him back to the reality of the moment.

"My God, Marjorie…Jenny, is in the care home critically ill and here I am feeling sorry for myself. What's wrong with me!?"

His lackluster eyes began to flash once more. Henry jumped to his feet as a burst of adrenalin exploded through him. He quickly slipped on his shoes and grabbed his jacket as he raced to the SUV.

Within minutes, a trail of dust swirled behind him on the dirt road leading to the main highway. He unbuttoned the top two buttons of his shirt and fumbled for the pewter angel hanging at the end of the chain around his neck. It wasn't the angel he had in mind when he brought it to his lips and kissed it, it was Jenny's lips he was searching for. It seemed inconceivable that the angel he received from Jenny was identical to the angel he had given her.

Yet it had happened!

"Please hang on, Jenny, I'm coming," he whispered. "And, thank you, Julean, I know it is you along with Jenny's and my dear guardian angels who are making this all happen. Thank you for bringing us back together fulfilling our heart's desire!

This is all so unbelievable!

Buying the house with everything in it…I just knew it was a special spirit who owned it.

It was my heart, though, that knew it was you, Jenny!"

Henry turned onto the main paved highway and stomped on the accelerator. The front end of the SUV lifted as it shot down the highway leaving a layer of scorching rubber on the pavement. Within seconds, the speedometer had launched past the posted 110 km/h limit, trembling.

"Ease up, for God's sake, Henry, or you're going to end up where Marjorie is heading before she does." The thought only made him press the accelerator harder.

It would be a catastrophe if Jenny died before he saw her!

Father Engelmann! Maybe he could help Jenny! As he weaved dangerously between lanes and zoomed by frustratingly slower vehicles, Henry flipped open his car phone and called Father's direct line.

FATHER HAD RETURNED from the hospital over an hour ago and tried to rest, but he was just too distraught. He finished reading his breviary and was now on his knees asking the Lord for forgiveness. Ever since Jenny gave him the envelope to deliver to her lawyer, he was tempted to open it to learn the identity of her daughter and first love. He so wanted to grant Jenny's final wish, yet he knew it was wrong to open someone's mail. Even a venial sin was mortal to him, and was deeply sorry for entertaining the temptation and not trusting his Lord to deal with the matter.

"Trust in the Lord with all your heart and do not lean on your own understanding," was a passage Father uttered under his breath when the phone rang.

"It will be the hospital. My dear Jenny must be gone."

Father hesitantly picked up the phone and braced himself for the worst.

"Father!"

Father jerked his head back, as his ears rang with Henry's voice.

"Yes, yes, what is it, Henry?"

"The lady whose house I bought on Hill Avenue is really Jenny Sarsky. I'm on my way to the Santa Maria Home to see her. I found Marjorie's diary in the house, yesterday, and have been reading the entries and just this morning I read how we met in your store and the summer we spent together before she left for Ottawa. Last night, too, I had a dream that Marjorie was Camilla, but really she is Marjorie, I mean Jenny, they just look like Camilla. And…and then the thought to quickly hold her hand popped into my mind…That's what Jenny always used to say to me when we took a walk over 30 years ago, and…it was Julean who reminded me of it…"

"Hold on, Henry." Henry seemed incoherent; all tangled up in his words and wasn't making any sense. All this talk about dreaming, thoughts popping into his head that were 30 years old. When he and Henry had talked, the other day, Henry had admitted that he might be losing touch with reality. And now he was making the lady who used to own the house on Hill Avenue to be Jenny.

Has he lost his mind?

"Henry," Father finally said, "what is this about a diary and who is this Marjorie?"

"That's the lady that owns the house on Hill Avenue, or used to own the house, until I bought it." And before Father could ask another question that might snap Henry out of this foolish talk, Henry prattled on.

"The entries in the diary confirm that she really likes to be called Jenny rather than Marjorie. Jenny is her middle name. I now know what the J stands for. Her husband always liked her first name, Marjorie, and said she should always sign her legal documents as Marjorie and not Jenny. That's why on the deed she used her first name, Marjorie. Marjorie Hamilton."

Out of all that, only the name Marjorie Hamilton got Father's attention.

"Who did you say, Henry?"

"Marjorie. Marjorie is Jenny."

"No, no, her last name."

"Oh, Hamilton, it's Marjorie Hamilton."

"Jesus, Mary and Joseph, pray for us," Father whispered. "Henry, that's the lady I am seeing at the Santa Maria Care Home! I remember seeing it on her chart when I first visited her. I started to call her

Marjorie, but she wanted me to call her Jenny. And… Ach, mein lieber Gott, my good Lord, Henry, something has always bothered me about her. She always looked so familiar, like I knew her from the past. Her eyes, the sparkle in her soft blue eyes, yes…perhaps it is her."

"You mean you have been visiting Jenny and you didn't know it!? And you didn't tell me!?" Henry exclaimed, almost jumping through the phone.

"Henry, people change, and she is so sick and has lost her hair and… who would even suspect or remotely think that this same lady could possibly be the girl of your youth, your Jenny?"

Oh, Lord, it is Henry whom she desires to kiss. There was no need to look into the envelope!

Forgive me for doubting and thank you for sparing me from sin. Your ways are not our ways and I trust this whole matter will turn out for the good!

"Father, Father, are you still there?"

"Yes, yes, Henry, I am still here, I am listening…"

"Oh, Father, everything is making sense, now. When I took Jenny to Balfour Collegiate that very first day I met her, to register for high school, the secretary couldn't find her application form because it was not under Jenny Sarsky, but her first name. Jenny told the secretary she preferred to be called by her second name. I meant to ask her what her first name was, *but I forgot to.* Now after all these years, I know. It was Marjorie Jenny Sarsky! Had I known her name was really Marjorie, I might have made the connection sooner."

Goose bumps prickled up and down both Henry and Father's spines.

"And, don't you see, Father, how Julean and our guardian angels brought us together? How I bought the house rather than Jeremy. How everything in the house appealed to me as if I had purchased almost every item. And the books she read, Father, well, I have most of them on my bookshelves.

"But it was the angel in the backyard that I just know is a miracle, Father. The other day I noticed a bouquet of flowers in it and they were as fresh looking as if they had been picked that day and placed in there!"

Father was still reeling from the fact that he had visited Jenny for months and never realized that it was Henry's Jenny.

Oh, let it not be too late.

He had already administered the last rites and for all he knew she may already be in God's care.

"Henry!" Now it was Father who shouted into the phone.

Henry almost dropped his car phone.

"What is it, Father?"

"You must go at once and see her. So often she spoke of her first love and prayed fervently to be kissed before she passed on. It is you, Henry, she so desires. *If only I would have known.*"

Tears rose in Henry's eyes. "Please pray, Father, that it is not too late."

It suddenly occurred to Henry to ask about her husband. She is married and has a son. "What is her husband like, Father? Have you met him?"

"No, no, Henry, that's fine, she is not married," Father quickly replied wanting to reassure Henry that his hopes and thoughts were fine.

"But, Father, Elaine told me she is married! Oh my God, Father, for a moment there I was confused. Just the other day I read that Marjorie divorced her husband. But it was really Jenny."

"Yes, that is correct. She was married and after they divorced she moved to Regina."

Father could only imagine the expression on Henry's face turning from total dejection to one of elation. The sudden roar of Henry's engine on the phone confirmed Father's instincts.

"My God, Father, this is all so incredible. When did she move back to Regina?"

"I believe she said last spring."

"Did she come into my gallery or café?"

"I don't know, Henry, she never said."

"She probably didn't. I would have known if she had."

"I am glad you are going directly there. She is gravely ill, Henry," Father added, to stress the urgency of the situation and yet hesitated, not wanting to squelch Henry's hope. "She is on the fourth floor, room 455, if you have trouble getting in, have the nurse call me."

And then it hit Father like a thunderbolt. Camilla! Camilla, Jeremy's wife, Henry's daughter-in-law! Our Camilla is also Jenny Hamilton's daughter! That is what his mind struggled to connect together when he saw Camilla the other day! Camilla too is in search of her real mother!

"Ach, mein lieber Gott,"

"What did you say, Father?"

Jenny so desired to be re-united with Henry and Camilla. That was her wish! Oh Lord, grant Jenny her heart's desire to see the loves of her heart.

"Father, are you still there?"

"Yes, I was just thinking on something else but I believe the Lord has it all under control. I will leave it in His Hands."

"But what is it, Father? Don't leave me hanging!"

The Lord had already summoned Henry, her daughter is sure to be close behind. Yes, yes, trust in the Lord and let life take its course. He was just too tired and weary to deal with another matter.

"Father, Father, are you still there?"

"Yes, Henry, just go, your sweetheart waits for you."

"But what is it that you want to tell me...?"

"Henry, you will know soon enough."

"Okay, then. I'm just entering the city limits only fifteen minutes away from the care home. Thank you, Father. Please pray for us, pray for God's mercy and understanding, pray for a miracle. Good-bye, Father. I will call you later, today. I should know the answer to everything then."

"Yes, good-bye, Henry."

Chapter Seventy-Seven

Father hung up the phone and stood in the silence of his room still in awe at the amazing developments. He was certain that Jeremy's wife, Camilla, was Jenny's daughter as bizarre as that might be.

'My ways are not Your ways' is certainly true, oh Lord.

Henry and Camilla were right under his nose and he didn't connect either to Jenny's prayer to see them before she died. As he looked back he could see how the Lord and his messengers tried to make both Henry, him and even Camilla aware, but none of them saw it.

What possibly have you in store for us, Lord?

Our sweet Jenny is at your door, perhaps already cradled in Your arms.

Two scriptures popped into Father's mind. "Trust in the Lord with all your heart and lean not unto your understanding." It was the same thought the Lord had given him earlier, but it was the second passage – John 10:10 – that puzzled Father, "Christ has come in order that ye may have life and that ye may have it abundantly."

Father pictured Jenny lying in her bed as he gave her feeble body the last rites. *What life?* Father dared to think for but a moment before it was immediately erased by the thought…*all things are possible through Christ.*

Father hung his head and let out a long weary sigh. "Not my will, but Thy will be done," he whispered. "Please help me to bear it all."

For several days, Father David Engelmann had noticed a bright light around him. At first he thought it was his eyesight, but soon realized that his vision was fine, in fact it seemed to be improved. The light gave him a sense of peace and warmed and comforted him. If it were not for this godsend, the drain and exhaustion of the past few weeks would have consumed him. He recalled how a few days before Anna's passing, she too talked to him about the bright light she saw.

Father sat back on the edge of his bed. He rested his elbows on his knees and slowly lowered his head into his cupped hands before him.

"Lord…perhaps, my hour has come, as well. I showed your glory on earth as best I could. I finished the work you gave me to do. There are many who can carry on your purpose."

David could feel the lassitude in his spirit dragging him down. He never allowed himself to sink or stay in that state. The scriptures he quoted earlier were usually sufficient to sustain and lift his spirit, but he realized he needed more. He reached for the Bible on the end table and let it fall open on his knees. At once his eyes fell on the words of John 15:12 and 13 that confirmed what was already heavy in his heart when he gave the last rites to Jenny:

"This is My commandment, that you love one another as I have loved you. Greater love has no one than this, than to lay down one's life for his friends."

David's eyes brightened, he suddenly realized his petition for the Lord to take him out of weariness was not his true motive.

"Yes, yes, Lord, that is my supplication. You have granted me a long life; my cup has overflowed with joy in serving you and carrying out Your will. It is time to give this joy of life to my dearly beloved. Yes, this is how we can give Jenny the abundant life You intended."

Rejoicing filled his heart as he seized the opportunity to exemplify that same kind of sacrificial giving toward another that his Master had shown on the cross.

Raising his head and hands towards heaven he uttered a heartrending cry, *"I now come to you, Father, through Your son Jesus, my Lord and Saviour, to grant my heart's prayer. Take my life and restore Jenny's. Give her and my son, Henry, the happiness of marriage. Oh, Father! Allow me to give you glory in your presence now to fulfill your command, give me the honour to lay down my life for my friends as Your son did for us."*

For the first time in days, David's spirit enhanced and a gentle peace overtook him. The Lord had brought him to his ultimate purpose. He looked across the room at his tan wedding suit hanging in the open closet, illuminated by a ray of sun, which found its way into the room between a slight opening in the window curtains. As the warmth of the light came towards him the peace growing within him elevated.

"Yes, perhaps my time is at hand, perhaps the Lord shall give me the privilege to love completely."

Father rose and walked slowly over to the closet and took his tan suit off the rack. "Yes, today is a good day to wear my suit. It feels like the right thing to do." After laying the suit on his bed, he returned to the closet and got his white shirt and tie and laid them on top. He slipped off his black trousers, his vest, and finally his white collar that identified him as a priest. How he loved that collar, so proud to wear it, to let all the world know that he was the Lord's shepherd, charged with looking after His flock.

He put on his tan suit – his wedding suit, the suit he'd worn when he and Anna married and the suit he had said he wanted to wear at his funeral. Like Anna, at her funeral, had worn her wedding gown to symbolize her new marriage with the Lord, Father wanted to wear his wedding suit for the same purpose. The buttons on his shirt were not as easy to do up as his vest. He fumbled with them then tucked the shirt tails into his trousers.

The full-length mirror attached to the front of the door reflected his image as he closed the closet door and looked at himself. He reached back onto the bed for his tie that still had the knot in it. He'd never untied the knot, just loosened it and slipped it on and off. Father had always maintained that like the knot in his tie, his marriage with Anna would never come undone. If the full truth be known however, he could never remember how to loop it all.

After tightening his tie, he turned his shirt collar over it and slipped on his suit jacket. He looked at himself in the mirror, shuffling his shoulders, settling the jacket until it fit his body comfortably. He could easily have married again after Anna died; outlived two or three wives by the looks of it. But, he chose to marry his Lord and he saw the results of his choice reflected in the mirror.

"Oh," said Father, as a thought came to him.

He went over to the window sill and snapped off a bright yellow geranium and then stuck it into the hole of his lapel. He walked back to the full length mirror and looked at himself, again. He smiled and winked at his image, "Not bad for a man of 100." Father looked incredibly good for his age, but he could see the growing weariness in his eyes the only evidence of his aging.

"Well, Lord, I am ready if you are, my will is your will. Yes, today seems like a good day for another wedding."

COMING SOON

THE ANGELIC LETTERS SERIES

Book Five
—✳—

ANGEL PROMISES
FULFILLED

1988–1989

HENRY K. RIPPLINGER

The following is a preview of Chapter One

Chapter One

H ENRY SPED DOWN Pasqua street heading south. His heart was racing and pounding so hard he thought for sure it would explode out of his chest. Beads of perspiration were beginning to roll down his forehead trickling into his eyes. He brushed them away with the back of his hand.

"Oh, Jenny, please hang in there." Geez, for months already he could have been seeing her. Marjorie's house was less than a mile away from the Santa Maria Home, for Pete' s sake. He remembered when he called the care home and asked about her. If only he had challenged the nurse on duty at the time. That he was more than family and had every right to see her. Perhaps if he had gone down there and pleaded with them or had asked them to ask Marjorie if she would see him,

But that's the past, Henry. What's done is done. Henry reached up and clutched the angel once again.

"Oh please, guardian angel, get me there on time."

The light had turned yellow as he approached the intersection of Dewdney and Pasqua. He hit the gas and sped through but rather than slow down he kept increasing the gas…

"Oh, no…he heard a siren and looked into his rear-view mirror and saw a patrol car almost touching his bumper.

Henry slowed and pulled over. His heart almost in his mouth. He knew better than to speed, but it's… a life and death situation.

Henry rolled down his window as the officer approached the car.

"Can I see your driver's license, sir," the officer asked.

Henry already had his wallet out in anticipation of the question. He deserved a ticket and wanted to get it over with as quickly as possible.

"Did you know you went through a late yellow light. It was well into the red by the time you got through the intersection."

"I'm sorry, officer I was so close to the intersection I decided to go through… I was going quite fas…"

"That's exactly right. You were going fast; too fast. I was sitting on Dewdney waiting for the light to change and saw you barreling down Pasqua and after you went through the light you didn't slow down either. Seems to me you went still faster."

"I know…but I can explain. I just learned that a girl I knew and was very fond of 30 years ago is very ill at the Santa Maria Home and apparently her case is terminal. I was hoping I could see her before… well before something happens to her…" Henry didn't even want to think that Jenny might be dead.

"That may be, but in trying to get to her before she may pass away you are putting yourself and others in danger."

Henry nodded, clearly guilty, yet hoping the officer would simply give him his ticket and let him go.

The officer turned to go back to his squad car and write up a ticket when he noticed who Henry was. He came back to the car.

"Say, are you Henry Pederson the artist?"

"Guilty again, officer, I am."

"I can't believe this. We have one of your prints hanging in our living room. My wife and I got it when we married five years ago. It's the one of a boy and his dog standing beside a dugout behind the barn in a farm yard. He's tossing a stone across the water to make it skip on the surface. I used to do that all the time."

Henry appreciated the fact that the police officer had a piece of his art but desperately wanted to go. He simply smiled and nodded not wanting to get into a conversation."

"I know you're in a hurry…look, I'll give you a warning this time."

The officer tightened his lips and tilted his head as a sign he could change his mind but before he could, Henry said, "I promise officer I'll be more observant of my speed. Normally I am, it's just that I want to see Jenny before it's too late."

"You said she is in the Santa Maria Home?"

"Yeah." Henry nodded.

"Okay, look …follow me."

The officer hurried back to his car. No sooner had he started the vehicle he turned on the siren and proceeded down Pasqua towards the care home. Henry followed and waved to the officer when they got there.

Just as he pulled into the Santa Maria parking lot, he saw Camilla run out of the care home crying. She looked so upset… She ran to her car and before Henry could even get out and run to her, she sped away even more in a hurry than he was to get here.

What was she doing here? Who was she visiting or seeing?

He wondered if she had ever found out if she was adopted or not.?

Henry thought about going after her and explaining what he just found out about Marjorie but he was more torn to see Jenny.

He hoped that Camilla would drive more carefully and slowly and not get caught speeding like he did. Geez wouldn't that be something if she got caught by the same officer…another dangerous Pederson!"

The lady at the reception desk looked up as Henry burst through the door. He slowed to barely a walk.

"Good morning," he said, as he resolutely walked past the desk. He was already detained once and he couldn't deal with another interference. Henry caught his breath and blurted, "I know the room number of the patient I want to see."

He was glad Father had given him the room number otherwise he might have been held back again or told only relatives were allowed. The elevator doors opened up just as he got there. He stepped inside and hit the number four button several times.

"Who are you going to see?" the lady at the reception desk hollered, as she chased after him.

"A very close friend—."

The last part of the sentence was cut off by the closed doors and simply echoed within the confined elevator. Henry shifted from one foot to the other, wanting to help lift the slow elevator as it climbed past the second and third floor. His heart hammered inside his chest. Beads of perspiration formed on his forehead and sweat under his armpits rolled down his sides joining the wetness of his undershirt soaked from the sweat off his back. It was as if he stepped out of the shower and put his clothes on without drying first. He pulled on the back of his sports jacket to free his back from sticking to his clammy shirt. Exhaustion from the roller-coaster of emotions was closing in. He breathed deeply to ward off a dizzy spell.

Finally, the elevator bounced to a stop and the doors opened none too soon. Cool air from the air conditioner on the fourth floor gushed into the stuffy elevator, offering Henry some relief. He grabbed the lapels of his jacket with both hands and flapped them back and forth. Along with the cool blasts of air to his face and chest came a growing nervousness.

"What if she doesn't recognize me or is upset with me for not writing." Hopefully she got his letter like he got hers. He recalled Mr. Sarsky's secretary saying she sent his letter to Jenny at the same time.

One thought after the other buzzed through his mind…

He shivered.

Only one nurse seemed to be on duty at the nurse's station, and she was busy writing something behind the raised counter. Henry slowed down and tried to soften his footsteps checking the room numbers as he proceeded down the hall. Room 453 was just to his right so room 455 must be at the end of the hall.

As he passed the station he sped up, the nurse looked up and called out, "Sir, excuse me, sir."

Henry pretended not to hear her and quickened his pace as much as he could. He heard her bumping into her desk and a chair tipping over. To see Jenny was his mission, he'd deal with the protocol of patient visits later. He read the number outside the room; 455.

As he turned in, another nurse was coming out carrying linen. Henry bumped into her, almost knocking her over in the doorway.

"Oh, I am so sorry," he whispered.

He rushed into the room and looked over to the bed.

Instant panic swept through him. He staggered backwards and once again bumped into the other nurse from the nurse's station who had finally caught up to him.

"Oh no," Henry cried, "I'm too late."

His heart thumped, ready to burst. The sight of seeing an empty bed was too much…

Jenny was gone!

About the Author

HENRY RIPPLINGER IS the bestselling author of *Pewter Angels. Another Angel of Love,* and *Angel of Thanksgiving,* the first three books in the six-book series "The Angelic Letters." The overwhelming response by readers to Henry's novels gives testimony to Henry's gifts as an author to write books that touch human hearts and offer direction to their lives.

Henry's empathetic abilities, combined with his lifelong experience and eclectic career as a high school teacher, guidance counselor, professional artist and businessman, prepared him to craft this inspirational christian romance series and indirectly realize his aspirations of writing a self-development book.

Henry is also one of Canada's foremost prairie artists. His work is on display at private and corporate collections across Canada, most notably in Saskatchewan, his home province, and can be seen in the critically acclaimed book, If You're Not from the Prairie.

He resides with his wife in the panoramic valley setting of Lumsden, Saskatchewan, Canada.

Please e-mail Henry at: **henry@henryripplinger.com** or visit **www.henryripplinger.com** for more information about Henry's work and art. He would love to hear from you!

ALSO BY HENRY RIPPLINGER

PEWTER ANGELS
BOOK ONE OF THE ANGELIC LETTERS SERIES

*"He hath given his angels charge over thee; to keep thee
in all thy ways…In their hands they shall bear thee up:
lest thou dash thy foot against a stone."*

PSALM 91:11-12

…Suddenly, she turned to Henry as if to speak, catching him off
guard. He didn't have time to pretend he wasn't staring at her. He'd been
caught. Their eyes met now for a second time and although he felt his face
warming again with a blush, this time he couldn't turn away. Her gaze
locked with his and his with hers. They rose from their knees simultaneously, as if lifted, and were at once standing, facing each other.

Nothing existed except this moment and this place.

A charged, earthly attraction united their hearts while a spiritual
energy traveled the length of the gaze they shared, drawing their souls
from their bodies and joining them at the halfway point. The aura around
them brightened…enclosing both in the surrounding glow of their celes-
tial connection.

Time stood still…

Pewter Angels will grab your heart, squeeze it
and hold it to the very last page.

ANOTHER ANGEL OF LOVE
BOOK TWO OF THE ANGELIC LETTERS SERIES

*"God causes all things to work together for good to those who
love God, to those who are called according to His purpose"*

ROMANS 8:28

It was as if Jenny had vanished from the face of the earth. Two years
after she and her family moved out of Henry's life, Henry still longs for
her, their whirlwind romance gone from his life but not his heart. He was
certain she would respond to his last letter, a pewter angel tucked inside
—but there have been no letters, no phone calls. Nothing. A country
apart, Henry and Jenny are unaware Jenny's parents have burned all the
letters but the last... it is protected, it seems, by an angelic power.

Henry continues to rely on the love, support and powerful insights of
his mentor Mr. Engelmann, and his secret plan to seek Jenny out sustains
the hope that one day his love will return—until he meets Julean Carter.

But, is their new-found love deep enough and strong enough to overcome the heavenly touch that entwined Henry and Jenny's spirits when
they first gazed into each others eyes?

Another Angel of Love...glows with moments of tenderness...
deeply inspirational....will captivate the heart of every reader!

ANGEL OF THANKSGIVING
BOOK THREE OF THE ANGELIC LETTERS SERIES

This may be the single most moving book you will read this year—or in your life time.

Henry and Julean couldn't be happier. With a new baby, a new home and Henry's new job, everything is turning out perfectly for the young couple. Or is it? Henry can't seem to shake the memory of Jenny from his mind or the love he still feels for her. Little does he know, his wife is all-too-aware of Henry's hidden thoughts and feelings. Meanwhile, Father Engelmann, back from seminary school and creating a sensation as the new parish priest, is caught in the middle when both Henry and Julean confess to him about Jenny.

Will Jenny finally give in to James' persistent proposals, knowing that once married her chance to reunite with Henry would be gone forever? Spanning two decades, Angel of Thanksgiving takes the reader on an incredible journey of faith, hope and love. As we see Henry and Jenny's lives unfolding separately and so far apart, w*ill destiny bring them together again?*

Timeless Biblical themes as surrendering to God's will, forgiveness, and unconditional love are beautifully portrayed through unforgettable, real-life characters in this compelling, hard to put down novel.

Make a huge space in your heart before you begin to read Angel of Thanksgiving as it will quickly fill with love's beauty and wonder.

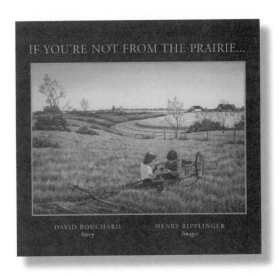

If You're Not from the Prairie, written by David Bouchard and illustrated by Henry Ripplinger, is a poetic and visual journey depicting the prairies and the people who have made this diverse land their own...a treasure for the mind and soul.

To contact the author and for further information about these books as well as other artwork, limited edition prints and other products, please visit:

www.henryripplinger.com